What Readers Are Saying About

KAREN KINGSBURY FICTION...

"Karen Kingsbury has been such a godsend. Her books have brought me to God and have motivated my husband and me to remarry after a bad divorce. After not being able to have kids, we now have an adopted boy and are trying to adopt another. Your books show faith, love, and tenderness, and I love them."—KATHY, Rancho Santa Margarita, CA

"I just love all of Karen Kingsbury's books. Every one has touched me in a very deep way, relating to one or another 'storm' I have gone through and yet giving me hope that God is always there, carrying us when we don't care anymore whether we live or die. I have been to that place, and God did lift me up from the depths of sorrow and pain! Thank you so much!"—HENRIETTA, British Columbia, Canada

"Karen Kingsbury's fiction has changed my life by reminding me that there is hope amid seemingly hopeless circumstances and that faith in God's redemptive plan is the anchor I can hold on to when life's compasses fail."—AMY, Lawrenceville, GA

"Karen Kingsbury's books have touched my life in many different ways, but *Where Yesterday Lives* really helped me in the death of my father-in-law... Thank you for the great stories."—CHRIS, Zeeland, MI

"The Lord prompted me to find a Christian author I enjoyed, and I found Karen Kingsbury. I have struggled with depression to a certain degree all my life, but when I read her book, I was at the bottom. This was the beginning of a wonderful journey to recovery for me."—DANNELL, Brawley, CA

"From Karen Kingsbury's very first book to her most recent, she has inspired me to be a better person, have a stronger faith in God, and to question how I am raising my family in a world filled with hate and evil."—PATTIE, Oceanside, CA

"When I went off to college, I fell into a dark depression but convinced myself that Christians not only don't suffer depression, but that it is inherently un-Christian to be depressed... I bought *When Joy Came to Stay* and read it in one sitting... I was able to receive treatment for my illness and work on dealing with events and behaviors that led to this depression. The book made it easier for me to see that God can use even dark times to bless us and help us grow."—DEIDRE E.

"Karen Kingsbury's fiction has helped me with my family problems. Karen's books have taught me how to stick together with my family through thick and thin. They have taught me that even when your family may be having a tough time, never give up."—ASHLEIGH, Fairfield, CA

"My grandmother has been diagnosed with dementia... Right after her diagnosis, she asked me to bring her some books. I took her everything I own by Karen Kingsbury, which is about ten books. She devoured them! They encouraged her and gave her hope."—DONNA I.

"I can't tell you how much Karen Kingsbury's books have blessed my life. The novels make me think seriously about what commitment means, sticking it out even when all seems gloomy, and understanding the covenant of marriage."—NATA, Nigeria

⤞⤝

NOVELS BY KAREN KINGSBURY

www.karenkingsbury.com

A KINGSBURY COLLECTION

THREE NOVELS IN ONE

KAREN KINGSBURY

Multnomah Books

A KINGSBURY COLLECTION
published by Multnomah Books
A division of Random House, Inc.

© 2005 by Karen Kingsbury
International Standard Book Number: 978-1-59052-521-0
Published in association with the literary agency of Alive Communications, Inc.
7680 Goddard St., Suite 200, Colorado Springs, CO 80920
and in association with the literary agency of Arthur Pine Associates.

Compilation of:
Where Yesterday Lives © 1998 by Karen Kingsbury
ISBN: 978-1-57673-285-4
When Joy Came to Stay © 2000 by Karen Kingsbury
ISBN: 978-1-57673-746-0
On Every Side © 2001 by Karen Kingsbury
ISBN: 978-1-57673-850-4

Unless otherwise indicated, all Scripture quotations are from:
The Holy Bible, New International Version © 1973, 1984 by International
Bible Society, used by permission of Zondervan Publishing House
The Holy Bible, New King James Version © 1984 by Thomas Nelson, Inc.
Excerpts from the hymn "Great Is Thy Faithfulness" by Thomas O. Chisolm
© 1923, Ren. 1951 Hope Publishing Company, Carol Stream, IL 60188.
All rights reserved. International copyright secured. Used by permission.

Multnomah is a trademark of Multnomah Books,
and is registered in the U.S. Patent and Trademark Office.
The colophon is a trademark of Multnomah Books.

Printed in the United States of America

For information:
Multnomah Books • 12265 Oracle Boulevard, Suite 200 • Colorado Springs, CO 80921

07 08 09 10—10 9 8 7

[Book One]

Where
Yesterday
Lives

Dedicated to Dad, that in seeing today what could be tomorrow, you would never wonder how very much you are loved. Mom, for being forever dependable. Your love has no limits.

My husband, my best friend, whose Bible is anything but dusty. Walking through life by your side is the greatest thing this side of heaven. Thank you for loving me enough to tell me the Truth. I love you always.

Kelsey, my sweet daughter. Your love for Jesus is as beautiful as the light in your eyes, the warmth in your smile.

Ty, my tenderhearted boy. I treasure watching you walk and grow in the image of your daddy, as he continues to walk and grow in the image of our heavenly Father.

Austin, our little Isaac. God blessed us with you not once, but twice. You will always be a living reminder that God still works miracles among us. I can't wait to see the great things He has planned for you!

And to God Almighty, who has for now blessed me with these.

ACKNOWLEDGMENTS

Like any writer, I draw from my experience and the experiences of others when I bare my heart in a work like *Where Yesterday Lives.* And so I thank these who make up my own yesterdays…Donald, of course, and Dad, Mom, Sue, Chris, David, Tricia, Lynne, and Todd. Reporter friends I have known and worked with, and my longtime friend, Lisa. Also thanks to those others who played an integral part in building my scrapbook of rainy-day memories. I remember you fondly.

This book could not have come together without the talented efforts of one very special editor and friend, Karen Ball. Thanks for believing in me and *Where Yesterday Lives.* And thanks for making me a better writer in the process. I'm excited about what God has planned in all this.

Thanks to Dad, Tricia, Gina, Sherri, Michelle, Natalie, Rene, Wendy, and Betty for your feedback and encouragement in the initial process of writing this book. And finally, a special thanks to Rene, Dawn, and Amber for watching my little ones while I snuck an hour or two to write. May God bless your servant hearts.

PROLOGUE

The first wave of pain seized his chest like a vice grip so that his hand flew to his heart and he gasped for breath. The second wave sent him to his knees. He felt his face contort from the pain, and he forced himself to concentrate on surviving.

Help! The word formed on his lips and died there.

Air refused to move in and out of his body, and his lungs screamed for relief. The pain intensified; the grip tightened. There was tremendous pressure now, as if a cement truck had stalled directly over his heart.

He clutched harder at his chest, ripping a button from his shirt. In the recesses of his mind, in the only place that was not consumed with pain, he knew what was happening.

His body crumpled slowly onto the matted brown carpet that lined the hallway. *Get up!* his mind screamed. But he remained motionless, every muscle convulsing in pain. Sweat beaded up on his forehead and his face seemed surrounded by flames. Frantically he gazed upward until he found the photographs that lined the walls.

His eyes darted across the familiar faces.

Another wave hit, and he squinted in agony, staring at the people in the photos, seeing them when they were young. When they still liked each other.

He wondered if they knew how much he loved them and suddenly a million memories fought for his attention. Once more he tried to speak, to summon help, but no sound escaped and his eyelids grew heavier.

The strongest pain of all hit then, and in the haze of agony he calculated how much time had passed. How much remained.

He could no longer keep his eyes open—a fact that brought overwhelming sadness. He wanted to see them once more, the photographs…the people who lived in them. He struggled with every bit of his waning energy, but his eyes remained closed.

There was a ringing sound in his ears now and he became light-headed. He was fainting, losing consciousness. He told himself that perhaps he was no longer having a heart attack but rather giving in to an overwhelming urge to sleep. He relaxed and let himself be sucked into the feeling.

Then one last time searing pain coursed through his body, and he remembered what was happening. Someone seemed to be shouting at him now.

Wake up! Wake up! Wake up!

He tried to move, to open his eyes. But he was slipping further away and it was too hard to come back. For the briefest moment, he thought again of the people in the photographs…and he prayed they would forgive him.

As he did so, the pain eased dramatically.

Then there was only darkness.

I

A dense blanket of heat and humidity covered the Florida peninsula the afternoon of July 10, but at the climate-controlled offices of the *Miami Times* the unending process of news-gathering continued at a frenetic pace.

That Friday afternoon, while the city sweltered under record-breaking temperatures, the editors sat quietly at their desks in the center of the newsroom and Ellen Barrett, back from a morning of interviews, worked intently at her computer several feet away.

"Jim, tell me there's not something more to this murder." She held up a news clipping and strained to see Jim Western. Jim sat in the cubicle immediately in front of her and worked the environmental beat, dealing with illegal chemical dumping and polluted harbors. He was not interested in homicides.

"Sounds fishy." His eyes remained focused on his own computer screen and the story he was writing. Ellen watched for a moment, fascinated with his neatly arranged notes, his clean desk, and the way he typed using only his index fingers.

"More than fishy." She reached for her coffee and took a sip, wiping the moist condensation off the notepad where the cup had been sitting. Her eyes traveled across her desk, searching for a clear spot. She alone could make sense of the disaster that was her work area. Somewhere, buried under layers of rumpled notes, was a picture of her and Mike on their wedding day and a Bible he had given her three years ago. It was dusty now, though its pages were stiff and clean—much as they had been when she received it.

Ellen studied the heap of papers and, as she had once a month for the past year, made a mental note to get organized. For now she pushed her keyboard back and set the hot drink in the space it created.

She looked at Jim again. "Guy lives his whole life in his father's shadow, tells his friend he hates the old man, and next thing we know Dad opens the door and gets blown away by an AK-47 on the Fourth of July."

"Some holiday."

"Neighbors think it's fireworks and no one sees a gunman. What does the grieving son do? Hops in Dad's shiny, new Corvette and shows it off to half the people in town."

"Fishy."

"Not to mention the tidy insurance settlement sonny boy figures to get now that Dad's gone."

"Very fishy."

"Know what I think?"

Jim sighed. "What?"

"Prison time for sonny boy."

"Hmm, yes." Jim continued to type, his index fingers moving deftly across the keyboard.

"And won't that be something after everyone's been busy doling out sympathy cards to the guy like he's some kind of forlorn victim? Truthfully, I can't understand why he hasn't been arrested. I mean, it's amazing, how obvious it is."

Jim sighed once more, and this time his fingers froze in place as he looked up from his work. "That all you and Mike talk about at home? Homicide investigations? Must make great dinner conversation."

Ellen ignored him, but she was quiet for a moment. She didn't want to think about Mike and the dinner conversations that were not taking place. She glanced once more at her notes.

"Well, I think the kid's dead in the water. No doubt in my mind. He'd better enjoy the Corvette while he still has his hands free."

Jim continued typing and the conversation stalled. Ellen settled back into her chair and glanced around the office. The newsroom was a microcosm of the outside world and it pulsed with a heartbeat all its own. If a story was breaking anywhere—from Pensacola to Pennsylvania, Pasadena to Pakistan—it was breaking at the office of the *Miami Times*.

The room held twenty-four centers, each with eight computer stations manned by hungry reporters. By late afternoon, most of the reporters were seated at their desks, tapping out whatever information they had collected earlier in the day.

Like the product it produced, the newsroom was broken into sections. News, sports, entertainment, religion, arts, and editorial. Each department had its physical place in the office and operated independently of the others but for the constant relaying of information to and from the city desk located at the center of the room.

Despite the hum of activity from the other sections, Ellen knew it was the editors at the city desk who ultimately made up the life force behind the paper. They had the power to destroy a local politician by placing his questionable use of campaign funds under a banner headline on the front page instead of burying it ten pages into the paper. A plan to expand the city's baseball stadium could be accepted or rejected based on the way the editors chose to play it in print.

Stories from around the world poured into the office through computerized wire services while editors sorted through reams of information and argued about whether children starving in Uganda was a better lead story for the World News section than Saddam Hussein's latest threat against American armed forces. Whatever was deemed worthy of writing was passed on to the other reporters.

It was a powerful job—one where perspective was difficult to maintain. At the *Miami Times,* editors did not walk in the same hurried fashion as reporters. They sauntered, carrying with them an unmistakable aura of importance and often causing reporters to shrink in their presence.

Except for the editors, Ellen's peers at the *Times* generally enjoyed their jobs, thriving on the kind of pressure that causes stress disabilities in other people. Angry sources, missing information, daily deadlines, mistakes in print...the reporters would have taken it all in stride if not for the wrath of the *Times's* editors. Among media circles, the *Miami Times's* editorial staff had a reputation for being demanding and difficult to work for.

Reporters at the *Times* credited one man with earning that reputation for the paper: managing editor Ron Barkley.

For three years Barkley had been in charge of the *Times's* news desk. Every section of the paper had at some time come under his scrutiny, but he paid particularly close attention to the front section. Stories that made the front section were produced by Barkley's general assignment reporters, a handful of the paper's best writers who gathered and crafted stories that did more than entertain readers. Front-page news changed lives. The *real* news, Barkley called it.

If anyone knew Barkley's wrath, or the impossibility of his demands, it was the general assignment reporters. His presence among them had caused more than a little grumbling in the newsroom. Ellen had even heard talk of a union forming to combat what some reporters considered inhumane treatment.

Ellen had once interviewed J. Grantham Howard, the paper's owner, for a piece about the *Times's* evolution over the years. Howard had acknowledged the friction between Barkley and his staff and told Ellen he kept himself apprised of the situation. Certainly the owner understood that Barkley did not make conditions pleasant for his reporters. But Howard was a multimillionaire with a keen business sense and he readily admitted he was not about to disturb the very successful chemistry in the newsroom.

Howard told Ellen he'd kept a close eye on Barkley and found him to be as brilliant as he was demanding. In the years since Howard had hired the managing editor, circulation numbers had reached more than a million on Sundays and advertisement rates had nearly doubled. The same thing had happened at the paper Barkley had run in New York, and Howard believed the editor was the common denominator. Still, whenever Howard would visit the newsroom, Ellen had seen him cringe at the way Barkley treated the staff. Especially her.

"Barrett!" Barkley would boom across the newsroom on occasion, shoving his chair away from his desk and rising to his full height of six feet, four inches. His eyes would blaze as he pointed toward his computer screen. "Get over here! We can't run that story unless you verify those things Jenkins told you. You wanna spend the rest of the year in court?"

His voice would echo off the fiberboard walls of the newsroom as other reporters busied themselves in their notes. Ellen knew they were empathizing with her and envying her at the same time. For all the grief she took from Barkley, Ellen knew the position she held at the paper. She'd heard it too often to doubt it: she was unquestionably the *Miami Times's* best reporter.

Ellen smiled, and glanced toward Ron Barkley's office. He thought Ellen feared him much the way her peers did. Her smiled broadened. Poor Ron would have been shocked had he known that his prize reporter really thought he was an emotional kitten of a man, a fifty-six-year-old gentle giant, whose rough exterior was only a cover-up for who he really was inside.

Ellen had been at the paper before Barkley's arrival. She had moved to Miami four years after earning her journalism degree from the University of Michigan and had been a sportswriter for a year before being promoted to the front page. When the *Times* hired Barkley, she heard rumors that he was hard to work for. She researched his background and found the names of several reporters who had worked for him in New York.

"Tough as nails," a senior reporter told her. "He'll yell and scream and throw a fit until you get the story perfect. But don't let him fool you."

And then the man told Ellen a story she had never forgotten. Ten years earlier Barkley's son had been a bright investigative reporter with a brilliant future in the business. The young man was driving home from the office one night when he was hit head-on by a drunk driver and decapitated. After that, there had been something different about Barkley's presence in the New York newsroom. He still sounded loud and acted angry, but there were times when he would be reading a story about somebody else's tragedy and suddenly start coughing.

"I'd catch him swiping at a tear or two when he thought no one was looking," the reporter said. "Eventually the memories were too much and he needed out of New York."

"You liked him?"

"I understood him. The man knows the stuff we write about is more than a way to fill a newspaper. Another thing. He's the best editor you'll ever work for. Ignore the rough package and listen to him. He'll make you a better writer than you ever dreamed."

That had been three years earlier, and Ellen had taken the reporter's advice to heart. When other writers fought with Barkley, Ellen Barrett gave in. When he demanded, she produced. When he screamed, she produced faster, nodding in agreement and accomplishing all he asked of her. She learned to rely on the man, ignoring his outbursts and allowing him to fine-tune her journalistic talent with each story. As a result, if Barkley got wind of a sensational tip or a front-page lead, he would always pass it to Ellen.

For her part, the effort paid off immensely. She was the highest paid reporter on staff and her name was known throughout Miami. Twice she had worked on Pulitzer-prize-winning articles and she was only thirty-one years old. She had no problem with the fact that the crusty veteran editor credited his editing practices as the cause of her success. Whatever the appearance of their working relationship, Ellen was not looking for sympathy. The situation suited her perfectly.

She flipped through her notepad and considered the homicide story on the screen before her. She wanted to scrap the whole thing and write a story blasting the dead man's son, painting him as the primary suspect. But that was impossible unless the police were at least headed in that direction. If only they'd arrest him and make it official.

She tapped her pencil on her notepad and wondered whether she should call Ronald Lewis, the sheriff's homicide investigator. Earlier that morning she'd visited his office and he'd told her there were at least a dozen leads on the case.

"What exactly are you looking for, Lewis?" Ellen had asked impatiently. "The guy's son did it, and you know it."

Lewis had studied her thoughtfully for a moment. He trusted her. She was thorough and truthful and careful not to burn her sources, and he knew that. She'd made sure that when someone talked off the record with Ellen Barrett, the information never appeared in print. It had been a long road, but she had earned the department's respect—and Lewis was no exception. There were things he would tell her that he wouldn't consider sharing with another reporter.

"Listen, you're probably right," he had admitted finally. "But let me make the arrest first, will you?"

That was six hours ago, and now Ellen stared at her story knowing it was noticeably vague and really only half written. She reached for the telephone just as it rang. "It's about time, Lewis," she muttered, picking up the receiver. *"Miami Times,* Ellen Barrett."

"Ellen, it's me."

It was Mike. She relaxed and glanced at her watch. Five-fifteen. He would be home wondering when she was leaving work. Lately their schedules had been hectic; sometimes weeks passed without a single dinner shared together. But that was the price of being successful reporters, she supposed. The success they both had achieved before they married had continued and grown after the marriage. Mike knew the business well, and so had understood the long hours. He'd even been the one to encourage Ellen to keep her maiden name since that was the name people in the industry knew.

"Hey." She softened her tone. "How was your day?"

"Ellen…" There was a long pause. "Ellen, I have bad news. Your dad's had a heart attack, honey. Your mom wants you to call right away. She's at the hospital in Petoskey."

Ellen felt the blood drain from her face and she hunched over in her chair, elbows on her knees, feeling like she'd been punched. A heavy pit formed in her stomach, and she pressed her fists into her midsection in an effort to make it go away. She felt nauseous. *Dear God, help me. Deep breaths, Ellen. Take deep breaths and stay calm.*

She had expected this phone call for as long as she could remember.

"He's alive, right?" Her voice betrayed none of what she was feeling.

"Sweetheart, I don't know anything. Your mom said for you to call her. I think you should come home."

She was silent a moment and Mike exhaled softly. "I should have waited until you were off work—" He broke off, then, "Are you okay?"

Ellen squeezed her eyes shut. "Yeah. I'll be home in a few minutes."

Friday was the day Sunday's front-page stories were filed and approved by the city desk. None of the general assignment reporters dared ask Barkley if they could leave before he cleared their Sunday stories. Even so, Ellen stood up, gathered her purse and her notes, and moved mechanically toward Barkley's desk.

He looked up as she approached. "What is it, Barrett?" he barked.

"Something's come up and I need to leave. My story's finished; it's in your file. I'll be at home."

Ellen studied Barkley, waiting, and she thought she saw a flicker of compassion. Maybe losing his son had enabled Barkley to tell when something equally devastating had happened in another's life. His response surprised her.

"Fine." Barkley's tone was almost gentle. He returned his eyes to the computer screen and stretched his long legs beneath his desk. "I'll call you."

Ellen turned, barely aware of her surroundings. She made her way to the elevator, and then to the parking garage outside where she climbed into her dirty, black convertible BMW. Vanity plates on the front and back read, *RTNBYEB:* "Written By Ellen Barrett." She switched off the car radio and screeched out of the parking lot, intent only on getting home.

"Please let him live," she whispered. "Please, God."

When Ellen pulled into the driveway of the two-story house she and Mike owned near the beach, he was waiting on the porch.

Even masked with deep concern, her husband's face was strikingly handsome. Marked by masculine angles and high cheekbones, punctuated with piercing pale blue eyes, Mike Miller's face looked like it belonged in a high-fashion advertisement or a cologne commercial. For some reason it seemed unfair that he should look virile and healthy when her father was fighting for his life eighteen hundred miles away.

"I'm sorry." He met her halfway down the sidewalk and nervously pulled her close, stroking her hair. "I've been praying."

Ellen remained stiff, unwilling to be comforted. Mike had never known how to deal with the emotional moments in their marriage, and she didn't want him practicing at a time like this. She refused to allow herself to break down. Her father was sick, but he was alive.

There would be time for tears later.

She pulled away. "I need to get inside and call."

Mike followed lamely behind her, and as they entered the house he sat on the couch and buried himself in a magazine. As usual, he would let her take care of making the call. Ellen clenched her teeth, but she couldn't exactly blame Mike. Her father, John Edward Barrett, was fifty-four that year and had undergone triple-bypass surgery the previous summer. Since then he had ignored doctors' warnings and continued to smoke three packs of unfiltered Camels a day. He ate eggs and buttered toast for breakfast, juicy beef hot dogs for lunch, and pizza for dinner. It was fairly certain the news would not be good.

Ellen kicked off her heels and picked up the cordless phone, collapsing in a cross-legged heap on the floor as she studied the message Mike had taken. As quickly as her fingers could move she punched in the numbers for Northern Michigan Hospital in Petoskey.

"John Barrett's room, please." She dug her elbows into her knees and rested her forehead in her free hand.

"Nurse's station," a woman announced.

"Yes, John Barrett's room."

"Who's calling?"

"This is his daughter, Ellen. May I speak with him please?"

"Just a minute, ma'am. Let me get your mother."

Ellen waited, praying against all odds that she was wrong, that the news would be good. Her father's health was poor but he had never suffered a heart attack. There was a chance he might recover completely if he had made it to the hospital in time.

"Ellen?" Her mother's voice was raspy and tired, and Ellen could tell she'd been crying.

"Mother, is he okay?"

"No." A single sob escaped from her mother and for a moment she was unable to continue. Ellen waited breathlessly. "He didn't make it, honey. I'm so sorry."

Ellen could feel the floor drop away from beneath her. She refused to believe it. "No, Mom, that can't be true. People live through heart attacks all the time. He was—"

"Not this time," her mother cut in. "He died four hours ago. Ellen, he's gone."

"No! Mom, please! He…he can't be gone."

"I'm sorry, honey. He loved you so much. You know that."

Ellen was silent as the truth coursed through her veins, searing her, weighing her down. Her father was dead. "Ellen?"

"Mom—" her voice was barely a whisper—"what are we going to do?"

"We're going to survive and we're still going to be a family."

Ellen nodded and fought a wave of anxiety. "Are you by yourself?"

"No, Megan and Aaron are here with me, and Amy's on the way. I've called Jane. She's coming out Sunday afternoon."

"How are they handling it?"

"Not well. Especially Aaron. He hasn't said a word since it happened."

A thousand memories crowded out Ellen's ability to speak, and she realized there was a lump in her throat. Her father was gone, and she hadn't gotten to say good-bye. Certainly Aaron, her only brother, would be devastated. The others, too. *He's in heaven. He's still alive, just happier now.*

Ellen thought about the last time she'd talked with her father, only a few days earlier. He had sounded fine. There had been no warning that it was the last time she'd ever talk to him. She called him often, keeping him up-to-date on her latest assignments. He had always been interested in the little-known details and behind-the-scenes anecdotes that went into her reporting. Now he was gone, and Ellen wondered if she would suffocate from the shock.

"Are you okay, honey?"

Her mother's strained question pulled her back. "Mom, what happened?"

"Well," her mother drew a ragged breath. "He wasn't feeling well when he woke up this morning, and he took a long nap in his chair until about one o'clock. Then he got up and had something to eat. He was walking back to take a shower when he collapsed in the hallway."

Ellen closed her eyes, picturing the familiar house, its aging dark brown carpet and narrow hallways.

"He didn't have a chance. We lost him before the paramedics arrived."

Ellen was quiet for a moment. "When do you want me home, Mom? When's the funeral?"

"Oh, honey, I don't know. I guess we'll have the funeral next Saturday. That's when your father's sister can get here from California. I don't know, it's all happening so fast." Her mom's voice cracked and she began to cry. "I guess none of us should be surprised, but it doesn't make it any easier."

Hearing her mother cry triggered something in Ellen and she felt her eyes well up with tears. Her parents had been married thirty-two years. How did one let go of something like that?

"Mom, you sure you're all right? You shouldn't be alone."

"I'm okay and I'm not alone. Listen, why don't you try to get here Sunday. Jane's plane is coming in around noon at Detroit Metro. If you and Mike could get here about the same time you could all ride up to the house together. Then we'd have a week to take care of everything."

"Okay. I'll make the plans and call you back. Where will you be?"

"At the house. I've already signed the death certificate so there isn't much else I can do here." Her mother sobbed softly and struggled to speak. "Dear God, Ellen. How on earth am I going to get through life without him?"

Ellen had no answers. She was too busy asking herself the same question.

She finished talking with her mother and then moved into the next room. A shaky sigh escaped her and she stared at Mike. His long body was stretched out on the couch, his feet dangling over onto the floor. He had fallen asleep, still dressed in his designer shirt and tie, the magazine clutched in one hand. She wiped her tears and wondered why she was angry with him.

"Mike." The word came out flat, cool.

He stirred and instantly sat up, wiping a trace of saliva from the corner of his mouth and trying to look awake. "Sorry, honey. What happened? How is he?"

Ellen sat down in a chair across from him and leaned back, staring at the plant shelves that lined the high walls of their living room.

"He's dead. Died before the paramedics arrived."

Mike leaned back and sighed. "Ellen, I'm sorry." He loosened his tie. "Come here."

She paused a moment. Mike had never made an effort to be close to her father, and now that he was gone, she was angry with Mike for not trying harder. He didn't understand what she had just lost—and with all her being she wanted to refuse his comfort.

Instead, she fell slowly to her knees and crawled the few steps that separated them. Then she dropped her head in his lap and gave way to the despair that gripped her.

"Why didn't he take better care of himself?" Her anger brought fresh tears, and they spilled from her eyes. "It makes me so *mad* at him."

Mike stroked her hair and said nothing. Finally, Ellen wiped her eyes and looked wearily up at him. He was her husband, and she believed God had brought him into her life. She loved Mike whatever his shortcomings, but she did not always feel loved by him. He rarely made an effort on her behalf—especially where her family was concerned. Now his attempts to ease her grief seemed too little, too late.

"My mom wants us to be there Sunday afternoon." She leaned up and away from him. "That's when Jane's coming in. The funeral will be later that week, Saturday morning."

"A week from now?" He sounded incredulous.

Ellen blinked twice. "Yes. That's the soonest Aunt Betsy can get there. Is that a problem?"

She saw Mike's hesitation, watched his eyes look away from her, as though he were trying to think of the right way to say something he knew she wasn't going to like.

"Honey," he started, shaking his head, "I've got a baseball game to cover that Saturday. I don't know how I can find a replacement on such short notice."

There was more to it than that, Ellen was sure. She knew Mike wasn't comfortable at funerals, knew he wouldn't be looking forward to spending a week at her parents' house in Petoskey. She loved her family, but she was aware that they had their problems…that there would be bickering even as everyone pretended to get along.…

Still, the least he could do was be there for her. "A baseball game?"

"Honey, maybe it'd be better if you went by yourself." He searched her face for a reaction. "I could always join you later when I can get away."

She burned with anger and she didn't even try to hide it. Drawing herself up onto her knees, she stared at him. "No, that *wouldn't* be better, Mike." Her voice was even and measured, a study in controlled fury.

"I have a game Saturday. Come on, Ellen, you know how the producers are about last-minute changes."

"Wait a minute. I don't believe what I'm hearing." Ellen's temper blazed. "This isn't some friend's wedding or a class reunion where you can back out and blame it on your work. My father is *dead.* My mother wants us both to come out for the week. Can't you understand that?"

"I'm not married to your mother." Mike looked like he regretted the words as soon as he said them, but it was too late.

Ellen's mouth dropped open. "Fine. *I* want us both there. Okay?"

"Ellen, you know I can't take a week off without any notice. Work is a fact of life." He paused. "Besides, I don't like funerals. I never know how to act."

Ellen's eyes grew wide, full of disbelief and accusation.

He cleared his throat before she could speak. "You'll have your family there," he insisted. "It's not like you'll be all by yourself." Mike shook his head. "Oh, forget it! You don't understand."

"You don't like funerals!" Ellen stood up and paced the floor. "No kidding, Mike—" She stopped and stared at him. "Me, neither. I don't like *death,* for that matter. But my dad is dead, and I need you there. So don't tell me I don't understand!"

"Don't yell at me. I don't deserve that."

"*What?* I deserve a husband who has complained about attending social events with me since we got married? A husband who doesn't want to go with me to my own father's funeral?"

"It's not that I don't want to go, Ellen. I told you I can't get away. Not on such short notice."

"What if it was *you* who died, Mike? I bet the station could get by somehow without folding."

She went to slam the cordless phone back onto the receiver.

She was so furious she was shaking. She turned to face him, and when she spoke, even she heard the hatred in her voice. "What is it, Mike? Some ditzy little news anchor have your attention?"

He stood up, recoiling as if he'd been slapped.

"That's unfair."

"Is it?" Her voice was still angry, but softer now. "Is it really, Mike? My dad dies and you won't take one lousy week off work for me? What am I supposed to think?"

Mike looked past her then and reached toward the fireplace mantel for his car keys.

"I don't know what you're supposed to think," he said, pausing by the front door.

Ellen was speechless.

"Listen," Mike's voice was calmer as he continued. "I'm sorry about your dad. I loved him, too."

"Oh, don't give me that! Not now. You never even knew him, Mike. You never *tried* to know him. And you certainly didn't love him. Not enough to take me to his funeral, anyway." She snorted sarcastically. "I get the worst news of my entire life, and *you* can't think of anyone but yourself. What's happened to you, Mike? You're supposed to be a *Christian,* remember? The spiritual leader of the household?"

Mike shook his head. "Oh, don't throw that in my face. Not this time. Besides, I don't exactly see you rushing to the Bible for comfort."

"I'm not talking about comparing my walk with yours. I'm talking about you and me. You're supposed to love me like Christ loved the church, give up everything for me. But not you, no sir. You won't even take a week off work for me. What kind of Christian love is that?"

Mike's shoulders sagged and he sighed loudly, dramatically.

"Ellen, I won't let you guilt me into going with you to Petoskey when I have work here in Miami. I could meet you down there the day before the funeral, but I can't possibly get a whole week off with no notice."

"Forget it, Mike." She turned her back to him.

"Look at me, Ellen," he demanded.

She whirled around and put a hand on her hip. "What?"

"You obviously need time to accept the facts." Mike's voice was measured and forced. "Your dad's dead. Nothing I can do can bring him back. You have family and friends in Petoskey, and you don't need me tagging along for a week of funeral preparations. I can probably get out there for the funeral. But that's all. Otherwise the topic's closed."

"Fly out for one day? I need you all week." Her icy anger melted and she began sobbing softly as she turned away from him again. "Forget it. I don't want you there."

Mike was silent, then his voice came from behind her, cold and hurt. "Fine. I won't go at all." He strode across the room, and flung open the door.

"Jerk!" she shouted, glancing at him over her shoulder so that their eyes met for an angry moment. Then he stepped outside and slammed the door.

She stood frozen in place, studying the door and relishing the distraction of her renewed anger. At that moment it seemed Mike had always been like this, and she cursed herself for marrying him.

"Jerk!" She said it louder this time, even though no one was there to hear her.

She marched across the living room, picked up the telephone, and sat down at the kitchen table. She dialed the *Miami Times,* and in a voice that was almost unrecognizable, she told Ron Barkley that her father had died.

"I'll need a week, Ron."

"Listen, I'm sorry, Barrett." Barkley's voice was soft. "Call us if you need more time."

She hung up and dialed the airline, scribbling flight numbers on a pad of paper and making reservations to fly to Detroit without Mike. When she was finished, she folded her arms on the kitchen table, laid her head down, and sobbed until she thought her heart would break.

Of course she had seen it coming. Her father had heart disease and diabetes, and if high blood pressure and excess weight were any indication, he should have died more than a decade ago. But that didn't make his death any less painful.

"So, this is it, huh, Dad?" she whispered, her eyes closed. "Time to say good-bye."

She silently summoned a strength she had not known she possessed, one she would certainly have to draw on in the days to come. She would go home and face her four younger siblings, all of whom had been unable to get along for years. She would help her mother pick out a casket and plan a service. Then she would see that her father was buried. She would remember the past, walk through it, relive it, and try her best to put it behind her.

"God, help me get through it." But the whispered words felt foreign, as if praying was something she had forgotten how to do.

She sighed and wiped her eyes. How could he be gone, the father who had shared so much of her life? How could she bury the one person who had always believed in her? He was the man who had attended football games with her, teaching her the rules of play even after she'd been hired as a sportswriter for the *Detroit Gazette.* There was nothing he would not have done for her, and now she would have to learn to live without him.

Never mind about Mike. She would be on a plane soon enough and then she would have one week before she would see him again. Meanwhile, she had a lot more to think about than what was wrong between the two of them.

Ellen lowered her head back down onto her arms. There had been a time when she thought the world revolved around Mike Miller, a time when she couldn't have imagined a scene like the one that had just taken place. Back when they spent Saturday mornings laughing at *I Love Lucy* reruns and Sunday mornings at church. But somewhere along the path of deadlines and breaking stories and babies that would never be, something had changed.

She tried to think back to the beginning, to the days when she and Mike couldn't stand to be away from each other. Images drifted through her mind.... Mike bringing her breakfast in bed on their first anniversary and the two of them giggling for hours because the eggs were rubbery and the toast like cardboard.... The birthday when she left work to find her BMW plastered with flowers and balloons, a task that had cost Mike a double lunch break....

It felt good to remember those things—and it forced her to think of something other than her father. The memories raced through her mind like a highlight film and, despite herself, the corners of her mouth lifted as she remembered.

Mike Miller was handsome and intelligent, a Christian man with morals and a sense of humor. He had completely swept her off her feet. But too many times since then he had left her alone when she needed him. If he could let her face the week ahead by herself, then what strength did their marriage have?

Ellen dried her cheeks with the backs of her hands. She would go back to beautiful Petoskey, to the shores of Little Traverse Bay along Lake Michigan, to her childhood home. She would say good-bye to her father, then she would come back to Miami and see if there was still a heartbeat in her marriage… or if that, too, had grown ill and died.

Ellen sighed. Every muscle in her body ached. She barely had the energy even to stand. Rising from the chair, she stretched and headed toward her bedroom. She peeled off her clothes, leaving them scattered about the floor, and slipped into a long T-shirt. Then she pulled back the covers and slid between the cool sheets.

She did not often dream and that night was no exception. But in the hours before she finally drifted to sleep, she found herself remembering a time when her father was still very much alive. A time when she and Mike were just starting out… when Mike had loved her completely and had done something no one else had been able to do.

He made her forget about Jake Sadler.

As she closed her eyes, she found herself there, immersed in the vivid memories of a time that would never be again.

2

For as long as she could remember, Ellen Barrett had known what she wanted to be when she grew up. She was not like other little girls who talked of being princesses or famous ice-skaters. Ellen was a writer. It was something that grew from her heart and worked its way through her very being.

As a child Ellen spent hours writing short stories and poetry. Her mother took her for a silly dreamer, but Ellen was nothing of the sort. She was merely a single-minded young girl honing a skill she was certain to draw from in years to come.

When she was ten years old, Ellen first understood her need to place on paper all that already existed in her heart. It was then that she made her decision. One day she would write for the *Detroit Gazette*.

The *Gazette* was the biggest newspaper in Michigan, and after high school, when Ellen began plotting her way toward a journalism degree, it was with the sole purpose of one day being employed by the *Gazette*. A position on staff would mean living in a small apartment by herself, four hours away from her family and the small town she loved. But Ellen wanted a staff position desperately. She would have lived on the moon if it meant working at the *Gazette*.

In 1990, she was in her final semester at the University of Michigan when she was selected to do an internship for the *Gazette*. She was a Christian by then, and many of her childhood plans had undergone significant changes—but not the dream of working for the *Gazette*. From the beginning she saw the internship as an answer to prayer.

"Ms. Barrett," the sports editor said when he called her at her dormitory that January. "We've reviewed your application and selected you as one of our sports interns for the coming semester."

"Sports," she repeated blankly. She had requested an internship in the news department, but her hesitation lasted only a moment. "Fantastic. That'll be perfect. What will I be doing?"

"You'll be taking scores over the phone several nights a week. Of course, you'll need a complete understanding of most of the major spring sports. Baseball, track, softball, volleyball, wrestling, tennis, swimming. And the city league sports, bowling and high-pitch softball. That kind of thing."

He droned on about the details. The job involved taking hundreds of scores and statistics from local sporting events and turning them into brief copy for the scorecard in the back of the sports section.

"Sound okay to you?"

Ellen thought quickly. She didn't know the first thing about the rules of sports. She wasn't even sure she knew how to keep score. "Definitely," she said before she could stop herself. "No problem. When do I start?"

"Next week. Stop by the office and pick up your schedule. You can fill out the paperwork then."

When Ellen hung up the phone, she let out a shriek so loud it brought students from several rooms away rushing to see what the problem was.

"I got the internship! I can't believe it! I'm on staff at the *Gazette!*"

The other students rolled their eyes and returned to their business, unaware of the significance of the moment. Within two minutes Ellen was on the phone with her father.

"Way to go, Ellen! That's my girl! I knew you could do it, honey." Ellen could see his smile as clearly as if he were standing in front of her. "This is only the beginning."

"There's one small problem, Daddy. I've been assigned to the sports department."

"Sports?" John Barrett laughed out loud. "Honey, you wouldn't recognize the difference between a ball and a strike. Why would they put you in sports?"

"My clip file included a few sports features I did. Remember?"

"You don't need to know sports to write about the Michigan quarterback's asthma condition. Didn't they ask you if you'd ever covered a game?"

"They asked me if I understood the games."

"What did you say?"

"I said yes."

"Oh, honey," John muttered. "When do you start?"

"Next week. But I don't have classes until then. I could get time off from the restaurant and I was thinking, maybe…"

"Get in your car and get here as soon as you can. We haven't had snow in a while so at least the roads are clear."

Her father's voice was kind and understanding. He was a professor at North Central Community College in Petoskey and spring classes didn't start for another two weeks. "I'll give you a crash course on everything you'll need to know. Maybe between the two of us we can fool 'em."

Ellen broke into a smile. "Thanks, Daddy. I'll be there in time for dinner. One thing though." She paused. "If Jake calls, don't tell him I'm coming up. I don't want to talk to him."

"I won't say a word, but he's got it bad for you, Ellen. I'll never understand you two."

"I don't want to talk about it."

She and Jake had dated for six years. But they had been broken up for ten months and the subject was closed.

"Okay, but you're breaking his heart." Her father sighed dramatically. "I'm sure you have your reasons."

I do, Ellen had thought. *Jake Sadler broke my heart first.* "It's nothing I want to get into. Just don't tell him, okay?"

"Okay, okay. Get your things together and get down here. I'll have Mom fix something special for dinner."

The week flew by in a blur of guidelines and rules and scoring methods. She memorized player positions, team violations, and rules of play. She learned the difference between the higharc and windmill softball pitches and that a slider was a type of baseball pitch, not to be confused with sliding into base. There were the spikes and sets and digs in volleyball, and whereas baseball gave its batters three strikes to get a hit, volleyball allowed three hits to form a play. She learned about the pin in wrestling, the splits in swimming, and the triple jump in track until finally the rules and terminology didn't seem quite so foreign.

Once in a while they'd be working and the phone would ring. Her mother would answer it.

"Just a minute, Jake," she'd say. Then in a whispered voice, "Ellen, it's Jake. He talked to your roommate and he knows you're here."

Ellen would look up from her pages of sports notes and shake her head. "Tell him I'm out."

Then she and her father would exchange a glance and Ellen would direct their conversation back to sports. She hated to lie, but where Jake Sadler was concerned, the greater evil would have been giving in to her feelings and seeing him. Jake was the only boy she had ever loved and now she could never, ever see him again. There was too much at stake. *My life depends on it. My spiritual life.*

"I'm sorry, Jake," her mother would say. "Yes, we're all doing fine. Yes. Well, I'll certainly tell her you called."

At week's end Ellen was certain she knew at least enough about sports to take phone scores at the *Detroit Gazette.* Her father had been so thorough that she even had time to spend with her sisters and brother.

There were long talks with nineteen-year-old Megan about her troublesome boyfriend, and time spent helping Amy with her homework. Amy was seventeen that year, the quietest of the Barrett siblings, and Ellen enjoyed her company.

On the last day of her visit, Ellen, Amy, and sixteen-year-old Aaron, the only boy among them, played Password until they were laughing so hard they had to quit. Later Jane stopped by and the seven Barretts gathered round the worn oak dinner table as they had done every night before Ellen moved away.

Jane was twenty-one then, two years younger than Ellen. Growing up, the two had been inseparable, but in recent years they had grown strangely distant. Ellen searched for something that would explain the change in their relationship, but there seemed to be no answer. *When I finish school,* she told herself that night after Jane left, *everything will be like it was before.*

The next morning she leaned up and kissed her father on the cheek. It was time to get back to the city. "Thanks, Daddy." Their eyes met and held for a moment.

"Ah, honey." He pulled her into a hug. "You're so grown up now. I can't believe this is your last semester."

"Yeah, I might even pass, thanks to you." Her eyes twinkled as she pulled away and grinned at him.

"It'll be our little secret. Deal?"

"Deal!" Ellen's eyes grew watery. "I love you, Daddy."

"I love you too, honey. Let me know how it goes."

"Ellen?" Her mother had called from the other side of the house. She'd been packing Ellen a sack lunch for her trip back to Ann Arbor and was a blur of motion, moving across the kitchen, reaching into the refrigerator, then up into the cupboards and back to the refrigerator again.

"Yes, Mother?"

"Now, Ellen, remember to eat these sandwiches in the car while you're driving," she said in a pleasant, breathless voice loud enough to reach across the house. "You don't want to pull off I-75 and risk getting abducted by some stranger at a backwoods gas station."

"Yes, Mother," Ellen said obediently, raising her voice so her mother could hear her.

"And whatever you do, be sure to fill that car of yours with gasoline before you leave Petoskey. You should probably stop at Mr. Gardner's station, right on the way out of town. You remember Mr. Gardner's station, don't you, dear?"

"Yes, Mother."

"He's been asking about you because he wants to send his son, Travis, to U of M next year. He'd love to see you, maybe hear a little bit about campus life and all. Could you do that for me, dear?"

"Yes, Mother."

"You know, that Travis of his is certainly a smart one. He won't have any trouble getting into U of M if you ask me. Of course Travis always did have a secret crush on you, Ellen. He was always…"

She continued on. Ellen and her father exchanged a conspiratorial grin and he hugged her once more.

"Go get 'em, honey. You want to know something?"

"What?"

"You're going to be a great writer one day."

Ellen nodded, too choked up to speak.

Her mother rounded the corner with the lunch sack and presented it to Ellen as she caught her breath.

"Don't forget what I said, dear." She leaned over and pecked Ellen quickly on the cheek. "Drive safely and don't take any chances in those small towns along the way. And that sports department is bound to be full of men. I guess there's nothing we can do about that. But don't you let them corrupt you. You're a good girl, Ellen. I understand that this is an important break for you, but I'm concerned all the same. I don't care what the modern school thinks of such things. A sports department is no place for a young lady, so watch yourself and be careful."

"Okay, Diane, okay," Ellen's father said gently. He placed his arm around his wife and pulled her toward him. "Let the poor girl get on the road or she'll never make it back before dark."

Five minutes later Ellen was on her way. Her first night shift at the *Gazette* was two days later and suddenly she was busier than she'd ever been in her life. Her hours were filled with senior level courses, labs and lectures and on-campus reporting. She would finish her course work, grab an apple and a bagel, and fly out the door for the *Gazette*. The days became weeks, and before Ellen realized it the semester was half over.

Once in a while she was allowed to forgo phone duty and cover a high school game in person. But most games were played on the weekend and Ellen's Friday and Saturday nights were spent at the *Gazette,* manning the phones in the sports department. The paper had a system whereby coaches would call in their scores when the games were finished. Ellen took scores from dozens of coaches of sports ranging from track to T-ball, bowling to baseball.

The paper received hundreds of calls each weekend and interns worked the phones until midnight. No exceptions. Ellen was thankful for the work because it left her little time to think of Jake.

"*Gazette* Sports, what team are you reporting?" Ellen would say as she answered the phone and prepared her fingers for action. Then she would cradle the receiver against her shoulder while her fingers flew across the keyboard, transferring the details as accurately as possible into the computer. When the call was finished she would organize the information and file it to the sports desk.

"*Gazette* Sports, what team are you reporting?" The calls continued through the night.

The questions became part of a formula. Who was the winner, what was the score, where was the contest played, why was the game important, when would the teams play again, and how did the winning team manage to win. Space was tight, and details beyond that had no chance of making the paper.

A few interns complained about being used by the paper. There was no pay, no bylines, and no promise of promotion.

The hours were long, and Ellen's neck grew stiff while she typed in details about park league T-ball games and high school volleyball matches.

She wouldn't have traded a minute of it.

She had waited tables in Petoskey and then in Ann Arbor for five long years while she earned her journalism degree. Now she was working for the *Gazette. Staff mem-*

ber, her employee badge said. Ellen took the words to heart.

As the semester drew to an end the *Gazette's* assistant managing editor John Dower spoke to Ellen's advanced news writing class. Dower was in charge of the news desk. He was pompous and condescending and had all the compassion of a frustrated drill sergeant. Ellen watched him size up the class of seniors and was silently thankful she worked in the sports department.

"Right now all of you are sitting there thinking you're hotshot reporters about to take the world of journalism by storm." The editor sneered, pacing before the class of fifty senior journalism students. "You think you'll breeze out of here with your University of Michigan degree and waltz your way on to the staff of some big paper like the *Gazette.*"

He stopped and stared at them. "You're wrong. Let me tell you how it's going to be." He began pacing again. "When you leave here you'll move off to a small-town paper, which, if you're lucky, might publish three times a week. You'll work every department, every beat, and make half of what it costs to survive." He stopped and smiled sardonically. "You'll do that for five years before anyone at the *Gazette* will even consider bringing you in for an interview. Any questions?"

Only one student in the room dared to raise a hand.

"Does that apply to interns at the *Gazette?*" Ellen asked.

The editor leveled his gaze in her direction and vaguely recognized her from the batch of interns currently doing time at the paper. "It *especially* applies to interns at the *Gazette.*"

Ellen began brainstorming ways to be more valuable to the *Gazette* staff. Instead of asking only the routine questions when scores came in, she asked a few more, searching for news worthy of more than merely a box score. She hit pay dirt a week later, four hours into a Friday night shift.

She was filing the information from the previous call when a score came in from a young boy named Chin Lee wishing to report the results of a junior-high basketball tournament. As Chin Lee rattled off the score, Ellen saw that the boy played for a school located in a neglected part of town. Most of the players had Asian names. *Strange. Usually the coach calls in.*

Ellen took down the usual information and then paused a moment. "Who's your coach, Chin?"

The boy was quiet a moment. "Uh, well, we don't have a coach. Is that okay?"

Bells went off in Ellen's head.

"Sure, but who works with your team, who makes up the plays for you?"

Chin hesitated. "We, uh, we get together a few times a week and watch tapes of the Los Angeles Lakers. We see their plays and we learn them. Then we use them in games."

Twenty minutes later Ellen had the phone numbers of the other players on Chin's team and enough information to write a magazine article on the boys.

She stood up from her desk and located the sports editor, Steve Simons.

"What is it, Ellen?" He looked up from his computer screen.

Ellen cleared her throat and proceeded to tell him. Three hours later she had written her first feature story for the *Gazette*. Simons told Ellen it would probably run in Sunday's paper.

On Saturday night Ellen could barely sleep. It was like being a little girl, waiting for Santa Claus to come. Only this time he rode a bicycle and his knapsack carried nothing but a stack of newspapers. The moment she heard the paper smack against the sidewalk outside her dormitory, Ellen rushed outside and tore it open. What she saw made her gasp aloud.

The *Gazette* had played her story on the front page.

After that there were other stories. A ninety-year-old runner attempting a final race in memory of her recently deceased husband; a Little League coach who had taken three boys from his son's team into his home when their parents turned out to be drug dealers. The list grew.

Two weeks before graduation Ellen learned of an entry-level opening in the sports department at the *Gazette*.

"They told us we'd need more experience, but I'm going to go for it, Daddy," Ellen told her father that night on the telephone. "Think I have a chance?"

"Are you kidding, honey? They're probably hoping you'll ask for an interview. Otherwise they might lose you to the competition."

"Pray for me, will you?"

She knew the request would make her dad smile. He had raised them in the Catholic church, and at first when Ellen started attending a Protestant church he had been discouraged, disappointed in her decision. But he was used to the idea now and seemed to enjoy her open discussion of prayer.

"I'll pray, honey. Now get back to school and get that job."

The interview came one week before graduation. Ellen bought a new skirt and jacket for the occasion and then worried that she was overdressed. She was the picture of professionalism as she walked up the marble steps and went inside, but she was assailed by doubts. *I'm too young...I don't have enough experience...They don't want a woman sportswriter...I should turn around and go home...Who am I kidding?*

She made her way through the newsroom and into the sports department just as she remembered the words John Dower had spoken to her senior class: *"When you leave here you'll move off to a small-town paper, which, if you're lucky, might publish three times a week. You'll work every department, every beat, and make half of what it costs to survive. You'll do that for five years before anyone at the* Gazette *will even consider bringing you in for an interview."*

Ellen entered the sports editor's office and the first person she saw was John Dower. He smiled kindly and motioned for Ellen to sit down. There was no mention of her inexperience.

An hour later she left with her first job offer.

She called her parents with the news.

"I don't know, Ellen," her mother said, her voice filled with concern. "I'll worry about you out late at night covering sports games in a city like Detroit. Working with all those men. You'll have to be so careful, dear. Are there any other women in the department?"

"No, but I've made a lot of good friends, Mom. I'll be fine."

"I just wonder if it's smart for a young lady to be involved in a job surrounded by men."

Then her father got on the line. "Honey, I knew you could do it!" He was bursting with pride. "Aaron and the girls will be so happy when they hear about this."

"I'll be covering high school sports for a while, but that's fine with me. Can you believe it, Dad? Me? A full-time staff reporter for the *Gazette?*"

"It's what you've always wanted, honey."

"As far back as I can remember."

"Before you know it you'll be covering U of M games. Then I'll be down every week."

Ellen laughed. The Barretts had lived in Ann Arbor fifteen years earlier and her father was fanatical about Wolverine football. "So that's why you taught me all that stuff about sports."

"You better believe it. I'll expect sideline passes to your first U of M assignment."

Graduation came and went, and Ellen began working sixty-hour weeks. She covered more high school sports than she thought possible. Newspaper copy was measured in column inches, and most of Ellen's assignments carried a maximum length of twelve inches. But there were times when she was given more in-depth projects, feature pieces on high school coaches and star prep players.

Two months passed. Ellen found a simple, one-bedroom apartment five minutes from the office and bought a few meager furnishings. Occasionally she ate a late meal with the sports staff after deadline on Friday nights, staying out until long after midnight swapping anecdotes and unwinding after an evening of tight deadlines.

Now and then she was asked out by one of her coworkers, but Ellen was adamantly opposed to the idea. There were nineteen writers and a dozen part-time reporters working for the *Gazette* sports section. As the only woman among them, Ellen would not consider being anything less than professional in their midst.

She spent most of her free time on the telephone with her parents and her sisters. They talked about a hundred different things from boyfriends to schoolwork to part-time jobs, but they respected Ellen's wishes and none of them ever mentioned Jake Sadler.

One day Simons asked to see Ellen in his office. He was an intelligent man in his late fifties with two young grandchildren. Ellen thought he was the kindest editor at the paper.

"The Wolverines have their first scrimmage of the season this Saturday," he said. "We want you there."

Ellen was stunned.

"We'll have a senior writer cover the game, but we'd like to try you on a few U of M sports features and see how you do." He grinned. "Congratulations, Ellen."

The day before the game she was given her press credentials. Ellen stared at them and remembered the long hours taking scores over the phone. She was twenty-three and she had arrived.

Her assignment was a simple one. Interview the offensive coordinator and determine the Wolverines' approach for the coming season. They had a freshman quarterback known throughout the country for his passing ability. Would Michigan stick to its ground game with such a talented athlete leading the offense? Ellen's story would answer that question and reveal the personal side of the coach.

Game time was ten o'clock Saturday morning, and Ellen's apartment was thirty miles east of the stadium. She planned to be there at seven, eat breakfast somewhere off campus, and go over her list of questions before arriving at the stadium at nine. That gave her fifteen minutes before her interview with the coach.

Ellen was aware that this would be her first time to work an event alongside male sportswriters who were far more accomplished than she. Certainly the broadcast journalists would be there. Joe Stevens from WGRT, a grizzled veteran with years of sports experience, and Mike Miller from WCBS, a handsome newcomer who had played tight end for Michigan before suffering a career-ending knee injury. Mike was also actively involved with a Christian Athletes' Fellowship and helped out at the local Children's Hospital. He had a promising career in broadcasting, and Ellen admired his work.

She prayed she could earn their respect and come across confident and capable. She planned to work among them often.

The morning began badly. She overslept and couldn't decide what to wear. She finally pulled onto Interstate 94 at 6:45, telling herself she would skip the leisurely breakfast and stop for fast food in Ann Arbor. Half an hour later she was minutes from the stadium, driving along State Street looking for a place to stop.

At the intersection of State and Stadium Way she stopped at a red light and glanced at the seat beside her to check how much cash she had. But her purse wasn't there. *Strange.* She looked nervously up at the light. Still red. She scanned the backseat of her four-door compact and again found nothing.

At that moment the white van in front of her began to move. *Green light.* She pressed her foot onto the accelerator and scanned the floor of her car once more, desperately hoping to find her purse.

The crash came almost immediately. She jolted up against the steering wheel and then back against her car's headrest.

"Green means go, buddy," she mumbled. Then she looked up at the light and felt her heart sink. It was flashing red. The van in front of her had moved forward only one car-length. She had presumed the light was green and that it was moving on through the intersection.

The van turned slowly into a gas station, and Ellen spied the letters on the side of the vehicle. WCBS.

Oh no. Ellen's heart sank. *They're on the way to the game. Please God, don't let Mike Miller be inside.*

She followed the van into the station and killed the engine just as two men stepped out. One of them was Mike Miller.

Ellen forced herself to get out of the car, furious with herself and the way her face was blushing a deep red.

"I'm so sorry! I thought the light was green and then you stopped and I guess I just didn't see it coming. I mean I've been down this street a hundred times and I've never seen that light flashing red before."

Great. I sound like my mother.

While she spoke, the driver of the van checked out his bumper and brushed off a few chips of paint that had come from the front of Ellen's car. Meanwhile Mike moved closer to Ellen. He seemed to be staring at her shirt and she finally grew flustered.

"Do you mind if I ask what you're looking at?"

Mike straightened and Ellen saw that he was easily six-foot-three. He grinned at her—and for the first time in Ellen's life someone other than Jake Sadler made her heart skip a beat.

"Sorry, miss," Mike said. "It's just, well..." He pointed toward her blouse and Ellen followed his gaze. The buttons were fitted into the wrong holes all the way down so that the left side of her rayon blouse hung four inches lower than the right.

Ellen quickly shoved the longer piece of rayon into her slacks. As she did, she bared a layer of white lace that ran along the top of her camisole. Mike raised an eyebrow and smothered a smile.

"Oh!" Frustrated at herself, Ellen yanked the blouse back into place and folded her arms over the section that was now, once again, hanging outside of her slacks.

"In a hurry this morning?"

"Yes, in fact, I am." Ellen was totally flustered and she prayed neither of them would figure out who she was. Perhaps Mike wouldn't see her at the game. With any luck he'd be transferred to a different department or hired by another city.

The driver of the van smiled in her direction. "No harm done, ma'am. Looks like you've got a pretty good dent, but nothing you can't drive with."

"I have my insurance information if you'd like it." She did her best to ignore Mike Miller's partially concealed grin.

"Sure," the driver said. "Never a bad idea after a fender bender."

Ellen opened her car door and searched frantically for her purse. It contained her insurance card, her driver's license, and her press credentials. Suddenly she knew with sinking certainty that it was back at her apartment.

She pulled out of the car slowly and put her hands on her hips, exposing her uneven blouse once more. "I'm sorry. I can't seem to find my purse. It has everything, all my information."

The driver of the van nodded and Mike tried to contain a chuckle.

"No problem. Everything's okay on our end, right, Mike?" Mike cleared his throat and tried to look serious. "Well, my neck's a little sore…" He rubbed his hand along the base of his skull. He wore leather loafers, dark wool slacks, and a starched white button down which contrasted sharply with his paisley silk tie. He was the picture of cool confidence.

Ellen stared at him beseechingly.

He caught her glance and smiled warmly. "No, I'm just kidding. But you better retrace your steps and see if you can find your purse. That could be a real disaster."

Everyone laughed, though Ellen's sounded a bit hollow, and the men bid her farewell as they climbed into their van. Ellen watched them disappear, then quickly got into her car and headed back toward Detroit.

She had ninety minutes until her appointment with the coach.

Two hours later, still breathless from the morning's events, she walked out of the offensive coordinator's office. She did not have a front-page story, but she had enough information to pull a feature together. The stairs to the press box seemed to go on forever and she was weary by the time she located her seat. She filed her notes and began checking her purse for a pencil.

"I see you found it."

Ellen looked up and found herself staring into Mike Miller's teasing blue eyes. Seating assignments for members of the press were made long before game time, and he was seated right next to her.

Ellen sighed and dropped her head in her hands. "Why can't this day end?"

"Hey, why didn't you say you worked for the *Gazette?*"

Ellen peered at him through the spaces between her fingers. "I was hoping once I fixed my buttons you might not recognize me."

Mike laughed. For the rest of the game he teased and talked with her, and the morning flew by. She had expected him to be ruthless—condescending and unforgiving of the mistakes she'd made earlier in the day. Instead he was helpful. He treated her with respect and consideration and was careful to avoid discussing the accident.

When the game was over Ellen gathered her things. "Guess I'll see you next week." She smiled at him.

"Hey, Ellen, you mind if I get your phone number?"

Ellen felt the heat flood her cheeks. "Oh, the accident. Right. I've got my insurance information here somewhere." She began digging through her purse, suddenly nervous. "I have insurance, really, I do. I just didn't have my purse with me. But I guess you know that, don't you?"

Mike placed his hand gently on her arm so that she stopped talking and looked up at him. He had the palest blue eyes she'd ever seen.

"I don't want your insurance information, Ellen. I asked for your phone number." His smile warmed her all the way down to her toes. "I was hoping you might have dinner with me sometime…"

The memory of that smile tugged at Ellen's weary heart, and she rolled over in bed, squeezing her eyes tight against the tears that threatened to fall. If only things had stayed that way…if only she and Mike had found a way to hold on to the wonder they'd found together…

If only life had turned out differently.

3

There was no break in the heat that weekend and Ellen stayed inside where it was cool, sorting through scrapbooks and boxes of tattered memories, drifting back in time. She wanted to find her prayer journal, the one she had kept when she first became a Christian. There she would find the words she'd written after she and Mike first met. And maybe then she would remember the reasons they married, the reasons they should fight to keep their marriage from falling apart. Besides, the task kept her from thinking of her father's death. Right now it was easier to believe she was headed back to Petoskey for a reunion with her siblings than to accept the fact that her father was no longer alive.

Ellen rubbed her weary eyes and gazed at the clock. She had the afternoon ahead of her. Mike was covering weekend sports. When he'd been home earlier their conversation had been stilted, forced. She sighed and reached into a torn cardboard box, sifting through the contents of what once had consumed her heart.

The box contained half-filled journals and what seemed like hundreds of letters. Peering inside, Ellen saw a series of inked-in hearts doodled painstakingly across the top of folded, yellowed notebook paper. She lifted the paper from the others and unfolded it gingerly so the creases wouldn't tear.

It was a letter from Jake.

She sighed. The words had nearly faded from view, the way everything else about Jake already had. She ran her fingers over the wrinkles, glanced at the date and quickly figured Jake must have written it in his junior year at Petoskey High.

"Hey Bucko, what's up?" Ellen read the words silently, and for the first time in years she could hear his voice.

> You probably already know this but I've got basketball practice after school. That's a big-time bummer. Know why? I'll tell you. Cuz I'd rather clean my garage or straighten my books. (J.K.) Truth is I'd rather spend the afternoon with you. I know that shocks you what with the hordes of girls flocking

around my locker. (Right!!!) Serious now. You're the only one I want to see, Ellen. I mean it. Even if you do like raisins on your salad (sick!) and drive that ugly burnt orange tank. (I made a mental note to never let you drive again. My Bug's the only way to go!) Speaking of which, you and Leslie and Rick HAVE to go to the game Friday night. I think I'll score the big 3-0 and then wink at you like they do in the pros. Plus, we could probably sneak a kiss at halftime. I know, I know. If I'm lucky. Let me know if you can come. Catch you after fifth period. Don't think you can avoid me, either. I'll follow you to the ends of the earth if you ever leave me. You're my future, babe. ILYADYFI, Jake.

ILYADYFI. *I love you and don't you forget it.* Her eyes grew dim and she smiled absently at the long-ago phrase. Last she heard, Jake was still living in Petoskey. For a brief moment she allowed herself to wonder whether he had gotten married, whether he still thought of her.... Then she folded the brittle paper and reached back into the box, sorting through dozens of similar notes until she found what she was looking for. Her prayer journal, the first one she'd ever kept. It was dated Spring, 1990.

Humidity had warped the pages, but Ellen could read the entries as clearly as the day they were written. She flipped toward the back of the floral cloth-covered book until she found September's passages. She saw it then, the lengthy entry she had written the night she first dated Mike Miller. Even now the words seemed to dance on the page, filled with the excitement she had felt that faraway day.

Well, I did it. I finally went out with Mike Miller. Ever since we met, our schedules have been too busy to get together. Not that I haven't thought of him and watched WCBS sports more than usual. Anyway, tonight he took me out for pizza and afterwards we walked around the Michigan campus and talked.

We want so many of the same things it's almost scary. He's a broadcaster so naturally we have sports in common. But it's so much more than that. He's a Christian. Raised that way. He said he hasn't had a serious girlfriend since high school because it's hard to find someone who loves God and wants the same things he wants. It's like he's perfect for me. Like God himself brought us together. We even talked about marriage, how it should be forever... between a man and a woman equally yoked, people who want to love the Lord, build a family and a home where Christ will be honored. I've only been out with Mike once and somehow I can't imagine marrying anyone else. Of course, I didn't tell him that. I'll wait till the second date at least. Maybe I should pray about it.

Dear Lord, I don't know why you've brought me and Mike together, but I need your help on this one. Is he the man for me, the man I might marry?

I need to know. There's something very special about him, something I can see in his eyes. Oh, Lord, help me to be careful around him and take things slowly. And thank you for his faith, his love for you. I pray that you will bless our relationship, whatever it may become. I love you, Lord. Amen.

Ellen remembered how it felt to write those words. She had fallen hard for Mike. *Give me a sign, Lord,* she remembered praying before each date. *Show me if there's some reason I shouldn't give him my heart.* And each time they went out, Mike exceeded both her expectations and her dreams.

"There's just one thing," Mike had told her tenderly when their dating became more serious. "I don't want to sleep with you, Ellen. Not until we're married. I really believe God won't honor our relationship unless we honor him."

Ellen had been stunned. She understood perfectly well that sex before marriage was wrong in God's eyes, but that hadn't stopped her where Jake was concerned. Indeed, she had always felt somewhat self-righteous for waiting three years after she and Jake began dating before giving in to her desires.

When she and Jake broke up and she became a Christian, she understood far better why God asks people to wait. There was a bond between her and Jake that should never have been there, a part of her that she could never get back.

Mike had been honest. He told her he had dated several girls through college and had been sexually intimate with three of them. "It was wrong, and the relationships were empty. A few years ago I made a promise to the Lord. Next time I'd do things his way."

Ellen could still remember how difficult it had been to stay within the physical limits of the dating relationship with Mike. He set a curfew for himself and was out the door of Ellen's apartment no later than ten o'clock each evening. Finally, a year later, they were married. The wedding was beautiful and their honeymoon on a beach near Manzanillo, Mexico, was truly blessed by God, beautiful beyond anything either of them had ever imagined.

Ellen smiled at the memory. There were no words to describe the depth of love they had shared physically and emotionally. They believed God was rewarding them for their obedience, and in those early years it seemed the honeymoon would never end.

Ellen ran her fingers over the words she had written and flipped through the pages of the journal. Mike had been so strong in his faith back then, so sure. Now it had been years since he had talked to her about his love for God…months since they had even discussed going to church.

Mike wasn't the only one to blame. She remembered a line from Psalm 51: *Restore to me the joy of your salvation.* Where was that joy now? She closed her eyes and felt the sting of tears. She and Mike were a mess, her father was gone forever, and everything that was ever good about life had changed. The Lord seemed a million miles away.

The phone rang, interrupting her thoughts. Ellen stretched her legs and reached across the bed for the receiver.

"Hello."

"Hi, it's me."

Jane sounded annoyed, and Ellen braced herself. Her sister had called twice already that weekend to make sure of Ellen's arrival time in Detroit and to report that the other family members were not doing well.

"I think we should have gone today instead of Sunday. You know, I wanted to switch to Saturday, but you and Mom said to wait until Sunday. I think it's a waste of time."

"It's the best we can do, I guess." Ellen stared out her bedroom window at the deep blue-green of the Atlantic Ocean. They were two blocks away from the beach and she never got tired of the view.

Jane was silent for a moment. "What's that supposed to mean?"

Ellen rolled her eyes. Jane had become so testy lately almost anything set her off.

"Nothing, Jane. I'm just saying we'll be there soon enough. I'm not exactly looking forward to this week."

"All you ever think about is yourself, Ellen. I mean it. That's the trouble with you. The world doesn't revolve around what you want. Mom needs us there."

"I know." Ellen tried to keep the fatigue out of her voice, and failed. "Forget it, Jane. Forget I said anything. You're right. We should have gone today instead of tomorrow. Will you forgive me?"

Jane released a short burst of air. "Whatever."

In the uneasy silence that followed, Ellen struggled, wondering what she could say to ease the tension between them. The last thing she needed was to spend a week in Petoskey fighting with Jane. She'd rather not go. Her mind grasped for something neutral to say. "Well, I still have a bunch of things to pack."

Silence.

"So, I guess I'll see you tomorrow, okay?"

Silence.

"Have a safe flight."

Jane sighed loudly. "Sure, whatever. See you later."

Ellen hung up the phone and leaned back against her pillows. She remembered how it had been when she and Jane were kids, before they graduated from high school. They had shared a room together, giggling about the boys they knew and telling each other a hundred different secrets. Regardless of their disagreements during the day, each night before falling asleep they would whisper the same words to each other.

"Good night, Jane. Love you. See you in the morning."

"Good night, Ellen. Love you. See you in the morning."

Ellen's eyes burned at the memory. She couldn't remember the last time they'd said those words.

She thought of the others then...Megan, Amy, and Aaron. The five of them had been so close as children. Eventually she and Mike had distanced themselves from her family by moving to Miami. Now Jane was angry most of the time; sweet Megan was twenty-seven and had gotten involved with an abusive, controlling drug dealer; twenty-five-year-old Amy was busy with her own life and never called or wrote to the others; and Aaron, at twenty-four, was unemployable because of a temper so fierce most people were afraid of him.

More than a decade had passed since the Barretts had lived under one roof. Gradually the family had stopped attending Mass regularly, and eventually Ellen's faith had led her away from the Catholic church. Now even that seemed like a lifetime ago. Ellen wished she could remember when they had stopped being the family everyone else envied.

Saturday passed slowly so that by early Sunday Ellen was packed and anxious to leave.

"Have a safe flight," Mike said, pecking her on the cheek as he glanced at his watch.

"Right." Ellen's voice was flat and she refused to look at him.

"Ellen." Mike placed his hand gently underneath her chin and tilted her face toward his. "I love you. Don't let yourself get confused about that just because your dad is gone."

"If you loved me you'd make an effort for me." Ellen's eyes were dry. She was emotionally drained and the week hadn't even started. "I told you I wanted you with me this week. It was important to me, Mike."

"We've been through this before. I can't get the time off and you know that. You knew that when you married me."

"If it was important to you, you'd get the time off."

Mike drew a deep breath. "Anyway, have a safe flight. I do love you and I'll call you in a few days to see how it's going."

Ellen waited until his car disappeared down their street. Then she reached for the telephone and called a taxi. Twenty minutes later the cab pulled up out front.

Grabbing her suitcase, she studied the picture of Mike and her over the fireplace, then headed for the door.

The taxi made its way through the city toward the airport, and again Ellen caught herself swimming in a sea of memories. Like scenes from a movie, flashbacks from her childhood filled her mind and it was all she could do to stop them.

She looked at her watch. Her flight was scheduled to leave at 10:30. She would travel three hours nonstop and land in Detroit just before two o'clock. Jane's plane would arrive twenty minutes later. Megan had arranged to pick them both up and drive them back to the house, four hours north of the city.

The taxi swung into the airport and pulled up along the curb in the area designated for passenger unloading. Ellen moved slowly as she paid the driver and checked her bags with the airline. She wore a simple navy rayon dress that fell nearly to her matching pumps. Her hair was pulled back from her face, tied in a navy silk scarf, and she wore round, dark-rimmed sunglasses that covered nearly half her face. With a lifetime of memories threatening to break free at any moment, she had no room for casual conversation on the flight. Regardless of the people around her, she intended to be alone. The glasses would stay.

"When can we board?" she asked a flight attendant at the gate.

"Go ahead and board now if you'd like."

Ellen made her way down one of the narrow aisles of the Boeing 747, relieved to see that she had a window seat. Three hours alone in the sky. Maybe that would help make sense of her feelings. She sat down, slid the window shade up as far as it would go, and stared at the airline personnel working like so many cogs in a machine to prepare the airplane for takeoff. Ellen wondered if any of them had adult siblings who no longer liked them.

She took a deep breath and realized how tired she was. Because of her early flight she had gotten up at five-thirty. She leaned back, and in less than a minute she was asleep.

"Excuse, me." The flight attendant's voice woke Ellen instantly. "We're about to serve breakfast. I thought you might like to know."

"Yes. Thank you." Ellen straightened herself and looked out the window, amazed she had slept through takeoff. She studied the ground below and saw they had nearly crossed the Florida peninsula and were headed for the long journey north across the states. Her eyes narrowed thoughtfully as she gazed upward into the endless blue sky. She couldn't have been sleeping long, but she had been having the strangest dream....

Jake Sadler had been beside her on the plane holding her hand, but instead of being in their early thirties they were teenagers as they had been when they were in love so long ago.

She smiled and closed her eyes. Jake Sadler. She could see his dark brown hair, his tan face, and laughing deep, blue eyes. It felt good to remember him. As she had the day before, she wondered what he was doing, what life had dealt him.

Somewhere, deep inside her, she felt a tug. A nudging. She frowned. Almost a warning. A verse drifted into her mind: *Do not let your heart grow hard to the Spirit's voice....*

Ellen shut her eyes and drew a deep breath. Why on earth had she thought of that verse? She was so tired, she was making no sense at all. There was nothing about her actions or thoughts that need concern her in the least. All she was doing was remembering the past...wondering what had happened to an old friend....

And what life would have been like if somehow they'd stayed together.

4

Jane Barrett Hudson was at home when she received the news that her father had died from a massive heart attack. As was often the case, her husband, Troy, a marketing executive, was away on business. Jane had been forced to deal with an array of feelings while changing diapers, preparing snacks, and wiping runny noses.

Koley, her six-year-old, was astute enough to understand that his mother was distracted. But three-year-old Kala, and Kyle, who was barely one, remained demanding as ever, unaware of their mother's emotional state.

Because of the children Jane did not immediately have a chance to break down and grieve her father's death. This was not entirely a bad thing because among the emotions that had assaulted Jane since she'd heard the news was one that definitely was not grief.

She was frustrated that her father had not taken better care of himself, angry that he had left their mother alone, and annoyed about having to leave her small, central Arizona town to spend a week in Petoskey pretending to be grief stricken. But the emotion she struggled with most of all, the one she knew she would have to hide if she was to survive the trip to northern Michigan, was her indifference.

Certainly none of the other adult Barrett children would be indifferent in the wake of their father's death and they would not understand Jane's reasons for feeling so. Therefore, Jane knew she would have to work through her feelings by herself.

She was well aware that indifference over the death of her own father was not normal.

I'll be guilty the rest of my life for feeling this way. If only Troy were home. He would know what to say to help me through this.

When Saturday night arrived, Jane sat stiffly in a worn-out recliner, rocking out an anxious rhythm as she waited for her husband's arrival. Nearly two days had passed and she still had not shed so much as a tear.

"Get home, Troy," she whispered. "Please, get home."

Gradually her rocking slowed and her mind wandered as she stared into a blur of yesterdays. Her entire life had been wonderful because of Troy.

The rocker came to a stop and suddenly Jane was no longer in the living room of her Arizona home. She was two thousand miles away in Petoskey, Michigan, working at the Pizza Parlor, meeting Troy Hudson for the first time.

The Pizza Parlor was a noisy restaurant filled with miniature carnival rides, flashing lights, and children's music. While customers ate pizza, a gigantic costumed mouse paraded through the dining area delighting children and adults alike. Every weekend the place handled dozens of children's birthday parties, each of which was conducted by a teenage party host or hostess. Parents left generous tips in return for having someone else manage their children's parties.

Jane met Troy one afternoon at the end of her first week of work. Noise was so much a part of the Pizza Parlor that by then Jane no longer heard it. The tips weren't half what she'd expected and she was in the middle of what seemed like a nightmare birthday party. The birthday boy was a six-year-old monster who screamed at his mother and pinched his party guests. He grabbed pizza off other people's plates and threw a tantrum when he didn't get his own way. He was finally opening presents, and Jane couldn't wait for the day to be over. "Yuck!" the child shouted as he ripped open another carefully wrapped gift. "More books. I *hate* books!"

"Joey! Be nice to your friends." The child's mother was embarrassed but she clearly had no control over the boy. "Say thank you, Joey."

"No!"

And so it went until Jane thought the party would never end. She was about to rip off her badge and leave without looking back when a large, furry hand tapped her on the shoulder.

Jane whipped around and saw a six-foot mouse standing before her.

"Lucky!" She forced herself to sound excited. "Okay, everyone. Look over here. Lucky's come to wish little Joey a happy birthday."

Lucky bent into a sweeping bow and took Jane's hand in his, bringing it to his oversized head in a mock kiss. The children giggled.

"Come on, Lucky." Jane pulled the creature's synthetic paw toward Joey. "Come meet the birthday boy."

The mouse nodded enthusiastically and allowed Jane to lead him to the child.

Joey stood up, looked Lucky up and down, and kicked the mouse on his fur-covered shin.

"You're a fake!" The boy turned to his mother. "You said Lucky was a *real* mouse. I want a real mouse, Mommy!"

"Joey! That's not nice!" His mother was mortified.

The child swung his leg and kicked Lucky harder than before. "I don't care! I hate that stupid mouse! He's a fake!"

Jane expected the mouse to walk away before he got kicked again. Instead, the creature patted Joey on the head several times— Jane noticed the pats were a bit more...*enthusiastic* than normal.

Joey yelped, but the noise was so great no one heard him.

Lucky pretended to see someone across the dining room and he waved excitedly.

Then he headed in that direction, effectively bumping little Joey out of the way.

"Mommmm! That mouse knocked into me!"

Again no one heard the boy's cry.

"Better watch out!" Joey shouted in Lucky's direction. "Or I'll kick you again."

Jane giggled secretly as the mouse turned around and came back toward Joey. As he did, he bumped once more into the child, as he pretended to look for someone. Several seconds passed before he shrugged and headed back across the diner.

Joey ran toward his mother. "Mommmmm! That mouse pushed me."

Jane had no idea who was playing Lucky that day but she hoped she would have a chance to thank him. She helped the children sit down and ten minutes later she had just served them cake and ice cream when she spotted Lucky making his way back toward their table.

"Look, boys and girls," Jane said, grinning. "It's Lucky come back to have some cake with us!"

Lucky tiptoed up to Joey's birthday cake. Then, raising a single finger to his mouth, he picked up the leftover cake and acted as if he was going to leave with it.

"That mouse stole my cake!" Joey whined. "Mom, stop him! That's my cake!"

"Don't whine, Joey," his mother said meekly.

Jane concealed a smile. "Yes, Joey, Lucky's only teasing you. Right, Lucky?"

Upon hearing his name, Lucky turned and nodded, balancing the leftover cake in one hand and placing the other over his belly as he shook with mock laughter. He was three feet from Joey and he put one foot in that direction. Then suddenly he tripped over something and lost his balance. Teetering back and forth, Lucky struggled to regain his grip on the cake, but he began to fall.

Momentum carried the great mouse the remaining two steps that separated him from the birthday boy. Suddenly what remained of the cake hit Joey square in the back of the head. Chocolate icing covered the child's blond hair and cream-filled cake slid in gooey chunks down his back. Joey burst into tears.

Lucky brought both paws to his mouth and looked from Jane to Joey's mother and back to Jane. She took the cue.

"Oh, dear! Lucky has had a bad fall, boys and girls. I hope he's okay!"

Lucky nodded emphatically and puffed out his chest. Then he waved politely to Joey and shook the stunned mother's hand. Raising a paw in the air he bid the party farewell and strode across the room the same way he'd come.

As Lucky left, Jane glanced at the spot where the mouse had tripped. There was nothing there.

Jane was doing her party paperwork later that afternoon when a boy with dark red hair and bright blue eyes approached her.

"Hope I didn't cost you a tip on that party today." He smiled.

Jane thought a moment and then her eyes flew open. "You were Lucky?"

"Yeah. I'm new. Troy Hudson."

"Hi, Troy," Jane grinned. "I'm Jane, and yes, you cost me the tip."

"You're not mad are you?"

"Are you kidding? It was all I could do to keep from laughing out loud. I'd have paid you myself to get back at the brat. That cake thing was great."

Troy's eyes twinkled. "Yeah, well, it was just a little leftover cake. Besides, accidents happen." He paused. "Hey, if you're not doing anything Friday night, want to go to the show? My dad's letting me borrow his car."

Jane considered him for a moment. "Sure. I guess you kind of owe me after treating my party to the psycho Lucky act."

"Yeah, well look at this." He lifted his pant leg to reveal a colorful bruise where Joey had kicked him. "Even a friendly mouse like Lucky can only take so much."

Troy was the first boy Jane ever kissed. He was seventeen, funny and impetuous, and determined to remain unattached.

"It's stupid for kids our age to get into these serious relationships," he said during one of their walks home from the Pizza Parlor. "Don't you think so?"

Not anymore, Jane thought, but all she said was, "Of course. There's plenty of time for that when we're older."

"Yeah, like thirty years older." Troy laughed and Jane felt her heart lurch. She had never met anyone like Troy. He liked her the way she was, regardless of whether she ever grew up to be like Ellen.

Summer ended a few weeks later and Troy quit his job at the Pizza Parlor so he could concentrate on senior prep classes at the private high school across town. His phone calls came less often and eventually stopped altogether.

"Someday, Jane, I'll grow up and be ready for you," he said during one of his last phone calls. "But I won't ask you to wait for me. Life goes on. I understand that."

Three years passed and circumstances caused both Jane and Troy to grow somewhat wise and worldly. At the end of that time, Troy finally called.

"Told you I'd call."

Jane grinned madly on the other end. Life had not been kind to her since she'd last seen Troy, but in an instant he infused hope into her heart. They were nineteen and twenty now and Jane believed they were plenty old enough. "Are you a grown-up now, Troy Hudson?"

"I was hoping you might want to go to dinner Friday night and see for yourself."

They picked up where they left off and this time Troy had no aversion to being serious. They dated for the next three years and were married at St. Francis Xavier Catholic Church in the spring of 1991.

Troy knew her like no one in her immediate family ever had. Except Ellen. But that had been when they were little girls. Before their father had let Jane down in a way that none of the others knew anything about. As time passed, Jane built her world around Troy. In the process, she willingly became something of a stranger to her family.

"Ellen's only interested in herself and everyone else has changed. None of us get along," she complained to Troy. "I'd rather spend time with you and our friends than sit around a table listening to one of Aaron's temper tantrums or hearing the latest great news about Ellen."

Troy watched her silently for a moment. "You're jealous of her."

Jane looked at him, incredulous. "Of Ellen?"

Troy nodded thoughtfully.

"I'm not jealous, Troy, I'm disgusted. Everyone thinks she's got her life so together but what they don't see is how selfish she is. All she thinks about is herself."

For the next two years Jane talked constantly about moving away from Michigan, out west.

"Just think, Troy, we could be done with winters and ice storms and snow-covered driveways."

Jane's enthusiasm was contagious and Troy, who was a high-level sales representative, began sending out résumés. Eventually he received a considerable offer to work as a senior sales representative for a stereo distributor based in Cottonwood, Arizona.

The other Barretts cried and hugged them both as they packed up their things and headed west. But Jane remained untouched by the event.

"I'm going to miss your dad's barbecues," Troy said idly as they drove across country.

"Hmm." Jane was staring out her window.

"They sure seemed sad to see you go."

"That's how people are supposed to act when someone moves away."

Troy took his eyes off the road and for an instant turned to face her. "That's not a very nice thing to say, Jane. Your family wasn't putting on an act when we left. They're really sad. They love you a lot."

She huffed slightly and her eyes met his. "I've known my place in my family for years now, Troy. I appreciate what you're saying, but believe me, they aren't going to miss me when I'm gone. We're doing the best thing by moving away."

His forehead creased, and she saw the concern reflected in his blue eyes. "As long as you're not running away from something."

"I'm not," she lied.

Over the years, Jane and Troy built a home for themselves in central Arizona. They camped among the pine trees on Mingus Mountain and climbed rocks overlooking the Verde Valley. They hiked Sedona's North Fork Trail and picked wild blackberries along the Verde River. They swam in Oak Creek and marveled over the breathtaking red rocks that brought tourists from all over the world.

Over the next few years they raised a family, and when the children were old enough Troy taught them how to avoid rattlesnakes. They found a local Christian church and Jane headed up the women's group. On summer nights, when Troy wasn't traveling, the two of them would sit on their back porch and watch dazzling sunsets as their children played in the yard.

Occasionally Jane and Ellen would call each other and spend half an hour on the telephone making small talk. Jane remembered once, after such a conversation, Troy had walked into the room and found her crying, her face buried in her hands.

"Honey, what is it?" He was at her side, sliding his arm around her shoulders, holding her close.

Jane drew a ragged breath and shook her head. "It's Ellen. She called."

"Did you two get into it again?"

"No." Jane was still crying, but she fought to regain her composure. "It's just that she and my dad are so close and...I don't know, maybe I am jealous of that."

She fell silent, but she saw Troy studying her closely, watching her face.

"You sure nothing else is bothering you, honey?"

"No, really. I'm fine." Jane forced a smile and patted Troy's hand. He seemed satisfied that she was telling him the truth and he got up and went back into their home office.

Jane remembered watching him go and feeling a stab of guilt. The rest of that evening she had wondered if she would ever have the strength to tell him the truth about that terrible, painful dark night. The night her life changed forever.

5

The plane rumbled monotonously and Ellen drew a deep breath, fighting to clear her head. Nine years had passed since she had seen Jake Sadler. There was no reason why he should be making appearances in her current thoughts as if they'd only broken up yesterday.

The flight attendant arrived and handed her a tray of food which she ate absentmindedly. When she finished she looked out the window.

Jake had been there for the good years, the times when her father was strong and healthy, and she and her sisters and brother got along with each other. Maybe that's why he was on her mind now. Jake would understand what the years had stolen from her. He'd understand more than Mike ever could.

She leaned her head back wearily. Even Jake didn't know about the early days, when the Barrett family was just beginning. Back then her father had worked for IBM, which everyone in the family always took to mean "I've Been Moved." They lived in seven different cities in seven years and never had time to build relationships with anyone except the people who shared their breakfast table.

I wonder if Aaron and Jane and the others remember how good those times were? Ellen squeezed her eyes tightly closed, freeing two errant teardrops. She knew what she needed to do…what she needed to allow.

She needed to remember.

The tears flowed freely now, and she was thankful for the dark glasses. Allowing the memories meant going to a place where her father still lived and laughed, where he still shared his contagious enthusiasm for life. She was afraid that once she found that place, she would never want to leave.

Normally, Ellen did not believe anything good could come from wallowing in days gone by the way some people did, spending a decade recounting it and paying a stranger to analyze it. Still, just this once, as she hung thirty thousand feet in the air, suspended between her present and past, she would go back. She would allow herself to find that faraway place where families are born and love begins. Perhaps if she spent some time remembering her past she would find answers for today and tomorrow. She closed her eyes and savored the moment, slipping slowly into a cavern of scenes from a hundred yesterdays, drifting back to a handful of cities across the country.

Fairfax, Detroit, Jamestown, Kansas City, Dallas, Livonia, and finally Ann Arbor. Ellen had been born in Fairfax; Jane and Megan, in Detroit. The three girls were barely school age when the Barrett family moved to Jamestown, a small country town in upper New York where there had been a hundred things for a child to do. Ellen kept her eyes closed until finally she could hear their voices....

"Ellen, look what I found!" A towheaded Jane, barely four years old, came bounding up the hillside, her small hands cupping the body of a bumpy, brown toad.

"Let's find him a box." Ellen motioned for Jane to follow and the two girls ran as fast as they could back to the house. Gasping for breath, Ellen ran inside and came back with a dilapidated cardboard container.

"Should we put grass in it to keep him happy?" Jane's innocent blue eyes gazed admirably at her older sister.

"Okay." Ellen helped Jane lower the toad into the box and grabbed fistfuls of grass. "I know he's your toad, Jane. But let's say we're both his parents."

"All right. That way he'll have two people who love him."

"Hey, what do you girls have there?" The voice was her father's. Clear, strong, vibrantly alive. He walked toward them, his whole face smiling.

"A toad!" they shouted in unison.

Their father, a systems analyst and one of the most brilliant men to enter the booming new frontier of computers, stooped down and patted the homely creature. "A fine toad, I might add." He glanced around. "What if we find another one? So that this one will have a friend."

Jane wrinkled her small nose. "No, Daddy. I think one's enough."

He sat back on the grass and looked at Jane thoughtfully. "Well, now, you and Ellen are sisters, but you're friends, too, right?"

Jane smiled at her big sister. "Right."

"Think how you'd feel if someone put you in a box and took you away from Ellen."

Jane's face fell and she reached for Ellen's hand. "I would be sad, Daddy."

"That's how your toad feels." He stood up and swung Ellen onto his shoulders, taking Jane's hand in his. "Come on, now. Let's go find ourselves another toad so that the little fellow won't be so lonely."

The voices grew dim and Ellen opened her eyes slowly, staring vacantly into the sky, wishing she could remember whether they had ever found another toad. Instead, a different scene began taking shape.

Kansas City, late-afternoon. Their mother was seven months pregnant with Amy and had taken Ellen, Jane, and Megan outside their rented townhouse to wait for their father's return from work. Dark clouds filled the sky and there was lightning in the distance. It was tornado season, and the weather bureau had warned that conditions were right for a twister.

Blissfully unaware of the weather, the girls giggled and sang silly songs, watching intently until finally they saw the green Ford sedan round the corner.

"Daddy!" Their delighted squeals rang out, and they jumped up and down as their father parked the car and climbed out. Dressed in a suit and tie, he bounded toward them, a blond, six-foot-two, former football player with bulky shoulders and arms of steel. He swept each of the three girls into his arms, one at a time, tossing them into the air and making them laugh so hard they could barely breathe.

"I have an idea!" He grinned at his wife and leaned down to kiss her.

She smiled. "That's what I love about you, John."

"What's that?" He traced a finger along her cheek and stooped to tousle Jane's hair.

"Never a dull moment. I'm married to the chief memory maker in all of Missouri."

"Tell us, Daddy. Please! Tell us." The girls jumped up and down, tugging on their father's coat sleeves and waiting to hear his plan for the afternoon.

"Let's take a drive." He pointed toward the menacing storm clouds. "Maybe we can get a better view of the storm." Ellen's face grew troubled. "Daddy, is it safe?"

She was always the worried one, doubting whether the car was working properly and making sure the doors were locked. She was especially nervous about storms, even as a six-year-old. Her father looked sympathetically at her and tousled her hair.

"Of course it's safe. I wouldn't do anything that might hurt my girls."

"It hurts to move away from our friends, Daddy," Ellen said then.

Her father frowned and lowered himself to his oldest daughter's level. "I know that, honey. It hurts me, too. But right now we don't have any choice."

"Will we move again?"

"Probably. But wherever we go we'll be together and we'll always have each other."

Her father's words rang in Ellen's mind, and she glanced out the window once more. What he'd said was true. Ellen and her sisters and mother had grown to depend on each other because they were never sure of anything except the family to which they belonged.

Another memory began taking shape, and Ellen could see herself holding a bulky, oversized chalkboard. There was something scribbled on it, and she was shouting at cars that drove by.

"Park here! One dollar. Park here!"

The image was clear now. The town was Ann Arbor, where the Barretts had lived just eight houses away from the University of Michigan football stadium. Each Saturday when there was a home game, fans would cruise up and down the neighboring streets looking for a place to park.

Nearly everyone on Keech Street parked cars in their driveways and even on their front lawns. Ellen was eight and all week she looked forward to the frenzied excitement of football Saturdays. She would wave the chalkboard to gain the attention of passing motorists. Park here, $1, the sign read. Anxious fans would pull into the yard, and her father would collect the money.

At halftime the family would walk toward the bright, yellow gates of the stadium, and her father would wink at the ticket taker.

"Residents get in free at halftime, right?"

The attendant would smile, size up the trail of children that tagged behind the man, and wave the group inside. They would sit as close as they could to the Michigan Wolverine marching band.

By then Amy was nearly two years old and the family finally included a boy, Aaron Randall Barrett. Even when the weather grew cold and snow covered the ground, their father would carry his infant son to the games, snuggling him tightly beneath his heavy brown wool coat. Their mother usually stayed home to work on dinner and get the house ready for weekend company.

"You're the littlest Wolverine of all," their father would say to the infant Aaron once they were settled into stadium seats. Ellen remembered watching with her sisters as their father tickled and cooed at their only brother. "One day you'll be a big Wolverine, Aaron, and Daddy will come watch you play football every Saturday."

"I'm going to be a Wolverine, too, Daddy," Ellen would say and her father would pull her close.

"That's my girl, Ellen. You can be whatever you want."

When Michigan scored a touchdown, as the team often did, the band would erupt into the familiar fight song and everyone in the Barrett family old enough to talk would sing along.

"Hail to the victors valiant, hail to the conquering heroes, hail, hail, to Michigan..." Even little Amy knew to raise her right fist whenever the word *hail* was sung.

Ellen sighed as the memories blended in her mind. Dozens of Michigan games. Every Saturday of the football season for two years.

The plane moved along effortlessly as Ellen tried to capture a glimpse of her father and savor it. She could see him sitting in Michigan Stadium, eyes wide with excitement, cheeks red from the chilly air, cheering the Wolverines to victory. How he loved Michigan football.

Twelve years later, when Ellen was accepted into the university's journalism program, no one was more thrilled than her father. Aaron had not pursued football beyond his sophomore year in high school. But Ellen knew she had been her Dad's kindred spirit, a child who shared the desires of his heart.

The plane rumbled as it passed through turbulent air, and suddenly Ellen remembered the football season just ten months before her father's death. Michigan had played Notre Dame in a spectacular contest. She'd known he would be watching the game and had called him from Miami during the third quarter to see if he'd caught one particularly good play.

But he was asleep. *Daddy, what's happening to you?* Ellen had wondered at the time.

"Your father's been so tired lately, Ellen," her mom explained when she got on the line. "His health really isn't that good. I'm sure he'll call you later."

Ellen shook off the image of her father sleeping through a Michigan football game. She refused to remember him that way and she drifted back once more to her childhood.

She and her siblings had thrived in Ann Arbor. Her dad had accepted a position with Parsons Engineering, and, thankfully, relocating was not part of the job description. Their family finally had a reason to develop roots and they did so in a matter of months.

With so many children under one roof, almost anything they did became an event to remember. In the winter they ice-skated at Almondinger Park and built snowmen families in the front yard. When summer came they picked blueberries at Hanson's Farm and swam at Half Moon Lake. Best of all was autumn and football Saturdays.

Their mother would easily go along with almost anything their dad wanted to do. But inevitably he was the parent who made things happen. He planned picnics at the local lakes, pajama parties at the drive-in theater, and birthday bashes for each of his children every year.

The family was fiercely Catholic, and their father believed his faith had to be alive to be worth anything. Once, when Ellen was in high school, he had stood for seven hours in the pouring rain before election day passing out Right to Life material.

"If we don't stand up for the rights of unborn children, who will?" he said to Ellen when she studied the pamphlets.

His convictions made him a doer among his peers. Ellen and her siblings had attended St. Thomas Catholic School on Elizabeth Street, and when the school board needed a chairman to raise money for extracurricular activities, John Barrett started a bingo program and ran it single-handedly.

The first Christmas Ellen's family was in Ann Arbor, a young couple from the church came caroling to the Barrett house as part of their holiday tradition. When they left, their dad's eyes lit up and he reached for their mother.

"Let's make that our family tradition, too." For the next twenty years the Barrett women designated a full day during Christmas week to bake holiday cookies, and then the entire family would go caroling.

Their father's favorite story of the holiday season was Charles Dickens's *A Christmas Carol,* and that first Christmas in Ann Arbor he found a brown suede English top hat with a high crown like those worn during the Dickens era. He wore it caroling every Christmas after that.

For two years they loved Ann Arbor as if they'd lived there all their lives. Their mother's sister, Mary, and her family lived three hours away in Battle Creek. Many weekends the Barretts would pile into the station wagon and set out for a raucous get-together between the two families.

It was during the Ann Arbor years that Ellen remembered her dad's football physique becoming soft, giving way to a lack of exercise and overindulgence. He had a voracious appetite for everything in life and food was no exception.

"You're the best cook in all of Michigan," he would tell his wife, kissing her on the cheek as she cooked up yet another gooey dessert or hot batch of cookies. "Keep 'em coming."

When the Barretts thought up fun things to do on the weekends, whether a Sunday drive or a trip to the lake, they always stopped for a treat.

"How 'bout a milk shake?" their dad would suggest, pulling the station wagon over in front of the local ice-cream parlor. If they were at the movies it was popcorn and licorice and frozen bonbons. At the lake it was cookies and rootbeer floats. The children were too active to be affected by the heavy foods, but their father spent much of his day sitting in front of a computer, and it wasn't long before his expanding midsection began to jeopardize his health.

Food wasn't his only vice. By then he had been chain-smoking cigarettes since he was fourteen years old. In the 1970s reports were released stating the dangers of smoking. Ellen's dad was one of the doubters, brushing off the reports as political posturing and premature hysteria. He kept his cigarettes in his shirt pocket, close to his heart, and smoked almost constantly. Smoking was a part of his image, his character. He had no desire to give it up.

Then in late February 1977, the Barrett world changed completely. One night Ellen overheard her parents talking to their Aunt Betsy in California.

"No, we haven't told the children yet," her father said quietly.

"It's not going to be easy for them." It was her mother's voice, and Ellen crept out of bed and sat at the top of the staircase where she wouldn't be seen.

"Yes, it's final." Her father's again. "We'll move to Petoskey before the spring semester. Yes. That's when the job wraps up here. Right. I'll be teaching a full load of computer courses at the community college. I know. It's a dream come true."

Tears sprang to Ellen's eyes. They couldn't possibly leave Ann Arbor. She and Katy Bonavan were best friends and they'd promised to stay that way forever. She gulped back tears as she stood up and tiptoed back into her bedroom. Jane was still sleeping.

"Jane," she whispered. "Wake up."

Jane was eight that year and she opened her eyes, looking disoriented and afraid. "What?"

"Jane, we're moving."

"We are?"

Ellen nodded quickly. "Yes. To somewhere called Petoskey."

Jane's eyes grew wide with concern. "You mean we're moving to another country?"

"Yes. I think so."

"When are we going?"

"In a few months."

Jane raised up onto her knees, still half-asleep, and hugged her older sister tightly. "It's okay, Ellen. We'll still have each other. I'll be your best friend wherever we go."

Ellen smiled through her tears. "I know. Love you, Jane."

"Love you, too." Jane collapsed back into bed. "Good night."

A month later they watched their belongings disappear on a moving van headed for Petoskey. Then they climbed into a station wagon loaded with pillows and suitcases and drove away. The neighbors lined up along the street to say good-bye, many with tears in their eyes.

"Come back and visit!"

"Don't forget to write!"

Ellen was ten and old enough to know that people would forget and visits would be rare, if ever. She began crying as they passed Almondinger Park and she didn't stop for three hours. Petoskey, with its shoreline community and Victorian houses, was not in another country, but it might as well have been.

Ellen's father was quietly understanding. He had promised his children they would not move again, but this time there had been no choice. The Parsons plant in Ann Arbor had closed down and he had accepted a teaching position at North Central Community College in Petoskey. By June that year they had settled in a neighborhood just west of the college. They bought a four-bedroom, corner house with towering maple trees, a wraparound porch, and a fenced backyard.

While her siblings adjusted quite naturally to the move, Ellen began eating to appease her loneliness. By the time she was in junior high she was a hefty twenty pounds overweight.

She began spending more time writing. She kept a journal and wrote poems, which she shared with her parents.

"Hmm," her mother would say thoughtfully. "I guess I don't really understand it."

Ellen would take the poem to her father. He would shut out the rest of the world and read it thoughtfully, sometimes with tears in his eyes.

"Sweetheart, it's wonderful," he would tell her. "Someday you're going to be a famous writer."

"Oh, Daddy!" Ellen would blush. "Do you really like it?"

"It's fantastic. Can I keep this copy for myself?"

The first four years in Petoskey were innocent and carefree, despite her struggle with weight. In summer their dad would get off work, squeeze into his swimsuit, and take the family for a late-afternoon swim at Petoskey State Beach. The sand stretched for what seemed like miles, and Ellen and her brother and sisters would play volleyball in the shallow pools near the shore. Despite his own worsening problem with weight, Dad could still palm a volleyball and rise halfway out of the water for a serve. Mom would laugh and wave from a nearby blanket, thoroughly content to watch the others play.

The summer after she turned fourteen, Ellen began noticing boys. She became keenly aware of the way they paid attention to other, thinner girls. One afternoon she went home, rummaged through her parents' bookcase, and found a dusty old paperback called *Dr. Stillman's Quick Weight Loss Diet*. The front cover promised a fifteen-pound weight loss in one week. Determined to keep her plans private, Ellen whisked the book into her bedroom and studied the doctor's diet plan.

The next morning Ellen ate three eggs for breakfast, cottage cheese for lunch, and only the meat from her dinner plate. No fruit, vegetables, bread, or sweets passed her lips, and in three months she went from size twelve jeans to an eight. The diet was neither balanced nor healthy, and twice she nearly fainted because of low blood sugar. But it worked, and that summer she slimmed down even further when she sprouted three inches, seemingly overnight. By the time she started high school that fall she had been approached more than once by a representative from a local modeling agency.

"Daddy, please, can I get new clothes for school?" she asked her father one night.

He smiled at her. "Of course, honey. I'm so proud of you for losing weight. Pick out whatever you want. By the way, maybe you can share your secret with me sometime." He patted his stomach, which had continued to grow.

"Ah, Dad. That's just you. Don't worry about it."

He didn't.

Ellen had fairly danced through her first year at Petoskey High School, thriving on the attention she received from her classmates. That year in physical education class Ellen met a girl named Leslie Maple, and the two were instant friends. They both rode skateboards and wanted to try out for Petoskey's cheerleading squad. They had shoulder-length dark hair and light green eyes, and they were both tall and slender. They even lived in the same neighborhood, just around the corner from each other. From the beginning, people mistook Ellen and Leslie for twins, and the girls delighted in letting people believe it was true.

It was a perfect year except for one thing. She and Jane had grown apart. Her father pulled her aside one day to share his observations about the situation. "Honey, I think Jane's feeling left out. Why don't you spend some time with her."

Ellen realized her father was right. She had been so busy making friends and celebrating her new popularity that she hadn't made time for Jane. She felt bad about Jane's hurt feelings and even tried to talk to her once. But Jane would be at Petoskey High in a couple years and then they would have more time together. Sure enough, when Jane entered high school, she spent most of her time with Ellen and Leslie and the problem seemed to dissolve.

Besides, Ellen was too caught up in her own life to worry about Jane. There were football games and cheerleading practices and Friday-night parties to attend. The next year, Ellen discovered the greatest distraction of all, one that would change her life forever. Jake Sadler.

Until that time Ellen's father had been the only man in her life. But Jake was like an unquenchable thirst—he consumed her from the moment they met, leaving little room for father-daughter talks.

⸻

At the thought of Jake, Ellen drew a deep breath and stretched her legs. She checked her watch. The plane had been in the air for two hours, which meant they still had an hour to go. With a sigh, her thoughts returned to Jake.

They had dated six years before breaking off their relationship, and even then it was another two years before they learned to live without each other. They dated throughout Ellen's three years at North Central. The same time period when her father lost his job and did something no one ever thought he would do—wrote a note to his family, pulled together a few belongings, and left.

The memory brought Ellen instantly back to reality. She sat up straighter, took a magazine from the back of the chair in front of her, and flipped through the pages.

Some things were better left in the past.

6

*I*t was nearly midnight when Jane heard the front door open. She was sitting in the recliner, rocking slowly, hypnotically, staring at a blank television screen.

"Sorry I'm late." Jane watched Troy drop his things near the front door. He came to sit on the arm of the chair and put a hand on her shoulder. "I wanted to be here. I can't imagine how you must feel."

Jane looked up at him without expression. "I'm not devastated, if that's what you mean." Her eyes were dry. "I haven't been close to my dad in years. You know that."

Troy raised an eyebrow. "Okay. But he was your dad, after all, and now he's gone. That has to hurt, Jane."

"It's *supposed* to hurt. That doesn't mean it does."

"Jane, don't be strong at a time like this. It's okay to cry."

"Why should I cry, Troy? My dad didn't love me. Why should I act like I'm suffering now that he's gone?"

Troy stood up and collapsed in a heap on the couch a few feet away. "Here we go," he muttered. "What do you mean he didn't love you? Of course he did. I saw how he treated you."

"Did you see how he treated Ellen? I'm not blind. He didn't love any of us the way he loved Ellen."

Troy shook his head and stared at his brown loafers. "Jane, you're wrong. You're forgetting the good times. Your dad loved each of you five kids the same."

Jane resumed her rocking and turned to stare at nothing in particular. Troy did not understand because he did not know everything about her past. He knew neither the facts nor the way they had affected her life. She took a deep breath and stopped rocking.

Perhaps it was time.

"Troy, there's something I want to tell you, something I never wanted you to know. But it's been inside me for so many years that if I don't let it out, especially now with my dad gone, it's going to kill me."

Troy leaned slightly forward. "All right. I'm listening."

"Promise me it won't change anything."

"I love you, Jane. Nothing could change that."

"All right, then. It goes back a long way. I'll try to take it from the beginning."

Jane drew in another deep breath and closed her eyes. "As far back as I can remember I was part of a pair, of Ellen and Jane. We shared a room, played together, fought together, and got in trouble together. At Christmas we received duplicate presents. We wore identical clothing. We were inseparable."

Jane smiled at the memory. Of course, there had inevitably been a leader among the two: Ellen. She decided what games they would play, what songs they would sing, and which programs they would watch on television. Because Jane was always seeking Ellen's approval, she was compliant and went along as she was expected to do. She never considered crossing Ellen or suggesting something that Ellen might not agree with.

Over the years that relationship had produced two very different personalities. Ellen was outgoing, gregarious, and a natural leader. Jane had always been considered the quiet one, shy and unsure of herself in public situations.

Jane shook her head. "Even when Ellen went through a period of being overweight," she said quietly, "she seemed to have more friends and more self-confidence than I did. So I suppose it only made sense that Ellen gained Dad's attention, his praise and admiration. Whatever I could do, Ellen could do better." She gave a hoarse laugh. "Once, when I was seven, I realized how much approval Ellen received for writing poetry. So I tried to compose a poem of my own. I brought it to Daddy, timidly making my way to where he sat watching a football game in his easy chair."

"'Daddy, look,' I said, handing over the scribbled prose. 'I wrote this for you.'"

"What did he say?" Troy asked softly, and Jane looked away.

"He read the piece and smiled at me and said it was wonderful." Emotion burned deep inside her at the memory. "I was so thrilled. I really thought he was talking about my poem." Her voice broke, and she had to wait a moment before she could go on. "But before I could thank him he told me it was wonderful I wanted to be a writer like my big sister. 'Have you shown this to Ellen? She could probably help you put it together, honey. Make it into a *real* poem.' I was crushed, but Dad had already gone back to watching television and he didn't even notice. I just walked to the kitchen, opened the cupboard, and pulled out the trash basket. Then I ripped the poem into a hundred pieces." She sighed and studied Troy.

"Go ahead," he said softly. "I'm listening."

She drew a deep breath and continued talking.

There were other times she'd been hurt. While going through puberty she gained eighteen pounds. She'd been chubby, but not nearly as overweight as Ellen had been. When Jane reached her highest weight, Ellen had already lost hers. One Saturday afternoon the summer before Jane started at Petoskey High, she and her mother purchased school clothes and then staged a fashion show for her father. When it was finished, he pulled Jane close beside him and smiled at her.

"You look beautiful, honey. The clothes are really nice."

Jane smiled, allowing the praise to warm her body. Her father was pleased and all was right with the world.

"And don't worry about your weight. Ellen lost hers at about this age. I'm sure you'll slim down, too, and then you'll be just as popular as your big sister."

Jane had felt her face flush with embarrassment. She'd been very sensitive about her excess weight and her cheeks had burned in shame. Again, her father didn't notice.

"You're lucky to have Ellen. When you get to Petoskey she'll help you make a bunch of new friends. You're a lucky girl, Jane."

Jane nodded and stared at her shoes. She suddenly felt uncomfortable in the new clothes and she wanted to get far away from her father and his hurtful comments.

"Hey," he continued, "don't worry about how you look now. When you lose weight, I'm sure you and Ellen can go shopping and get some real nice skinny high school clothes."

Jane nodded again and turned away so her father wouldn't see her tears. Then she ran into the bedroom she shared with Ellen and ripped off the new clothes, stuffing them into her closet. For the next two days she ate nothing. She wanted desperately to be rid of her plump figure before the week was through.

Instead, on the third day she found a freshly baked batch of cookies in the kitchen, grabbed two handfuls, and ate them in her room. She would eat whatever she wanted even if she never looked like Ellen.

High school was more of the same. She'd been cast immediately into the role of Ellen Barrett's little sister. "At first I didn't have or desire a separate identity." She frowned. "But Ellen ignored me when we were at school. She seemed almost embarrassed of me."

"How so?" Troy asked, and she told him of one incident in particular.

Jane had worn a light blue, oversized nylon windbreaker to school nearly every day that year. The jacket gave her a way to hide her less-than-perfect body, especially in light of Ellen's slim figure. The last thing she needed was people comparing her and Ellen at Petoskey High the way they did at home. But one day Ellen pulled Jane aside and fingered the jacket in disgust.

"Jane, you've got to get a new jacket. You wear this thing every day. Everyone's talking about it."

Jane struggled for an answer, her cheeks red hot with shame. "I like it," she said finally.

"Well, I think it makes you look fat. If you want people to like you, you need to wear something else."

A few days later, Jane overheard Ellen talking to their mother.

"Mom, pleeease!" Jane peeked into the room and saw that Ellen's arms were crossed and one hip jutted out in frustration. "You have to make her wear something else. It's embarrassing."

"Ellen, you should be talking to her about this. It's between you and her."

Jane was furious as she listened, but she was afraid to say anything. She needed Ellen if she wanted to survive at Petoskey. Her eyes stung as she ran out of the house and slammed the door. The noise brought Ellen and Mom into the foyer and Jane heard them calling her. But it was too late. She walked through the quiet, tree-lined streets of Petoskey for an hour. Then she came home and shut herself in her room.

Jane fell silent for a while, then shrugged. "Things were never the same again between me and Ellen."

"I'm sorry."

Troy's quiet sincerity touched her deeply, and Jane bit her lip, then went on. "Mom must have said something to Ellen because she didn't say another word about the jacket. I still hung around with Ellen, but by that time I was making friends of my own. Friends who were outside the circle of popular kids Ellen associated with. By the end of my sophomore year, I'd made friends with a group of quiet, studious types who didn't care about the clothes I wore. I could tell them secrets about Ellen, things I would never have shared with my family."

Jane's comments came back to her as though she'd said them just yesterday. "I told them Ellen was a snob. I told them she was stuck-up and self-centered; and that all she ever thought about was herself. I said I could barely stand living with her."

She swallowed painfully, then looked at Troy and smiled weakly. "It was about that time I met you. I knew I'd never love another boy like I loved you. But then you were gone and I had no idea whether I'd ever see you again. By the beginning of my junior year I had grown taller than Ellen and lost twenty pounds so that I was actually quite thin. I was pretty enough—"

"You were beautiful," Troy broke in. "You still are."

She smiled at him. Her father had said the same thing, but she hadn't believed him, either. Unlike Ellen, Jane had lacked confidence and charisma and therefore still could not compete with her.

Her lips pressed together. Of course, on the heels of telling her she was beautiful, her father had gone on to add something about Ellen giving her makeup tips.

Finally, in her senior year, Jane was free of Ellen's shadow. That was when Jane began doing things she had never done before. She went on dates with older boys and came home well after the family's midnight curfew. She bought a bicycle and rode through the dark streets of Petoskey to Magnus Park on Friday nights. There she would meet her new friends and drink beer. Eventually her parents forbade her from going out. Jane still found a way to do what she wanted, only now she no longer asked her parents' permission.

She stopped studying and her grades plummeted. The conservative outfits she had worn in her first three years of high school were replaced with tight, black outfits borrowed from her new friends. She wore heavy mascara and carried an air of defiance that caused her parents great concern.

At one of the parties Jane attended that year she had met a long-haired man in his midtwenties named Clay. He was the leader of a local rock band, Jungle Fever, and Jane began dating him secretly.

By that time Ellen was involved with Jake Sadler. Popular, handsome, basketball-hero Jake. Everyone liked Jake. But Clay was hard and mean looking, with a viper tattoo that wrapped around his left forearm. He was a rebel, and Jane knew better than to bring him home. Her mother might have made an attempt to be nice to him, but the comparisons between Clay and Jake would have been too tempting for her father to resist.

"I didn't know any of this." There was a kind of shocked sadness in Troy's eyes. "I'm surprised your parents put up with it all."

Jane shrugged. "They didn't. Not for long."

She could still hear the tone of her father's voice when he'd finally confronted her. She had broken the rules and ridden her bike to a party. When she came home, it was two in the morning.

Her father was waiting. He'd stared at her with an expression she'd never seen before.

"Jane, you're being disobedient and rebellious and we cannot tolerate it any longer."

Ellen was gone that night, sleeping over at a girlfriend's house, but that hadn't kept Dad from making a comparison. "When Ellen was your age, she would never—"

"Stop!" The shout came out before Jane could think, and Dad raised an eyebrow. Well, she'd started it so she might as well finish. She met his surprised gaze. "I don't want to hear about Ellen. All I've heard since I was a little girl is how Ellen does *this* better and Ellen does *that* better. Well, Ellen's no saint, Dad. She's probably spending the night with Jake Sadler instead of staying at Leslie's house. She lies to you all the time, but you don't see it because you think she's so perfect. She's not! She never has been!"

Her father had been stunned. It was completely out of character for her to accuse Ellen of such a thing.

He shook his head. "I don't think Ellen's a saint. I think my children are wonderful people, fully capable of making wrong choices. We've certainly seen that these past few months. Besides, this isn't about Ellen. It's about you. I want you to stop coming home whenever you please and start respecting our curfew. Do you understand?"

"I understand." Sarcasm dripped from her words. "But Daddy, don't tell me that each of us is wonderful. You love Ellen more than you love me. You always have."

Dad's face grew angry at the accusation. "Listen, Jane. I do not love any of my children more than the others. I am proud of Ellen, yes. She was an honor student, a cheerleader, an editor on the school paper. I'm her father and I have a right to be proud of her, don't you think?"

Jane rolled her eyes.

"I'm just as proud of you, young lady. But I won't tolerate excuses for bad behavior. You will obey my rules or you will be punished, do you understand me?"

Jane's eyes grew damp and she ignored his question. She ran to her room and slammed the door.

The next day, before Ellen returned home from her friend's house, Jane packed some belongings into a knapsack, flung them over her shoulder, and set off on her bicycle. She rode four miles to the house where Clay and the other band members lived. They were having a speed party and Jane was invited. The idea was completely new to Jane. She and Ellen sometimes drank at parties, but they had never dabbled in drugs. For that reason alone, Jane decided to attend the party. She would be different from Ellen if it killed her.

But that night she had more in mind than the drugs. Jane had experimented sexually with Clay but had not yet lost her virginity. Now she'd made up her mind. She would stay at Clay's house for a week and spend much of it in bed with him. So what if it went against everything her parents had taught her, everything she had learned at church over the years? So what if Clay didn't love her? Neither did her father.

But that night after taking one hit from a cigarette dipped in liquid speed, Jane grew violently ill and threw up on the living room rug. Looking disgusted with the mess and frustrated by her inexperience, Clay relegated her to a back bedroom.

"Lotta fun you are. Stay there until you can party like the rest of us." He slammed the door.

Her heart raced and she could barely catch her breath. She struggled for an hour to stop vomiting. When she felt better she climbed out the bedroom window, crept around the house to where her bicycle was parked, and sped off. She spent that night and most of the next day at her friend Rochelle's house, sorting through her feelings. Rochelle had seen the changes in Jane and was thankful she had come to her senses before making a grave mistake.

"Clay is worthless, Jane. Let him go."

Jane nodded and suddenly Troy's words had come back to her: *Someday, Jane, I'll grow up and be ready for what we have between us.*

"Thinking of Troy?" Rochelle had asked.

"Yep."

The two girls stayed up into the early hours of the morning talking. Jane promised Rochelle she was through with Clay and the fast crowd, but she could not bear any more comparisons to Ellen. She was determined to explain this to her father.

When she phoned her parents they were frantic. They had contacted the police and searched for her throughout the night.

"Jane, where have you been? We've been so worried."

"Never mind, Dad. I have something to say."

There was an uncomfortable silence and Jane knew her father was probably at a loss for how to deal with her. Ellen had never challenged him this way, she was sure. But she was equally sure the time had come to make her feelings clear.

"What?" His voice was gruff with disapproval.

"Dad, don't ever compare me with Ellen again. Please."

"Jane, I never meant—"

"Dad, please. Don't talk about it now. I've thought things through and I'm ready to start living the way you want me to live. I'm sorry about the past. Just don't ever compare me to her again."

Dad was silent and Jane wondered if maybe he was crying. "I won't compare you," he said finally. "But I will insist that you come home now and start acting like the responsible young lady we've raised you to be."

Jane was satisfied with that. The trip away from home was worth every minute if it had finally made him aware of her feelings.

After that Jane still felt she didn't quite measure up in her father's eyes. But at least her shortcomings were no longer verbalized.

Jane paused a moment, catching her breath and collecting her thoughts. "Is there more?" Troy asked, taking her hand.

A sadness fell over Jane then, and for the first time there were tears in her eyes. She tightened her grip on his hand.

"You okay?" He moved closer, and she fell into his arms.

"Hold me," was all she could manage between sobs. "There's more."

The worst was yet to come.

7

*J*ane sat back against the cushions. "Are you okay?" Troy asked. "You don't have to do this, hon."

She nodded. "Yes, I do." Reaching out, she took his hand, then closed her eyes, letting her mind drift back. Back to the events that took place after her graduation from high school. She held Troy's fingers tightly, grateful for his love. For his support. She needed both desperately if she was going to finally tell him the truth.

"It was the summer of 1986." She paused. "The summer Daddy lost his job."

Jane remembered the details of that ordeal like it was yesterday. Her father had left the security of his long-time position as professor at North Central Community College for a lucrative offer with a promising new company in Traverse City. It was a forty-five minute drive one way, but the company offered him nearly twice his previous salary and a benefit package that included a pension plan and complete medical coverage. It was an offer too good to pass up, and her father took it willingly.

"Up until that time, things had been modest. Oh, we never had to do without. But my parents did what everyone did those days: they used credit cards and second mortgages to buy material goods. They bought our Petoskey home for only $39,000, and by 1980 it was worth three times that. Each time the value of the house grew by $20,000 or so, Mom and Dad borrowed against it and paid off the cards." She shook her head. "Dad's new position could have offered him a chance to finally pay off their debts and reduce their mortgage payments."

"Could have?"

"Yeah, but Daddy didn't have the job five weeks before he and Mom bought a new van, new clothes for all five of us kids, and a time-share vacation condominium in Lake Geneva. There were dinners on the town, steak barbecues, and personal computer components." She grinned. "It was like Christmas every day.

"One night we were all gathered at the table for dinner and Daddy got this funny-looking grin on his face. He pulled a box from his suit coat and gave Mom the most beautiful string of diamonds you ever saw. No one could believe it."

Troy looked surprised. "I'll bet."

"He told Mom he'd never been able to shower her with gifts. If money weren't a problem, he said, he'd give her gifts like that every day."

"It must have felt good for him to do something like that."

"It didn't feel so good when the debts piled up. I heard Mom ask Dad once if we could afford everything, and he just assured her that his new job would take care of all our financial worries."

"Sounds like an exciting time," Troy remarked, and Jane gave him a grim smile.

"You have no idea. Four weeks later, on a Monday at the end of June, Dad's supervisor approached him with bad news. They had lost one of their most lucrative contracts, an oil deal with Saudi Arabia. The company was downsizing. They had to let Dad go. And there was no severance pay."

Her father had been stunned. He spent the rest of the week waking at his usual time, dressing and pretending to go to work while he looked desperately for a new job.

He approached his previous employer and spoke with the president of the college.

"They said they'd love to have him back, but they were filled for the semester. They couldn't get him on staff until January." She paused, closing her eyes. "It was June. When nothing else seemed immediately available Dad began to panic. On Thursday night he wrote a letter to us." She opened her eyes and met Troy's stunned gaze. "I know it by heart.... 'Dear Diane, Ellen, Jane, Megan, Amy, and Aaron. I have failed all of you miserably. My company lost a contract and let me go last Monday. I have looked for a job but there is nothing. The college can't take me back for seven months so I have let you down and I am sorry.

"'You will notice that the computer from the back bedroom is gone. I hope to sell it. I'll send money when I do and there should be more money later; I'm sure you'll know what to do with it. Diane, my life insurance policy is in my top drawer. I love you all. Please forgive me for what I must do. Your loving husband and father.'"

"Did you find the letter?" Troy's question was filled with sympathy.

Jane shook her head. "Mom did. It was in a business envelope propped up on Dad's pillow. She told us about it that afternoon. She said Dad had lost his job and gone away for a while. We were stunned. We just sat there, staring at her." Jane grimaced. "Of course, Ellen was the first to recover. She asked where Dad was. Mom sighed and said she wasn't sure. That he'd send us some money soon."

In her mind's eye, Jane could still see the loss on her mother's face, the confusion in her brother's and sisters' eyes. "Maybe he's trying to find work," her mother had finished.

"How could he do that?" Ellen asked and she closed her eyes so the others couldn't see her tears.

"Maybe it's just a vacation," Megan had mused. She was fifteen and always the optimist back then. "Maybe he needs a little break so he can work things through."

"Why didn't he take us?" Amy asked. She was thirteen and there was naked fear in her green eyes.

Aaron said nothing. He folded his arms across his chest and stared at the floor. Jane remembered studying the others and rolling her eyes.

"He didn't take us because Megan's right." Mom had tried so hard to sound reassuring. "It's something like a vacation, except this time he needs to be alone. Sometimes adults need time to themselves." She looked at the other children and tried to assess their feelings. "Jane, do you understand?"

"Sure." She'd allowed hatred to fill her eyes. "Dad doesn't love us so he left."

"Jane!" Her mother reached gently toward her and touched her cheek. "That's not what's happened at all. Of course your father loves you and all the rest of us. This must be very hard for him."

"Yeah, Jane, why don't you just shut up!" Ellen had shot back, tears spilling onto her cheeks. "You're always so rude to Dad. Why don't you give him a chance. He'll be back anytime and then he'll explain the whole thing."

"He'll explain it to you, maybe, because he loves you. But he doesn't care if he leaves me, and that's the truth."

Ellen clucked her tongue against the back of her teeth. "Not another poor Jane story. You always think people love you less than everyone else. It's all in your head, Jane. Why don't you grow up?"

"Girls!" Their mother's voice was loud and it stopped the argument. "We all need to stick together. I won't have any more arguing." She paused. "There's something else."

She dismissed the younger children and asked Ellen and Jane to remain. Their dad had never done anything like this before, she said, so there was no telling when he might come back. She told Jane and Ellen that she was planning to find a job and begin working immediately, but several weeks might pass before she received a paycheck.

"We have a house payment coming up. You both have jobs this summer and I may need your help." There was shame in her eyes and the girls had to strain to hear her. "I hate to have to ask, but we don't want to lose the house."

The girls nodded, stunned by their mother's request. They had never considered their parents' finances before. Suddenly their firm foundation was shifting badly.

"What did you say?" Troy asked quietly, breaking Jane's flow of memories.

"We said we'd do whatever we could to help." Jane shifted, restless.

"You don't have to go on, hon. Not if it's too hard."

She reached out to touch his face. "Yes, I do. You need to know this. We heard nothing from Dad that night, and early the next morning Ellen left the house. She said she'd be back later and not to worry about her."

"Did Ellen ever tell you where she went?"

Jane nodded. She had, indeed.

With the sun still making its way into the sky, Ellen had driven to Magnus Park and found it empty. The tourists had recently returned to their homes in Chicago and Detroit and the town was noticeably quieter. She walked through the thick grass toward a shady knoll overlooking the water. No one would bother her there.

She stared at the blue-green bay and thought about the position her father had left them in. His actions tore at her loyalty to him as nothing else had.

After a while, her thoughts drifted and she considered her own life. She had missed so many classes at North Central the year before that she had been placed on academic probation.

"You're a smart girl, Miss Barrett," the dean had told her. "We would welcome you back should you change your study habits. But we will have to limit your course load until you can show an improved attendance record."

The probation was her fault. The reason, of course, was Jake Sadler. When he wanted to see her, she went regardless of her schedule. What was a history class when she could spend an afternoon with Jake?

After being put on probation she figured that perhaps she did not need a college degree, after all. She had not told her parents, but she planned to drop out of school and enroll in a course for legal secretaries. But her father's disappearance had changed everything.

A gentle breeze blew off Lake Michigan that day, and Ellen stared beyond the bay toward the open water. For the first time in her life she realized how utterly dependent the six of them were on their father. She thought about Jake and their plans to marry someday. Certainly she relied on Jake and would do so even more if they married. If he left she would be heartbroken.

But she would not be broke.

She later told Jane that in those solitary moments she decided she would never be financially dependent on Jake or any other man. She would never wonder where the next house payment was going to come from.

Suddenly the idea of quitting college seemed utterly ludicrous. She would reenroll at the community college. She would attend her classes, regardless of Jake's persuasive invitations. She would work harder than ever to earn high grades and then she would transfer to the University of Michigan where she would work until she had her bachelor's degree. Jake had made her forget her dreams, but now they were convincingly clear. She would study journalism and become one of the best reporters ever.

When she married, she would never place her husband under the financial strain her father had been living with. She stood up, brushed the sand off her shorts, and headed for her car.

"It was a turning point for Ellen." Jane turned to meet Troy's eyes. "She told me she knew it with everything in her. Even her walk was different, more confident, the picture of determination." A wry smile tipped her lips. "She said there would be no notes left on bedroom pillows for Ellen Barrett. No matter what happened with Dad, she was sure of that much."

"Sounds like a defining moment for her," Troy said, and Jane nodded.

"It's strange, though, how the same event affected each of us so differently." She sighed and forced herself to continue.

When her father didn't return home by Saturday evening Jane did something she hadn't done in months. She called Clay's friend and found out where the band was playing that night. By then she had saved up enough money to buy a small used car. After dinner she drove ten miles along the shore of Lake Michigan to Charlevoix where the party was already underway.

"I moved through the crowd of drunken, drugged partygoers and wondered what I was doing. I thought about my father and his eternal comparisons and I had the strange sensation that I was someone other than Jane Barrett, almost as if I no longer had any attachment to the Barrett family whatsoever."

She closed her eyes, fighting the tears. Troy squeezed her hand, offering her silent encouragement as she went on.

"This tall, dark-haired stranger with bloodshot eyes came up to me then. He looked me over, and I could tell by his expression that he liked what he saw. I guessed he was about twenty years old, completely stoned. But his approval fed something…a hunger, I guess, deep inside me. He was handsome in a dangerous way and he dressed like one of the band members even though I had never seen him before. I—I smiled at him."

How she regretted that smile. Even now, so many years later, she wished desperately that she'd just turned and walked away.

"I'm the new drummer, and you're Jane Barrett, right?" His words had been slightly slurred.

"How do you know?" Jane had batted her eyes, playing with him.

"Everyone knows about Jane Barrett. Used to be Clay's girl. The only blond who ever dumped Clay on his royal behind."

He laughed at the thought and put his hand on Jane's bare shoulder. She savored the sensation and felt a stirring in the pit of her stomach.

"It's warm in here." His voice was husky. "Let's take a walk."

Jane had looked into the young man's red-rimmed eyes and decided no harm could come from taking a walk with someone who thought she was beautiful. She nodded and allowed him to slip his fingers between hers as they turned and headed for the door.

"Hey, Squid-man, where you headed?" The voice could barely be heard above the din of the party, and Jane turned to see another band member making his way toward them.

"Taking a walk," the dark-haired stranger shouted in reply, squeezing Jane's hand tighter. "Be back before the next set."

The band member smiled and flashed an okay to the couple as they headed out the door. They walked more quickly than Jane would have liked and headed away from the party, down a narrow sidewalk that led to a private beach. In a matter of minutes the roar of the party had disappeared, and Jane felt suddenly awkward in the silence between them. She wondered if she was crazy, walking hand in hand with a perfect stranger, someone so stoned he probably didn't remember his name.

He glanced at Jane, tripping and nearly pulling her down on top of him. As he struggled to regain his balance he laughed. "You sure are pretty, Jane. Clay must have been messed up for weeks when he lost you, huh?"

Jane wrinkled her eyebrows, not sure what he meant. "Clay was a jerk, to be perfectly honest."

"Yeah," the young man laughed as if he'd heard the funniest line ever. "Right. A jerk."

They stepped off the paved sidewalk and began walking on the sand. There were clusters of bushes and trees along the beach and dozens of dark places.

"Let's go back." Jane tried to twist her hand free from the stranger's. "I'm cold."

He stared at her, the laughter gone, and tightened his grip. "We can't go back now, we haven't had any fun yet." He turned toward her and pulled her into his arms, holding her fast, kissing her hard.

Jane pushed him away and wiped her face with the back of her hand. She was suddenly terrified. "We took our walk, now it's time to go back."

Suddenly the stranger shoved her hard with both hands so that she fell backward onto the sand. The spot was pitch dark, surrounded by dense brush. In the distance she could hear water lapping softly against the shore. A faint scent of honeysuckle from a nearby garden mingled with the smells of the bay.

"Hey!" she cried. "What do you think—"

"Shut up! Don't pretend you don't like it. I heard all the stories from Clay. You'd tease him all night and never give in. Well, you're gonna give in tonight, baby. Right now."

In an instant, he ripped at her clothes.

"No! Get away!" Suddenly she thought of the one person who had always saved her from trouble and she screamed his name. "Daaad! Help!"

The stranger laughed at her as he pinned her to the ground. "Your daddy's not going to help you now."

She screamed again and fought to be free of him. But she was no match for his strength and he slammed his hand over her mouth.

"Don't say a word, or you're dead. Got it? Just relax and enjoy it. Let old Squidman teach you a thing or two about teasing."

For what seemed like an eternity the stranger savagely raped her. When it was finally over, he stood and kicked her in the ribs. "You look like something a cat would bury." He laughed cruelly, then bent down, picked up a fistful of sand, and threw it at Jane's face. "Good for nothing witch," he snarled. "You tell anyone about this and I'll say you begged me for it."

Jane waited until the sounds of the party began to fade before she crawled back into her torn clothing. She wiped the sand from her eyes and mouth and made her way through the shadows back toward her car. When she got home, she slipped into her room, changed her clothes, and ran a finger over the painful bruises on her arms and legs. There was blood on her underwear and she stuffed them in a bag, which she buried quietly in the trash.

Then she stared in the mirror at the woman she had become that night and wondered at the lengths she had gone to convince herself she did not need her father's love.

"Daddy," she whimpered at her reflection. "I only wanted you to love me for who I am. Oh, Daddy, I miss you."

She cried herself to sleep that night and every night for a month.

Jane fell silent, hanging her head. Twelve years had passed since that horrific night, but she could still feel the pain, still smell the musty wet sand and the sickly sweet honeysuckle.

What must Troy think of her? Fear filled her, but she pushed it aside and turned to look at him. He watched her, his eyes filled with pain and compassion. He opened his arms, and with a sob of relief Jane collapsed in his embrace. She cried deep, gut-wrenching sobs.

"Th-that," Jane said when she could speak again. Tears streamed down her face as she lifted her head and stared into her husband's eyes, "was how I lost my virginity. The same week my dad left."

She sobbed loudly, painfully.

"Shhh, it's okay, honey." Troy stroked her back, speaking words of love, telling her how proud he was of her for finally trusting him with the truth. "I love you, Jane. I'll always love you."

"I loved my dad. I wanted his love," she cried. "I wanted it so badly. Then he left, and I tried to find it somewhere else. Instead I got raped."

With a shuddering sigh, she straightened. The memories had left her exhausted, almost dizzy. "Dad came home a week later and found another job. Six months after that, he was rehired by the college."

Troy's arms came around her and he held her tightly. Jane would always remember the expression on Troy's face. He obviously understood now. By the time her father had returned home, the damage was already done. How could she grieve his death, when, in her mind, her father hadn't existed for more than a decade. He had died twelve years earlier on a musty, sand-covered beach in Charlevoix, Michigan.

8

$\mathcal{O}$n Sunday morning, two days after her father's death, Megan and her mother attended an early church service. For forty-five minutes the priest droned on about being a servant of the church and how best to imitate the lives of the saints. Not once did he make reference to their father's death.

Afterwards, arms linked, Megan and her mom made their way back to the family van where they were silent for a moment. The service had been a disappointment for her mother, Megan could tell. The poor woman had hoped to receive some comfort from her church family. After all, they had belonged to St. Francis Xavier Catholic Church for twenty years.

"That was terrible," Megan said quietly as they drove out of the church parking lot.

"It was a bit disappointing," her mother conceded, keeping her eyes on the busy tourist traffic that congested State Street. The church was located in the Gaslight District where dozens of quaint shops added to the annual draw of tourists. July was the busiest month of all.

"It was more than disappointing. It was sinful. That priest knew we were upset and he didn't even acknowledge us." Megan fumed as she tightened her seat belt. Certainly the priest knew who they were and what had happened! Mom had spoken with him the day before to arrange a date for the funeral. "Dad took us caroling to that priest every Christmas for the past twenty years." She turned to stare out the van window. "And not even a smile or a hand on the shoulder, nothing to help us believe we'll get through this."

Megan and Amy had attended the church's grade school, and their mother volunteered her time as a catechism teacher. The Barrett family had sat in the same pew every Sunday for two decades, Megan thought angrily. But still the priest had failed to help them in their time of need.

As they drove, Megan remembered an incident two years earlier when her father was in the hospital with circulation problems. Mom had called St. Francis Xavier and requested that the priest visit John in the hospital.

"I'm sorry," she was told. "That hospital isn't in our area."

"What? It's only three miles from the church," her mother had protested.

"I'm sorry. You'll have to contact the priest of a church closer to the hospital. I believe that would be the Catholic church in Charlevoix. That's the way the system works."

Overall, Megan believed St. Francis Xavier was undeserving of John Barrett. When they moved to Petoskey her father had offered his assistance in fund-raising, but he was told the church had all the help it could use. Her father never forgot that, and in Megan's opinion, he never viewed St. Francis the same way he had once viewed St. Thomas in Ann Arbor.

The women drove home in silence and sat outside for a moment.

"I need you to help me clean the house, Megan." Her mother looked weary, and Megan was worried about her. "We'll have the girls home tonight, and in a few days people will arrive from out of town. I want the house ready."

"Fine."

"And don't worry about what happened at church today. I'll be all right. Grieving is a private matter for me, something between God and me. I don't need a priest hugging me and telling me everything will be okay."

Megan nodded, and the two went inside. The cleaning started in the kitchen.

"I think Ellen's right," Megan said thoughtfully as she worked alongside her mother. Ellen and Jane had both left the Catholic church years earlier and attended small, nondenominational Christian churches in their separate communities. "Ellen says the Catholic church isn't concerned with people's private lives and that—"

"That's her opinion," her mom cut in, making it clear to Megan that she did not want to talk about the ways in which the Catholic church, according to Ellen, might be lacking. Megan knew her mother had participated in very few religious discussions since Ellen and Jane had abandoned their Catholic upbringing. Still, she'd always made it clear she accepted their decisions and believed there were good things about the churches they attended.

Mom also made it clear that she was aware that St. Francis was not a perfect church, but that did not change her opinion of the Catholic church as a whole. Besides, she had been Catholic as long as she could remember and she would be Catholic until the day she died. Regardless of what anyone thought.

"But, Mom, don't you think that was cold? It's like no one even knew Dad existed at that church. Even after twenty years."

"Your father loved being Catholic. He understood that the priest at St. Francis is a busy man. Now I think that should be the end of the conversation."

Megan shrugged. "At least at Ellen's church everyone cares about each other. When someone dies they pull together and—"

"Megan, that's enough. Now check the calendar and tell me what time the girls' flights are coming in."

Megan stared at her mother. All their lives she had refused to talk about contro-

versial matters. Whenever the discussion made her mom uncomfortable she changed
the subject, as she had just done. Megan let it go and checked the calendar.

"Ellen's in at 1:30, Jane's in at 1:50. I need to leave here no later than eight-thirty."

"Well," she wiped her hands on a towel and rubbed her eyes. "I hope the girls
won't bicker this week. The rest of you either. Your father would have wanted everyone to get along."

Megan rolled her eyes. "Mom, don't even say such a thing. Of *course* everyone will
get along. We haven't been together since the reunion two years ago. Everyone will
have a lot of catching up to do. Besides, we have Dad's funeral to think about. You
don't think planning a funeral is going to cause us all to start fighting with each other,
do you?"

"It could."

"Mooooom. Please. We're adults, after all."

"Honey, you don't know your sisters as well as I do. I'm just going to say a special prayer that Ellen and Jane get along. I'm worried about them the most. It's
important to me."

"If you think it's necessary."

Her mother sighed. "You know, sweetheart, you missed a lot all those years you
dated Mohammed. Sometimes I think they created a vacuum in your life."

"Meaning what?" Megan knew she sounded defensive.

"Meaning you have a tendency to see your brother and sisters the way they were
when they were all very young. Things have changed since then, Megan."

Megan watched her mother as she continued scrubbing the kitchen sink. She felt
tears forming in her eyes. "We still love each other, Mom."

"I know, dear, I'm sorry. I didn't mean to say you don't love each other." She was
quiet a moment. "I hope you have time to really help each other this week, maybe
cry together. I think that would be good."

They heard Aaron lumbering down the hallway toward the kitchen. Megan
swiped at an errant tear and sniffed loudly, composing herself. "Mom, you think
Aaron would want to go to the airport with me?"

Diane picked up a wet pan and began drying it. "Well, dear, probably not. He
hasn't said much since Friday and I don't think he'd be very good company."

Aaron walked into the kitchen, opened the refrigerator, and grabbed an apple. He
looked tan and freshly showered, and Megan wondered what he was thinking, how
he was handling their father's death.

"What'd you say?" he mumbled.

"Hello, dear."

Megan glanced at her mother. She always made an effort to sound cheerful when
she talked to Aaron, almost as if she was afraid to make him angry.

"Megan wanted to know if you'd like to go to the airport with her."

Aaron grunted, rubbed his apple on his jeans, and left the room.

"Would that be yes or no, Aaron?" Megan called after him.

"I said no!" Aaron's voice boomed through the house from his back bedroom.

"He's going to be great company this week," Megan mumbled.

Sometimes she wondered if Aaron was still angry with her for dating Mohammed. But how was she to know he was a drug dealer? It wasn't until they'd been together a while that she found that out. And by then it was too late to leave him....

Once Aaron had pulled her aside and snarled at her, "That idiot is worse than the slime from a septic tank. And you're nothing but a scumbag for dating him, Megan. Don't give out your last name. I wouldn't want anyone to think we're related."

She had long since forgiven him for his harsh words. She realized that essentially her brother had been right. Dating Mohammed had been a crazy thing to do. But she couldn't help but wonder if Aaron still held a low opinion of her for those wasted years.

She looked at her mother. "I'll assume he doesn't want to go. "

"Now, Megan," her mom pleaded. "Don't be sarcastic. He's going through a hard time right now, like all of us. Try and understand."

"Oh yes, I know the story. Aaron's had such a hard life and so on and so forth. You'd think he was raised in an orphanage the way people talk about him sometimes. 'Poor Aaron. Raised in the same house as all those girls.' I guess they don't know that he was the only one who had his own room and the only one who went golfing on Saturdays with Dad while the girls stayed home and did the housework."

"Megan, dear. Be nice."

"I will," she said sweetly, brushing a single lock of hair off her damp forehead. "Don't worry. We wouldn't want to make Aaron angry, now would we?"

Aaron always blamed his temper on the fact that he was raised with four sisters, as if that alone was enough to drive someone insane. Megan clenched her teeth, not wanting to let her frustration with Aaron spill over onto her mother. "I'm sorry." She closed the dishwasher and pushed a button to start the cleaning cycle. "I'll try to be nice."

"Thank you, Megan. It means a lot to me. I really don't think I can make it if you children don't get along this week."

Megan took out the broom and tilted her head thoughtfully as she swept the kitchen floor. After all these years their mother still referred to them as children. She glanced at her watch and saw that it was eight o'clock.

The front door opened, and they heard Amy's voice.

"Hi." Amy rounded the corner, her husband, Frank, by her side. Her eyes were bloodshot and she looked like she hadn't slept. "We're here."

Frank sat down immediately and began thumbing through a computer magazine. Amy remained in the kitchen. She leaned against the counter and stared at her mother and sister working together.

"Is there anything I can do?"

Their mother smiled warmly at her youngest daughter. Amy had always been quieter than the other Barretts. Family theory had it that since her older sisters were so busy talking, she never had a chance to say anything. But Megan didn't buy that. She was convinced Amy didn't want to talk about her life. She was a private person. When she finished her child development courses at North Central in 1992, she'd married a computer wizard. They were a reserved couple who preferred to spend their time alone. Megan considered her sister. None of them really knew or understood Amy— and that seemed to be fine with her.

The one member of the Barrett family who seemed to understand Amy perfectly was their mother. According to Mom, Amy was much like she had been at the same age. Amy was the only Barrett daughter with their mother's jet black hair and green eyes. Megan smiled. The similarities did not stop there.

Mom had always admitted she desired little in life except to be John Barrett's wife and the mother of his children. She did most of the cooking and cleaning, even after taking a full-time job at the telephone company. She never complained. In her opinion a woman should take care of the home, regardless of her busy schedule.

Of all her daughters, only Amy was the kind of wife their mom had been as a young married woman. She met her husband's needs much the way Mom had always met Dad's needs, right up until his death. Amy would never cause a conflict, and for that reason their mother was especially proud of her youngest daughter. Amy had been a simple child and now, though she was married and working at a local day care, Megan saw her as a simple woman.

"There's a load of laundry in the dryer if you wouldn't mind folding it," Mom said, hugging Amy close.

Amy nodded and did as she was told.

"Want to come to the airport?" Megan put the broom away and helped Amy carry the laundry into the living room where they dumped it on an oversized chair.

"No. You guys don't need me."

Megan looked at her younger sister strangely. "What do you mean we don't need you? We're all in this together. He was your dad, too."

"I know. I just mean they'll probably feel more like talking if I'm not around."

Megan's eyebrows came together in a puzzled frown and she glanced at Amy's husband. "I'm glad you understand her, Frank. I sure don't."

For several minutes she helped fold laundry, making small talk with Amy and Frank. Then she picked up her purse and kissed her mother on the cheek.

"Bye." She studied her mother's face, then added softly, "Why don't you get some rest, Mom? We'll probably be up late tonight."

Her mother nodded absently. She folded the kitchen towel, set it on the counter, and looked up. Megan saw the tears in her eyes.

"It's hard to believe he's gone, isn't it?"

"I know." Megan felt tears of her own. "Sometimes I wonder how we can all be a family without him."

Her mother sniffed, wiping at her eyes. "I keep thinking I've got to stop crying.

I won't be able to get through the week if I don't get a grip."

"No, that's not true. You go ahead and cry." Megan put an arm around her mother. "You were married to him forever. You can cry for a year if you want."

Her mother uttered a short laugh, and Megan hugged her tight.

"It's so good to have you back, Megan," Mom whispered into Megan's hair. "My sweet, sweet girl. There were times when you were dating Mohammed…" Her voice trailed off, choked by deep gratefulness. "Thank God he brought you back."

"I know." Megan sobbed softly and allowed herself to be hugged like a little girl. "I'm glad Daddy lived long enough to see me come to my senses."

"He prayed for you every day." Her mother pulled back and studied Megan's eyes. "We got through that time, and if we all pull together we'll get through this, too."

Megan nodded, tears still streaming down her face. Wracked by the ache in her heart, she prayed her mother was right.

9

*T*raffic at Detroit Metropolitan Airport did not hold to a specific rush hour. Regardless of the time of day, bumper-to-bumper cars snarled and knotted around the airport's massive loop causing delays for weekend and midweek travelers alike. Megan Barrett fought for position amidst hundreds of motorists and parked her compact car not far from the terminal where her sisters would be arriving.

It was ninety-two degrees and the humidity hovered at just above 80 percent, trapping the city's pollution so that the skyscrapers pushed their way through a murky brown layer of smog. Megan glanced at her watch and picked up her step. It was nearly one-thirty; Ellen's plane would be landing any time now.

The jet was gradually descending, and Ellen peered out the window, scanning the aerial view of the city. The air around the plane had become thick and dirty, and she wondered how she had ever enjoyed living in Detroit. At least in Miami breezes off the ocean kept the city air relatively clean.

She lifted her gaze through the hazy sky toward upper Michigan. Interstate 75 made an almost direct route from Detroit to Petoskey, north up the center of the state. It took between four and five hours to reach Petoskey from Detroit, but as long as it wasn't snowing, the Barretts had never minded the drive. The countryside was quietly rugged with deep green pastures, towering Ponderosa pines, and shimmering picturesque lakes.

Years earlier when her family had made the drive, her father would comment on the lush groves of pine trees or the endless sea of wild grass or the glassy lakes along the way. His favorite part of the drive was just before they reached home, as Highway 31 curved along Lake Michigan and dipped down along the water for a breathtaking view of Little Traverse Bay and the Petoskey shoreline.

"Behold," he would say, sweeping his arm grandly across his bod,. "the beautiful bay."

The pilot lowered the landing gear and Ellen put her seat in an upright position. She had flown into this airport a dozen times, and each time her father had been waiting when she got off the plane. Even once when she flew for business and had access to a rental car, her father insisted on meeting her.

"If a father can't meet his daughter at the airport, then things have gotten pretty sad," he'd say with a smile.

"I don't know, Dad, it's a long drive."

"Don't worry about it, Ellen. It's not a problem. I enjoy it."

She closed her eyes and sighed, wishing with all her heart that he could be there now, at the end of the ramp, peering over the heads of strangers as he searched for her face. Just one more time.

The three-hour flight from Phoenix to Detroit was relatively easy for Jane, despite the fact that she had the children with her. Troy had a sales convention in Los Angeles and would join her Friday morning, the day before the funeral. Jane was used to Troy's traveling and she never even considered asking him to cancel the convention and spend the week with her in Petoskey. She and her siblings would have to choose a casket, plan the service, and help their mother survive until the funeral. Troy would have only been in the way.

Jane glanced at her pretty, blond children sleeping in the row beside her. She could picture having more babies. She was patient and fair and had long since learned the art of listening to her little ones.

"Mommy, know what?" one of the children would ask.

Jane would stoop down and look the child in the eyes as if there was nothing in the world more important than the words he was about to say. "What is it, honey?"

The child would smile and proceed with a story while Jane remained captivated until he was done. Her response was something she had learned in her weekly care group at Verde Valley Christian Church. Growing Kids God's Way, the program was called. Through it she and Troy had learned dozens of parenting skills. Listening to a child, they had agreed, was often the most effective way a parent could communicate love. More than anything, Jane and Troy wanted their children to feel loved.

She smiled at them now, absently running her hand across each of their three foreheads. They would miss Papa, as they called him. He had been a hands-on grandfather. He bounced them on his knee, read them bedtime stories, and played silly games with them. It had been during their recent visits, when her father would spend time loving her children, that Jane had actually felt close to him. There were no Ellens in John Barrett's life once he became a grandfather.

As the plane landed, Jane wondered how Ellen was handling their father's death. She was probably devastated. For a moment, Jane felt guilty for being gruff with her on the telephone. There seemed no way to bridge the gap that lay between them.

She ran a hand through her short-cropped blond hair and silently asked God to help her get through the coming week. She was not looking forward to seeing Ellen so upset. It would only make Jane more aware of the relationship she had never shared with their father.

The plane landed gracefully, gliding down the runway and turning toward the proper terminal. Jane glanced at her watch.

Ellen's plane would have already landed, and she and Megan were probably comforting each other.

Jane stared out the window of the plane, her teeth clenched. *Just as well that I'm arriving a few minutes later.*

Still wearing her round-rimmed sunglasses, Ellen exited the plane, her leather bag slung over one shoulder. She searched the crowd for Megan and finally spotted her waving, working her way through the crowd.

"Ellen!" Megan's arms were around Ellen's neck and her eyes stung with tears. Ellen hugged her sister tightly. They stayed that way for a while, unaware of the people streaming past them.

"He usually meets me at the airport and—" Ellen's voice broke. "He should be here, Megan. I can't believe he's gone."

"He had a good life, Ellen, we have to remember that." Megan was crying, too, and she kept her hands on Ellen's shoulders as she pulled away and looked intently at her. "He loved us with all his heart."

Ellen nodded. "I know," she sniffed. "But I miss him so bad it hurts."

"Me, too." Megan handed her a tissue and picked up her bag. "Come on. We have to meet Jane in a few minutes."

Jane had taken the same airline and would arrive just two gates away.

"You look good, Megan," Ellen glanced at her sister and thought how much more attractive she was than…before. Megan was thin and curvy, with long legs that had finally stopped growing when she reached five-foot-ten. She wore her dark blond hair much like Ellen's: cropped to her shoulders and fashionably styled. Ellen smiled as she noted the masculine glances being directed at the two of them. Despite their tearstained faces, they made a striking pair.

"How's Mom doing?" Ellen asked as they found seats near the gate where Jane would be arriving. "I've talked to her ten times since Friday but I can't really tell without seeing her."

Megan nodded. "She's handling it. Aunt Mary's been over a lot cooking and spending time with her. Mom's been expecting this for a long time, you know."

"We all have. I used to think of Dad as being terminally ill so that it would be easier when he died."

"Did it help?"

"Not at all. There's no way to be ready for news like this."

"I knew his health wasn't good, but I thought he'd live another twenty years. Wishful thinking I guess."

"Remember when he lost his job and left for that week?" Ellen adjusted her sunglasses.

"Yeah. Vaguely." Megan leaned back in her chair and crossed her arms over her stomach. "That was a bad time."

"After that he was never the same."

"Healthwise, you mean?"

"Everything. But especially his health. Even after he got another job there was one problem after another."

"The blood clots."

"Blood clots in the lungs, blood clots in the heart, blood clots in the legs. Phlebitis put him in the hospital every ten months until he had his veins stripped. Then there was the high blood pressure, and by then he was probably a hundred pounds overweight."

Megan nodded. "At least." She paused a moment. "He was a tall man, but that's too much for anyone."

"I remember taking a health class in college and the professor told us the warning signs for a heart attack. Male, over forty, obese, smoker, high blood pressure, stress, diabetes. When Dad was diagnosed with diabetes four years ago, he was like a loaded gun ready to go off. It was just a matter of time."

Megan sighed. "I know. But he defied the odds for so long I kept thinking he'd get one more chance. Even when I got the call at work that he'd had the heart attack I thought he'd be okay."

Ellen swallowed the lump in her throat and nodded. "Me, too. Just like last year when he had the bypass surgery. Remember when he had the angiogram to see how badly blocked his arteries were?"

Megan nodded. "I was there. They had him laid out on this cold, steel table with technicians and doctors buzzing around doing the test and putting nitroglycerin under his tongue. 'His heart's not gonna make it if we don't do surgery right away.' That's what the doctor said."

Megan shook her head, and Ellen reached out to take her sister's hand.

Drawing a steadying breath, Megan went on. "I remember looking at this huge screen where Dad's heart was on display for everyone to analyze. You know what I thought? With all their technology those people didn't know a thing about Dad's heart. He was more than another heart patient and I wanted to tell them so. For some reason that scene always stays with me."

"I didn't think he'd live through the surgery." Ellen recalled her fear that day. "But when he did I guess I thought he was finished with heart trouble."

"I know. I was sure he'd die on the operating table," Megan admitted. "We all sat there in that waiting room crying and thinking we'd never see him again."

Ellen sniffed and sat straighter in the padded airport chair. "At least we got another year, right?"

"But I wanted *ten* years. Twenty—" Megan's voice broke again. "I wanted him to walk me down the aisle when I get married someday. Like he did with you and Jane and Amy."

"I know." Ellen squeezed her hand. "Me, too."

They were silent then as Jane's plane pulled into position and passengers began streaming off. Ellen and Megan stood up and searched for their sister and the children.

She appeared carrying baby Kyle and holding three-year-old Kala's hand. Koley walked along beside them, handsome in a pair of shorts and an Arizona tank top. Megan waved, and Jane and the children headed toward them.

"How was your flight?" Megan hugged Jane and bent over to tousle the children's hair.

Jane set several bags down and took a deep breath. "Good, actually. The kids slept the whole way."

Ellen moved closer and hugged Jane. "You doing all right?"

Jane returned the hug, but Ellen didn't miss that she seemed slightly stiff. As she pulled away Jane smiled sadly. "Yeah. It's not easy but I'm surviving. You guys okay?"

Ellen nodded, and Megan began crying again. She put an arm around each of her sisters. "We have to be there for each other now that he's gone."

Ellen said nothing but noticed that Jane seemed to ignore Megan's statement as she pulled her children close and struggled to pick up her bags.

"Let's get the luggage and get home," Jane said. Her eyes were cool and dry. "It's a long drive, and I'm sure Mom needs us."

They collected their bags and returned to Megan's car. The children were buckled into the backseat so the adults could share the front and catch up on the latest details.

"So, what happened?" Jane asked when they were all in the car. "Was there any warning?"

Megan shook her head, looking over her shoulder as she backed out of the parking space and merged with the airport traffic. "He seemed perfectly normal the day before. In fact, I got home from work early Thursday and spent an hour telling him about all the personality conflicts at the office. He was a little sleepy, but other than that he was fine."

Ellen, too, wondered what her father's last days were like. Her mother had been too distraught to talk about anything more than the bare details, and Ellen was hungry for more information.

"No chest pain?" she asked.

"Nothing." Megan steered the car out of the airport and west onto Interstate 94. "Then on Friday morning he was supposed to play golf with Aaron but he was too tired. After breakfast he fell asleep in his old easy chair. When he got up and walked down the hallway to take a shower, he collapsed."

"Who was home?" Jane turned around and gave the baby a pacifier. The other children had fallen asleep.

"Just Mom. She heard him fall and knew right away that he'd had a heart attack. She called an ambulance and tried to wake him up, but it was too late."

Ellen felt the tears again as she pictured the scene. She was thankful she hadn't been there.

"How long did it take the paramedics to arrive?"

"Not long." Megan kept her eyes on the road as she talked. "Mom tried to do CPR after she called for help, but on a man Dad's size it's pretty hard. He was already dead when the ambulance got there."

"It wasn't up to Mom to do CPR. That's the paramedics' job. They should have at least tried." Jane crossed her arms and looked suddenly angry. "People can be brought back from that point, you know."

"Jane." Ellen turned so she could see her sister plainly. "His heart quit. There wasn't much they could do about that."

Jane's eyes were hard. "You don't know everything, Ellen. I worked in the medical field and I know for a fact there are things they can do even after a person's heart has stopped."

"You were a dental hygienist, Jane. Most people would not consider that 'working in the medical field.' It's not like you were a nurse."

"I know more about medical issues than you do, okay?" Jane sat stiffly between her two sisters and snorted angrily.

Ellen wanted to argue, to force the issue, but instead she just drew a calming breath. "Well, either way, he's gone." She leaned forward looking past Jane to Megan. "He didn't have any symptoms or anything?"

"His neck had been bothering him, but everyone said that was just muscle tension. Dad thought he'd injured it playing golf."

"Didn't his neck hurt right before the bypass surgery?" Ellen asked.

"That's what I said. But the doctors swore the neck pain had nothing to do with the heart."

There was silence for a moment.

"Well, like you said, Megan, they didn't know anything about Dad's heart." Ellen's voice was noticeably softer. "Only we know what kind of heart he really had."

"Here we go," Jane muttered.

Ellen turned toward her. "What?"

"Nothing."

"No, tell me. What do you mean, 'Here we go'?"

Jane looked like it was all she could do to tolerate Ellen. "It's just that you're so dramatic, Ellen. The rest of us have been expecting Dad's death for years. You can't tell me it caught you by surprise."

Heat flooded Ellen's face, and she drew back as if she'd been slapped. "No, I'm not surprised. I'm *hurt*. And I want to remember who he was as a person and not just his health problems."

Jane's lips thinned. "You're right. Sorry for bringing it up." She looked straight ahead, and Ellen exchanged a quick look with Megan.

Ellen changed the subject. "Anyway, what are the plans so far for the funeral?"

"Nothing, really. Mom's waiting until we're all together so we can decide what to do."

Ellen leaned back against the headrest and closed her eyes. An hour passed in silence.

"Megan, when was the last time you talked to him?" Ellen finally asked. She remembered her last words with her father. Surely her sisters and brother did as well.

"It was Thursday night. He was watching TV with Mom and me, and I had to be up early in the morning for work. I kissed him good night just like I would any other time, and he smiled at me. You know that smile where you can see that he loves you and he's proud of you?"

Jane looked away.

"Yeah." Ellen smiled and nodded. Her eyes glistened with fresh tears.

Megan's voice was soft. "It was that smile. 'I love you, honey,' he told me. I told him I loved him, too. And then I drove home to my apartment and went to bed. That was the last time I saw him."

Ellen squeezed her eyes shut and hugged herself tightly. She did not regret moving to Miami, but she would have given anything to have been there that night. She could picture her family, watching television and swapping commentaries on the program. What would she have said if she'd been there and known it was his last night?

"How 'bout you? Do you remember the last time you talked to him?" Megan switched lanes and then looked questioningly at Ellen.

Ellen nodded. She wiped at her tears and struggled to speak. "It was Wednesday. I was working on this murder case and I thought I had it figured out before the police. I called and told him the details. He listened and asked questions, like he always does. Then I asked him how he was feeling and he said he was fine. The doctors had given him a clean bill of health not too long ago and he and Aaron were going to try and get back into golf so he could lose some weight."

"Same old story." Megan smiled.

Ellen tossed a quick glance at Jane. She didn't seem to be listening to their conversation. Instead she stared blankly at the road before them. Ellen shifted restlessly, wondering if her sister was aware of the uncomfortable feeling her silence was causing. She turned back to Megan.

"Same old story, all right. He even said he had picked a date toward the end of the year when he was going to stop smoking…"

"Again." Megan finished.

"Again." Ellen sniffed, grinning sadly at the memory. Their father had tried to stop smoking so many times it had become something of a hobby. After his bypass surgery he refrained for several months, but once he started up again his children refused to believe he would ever stop.

"Anyway, he seemed upbeat, and we talked maybe thirty minutes. Then he told me to keep up the good work and send him the article when it ran in the paper. I usually send him copies of my big stories, so I told him I would. He told me he loved me and that he was proud of me for my work on the paper—" Ellen's voice cracked. She cleared her throat, and went on. "I told him I loved him, too, and that was the end of it. I never found out the information I needed and I was going to call him Friday to see if he had any ideas. A lot of times I would call and pick his brain. Sometimes he helped me find a lead when nothing else worked." She shrugged. "You know the rest. By Friday night it was too late."

"At least we both told him we loved him," Megan said. There were more cars on Interstate 75 heading north than usual and Megan remained focused on the road. They had just passed Flint and had two more hours until they reached Petoskey. "I'll bet Aaron hasn't said those words to Dad in years. I wonder how *he's* feeling."

"Has he said anything to you?" Ellen hadn't spoken to him since their father's death. Aaron usually spoke in one-syllable words and seemed to have two basic personalities: bored or on the brink of losing his temper.

"No. He hasn't talked to any of us, really."

Ellen settled back against the headrest and stared out her side window. Another hour passed and she thought about her brother. There was a time when Ellen had made an effort with Aaron. She had sent him encouraging Bible verses and occasional letters. But sometime later she heard through her father that Aaron did not appreciate her efforts at correspondence.

"He thinks you're preaching to him," her dad said gently. "I know you're trying, honey, but maybe you'd be better off to just let him be. You can't change him, you know."

The news hurt, and for months Ellen considered calling Aaron and explaining that she had written the letters only because she cared. But she never called and she stopped writing after that. Although there was no tension between she and Aaron, they hadn't said more than ten words to each other in the past two years.

"What about you, Jane?" Megan broke the silence. "You remember the last time you talked to Dad?"

"I didn't talk to Dad much. Whenever I called I talked to Mom."

"I know, but do you remember the last time you talked to him?" Megan pressed, clearly frustrated and determined to work Jane into the conversation.

"No, I guess not. He probably told me to give the kids a hug and kiss or something. That's usually what he'd say."

Ellen sighed and turned to Jane. "He loved *you,* Jane. Not just your kids. Sometimes you act like he didn't."

"You don't need to tell me that. I know he loved me. But he and I weren't close like you two, or like he was with Megan. And that's something *you* don't understand, Ellen."

"That was your choice." Ellen raised her voice. "You never spent time with him or talked to him or sat down to keep him company. What did you expect, Jane? You have to be around someone if you want to be close to them."

"Well, it didn't seem to matter how far away *you* were. You moved eighteen hundred miles south and you were still closer to him than any of the rest of us."

Megan sighed. "Come on, you guys, don't fight. Dad loved us all. We have to lean on each other now and get through this together. The past is the past."

"I'm not fighting." Ellen returned her gaze to the road. "I just don't want her making Dad out to be some cold-hearted guy. It's time to say good-bye to him and I don't need her cheapening it."

She glanced at Jane again. "Maybe you two weren't close but don't go talking about it. The rest of us want to remember him in our own ways this week. Understand? I mean, you did love him, didn't you?"

Jane held her head a bit higher and clenched her teeth. Ellen was surprised to see tears fill her eyes, but they didn't spill over. It was as though Jane was refusing to cry. Like so many times before. Ellen longed to know what it was that troubled her sister so deeply, why she seemed so set on believing the worst about their father.

"Of course, I loved him," Jane said finally.

"Well, then, let's focus on that. All of us, all right?"

They continued north along Interstate 75 through the Mackinaw State Forest, past Higgins Lake and the Alpine town of Gaylord, on up to Highway 68 past Burt Lake and then to Highway 31. They drove over the slight grade and finally saw water as the road curved left and headed along the shore of Lake Michigan and Little Traverse Bay.

"Behold, the beautiful bay." Ellen could hear her father's proud words.

He had been right. The bay held the deepest, clearest blue water Ellen had ever seen. Even the Atlantic Coast could not compare with the pristine, majestic beauty of upper Lake Michigan.

In a matter of minutes they passed the summer community of Bay View. The social and financial elite from Chicago and Detroit owned the homes in Bay View. They were summer homes, supplied with electricity and water from May through August only.

Megan braked for a light, and Ellen studied the grand houses, their intricate Victorian designs and double-wraparound covered porches. Many of the homes were more than a hundred years old, but most had been completely restored to their original color and design. The neighborhoods swarmed with luxury cars while homeowners sat outside in porch swings, enjoying the *dazzling* view of the bay.

"Dad loved those summer homes," Ellen whispered.

Traffic was thick, and every other car on the road seemed to carry tourists. During most of the year, Petoskey had a population of six thousand. In the summer, that number doubled. Ellen remembered how exciting the tourist season was when she was a teenager. She would sit at the beach with her family and watch all the new boys playing touch football and volleyball on the sand.

The town put its best foot forward during the summer months and there was something exciting about the increase of traffic each June. Of course, some residents hated the tourists, cursing them for clogging up the city streets and making downtown Petoskey's Gaslight District nearly impassable.

But tourism was the leading industry in Petoskey, and everyone in town benefited from a strong summer season. Those who grumbled knew enough to keep their feelings to themselves. After all, the inconvenience lasted only three months.

There was something comfortable and reassuring about August, when the summer residents went home and the town returned to its simpler ways.

Megan drove up Spring Street over Bear River and turned left on East Mitchell Road. She continued past Stone Funeral Home into a sprawling subdivision of country homes and restored turn-of-the-century farmhouses. She turned right on Lake Avenue, drove past five houses, and then finally there it was: the yellow-and-brown two-story house where the Barretts had lived for twenty years.

Built in 1954, their house had been restored gradually over the past several decades. The covered porch had been used for everything from first kisses to card games, heart-to-heart conversations and family sing-alongs.

Ellen was glad the house looked the same. The willow trees still anchored it on either side. The interior would be the same as well, just as it had been when she lived there. Vaulted ceilings in the foyer, walnut railing up the stairway to the bedrooms on the second floor, dark brown carpeting throughout, a spacious country kitchen with a faded yellow-tile countertop.

They turned into the gravel driveway and parked behind the other cars. Their parents owned two acres of rolling grassland. After living in a Miami subdivision, she thought her family's backyard seemed to go on forever. They climbed out of the car and helped the children out of their seat belts as Mom walked out to meet them.

Jane was instantly at her side. "Mom, I've been so worried about you."

Ellen and Megan lagged behind with the children, and for an instant Ellen felt a pang of jealousy as she watched Jane and their mother embrace. Jane had always been a kindred spirit with their mother, while Ellen struggled to gain her approval. Ellen wondered if their mother had seen how much Dad loved her and Megan and had compensated by giving more of herself to Jane and Amy. Or perhaps her mother was still upset that Ellen was the first to leave the Catholic church. Either way, now that her father was gone she felt suddenly alone, without an ally.

Ellen studied her mother. She looked too thin and her face was drawn and pale. There was more gray in her hair than there had been two years earlier when Ellen was last in Petoskey. Her mother's eyes had dark circles beneath them, and every move she made looked painful.

Jane must have noticed the changes, too, for she looked worried. "How are you, really, Mom?"

"I don't know." She started crying softly and she put her arms around Jane's neck. Megan and Ellen quietly rounded up the children and joined Jane and their mother on the sidewalk.

"I'm sorry, Mom." Ellen placed a hand on her mother's back. "I wish he was here so he could say something to make us laugh again."

Her mother nodded and straightened, wiping her tears. She leaned over and hugged Ellen. "We'll be all right. We're together now. Come on, let's go inside. We can talk there."

Inside, Amy and Frank sat on the living room sofa and Aaron filled the matching oversized chair. His legs took up half the floor space in the room. He wore dark sunglasses and his arms were crossed tightly in front of him. Ellen thought he looked like an angry prisoner, daring anyone to get past the walls that surrounded him.

Amy stood up and hugged her sisters, then leaned over to kiss the children.

"Where's Papa?" Kala asked. She was still half asleep, her wispy blond hair pressed against her face from the long car ride.

"Oh, honey," Amy said and her eyes grew damp. "He's in heaven now. But he's very, very happy there and you know he still loves you, right?"

Kala started to cry. "I want my Papa." Jane lifted the child into her arms to console her.

Amy turned to Ellen, and the two hugged while Aaron remained motionless in the chair.

"Hi, Aaron." Ellen positioned herself so her brother could not help but see her.

Aaron grunted, which told Ellen little had changed. She wondered what kind of war was raging inside his head and heart that he had to work so hard to hide his feelings.

"Did you bring your bags in?" Her mother glanced at Ellen as she shut the door and searched the living room.

"No. I think we're staying at Megan's. Is that right?" Ellen didn't want to assume anything. Not with Jane on edge and their mother an emotional wreck.

"Right." Megan looked at their mother.

"Well, I suppose." Mom shrugged. "I just thought we could all stay here and be a family again. Like old times."

Ellen cringed inwardly as she imagined trying to share a shower schedule with Aaron and Jane.

"Mom, I think we need more space. Especially for the children."

For once Ellen agreed wholeheartedly with Jane. "We'll just be at Megan's at night so we have a place to sleep and shower."

"Oh. Well, I guess." Their mother looked slightly put out. "Your Aunt Mary is staying with me so I guess I'll be okay."

"Mom, if you want us to stay here, just say so," Ellen jumped in. She felt pierced by guilt.

"No, no. That's all right. You go on ahead and stay with the girls. Amy and Frank will be at their house so we wouldn't have all been together anyway. It's fine."

Everyone found seats around the living room, and Jane put the children in the den to watch cartoons. When she returned they rehashed the events that led up to their father's heart attack. They talked about his unhealthy eating habits, his lack of exercise, and his habitual smoking. Everyone agreed that certainly his death was not

a surprise. They talked about how much better it was that he had died quickly without any pain or suffering and how terrible it would have been if he had died from
diabetes complications.

"He could have lost his legs or his kidneys," their mother said.

"Or worse, his eyes. That would have been so hard for your father."

Ellen felt sick as she pictured her father blind or without legs. Mom was right.
Had he lived much longer the amputation of his lower limbs would have been a very
real possibility. He had varicose veins and terrible circulation. Over time the diabetes
would only have made the problem worse.

Ellen sat in silence as the others talked about how their father was in a better place
now.

"He knew he didn't have long," her mother said quietly.

"What do you mean?" Ellen looked at her mother in surprise.

"When we were in Las Vegas last spring he told me he didn't think he'd live much
beyond the end of the year."

"What? Why didn't he tell *me* that?"

Jane rolled her eyes but Ellen ignored her.

"I don't know. I guess he realized he hadn't followed the doctor's advice after his
surgery and he figured he was using up his last chance. He told me his quality of life
had slipped and he didn't want any more surgeries or any drastic measures taken. He
was at peace with God and himself and he was ready to go."

"Mother, he was only fifty-four!" Megan said angrily. "He should have been
thinking about how he could change his life and get himself healthy again."

"Megan," their mother said softly. "It's been a long time since he was healthy. You
know that."

There was silence and then the reminiscing started again, as though they had to
talk about every memory, every recollection they could think of—as though that
somehow kept him alive and in their midst.

When they had exhausted every subject concerning their dad's poor health, they
started over and talked about his last day again. Through it all, Aaron sat stone silent,
unmoving and apparently detached from the others.

Finally at six that evening, during a lull in the conversation, Megan stood up and
massaged her temples.

"I'm going for a walk," she announced. "Anyone want to come?"

Ellen rolled onto her feet and stretched her hands over her head as she yawned.
"I'll go. Mom, what are we doing for dinner?"

"Pizza. It'll be here in about thirty minutes."

Ellen looked at Jane, determined to make an effort. "Wanna come?"

Jane shook her head quickly. "No. That's all right. I need to change the kids and
get them a snack. The cartoons are over and they need some attention." She hesitated.
"Besides, I'm sure you two will have plenty to talk about without me tagging along."

Ellen ignored the comment. "Aaron?"

He uttered an imperceptible sound.

"Aaron, would you like to take a walk?" Ellen could feel the rising tension but she was determined to get an answer from him.

"I said, no! Are you deaf?"

Ellen turned, ignoring her brother's outburst. "Mom, we'll be back in a while."

She joined Megan outside, leaned against the front door, and sighed. She had never worked so hard to be kind to people in all her life.

"Wonderful, isn't it?" Megan seemed to read her mind and grimaced sadly.

"You feel it, too?"

"The tension? Of course. Aaron and Jane are like time bombs, and who knows what Amy's thinking."

"Tell me something, Megan." Ellen walked down the stone sidewalk toward the road and Megan fell in alongside her. "I know I've been gone four years and things change for everyone..."

"That's for sure."

"But what in the world happened? When did we all get to be strangers?"

Megan's eyes narrowed and she stared upward, still walking. When she spoke her voice was a strangled whisper. "I don't know, Ellen. I just don't know. But it's something we've got to figure out, or I'm afraid we'll never get back to being a family again."

10

There were no sidewalks so the girls walked on the right side of the worn road. The temperature had dropped considerably and a cool breeze filtered through the ancient maple trees that lined the street. Megan and Ellen rounded the corner.

"Gosh, what's wrong with Jane?"

"Oh, you mean Miss Congeniality?" Ellen uttered a short laugh. "I've been trying to figure that out for years."

"She's not being fair to Dad, do you think?"

"I don't know. She thinks Dad didn't love her like he loved you and me."

"That's crazy." Megan slowed her pace, clearly frustrated.

"I agree." Ellen shrugged. "But those are her feelings. I just wish she could remember the good times."

Megan kicked up a piece of asphalt. "I keep thinking of that Thanksgiving several years ago before she and Troy moved to Arizona. You were in Miami, but everyone else ate dinner at Mom and Dad's. All through the meal Dad kept saying how we should consider all God had given us and be thankful for what we had."

Ellen gazed at the treetops, remembering. "He loved the Lord, that's for sure."

"Always did." Megan paused. "Anyway, that evening when we were done eating he found one of those heavy paper plates Mom keeps around. He piled it high with turkey and potatoes and lime salad and pumpkin pie and then he wrapped it up in clear plastic."

Ellen stopped walking and looked at her sister. "I never heard about this."

Megan sighed. "That's because Jane never talks about the good times. She remembers things the way she wants to remember them."

We all do, Ellen thought. She started walking again. "So, what happened?"

"Well, Dad and Jane left the house and went driving around the Lamplight District looking for one of Petoskey's two wandering alcoholics. It wasn't very long before they found that older guy draped across the sidewalk in front of Michael's Doughnuts."

"What happened?"

"Dad and Jane got out of the car and walked up to the guy. Dad handed him the plate, wished him a happy Thanksgiving, and told him to remember how much God loves him."

Ellen smiled warmly, imagining the scene. "How'd you hear about that?"

"I was there when they got back and Jane told me all about it. She said Dad had tears in his eyes when he handed the man the plate. When they got back in the car, he told her he was proud of her for being a wonderful daughter and a terrific mother."

"Maybe we should remind Jane of that when we get back," Ellen offered. They walked past a sprawling farmhouse that had been renovated the year before. "At least she'd have one good memory."

"I don't know. She'd probably get mad at us for talking about her behind her back. That's how she's been lately."

"You think so, too?" Ellen folded her arms and glanced at a barking dog across the street. "I thought it was just me."

"No, I've seen it. I just don't say anything." Megan hesitated. "I want everyone to get along so badly. I missed a lot of years when I—when I was gone. Now I'm back. You and Jane have your husbands and your own lives far away from me. But you two, and Aaron and Amy and Mom are all I have. I think it's about time for us to be a family again."

Ellen sighed. "It's not that easy, Megan. Time passes, things change. I can't explain it but I can feel it. We're all different and we can't go back to being something we were twenty years ago."

Silence settled over them as they walked.

"How's everything with Mike?" Megan said after a while. Ellen laughed, but she knew it sounded bitter. "I'm not sure I want to talk about it."

Megan studied her older sister carefully. "I thought something might be wrong. Mom said Mike was coming with you. When I found out you were flying by yourself I thought it was strange."

"He has to work. At least that's what he says. He also says he doesn't care for funerals."

Megan cringed.

"Yeah, tell me about it. He actually told me I didn't need him, that I'd have lots of people around for support."

"Let me guess…you don't agree?"

The sun was setting, splashing brilliant hues of pink and orange across the northern Michigan sky. Ellen stopped walking and allowed her eyes to drift. When she looked back at Megan she shook her head angrily.

"No, I don't agree! I wanted him to come with me and he refused." She was quiet a moment. "That's how Mike and I are doing."

Megan was pensive as they resumed walking. "Mike's a great guy, Ellen. Don't judge him on this. You know he loves you."

Ellen shrugged. "I used to think so. But it's not just this. Weddings, concerts, social events, lots of times he doesn't want to go with me. What kind of love never makes a sacrifice for the other person?" She studied her feet and kept walking. "I don't know. Sometimes I think we're drifting apart."

"You guys going to church?"

Ellen shook her head. "That's a big part of it. How can God bless our marriage when we've all but forgotten about him?"

"I can't believe you guys aren't going to church. I always thought you were the perfect Christian couple."

"No one's perfect, Megan. Least of all Mike and me."

"Did something happen? At church I mean?"

"No, nothing like that. We just got busy. One thing led to another and now it's something we don't talk about. Like we're too far away from it all to go back." A lump formed in her throat and she had to fight a wave of tears. "I think I'm starting to feel that way about Mike, too."

"He is coming for the funeral, right?"

"We left it up in the air. I told him I didn't care if he stayed home, and he told me that was fine with him. I guess I'll have to talk to him sometime this week so we can decide what to do."

They turned a corner and headed back toward the Barrett home. Megan thought a moment and then glanced at her sister. "Know who I saw the other day?"

"Who?"

"Jake Sadler. Over at the hardware store buying lumber. He's building a fence for his parents or something."

Ellen's stomach flipped. She forced her voice to remain unchanged. "How's he doing?"

"Same as always. Single, tall, beached-out, and gorgeous. Guys like Jake never change."

Ellen's eyes narrowed. "I haven't seen him in so long. Probably ten years, I'll bet. Eight at least."

"He asked about you, wanted to know if you were still happily married, the whole nine yards."

"What'd you tell him?"

"Ellen! What do you think? I told him of *course* you were happily married." She hesitated. "You are, aren't you? I mean there's nothing really wrong with you guys, is there?"

Ellen picked up a loose rock, took aim, and threw it at the trunk of an old maple tree. She stared at her sister. "I guess not. I just wondered what you told him." She fell quiet then, but warning bells sounded deep inside her.... *Don't do it. Don't go there!*

She pushed her thoughts aside impatiently. It only made sense that she was thinking about Jake a lot lately. After all, her father's death had made her think about the past, hadn't it? That's all it was. Remembering a time gone by...a love that could have been...

The bells grew louder—and with them, Ellen's determination to ignore them.

കൈറ്റ്

The sisters stopped in front of the aging yellow Victorian, the home they had shared for so many years.

"I look at the old house and I can still see Dad sitting on the porch, smoking, waiting for us to come over for dinner. That year before we moved we probably ate here twice a month." Ellen stared at the house and saw it as it had been a decade earlier.

"Yeah, I know what you mean. I see him sitting beside the front door in that heavy jacket and that old caroling hat, handing out Halloween candy and pretending to be scary. He must have given out more candy than anyone on the block."

"And the kids knew it." Ellen tilted her head, smiling despite the tears that filled her eyes.

Megan laughed softly. "He did that every Halloween for as long as I can remember."

"And then in December he'd be there climbing up that old broken-down stepladder, covering the house in lights. He sure loved Christmas. Remember that time when someone stole the lights from Candy Cane Lane?"

Megan nodded, a sob lodged in her throat, as Ellen reached over and gently squeezed her sister's hand. Candy Cane Lane was an upper-class neighborhood that ran along the lake in Charlevoix. Twenty years earlier residents there agreed to erect stunning Christmas displays, complete with thousands of lights, moveable figurines, piped in music, and special effects. Three streets participated, and each was given a different name for the Christmas season. Carolers' Lane, Bell Lane, and Candy Cane Lane. The Barretts visited the neighborhood every Christmas as part of their holiday traditions.

Then one year vandals struck and stole the lights from several houses. For the first time ever, the homeowners talked about stopping the tradition. Determined to show his appreciation, Ellen's father went to the store and purchased dozens of light strings. He put them in a bag and left them on the porch of a Candy Cane Lane homeowner. He taped an anonymous note to the bag: "We enjoy what you do. Please don't let one Scrooge ruin it for the rest of us. God bless you."

The newspaper got wind of his act and ran a story. After that, others followed John Barrett's example until the homeowners along the three streets had more than enough lights to make up for what had been stolen. The tradition continued.

"He was something else, wasn't he?" Megan finally said.

Ellen nodded and put an arm around her sister, hugging her close. "Come on. Wipe your tears. Let's go in and see if Aaron's still glued to that chair."

feeling of doom hung over the house Sunday night when Mike Miller returned from covering the baseball game. He'd done a particularly professional job of reporting the close contest that night, both throughout play and later during postgame interviews. Before he left the field, one of the producers had approached him.

"Mike, they say you're a natural. You have national sports written all over you, man. You must be living right or something."

Normally the producer's comments would have sent Mike sky high and he would have sped home to share the news with Ellen. But she was in Petoskey, and ever since their disagreement on Friday, nothing felt right to Mike. He was jumpy, nervous, and there was a hard knot in his gut that wouldn't go away. Dread, deep and frightening, burned at him.

He was afraid his marriage wasn't going to survive.

"How'd everything get so messed up, Lord?" He wandered about his living room. Almost in answer, he paused by the bookcase and found himself staring at the binding of his leather Bible. *Maybe later. After I eat. Maybe it's time to get back into the Word.*

He tossed his jacket on the back of the chair and glanced at the clock in the kitchen. It was just after nine. Ellen and the others would be together now, probably seated around the Barrett dining room table.

Mike sat down at his own empty table and stared at the portrait of Ellen and him that hung over the fireplace. As he had been doing since Friday evening, he second-guessed his decision to let Ellen go by herself to Petoskey. He could have found a replacement to cover the game. So what if he didn't care for funerals? Ellen was right: *no one* enjoyed funerals.

But he still could not stomach the idea of spending a week watching the adult Barrett children tear each other apart. Ellen always talked about how close she and her sisters and brother had been growing up, about the memories they'd made together. But based on what he'd seen of her family, Mike wondered if she wasn't imagining things that had never happened.

He remembered a dozen times when he and Ellen had been at a Barrett family gathering only to leave early because of the tension that all but crackled in the air. In some ways that was why they had moved to Miami. Yet, when Ellen was away from them she called often, wrote once a month, and there seemed to be no conflict at all.

"We get along better when we're two thousand miles apart," Ellen had often told Mike. "I think that's the secret."

Especially when it came to Ellen and Jane.

The strangest thing about Jane, in Mike's opinion, was that away from Ellen she was a wonderful person. Sadly, Ellen knew it, too.

"Have you ever seen how her friends treat her? How she treats them? They love her, Mike. She's bubbly and funny and happy. She's the greatest in their eyes."

Mike listened sympathetically.

"Why can't she be that way with me? I'm her sister, after all. I love her more than any of them, and she treats me like dirt. Sometimes I feel like walking up to her and saying, 'Hi. I'm Ellen. Let's be friends.' Maybe if I pretended to be a stranger, she'd be nice to me."

Mike was puzzled by Jane's attitude. Especially after Jane and Troy were married and began having children. Koley was born in 1992, and Ellen tried to make herself available on the weekends to help Jane when Troy was on business trips.

Mike recalled the time Ellen stayed at Jane's home and watched the newborn baby one Saturday so Jane could sleep. Mike had come to pick Ellen up just as Jane trudged wearily from her bedroom.

"How was he?" she asked.

"Just fine," Ellen cooed at the baby and tickled his cheek. "Get any sleep?"

"Yeah. Thanks."

Ellen studied her sister. "You know, Jane, you look really good. You'd never know you had a baby two weeks ago."

Mike had been surprised at the cool look in Jane's eyes.

"What's that supposed to mean?"

Ellen paused, clearly at a loss. "Nothing. Just what I said. You look good."

"Listen, don't make fun of me," Jane barked. "Just because you're Miss Cosmopolitan with the sleek figure doesn't give you the right to comment about me—"

"Whoa, Jane, Ellen was just being nice," Mike broke in.

She ignored him. "Just wait, Ellen. Your turn will come. You'll get stretch marks on your stomach and crease marks on your chest and you'll be struggling to find your old shape. I can't wait for that day. Imagine, Ellen Barrett, chunky and out of shape. That'll be a sight I definitely don't want to miss."

Tears welled up in Ellen's eyes and she stood up, passing the baby to Jane. "I have things to do, Jane. Call me if you need me."

"Are you trying to say I can't do this on my own?"

Mike wondered if he had missed some segment of their conversation. He could not understand what had triggered Jane's anger.

He took Ellen's arm and led her across the living room to the door, growing angry himself when he felt how Ellen was trembling. Jane followed after them, crying and waking the baby with her shouting.

"Don't worry about me, Ellen! I don't need you. I can handle this mothering thing all by my—"

Mike closed the door on the rest of the sentence. They walked to the car in silence, then drove straight to Ellen's parents' house where they were staying for the weekend.

"It's like she hates me and I don't even know what I've done wrong," Ellen cried when they were in their room.

Mike had his opinions about Jane but he kept them to himself. That afternoon he convinced Ellen that Jane must have been suffering a hormonal imbalance. "You know, that baby blues thing, postportem or something. I heard about it on *Oprah* once."

"Post*partem.*" Ellen sniffed. "Maybe you're right."

"Come on, honey. She'll be fine in a few weeks. Don't take it personally."

But privately he didn't think hormones could excuse Jane's actions toward Ellen. They certainly could not explain her bitter attitude before the baby was born.

Through the years Ellen had found several opportunities to address the issue directly with Jane.

"Why do you hate me, Jane?" Ellen would ask. "What have I done to hurt you? What can I do to change so that you'll be civilized when we're together?"

Whenever Ellen asked such a question Jane would do something that completely baffled Ellen. She would cry and accuse Ellen of saying hurtful things and trying to upset her.

"Do you think *your* words don't hurt *me,* Ellen?" she'd shout, tears coursing down her face. "You have a wicked tongue and you don't care how it hurts people."

Inevitably Ellen would apologize. For six months or a year the sisters would get along, visiting by phone from their separate homes and talking about surface subjects.

Mike shook his head. Problem was, they never discussed the real reason behind Jane's resentment. Mike thought it was almost as if Jane was hiding something from Ellen.

The cycle made Mike tired just thinking about it. He could only imagine how it had taken its toll on Ellen over the years.

Poor Ellen. She had been so close to her father and Jane had been so distant. Undoubtedly, now that he was dead, Jane would be upset with Ellen over that fact, too. She would probably accuse her of being their father's favorite. If Jane did that, Mike could only imagine the friction that would develop between the two oldest Barrett daughters that week.

As if the tension between Jane and Ellen wasn't enough, Ellen's other siblings had problems of their own—some considerably more serious than Jane's anger.

There was Megan, who at twenty-seven was finally beginning to live again. For a five-year period, from age twenty to twenty-five, she had spent much of her time dating a drug dealer. The man had convinced her that her family didn't care about her and that Ellen, especially, was trying to change her into something she could never be.

As a child Megan had looked up to Ellen. She imitated her and planned to be just like her when she got older. Megan was a brilliant writer with an art for communication. Like Ellen, she was a natural leader and had dozens of friends. She was also, unquestionably, the best looking of John Barrett's daughters. Whereas Ellen was beautiful and Jane quietly pretty, Megan was gorgeous. She had blue eyes big enough to fall into and cheekbones that seemed carved by an artist. Her skin was the color of pale honey and her dark hair hung halfway down her back. On top of that she was gifted with the voice of an angel. When she entered a room, her presence demanded the attention of every person there.

When Megan was in eighth grade Ellen gave her a handwritten book with personal advice on how to survive high school. Megan read the book hungrily, fascinated at the advice Ellen had written for her. She wanted to be everything Ellen had been and more.

Then, unexplainably, she dropped out of cheerleading in her junior year and began dating loner types. When she was twenty she met Mohammed, a Goliath of a man with Middle Eastern roots and a forest of dark hair that covered his body. The few times Mohammed visited Megan at the Barrett home he never wore shoes or spoke directly to John or Diane. His eyelids remained half closed and there was something condescending in his attitude toward everyone in the Barrett family. Especially Megan.

Mike remembered the first time Mohammed visited the Barrett family. It had been a big family get-together.

"So, what is it you do for a living, Mohammed?" John had asked, spreading a thick layer of butter on his bread and helping himself to an extra serving of gravy.

"Things." It had bothered Mike, the way Mohammed refused to make eye contact with John. Several others at the table had exchanged curious glances.

It made sense now, but at that time none of them—except Megan, of course—knew that Mohammed was a pusher. Everywhere he went he carried a briefcase packed with marijuana, cocaine, and two loaded pistols.

Mike learned later how Mohammed had taught Megan to listen to blank cassette tapes for subliminal messages from "helping-demons," and when Megan didn't cooperate, he'd beat her or put his fist through the windshield of her car.

"If you leave me I'll kill your parents," Mohammed would threaten her. He was five years older than Megan and she believed him completely. The relationship continued.

For years, Mike had watched as Ellen tried unsuccessfully to bring Megan to her senses.

"Don't preach at me, Ellen!" Megan would scream. "Not everyone is perfect like you. Besides, I don't do drugs and I'll date whomever I want, so don't try to run my life. At least Mo isn't some plastic phony like Mike!"

Long after Mike and Ellen moved to Miami, Megan was still caught up in the destructive relationship. By the time she finally broke it off with Mohammed, so many years had passed that the chasm between Megan and her sisters was almost too vast to cross. Mike had seen firsthand at family get-togethers how the tensions remained. This week would be no exception.

Then there was Aaron, the only son. His father's pride and joy. Aaron was strikingly handsome and had always boasted a string of girlfriends. But he was *lazy* and utterly dependent on his parents for survival. By the time he was twenty-two he had been fired from seven construction jobs. He was six-foot-four, built like a professional linebacker with the strength of five men his size. Once his temper flared in the workplace most employers found it simpler to let him go than to deal with his outbursts.

Mike remembered once when he and Ellen had flown back to Petoskey for a family reunion. A dozen or so family members had gathered at the Barretts' house for a barbecue and spirits were high. They were seated around the dining room table when Aaron waltzed in after work and helped himself to two hamburgers and a full plate of fixings.

"It's a potluck, Aaron. Did you bring anything?" John Barrett had asked when Aaron pulled up a chair and sat down.

Aaron slammed his fork down and threw his plate across the room. Diane gasped as the burgers fell apart and landed on the carpet, splattering ketchup on the dining room wall. Aaron glared at his father, stood up, and went into the kitchen where he slammed the dishwasher shut breaking dozens of dishes.

"Aaron!" Diane had gasped.

Unrepentant, Aaron glared at his father and stormed down the hallway toward his bedroom. Mike remembered John Barrett's expression as he looked at the others, clearly shocked and embarrassed by Aaron's actions. Then he excused himself and went back toward Aaron's room to deal with the situation.

The exchange could easily be heard by everyone at the dinner table.

"We cannot tolerate that behavior, son," John had said, his own voice trembling with controlled rage. Aaron was two inches taller than his father and fifty muscled pounds heavier.

Aaron responded with a string of profanity, telling his father to mind his own business. Then, as was too often the case, he blamed his parents for treating the girls better than him over the years.

"I always got in trouble for things they did!" Aaron's voice echoed through the house. Mike pushed his plate aside. Another meal spoiled by Aaron's tantrums. "Do you know what it was like growing up in this family and being the only son?" Aaron shouted. "I bet you didn't ask *them* to bring anything to the meal. They do whatever they want, and I'm the one who gets the shaft!"

There were more profanities then and finally Mike walked purposefully down the hallway and put himself between John and Aaron.

"Come on, Aaron, let's take a drive and talk this through," Mike said.

Aaron glared at Mike and swore at him, accusing him of being a meddler and reminding him that he was not part of the Barrett family. Then in a sudden burst of intense anger he lifted his fist and held it inches from his father's face. Diane, who had come to see if she could help, screamed. "Someone call the police!"

Aaron swung his fist furiously, but at the last moment he turned his body so that his hand slammed completely through his bedroom door instead of hitting his father. Pulling it free from the splintered wood, he continued to swear at his parents, punching a series of holes in the door.

"Aaron, stop it!" John tried to wrestle him away from the door, but Aaron was out of control. He jerked away from his father's touch.

"John!" It was Diane's voice. "Leave him alone. You'll have a heart attack!"

"That's all right!" Sweat dripped from his face as he struggled to stop Aaron's destructive temper tantrum. "He's my son and he's not going to behave this way in my house."

Mike had watched, ready to step in if necessary, amazed at Aaron's strength as he ripped his bedroom door completely off the hinges.

"I hate all of you!" he screamed.

He pushed his father out of the way, shoved past the others, and stormed out of the house. The Barrett family stood motionless, stunned, as they heard Aaron screech away from the curb in his pickup truck.

It was neither the first nor the last example of Aaron's explosive behavior.

Mike remembered a time when Amy, then eighteen, had told Aaron he was a loser. "When are you going to get a real life?" she had asked.

In response, Aaron had walked out to her brand-new car and kicked his work boot deep into the passenger door. As far as Mike knew, the damage had never been repaired.

Mike had leveled with John Barrett one day. "He's making your life miserable. Maybe it's time he found his own place."

"Well, Mike, I'll tell you. There are times I wonder what I did wrong with Aaron. Sometimes I think he's still a little boy trapped in a man's body. But we have our good days, the times when we go golfing and get along." John took a deep breath and slowly released it. "Besides, we have no throwaway kids. Aaron can stay here as long as he needs to. That's what family is all about."

Mike had his own opinion about what Aaron needed, but since the conversation with John had proven fruitless, he'd decided to keep his thoughts to himself. With John. With Diane. Even, most of the time, with Ellen. Shaking off the sour memories, Mike stood up slowly and headed into the kitchen for something to eat. The more he thought about the Barretts and their assorted conflicts the more he was thankful he hadn't gone to Petoskey.

I love her, Lord. You know I do, with my very soul. He passed a hand wearily over his eyes. *But I can't spend a week with her family. Not even for this.*

He took a hot dog from the refrigerator, heated it in the microwave, and placed it in a cold bun. Then he looked at the telephone. He should call Ellen. He sighed and stuffed one end of the hot dog into his mouth.

No, it would be better to wait a few days—give her time to forgive him for not going with her.

He walked past the phone, past the portrait of him and Ellen, past the bookcase and the unopened Bible, and found a comfortable spot on the sofa. Then he kicked up his feet, grabbed the remote, and ran his finger deftly over the power button. Before flicking on the evening news he wondered once more whether Ellen was still mad at him. He thought again of Jane and Megan, Amy and Aaron, and he shuddered.

He was glad he had stayed home. Ellen would simply have to understand.

12

By the time Ellen and Megan came back inside, forty minutes had passed and two half-eaten pizzas were laid out on the dining room table. Their mother was on the telephone, talking in hushed tones, and Jane was in the den reading a book to her children. Amy and Frank had gone home for the night. Only Aaron remained in the living room, positioned in the chair as he had been when they left.

"How's it going?" Ellen sat down near him and leaned over her knees, studying him. Megan took the cue and left the room for a slice of pizza.

Aaron turned and stared at the wall.

"Aaron, you'll feel better if you talk about it. We're all going through the same thing."

Aaron smothered a sob and wiped a tear as it fell from beneath his dark glasses. He stuck his chest out and crossed his arms more tightly around his body. He had always absolutely refused to cry. He wasn't going to give in now, Ellen guessed, especially not in front of her.

"He-*llo?*" She held out the last syllable, aggravated. "Aaron? I'm trying to talk to you."

"Don't want to talk." Aaron rose to his full, towering height and hitched up his jeans. Then in one movement he grabbed his keys from the ledge near the front door and left without saying a word.

"Who's here?" her mother called from the kitchen as the door slammed shut.

"No one. Aaron just left." Ellen wandered into the kitchen and took some pizza. Her mother was still on the phone and she raised her hands, silently asking Ellen where Aaron had gone.

"I don't know. He's not talking to me."

With a sigh, her mother returned to her conversation. Ellen moved in beside her and began helping with the few dishes from dinner.

Aaron climbed into his full-size, silver-and-black pickup truck and headed down Mitchell. In a matter of minutes he reached Spring Street and turned right toward the water. He slipped a Garth Brooks CD into his car stereo and blasted the music—as if that could take away the pain in his heart.

He drove, unsure of where he was headed until he pulled off Highway 31 and turned right on Country Club Road. Suddenly he knew where he had to go. He headed the same way he had a hundred times, making the necessary turns and stops until the street came to a dead end on a hill overlooking the Bay View Country Club. He turned the music off and stared over the golf course, across the eighteenth hole, out toward the bay.

The clubhouse was just to his right and although it was after eight, there were still people leaving, heading for their cars. During July, Petoskey stayed light until nearly ten. He shifted his foot to the gas pedal and drove through the parking lot toward the roadway that divided the course's front and back nine. He passed what was probably the last cart of the day heading back to the clubhouse, then he pulled into a gravel area just off the road so that he faced the golf course. Trees on either side made the spot private, and Aaron killed his engine.

The only sounds were the gentle rustling of trees and the distant traffic on the highway. Over the tops of the trees that lined the ninth fairway, the bay was still visible, and Aaron saw that the sun was moving slowly toward the water. The course would be closed in a few minutes. He could be alone here.

He took a deep breath and then, surrounded by the silence of the empty golf course, he gave himself permission to feel.

Bitterness and anger flooded him. How could his father have done this? How could he have left him?

His anger swelled as he unleashed it and memories ran rampant…memories of times he had been mad at his father, times when he had been punished more severely than his sisters, times when he had hated his father for being so hard on him.

"Son, don't tell me they hit you first," he could hear his dad say. *"You're a boy and no matter what happens you don't hit girls."*

As far back as Aaron could recall, his sisters had ganged up against him. They had teased him and threatened him and once they even put eye shadow on twelve-year-old Megan's cheek so that their father would believe Aaron, three years younger, had hit her.

Aaron closed his eyes and remembered the hard spanking he'd gotten for that.

"Dad, I swear I didn't do it," he had yelled throughout the punishment.

But John Barrett was not a man interested in excuses. He punished Aaron and let him know in specific terms the extent of the punishment he would receive if he ever hurt the girls again.

Even after he had received the unfair punishment, the girls did not let up. He remembered a little miniature wind-up robot he'd bought with his own money when he was seven. The girls found it and placed it in the ice-cube tray so that it froze under water. Aaron searched the entire house before finding it in the freezer. The girls had thought it was the funniest thing ever.

Seventeen years later he could still hear their cruel laughter. The afternoon breeze had stilled and the trees barely rustled. Aaron kept his eyes on the golf course, his anger building with each memory. There was another incident, when Aaron was eight. He had been given his own pack of gum and did not want to share it. Led by Ellen and Jane, his sisters had taken out each piece, chewed it, and rewrapped it. Then they placed it back in the package with a handwritten label across the front: ABC Gum. Give it a try.

Aaron's eyes narrowed angrily and his grip grew tighter on the steering wheel. Already Been Chewed. *Ellen probably wrote that.* Ellen, who pretended to care about him these past years, but who had treated him miserably when he was little. Ellen, who had stolen John Barrett's attention away from him.

There had been a time when he didn't care about Ellen and her relationship with their father. No matter how much Ellen did right, she couldn't play football. When Aaron was a young teenager, football had been his surefire way of winning his father's attention.

Aaron played offensive lineman for Petoskey, and John Barrett was at every game. He cheered louder than any parent and was quick to compliment his son's burst of speed off the line of scrimmage. But after two years on the varsity squad Aaron could no longer fool himself. He had the size and speed to be a college player but he had one very big problem. He didn't like the game. He was only playing for his father's approval and after his sophomore year, he could no longer pretend.

"Son, is it true?" Aaron could still hear the disappointment ringing in his father's words. "You quit the team?"

Aaron remembered hanging his head. "Yeah, Dad, it's true. I'm really not into football." He had looked up then, expectantly. "You're not mad, are you?"

"Son, of course I'm not mad. I'm disappointed. Not for what I've lost, but for what you've lost. You were really something out there. You can quit the team and it won't change how I think about you. But maybe you should give it some more thought. You could play college ball with your size, son."

"Dad, I'm done with football. That's the end of it. All right?" Aaron spent the rest of the evening in his room certain that his father would never again view him the same way.

That was 1990, when Aaron was sixteen and Ellen had just graduated from college with her journalism degree. She was hired to work for the *Detroit Gazette* sports section and cover high school football games. That season instead of watching Aaron play, John helped Ellen. He gave her pointers and helped her understand football so that she could write better stories.

With Ellen and their father spending so much time together talking about football, both in person and on the telephone, Aaron felt as if he had ceased to exist in his father's eyes. As long as there wasn't a blizzard, Ellen would come home each Saturday and watch football with their father. They talked about first downs and reception averages and kickoff returns while Ellen hung on every word the great John Barrett said.

The whole thing made Aaron sick. There had been a time when he cherished taking in a football game with his father. After Ellen's indoctrination into sportswriting, Aaron no longer wanted anything to do with the game.

"Aaron, come on out here and see this." His dad would wave to him from his easy chair. "It's the big game. Michigan and Ohio State. We're about to score."

"I'm busy," Aaron would shout from the next room. "Maybe later."

Why bother? He'd figured there was no point. Ellen so monopolized their father's attention that Aaron no longer had any interest in watching sports with his father. In fact, he had no interest in doing *anything* with his father, and for years there seemed to be a distance between them no bridge could span.

Then Ellen moved to Miami, and the relationship between Aaron and his father improved dramatically. Overnight the two men discovered they had something in common: golf.

Until his father's triple-bypass surgery the year before, the two of them had spent four or five mornings a week shooting nine holes before work. They would be at the course by six and finish before eight. They golfed in Harbor Springs and Charlevoix, and sometimes even Traverse City. But their favorite course was the grassy, tree-covered spread at Bay View Country Club.

Aaron allowed his eyes to scan the greens. They sloped gently downhill from the road in a velvet carpet that seemed to extend all the way to the bay beyond. How many memories had he and his father made here? It had been on the neatly mowed grass below that he had told his father his girlfriend was pregnant. Aaron would never forget the pain in his father's face that morning.

"I won't tell you I'm not disappointed." He paused. "But son, you need to do the right thing and stand by the girl. She's going to have the baby, right?"

"Right. She doesn't want an abortion."

"Well, let her know that we'll do whatever we can to help."

Three months later they were on that golf course again when John asked about the girl, and Aaron broke down.

"She lost the baby, Dad." Aaron had swiped at his tears, embarrassed at the show of emotion.

"I'm sorry, son." His father had faced him and put an arm on his shoulder.

"I know it wasn't right what we did." They were far out on the seventh tee where no one could see them at that early hour of the morning. "But I was ready to love that child. I don't know, Dad. It's like I miss him. Even though I never knew him. Do you think I'm crazy to feel that way?"

Aaron would always remember the compassion in his father's eyes at that moment. "Son, an unborn child is a child nevertheless. I understand your pain."

No one but he and his father knew about the lost child. And that morning his dad shared something with Aaron that he said he hadn't shared with his other children.

"Your mother had a miscarriage once, too," he said softly. "It was two years after

Megan was born and your mother was already five months pregnant. The baby was a boy."

There were tears in his father's eyes. The two hugged and Aaron felt like a little boy again, safe in his daddy's arms.

When they pulled apart, his father smiled sadly. "Believe me, I understand how you feel. A week doesn't go by when I don't think about your brother, how old he would be, what he'd be doing now."

Aaron thought of a hundred other such moments he and his dad had shared on the golf course. Even when he began having bouts of rage and punching holes in his bedroom door, his father would forgive him and in a few days the two would be back out playing golf.

On the course, Aaron would apologize and his dad would shrug. "Forget about it, son," he would say. "I love you. I always will."

Then he and Aaron would spend another morning talking and teeing off.

But there was something Aaron never said to his father, and the knowledge of that omission burned at Aaron's soul. He had run out of time. His father was gone, and in all their years together, through all the feelings Aaron had shared with no one else, he never once had the courage to tell his father the most important thing of all.

It was growing dark and the course was becoming more difficult to see. Finally, knowing that he would explode if he didn't give in to his desperate grief, Aaron grabbed the steering wheel and laid his head on his forearm.

There, finally, he cried.

Torrents of angry tears spilled from his heart as he remembered the man he had loved and admired, the man who had known him as no one else had. He would give anything, he thought, to be here in the morning with his father preparing to shoot nine holes of golf. Just once more.

He sobbed violently, remembering the hateful things he had said in anger, wanting desperately to take them back. He remembered the last thing he had said to his father...

Thursday night Megan and his parents had been watching television. For once he didn't have a date so he'd gotten dressed in his jeans and boots and made plans to meet his buddies at Denim 'N Duds, a country dance club just out of town. He was running late and as he headed for the door he did not intend to waste time telling his parents good-bye.

But his father heard him leaving.

"Son? You going out?" Dad called from the den, his voice pleasant.

"Yeah. Dancing." Aaron leaned into view and cast an impatient look at his father.

"Okay. Have fun." Just before Aaron turned away he caught his father's smile. That warm, full-faced smile that assured Aaron he was loved beyond anything most sons would ever know.

He could have stopped then and said good-bye or wished his father a good night in return. But instead he turned away and walked out the door. That was it. The last time he saw his father alive. His last chance to say the most important words…words he had never shared with his father.

Aaron squeezed his eyes tight, but he could not shut out the truth. His father was gone and there was no more time. No time to say the one thing that should have been said.

"Why?" Aaron shouted, slamming his hands down on his steering wheel. There was a cracking sound and he looked at the wheel. A hairline split ran along the top.

Good. Who cares? Who cares about anything?

He climbed out of his truck then, walked around to the back, and jerked open the tailgate. There inside were his golf clubs, a complete set that his father had given him four years ago for Christmas. Angry, nearly blinded by his tears, Aaron pulled the bag from the truck bed and flung it toward the edge of the hill overlooking the course. He strode angrily toward the fallen clubs and then, one at a time, he hurled them with all his might toward the ninth fairway.

When he was finished, when the bag he had toted alongside his father's was completely empty, he sat down on the grassy hill and sobbed. The rage was gone. Minutes became an hour until finally he gazed out toward the golf course again and pulled himself up. For a moment, in his mind's eye, he thought he could see his father in the shadows. Yes, there he was. Waving to him, calling him to come down and play some golf.

"Dad!" Aaron yelled. "Daaaaad!"

"Son?" The image was fading and his father seemed to be having trouble hearing him. "What are you saying, son?"

"Daaad!" Aaron shouted as the image faded completely. "Dad…I love you!"

His words echoed over the empty golf course, ricocheted off the sturdy maple trees, and faded softly into the gentle breeze that drifted off the bay.

13

*N*o one said anything to Aaron when he returned to the Barrett home that evening. Instead, his arrival at just before eleven o'clock gave the others a reason to turn in for the night. At Megan's apartment, Ellen and Jane were politely civil but the strain between them was mounting. When they made it through the night without an argument Ellen sank onto her bed with a relieved sigh.

The next day their mother had plans with Aunt Mary, so the three oldest sisters took the children to the park, talked about their father, and shopped for the week's groceries. Remarkably, there were no blowups between Ellen and Jane. It was late afternoon before they reported back to their parents' home. Amy and Frank arrived moments later.

"I brought dinner," Amy said as she struggled through the doorway. She and Frank carried sacks of submarine sandwiches and potato chips.

Her mother hugged her gratefully. "Thank you. This is wonderful." She took the bags and moved them toward the dining room table. "Perfect timing. I had no idea what to fix tonight."

Jane busied herself feeding the children while Ellen, Megan, and Aaron silently helped themselves to a sandwich and found a place in the living room. Amy and Frank passed out drinks and then sat down at the dining room table, turning their chairs to face the others.

"Do we know what we're doing for the service?" Amy's tone was soft. "I have a few ideas."

Ellen studied her youngest sister. Amy's comments were always made tentatively. She was extremely sensitive to what others thought of her opinions and she had been known to suddenly leave a gathering if she felt offended. As far back as any of them could remember, Amy rarely interjected her opinion in a conversation, and now that she wanted to talk everyone sat a bit straighter and gave her their attention.

"We have a lot to discuss and I want input from all of you children." Their mom had fixed a plate and joined Amy and Frank at the table. "I thought we could get together tomorrow and spend the day working out the details."

"Fine," Ellen and Megan said in unison, and Aaron grunted his approval.

"Of course…" Jane said, "I don't know what I'll do with the kids. They're good, but they can't sit still for most of the day while we talk. I guess I'll—"

"Jane," their mother interrupted. "Relax. Aunt Mary will watch the children. She told me she'd be at Megan's apartment first thing in the morning and stay with them all day if necessary."

Jane's chin lifted defiantly, and Ellen and Megan exchanged a quick glance. "Well, if that's in order," Jane said, "then fine." She placed the rest of her sandwich on the plate and stood to gather her things.

"Where are you going?" Amy looked at her.

"If we're going to be here all day tomorrow I think we should make it an early night. I want to spend some time with the children."

"Yeah, but I wanted to talk about music. I remembered last night that Dad really liked that one song, you know, about the rugged cross, the one where—"

"Amy," Jane looked down at her youngest sister as if she were a small child in need of a reprimand. "That's why we're getting together tomorrow. To talk about rugged crosses and everything that goes with them."

Amy was quiet for a moment, and from where she sat across the room Ellen knew instinctively that Jane had gone too far. The youngest Barrett daughter turned to her husband and nodded. In an instant they were on their feet, headed for the door.

"Amy, you don't have to go just because Jane's leaving." Their mom stood up too. She put a comforting arm across Amy's shoulders.

Ellen raised her eyebrows and stared at the floor. She hated the way their mother treated her youngest sister like a baby. Amy was twenty-five years old and a married woman, after all. Still, the moment things didn't go Amy's way, Mom was immediately at her side, making her feel better.

"I'm leaving," Amy announced to her mother. "If Jane doesn't want me to talk about the service, I won't talk at all."

"*What?*" Jane shrieked. "I didn't say anything to make you leave. Don't blame *me* for your weird behavior."

"See!" Amy said to her mother. Tears filled her eyes and she looked overwhelmed. "We can only talk about something if it's okay with Jane." She wheeled around and faced Jane, who was standing nearby with her mouth open in mock astonishment. "Jane, nobody made you the boss of this family. Why don't you keep your opinions to yourself?"

"What*ever!* I was only stating a fact. This isn't the time to talk about rugged crosses. That's why we're getting together tomorrow."

"But if I want to talk about rugged crosses today, then I'll talk about rugged crosses today!"

Jane's hands flew to her hips and her face grew red. "That's right, Amy. I forgot you were so sensitive about every little thing. I guess we should all just walk around watching what we say. Wouldn't want to hurt little Amy's feelings, now would we?"

Ellen cringed and glanced into the kitchen, wishing she could escape. Jane had definitely stepped over the line with that last comment. Megan and Aaron had moved to the table and were busy eating their sandwiches, pretending not to hear.

"Jane!" Mom fired a scolding look at her second daughter. She had positioned herself between the two sisters, ever the peacemaker. "That wasn't very nice."

"Come on, Frank." Amy took her husband's hand and turned to her mother. "Forget about tomorrow." She looked angrily at Jane. "I won't be where I'm not wanted."

"Amy, don't say that." Their mother followed Amy and Frank to the front door and out into the warm evening. "I want us all here tomorrow. It would mean so much to your father and—"

Her voice grew faint as she trailed after them, leaving an uncomfortable silence in the Barrett home. Jane remained in the center of the room while the others looked at her expectantly.

"Well, what's everyone looking at?" she demanded. "Come on, Megan, Ellen. Let's get the kids and go. Obviously I am not wanted around here."

Ellen stood up and stretched, hoping some of her anxiety would dissipate when she got back to Megan's apartment. Then she gathered her things and those of the children. Just as they were about to leave, their mom returned. Everyone could see she had been crying.

"Don't worry, Mother, I'm leaving." Jane spat the bitter words as she moved toward the front door, the baby on her hip. "I wouldn't want to upset your precious Amy."

Ellen wanted to kick Jane, to make her think about what she was saying. She looked at her mother, worried, but Mom just drew closer to Jane and took her daughter's face in her hands. "I love *all* of you girls very much, Jane. But I wish you could make more of an effort to get along. You know how sensitive Amy is."

"I know, but I think we need to stop babying her. It's a bit ridiculous."

"Maybe you're right. But there must be a better time to deal with her than the week of your father's funeral. We have a lot to do tomorrow, and I want all of you here."

"Is she coming?" Jane's disgust was clear in her voice.

"I hope so. But please, girls—" Mom looked at Ellen and Megan—"try to get along tomorrow."

"Don't look at me, Mom, I'm doing everything I can," Ellen said. She was carrying Kala and hoped they could get out the door soon. "Why would I come all the way from Miami just to fight with everyone? I want us all to get along, too."

"Right." Jane muttered under her breath, casting a look at Ellen.

Ellen stared at Jane, wondering yet again what she had done to make her sister so angry, so resentful of her.

She glanced at her mother to see her eyes had filled with tears once more and she seemed on the verge of losing control.

"See, Jane?" Mom pointed out. "That's what I mean. That wasn't necessary.

Comments like that tear us apart at a time when we should be holding each other up."

Jane sighed and looked suddenly sheepish. After several seconds she spoke and this time her voice was humble. "You're right. I'm sorry. I guess I must be tired. Besides, no one ever sees any of this from my point of view...."

Ellen exchanged a knowing glance with Megan. Jane's behavior could not be written off just because she was tired. She had been rude and unkind through much of the evening and there was no excuse for her attitude. Ellen shifted her weight, adjusting the child she still held in her arms. She watched Jane impatiently and waited for her to finish so they could leave.

"I didn't mean to upset Amy," Jane continued. "But it'll be hard enough for everyone to spend an entire day planning Dad's funeral. The last thing I want to do is spend tonight talking about it, too."

Mom nodded and put her arms around Jane. "I understand. It's hard for me, too. He was my husband, remember?" She looked at Ellen and her sisters. "I'm going to ask that you girls do everything you can to get along tomorrow and the rest of the week. Understand?"

Jane nodded and returned her mother's hug.

"Ellen?" Mom asked.

"Sure. I'll try. That's all I can do."

While they were saying good-bye, Aaron stood up and left. "Honey, are you going somewhere?" Mom asked as he slipped past them and headed for his truck.

"Out."

The Barrett women watched in silence as he drove away. "He probably just needs time alone, Mom," Jane said. "Don't worry about him."

"I know. Go ahead now, go home and get some rest before tomorrow."

The moon was full and there was a warm glow over the sleepy neighborhood as Megan, Ellen, Jane, and the children left for the night. Diane watched them go and then went back inside. She shut the door and locked it. Her sister, Mary, had a key and would be over later to spend the evening with her.

She closed her eyes and realized how consuming silence could be. That was one sound that had seldom filled her home. There had always been family parties, barbecues, jam-making sessions, and dozens of kids filling the halls with laughter. Life at the Barretts' had been a whirlwind of activity, with John always at the center.

Diane looked at the empty living room and thought how sad and lonely a house full of memories could be. She picked up a photograph of her and John at Amy's wedding and studied it. She could still picture him as he walked Amy down the aisle. And Jane, and Ellen before that.

For just an instant she was angry with John, angry that he hadn't heeded the doctors' warnings and given up smoking, angry that he hadn't changed his eating habits.

If he had loved them, why hadn't he taken care of himself? He would be alive today if only he'd had the will to change.

Then, just as quickly the anger disappeared. Diane's tears fell onto the glass frame and she carefully rubbed them off with the edge of her faded cotton blouse.

"John, my love," she whispered. "What am I going to do without you?"

That night in a small house three miles away, Frank was doing all he could to comfort Amy, but he was having little success. She had locked herself in the bathroom and was sobbing so hard Frank thought she might pass out. She had already vomited twice, and Frank wondered if she was having a nervous breakdown.

"Amy, please! Come out here so we can talk." He had been trying to get her out since they got home. His voice was gentle but firm. "We can't talk about it while you're in there."

"No! It's my problem, Frank! My family has always treated me this way. There's nothing to talk about."

"But I love you," he said softly. "I want to help. Come out so I can hold you."

Finally, after fifteen minutes of pleading with her, Amy opened the door and collapsed in Frank's arms.

"I'm sorry," she sobbed. "I didn't mean to shut you out."

He led her to their bed in the middle of the room and with one arm around her waist he sat down beside her. "Tell me about it, Amy. I'm here for you. I'll listen."

Amy struggled to calm herself. "It's been like that for years." Her breathing came in short, fast bursts. "Wh-whenever I say anything or try to make a suggestion, someone cuts me off. It's…it's like my opinion isn't worth anything because I'm the youngest."

"Aaron is the youngest," Frank corrected gently.

"Oh, I know that." Amy was frustrated as she reached for a tissue and blew her nose. "But I'm the youngest *girl*, and Aaron doesn't talk to anyone, anyway. So I might as well be the youngest."

Frank was silent, encouraging her to continue.

"All my life they've shut me out of their little threesome. Ellen, Jane, and Megan. I was too young to go to the movies with them, too young to go to parties with them. And to tell you the truth, Frank, after a lifetime of sharing a house with them, I don't even really know them."

A sob caught in her throat. "I love them, Frank. They're the only family I have besides you. But when I'm with them I feel like a stranger. They don't call me or write to me or ask me about my life. It's like I'm some kind of fixture in the room. They expect me to be there but they don't expect me to say anything important or to feel hurt when they leave me out."

"Amy, I'm sure you don't feel that way all the time. This is just a hard week. You're all under a lot of pressure."

Amy shook her head fiercely. "No, it's more than that. My father treated me the same way. Like a tagalong. You know, I tried to think of one time when Dad and I did something special together by ourselves, without any of the others, and I couldn't remember one. Not one single time. I never said anything, never complained about being left out. So no one thought I had needs and hurts and feelings. Now I'm all grown up and I feel like an outsider in my own family."

"They love you, Amy. Really, honey." Frank stroked her shiny dark hair.

"I don't know, Frank. Look at Jane, the way she treats me. You can't think she really loves me. And Megan, she's too caught up in her own life, just like Ellen. Aaron practically hates me because I stand up to him."

"Your mother loves you. Don't forget how much she cares."

"I know." She seemed calmer as she turned to Frank. "You know something strange? Even though I can't think of any special times alone with my dad, he's at the center of every happy childhood memory I have. I was such a serious kid, I might never have learned to laugh if it wasn't for my dad."

Suddenly she was crying again, and he pulled her close. "Oh, Frank, I'm going to miss him so much."

"I know, honey, I know."

"Do you think he knew how much I loved him?"

"Of course, sweetheart. Of course he knew."

"But I'm not sure I ever really told him. You know, in those exact words."

"Amy, he knew. Believe me."

She struggled to speak. "I loved him with all my heart. He was bigger than life, my hero, my daddy. Frank, he was my laughter. How am I going to live without him?"

Her sobs grew harder and Frank understood. They were coming from a place Amy did not visit often. And so it continued.

Hours after the others had forgotten about Amy's hurt feelings, Frank held his wife close while she cried for the man who, long ago on a carefree yesterday, had taught her to laugh.

14

uesday morning a thick layer of gray clouds came off the bay and covered Petoskey, making it unseasonably cool for July—and appropriately dismal. Just before eight o'clock Aunt Mary arrived in typical timely fashion, chattering about how good it was that everyone could be together to make plans for the funeral and what a wonderful support system they were for each other.

"I just know your mother will be so pleased, what with everyone back together under one roof. I'm sure you'll all work well together, planning the service and making decisions for your mother. You know, this is one of those things where everyone really needs to make their suggestions and see them carried through because, well, after all he was…"

Ellen stopped listening and returned to the bathroom to finish her makeup. Aunt Mary meant well. It was just that the woman was hopelessly out of touch with the way they were feeling. Until Aunt Mary arrived, the three sisters had been lost in their private thoughts, savoring the heavy solitude and the relative lack of tension it afforded them.

Running a brush through her hair, Ellen stared at herself in the mirror. For an instant she wondered how much she had changed since she was in high school…back when Jake thought she was the prettiest girl in Petoskey. She dismissed the thought as quickly as it had come.

She had long since perfected the art of disregarding thoughts about Jake. In the early days after she embraced Christianity, Ellen learned from Scripture that the best way to steer clear of a weakness was to never entertain thoughts about it. Jake was her strongest weakness back then, so when thoughts of him came she refused to entertain them, recalling instead specific memory verses from the Bible.

Memory verses. Ellen met her reflected gaze thoughtfully. *It's been years since I've even tried to commit a Bible verse to memory.*

For an instant she was pierced with guilt, but she shrugged that off as well. *Later. When I'm back home and things are settled. Then I'll get back into the Word.*

She ran a dab of clear gloss over her lips and when she was satisfied with her appearance, she gathered her purse and a pad of paper. They had a long day ahead of

them. It was one thing to make suggestions, and quite another to plan a funeral service. Ellen intended to take notes and help them stay on track so they could finish by
the end of the day.

Her sisters were ready to go when she walked back into the main room. Jane was
rattling off instructions for the children, advising Aunt Mary to call if there were any
problems.

"We'll probably come back for lunch, at least I will if I can get a ride." Jane
glanced at Megan. "Is that okay?"

"Sure, we can all come back for lunch. We'll probably need a break by then, anyway."

Ellen nodded. "Sounds good."

She was not about to disagree over lunch plans. Not when they had so much to
work through that day. The three sisters bid their aunt good-bye and left.

"She's a talker," Megan said as they walked to her parking space outside the building.

"Yes, that must be where Ellen gets it," Jane added. Normally Ellen would have
laughed. There was no secret in the fact that she was a talker or that she had received
a fair amount of teasing for it over the years. But in light of Jane's attitude the last few
days, Ellen felt attacked. Still, she said nothing. There was more satisfaction in keeping peace.

Ellen looked at her sisters. "Is Amy coming? Did anyone call Mom and find out?"

Megan shook her head, but Jane snorted sarcastically. "She'll be there. That whole
little demonstration last night was just a big play for attention. When Amy wants
attention, Amy gets it."

Her comments were met with silence. There was no point defending Amy when
to do so would just bring further conflict. The ride to the Barrett home was quiet,
and Ellen wondered if that was the secret to peace with her sisters. Simply stop talking.

They arrived at quarter past eight, just as Aaron appeared from his bedroom,
shaved and showered. For the first time in two days he was not wearing his dark
glasses. Five minutes later, Amy and Frank pulled up.

"Oh, thank God," Mom muttered quietly. She settled into one of the dining
room chairs and watched the couple make their way up the walk and into the house.

Ellen studied the room. Mom had arranged a circle of seating for the occasion.
Aaron claimed the oversized stuffed chair, the one their father had always used, while
Amy and Frank shared the sofa with Megan. Jane sat on a chair in the corner of the
room and Ellen completed the circle by taking the chair between Aaron and their
mother.

It felt good to gather for a reason, Ellen realized. It almost seemed to give them
some sense of purpose. Since Sunday night she and the others had been helpless to
do anything but talk about John Barrett's terrible health and how his death could
have been prevented and how relatively wonderful it was that he hadn't suffered.

Now…she studied the faces around her. Now they were ready to take action.

"Well." Her mother's voice was shaky but she managed a weak smile. "I'm glad you're all here. We have a lot to plan and I want us to do it together. Your father would have wanted it that way."

Ellen prepared to write as her mother flipped through several pages of notes and turned to the first page of a small booklet.

"The priest told me we can plan whatever kind of funeral service we want. I had no idea where to start so that's one of the reasons I wanted you all here."

Silence.

"Father Joe gave me this little book." She held it high. "It gives us a guideline we can follow as we make decisions."

"Father Joe?" Ellen asked.

"Yes. He's new at St. Francis."

"He's not officiating at the funeral, is he?"

"I don't know, Ellen. Do you have a problem with Father Joe?"

"Dad didn't even know him," Megan cut in.

"Yeah," Ellen agreed. "Father Jim is the one Dad knew. He's the one we brought cookies to when we went caroling, right?" She looked at Megan for support.

"Right, Father Jim. Mom, the funeral should be led by someone who knew him."

Jane clucked her tongue. "Like it matters. The people at St. Francis don't know each other, anyway."

"It *does* matter," Ellen said softly. "We don't want some guy up there saying how sad it is that John Barrett died, and, gee, it would have been nice if he'd known him. The minister in charge of a funeral should at least know something about the deceased."

"He's not a minister, he's a priest," Mom corrected.

"That's not true, Jane." Amy met her sister's gaze. "I happen to know many of the people at St. Francis quite well."

"Oh, sure you do." Aaron shifted positions restlessly.

"Who cares who knows each other at St. Francis?" Jane's eyebrows met in the middle of her forehead and she glared at Amy. "I was just saying that it doesn't matter who says the funeral."

"I think it does." Ellen was quiet but firm.

"Well, excuse *me,* Ellen." Jane crossed her arms angrily and sat back hard. "Forget I said anything."

"Come on, Jane." *Control my tongue, Lord,* Ellen prayed. She waited a moment, calming herself. "Don't take it personally. It's just that we should do our best to have Father Jim officiate the funeral because Dad knew him. I think it's only right."

Their mother wrote something on the pad of paper. "What about you Aaron, Amy? Do you think it matters who says the funeral?"

"Dad's dead," Aaron said simply. "He won't know whether it's Father Jim or Father Joe or Sam the Barber."

Amy was silent.

Ellen looked at her brother curiously and was struck again by the emotions that must be warring inside of him.

"At least I'm not the only one," Jane muttered. "I agree with Aaron. Who cares which priest says the funeral?"

Ellen looked around the circle at the faces of her family. "Whatever. If that makes everyone happy." She stared at her blank notepad and tapped her pen nervously. *Well, Lord, I'm obviously not prepared for this . . .* She had expected resistance from Jane, of course, but she had not planned on Aaron siding against her, too. "I just thought it would be nice to have someone who knew Dad say a few words at his funeral."

"There's nothing wrong with having someone who knew your father speak about him at the funeral," Mom said. "In fact, that's something else I want to talk about. I think it would be wonderful if each of you could write something and read it at the funeral. We don't have to discuss it yet but be thinking about the idea."

"I'm not getting up in front of a bunch of people and reading something," Amy announced. "No way."

"Me, neither," Aaron said. "What's the point?"

Their mother sighed. "It's a chance to tell the world about your dad, who he was in your life. Maybe by doing so it'll be easier to let him go."

"I could write a book about him and it wouldn't be easy to let him go," Ellen said lightly. "But if you want us to do something like that I'm in. I love putting my feelings into words."

Jane sneered. "I think we know that, Ellen." She took on a high-pitched voice. "'Ellen Barrett, the great writer.' I'm sure you'd love to write something about Dad and I'm sure you'd enjoy making the rest of us look bad while you were at it."

"Jane! Stop that!" Mom ordered.

Ellen stared at Jane, astonished. Only a blind person could miss the hatred in her younger sister's eyes. *Jesus, help us! This is such a disaster.* She drew a deep breath, then put a hand on her mother's arm. "It's okay, Mom. I'm under no delusions here. I know how Jane feels about me."

Jane glared at Ellen but remained silent.

Their mother looked at each of them as they sat there. "What I'm saying is that, rather than having a priest do all the talking, I'd like you five children to help us remember who your father was and why we loved him. Don't make any decisions about my idea one way or the other. Just think about it."

Thankfully, the disagreements seemed to ease after that. They spent two hours discussing which Bible verses best reflected their father, when they should be read during the service, and who should read them. They decided to stay with the Twenty-third Psalm, a favorite of their father's since he'd recited it aloud as valedictorian of his graduating class in college. Megan would read that passage.

"What about the Serenity Prayer?" Ellen asked. "Dad always liked that."

"That's not a Bible verse, Ellen. The priest wanted two Bible verses." Jane's tone was condescending, and Ellen had to fight the urge to slap her.

"Mom, did the priest want us to plan the service or not?" Ellen asked.

"Yeah," Amy interjected. "He said we could plan it ourselves, right?"

Ellen realized that Amy was probably taking her side to annoy Jane, and the thought only raised Ellen's anxiety level. Amy didn't hold a grudge so much as she nursed it, breathing life into it as long as possible. After the fiasco the night before, Amy would be upset with Jane for months.

"Yes, Ellen, that's right." Mom's tone was even as she answered. She seemed determined to remain unaffected by the tension in the room. "We can read whatever prayer or poem or Bible verse we'd like. Ellen, why don't you read that prayer to us. Do you have it handy?"

"Yes, I jotted it down over the weekend in case we could use it." She flipped through her notepad. "Here it is. 'God grant me the serenity to accept the things I cannot change, the strength to change the things I can, and the wisdom to know the difference.'"

There was a moment of silence.

"That sounds like Dad," Aaron said finally, and Ellen raised an eyebrow in surprise. She had heard her brother talk more that morning than in the past four years combined.

"Okay, then. Unless someone objects, I think maybe Ellen should read that at the service."

"What if *I* want to read a Bible verse?" Jane's eyes were hard, her tone defensive. "Why should Megan and Ellen be the only ones to read something?"

"Well then, pick something," Mom said pleasantly. "Everyone can read a verse as far as I'm concerned."

"No, that's all right." Jane looked away, the picture of persecuted martyrdom. "It's probably better this way. Ellen and Megan are better in front of people. Dad would have wanted them to read."

"Well," Megan stood up and reached for her purse. She looked and sounded disgusted with Jane's attitude. "I've had about enough for a while." She turned matter-of-factly toward Jane. "You said you wanted to go back for lunch. It's eleven-thirty. I'm ready if you are."

"Oh." There was obvious hurt in their mother's voice. "I thought you could all have lunch here. We're finally together and getting something done. Why don't you stay and I'll fix something for everyone?"

"We could," Jane said as she collected her purse and headed for the front door. "But I need to get back and see the kids."

Ellen was torn. She didn't want to spend any more time with Jane than was absolutely necessary, but she agreed with Megan that they needed a break from the discussion. She hoped their mother would not be too disappointed.

She shrugged. "I guess I'll go with Megan and Jane. Is that all right, Mom?"

Her mother's crestfallen expression belied her words. "I suppose. I just thought we could spend the entire day together and continue the plans while we ate."

"We'll be back right after lunch. And don't worry—" Jane crossed the room and hugged her mother—"we're working things out, and I think it's going very well so far. Dad would approve."

Ellen stared in stunned confusion. How could Jane be so thoughtless one minute and so gentle the next?

"Think we'll be done before dinner?" Jane asked as she headed for the front door.

"I hope so. This is exhausting." Mom stood up and stretched. "Maybe I'll take a nap while you're gone."

"Good idea," Jane hugged her again.

"Be nice…" Their mother's voice broke. "Please, Jane."

Jane pulled back, studied Mom's face, then nodded slowly. "I will. I'm sorry."

Quick tears stung Ellen's eyes. *Lord, I will never understand Jane. Not for as long as I live.* A sad desperation filled Ellen as she followed her sisters to the door.

After the three sisters were gone, Diane Barrett gave a small sigh. *Oh, John, what's happened to our family?* She wasn't sure how much more of this tension she could take.

Amy and Frank rose from the sofa and moved toward the front door.

"Frank and I are gonna get some hamburgers. You want one, Mom? Aaron?"

Diane smiled at her youngest daughter. "Sure, honey, thanks. Let me give you some money."

"Aaron?" Amy looked at him expectantly.

"A double. No onions." Aaron stood up and lumbered into the den where he flipped on the television. The others could hear what sounded like a golf competition underway. Aaron watched for a moment and then turned the channel.

"Talkative, huh?" Frank broke the silence Aaron had left in his wake. Frank managed a plastic smile from behind his thick, round glasses. There were beads of perspiration forming along his thinning hairline, and he looked especially tense.

"I'm sorry, Frank," Diane patted his shoulder as he and Amy prepared to leave. "Don't take it personally."

Frank shrugged and shook his head quickly. "He's very immature. That's not something I take personally."

Diane bid them good-bye, thankful that Frank was an intelligent man. He was thirty-eight and had come into Amy's life at a time when she was trying to decide what to do with her future. She was a pretty girl with a fuller figure than her sisters. She hated the way men ogled her chest whenever she went out. Before meeting Frank she had confided in Diane that she was seriously thinking about becoming a nun.

In response her father had taught her how to use his computer to tap into electronic bulletin boards. After that, Amy spent hours chatting with people she could neither see nor hear. Until then, she had never found a social niche that suited her. But when her fingers made contact with the computer keyboard, she entered a world that seemed custom-made for her alone. It was a world in which she had thrived.

A few months later she began having nightly computerized conversations with a man whose screen name was "Franco." She was going by the name "Aimless," something her friends had called her in high school. After exchanging photographs in the mail, they finally agreed to meet one afternoon at a busy restaurant. Six weeks later they were engaged, and Frank quickly found his place in their family. He and John could talk for hours about computers. John had even said that, in Frank, he saw himself as a young man: intelligent, idealistic, and replete with limitless energy.

Frank ran his own business assembling computers and selling them through mail-order advertisements. He easily earned enough money to keep Amy quite comfortable. After they were married Amy continued working at the private day care, but they certainly did not need her income to make ends meet.

Frank was slightly plump and more than a little balding. He had almost white blond hair and was only an inch taller than Amy. From their first meeting, Frank doted on Amy and gave her the security she craved. Diane thought they were a perfect match.

She watched them now as they drove away, and suddenly she felt exhausted. The sadness was so tiring, so gut wrenching. She wondered if she would ever wake up feeling refreshed and free of the burden John's death had placed on her. She closed her eyes and rubbed her neck. Then she padded slowly down the hallway, past the spot where John had died, back to the bedroom they'd shared for twenty-one years. The pillows still smelled like him.

In two minutes she had cried herself to sleep.

15

Back at Megan's apartment, the sisters found Aunt Mary struggling with the children. Kyle had refused his bottle and spit up his applesauce on Megan's living room floor. Kala and Koley had fought all morning over what toy belonged to whom, who had played with it longest, and whose turn it was now.

Aunt Mary looked on the verge of a breakdown.

Jane stepped into the middle of the chaos and calmly directed her children. In minutes there was peace again.

"Kyle, get your pacifier," she told the young boy. She walked to the spot where his playpen was set up. "Now lie down on your blanket and close your eyes." She knelt beside him, stroked his forehead, and hummed softly. The child was asleep almost instantly.

Next she looked at Koley. "Were you mean to your sister?" she asked softly. Megan disappeared to her room and Ellen found a chair off in the distance where she could watch Jane interact with her children.

"Yes, Mommy." Koley's deep brown eyes were remorseful, full of shame.

"Was that the right thing to do?"

Ellen wondered if Jane caught the irony in her statement. After all, she hadn't exactly been kind to *her* sister that morning. "No, Mommy."

"Well, I want you to go give Kala a kiss and tell her you're sorry."

The little boy did as he was told, hugging his small sister so tight she could barely breathe.

"That's fine." Jane motioned her children closer and kissed each of them on their foreheads. "I love you both very much and I know you're going to behave better for Aunt Mary this afternoon while we're gone. But right now I want you to find a spot on the floor and lie down. It's nap time."

Ellen watched, amazed. Jane made parenting look easy, and Ellen wondered whether she would be so patient if she had children.

Once the children were settled Jane fixed herself a sandwich. Megan joined Ellen at the small table, and Aunt Mary rested on the couch, exhausted from the morning.

"Are you sure you can stay and watch them this afternoon?" Jane asked. "If it's too much I can probably take them to Mom's."

"No, no—" Aunt Mary straightened herself and tried to smile—"really, it's all right. I think after they have a good nap everything'll be just fine. In fact, I think I'll go out and pick up something to eat before you leave."

Jane nodded. "Don't rush. And thanks again, Aunt Mary. I'm sorry they were such a handful."

"Oh, it's no problem. You all have a lot to work out and this is the least I can do for your mother."

Aunt Mary and the girls' mother were very close; they had been for as long as anyone could remember. Like Ellen and Jane, they were only two years apart, but somehow through the years they had forged a camaraderie that superseded petty resentments.

When Aunt Mary was gone, Ellen sighed. "She really seems frazzled. Too bad we can't just take the kids back to Mom's with us. I think she could use a break."

Jane lowered her sandwich and stared at Ellen, her eyes glittering.

"If you're trying to say that my children aren't well behaved, then maybe you'd better keep your comments to yourself." Ellen threw her hands in the air in mock surrender. She had tried unsuccessfully to ignore Jane's comments all morning, but this was it. She'd reached her limit.

"Jane, no matter what I say you take it wrong."

"Well, then, here's some advice, Ellen. When it comes to other people's kids, keep your mouth shut." She snorted. "Of course, you've never been able to keep your mouth shut about anything."

Ellen stood, her body shaking with anger, and stared down at her sister. "What *is* with you, Jane?" She realized she was shouting, but she didn't care. Across the room one of the sleeping children stirred. She struggled to regain her composure. "Exactly why is it you hate me?"

"Be *quiet*, Ellen," Jane hissed. "You'll wake the kids."

"Oh, now it's the *kids* again. *Listen* to yourself, Jane. Listen to how you talk to me whenever the kids are involved." Ellen lowered her voice, but she couldn't hide her rage. She was losing control. "You treat me like I'm some inept, brainless woman who has no idea what to say or do around someone younger than eighteen. Well, get off your high horse, sister *dear*. You're a wonderful mother, but just because I don't have children doesn't mean I don't know anything about them."

Jane raised her eyebrows sarcastically and picked up her sandwich. "If you knew anything about children, you wouldn't have chosen a career over motherhood. But that's just my opinion."

The words were a slap that took Ellen's breath away. Her eyes filled with tears; her face twisted in pain. "Grow up, Jane! You're so caught up in your own little bitter world that you don't even know what you're saying—" Ellen broke off, and two tears trickled down her face.

Megan dropped her head in her hands and sighed. "You guys, this is so stupid.

You know you love each other, so why don't you just apologize and get over it."

Ellen spun to face her. "Megan, this has nothing to do with me. I've done every-thing humanly possible to get along with Jane, but she's determined to make life miserable for me. Am I the only one who sees it?"

"I don't know." Megan stood up abruptly. "You guys'll have to work it out on your own. I'm not taking sides." With that she headed for her bedroom.

"I'm leaving," Ellen announced.

"We'll leave together. In about thirty minutes."

Ellen looked at Megan. "No. We won't. I'm walking back to Mom and Dad's." Ellen swung her purse over her shoulder and marched toward the front door. The Barrett home was two miles away, but Ellen would have walked ten rather than spend another minute in the same room with Jane. She stared at Megan before she left. "I'm not mad at you. I just can't take her abuse anymore."

Jane shrugged, took a bite of her sandwich, and watched unsympathetically as Ellen walked to the door. "Get over it," she muttered. And then to Megan, "She's always overreacting about something."

It was a thick, humid afternoon and Leslie Maple wandered outside her Pennsylvania house toward her mailbox. She sorted through a stack of items as she made her way back in. Credit card offers, advertising, an insurance statement. Then she saw it. A hand-addressed, pale blue envelope postmarked Petoskey, Michigan. The town where she'd grown up. She set down the other mail and carefully ripped open the blue paper. Inside was a brief note and a newspaper article.

"Thought you'd like to know about this," the note read. "Take care and drop me a line sometime." It was from Carolann Hanson. Carolann had graduated from Petoskey the same year as Leslie. And Ellen Barrett. Leslie smiled at the thought of her best friend from high school. When Ellen moved to Ann Arbor, Leslie had been devastated, but it had helped that she and Carolann began attending Bible studies together and meeting once a week for prayer. Leslie and Carolann still exchanged Christmas cards and remembered to pray for each other's families.

Leslie opened the clipping and saw that it was an obituary. Her heart sank and tears flooded her eyes. John Barrett, Ellen's father, had suffered a heart attack and died. Leslie remembered Mr. Barrett vividly, his broad smile and the way he made Ellen's friends feel so welcome in his home. She and Ellen's other friends had loved Mr. Barrett and even called him Dad when they stopped by to visit. He was just that kind of parent.

She sighed and thought of Ellen, of how devastated she must be. Then as natu-rally as she lived and breathed, Leslie bowed her head and began to pray.

By the time everyone was back in place at the Barrett home it was one-thirty. Ellen sat in stony silence, not even looking at Jane. The anger between them was palpable, and the room was almost electrically charged with tension.

Their mother studied the faces before her, and sighed. "First, I think we need to take care of whatever happened between Ellen and Jane."

"No problem here," Jane said flatly.

Ellen stared at Jane. *Two could play that game.* She turned and smiled at their mother. "Everything's fine."

Their mother looked skeptically at her daughters. Across the room, Frank yawned and checked his watch.

"Well," she continued, "I know there's a problem between you two, but if you don't want to talk about it then let's get on with it. We still have a lot of planning to do."

"About the music," Amy jumped in. "Like I was trying to say last night—" she cast a disgusted glance toward Jane—"I think it would be nice if someone played that rugged cross song."

"'The Old Rugged Cross,'" Jane snapped, providing the title of the song self-righteously.

"The church has offered its organist and soloist for Saturday if we're interested. So maybe we could make that a solo number early in the service," their mother said. She wrote something down.

"You're right, Amy," Megan said. "Dad loved that song. I think we should ask the soloist to sing it."

Mom nodded. "What do you think, Aaron? Girls?"

"Fine." Aaron was wearing his dark glasses again, and Ellen thought his cheeks looked tearstained.

"Fine," Jane added.

"Ellen?"

"Sure."

"Sure? Does that mean you'd rather have a different song?"

"No, Mom." Ellen was drained, and she felt almost sick. The walk had done little to ease her anxiety. She'd been too angry to feel like praying, so she'd spent the time thinking about her father first, and then about her marriage. In her haste she had forgotten her notepad, and she felt helplessly unorganized and a bit adrift without a distraction should the conversation become too heated. *If Dad were still alive I'd be able to count on his support.* But her father wasn't alive. He was gone. Forever. And Ellen felt his absence more keenly with each passing moment.

"Ellen?" her mother asked again. "Would you rather have a different song?"

Wearily, she tried to explain herself. "I don't want a different song. It's just hard for me to get excited about songs that will be sung at Dad's funeral."

Her mother sighed. Ellen thought her mother had sighed more these past days than in her whole life.

"Ellen, dear, no one's asking you to be excited. It's a fact of life. We have to plan his funeral service or it won't get done. Try to understand."

"I know. I'm sorry."

Mom looked at her notes again. "Now, Megan. Have you considered singing at the service?"

Megan stared at her feet and fumbled her fingers uncomfortably. Ellen wondered at the hesitation. Everyone knew her sister had a beautiful voice, so much so that she was a favorite at local weddings and Christmas pageants. "I've thought about it." She hesitated. "I just don't think I could pull it off, Mom."

"Are you sure, honey? Your father loved to hear you sing."

Megan nodded. "I'm sorry. It would be too much for me."

"Okay, then, I think other than that we'll just let the organist choose whatever music she wants."

There were nods of approval around the room.

And so it continued.

Their mother led them from one topic of concern to another. They decided to use roses throughout the church since their father loved red, and they agreed on a time for the service. Next they spent an hour discussing whether to use a two-page program with their dad's picture on the front or stick with tiny prayer cards. Once they decided on the two-page program, they worked another two hours on the contents.

They agreed to pick out a coffin on Thursday and to make Friday the private and public viewing day at the mortuary. Ellen and Aaron were opposed to the viewing, but their mother was adamant.

"It's important that we have a chance to say good-bye and see him as he'll be when we bury him. It makes it more real."

Ellen shuddered at the thought. "He's already gone, Mom. I mean, we can look at his dead body but we won't be looking at him. That's just a shell of who he was."

"Mom isn't interested in your theology lesson, Ellen." Jane's tone was typically dry.

"Girls! That's enough. We're having a viewing and that's final."

Their mother sorted through her notes and glanced at her watch. Ellen followed suit. It was five-thirty. There were cold cuts and various breads and salads in the refrigerator and they had planned to eat no later than six. They weren't finished, but Ellen hoped they would take a break soon. They could always finish after dinner if necessary.

"Okay." Mom glanced at her notes once more. "We still have to decide whether we want a full Mass or a shortened service where we do more of the talking."

"A Mass is too impersonal. Especially at St. Francis," Megan said. "Besides, I thought we were each going to write something about Dad and read it at the service."

"We talked about it but we didn't decide anything." Amy glanced around the room. "I couldn't get up in front of that many people if my life depended on it."

"Same here," Aaron grunted.

"I think I've changed my mind on that. I agree with Amy and Aaron." At this pronouncement, everyone in the room turned and stared at Ellen.

"You don't want to write something about Dad?" Megan was clearly shocked.

"Not for his funeral." She had thought about reading a eulogy and decided against it during the walk from Megan's apartment. "I've written him a thousand things in the past. He's gone now. I can't imagine summing up a lifetime of feelings in a two-minute eulogy. It'd be impossible. Let's forget it."

Jane cocked her head to one side and considered Ellen's statement. "I think we should do whatever Mom wants. Regardless of how Aaron and Amy—" she hesitated for effect— "and *Ellen* feel."

"Well, then—" Ellen stood—"maybe it's time to wrap things up for the night and get back to the apartment." It was all Ellen could do to keep her tone civil. It was obvious that Jane had agreed with the idea of individually prepared eulogies to spite her. Ellen was sick to death of her sister's petty behavior. She just wanted to get back to Megan's before she unleashed her rising anger on Jane, despite her mother's request that they get along.

"Sit down, Ellen," Jane ordered. "We're right in the middle of trying to work this out. We all heard what Mom said. She wants us to write a eulogy, however brief, and read it at the funeral. I think we should at least give her idea a chance."

Ellen pinned her with a glare, then smiled sweetly. "And I think Aunt Mary's probably ready for a break after watching your children all day. Why don't we stop for now, pick up the kids, and come back later?"

Jane's face grew red. "I don't need *you* telling me when to give Aunt Mary a break. I can handle my children perfectly fine, thank you. That is one area where you can't possibly know more than I do."

"Here we go," Megan muttered under her breath while the others squirmed uncomfortably.

"Jane, hear me out." Ellen's words were carefully controlled, but they did not hide her frustration. "You know the kids gave Aunt Mary a hard time this morning. Why make her work longer than she has to? Let's take a break, get the kids, and come back."

Ellen clenched her teeth so hard they grated together. Being around Jane was like being subjected to mental torture—and she wasn't finished yet.

"My kids are not the big problem you make them out to be." Jane raised her voice. "What would *you* know about raising kids? Like I said earlier, anyone who would choose a career over motherhood certainly has no room to comment about another person's children!"

Ellen felt her control dissolve. Angry tears filled her eyes and she clenched her fists, driving them into her knees. "Jane, you are the coldest person I know! What happened to you? You and I used to be best friends when we were little and now look at you!"

"We aren't little anymore!" Jane spat.

Aaron got up and headed outside. The others left the room one by one until finally there was only Ellen and Jane, staring angrily at each other.

"No, we're not little anymore," Ellen said. "That's true. But we're still sisters and nothing can change that." Ellen began to sob. The fight was gone from her voice and in its place was a terrible sadness. "I'm sick of you treating me like some kind of cosmopolitan ice queen. I have feelings, too."

Jane remained silent while Ellen's sobs became more convulsive. "Mike and I…we've tried to have children—" She broke off.

I can't, God. I can't tell her this.

But she knew she had to. When she tried to speak, the words came out in grief-stricken sobs. "I've…I've lost two…babies, Jane." She tried to catch her breath but the sobs continued to wrack her body. "Do you have any idea how that feels? To know there's a life inside you, and then…then…it's gone?" She drew in several quick, jerky breaths and then exhaled slowly, trying to compose herself. "Right now…I'm…I'm just not ready to try again."

Jane's lower jaw dropped and her eyebrows raised slightly. She looked instantly remorseful. Ellen wrapped her arms around herself protectively, and suddenly her mother and Megan were there, putting their arms around her.

"Oh, sweetheart, I didn't know," her mother said. "Why didn't you tell me?"

"Dad knew. He told me not to say anything to anyone else if I didn't want to. It was too hard to talk about it."

"Honey, I'm so sorry." Mom hugged her.

"Ellen." Jane's voice was low, full of misery. "I'm sorry, too. I never guessed… And I've been such a jerk today. I don't know what's wrong with me." She looked away quickly, but not before Ellen had seen the look in her eyes. Jane was lying. There was a reason why she'd been behaving so terribly but she was refusing to tell them.

Why won't she tell me, Father? Ellen's heart cried. *How long will this go on?*

When Jane turned back to her, there were tears in her eyes, too. "I'm—I'm sorry about your miscarriages. I didn't know."

Ellen's anger rose again. "Of *course* you didn't know. How could you? You hardly talk to me anymore. But does that give you license to be angry with me for being childless? I swear, Jane, you think you're the only one in the world who's hurting."

Ellen pulled away from the group and headed for her parents' bedroom. "I need to be alone for a while."

No one followed her.

Once inside she shut the door and sat down on her father's side of the bed. She stared at the telephone through a blurry veil of tears. Since Sunday she had been so busy defending herself and avoiding Jane's wrath that she hadn't called Mike.

She remembered their argument the night before she left, and she was angry all over again. She wouldn't call him. Not now when she was so upset. He would only think he was right about not coming to Petoskey.

She took a tissue off her father's nightstand and blew her nose.

"Why, Dad?" she whispered brokenly.

She missed her father so badly. And now she was trapped in his house, surrounded by reminders of him, and faced with at least one sister who didn't even like her. She clenched her jaw.

"I want out of here." She glanced around the room, desperately seeking an escape.

She had no car; she would probably be stuck at the house until late that night. Her eyes fell on the Petoskey area White Pages. Suddenly an idea hit her.

It was crazy…or was it?

She picked up the phone book and considered what she was about to do. She thought about the way Jane had made life miserable for the past three days. Then she thought about Mike and how he had refused to make even the smallest sacrifice for her sake.

With angry resolve, she took a deep breath and thumbed through the book to the *S* section. Scanning the columns of names and numbers she finally found the one she was looking for.

Jake Sadler.

She picked up the telephone and dialed his number. Then she held her breath and waited.

That night, in the brand-new wing of the First Baptist church fellowship hall in Pine City, Pennsylvania, Leslie Maple and twenty other women were meeting to discuss the need for a church prayer line. The conversation was heated.

"If someone wants prayer they can call their closest friends and ask for it," Erma Brockmeir said. She sounded self-righteous and she knit her brows together in distaste.

"That's right," someone else spouted. "Anything more and we'd have ourselves a full-fledged gossip channel."

Leslie Maple stood up and waited until the chatter died down. "If we are to believe in the power of prayer," she began softly, "if we are to take the Lord at his word and lay our requests at his feet, then we have no choice. We must pray when we are alone and when we are together. We must pray constantly and we must pray as a body. A prayer line is the best, most efficient way to let the congregation know when someone is in dire need of prayer."

She stared beseechingly at the women. "If we are not willing to be part of that kind of prayer," she hesitated, "then we are failing to do what Jesus wants. We are failing him."

Several of the faces about the room softened and Imogene Spencer positioned her aluminum cane and slowly struggled to her feet. "As the church secretary at First Baptist, I, for one, think Leslie is right. Sometimes we older women need to listen to the younger set. Their ideas may be different than what we're used to, but it is a disgrace to think we have grown so deaf to the Spirit of God that we cannot hear his wisdom in their youthful words." She paused. "I say we start the prayer line today. As soon as we can find people who will make it work." She studied the women and cleared her throat. "Now, can I see a show of hands." She raised hers high over her head. "Who else is willing to join the prayer line?"

The ladies looked from one to another, then slowly a teary-eyed Erma Brockmeir rose her hand. Two women in the back row added their hands, and in the front row an entire section lifted theirs. Leslie grinned and pulled Imogene Spencer into a hug as the remaining ladies raised their hands.

"Well, my dear," Erma said. "Let's get busy. How exactly do we start a prayer line, anyway?"

16

*J*ake Sadler twisted the cap off a cold bottle of Pepsi, sank deep into his leather sofa, and closed his eyes. He had taken orders for more than a hundred windows that day and he was exhausted.

He reached down, picked up a week-old copy of the *Petoskey Times* and flipped to the Lifestyles section. There, sprawled across the top of the page, was an article about his company.

"Sadler's personal touch is the best thing to happen to windows and doors since the discovery of wood," the article stated. That explained the high number of orders he was getting. A person couldn't pay for that kind of advertising. Odds were good he'd reap the rewards for weeks to come. Jake studied the news clipping, remembering how it had been at the beginning. Sadler Custom Windows and Doors had been born in the early 1980s, after construction in Northern Michigan had slowed and often left Jake unemployed. Quick research told him that thousands of homes were nearly thirty years old and in need of renovation. Especially the custom homes that lined the shores of Harbor Springs, Petoskey, and Charlevoix. He tinkered around with several French and Victorian designs and finally launched his own business. Thereafter, his company supplied custom windows and doors specifically for those homes.

That was six years ago and now his business had grown beyond anything he had imagined. It brought him a hefty six-figure income and required him to employ three additional men.

Jake lived like a man who knew the definition of success.

He owned a large split-level home in Harbor Pointe, a premier, gated community situated on the northern peninsula of Little Traverse Bay. Technically the home was in Harbor Springs, but through windows of his own design he could gaze across the bay at the shores of Petoskey. The city limits were barely twenty minutes away.

He had a new boat, a new truck, a self-employed pension plan. Even before the article in the *Times,* his business had been thriving, gaining notice throughout Northern Michigan.

Still, Jake was restless, vaguely dissatisfied with life. He was busy at work and sometimes went out socially, but there was no one special. There hadn't been since Ellen Barrett.

"The business needs me," he told the women who had come and gone over the years. But he knew that wasn't completely true. Every now and then when he'd walk through his neighborhood or relax on his back deck, staring at the bay, he would think about Ellen...and wonder.

Tonight was one of those times.

John Barrett had died that past Friday. Jake heard the news hours later from his high school friend, Andy Conover. Andy worked as a technician in the hospital emergency room and was on duty the day John Barrett had suffered his heart attack. When a nurse mentioned the patient's last name, Andy became curious. He called Jake as soon as he got home.

"What was Ellen's dad's name?"

"Ellen Barrett?"

"Yes, what was her dad's name?"

"John. John Barrett." Jake was struck by the urgency in Andy's voice. "Why?"

"Oh, man, I thought so. We had him in ER today." Andy paused. "Jake, he's dead. Massive heart attack. Guy didn't have a chance."

The news hit Jake hard, and he hadn't stopped thinking of Ellen since. Certainly she would come out for her dad's funeral. She was probably already in town. She and Jane and the other Barretts.

Jake took a swig of his drink and wondered if there were still problems between Ellen and Jane. Back when he and Ellen were together it seemed he was constantly acting as referee for the sisters. In the end they had always worked things out, but Jake's last year with Ellen had been one of the worst.

That year Jane and Ellen had shared an apartment a few miles from their parents' house. It was 1988 and Troy was not yet back in Jane's life. Somehow, Ellen managed to look back on that year as a happy one. Jake remembered differently.

Jane was forever upset with Ellen for leaving dirty dishes in the sink or piling the trash so it overflowed. Ellen often forgot to tidy the living area and was, in general, a poor housekeeper. She planned too many activities for too short a time and inevitably her house was the first thing to suffer.

Ellen's messy habits had not been a problem outside of home. But as a roommate, Ellen's messiness was wearisome and Jake thought Jane had every right to express her concern. What bothered Jake back then was Jane's tone of voice when she spoke to Ellen. Jake would listen between the lines and what he heard was a lifetime of hate and resentment there.

The strangest part of all was that somewhere behind intricate layers of unexplained bitterness, the sisters really did love each other. Jake was sure of it.

He drew a deep breath and set down his drink on the varnished maple coffee table. Ellen. It had been years since he'd seen her but he had never stopped thinking of her. Her memory was so real he could almost touch her.

You blew it, he told himself. *You let her go and now you'll spend a lifetime regretting it.* He sighed and reached for the remote control just as the telephone rang.

He reached out to lift the receiver. "Hello?"

Silence.

"Hello?" Still nothing.

He was about to hang up when a familiar voice said, "Jake? It's me. Ellen."

Jake sat up straight, his eyes wide, his heart suddenly beating faster. "Ellen...how are you?"

"Well, not too good, really." He thought he heard tears in her voice. "My dad died...last Friday."

"I know. Andy was at the hospital. Andy Conover. He called me that night." She didn't say anything, but he heard her sniffing. "Ellen, hey, are you crying?"

She still didn't answer. Memories of her flooded over him, of her tender heart, her love for her father. This had to be killing her.

He tried again. "Where's your husband? Isn't he there?" She released a single sob. "No. He didn't come."

"You're not doing well. I can tell."

There was no response. Only the muffled sound of Ellen's cries. Jake stabbed his fingers absently through his hair. Her crying made him ache, made him willing to do anything to take the hurt away. "What can I do, Ellen? Tell me."

She sniffed loudly and regained control of her voice. "I...I don't know. I mean, that's why I called. Everything's kind of crazy around here and...well, I guess...Could you come over and pick me up? Take me somewhere so we could talk?"

"Sure." He looked at his watch: eight-thirty. "Let me change clothes and I'll be there at nine. Okay?"

"Okay. I'll be out front."

He hung up slowly, then sat there, staring at the phone, dazed. Had that just happened? Had Ellen just called him?

He exhaled a long, slow breath. Yes, it had happened. And he knew, as clearly as he knew anything in his life, that Ellen needed him. And he would be there for her.

Ellen hung up the phone and stared at her wedding ring. What in the world was she doing making plans to spend an evening with Jake Sadler? She didn't know...and right now she didn't care. She needed someone...someone to listen, to care. She left her parents' bedroom and headed for the front door.

"Where are you going?" Her mother looked at her, surprised.

"Out."

"You didn't eat and you don't have a car. There's nowhere you can go on foot at this hour of the night, Ellen. It wouldn't be safe."

Ellen released a short laugh. "At this point anything would be safer than here."

"Ellen, please—" Mom began, but Ellen stopped her.

"No. I called an old girlfriend." *Why am I lying? Why not just tell the truth? I'm not going to do anything wrong, for heaven's sake!*

But she couldn't tell them. She didn't want to deal with their reaction if she did. "She's picking me up and we're going for a drive. I'll have her drop me off at Megan's apartment later on. Don't worry about me."

"What about the funeral service? We didn't figure out about the eulogy. Whether you five kids will each read something." Clearly Mom was tired and frustrated. She wanted them to stay together until the plans were finished.

"Whatever you decide is fine with me." Ellen walked outside and shut the door behind her.

She was dressed in denim shorts and a white T-shirt, and suddenly she felt six years younger than her age. She found a place on the cool grass and sat down to wait for Jake. Then she tried not to think about how she'd done that very thing at least a hundred times before, long ago, when life had seemed so much simpler.

So much happier.

Inside the Barrett home, Jane heard the front door close and looked up from her dinner.

"Who was that?"

"Ellen. She's going out with a friend. She'll meet you and Megan back at the apartment later."

"That's nice." Jane had really tried to be more civil since Ellen had told them about the miscarriages, but she couldn't keep the tinge of sarcasm from her voice. "Shouldn't she be here? We haven't finished working out the funeral plans."

Their mother shrugged. "She said she'd go along with whatever we decided. I think she needs time away."

"Well, then, let's decide whether or not we're going to write separate eulogies and read them at the funeral. I think we should do it because it's something Mom wants."

Jane looked around the table, waiting for a response. "Well?" she said when they were silent.

"I don't like it, but I'll do it," Amy said finally. "Mom, it doesn't matter if it's short, does it?"

"No. Make it as long or short as you like."

Aaron shook his head. "I can't write something like that, Mom. You know how I am."

"I'm not asking you to write an essay, Aaron. Just a few words about your father and what you'll miss the most."

Aaron was quiet a moment and Jane wondered if he might actually cry. He nodded abruptly, then rose from the table. "Fine. I'll try."

Megan wiped her mouth with a napkin. "I already said I liked the idea."

"And Ellen said she'd do whatever we wanted, so I guess that settles it. Right, Mom?" Jane looked at her mother expectantly.

"Seems like it. You'll have to let Ellen know tonight. Other than that, I think we're about done."

"I'm going to bed," Aaron announced.

"So early?" The disappointment was evident in Mom's creased forehead, in her pained expression.

"Yes." Aaron's voice was defensive. "I need to work on what I'm going to say. Is that all right with you?"

True to form, Mom backed down. "Sure, honey. I'm sorry. We'll see you tomorrow, then."

The others finished their dinner and gathered in the den to watch television. Since that didn't interest her, Jane borrowed Megan's car and set out to relieve Aunt Mary of her children. As she walked across the front yard she passed Ellen. She said nothing to her then or ten minutes later when she returned with the children in tow.

What Ellen had told her had struck deep. Had it been any other person, any friend, who had shared such a struggle, Jane would have known what to say, what to do. But this was Ellen. And with Ellen, Jane simply didn't know any way other than anger.

Silence seemed the greatest kindness she could extend.

Ellen watched Jane as she left the house, then returned later with her children. Twice Jane walked right past where she sat waiting. Both times she hadn't even looked her way, hadn't said a word.

Even strangers say hello.

She stared down the street, disgusted, hurt. Why had she even bothered to tell Jane anything? Why had she thought it would make a difference? They were sisters, but that didn't seem to matter. They couldn't even get along in the wake of their father's death. No, nothing mattered between her and Jane anymore. Nothing but the anger.

Ellen looked at her watch and saw that she had fifteen minutes until Jake would be there. Forget Jane. Think about something else.

For a moment, her thoughts drifted to Mike, but she shut that down. The last thing she needed after the unceasing doses of Jane's anger was to think about her fights and struggles with Mike.

She looked up at the sky, closed her eyes wearily, and let her mind wander....

What would Jake look like after so many years? Would he still have that same smile, the one that had always warmed her all the way through? Would his eyes still sparkle? Did he still have that deep and unrestrained laughter?

Stop! Her conscience jabbed at her, and she sighed. It was wrong to think about him that way. She had loved him, truly she had. But that was another time. He was coming to meet her as a friend. Nothing more. And that's all she wanted. A friend. Wasn't it?

She sighed softly. At that moment she was too tired, too weak not to miss Jake and the way life had been when they were together. Back then everything had seemed so...right. Her father was well, she and her sisters got along, and she hadn't a care in the world. Everything about those years was peppered with Jake's presence.

Finally, like dear, long-lost friends, the memories came flooding back—and Ellen entertained them willingly. She ignored that still, small voice warning her to take every thought captive for Christ, and she drifted back to a breezy afternoon at Petoskey High School.

The day she first set eyes on Jake Sadler.

17

It was the fall of Ellen's sophomore year in high school, and cheerleading practice had just started. That afternoon Ellen and her best friend, Leslie Maple, were working out with the squad in the physical education area when Stacy Wheatley appeared fifty yards away with a boy Ellen had never seen before.

"Isn't Stacy supposed to be practicing?" Leslie asked quietly. Their cheerleading coach, Mrs. Black, was a stickler for punctuality; Stacy was already ten minutes late.

Ellen ignored Leslie's comment. She was too busy staring at the boy to answer. "Who's *that?*"

Leslie squinted across the field, shaking her head. "I don't know."

The boy was tall, with dark brown hair cut close to his head. He wore only his athletic shorts, and his tanned and toned stomach was attracting the attention of several cheerleaders. He looked like he belonged on a tropical island as he teased and flirted with Stacy.

"I think that's Jake Sadler," Leslie said after a moment. "He's new."

"Freshman?"

"Yep. Came from the middle school across town."

"Sure beats anything the sophomore class has to offer."

"That's what everyone's saying."

Stacy and Jake walked closer. He lifted her hand, kissed it, and bowed like a Renaissance man before winking at her once and turning to go.

"Oh, *brother,*" Leslie whispered.

"Stacy!" Mrs. Black's voice boomed across the field. "Stop messing around and get over here where you belong. You have two minutes to get that uniform on."

Red-faced and giggling, Stacy ran into the girls' locker room to do as she was told. When Jake turned around to wave one last time he caught Ellen watching him instead.

For a long moment Ellen was caught in Jake's curious stare. He studied her, almost as though trying to remember where he'd seen her before. Then he flashed her a wide grin and winked, the same way he'd winked at Stacy. In an instant he rounded the corner and disappeared from sight.

Ellen felt herself blush and she couldn't hear Mrs. Black's instructions. With all her might she tried to concentrate on the routine but she kept seeing Jake Sadler's blue eyes instead.

"Ellen?" a voice boomed. "I said move to the grassy quad with the other girls and stretch out. Are you awake?" It was an Indian summer afternoon and Mrs. Black was hot and frustrated. "If I could only get you people to listen."

Ellen moved sheepishly toward Leslie.

"You okay?" Leslie nudged her. "You look spaced out or something."

Ellen nodded and Leslie raised a single eyebrow. "It's that Jake guy, isn't it?"

Ellen said nothing and pretended to concentrate on stretching her right hamstring. She lowered her upper body over her leg and avoided Leslie's probing eyes.

"Ellen, that's it, isn't it? Tell me I'm right. You're thinking about Jake Sadler."

"Of course not," Ellen hissed. She would be mortified if Mrs. Black heard them. "He's obviously dating Stacy. Why would I be interested?"

"Right. I'm your best friend and you expect me to believe that. Come on, Ellen. I can see it clear as the nose on your face. He knocked you flat out, didn't he?"

"Stop! We're gonna get in trouble."

"No sir, Ellen," she whispered loudly. "We're not going to get in trouble. *You* are. Especially if you get your heart set on Jake Sadler. He's had a different girl on his arm every day since school started. And school only started two weeks ago. Forget him."

Ellen nodded. "Okay. Fine. Now let's practice."

"So you admit it! You have a thing for the guy, don't you?"

"Shhhh! Get to work."

Long after cheerleading practice was finished and Leslie had dropped Ellen off at home, the image of Jake Sadler consumed her and left her stomach a twisted mess of butterflies. The next morning before class she was talking to a group of friends when she spotted him, sitting by himself at the other end of the covered lunch area. He was watching her, and when she caught his gaze he grinned. Ellen squelched a smile and excused herself from the group. Despite her nervousness, she walked the twenty feet between them in an unhurried manner.

"Hi." His eyes danced with challenge and Ellen's heart skipped a beat.

"Hi." She sat down across from him and stared at him questioningly. "You're new?"

Jake nodded. "Jake Sadler."

"Ellen Barrett."

"I know."

"How'd you know?"

"Who doesn't know Ellen Barrett?"

"Apparently you know quite a few people. Like Stacy Wheatley, for starters."

Jake stretched, and Ellen noticed the muscle definition in his arms. "Stacy's just a friend. We knew each other in junior high."

"You guys looked pretty friendly yesterday."

Jake shrugged. "That's me, I guess. Can't seem to break the flirt image."

"Apparently not."

The bell rang then and Ellen stood to leave. "Well, see you around."

"You'll be over there at lunch, right?" He pointed to the spot where the cheerleaders and football players hung out. "Right."

"I'll look for you."

That afternoon Jake found her and gave her a note he'd written during class. She read it while he was buying milk and ended up spending the entire lunch hour by his side. They laughed and teased and kicked at each other's feet, so that by the time the bell rang half the school was talking about them.

"Okay, what's the deal?" Leslie asked in their sixth-hour English class. "Everyone saw you with Jake Sadler at lunch. I want every detail."

Ellen smiled. "He's cute, isn't he?"

"He's gorgeous. So what? I'm telling you he makes eyes at a dozen girls every day."

"Oh, Leslie, just because he flirts a little doesn't mean he's a bad guy. Give him a break."

"Okay, but don't say I didn't warn you."

Time and again over the next six years, whenever Jake broke Ellen's heart, Leslie would remind her that she had seen it coming.

"I warned you, Ellen," she would say. "Dump the guy. He's dragging you down."

But Leslie's efforts never changed anything. From that first day she saw him, Ellen was addicted to Jake the way some people are addicted to drugs. Even when she knew he was bad for her, she could not bear to be apart from him.

At first they'd decided to just be friends. They tickled and teased, but they kept their relationship platonic. Jake was just too popular with the girls. They hung on Jake's every word; they followed him to and from classes and giggled when he passed by. Ellen, too, received more than a little attention from the opposite sex. Neither of them was ready to be exclusive.

Still, they walked together between classes, sat together when her cheer squad took breaks at football games, and talked on the phone almost every night.

"Well, have you kissed the guy yet or what?" Leslie would ask and Ellen would shake her head.

"No, I told you. We're just—"

"I know, I know," Leslie interrupted. "You're just friends. But that's not how it looks. That boy's mad about you, Ellen. And I think the feeling's mutual. The whole thing spells trouble."

"I'm telling you, we're friends. Nothing more."

Then, things changed. Ellen had known for months that her feelings for Jake went deeper than friendship. And one evening, he told her what she'd been waiting to hear. They were walking together, and ended up in a small park. They found a bench and sat down. Jake had been unusually quiet, so Ellen turned to him. But before she could say anything he turned to her, his expression serious. "Something's happened."

She stared at him, and fear washed over her. Was his family moving? Was he in love with someone else, someone who didn't want them spending time together anymore? She was silent, willing him to continue.

He took her hands in his, slowly rubbing his thumb along her fingers. "I'm not sure how you're going to react."

Just say it! her mind screamed. For once she didn't have anything to say. She was too frightened at the thought of losing him.

"The thing is…I think I'm in love with you."

Ellen stared at him blankly. "What?"

He didn't reply. Instead, he held her gaze for a moment, then reached up to cup her face with his lean fingertips. Slowly he lowered his head and, for the sweetest minute of her life, pressed his lips to hers.

The memory of that kiss still took her breath away, still warmed her heart…

They'd both been breathless when they drew apart. They stared at each other, nervous about the line they had crossed, drowning in a sea of first-time emotions.

"I love you, Ellen," he'd finally said, and joy had coursed though her.

After that there was no turning back.

Ellen and Jake were together through the summer and her junior and senior year. She turned eighteen after graduation and he was seventeen with one more year left at Petoskey. That summer she camped with his family and spent half her days swimming with him at Magnus Park. They played Ping-Pong and Frisbee and backgammon and chased each other in the shallow water along the shore of the bay. They kissed and held hands and studied a hundred sunsets. The days wore on and they were inseparable.

When school started that fall everyone they knew felt shut out of their relationship.

"I don't know, Ellen," Leslie said. "I think it's all a little too good to be true. Let's see what this year brings, now that you're not on campus with him."

Ellen scoffed at her friend's warning, but Leslie proved to be right. Jake was a senior that fall and better looking than ever. Ellen, meanwhile, was miles away at North Central Community College.

Every girl at Petoskey knew that Ellen wasn't around to monopolize Jake's attention. As far as they were concerned, Jake didn't have a girlfriend. They chased him for all he was worth. He found notes on his car, notes in his locker, and mysterious phone messages on his answering machine.

One day Leslie called and told Ellen the news she thought she'd never hear.

"Ellen, I don't like to have to tell you this, but, well…it's about Jake."

"What about him?" Ellen had just walked into the house from a day of classes and was fixing herself something to eat.

"You sure you want to know?"

"Don't be so dramatic, Leslie. Whatever it is, just say it."

"Okay. Well, you know how my brother's a senior, right?"

"Right. So?" Ellen opened the refrigerator and pulled out a loaf of bread, stretching the phone cord to its limit.

"Well, I guess Jake's been spending a lot of time with Candice Conner. You know, the J.V. cheerleading captain."

Ellen's heart sank. She set down the bread and pulled out a chair from the kitchen table. Her lunch was forgotten.

"Are you sure?"

"Billy says you'd never know he has a girlfriend by the way he acts at school. It's been that way since September."

Ellen didn't want to believe Jake had betrayed her, but that night Jake told her the truth himself.

They'd decided it was better to see other people. Ellen refused to let Jake see how much the situation had hurt her. But after he left that night, she cried for two days straight. She listened to sad songs on the radio and stayed up late writing poetry about lost love.

Then one night after two weeks of hearing nothing from Jake she was watching television when she heard the sound of his car horn in front of her house. She ran to the front door and peeked through the curtains. It was Jake. He honked again and she went outside, running lightly in her bare feet to the driver's side of his Volkswagen.

He was crying and he reached for her hand.

"Jake, what's wrong?" She was suddenly worried something had happened to him or his parents.

"I'm so sorry, Ellen!" He slammed his right hand against his steering wheel.

Ellen was quiet. She hugged herself tightly to ward off the chill in the air and waited for an explanation.

"Candice chased me, Ellen. I swear. She wanted to go out and finally I thought what the heck. It might be fun." He dried the tears off his cheeks with the back of his hand. "I was wrong, Ellen. I don't want her; I want you. I've never stopped wanting you. The problem is sometimes I want to date other girls. It's like I can't make up my mind."

Ellen's knees were weak and she tried to think of something to say.

"I know you don't want me around, not now when I'm not ready to be your boyfriend again. But could you at least talk to me, be my friend like we used to be?" He looked up at her. "I need you, Ellen. I miss you so much."

Then he reached around to the backseat and pulled out a dozen red roses. He handed them to her and there were fresh tears in his eyes. "I love you, babe."

Ellen wanted so badly to tell him to leave, to never come back unless he was sure he wouldn't break her heart. But she knew as surely as she had the first time she'd seen him that she could not turn him away. She sighed and took his hand, fitting her fingers between his.

"Okay. But just friends." she said softly. It was a wish, a way of trying to save face. She missed him terribly and wanted to believe she could spend time with him even while he dated other girls. For an instant she thought about Leslie's warnings, but then she put them out of her mind.

She smiled and Jake's eyes lit up. "Park," she said simply.

He did, and they spent two hours on the porch swing in front of her house talking about the time they'd missed and savoring the fact that they were together again. When he stood up to leave, he pulled her into his arms as if nothing had changed between them. But before he could kiss her she leaned out of reach.

"Don't mess with my heart, Jake," she whispered. "If you're dating other people then we can't…"

"I know," Jake put a finger to her lips. "I'm sorry. It won't happen again."

But they both knew it would. The more time they spent together, the more difficult it became to remain platonic, and finally one night Jake told her he wanted things to be the way they were.

"What about the girls at school?"

"I want you," he insisted.

She sighed and twirled her finger through a lock of his shiny hair. "Ahh, Jake. How can I say no?"

"I love you, Ellen." He kissed her softly.

"I know. Me, too."

Their relationship deepened as they grew older. Soon the youthful romance became something much more serious. Finally, after being together for three years, though it went against everything she'd been taught, everything she believed in, Ellen gave in to her desires and Jake's and they began sleeping together.

From time to time guilt would stab at her and she'd close her eyes, fighting back tears. *Father, forgive me…*she'd pray. *But you know we love each other. And we're going to get married. Someday. I just know it. So it's not really wrong, is it?*

Her only answer was silence.

For three years their relationship continued. They slept together, camped together, and made promises to marry each other. But every time Ellen thought things were going great, Jake would break up with her because of another girl.

After six years of the roller-coaster ride with Jake Sadler, Ellen wondered what had happened, how she had fallen so hard and lost control of her life. She wondered if the reason she continued to go back to him was the challenge of changing him. She wondered if she was crazy.

One night she was lying in bed, agonizing over yet another letdown with Jake, when her heart suddenly began racing, thumping wildly about in her chest.

She sat up, struggling to breathe. *I'm dying!* Sweat began to bead along her forehead and she climbed out of bed, moving quickly down the hallway to her parents' room, where she knocked on the door. After a minute, the door opened slightly and her mother's bleary-eyed face appeared.

"Ellen? What's wrong?"

"My heart." She shivered as she put a hand to her chest. "It's racing a mile a minute and I feel like I can't breathe."

Her mother led Ellen out to the living room and sat next to her. "You need to relax, dear. Take a deep breath and hold it."

Ellen did as she was told.

"Now, let it out slowly."

The air seeped out of her mouth, and she felt slightly more relaxed. "Now what?"

"Do it again." Her mom rubbed her back, talking to her in a soothing voice. After five minutes, Ellen's heart stopped racing and she was calm again.

"Go get some sleep now, but I'll make a doctor's appointment for you tomorrow."

The doctor's diagnosis was simple: she had suffered a panic attack.

"Is there anything in your life making you feel out of control?" he asked.

Ellen thought of Jake and uttered a short laugh. "You could say that."

"A boyfriend?"

Ellen nodded sheepishly.

"Well, young lady." The doctor was in his late forties and had a fatherly way about him. "I'd say it's time you remove him from your life before the situation compromises your health."

Ellen nodded again.

After that she thought long and hard about her relationship with Jake.

They shared what seemed like a lifetime of happy memories and she loved him more than ever. They rode bikes along the shores of Mackinac Island, sailed on Little Traverse Bay, and cuddled together at Magnus Park under the shade of the leafy maple trees. They made fancy egg omelettes and laughed until Ellen thought her sides would burst. He was charming and romantic and the ultimate challenge. Jake Sadler was the only man she wanted in her life. But his unfaithfulness was affecting her health and something had to change.

The holidays passed and Ellen ushered in the New Year with a single resolution. She would give Jake an ultimatum. One more chance. If he couldn't be faithful, they were finished.

On a bright Saturday morning she drove to his house, prepared to share her decision. She was on break from the University of Michigan, but they hadn't talked much for the past week. They'd both been busy—she working at a steak house on the beach in Charlevoix and he working construction in the days.

Ellen pulled up in front of his house and saw that his parents' car was gone. She was slightly disappointed. She loved Jake's parents dearly and looked forward to seeing them. They had become like family to her.

Still, if they were gone that meant Jake was alone. Ellen smiled at the thought. She looked at her watch as she climbed out of her car. It was only eight-fifteen. If his parents were gone, Jake would still be sleeping. She walked up the front steps and knocked loudly. When no one answered, she knocked again.

"Come on, Jake, get out of bed," she whispered.

Suddenly the door opened and a leggy blond with tousled hair stood before her. She was wearing Jake's bathrobe. Ellen was too stunned to speak.

"Yes?" The girl had sounded annoyed, her voice raspy from sleep. She was definitely suffering the effects of a hangover. Ellen's heart began to race and she felt faint.

"Are you selling something or what?" the girl asked impatiently. She seemed anxious to be done with Ellen.

"No. Nothing." Ellen was in a fog of disbelief. She turned toward her car.

"Who are you?" the girl shouted after her.

Ellen ignored her and sped away. Angry tears streamed down her face as she drove aimlessly through the streets of Petoskey. She could not go home and face her parents' questions but her heart was racing so fast she thought she might have a heart attack. She wrestled with the idea of driving to the hospital, then convinced herself there was nothing physically wrong. She was having another panic attack.

She drove to Magnus Park and found a deserted plateau overlooking the freezing bay, a spot where she and Jake had parked a number of times over the years.

"I hate you, Jake!" Her heart responded by beating even faster.

She had trusted him, believed in him, given him everything she had to give. And he had betrayed her. No wonder her heart was racing. Her life was out of control and it was her own fault. She had stayed with Jake Sadler all these years, knowing that he wasn't faithful. Now she had no one but herself to blame for what was happening. She drew a shaky breath and decided that control was hers for the taking.

"It's over, Jake." She wiped her tears. It didn't matter that she had said the words a hundred times. She felt like blinders had been removed from her eyes. And there was too much at stake—primarily her health—to turn back. "I mean it this time."

With that declaration, Ellen's heart skipped a beat and then slowed considerably. The panic attack had left her tired and aching from the finality of her decision. Filled with a determination she had never known, she started her car and headed home. Her mother met her at the door.

"Jake called."

"Thanks." Ellen walked past her mother toward her bedroom. Her father intercepted her in the hallway.

"Ellen? You've been crying, honey."

"Yes, but I'm okay."

"Jake?"

Ellen rolled her eyes and released a sad, short laugh. "Who else?"

"Honey, you need to let that boy go. He's not ever going to change. Not even for you."

Ellen nodded and hugged her father. "I know, Daddy. Thanks."

When she didn't return his phone calls for two days Jake appeared at her house late one night. He tapped lightly on the door. Ellen saw who it was and she summoned her determination. The time had come to tell him good-bye. She slipped a parka over her turtleneck sweater and went outside.

"Hi." Their eyes met and she looked away. He was no longer welcome to see into her soul.

"Hi." He stuffed his gloved hands nervously in his pocket. Two feet of snow covered the ground even though the skies had been clear for a week. At that late hour the temperature hovered just above zero. "Ellen, what's wrong? You haven't called me in two days." Jake shivered and moved closer. "I've been calling you every few hours."

Ellen ignored him. She walked toward the porch swing and sat down. Jake followed. His eyes looked deeply troubled and Ellen guessed he probably knew what was coming. She thought about the years they'd been together, the memories they'd built, the love they'd shared....

She looked at him now and was still struck by the sight of him. *Will there ever be anyone like you, Jake?* They had planned to spend their lives together, raise children and take them fishing on the bay, camping in the wooded pastures of the Upper Peninsula. But now it was over. It had to be. Her eyes filled with tears and she stared at the ground between her feet.

"Ellen, what is it?" Jake put an arm around her shoulders and she recoiled as if he'd slapped her.

"Don't touch me, Jake. Not now."

"Ellen, I—"

"Don't." She held up a single hand and stared into his eyes. "I came by the house Saturday morning."

Jake's body jerked as if he'd been slapped.

"Don't defend yourself." Her voice cracked. She was neither angry nor hateful, only sad at what they were both losing.

"I can't keep doing this, Jake." Her eyes were full of pain, and Jake looked away.

"Ellen, I can explain. I was drinking with the guys and I had a few too many. It wasn't—"

She shook her head. She was twenty-one years old and she had listened to Jake's excuses for six years. "I should hate you for what you've done to me, Jake, but I love you too much. Isn't that stupid?" Fresh tears welled in her eyes. She brushed them away and shivered as she stared intently at him.

"I have something to say so listen to me, please," she said softly. There was silence for a moment. "We're finished, Jake. For real this time."

"Ellen, don't do this." His eyes grew watery. There was a fear in his eyes that Ellen had never seen before. "I can't live without you, you know that."

"Yes, but I can't live *with* you. I've tried, Jake. Really." She pulled one hand from her lined pocket and touched his cheek gently with her freezing fingertips. "I love you. I'll probably never love anyone the way I loved you. But you'll never change, Jake. It's time for me to go my own way."

"Ellen, why can't you believe me? She was nothing—"

"Jake!" Ellen raised her voice for the first time that evening. "Please. Don't." Tears streamed down her freezing cheeks but her voice remained unaffected, determined. "There's nothing you could say to change my mind. It's too late."

She stood up, and Jake rose to her side.

"Can't you just hear me out? Can't we try—?"

"Jake, go. Please."

He slumped in defeat. For a moment he stared at his feet, as though understanding for the first time the finality in her words. Then he came to her and circled his arms around her waist. For the last time she let him. "I love you, Ellen." He clung to her.

She could feel his heartbeat through their jackets, and suddenly she was terrified to let him go. She had to get inside before she changed her mind.

"I'm a jerk. I blew it and it's all my fault. But I'll never stop loving you."

Ellen felt his tears on her forehead and she ached to tell him it was all right, they could try again. She closed her eyes tightly and held him a moment longer. Then slowly, for the last time, she pulled away.

"Ellen, give me time. I'll change and then at least let me call you."

"I need to go on with my life. I've spent six years waiting for your phone calls. So, please. Don't make me promises. Not now."

"But…"

"Jake, go. Please."

He met her gaze, and it struck her that he looked as if he'd lost his greatest treasure. She understood. She felt the same way. In the end they had both lost.

Without Jake in her life, Ellen's panic attacks stopped immediately. She busied herself with extracurricular school projects and housecleaning. In the evenings, when she was sorely tempted to call Jake, she forced herself to visit her girlfriends, especially Leslie Maple.

That year Leslie had become a Christian and there was something undeniably different about her—a joy, a light in her eyes that hadn't been there before. Two weeks after the breakup with Jake, Ellen spent a weekend with Leslie. The two prayed and read Scripture, and for the first time in Ellen's life she understood that Christ desired a relationship with her. She cried, picturing Jesus on a cross dying a painful death while she, Ellen Barrett, was on his mind. That was a kind of love so real it was intoxicating. She had believed in God. She had gone to church and catechism and confession. But she hadn't really known the Christ. That weekend, in those quiet, prayerful moments with Leslie, she understood that the physical relationship she had shared with Jake was wrong, not because of a list of dos and don'ts, but because God had different, better plans for his children. And now Ellen wanted nothing more than to follow those plans. That Sunday morning she went to church with Leslie and afterwards she accepted Jesus as her personal Savior in a way she had never done before.

She'd never known the kind of joy that decision brought her. It surpassed anything she'd ever felt before. "Does this last?" she asked Leslie with a grin.

Leslie smiled. "As long as you keep Christ your main focus, yes. But there are a lot of things in life that can come between you and your faith."

"There's only one person who could come between me and the Lord," Ellen admitted.

"Jake?"

"Jake."

"Well, girl, let's pray about it." Leslie grinned and took Ellen's hands in hers. "God alone can help you where Jake's concerned."

They did so. Ellen took the lead and asked God to protect her heart and to forgive her for the physical relationship she'd shared with Jake. She asked the Lord to teach her, to guide her, to show her how to keep anything from coming between her and him.

When the prayer was over, Ellen and Leslie smiled at each other.

"There's a wonderful, Christian man out there for you somewhere, Ellen." Leslie's eyes were shining. "I'm sure of it."

Ellen joined a campus fellowship when she got back to the university and her heart soared with a joy she hadn't known before. God loved her deeply and in that there was a freedom she hadn't realized existed. She was his alone. There was comfort knowing that if she listened to his voice, he would lead her along the right paths. Her quiet moments talking to the Lord satisfied a need deep in her soul, a need not even Jake had been able to meet. She began telling her parents and siblings how powerful a relationship with Christ could be.

"I only wish you could both join a Bible-believing church, Dad," Ellen told her father one day. "The Catholic church has so many traditions and things that aren't in Scripture."

John Barrett raised an eyebrow and pulled Ellen aside. "Let's get one thing clear. We have no choice but to accept your decision about leaving the Catholic church, but don't expect us to leave just because you did. Catholics love the Lord every bit as much as Protestants."

"I'm not talking about Protestants *or* Catholics, Daddy," Ellen insisted. "I'm talking about Christians. Bible-believing Christians."

John Barrett smiled patiently. "Believe it or not, I, too, read the Bible. Nearly every day. It doesn't matter what label you wear. What matters is that you know Jesus and have a relationship with him. There is one faith and one Lord, after all." His voice had grown softer then. "You and Jake broke up and now you've found comfort in God's Word. I'm glad for that. If you think you can be closer to God at a different church, then we accept your decision. Every day since you were born I've prayed that you children would grow close to God. But don't go thinking your mother and I don't love the Lord as much as you do just because we're Catholic."

Ellen never again tried to convince her family to leave their church. Instead she prayed that their faith would be strengthened, and over the years she saw those prayers answered.

Weeks after the discussion with her father, Ellen was back in Petoskey for his crash course in sports reporting. Six months later she met Mike.

She and Jake saw each other just once after that, when they met by chance at Glen's Market in Petoskey. Ellen remembered her prayer and managed to leave the store after barely exchanging greetings with Jake.

That was nine years ago.

Ellen picked at the damp grass around her. She wondered if he had changed, if he still had a string of girls or if he had finally gotten serious about life.

A truck turned and headed down the street. Ellen's pulse quickened as the vehicle came closer and finally stopped in front of her house.

The truck was new, a full-size Chevy with an extended cab. A man climbed out slowly. Jake. She would have known him anywhere. He studied her as she stood up and brushed the grass off her shorts.

"Hi ya." The soft greeting was one she'd heard from him a thousand times before.

"Hi." She was thankful he couldn't see her red cheeks from across the yard.

He walked around and opened the passenger door, watching her carefully as she climbed in. He closed her door, walked around and climbed into the driver's seat. He drove several houses down the block, then pulled over.

"Ellen." He turned to her, searching her face. Gently, he took her hands in his, but he said nothing. There was no need. Ellen could read his piercing blue eyes as easily as she had the day they'd met. They were adults who had shared everything at a time when life was most impressionable and the memories were there for both of them.

"I know," she said quietly.

Then without a word they hugged each other, bridging the awkwardness between them and erasing the years in a single instant.

18

Ellen pulled away first, smoothing her T-shirt and wrestling with her emotions. Jake stayed close. He stared into her eyes, watching her carefully.

"Are you okay?" he whispered. "About your dad, I mean?" There was concern in his voice, and Ellen caught the scent of his cologne. Mixed with the smell of the truck's new leather interior it was enough to make her flustered, unsure of herself—and her motives for calling him.

Lord, what am I doing here? What am I looking for?

As had happened so often lately, the only answer she received was silence. Drawing a deep breath, she steadied herself. Jake had spent so much time with her family that he would understand what she had lost. He had loved her father, too.

And that, Ellen realized, more than any other reason, was why she wanted to see Jake after so many years.

She wiped at an errant tear. "I miss him, Jake."

"He was something, wasn't he?" Jake's eyes were distant and sad. He looked at Ellen again. "You okay?"

"I guess. It wasn't a surprise or anything. I just…I just needed to talk to someone who would understand."

"Well, I have all night." Jake started the engine and pulled back onto the street. "Why don't you relax a minute and you can tell me all about it when we get there."

"Where are we going?"

"You'll see."

She sank deep into the leather seat and studied him as he drove. He wore a blue tank top and athletic shorts, and it was easy to see that he was still lean, still remarkably fit. His hair was darker than before, cropped short at the neck and slightly longer on top. He was still tan, his eyes still as blue as the water in Little Traverse Bay. But there was something different. Something…more steady, more mature. He turned onto Mitchell, and Ellen saw he was heading toward the water. The silence between them was easy, and when she turned to watch him again he caught her gaze and smiled.

"I'm glad you called."

She shook her head, chuckling wryly. "I still can't believe I did it. I thought you'd think I was crazy, calling after all these years."

"Come on, Ellen. Did you think I'd forget you?"

She stared at her hands. "No."

"Well, that's good."

Ellen smiled to herself. Jake was trying to keep things on a surface level, and that *was* good.

"You have to admit it's a little strange, calling you out of the blue after nine years and asking you to come get me."

"You can always call me, Ellen. You know that." Jake's voice was kind, and Ellen felt it wrap around her, warming her wounded heart. Hot, unexpected tears pricked at her eyes at the compassion she heard in his voice, saw in his eyes. No doubt about it, Jake had been a head turner when they were younger. But this kinder, gentler manner…this sincerity and compassion that she felt from him…

That took him way beyond attractive—and right into dangerous.

They drove another ten minutes to the plateau along the beach at Magnus Park. A thicket of trees surrounded the secluded spot but opened just enough to offer a spectacular view of the bay. It was nearly nine-thirty and the sun was beginning its trek toward the water.

Ellen settled more deeply into her seat and sighed. She and Jake had parked here so often before. The plateau was where they had broken up and gotten back together a handful of times over the years. This was where she'd come after going to Jake's house that last time and finding another woman there.

How strange it was to be here again.

Jake turned off the engine and leaned back, facing her. He was silent, studying her. She laughed nervously. "Kinda familiar, huh?"

Jake didn't laugh. "That's not why I brought you here."

"I know. It just brings back memories, that's all."

"We can go somewhere else."

"No," Ellen said quickly. "This is fine. I like it here."

"So," Jake said. He folded his hands behind his head and leaned against the window of his truck. "I'm listening."

"Well, it's a long story."

"About your dad?"

"No. I mean, I'm dealing with my dad's death. At least I think I am. Actually I'm so busy fighting with Jane that I hardly have time to think about my dad."

Jake shifted so that he was slightly closer, and Ellen realized he could still make her feel safe and secure, still soothe away her pain without a single touch.

"I wondered how things would be between you two this week."

"They're terrible. Isn't that crazy? We come together for our dad's funeral, travel the country so we can be here in our hometown and bury this man we all loved, and we can't even get along with each other."

"Ah, just like old times."

Ellen stared at him. "Huh?"

"Come on, Ellen. You and Jane always fought. Don't tell me you don't remember."

Ellen was quiet a moment. She stared out the windshield at the waning sunlight. The bay had become a shimmering expanse of silver and gold. She drew a deep breath and turned to Jake.

"When I think about Jane I remember hanging around her at school and sharing secrets late into the night. Dancing on a flatbed truck one New Year's Eve. And a thousand happy memories growing up together."

"Those are all good, Ellen. But there were bad times, too. Remember the year you shared the apartment?"

Ellen frowned. She remembered. "We disagreed once in a while back then, but it's different now. She snaps at everything I say. It seems like she hates me. I don't know how to get along with her, I don't know what to say around her, and I don't know what I've done to make her so mad. When I couldn't take it anymore I called you. And here I am."

Jake inclined his head but said nothing.

Ellen went on. "I was closer to my dad than she was."

"I remember. You think that's the problem?"

Ellen stared out the windshield again. "I don't know. It seems like she's taking it out on me, like she resents me or something." Tears made their way quietly down her face. "She tells me I shouldn't talk about her children, and then she ridicules me for not having any of my own." She closed her eyes. "She accused me of choosing my career over having children." She gave a short laugh. "I can't believe she thought that. I want kids; for a while I wanted them more than anything in the world. But Mike and I have tried and it just hasn't happened." She opened her eyes and met Jake's gentle gaze. "I've had two miscarriages."

His eyes filled with sympathy. "I'm sorry, Ellen. Really."

She nodded and sniffled loudly. Jake handed her a tissue from his glove compartment and Ellen was thankful she had called him. There was still a certain chemistry between them, but there was no spark, no hint of anything less than proper. She was a married woman talking heart-to-heart with an old friend, with the one person who understood everything she was going through. It was nothing more than that.

"I remember once when we were having pizza at the Cookery with Leslie and some of the others," Jake said. "One of the girls was Cindy, that girl Jane hung out with once in a while. Remember?"

"I think so."

"You said something about sharing a room with Jane but being too busy to talk to her for the past week. Something like that."

"Right, I remember."

"And that girl, Cindy, she said she was surprised you two shared a room because

Jane had always talked like the two of you never got along. She told you Jane couldn't stand you. Remember?"

The memory came flooding back. Ellen sat up straighter and curled her legs beneath her on the seat.

"You were hurt for days afterward," Jake reminded her. He smiled gently, and again Ellen was glad she was with him. He did understand, even about her struggles with Jane.

Why can't Mike be more like that, Lord? The thought no sooner drifted into her mind than she pushed it away. She didn't want to think about Mike now.

"If I remember right, everything was fine in a week or so," he continued.

"I asked her to be honest, to tell me if she was upset and not talk about it with the kids at school."

"After that you were best friends again."

"You're right."

"And what about that John Bronson? That fireman guy you met at the health club one of those times when we were broken up? The two of you went on a date and you found out later that Jane had a crush on him. Remember?"

Ellen cringed. "That's right. She didn't speak to me for two weeks."

Jake nodded. "It hasn't always been rosy, babe."

The term of endearment caught Ellen off guard, and, from the look on Jake's face, it had surprised him as well. *Ignore it,* she told herself, hoping she was right. But still her composure was shaken. She forced herself to sound unaffected. "So you think Jane and I were never close?"

Jake leaned nearer still, shifting to a more comfortable position and stretching his legs. "No, that's not what I'm saying. You were close enough to fight and still love each other at the end of the day."

"And you think that's all it is now?"

"Probably. I'm sure she's upset about your dad. Maybe there's something else bothering her. I don't know, why don't you ask her?"

Ellen hesitated. "I guess I could."

"Just remember she doesn't hate you, Ellen. Not any more than she did when we were all kids at Petoskey High."

Ellen allowed a few moments of silence while she considered Jake's explanation. The sun was slipping beneath the horizon now and the sky across Lake Michigan was streaked with pink.

"Back then at least I knew why she was mad. Either I was too outgoing or too attracted to a guy she liked." Ellen kept her eyes on the sunset. "Now I don't know what's going on. If she has something against me, she sure hasn't told me about it."

"Yeah, but think about how unhappy she is. I mean, you probably had a chance to tell your dad you loved him before he died. I'll bet she can't even remember when she talked to him last. That's how it was back when I was around, anyway. She lives in Arizona, right?"

"Right."

"And I'll bet she usually talks to your mom when she calls home, right?"

Ellen nodded and cocked her head, smiling warmly. "How come you know so much when I haven't seen you in nine years, Jake Sadler?"

"I was there a long time, remember?"

His voice was soothing, the same voice she had been in love with such a long time ago. Despite her good intentions, Ellen felt her stomach flip.

"I remember."

"Then trust me. It's just a phase. It'll pass and everything will be fine again before you know it."

"Okay, but what about the others? Aaron and Amy are fighting, and Megan's filled with all these unrealistic ideas about us being a family still because that's what Dad would have wanted. Meanwhile Jane and I are about to tear each other's hair out, and I just want to go back to Miami. I keep thinking there's supposed to be all this love between us because that's what I remember when I think of our childhood. Mom and Dad and us five kids moving from place to place. We had no one else back then, Jake. We needed each other." She bit her lip. "Now I find myself sitting around a room with those same people and it feels like we're strangers, like everything's changed and we don't even like each other."

"Your dad hasn't been gone a week yet, Ellen. You're all trying to find a way to let him go."

"And that's why everyone's being mean to each other?"

"That's why nothing feels right. Your dad was a great man. It's going to take a while for everything to be back to normal. In some ways it'll never be the same again."

The truth of those words stuck her deep. Jake was right. Life was never going to be the same again. Fresh tears rolled slowly down her cheeks. "What am I going to do without him, Jake?"

"Ahh, Ellen." Jake leaned over and wiped two tears from either side of her chin. "I'm sorry. Really, I am."

"I want to see him so badly, just once more. So I can talk to him and ask him what to do about Jane. Sometimes I don't think I'll survive without him."

Jake watched her intently. "I know how that feels."

"Yeah, but your dad's still alive."

He paused a moment. "I still know how it feels."

Ellen did not examine his statement but reached for another tissue instead. "So, you think things will work out for me and Jane? You think we'll have an understanding between us again?"

Jake smiled and brushed a lock of hair off Ellen's forehead. "If there's one thing your father left behind, it's love. He loved his family the way some people never love in their lifetime. I watched him all those years. He was a wonderful dad, a real maker of memories."

Ellen sniffled again. "He was, wasn't he?"

"Yes. And everyone in your family loves each other with an intensity that goes beyond words. I've seen that for myself, too. No matter what Jane says to you or how she's been acting lately, I know she loves you, Ellen."

Ellen looked doubtful. "I don't know, Jake. You haven't seen her in a while. Something's changed. I know I said it already, but I don't know any other way to describe it. It's like she hates me."

"She doesn't hate you. The two of you have your differences, that's all. Maybe it's best that you live in Miami and she lives in Arizona. But that doesn't mean she doesn't love you."

Ellen sighed. "I don't know. These days it's hard to see any love in her at all."

"Give it time. Watch for a chance to reach out to her. Maybe she'll open up and tell you what's wrong. Maybe it's more than your dad's death, maybe she's dealing with something else."

Ellen nodded. "Okay. I'll try. At least I don't feel like jumping on a plane and heading back to Miami tomorrow morning." She looked at Jake and smiled, wiping her eyes with her fingertips. "Thanks. Somehow I knew you'd understand."

"No thanks needed, Ellen. I'm always here for you." His steady gaze held hers. "I hope you know that."

They talked a while longer, filling in simple details about the years that had passed. It was ten-thirty when they pulled up in front of Megan's apartment, and the lights were off inside.

Jake cut the engine and turned to face Ellen. His voice was soft, gentle. "Don't take this wrong, but it was good to see you again."

Ellen's eyes grew moist. "I know. After all these years, who'd have thought we'd ever have a night like this?"

"Yeah, you weren't exactly speaking to me last time I saw you."

"I spoke to you." Ellen pushed him playfully in the chest. "Just not any longer than you deserved."

"Touché." His smile faded then, and Ellen could see his regret. After nearly a decade they could kid about what had happened between them, but it still wasn't funny. Not really. It never would be.

"Ellen, I've always wanted to tell you—"

"Jake, don't say anything. I didn't call you looking for a bunch of apologies. The past is behind us."

He let it go, but he looked pensive. "Are you happy, Ellen? In your life, I mean?"

She sighed and ran her fingers through her hair nervously. She caught Jake's eye, saw him watching the gesture, and quickly dropped her hand. It was something she'd always done, and he'd know it wasn't a good sign. She shrugged. "Most of the time, but...oh, I don't know. Mike and I are having a little trouble right now, I guess. There's a distance between us. He doesn't like to go out of his way for me, and sometimes that gets old. Like staying home while I attend my dad's funeral."

Jake listened, but again he maintained his silence. Ellen appreciated that he didn't try to fix things, to offer her solutions or explanations. It was becoming more and more evident Jake's physical appearance wasn't the only thing enhanced by the years. Jake Sadler had learned that sometimes it was better just to be silent and listen.

Ellen settled into her seat again, feeling safe and free to talk. "Mike's a wonderful man and a brilliant broadcaster. But I miss the romance we had at first. Most of the time it's like we don't even want to be together anymore." She shrugged. "Just something we have to work out, I guess."

"Ellen." Jake looked anxious, like he wasn't sure if he should say what was coming. "Do you ever wonder?"

Again tears stung her eyes and she released a shaky sigh. "Oh, Jake. Of course. How could I not?" She leaned back against the seat and stared straight ahead at invisible memories floating in the summer breeze. "You were my first love. You took my heart by the hand and led me on a wonderful ride. And when I think about the bad times now, they're not so terrible. Just sad."

"Time does that, doesn't it? Makes the bad times not so bad after all."

Ellen nodded. "I wouldn't have stayed around if the good times didn't make up for it. I guess I always thought we'd stay together."

"Me too."

She hugged herself tightly and kept her gaze on the trees outside. "You know, Jake, there were times after we broke up when I could have killed you for not being faithful. You ruined all our plans." She glanced at him and saw that his eyes were wet, too. "I talked to your mom once after Mike and I were engaged and you know what she said? She said, 'Are you really sure, Ellen. I always hoped you would wait until Jake grew up. '"

She laughed self-consciously. "I had second thoughts about marrying Mike for more than a month after that. I kept wondering if she was right, if maybe it was only a matter of time before you really did grow up and everything could be like I always wanted it to be."

She fell silent, then nodded slowly. "Yeah, Jake. I wonder." She smiled sadly at him. "But I know what would have happened. In time we would have hated each other, because as charming as you were, as much as I was in love with you, you didn't have it in you to be faithful. And if we had gotten married, your cheating would have destroyed me." She drew a deep breath. "How are things for you? Megan says you're not married."

Jake shook his head.

"Seeing anyone?" She was ashamed of herself, but in some ways she didn't want to know, didn't want to feel the familiar pangs of jealousy where he was concerned.

"No. There's no one. I date once in a while, but nothing serious." His eyes narrowed as if he was trying to see into her soul, the way he had so easily when they were together. "I guess I'm still looking."

Ellen raised a wary eyebrow.

"I know what you're thinking, but it's not like before. Actually, I haven't been on a date in months. No time, really." He paused and seemed to struggle for a moment. "I'm not the same guy I was back then, Ellen."

She smiled. "We've both changed, Jake." For a moment she considered telling Jake about the biggest change in her life since they'd broken up, about becoming a Christian. In some ways she owed her conversion to him, since it had come in the wake of their breakup. She wanted to thank him for that…but if she told him about it, she'd also have to tell him she had prayed for God to keep him out of her life. And, somehow, it just didn't seem right to do that right now.

"Well, I know I'm different. I was a jerk, and I learned my lesson."

"At my expense."

He spoke slowly, deliberately. "At *our* expense."

Ellen sat up straighter and reached for the door. They had crossed into dangerous territory and she knew better than to stay. "Well, on that note I should probably go in. The week's pretty much planned for me. I told my family to work things out without me tonight so they'll probably have a whole list for me to do tomorrow."

"When's the funeral?"

"Saturday morning." Ellen stretched and then reached down to tighten the laces on her tennis shoes.

"Would you mind if I go? I loved him, too, you know."

She sat up slowly and studied Jake's face, remembering the reasons she had fallen in love with him. "You did, didn't you?"

He nodded.

Ellen smiled sadly. "I'm glad you want to be there. I could use the support."

"You don't think it'll raise any questions?"

"Of course not. You're a friend of the family, a friend of my father. Everyone would understand."

Jake nodded again. "All right. Then I'll see you Saturday."

"Okay." Ellen watched as he got out of the truck. He ambled gracefully around to her door and opened it so she could climb out. When she stood before him she saw he had grown several inches over the years.

"You're taller."

"Yeah, runs in the family. My dad grew a few inches in his twenties, too."

"It looks good on you."

"Thanks." He stared at her, his gaze intense. "The years look good on you, too."

They studied each other, and Ellen was keenly aware of the narrow space between them. A gentle wind sifted through the trees above them, and Jake's eyes grew soft as he stared into hers.

The sudden image of Mike's eyes, Mike's face, drifted into Ellen's mind. She stepped back. "I'd better go." It was hardly wise to linger in the moonlight on a summer night in Petoskey with the breeze from Lake Michigan dancing in the trees above and Jake Sadler so close she only had to lean forward to kiss him.

"I hope things get better with Jane."

"Me, too. Thanks again, Jake." She smiled, sadness filling her, then turned and ran lightly up the walk toward the apartment.

"Call me again if you need a break," he yelled softly after her. "I'm taking tomorrow off to catch up on things at home."

She nodded and waved once more before going inside.

When her eyes adjusted to the darkness she saw that Jane and Megan were sitting on the couch watching television. They turned and stared at her, and she felt like a schoolgirl caught out past curfew.

"Where were you?" Jane stared at her hard.

"Out." Ellen did not feel obligated to share the truth with her sisters. They probably wouldn't understand, anyway. "With whom?"

"A friend."

Jane cast a disgusted look at her older sister. "Fine. Don't tell us."

Megan seemed sad as she turned away from the program and looked at Ellen. "We missed you tonight. You should have stayed around."

"I needed a break."

Megan shrugged. "I know. Mom understood. It's just that the week is going fast, and I'd wanted us to spend as much time together as possible before we go our separate ways."

Jane snorted softly and Ellen forgot all the comforting words Jake had said. He was right. There had to be something else wrong with Jane. *Help me find out what it is that's destroying her, Lord. I can't do this on my own.*

"We made a decision about the eulogy." Jane turned to the television again.

"What?" Ellen remained by the door, her cheeks still flushed from the warm summer air and Jake's nearness.

"Everyone's writing something and reading it at the funeral. Just like Mom wanted."

Ellen felt her anger rise, but she stayed quiet. She could picture Jane gleefully orchestrating that decision to spite her. "Did you hear me?" Jane stared at her impatiently.

"Yes. Who decided that?"

"All of us. You went out socializing for the night so you'll just have to go along with it."

Ellen thought of a dozen smart comebacks, but she refrained. Jane wasn't going to ruin what had become a nice evening. Not this time. "Fine," she said when she had a handle on her temper. "I'm going to sleep. Good night."

Megan spoke up. "By the way, we're not planning much for tomorrow. Mom has some things she wants to do on her own. We're invited for dinner and I thought we could all hang out there during the day. Maybe go for a walk or something. Then Thursday we'll shop for funeral clothes and a casket. That's what Mom said, anyway."

"Okay. Fine." Ellen crossed the room in front of them and headed for the spare bedroom, which she and Jane and the children were sharing.

"Is there any other place you could sleep?" Jane called after her.

"You have a better suggestion? A hotel, maybe? A park bench?"

Jane swore under her breath. "You're so sarcastic, Ellen. I just wondered if you could please sleep on the sofa tonight so you don't wake the kids. *Last* night I didn't get any sleep with all of us crammed in there."

Now Megan rolled her eyes. "Oh, brother! The room's small. Deal with it."

"Whatever." Ellen sighed. "I'll sleep on the couch. But seeing as you guys are watching television, what am I supposed to do until you're ready to go to bed?"

Jane released a forced burst of air and stood up in a huff. "I'm going. Don't worry." She glared at Ellen. "Just like old times, huh, Ellen? When Ellen speaks, people move. Daddy's precious Ellen has to have whatever she wants as soon as she wants it." Jane picked up her pillow and stormed out of the room.

When she was out of earshot Ellen looked wearily at Megan. "What's the deal with her?"

"I don't know. You two get in a fight before Dad died?"

"Not that I can remember. But there must be something going on. I've never seen her like this."

Megan nodded. "I know. I see it, too."

Ellen remembered Jake's words earlier that night. *Maybe there's something else bothering her…why don't you ask her?* "Oh, well. Tomorrow I'll talk to her and get to the bottom of it."

"I hope so. Maybe she's just upset about Dad."

"That doesn't give her the right to act like this."

"I know." Megan sighed and rubbed her neck absently. "Well, I'm turning in, too. I'll get some blankets for the couch."

"Okay. Thanks." Ellen began moving pillows to make room.

"Hey, Ellen…"

Ellen turned, distracted by memories of the evening with Jake. "Hmm?"

"Let's hope tomorrow's a better day. Daddy wouldn't have wanted everyone fighting with each other."

Ellen sighed and flopped onto the couch, clutching a pillow to her midsection. "I know it. But things are different now, Megan. Everything has changed so much." *Even Jake Sadler,* she thought sadly. *Just a few years too late.*

"You're right." Megan hugged her rib cage. "But it's so hard on Mom this way, with you and Jane at each other all the time."

"I'm trying my best." The insinuation that Ellen was partially to blame for the problems was frustrating. "What more can I do?"

"It's Jane's problem. Everyone can see that. But try to get along. For Mom's sake."

Ellen nodded. "I'll do my best. Tomorrow's another day. Maybe we can talk things out, and she'll be back to her old self."

"I hope so." Megan turned toward her room. "Good night, Ellen. Love you."

"Good night. Love you, too."

Ellen watched her sister disappear into her room. When she was alone, her shoulders sagged slightly forward and she crawled between a pile of blankets. She wondered absently what Jake was doing, what kind of house he lived in. Then she pictured Mike, alone in their house in Miami. The two images were still battling for position as she fell into a restless sleep.

19

Mike was standing next to her, his eyes full of questions as he held a bouquet of red roses.

"Come on, Ellen, make up your mind," he said. Then he said it again.

Somewhere in the background Jake was laughing. He walked up, winked at Ellen, and took the flowers away from Mike. He kept his eyes on Ellen's as he ripped the flowers, one at a time, into a dozen pieces and dropped them onto the carpeted floor. But then the carpet changed and it was an endless field of lush green grass. She and Jake were sitting in wooden chairs, laughing about something.

Mike was there, too, crying softly as he leaned against a tree. He started to speak but no sound came out, and Jake asked him to leave. Before Ellen could protest, Mike's crying grew louder and louder.

Ellen opened her eyes, unsure where she was. She blinked, disoriented. She'd been dreaming...dreaming that someone was crying—

No. She listened carefully. Someone was crying. A soft, sobbing sound was coming from Megan's room. Or was it? Ellen sat up, breathless, and the last wisps of her dream cleared.

She waited a moment and when she was sure the sobbing was real, she stood up and padded quietly into Megan's room.

For a moment she watched her sister, not willing to intrude on her privacy. Megan had four photo albums spread out before her and she looked as if her heart were breaking. The albums contained pictures of the Barrett family, from their parents' wedding through Aaron's high school graduation.

Megan turned a page and ran her fingers gently over a photograph as tears streamed down her face.

"Megan?" Ellen said quietly.

Her sister jumped. She obviously hadn't expected anyone to be up for another few hours.

"You scared me."

"Sorry." Ellen went to sit next to her on the bed. She looked at the picture albums and saw a photograph taken at the Detroit Zoo. The five of them were lined up against a stone wall, oldest to youngest, with Mom at the end holding a squirming baby Aaron. As usual, Dad wasn't in the photo because he was behind the camera, making memories for another day.

"I miss them." Megan ran a finger over the faces of the small children.

"Me too." Ellen blinked back tears as she turned the page. There was a photo of her and Aaron with their brand-new bikes. Their birthdays were both in early July and their parties were usually on the same day. She flipped the page and saw her and Jane with their arms around each other. She and Amy holding hands. Megan and Aaron sitting in the same wagon, smiles on their faces.

One after another the pictures shouted the truth. Things had changed.

"Do you think Jane hates us?" Megan sniffed.

"I don't know. Nothing's the same with Dad gone, I guess."

"But Jane doesn't have to be so mean. I can't understand what's gotten into her."

"I don't have to what?" Jane leaned into the room and scowled. "What are you guys doing? Talking about me behind my back?"

"We thought you were asleep," Megan explained quickly. "Are the kids up, too?"

"No, don't worry. The kids won't bother you. They're asleep. So, why're you talking behind my back?" Jane stood in the doorway, her hands on her hips.

Ellen lost her temper. "You know, Jane, why don't you go back to Arizona if you can't be civil to the rest of us." Poor Megan had merely wanted a quiet morning to grieve the loss of their father and the family they used to be. Jane's selfishness wouldn't even allow that.

"Mind your own business," Jane sneered.

"Darn you, Jane!" Ellen stood up and yelled at her sister. "What happened to you? You're so full of hate you can't think of anyone but yourself."

"Maybe you just bring out the worst in me."

Ellen was silent, seething inside.

"Come on, you guys. You promised to get along today. Let it go." Megan was crying harder now, and Ellen caught the sound of a baby whimpering down the hallway.

"Way to go. Now the kids are awake!" Jane shouted at Ellen. "I hope you're happy."

"I'll be happy when you leave." Ellen muttered the words under her breath and Jane whirled around again.

"What?"

"I said—" Ellen raised her voice— "I'll be glad when you leave. I can't stand the way you're treating Megan and me. And Amy, too."

"I suppose that's what you were talking about when I walked in?" Jane ignored her crying child.

"No, in fact it's not. If I want to say something about you, I'll say it to your face. Are you listening?"

Jane glared at Ellen.

"I think something must be terribly wrong, Jane, something you're not talking about and I think it's time to get it out in the open."

Shock ran over Jane's face, and for a moment Ellen thought her sister was going to burst into tears. She didn't give her the opportunity.

"This is your chance, Jane. Are you going to tell us what's wrong or should we take turns guessing?"

Jane's features hardened again. "Fine. Know what's wrong with me? Very simply, it's you. Ever since we were kids you've bothered me, Ellen. I'm sick of you. You think you're better than everyone else and that everyone should bow at your feet." Jane moved a step closer. "I guess I just don't like you, Ellen. I'm having a hard time pretending that I do."

She wheeled around and stormed out of the room.

"Forget pretending!" Ellen shouted after her. "I'm leaving anyway."

Megan watched the argument from her bed and shook her head in frustration, angry tears spilling onto her cheeks. "You two are the most selfish people I know. Dad's dead! And you guys can't stop picking on each other long enough to love each other through the hardest week of our lives." She was sobbing so hard she sounded hysterical.

"Megan—" Ellen began, but her sister jumped up and stormed into the bathroom, slamming the door behind her and turning on the shower.

Left alone in Megan's room, Ellen stared at the phone. Jake's words came back to her. *Call me again if you need a break. I'm taking tomorrow off...tomorrow off...tomorrow off.*

I need to talk to Mike. She sat down on the bed and picked up the telephone, dialing quickly. The phone in her Miami bedroom rang five times before the answering machine came on. Ellen hung up and looked at the clock. 7:05. Mike was gone to work.

She tapped the phone with her finger and wrestled with her conscience. Then beyond the bedroom door she heard Jane shout at Megan, her voice shrill and angry. Ellen closed her eyes and wondered if she could stand another day with Jane.

Call me if you need a break. I'm taking tomorrow off.

Ellen reached for the phone and dialed a number she had memorized only the night before.

Jake was up early that day and had already shaved and showered when the phone rang. His work crew would be handling the office calls and he was in a particularly light-hearted mood. Seeing Ellen had always had that effect on him.

"Yup?"

"Jake...it's me."

Ellen. He sat down slowly, surprised to hear her voice again so soon. "Uh-oh. What happened? You and Jane again?"

"I don't know what to do! She's driving me crazy. I can't stand it."

Jake sighed. "Listen, you need to get away for a while. Get your thoughts together and let her do the same."

"Any suggestions?"

"I'll be there in thirty minutes. We'll go to Mackinac Island, rent bikes, and lay in the sun. Or just sit and talk."

"But you had some personal stuff to take care of."

"It can wait. Come on, no protests. You're gonna lose it if you don't get away for a while."

A sniff sounded. "Okay. I'll be ready."

Half an hour later Ellen walked out of Megan's room wearing a navy one-piece swimsuit underneath shorts and a T-shirt. She held a towel under her arms.

"Where do you think you're going?" Jane asked. She was spoon-feeding the baby and overseeing breakfast for the other two children. Megan was reading a magazine nearby.

"To the beach." Ellen grabbed her purse and headed for the front door. "I'm spending the day with a friend."

"No cares, no worries, right, Ellen?" Jane scowled. "Did it ever occur to you that Mom might want you around the house today?"

"You aren't really leaving, are you?" Megan was shocked.

"Yes. I really am. I'll be back for dinner. Tell Mom I'll see her then."

Without waiting for a response she walked outside and propped herself against a tree where she watched for Jake's truck. Ellen knew her sisters did not for a minute think the friend she spoke of might be Jake Sadler. As he pulled up in front of the apartment she hoped they were not watching.

She settled into the dark brown leather seat. It was like entering another world. *Forget Jane. Forget Mike. Forget everything.* After all, it wasn't her fault Jane was acting vicious or that Mike had forgotten how to love her. Maybe if she disappeared for a day, her sister would have time to think about her behavior and everything would make sense again.

Jake opened the sunroof and slipped a Chicago CD into the car's player. He raised the volume on the stereo as they drove. A warm breeze circulated through the car, and Ellen's anger dissolved like April snow. She leaned back into the seat, saying nothing, enjoying the easy silence between them.

After a few miles, Ellen raised her eyes and searched the tops of the towering pine trees that lined the highway. She had missed them, living in Miami. Somehow the sights and smells of the Michigan pines and Jake's nearness carried her back in time, back to the days when her father was still healthy and strong and she and Jake believed in forever. She closed her eyes and savored the sensation.

In thirty minutes they began seeing signs that directed them toward Mackinaw City's main strip and the ferry boats that made regular runs to the island and back. She drew a deep, cleansing breath and grinned at Jake.

"Feels good, doesn't it?" He returned the smile.

Ellen took another deep breath and nodded. "I miss Mackinac Island. The way it looks and sounds and smells. It's been a long time."

They were quiet again, and Ellen absently twisted her wedding band. What would Mike think about her spending a day with Jake like this? What would her father think? *Help me not to do anything I'll regret, Lord.* But even as she prayed she knew she was being double minded—and wondered if it wasn't already too late.

Her thoughts poked pins at her conscience and she closed her eyes again. When she opened them, upper Lake Michigan lay spread out before her and thoughts of Mike and Jane and her father, even of her faith, were suddenly a million miles away.

Today there would be only Jake.

That same morning, a thousand miles away, Leslie Maple was studying Paul's words in the book of Romans, but she couldn't get Ellen out of her mind. She had wrestled with whether to call Ellen or not. Years had passed since they had talked last, and Ellen might not feel like talking so soon after her father's death. Especially to someone she hadn't heard from in so long. Leslie wasn't even sure she had Ellen's Miami phone number.

She tried reading the Scripture before her again but it was no use. All right, all right, God, I'll do it. It's been a long time, but I need to call her. Maybe this afternoon. She felt a sense of urgency at the thought. Then again, maybe right now.

Leslie shut her Bible, found her address book, and thumbed through it. She remembered that, because of her position as reporter, Ellen still used her maiden name. She found the B section and scanned the page. There it was. Ellen's number in Miami. She was probably already gone, back home in Petoskey for her dad's funeral. Leslie thought of how Ellen and Jane had sometimes fought. If she were already gone, then she would be dealing with more than her father's death.

Poor Ellen. Leslie's fingers flew over the buttons. Please let me catch her, Lord. Let me pray with her before she goes to face her family.

Mike was on his way out the door when the phone rang. He lunged for the receiver. "Hello?"

A woman's voice responded, "Oh, I'm so glad I caught you in time."

Mike frowned. What on earth? Who is this?

"Leslie Maple, Ellen's friend from high school. I just heard about Ellen's dad the other day and I'm so glad I caught you before you left for Petoskey. Can I talk to her? Is she there?"

Mike glanced at his watch and knew he had to leave. He had only stopped home between assignments to change clothes. "Ellen left a few days ago. You can reach her at her parents' house. I can get the number for you if you'd like."

Silence. Then, "She went by herself?"

Mike's gaze drifted to the kitchen table and the unopened Bible lying there. Guilt seemed to be coming at him from all directions. "Yeah. Hey, listen, I've got to get going. Did you need that number?"

"No. No, that's all right. I have it. I was just hoping to pray with her before she left. How was she? Before she left, I mean? Did you guys get a chance to pray together?"

Mike sighed. The questions couldn't have been more probing if God himself had called. "No, not really. It all happened kind of fast, I guess."

There was a short silence. "When are you leaving, to join her?"

"The funeral's Saturday, if that's what you mean. I have to work this weekend so the plans are kind of up in the air."

Silence again. Apparently Leslie thought as much of that as Ellen had.

"Well, then. I guess I'll try to catch her at her parents' house. Thanks."

"Sure thing," Mike said. "Thanks for calling."

Leslie hung up the phone and took a moment to consider all she had just learned. Ellen's father's death had been sudden, no doubt leaving Ellen grief stricken. In the wake of the shock, she and her husband had neither prayed together nor taken the same plane to Michigan.

Which meant Ellen was back in Petoskey surrounded by her siblings, frustrated by her husband, and without a friend in the world.

Years may have passed since Leslie had last seen Ellen but some things did not change, and she knew that if things got too painful, too tense between Ellen and her family, too lonely without Mike, there was only one person she would turn to.

"No," she whispered aloud. "She wouldn't think of calling him. That was years ago."

Out of nowhere Ellen's heartfelt prayer that Sunday afternoon so long ago came back to her. "Jake is my strongest weakness, Leslie. Pray for me. Pray that we stay away from each other."

Suddenly she knew what she had to do. She picked up the telephone and dialed a local number. "Hello Martha, this is Leslie." She drew a calming breath. "I have an urgent request for the prayer chain."

20

Jake and Ellen parked in the lot at Shepler's Ferry and blended with a throng of tourists headed for the dock. People from all over the country came to Northern Michigan to see Mackinac Island's seventeen hundred acres and eight miles of shoreline. Ellen had always appreciated the island's historical background. She and Jake picked up a brochure as they boarded the boat.

"I didn't know Mackinac was founded in 1715," Jake said idly. There wasn't a cloud in the sky and the boat filled quickly with tourists headed toward the island.

They continued to read. Mackinac had at different times served as a fur-trading station, a military post, and a summer home for the East Coast elite. Cars were not permitted and travel was done one of three ways: on foot, by horse, or by bicycle. As they read, Jake strained to see over Ellen's shoulder. Occasionally, their elbows would touch and one of them would pull slightly away.

They sat on the boat's upper deck and laughed as the wind pulled at their hair and stung their eyes. The ride was exhilarating, and fifteen minutes later the boat docked along Mackinac Island's main thoroughfare.

Dozens of fudge shops and other specialty stores lined Main Street. At the end of the busy strip stood the famous Fort Mackinac, where an 1880s unit of American Soldiers once guarded the straits of Mackinac from enemy forces. The buildings had been restored to look as they had a century earlier, and authentic shooting demonstrations took place throughout the day on the quad.

Most of the tourists stayed on the main stretch, browsing through shops, eating fudge, and touring the fort. The remaining seven miles of island shoreline was relatively free of people. Jake and Ellen rented two bicycles and set off toward the quiet side of the island.

"Remember that time we were riding this path and that kid walked out in front of you," Ellen turned sparkling eyes toward Jake. They were out of the city and, other than an occasional cyclist, there was no one else around.

"He didn't even look. Just crossed the path right in front of me."

Instead of running over the child, Jake had ridden off the path and tumbled down a rocky embankment toward the water. His knee was skinned raw in the resulting fall.

"Still have the scar?" Ellen locked her elbows, enjoying the wind in her face as she steered her bicycle around a pack of tourists.

"Yup. It's faded, but it's still there. My battle with a bicycle."

They laughed and rode on, side by side leaving the tourists behind them. The deep blue water spread out a few feet to their right and a forest of evergreens towered to their left. It was easy to feel at least a little of what the early settlers must have felt: like they were the only people in the world.

"Life must have been hard for the people who lived here a hundred years ago."

"They didn't have fudge shops, that's for sure." Jake raised a teasing eyebrow and Ellen's heart soared.

On the heels of that elation came a Scripture verse flashing across her mind. Proverbs 4: *"Above all else, guard your heart, for it is the wellspring of life.... Make level paths for your feet and take only ways that are firm. Do not swerve to the right or the left; keep your foot from evil."*

Ellen swallowed hard. She stared at her feet and the firm, level path before her. Somehow she didn't think that was what the Lord meant by those words. *I'm not doing anything wrong,* she protested silently. *After all I've been through I deserve at least this.*

They rode nearly three miles, then pulled into an alcove and parked their bikes. A stretch of sandy beach lay just in front of them, hidden from the bike path by a thicket. Jake cast a questioning look toward Ellen.

"Ready for some sun?"

"If you don't laugh." She brushed her fingers quickly over his tanned arm. "Some of us work too hard to have much of a tan."

"Ellen! I'm surprised at you," Jake teased. "Living in Miami and missing out on the beach life. Maybe you need a vacation."

It was not yet ten, still too early for anyone else to have discovered the private beach. They found a spot near the shore and lay their towels side by side.

"It's beautiful here." Jake walked back toward the bicycles. He wore red swim trunks and as he walked he stretched and slipped off his T-shirt. Next he grabbed a miniature ice chest from his bike basket and carried it down near their towels.

He smiled, tossing her a bottle of suntan lotion.

"Do my back?" He turned around and positioned himself in front of her.

Ellen snagged the lotion and stared down at it. *What am I doing here? Alone on an island beach with Jake Sadler, about to rub suntan lotion onto his back?*

She drew a deep breath and slowly released it. *Don't let your paranoia run wild,* she chided herself. *It's just a day with an old friend.* She squeezed a handful of cool, creamy lotion into her palms and rubbed them together. Then, like a hundred times before, she rubbed it across the width of Jake's shoulders.

"Mmmmm," he said. "That feels good."

Ellen blushed. She wrestled with her emotions and she was thankful they were on a public beach in broad daylight, even if there wasn't another soul in sight. She continued to rub in the lotion, moving her hands in tight circles down the center of his back and toward his waist. His muscles flexed beneath her touch and Ellen noticed chill-bumps along the base of his neck.

He turned around then and his gaze caught hers. For a moment their eyes spoke a hundred things that neither of them was ready to say. He cleared his throat and took the lotion from Ellen's hands.

"Your turn."

Ellen stared at him, then looked down at the lotion in his hand. An image of those hands rubbing the lotion into her skin swam before her mind's eye…and those warning bells that she'd managed to ignore for the last day or so were suddenly clanging so loud she thought she'd go deaf.

Okay, okay, Lord. I get it. She gave a quick shake of her head.

"No, thanks. I'm…uh, I'm not ready to take my shirt off yet." Something akin to disappointment sparked in his eyes, but he just nodded and put the lotion away.

They lay down on their individual towels, but Ellen couldn't help being keenly aware of Jake's nearness. Five minutes passed and Jake shifted. As he did so, his elbow ended up touching hers. Had he moved that way on purpose? And were his senses, like hers, completely focused on the spot where their skin touched?

She closed her eyes and tried to listen to the gentle surf, tried to find a voice of reason within her. But there was no getting around the one pervasive thought that filled her mind: the chemistry was back, as powerful as ever, working on her heart and mind and soul. She tried desperately to think about Mike, but he seemed part of another life. The sun was warm, the breeze soothing. In all the world there was only her and Jake, side by side on a sandy, secluded beach on the distant shores of Mackinac Island.

An hour passed and suddenly there was something freezing cold against her neck. She jumped and Jake grinned. In his hand he held a wet can of soda he had taken from the ice chest.

"Come on, sleepy head. Get up," he teased. "You'll get sunburned. Especially with that working-woman white skin of yours."

"Ooooh!" Ellen stood up and adjusted her T-shirt. She grabbed a handful of ice cubes from the chest and ran after him. "I'll get you, Jake Sadler!"

She chased him toward the water and caught him just as he reached the shore. Grabbing his arm she rubbed the ice on his back and laughed when he arched from the chill.

"Got you!" She grinned.

He pulled away easily and she chased him again. Then suddenly he turned on her, picked her up by the legs, and moved unceremoniously into the water.

"Jake! Don't! It's freezing."

He continued deeper into the lake, still holding her around her thighs, until the chilly water was up to her knees. She placed her hands on his shoulders to steady herself.

"Tell me I'm the nicest guy who ever walked the earth," he shouted into the breeze.

"Ha! Name, rank, and serial number. That's all you'll ever get from me!" She was laughing so hard her words barely made sense.

"What's that? Does the prisoner dare speak against her captor?" He swung her precariously near the waves, threatening to drop her.

"Jake, put me down!"

"You got it." He let go and she fell directly into the lake. When she came up her shorts and T-shirt were drenched and she was intent on revenge.

"That's it, you've had it!" She spit water and brushed her wet hair off her face. She reached down, cupped her hands in the waves, and splashed Jake as fiercely as she could until he, too, was soaked.

"Now you're gonna get it!" He retaliated, and the game was on. With an almost reckless abandon, they chased each other along the shoreline, teasing and splashing—and all the while Ellen kept desperately reminding herself that they were no longer young and in love.

When they were exhausted and breathless, they lumbered through the warm sand and headed for their towels.

"I'm freezing." Ellen picked her towel up off the ground and wrapped her body tightly. They sat down together, and she tried to catch her breath.

"Wimp."

Ellen kicked a bit of sand at him. "Not."

For several minutes they were silent, enjoying the sun as it soaked through their freezing bodies. A group of noisy cyclists passed by on the path above them and then disappeared into the distance. There were dozens of small private beaches lining the shores of Mackinac Island and the one they'd chosen remained empty otherwise.

"Makes me wish we had a blanket and a backgammon game." Jake pushed his bangs off his forehead, pulled his knees up to his chest, and turned to face Ellen. He dropped his head onto his arm and stared at her.

"We had fun, didn't we?" She turned and gazed at the horizon as she tousled her hair and pushed it off her face. She refused to look at him, afraid of what she might see in his eyes.

"More than fun."

She nodded absently, busying herself by searching for the suntan lotion and reapplying it to her pale arms and face. He watched her the entire time.

"Good idea. I could use some of that." He reached for the bottle and touched her hand instead.

She nearly gasped. "Jake, I—"

He gave her a bland look. "I just want you to rub some more lotion on my back."

She nodded, feeling foolish for making more of his actions than he intended. She did as he asked, this time as quickly as possible. When she finished she handed him the bottle.

"Okay, Barrett, get yourself up and let's play a little Frisbee." He reached into his backpack and pulled out a white plastic disc.

Ellen was thankful for the distraction, thankful they hadn't discussed the feelings she knew had come alive again between them. She stood up and ran down the shore until she was positioned just right.

Jake tossed the Frisbee in her direction and she snagged it expertly, returning it to him in a single motion.

"You haven't lost your touch," he shouted. "Try this one."

He flung it into the air so that it hung on the breeze and floated gently toward her. She ran forward, concentrating on her timing. Then, just as she was about to pull it from the air, Jake picked her up around her thighs and threatened to dump her in the water again.

"Jake Sadler! Come on. I'm still cold from last time."

"Tell me I'm king of the beach!" He laughed and swung her precariously near the water.

"Not on your life!" She flailed at him, jabbing him beneath his upper ribs and trying to push herself free.

"Tell me I'm the handsomest man in the world!" He spun her around in the shallow surf, and she could feel the cold water on her feet.

"Get real!" She struggled harder, laughing at the same time.

Suddenly he stopped. With deliberate slowness, he lowered her in front of him. He placed his hands tenderly on either side of her face and his voice was soft when he spoke again. "Tell me you still have feelings for me, Ellen." His eyes searched hers and he wove his fingers into her hair.

"Jake…" She was having trouble breathing, and tears filled her eyes as she looked into his. Breaking the connection, she hung her head, wrapping her arms around herself protectively. "Jake, I can't."

There was silence for a moment, then Jake stepped back from her. "I know. I'm sorry." Ellen saw from the look in his eyes that the apology was sincere. "I shouldn't have said that."

"Sometimes I think you know me better than anyone," she said, tears spilling onto her cheeks. "What do you see when you look into my eyes?"

He spoke quietly, studying her face. "You still feel. For me."

She nodded. "A part of me will always love you. But that doesn't change the facts, Jake. I'm married. It's wrong for us… for me…"

"Don't say it, Ellen. I understand. I was wrong to push it." He reached out as though to touch her cheek, then let his hand fall to his side, a crooked smile on his face.

Ellen fought a sob. "I love my husband, Jake." At his steady look, she shook her head. "I know, I know. I called you. I agreed to come here with you. I...I don't know why. I wanted to find something, to feel something." She met his gaze again. "But I can't have some cheap affair on the beach while Mike thinks I'm here mourning my father's death." She moved away from him, angry with herself as she trudged toward her towel. He followed and they sat together in silence.

"Okay, then," Jake sighed and his sad smile nearly broke Ellen's heart. "Tell me about Mike."

Ellen drew a deep breath and stared at the endless deep, blue waters of Lake Michigan. It was colder and more intense looking than the Atlantic, and Ellen realized how much she had missed it. The breeze was stronger than before and clouds had formed in the west, blocking the sun.

"Mike is bright and funny and handsome. And a very good broadcaster. The execs at the network have their eyes on him for a national spot."

Jake's eyebrow arched slightly and he hesitated. "That's not what I mean, Ellen.... Tell me why you love him."

She sighed and hugged her knees close to her body. "Oh, Jake. Don't ask me that. Not now."

"I'm not trying to stump you. I just want to know what he has. What's so special about him? How come after you two met you were finally able to let go of us?"

Ellen pondered his question. What had been special about Mike? For one thing, he'd shared her faith and because of that she'd been certain God had brought Mike into her life. She was still certain. But after what had almost happened between her and Jake she was embarrassed to talk about her faith. She knew she wouldn't sound convincing. Not now when her faith was being tested and her feelings for Mike were so shaky.

After a while she turned her head and stared at Jake. "I trust him," she said simply.

Jake looked as if she'd taken a hammer to his gut. His face filled with regret and he turned away, gazing out at the water.

When he said nothing, she continued. "You let it happen, Jake. I was coming to your house that day to tell you I would be there forever. I only wanted to know I could trust you."

He lowered his head.

"Then that...that girl answered the door. Wearing nothing but your bathrobe."

He reached for her hand and squeezed it once before letting it go. "I'm sorry, Ellen. I've been sorry ever since. Really. You deserved better."

Ellen nodded. "You broke my heart, you jerk," she said softly. Her eyes were wet again. "All I ever wanted was to stay in love with you the rest of my life. But you weren't content with that. I wasn't enough for you, Jake."

He was silent, pensive as he watched her.

"That's what I love about Mike," she said finally. "I trust him. I'm enough for him." She paused. "And he won't ever break my heart."

Jake nodded. "Good. I'm happy for you, Ellen. Really, I am."

"I'm not saying it's perfect. But being with you these last two days I've really had to think about my life and what's important. There are reasons you and I broke up, and reasons Mike and I married. I can't forget that now that I'm here with you again." There was silence for a moment before she continued. "My marriage is important to me, Jake. I want it to work."

"I know. Forgive me?"

She studied him. "Forgiven."

"Let's forget about it, okay? I guess it's only natural for us to remember how we felt about each other."

"I guess."

Jake smiled at her. "Made you forget your family for a while, though, didn't I?"

She tossed a fist of sand at his feet. "Jake Sadler, I thought you'd grown up and quit your incessant teasing."

He grinned. "Some things never change."

She thought of the way he made her feel and she uttered a short laugh. "That's for sure."

For the rest of the day they kept their conversation on safer topics. Her job at the newspaper, his business. By midafternoon they'd caught up on nine years, all the while keeping a careful distance from each other. Finally, they climbed back on their rented bicycles and continued the rest of the way around the island. After they turned their bikes in, they walked along Main Street and sampled Island Almond Fudge and Northern Nutty White Chocolate.

At four o'clock they boarded a ferry headed back to the mainland. The air had cooled considerably and Ellen started when something came over her shoulders. It was Jake's shirt. He'd draped it around her without saying a word. She smiled her thanks, and he nodded. Though he didn't touch her, his nearness had an almost physical impact on her. The boat arrived at the dock and they walked across the parking lot to his truck. He led her to the passenger side, and before he opened her door, he wrapped his arms around her waist and pulled her close.

They had lost a great deal, and they both knew they could never have it again. The rules had been established. But for that moment they needed to say good-bye to what they'd found on a secluded island beach in the middle of Lake Michigan.

"Thank you," she said finally, tilting her head, looking up into Jake's face. "Thanks for today. Thanks for understanding."

Jake's hands tightened ever so slightly about her waist and their faces were inches from each other. If he lowered his head now, kissed her, Ellen didn't know if she could stop herself.

Don't let him do it, God. Please! I'm so weak and if he kisses me, I'll never go home again. Help me here, Lord.

Seconds passed and finally she saw him clench his jaw and pull back. He took her hands in his.

"It was a day from the past." He smiled. "I won't ever forget it, Ellen."

Thirty minutes later he dropped her off a few houses away from her parents' home.

"Just in case our being together might cause trouble with the others," he said.

Ellen smiled tenderly. "Thanks again for today," she whispered.

He squeezed her hands gently. "Don't thank me, Ellen. I never thought I'd see you again and…well…I'll always remember today. I haven't had a day like that in years."

"Years?" she teased.

He didn't laugh. Didn't even smile. "Nine years, to be exact."

She looked down at her hands, unsure of what to say. Her eyes fell on her wedding band.

"You go on," he said finally. "Call me if you need me."

Ellen nodded and reached for the door handle. "Thanks for understanding…about me and Mike. It was good for me to talk about him."

Jake smiled sadly. "Me, too. He's a lucky man, Ellen." He paused. "Don't think I wouldn't give anything to be in his shoes, because I would."

"Jake…"

"I know. We had our time. But don't ever mistake how I feel about you. No amount of time can change that. Now go inside before I drive away with you and whisk you off to some undiscovered island to live with me forever."

"You're crazy."

Again, there was no humor in his level gaze. "I'm honest. Now go."

She smiled, thanked him again, and said good-bye. After a few steps, she turned to wave again, but her hand froze at her side. She'd caught sight of Jake's face just before he drove away…and there had been tears running down his face.

21

Jane's children were down for a nap in her parents' spare bedroom and she was wandering around the hallway looking at framed photographs. Megan, Amy, and Aaron were in the den finishing lunch, trying to figure out what to say at their father's funeral. For that moment at least, peace reigned in the Barrett household.

Jane came upon an old, gold-framed photo and studied the roughly colored print of Ellen and her at four and two years old. Even back then Ellen looked confident while Jane looked uncertain. Jane noted how, in the picture, she had leaned on her older sister for support.

That had certainly changed.

Now her support came from Troy. She wished he were there so he could calm her down, make her less angry around the others. They had all misunderstood her. It wasn't that she was mad at them. She simply couldn't relate to their sorrow and so had become increasingly frustrated. She could hardly wait for the week to be over so she could return to her calm, peaceful life in the Verde Valley.

She heard footsteps and she glanced out the window to see Ellen, looking tanned and relaxed. Jane's mouth twisted. How was it that while Jane was wrestling with the memory of being raped, struggling with indifference over her father's death, Ellen was off sunning herself with an old friend on the beach all day?

Ellen flung her things on an oversized chair and smiled tentatively at Jane. She was still savoring her day and the last thing she wanted was another fight. "Hi, how's everyone doing?"

Jane uttered a short laugh. "Like you care."

Fine, Ellen thought. *End of discussion.* She shrugged and without saying another word headed toward the den where the others had turned off the television so they could talk.

"I can't think of what to write," Aaron was saying as she walked in.

He was stretched out in their father's easy chair, his mannerisms almost identical to those of their dad. Ellen sat next to Megan on a comfortable old sofa that had been in the family for years.

"What's the discussion?"

"Where've you been?" Amy asked. There was no accusation in her voice, but Amy looked nervous and intimidated by her siblings.

"The beach."

"By yourself?"

"No, with an old friend."

"Who?" Megan asked curiously.

"No one you'd remember," she lied. "So, what're you guys talking about?"

"Trying to figure out what to write for Dad's funeral." Amy studied a page of notes in front of her and wrinkled her face. "Any ideas?"

"Well, it's supposed to be a private thing. I mean, you're supposed to write what *you* remember about Dad. Not what any of the rest of us remembers. Am I right?" She looked to Aaron and Megan.

Aaron snorted in frustration and slammed his notes onto the table next to the easy chair. For an instant Ellen remembered that her father had kept his medicine on that table after his bypass surgery. For three months he convalesced in that chair until both thirty-six-inch incisions, one down the center of his chest, the other along the inside of his left leg, had healed. How could a person smoke again after that?

She brought herself back to focus on her brother. "What's wrong, Aaron?"

"You."

"Me?"

"Not you. What you said," he barked. "You say it's supposed to be our own writing, but I'm not a writer. I can't put things down on paper like you and Megan and everyone else. I need a little help. Is that all right with you?"

"I wasn't trying to start a fight, Aaron. I only want you to understand the purpose of doing separate eulogies. It's what each of us individually remembers about Dad. Not what someone else remembers."

"Okay, but what am I supposed to say?"

"Exactly," Amy joined in. "How are we supposed to come up with the right words? I want to write something, say something that comes from my heart. But I can't think of anything."

"Okay, tell you what—" Ellen looked at Amy, her mind racing—"start with you, Amy. Tell me what you loved most about Dad. What you'll always remember."

Amy squirmed uncomfortably. "Well, he was bigger than life, kind of like my hero, I guess." Her eyes grew damp and Ellen tilted her head in empathy.

"He was, wasn't he."

Amy nodded, wiping a stray tear.

"Okay. What else?" Ellen coaxed tenderly, aware that Aaron watched them intently.

"I remember when we moved to Petoskey and I was a little girl. I fell in the back-yard and cracked my chin on the patio."

"You were four, I think," Ellen said.

"Right." Amy's eyes grew distant at the memory. "Daddy picked me up in his arms and took me to the hospital. I don't remember how they fixed me up or what happened after that. Just that he took care of me."

"Okay, now you're getting somewhere. He was bigger than life, he took care of you. Jot those things down."

Amy did as she was told and Ellen turned to Aaron.

"Now, Aaron, you do the same. What do you remember?"

Aaron thought awhile, and Ellen could almost see the memories battling to take shape in his mind. But before he would give them a chance to materialize, he forced the chair's footrest down and stood up in a sudden burst of motion.

"Forget it!" He hitched up his jeans and turned to leave the room. "All I remember is how he paddled my butt while you girls got off easy."

Ellen stared at him, completely baffled. Not so much at what her brother had said as the fact that he seemed to believe it. "Aaron!" she called him back into the room. She did not expect him to return, and when he did, she pointed to the chair. "Sit down. We need to talk about something."

"What?" It was more of a grunt than a word but Aaron sat down and waited.

"Those things that happened to you when you were a child, they're in the past. They weren't Dad's fault, they were ours, mine and the other girls'. But I can tell you now, one adult to another, that everything we ever did to you was done in fun." She hesitated. "You might not have thought it was funny, you might have felt picked on. But you were our only brother, and we felt it was our duty to gang up against you. It was just a way of getting a few laughs."

"I didn't laugh then," he said, surprisingly articulate. "And I'm not laughing now. How would you have liked being the only boy with four girls picking on you all the time? And no matter what I said back then, Dad took your side."

"Is that the whole story, Aaron? Really?" She made sure she had his attention and she continued. "I remember things a little differently. Every Saturday you and Dad went out and had fun while Mom and us girls stayed home and cleaned the house. How do you think that felt? And what about your bedroom? Do you think any of us girls wouldn't have been thrilled with a room of our own?"

Aaron was quiet.

"Dad loved you, Aaron. You were his only son. Don't tell me about how bad you had it."

Ellen saw Amy and Megan stare at their brother. *Oh, please, Jesus. Don't let any of them jump in and say anything that will anger Aaron. Just this once, please, let things be peaceful.* Ellen knew they were all hurting now; it wasn't the time to fight about Aaron's leftover emotional baggage. The girls remained silent and Ellen breathed a sigh of relief.

When Aaron's anger seemed to subside, she continued. "Maybe you could write about something that happened in the last few years. Like when you and Dad spent all that time golfing."

Aaron put his elbows on his knees and covered his face with his hands. His shoulders sank but otherwise he was silent, unmoving. The others watched him carefully, and though he didn't make a sound, they could see huge tears dropping onto the floor. Ellen felt her throat constrict. The ice was melting.

Jane entered the room then and looked around at the faces of her siblings, unaware of the moment taking place. "What's going on?"

"We're trying to figure out what to write about Dad," Amy said quietly. "Thinking of memories."

"Hmph." Jane crossed her arms. "You have to have memories to think of them."

"You have memories." Ellen heard the weariness in her voice. "All of us have memories."

"Yeah, well some of us have better memories than others," Jane said pointedly. She sat down next to Amy and picked up a magazine from an end table. Thumbing through the contents she found an article and began to read, seemingly uninterested in the conversation around her.

"Aaron," Ellen tried again. "Pretend you're in a room all by yourself and an imaginary person wants to know what you remember about Dad."

Aaron grunted.

"Write down whatever you would tell that person. That's all you need to do."

Aaron nodded, sniffing loudly and discreetly wiping his eyes. "Okay. I'll try."

He stood up and lumbered from the room. It was just after six o'clock and he had a date that night with a girlfriend he'd seen the previous year. It was a date he'd clearly looked forward to. He picked up the phone and dialed.

"Jen, I have to cancel," Ellen overheard him say. "That's right. I need some time by myself. Right. Okay, talk to you later."

Aaron straightened himself up and there was an air of determination about him. He picked up some paper and a pen, grabbed his keys, and left the house without another word to his sisters.

When the door closed behind him, Ellen looked at the others. "I think he'll get the eulogy written."

Megan nodded. "His feelings are there, they're just buried so deep it's hard for anyone to find them."

"Yeah," Ellen agreed. "Even him."

Amy studied the notes she had written in the past few minutes and sighed. "Well, I guess I'll go home early tonight. I think I can work with these notes and put something together. At least I hope so."

"You'll do fine," Ellen said.

Jane looked up from her magazine. "Don't tell her how she'll do! She doesn't need your opinion to make her efforts worth something."

Ellen leveled an ominous glare at Jane as she stood and turned to Megan. "I'll be in Mom's room lying down. Wake me for dinner." She started to leave and then stopped again. "Oh, and another thing. Tell Mom I'm staying here tonight. It'll be easier on everyone."

Megan looked disappointed but she didn't argue. "You're probably right."

Jane watched Ellen go, angry that her older sister had given up so easily. If only Ellen cared enough to take her aside and ask what was wrong, Jane might consider telling her about the rape. Maybe then they could work through the barrier between them and find love again, even friendship. Tears stung at her eyes and though her vision was blurred, she stared down at the magazine and pretended to read so no one would see her cry.

22

Ellen was tired from the bike ride and her day at the beach with Jake. She lay down on her parents' bed and hugged one of the pillows to her stomach.

She thought back on the day, remembering how close she had come to giving in to Jake.

Then just as quickly another Scripture, this one from James, besieged her. *"Each one is tempted when, by his own evil desire, he is dragged away and enticed. Then, after desire has conceived, it gives birth to sin; and sin, when it is full-grown—"*

Stop! She shouted at herself. *Enough of that! I needed Jake today and besides, I didn't do anything wrong.* But the argument sounded unconvincing, even to her.

It was wrong. It was wrong to be with him, a voice within her said. *And dangerous.*

She pressed her lips together. If Mike had come with her this week, she would never have called Jake. And she certainly wouldn't be wrestling with old feelings that should have died a long time ago.

Mike. At the thought of him, Ellen had to fight off tears again. What had happened to them? Things had been so wonderful at the beginning. Their first date was a complete hit, and after that Mike had been full of surprises, like the time he took her to Canada for the day or out to dozens of wonderful restaurants. At their wedding Ellen remembered looking into his eyes and thinking she would love Mike Miller for the rest of her life.

The trouble had started a few years later. They lived in Detroit at first, and Ellen was used to making the trek back and forth to Petoskey. Especially during summer.

"Mike, my dad wants us to come up this weekend for a barbecue," she remembered telling him one summer.

"Sounds good."

The week passed, and when Friday arrived Ellen reminded him of their plans. "Are we leaving tonight or in the morning?"

"Leaving?" He sounded clueless.

"Yes. For Petoskey. Remember? My dad invited us up for a barbecue this weekend."

"Oh, that. Hey, hon, I don't think I'll go this time."

Ellen's mouth had dropped open. "What?"

"Sweetheart, I never really said I wanted to go." Mike looked suddenly pained. "I said it sounded good."

"When someone says something sounds good, it's typically safe to assume the answer is yes."

"Well, you go ahead and go. I have to research the games for next week."

"I won't do that to my father. He's expecting us and I want us there. You said you'd go."

"I did not. I said it sounded good."

"It's the same thing, Mike. Besides, you can do your research in the car. I'll drive."

Mike had exhaled dramatically. "All right, fine. I'll go. But it would be nice if one of these days you could see things from my point of view. It takes four hours to get to Petoskey and it wastes the whole weekend."

While Ellen talked with her parents and caught up on the latest, Mike grabbed a magazine and found a quiet corner. In the end, Mike made the trip miserable by distancing himself from the others and arguing with Ellen until they were back home again. There were a dozen such incidents like that in the early years of their marriage.

"Tell them I don't want to go," Mike would suggest.

"You don't understand, Mike. My dad really loves you. He thinks you *like* spending time with him. How do you think he'd feel if I called and told him you didn't want to come for a visit? That you had better things to do and wanted me to make the trip by myself?"

The worst part, Ellen thought now, was that whenever Mike did accompany her to Petoskey, he made sure she knew it was against his will. In doing so, he robbed her of the joy she might otherwise have felt about the trip. Mike had not pursued a relationship with her parents, and now that her father was dead Ellen was angry at him.

At least Jake knew and loved my dad.

She pushed the thought aside, feeling disloyal.

There were other problems that developed between her and Mike once they moved to Miami. Birthdays, for instance. Year after year she looked forward to Mike's birthday. She plotted and planned for a month until she had picked out the perfect gift. One year it was a surprise vacation to the Keys, another year it was tickets to Wisconsin so he could take in a Green Bay football game with his aging grandfather. She had created personalized wall hangings for his office and put his baby pictures together in a quilted scrapbook with his name embroidered on the front.

She loved Mike and she wanted her gifts to be a reflection of that love.

Mike's approach couldn't have been more different.

He generally did his shopping a day or two before her birthday and was usually gone not more than an hour. One year he gave her a bright orange nylon dress that she wore exactly once before giving it to Goodwill. Another year he bought her a bulky beige purse with double straps that looked more suitable for her grandmother.

But the worst birthday of all came four years ago. Ellen planned for them to spend the weekend at a hotel south of Miami. Friday night was wonderful with a walk along the beach and a shared bath later in their hotel room. Then, when her birthday dawned the next morning, Mike explained that he had not gotten her a gift.

"Honey, I've been so busy lately. You know how it is."

Ellen did *not* know how it was. She stared at Mike and tried to understand. "Did you get me a card?"

Ellen had always made it clear to Mike that in lieu of a present she would always be thankful for a handwritten card or letter. She was not interested in expensive baubles or costly floral bouquets. But a gift should be a reflection of love and to that end Mike was a dismal failure.

That weekend, after the shock wore off, Mike tried to sound hopeful. "Hey, Ellen. I can go sit on the patio right now and write you a letter if you want."

"No. I don't want a letter now that my birthday is already here. It's too late."

"Don't be mad. I meant to get you something. It's just that the days got away from me."

"Mike, it's very simple. May is followed by June, which in turn is followed by July. There is nothing random about the way we arrive at a given date. I don't understand how the days can 'get away' from you if you really love me."

"Ellen, don't make this an issue, darling. Of course I love you. Gifts don't reflect how much a person loves another person. Think about last night."

"They matter to me, Mike." She picked up her towel and headed for the door. "You know they matter and still you don't make an effort. How am I supposed to feel about that?"

If there had ever been a summer when she was tempted to call Jake Sadler, it was the summer of 1994. After the birthday incident, one of her fellow writers at the paper in Miami invited her to his wedding.

"I can't wait," she told Mike that evening. "We haven't been on a date in months and this will be even better. We can dress up and dance. Can you make sure you're free that afternoon?"

"Ellen," Mike moaned. "I can tell you right now I don't have a game that day. But I don't even know the people getting married. Why don't you go and use the time to catch up with some of your coworkers?"

Ellen could feel her anger rising. "Mike, this is a simple thing I'm asking you. I haven't been feeling great about our marriage and it is very important that you accompany me to this wedding."

They discussed it for weeks but in the end she attended the wedding alone and afterward came home and parked in their driveway. She sobbed angry tears for two hours before going in. Thankfully, Jake lived in another state because if she'd had somewhere else to go that night she would have gone.

There were other occasions after that. Concerts, get-togethers with friends. Mike would only go when Ellen badgered him. Even then he would let her know it was an effort.

She rolled over in her parents' bed and thought again about Jake. In some ways, he and Mike were complete opposites. Jake had brought her flowers and given her jewelry and surprised her with picnics on the beach and walks through Magnus Park. With Jake, Ellen never had to wonder if she was loved.

But she did have to wonder about other things.

Suddenly she pictured the blond in the bathrobe. Yes, Jake had been attentive, but he had also been dishonest and unfaithful. In the end she had been willing to let go of the romance in hopes of finding someone she could trust, someone with a love for God like she had known in those lonely days after leaving Jake.

Someone like Mike.

Mike did love her. He showed her in a dozen unique ways every day of their lives. He wrote songs for her and did the dishes when she was too tired to move after a day's work. He was loyal and fun loving and utterly faithful.

She rolled over once more and pulled the pillow more tightly to her body. *What is it, Lord? Why aren't things like they were between us?*

Again, no answer. Tears ran down Ellen's cheeks. Sure, Mike made mistakes, but his faithfulness had to mean something. He must love her, and more than Jake ever had.

She closed her eyes and tried to believe it was true.

23

For the first time that week, curled up in the king-size bed where her father had spent every night for the past twenty-one years, Ellen slept soundly. The room even smelled like him, and she fell asleep dreaming about being a small child, scurrying to her parents' bed for protection during one of the fierce Midwestern thunderstorms.

Sometime later, she grew vaguely aware of someone standing over her, touching her face gently, pulling the covers up over her. The sense she had was one of safety and care, and she burrowed deeper into the pillow with a sigh.

She awoke the next morning to find her mother lying beside her.

"Good morning, sleepy head." Her mother's smile was tender. Ellen smiled in return. "Morning." Then she stretched. "Sorry to take over your bed."

Mom plumped her pillow and sat up against the headboard. "You were sleeping so soundly when I came in last night, I knew you needed the sleep. I just pulled the covers over you and left you there."

Ellen glanced at the clock; it was still early. It would be some time before Aaron was up, before the family members and relatives started calling. For a while she and her mother said nothing, staring at the ceiling, comfortable in the silence between them.

"I still can't believe he's gone," her mother said finally. She kept her gaze on the ceiling, talking more to herself than to Ellen. "I wake up, ready to climb out of bed and make him coffee. Sometimes I even get halfway down the hall before I remember. Then it hits me. He's gone and he's not coming back."

Ellen felt her gut twist with her mother's words. She had been so busy that week, fighting with Jane, dealing with Aaron, angry at Mike…struggling with her feelings for Jake. It had almost been enough to make her forget why she was there. But the truth wouldn't go away. Not for long. She could ignore it, push it to the back of her mind, walk around it. But the fact remained. Her father was gone.

"I loved him, you know, Ellen. I wonder sometimes if I said that enough."

"Oh, Mom, don't be so hard on yourself." Ellen rolled onto her side and faced her mother. "Of course you said it enough."

"No, I don't mean to your father. I told him every day. But I wonder if you kids knew how I felt."

"We saw how you waited on him, if that's what you mean."

Mom shook her head. She turned onto her side and propped her head up on one hand. "That's not what I mean at all. I waited on your father because I loved him. Because he would have done anything for me through the years."

"We knew that. Otherwise you wouldn't have treated him the way you did. Still, I always thought he could have been a little more helpful, to tell you the truth." She paused. "It seemed like you had to do all the housework yourself. Especially after we girls were gone." She shrugged. "But that didn't change what was obvious about you and Dad. Everyone knew you loved each other."

Her mother sighed. "I didn't do that much, Ellen. Sure, I made him coffee and brought him a Diet Coke when he asked. I made dinner and did his laundry. But he did things that couldn't be counted or measured. He made a wonderful life for me. He made me laugh and made our marriage an adventure. Everything we ever did with you children was his idea." She was quiet then and Ellen saw her lip quiver. "He made us a family, Ellen."

Ellen reached for her mother's hand. Suddenly she knew she would always remember this moment with her mother. The thought brought a fresh pang of regret. If only they had shared more times like this over the years.

"We're still a family." Compassion swept her. "I guess that's his legacy, huh?"

Her mom looked unsure. "You children aren't what you used to be, you're not as fun loving and close. There was a time when you got along beautifully together."

Ellen thought of Jake's words and pursed her lips pensively. "I don't know, Mom. I think we always fought. Even in the best of times."

"Sure, but nothing serious. Nothing like you and Jane now."

Ellen sighed. "I don't like it any more than you do. But every time we're together she says something hateful. At least that's how I see it."

"I know. But couldn't you at least talk to her, ask her what's bothering her? She's always been moody, but Ellen, even you must admit this just isn't like her. It's obvious something is very wrong."

"I'll try, Mom. I've been trying since I got here. But she's been treating me different for a long time—long before Dad's death."

They were silent again. Finally Mom slipped out of bed, stood up, and stretched. She straightened her nightgown and checked her reflection in the mirror.

"I have more gray now, did you notice?"

"Not much. It's flattering."

"That's what your father said. Sophisticated, he called it." She took a deep breath and turned back to Ellen. "We're going shopping this morning at ten so we can find something to wear to the funeral. You're coming, aren't you?"

"Of course. I'll call Megan and make sure they're up and getting ready."

Mom looked pensive. "Ellen, have you talked to Mike?"

At Mike's name, Ellen felt the heat rise in her face. "Why do you ask?"

"I don't know. I just sense that things aren't great between you."

Ellen sat up slowly and hugged her knees to her chest, leaving the bed sheet tucked around her. "We had a fight before I left."

"Have you talked to him?" she asked gently.

"No. I've been too busy."

"You've had time to visit with friends."

"Mom," Ellen groaned. "I'm a grown woman. I can handle my marriage just fine, thank you."

"I know. But I think it's time you called him. You don't even know when his plane's coming in for the funeral."

"I don't even know *if* his plane's coming." Ellen instantly regretted making the statement.

Her mother raised an eyebrow. "Then it's worse than I thought." She waited a moment, appraising her oldest daughter carefully. "It's true, you're a grown woman, Ellen. You can make your own choices. But if you know what's best for you, you'll be on the phone sometime today patching things up."

Ellen was silent.

"The years go by too quickly to waste them in silent prisons of hate."

With that, she turned around and headed for the kitchen, leaving Ellen speechless and overwhelmed. All her life she had thought her father to be the poetic one, the parent who could best relate to her creative side. But once in a while her mother would surprise her by coming up with something meaningful enough to be remembered for a lifetime. *Silent prisons of hate.*

Ellen peeled back the sheets, stood, and stretched. If only Mike had come with her in the first place. She wandered absently toward her father's nightstand and opened the top drawer. Assorted pens and pencils, a calculator, and a couple of paperbacks. She shut it and pulled open the next drawer. Suddenly she caught her breath and stared. There was her father's old Bible.

Fresh tears stung her eyes. "Oh, Daddy," she whispered. "I knew you read the Word, but…I didn't know you kept it here…so close." She lifted it carefully from the drawer and ran her fingers over the worn leather cover. She traced his name, embossed in gold on the lower right corner. Holding his Bible made her feel nearer to her father than she had felt all week.

It also made her miss him more.

She opened it gingerly, wondering if he had written in the margins. Her eyes fell on the dedication page. "To my beloved John, on our first anniversary. Yours forever in love, Diane." Ellen felt a stab of regret for all the times she had questioned her parents' faith. She flipped gently through the text and saw that, indeed, he had written many notes alongside favorite verses. Her eyes fell on one that her father had highlighted and underlined: 1 Corinthians 10:12–13. *"So, if you think you are standing firm, be careful that you don't fall! No temptation has seized you except what is common to man. And God is faithful; he will not let you be tempted beyond what you can bear. But when you are tempted, he will also provide a way out so that you can stand up under it."*

Her father had drawn several asterisks near the verse and written his own comments. *"Hold fast to your faith. Temptation is a given; look for the way out! It is possible to fall!"* The words cut Ellen as deeply as if her father had been standing before her, saying them himself. She squeezed her eyes shut, and two tears fell onto the delicate paper. Dabbing at the page, she considered the message from her father—or her Father…? She was supposed to be looking for a way out, a way to withstand her temptations. Instead she'd been entertaining thoughts of Jake Sadler from the moment she'd boarded the plane to Michigan.

Oh, Lord, help me stand up under it all. She read the verses and her dad's words again through blurry, tear-filled eyes. She glanced at the nearby alarm clock. It wasn't yet seven in Miami so Mike might still be home. She composed herself so that he wouldn't know she'd been crying, then she picked up the phone and punched in the number. He answered on the second ring.

"Hello?"

She paused a moment. "Mike, it's me."

"Ellen." There was something stiff and unyielding in his voice. He was probably angry with her for waiting so long to call. "I wondered whether you were going to call me this week."

"Of course. I've just been busy."

"Are you okay? Is everyone getting along?"

"I'm fine, we're all fine." There was no need to get into it now. She could tell him the details later. "How's work?"

"Busy, but great. They've got me working another couple games this weekend. They both have national attention."

The hair on the back of Ellen's neck bristled. "This weekend?"

"Yeah. Is that a problem?"

"The funeral's this weekend, Mike. Saturday morning."

He hesitated. "You told me you didn't want me there. Right?…Wasn't that you?"

Ellen released a loud huff. "That's not what I meant and you know it! I was mad because you wouldn't come for the whole week."

"Well, I took you at your word, Ellen, and now I'm booked. It's too late to change my plans."

"I don't believe this. You couldn't possibly have thought I didn't want you here for the funeral. I need you."

"Look, Ellen. You told me you didn't want me there. Then you didn't call for almost a week. What was I supposed to think?"

Ellen was silent, furious with him. "I don't know. But I think it's pretty clear how much I mean to you if you can't even take time from your schedule to attend my father's funeral with me.

"You told me you didn't want me there," he insisted angrily.

"But if you loved me you'd have come—no matter what— I was angry. You know I didn't mean what I said."

"It's too late now, Ellen. Lighten up."

"Don't tell me to lighten up." Her voice was frigid. The sudden image of Jake sitting beside her on the shore of Mackinac Island flitted into her mind. "Forget it, Mike. I'll have plenty of support."

"Listen, Ellen, I'm sorry. Don't be so angry. I've missed you all week and I can't wait to see you. I even read my Bible last night. First time in a while."

"Good for you."

"Ellen, stop. I know this must be hard for you, but it would have been almost impossible to get the weekend off. Especially at this time of the year with the pennant race heating up."

"What exactly do you think it means to be married, Mike?"

"What kind of a question is that?"

"A pertinent one. Marriage should be more than a convenience, more than a body to warm your bed." Ellen closed her eyes and her mind filled with the image of Jake. When she spoke again there was a catch in her voice.

"When you love someone you do whatever it takes to be by their side." She was talking to Mike, but she knew deep inside she was describing Jake, the way he was now. "You stand by them and make yourself available when they need you."

"Come on, Ellen—"

She cut him off. "No. I mean it, Mike. That's what love's all about. But that isn't you at all. The pennant race is worth more than me."

"Oh, Ellen, come on. Stop being so dramatic. You know I love you."

Ellen felt the sting of tears. Her husband had rejected her when she needed him most; she had no desire to fight him now.

"No. I don't. And that's the saddest part of all. I need you, Mike." She uttered a short laugh. "And you're not here. How am I supposed to know you love me?"

Mike was quiet. "I don't know what to say."

She waited a moment and then reached into her purse beside the bed for her airline tickets.

"I'm coming home on Flight 252 at 5:30 Sunday evening." It was her professional voice, the one she used at work. Businesslike, without a trace of the pain that was strangling her heart. "Will you be there or should I take a taxi?"

"Of course I'll be there. I'll come straight from the game. Hey, when we get home let's go out and talk."

"Fine. Listen, I'd better go. We have things to do this morning."

"Ellen, don't be mad."

"I'm not mad. I'm hurt—" She broke off. "You don't understand me at all, do you?"

Mike sighed. It was a totally dejected sound. "I'm sorry, Ellen. I guess we need to communicate better."

"Good-bye, Mike. Do me a favor and don't call these next few days. I need some time to think."

There was a painful silence. "Whatever you want, Ellen. I'll see you Sunday."

"Fine."

As she hung up Ellen struggled with her anger. How could he be so insensitive? He knew how close she and her father had been. The urge to call Jake was strong, but instead she closed her eyes. *Help me, Lord. Help me before I give in to my heart and completely destroy everything you've ever given me.* She took a deep breath and as she did the phone on the nightstand next to her rang. Her heart lurched and she reached for it, wondering if maybe it might be Jake.

"Hello?"

"Ellen?"

"Leslie?" An answer to prayer, but not the one she'd been wrongly hoping for. "Somehow I'm not surprised you found me. How did you know I was here?"

"Mike told me. Ellen, I'm so sorry about your dad."

Tears filled Ellen's eyes and spilled onto her cheeks...tears of loss. But Ellen wasn't sure if they were over her father—or her marriage.

She talked then, telling Leslie how badly she missed her dad and of the struggles with Jane and the others. As they talked, Ellen quickly remembered why she and Leslie had been friends for so long. Nothing ever changed with Leslie. The two might not talk for years and still they could pick up where they left off. They had that kind of friendship. Especially after that weekend when Leslie led her to Christ.

When it seemed like their conversation was winding down, Leslie's tone of voice suddenly changed. "Okay, come on, Ellen," she sounded gently suspicious, almost parental. "What else?"

"What do you mean?"

"Please, Ellen. I've known you longer than that. I know you're upset about your dad, but there's something else going on. I can see it in your eyes."

"You can't *see* my eyes."

"Okay, then I can see it in your voice. But I *can* see it. Clear as if you were standing in the same room with me. Mike isn't there, and that's bugging you big time."

Ellen sighed. "Is it always like that? The person who leads you to the Lord can see right through you when you're blowing it?"

"Talk to me, Ellen. What's happening out there?"

"Oh, Leslie, I don't know. Everything's so mixed up right now."

"Can I tell you something?"

"Go ahead."

"When I found out you went to Petoskey by yourself I had this crazy thought that I should pray for you, that maybe, even though it'd been years, you might call Jake Sadler."

Ellen uttered a short laugh. "Well, that settles it."

"What?"

"God knows what he's doing. I mean, are you serious? You've been praying for me?"

"Mm-hmm. Hoping you wouldn't do anything you'd regret. Did you, Ellen? Did you call him?"

"Yes." The word came out hoarse. "But not because I wanted to get back at Mike. Nothing like that. Leslie, I keep thinking back to when my dad was healthy and everyone got along. I have a million happy memories, and Jake is right there in the middle of all of them. I had to call him. He's the only one who really knows how I feel."

"So you've seen him?"

"A few times. He's changed, Leslie. He's grown up and he's a wonderful man, honest and considerate. He's been there every time I've needed him."

"Is he married?"

"No."

Leslie hesitated, then went on, her tone cautious but firm. "Ellen, don't take this wrong. But you and Jake had something very special, beyond the usual high school romance thing."

"So?"

"So don't you think, if you're really honest with yourself, that it's possible Jake's still in love with you?"

"Have you been following me, Leslie?"

"Am I close to home?"

"Very close. I never would have thought it was true, but now that I've seen him I'd be lying to say he doesn't still care for me. He does."

"And you?"

"Well, you know that special something we shared in high school and afterwards? It's still there. Whatever it is it hasn't gone away with time."

"Okay, this is totally off the subject." Leslie paused. "And it might be a long shot, but how are you doing spiritually?"

Ellen had no response.

"I thought so." Leslie sighed. "Oh, Ellen, I feel so bad. I haven't called or prayed for you or done any of the things I should have done over the years."

"It isn't your fault, Leslie. Life goes on and people go their own ways. You weren't responsible for my walk with the Lord. I was."

"You still believe, don't you?"

"Of course. It's not that we denounced our faith or anything. We just sort of dropped out of the whole Christian circle." Ellen shifted to a more comfortable position, leaning back against the headboard as her mother had done earlier. "You wouldn't believe how easily it is to let that go when you're both working full-time during the week. It's like we convinced ourselves that the weekends were ours. We were too busy for church. Before long we were too busy to pray and too busy to talk about God. You think there's a connection, right?" She altered her voice so that she sounded like a newscaster. "Christian couple strays from God and winds up on the skids."

"Don't you?"

"I don't know. It seems more complicated than that. Mike doesn't love me like he used to. No one should have to stay in that kind of relationship forever."

"I don't care how far from God you are today, Ellen, God hasn't moved."

Ellen wanted to get angry, but there was so much compassion in Leslie's voice that she couldn't.

"God's there," Leslie went on, "and he expects you to honor your marriage vows. Satan would love to make you think you and Mike don't belong together anymore. He'd love to destroy the knot that God himself tied. I only wish I'd called sooner so we could have prayed about it before now."

"I don't know, Leslie. I don't think it would have helped. Mike isn't going to change. Not for me, not for anyone."

"So you've written off the Word, too. Remember Luke 1:37? Nothing is impossible with God." Leslie waited a moment. "I don't want to sound trite, like I'm giving you just another pat answer. But it's true. You loved Mike with all your heart, Ellen. You loved him for all the right reasons. Somewhere, buried deep within the man, those reasons still exist."

"And you think prayer will change him back to the man he was?"

"Or help you to see the man he still is, deep down. You should know how powerful prayer is, Ellen. You've seen God work in your life. You prayed about the job at the *Gazette* and got a position when no one else with your experience would have been considered. You prayed that God would help you forget about Jake and next thing you know you're dating the handsome *and* godly Mike Miller. Have you really stopped believing in prayer?"

Tears stung Ellen's eyes again and she blinked them away. She thought of her miscarriages and how things had changed with Mike. Her throat was thick when she could finally speak. "Maybe I have."

"What about Mike?"

"I don't know. He and I don't pray together, we don't read the Bible anymore." She bit her lip and the tears trickled down her cheek. "I guess neither of us should be surprised that we aren't doing well."

"So do something about it. Put Jake out of your mind and get busy."

Ellen's voice was barely a whisper. "What if I don't want to?"

"What do you mean?"

"I'm mad at Mike. I don't want to pray with him and work everything out. Right now I don't even care if I do something that'll hurt him."

"I can think of someone you could hurt more than Mike."

"Who?"

"God. Your Lord, your Savior. Remember him? Remember reading the Bible with me that day in my bedroom and realizing for the first time what Jesus suffered? Remember? When you finally understood that he took his place on the cross that day because one of the faces on his mind was yours? You couldn't stop crying. He loves you. And he's the one you will hurt the most, Ellen. He's the one you'll be unfaithful to." She paused, then asked softly, "Do you really want to treat God the way Jake treated you so many times?"

Ellen's shoulders sagged forward and the trickle of tears became a stream. She still wanted to call Jake, even now. Wanted to see him so badly, to spend time with him even though it would hurt Mike. Or maybe because it would hurt Mike. But picturing the Lord in pain because of her selfishness was almost more than she could bear.

Leslie's voice was thick when she went on, as though she, too, was crying. "Marriages take work, Ellen. Hours of communication, moments of honesty when needs are expressed and problems worked through. But most of all they take prayer, from both of you. If you and Mike aren't praying and worshiping together, then you don't stand a chance. None of us would. A cord of *three* strands is not easily broken."

Ellen sniffed and wiped her eyes. She hoped none of the others would look for her now that the morning was wearing on. She needed time to think.

"It-it kills me to think I might be making God sad." She sobbed softly. "Oh, Leslie, I've blown it so bad."

"No. That's where you're wrong. You haven't blown anything. Not yet. God is there with you. You can leave him but he'll never leave you, Ellen. Never. Remember that night when you asked Christ into your heart?"

"Mm-hmm."

"You prayed that God would keep you away from Jake. He was your strongest weakness then and he's your strongest weakness now. Pray it again, Ellen. Come on, right now."

Ellen was crying even harder. She couldn't bring herself to say the words. "I can't. You pray."

"Okay."

Ellen squeezed her eyes shut as her body shook with each silent sob. She listened intently to Leslie's gentle words.

"Lord, precious Savior and Father, we come before you and lift up Ellen. She's hurting now and she needs your touch. Give her peace and wisdom and comfort so that she will survive this week, the funeral of her father, the strained relationships with her family. The nearness of Jake Sadler. Lord, please keep her strong in the face of temptation. As she prayed so long ago, we pray again, Lord. Keep her away from Jake. And please restore her love for Mike. I pray that they will feel a desperate need to be back in your presence, in the shelter of your church, and the strength of your Word. Thank you, Lord. In Jesus' name, amen."

There was silence for a moment.

"Ellen, you okay?"

Her tears under control now, Ellen cleared her throat. "Thanks. Keep praying for me, will you, Leslie? I know what's right, but the only way I'll do it is if I keep my eyes on God."

"And off Jake Sadler."

Her heart constricted at the truth. "Right. Listen, I gotta go. I'll call you later and let you know how things went."

"Okay. Give my love to your family."

"Yeah. Thanks. And thanks for being there, Leslie. I needed you.

"Hey, I love you, Ellen. Mike loves you. I'll be praying for you guys. And you know what?"

"What?"

"Somewhere, I believe your dad is praying for you, too. When I think of people who lived their entire lives in faith, I think of him. Follow his example, Ellen. Please."

"Thanks. Talk to you later."

Slowly Leslie hung up the phone. Ellen's words, the pain in her voice, rang in Leslie's mind. Quickly she lifted the receiver again and dialed Imogene Spencer at the First Baptist Church office.

"Imogene, it's me, Leslie. About my friend, the one on the prayer chain, I want to make that prayer request a bit more specific."

Ellen hung up the phone, wishing she felt better.

Leslie was right, of course; there was only one right thing to do. But still Ellen was confused. In fact, nothing about that week's events made sense. Ellen fingered her wedding ring and knew one thing for certain. Her entire future depended on the decisions she would make in the days to come.

She pulled the sheets off her bare legs and climbed out of bed. It was time to get ready. The others would be there soon and she didn't want to hold them up.

She twisted out of her nightshirt and climbed into the shower. As the hot water ran down her body she struggled to clear her mind. But no matter how hard she tried, one question remained.

If you love me, Mike, why aren't you here?

24

*L*ater that morning everyone but Aaron piled into the family van and headed for the mall. After two hours of shopping only Jane had not found a dress for the funeral.

Ellen was ready to scream.

"What exactly are you looking for, Jane?" Mom tried to sound patient.

"I don't care; whatever I can find."

"Honey, we have a lot to do today and I wanted to take you girls to lunch. We've been to three stores and you haven't liked anything yet. I'm just wondering what you're looking for."

"In other words, could you hurry and find something," Ellen added. She had been on edge since talking to Leslie, as if the battle for her heart was intensifying with each moment. It was taking every fiber of her control to keep from calling Jake and spending the afternoon with him.

"Lay off, Ellen," Jane snapped.

Their mother placed a soothing hand on Jane's arm.

"Girls," she said, her voice calm. "Let's not get angry with each other." She turned to Jane. "I was only trying to help you narrow your options so we could finish up and get to lunch."

Jane stared at Ellen and then their mother, her face twisted in frustration. "You know, I'm doing my best. You'd have a hard time, too, if you were trying to find a dress with three children pulling at you."

"Here, dear." Mom reached down to take Koley's and Kala's hands. "Let me watch the children while you look."

"Fine," Jane snapped again. She turned around and walked toward the women's clothing, pushing Kyle's baby stroller while Koley and Kala linked hands with their grandmother and walked along behind her. Ten minutes later Jane had picked out a dress and paid for it.

"Satisfied?" She looked at Ellen.

Megan sighed impatiently and Amy remained motionless. Their mother looked at the faces before her and forced a smile.

"Well. Now that we're all getting along so well, let's go to lunch." There was not a trace of sarcasm in her voice.

Ellen marveled at her mother. The woman always had the ability to don a smile regardless of the circumstances. She and Jane used to accuse their mom of burying her head in the sand because she never wanted to discuss anything remotely controversial. Now she was starting to wonder if it wasn't just her mother's way of doing her best to hold her family together.

They moved silently through the mall, back to the car, and said nothing to each other as Mom drove to a nearby Italian restaurant. After the meal they headed home and rested until Aunt Mary arrived to watch the children. It was three o'clock and they had an appointment in thirty minutes. It was time to pick out a casket.

Three cars made the trip to Stone's Funeral Home. Ellen rode with Megan, Mom took Amy and Jane, and Aaron rode by himself. By that time their father's body had been embalmed, dressed in his best Sunday suit and tie, and made up to look "lifelike."

Ellen was thankful they wouldn't have to see him yet. That would come the following night, Friday, at the public viewing. Today was the final day of planning, of meeting with the director of the mortuary so they could choose a casket and coordinate the funeral plans.

The mortuary was conservatively set back from the road. It had beige siding and a black, shingled roof. Each window had decorative shutters accented in white trim. Stone's Funeral Home had been in business since 1899 and had a reputation for being one of the most capable in Northern Michigan. The grounds were a carefully manicured carpet of deep green, and not far from the main entrance an American flag flickered in the afternoon breeze.

Ellen thought it was probably supposed to look like a very large family home. It did not. For all its careful upkeep, it still looked like death.

They filed quietly into the somber building and waited in a lobby for someone to help them. Ellen glanced down and noticed a standing ashtray near the foyer. *For future customers.*

"Smells weird," Megan whispered, and Ellen nodded.

"Hello there." A thin man reminiscent of Ichabod Crane appeared and ushered them into a spacious office. He spoke in hushed tones, exuding an appropriate aura of respect for his clients' loss. "You're the Barrett family, I presume."

"Yes." Mom clutched her purse tightly.

"Fine. Take a seat." He motioned to the padded chairs around the room. "I've been expecting you. I'm Mr. Whitson."

Everyone in the Barrett family remained silent, waiting.

"Now—" the man said, reaching into his desk drawer and retrieving a leatherbound catalogue—"these are the coffins we can have available for the Saturday funeral. Whatever you choose, it can be here by morning. Of course…there's a wide price range."

He paused and looked at their mother. "Did you have some idea of your price range?"

Ellen squirmed and hugged herself tightly. Her stomach was beginning to hurt.

"Yes, we'd like to stay under three thousand dollars, if that's possible."

The man nodded quickly. "Definitely. Very possible." He flipped open the book and thumbed to the back section. "We have a wide variety of oak and walnut caskets in that range. Of course the price goes up depending on the definition and degree of difficulty in the engraving on the wood."

He flipped from one page to another, quietly allowing their mother to see for herself the many designs. Amy sighed softly and stared out a small window at the sunlit afternoon outside while Megan crossed her legs and nervously tapped her foot up and down. Each of them waited for their mother to say something.

Mom looked from one page to another and then directed Mr. Whitson to flip back to the first model he'd shown her.

"What's the difference, Mom?" Aaron's voice was loud and disagreeable as he broke the silence. He obviously did not care if he embarrassed her.

Ellen felt sorry for their mother. Mr. Whitson was too clinical, too businesslike. They weren't buying a new refrigerator after all, they were trying to bury their father and get on with their lives. A sales pitch on types of wood was unnecessary. Still, her brother's attitude was only making the task more difficult.

"No one's going to see it," Aaron continued. "What's the big deal?"

Mr. Whitson cleared his throat and discreetly excused himself for a drink of water. "I'll be back in ten minutes. Why don't you talk about it and we'll see what we can work out."

He disappeared and Mom looked wearily at Aaron.

"Your father was not a wealthy man, Aaron. He was not an important man by the world's standards and certainly not a famous man. But I'd like to see him buried as comfortably as possible."

"That's disgusting," Jane blurted. "He's dead, Mom. Good night! How can you talk about him being comfortable."

"That's not what I mean. I'm talking about his body. The coffin is his final resting place and I think it should be as nice as possible."

Ellen looked at her mother tenderly. "If that's what you want, Mom, and if you think that's what Dad would have wanted, I say get the best casket you can afford. It isn't time to be cheap."

"Oh, Ellen, that's ridiculous," Jane hissed. She turned to her mother, speaking like she would to one of her children. "I agree with Aaron. It's a waste of money. I say get the cheapest one there is and use the rest of the money to buy him a nice tombstone, something we could at least see. The coffin will be underground, for heaven's sake."

"With that logic, a tombstone's not worth wasting money on, either," Ellen mused aloud. "It's just an oversized rock. We don't need a larger one than normal to remember him. At least I don't."

Jane rolled her eyes. "Do you always have to have the last word, Ellen? Why don't you be quiet and let Mother decide for herself."

Ellen stared at Jane and stood up. Once again, Jane had pushed her beyond her limit. She searched her purse for a few silver coins, and then stared at her mother. "I'll be back. I have to make a phone call."

Mom gave her a knowing look. "Good, dear," she whispered in Ellen's direction. "It's time."

Ellen ignored her mother's comment and despite Jane's angry glare she turned and headed for the pay phone in the lobby. She had spotted it on the way in and made a mental note that if things got too tense she would excuse herself and make the call, regardless of her battered conscience.

Her mother didn't know about the earlier conversation she'd had with Mike. Apparently she thought Ellen was about to call her husband and patch things up. A wave of guilt assaulted Ellen as she arrived at the pay phone, and for a moment she almost turned back to join the others. Then she thought of Jane, how their relationship was unraveling faster than a half-made sweater.

She thought of Mike, too. *It's too late to change my plans… too late…too late….*
She picked up the phone.

Don't do it, a voice inside her head screamed. *You're married. You're a Christian. You're crazy. This isn't about Jane, it's about Mike. You've been looking for an excuse to call Jake ever since this morning. Come on, Ellen, remember what Leslie said.*

Her conscience challenged her and threatened her, tempting her to hang up the phone. Leslie's words came back to her.

Don't do it, Ellen. Don't do it.

She slipped the coins into the slot and dialed his number. "Hello?" Jake sounded tired and Ellen almost hung up the phone.

"It's me."

"Ellen," he said her name slowly and it sounded like velvet on his tongue. His voice was filled with concern. "I've been thinking about you. I wanted to call but I was afraid you'd be uncomfortable."

"I know. I've thought about calling you all day."

"Things worse?"

"Yes." Her voice was choked with emotion and not very clear. "I'm at the mortuary, Stone's Funeral Home on Mitchell Road."

"I know it."

"Please come, Jake. I need to talk."

Jake was quiet and Ellen knew his struggle. In that instant she was certain he still loved her. He was afraid to see her again, terrified that he couldn't keep his distance. Jake didn't have to say a word. Ellen knew what he was thinking because she felt the same way about him.

"What time will you be done?" There was resignation in his voice.

Ellen looked at her watch. It was four o'clock. "Around five-thirty. I'll send the others home without me and I'll wait here for you."

"Where should we go?"

"How 'bout back to your house. Just for a few hours."

"Are you sure?"

Ellen understood the deeper meaning behind his question. Perhaps they were asking for trouble, allowing themselves to be alone together at his house. If so, Ellen didn't care. Mike didn't want to be there. She and Jane were no longer on speaking terms. Worse, the constant friction between them made it impossible for her to think about her father. His funeral was in two days and she hadn't even had time to mourn his death. What did it matter if she spent a few more hours with Jake? The week would be over soon enough and they would return to their separate lives, thinking of each other only on occasion as they had before.

"Ellen?" His voice was a caress.

"Yes," she said quickly. "I'm sure."

"Okay, five-thirty. See you then."

Ellen hung up and returned to the office where the others had reached an agreement on an oak casket. It was lined with white satin and engraved with tiny roses around the base.

There were six brass handles stationed along the sides where the pallbearers would carry it from the hearse to the church and back.

"What do you think?" Mom pointed to the picture of the coffin in the catalogue. She had dark circles under her eyes and she seemed anxious to be done with the selection process.

"I don't know. It's a coffin." Ellen stared at the wooden box in the picture and thought of her father, full of life, sitting at a Michigan football game. She tried to imagine that same man lying in the carved oak casket and she shuddered. "It's hard to picture."

"I know, dear. I understand that. But I want us all to agree on the coffin and this is the one we've picked out. Could you please tell me what you think?"

"It's fine."

"Okay, then that's it." She turned to face Mr. Whitson, who was once again sitting patiently behind his desk while the family made their decision. "What's next?"

"We need to work out arrangements for tomorrow night's viewing and transportation to the church and cemetery. You do have a plot picked out?"

"Yes, that's taken care of."

Megan shut her eyes, and Ellen thought she was probably holding back tears. Amy stared at the floor, and Ellen clenched her fists, pressing them into her stomach to ease the knots that grew there. Aaron slipped on his dark glasses. Jane remained motionless.

The plot was located in St. Francis Cemetery, a small tree-lined park situated on a steep bluff overlooking Little Traverse Bay. The view was incredible from any spot in the cemetery, and there was a generous amount of space between plots. Earlier that week their mother had chosen a plot directly underneath a large oak tree. It was not far from the split-rail fence that bordered the edge of the cemetery and the embankment that led down to the water. Mom had not taken them all to see the plot. Ellen was just as glad. They would see it soon enough.

For an hour the five Barrett siblings sat quietly, together but very much apart, as their mother worked out the logistics of the viewing, funeral service, and burial. Ellen thought her mother was holding up remarkably well. She made notes and jotted down key details as they worked through the planning process.

Ellen watched and wondered if funerals were always like this. The planning took so much effort that there was no time to grieve. She had expected her mother to break down and cry, to be unable to get through this part of the week. Instead she was stoic and calm, well organized and efficient. Ellen wondered when the reality would hit.

"Well, that's all I have. I think we've worked everything out."

Mr. Whitson stood up and shook their mother's hand. He looked at the others and barely smiled. "We'll see all of you tomorrow night. You should get here at least an hour before the public viewing but you can come any time after two o'clock."

"Thank you," Mom told him as the group filed quietly out of the office. As soon as they were outside, she announced that they were all expected back at the house for dinner.

"Is that okay with everyone?" She held the keys to the van and looked at each of them expectantly.

"Uhh, I still have some work to do on that thing I'm writing for the funeral," Aaron mumbled. "I thought I might go to the beach and work on it."

Their mother's shoulders dropped in disappointment and she sighed heavily. "Aaron, I thought we'd all be together tonight."

"Mom, if you want me to get that thing done then don't complain about me missing dinner. Maaaaan, I mean it. Give me a break, will ya?"

Ellen cast a disgusted glance toward her brother and Amy rolled her eyes.

"Okay, okay," Mom smiled calmly, caving under Aaron's implied threat of a temper tantrum. "Go ahead, honey. Drive safely."

Aaron mumbled something, slid behind the wheel of his truck, and drove off. She looked at her daughters. "What about you girls?"

"I can come over for a little while but the children need to get to sleep earlier than last night." Jane crossed her arms impatiently. "Troy's coming in at 10:30 tomorrow morning so I don't want to stay up late."

"Amy?"

"Frank wants me to meet him for pizza with a few of his friends. We'll come back to the house later. Around nine or so."

"I'll be there," Megan said. She looked accusingly at her sisters. "This is a time when we should be together."

"Ellen?" Mom raised her eyebrows hopefully.

"I have plans, too. Sorry, Mom. I won't be late."

Her mother sighed, and Ellen was glad she seemed too preoccupied to ask what her plans were. "All right. Let's get going, then."

Her mother, Amy, and Jane piled into the van and drove away leaving Megan and Ellen. They walked slowly, silently toward Megan's car.

"I don't need a ride, Megan." Ellen tried to sound casual.

Megan stopped and stared at her. "Why not?"

"My friend's picking me up here."

Megan narrowed her eyes and studied her sister. Ellen could see the suspicion in her face. "What gives, Ellen? Who's the mystery friend?"

Ellen nudged the tip of her shoe at a few loose rocks on the asphalt. She refused to look at Megan. "Just an old friend."

Megan lowered her face so that she could see directly into Ellen's eyes. "I'm your sister, remember, Ellen? I know most of your old friends. Who is she?"

Ellen hesitated. "He."

"He?"

"Yes." She drew a deep breath. "Jake Sadler. We're getting together to talk."

"What?" Megan's voice rose.

"Shhh. You heard what I said."

"Why on earth are you doing that?"

"I've seen him twice this week. I called him that night when Jane told me I was stupid for not having any children. Remember?"

"You saw him that night, too?" Megan was clearly astonished and Ellen felt a twinge of guilt. "Is that who you went to the beach with?"

Ellen nodded. "Mackinac Island."

"Ellen, are you having an affair?"

Megan sounded as if she was about to collapse from the shock and Ellen took her arm and led her gently to her car.

"No, Megan. It's no big deal. Don't worry. Just a couple of old friends remembering the way things used to be. He loved Dad, too, remember?"

Megan emitted a brief laugh that was completely void of humor. "Who are you trying to kid? I might have been younger than you, but I wasn't blind. Listen, Ellen, you and Jake Sadler were *anything* but friends."

"That was a long time ago."

"Not long enough." She thought a moment. "Does Mike know?"

Ellen shook her head.

"You guys are fighting, aren't you?"

Ellen set her jaw. "Mike and I are fine. This has nothing to do with him."

"Then why, Ellen? I can understand Jake's motives, but what about yours?"

Ellen was immediately defensive. "That's not fair. Jake's matured a lot since high school."

"I don't care what he's done since high school. You're a married woman and you have no right spending an evening with Jake Sadler."

Ellen was silent, her arms crossed stubbornly.

"You know I'm right."

"I know that whatever you say isn't going to change my mind." Ellen was matter-of-fact. "Please, Megan, go home and spend some time with Mom. I can take care of myself."

Megan frowned at Ellen and turned away. She opened the car door, slipped inside, and started the engine. Then she rolled down the window and stared hard at Ellen. "Do what you want, Ellen," she warned. "But Jake Sadler is trouble. He's been trouble since the first day you met him."

"If anyone knows that, I do," Ellen replied quickly. "I said don't worry about it." She was beginning to feel nervous because it was almost five-thirty and she didn't want Jake to pull up and see them arguing about him.

"I think you're making a big mistake. Obviously I can't stop you."

"Good-bye, Megan," Ellen said simply.

Megan shook her head. "I have one more thing to say and then I'll go."

Ellen shifted her position impatiently.

"Please be careful." The accusation in Megan's voice was gone.

"Megan, don't worry. I told you there's nothing between us."

"Don't lie to me, Ellen. I know how you and Jake were. That isn't something that goes away with time."

"I know," Ellen finally conceded. "I'll be careful. I promise."

Megan nodded and then drove away. Ellen watched her go and then walked across the parking lot. She sat on the wooden bench in front of the mortuary and waited anxiously for Jake. She was restless, watching for his truck and feeling more nervous than she had all week. Not because of Megan's warning. She was not afraid of Jake Sadler's intentions.

She was afraid of her own.

25

Ellen heard the low rumbling sound of Jake's truck seconds before it pulled into view. He climbed out and walked toward her, hesitating for a moment before pulling her into a hug. She buried her face in his pullover.

I can't go with him. It'll just hurt us both. "Thanks for coming," she whispered.

Jake's eyes filled with concern, and Ellen's doubts dissolved like summer days. He was her first love, but he was also her friend. In all the world he was the only one she wanted to be with at that moment.

Unbidden, another verse drifted into her mind: *"The way of a fool seems right to him, but a wise man listens to advice."* She felt her cheeks go red.

He slid into the truck and put his seat belt on. "Everyone gone home?"

"Finally." She closed the door and was surrounded by the scent of leather and cologne. She sank into the seat and released a heavy sigh.

"That bad, huh?"

"Worse. I don't know, Jake, maybe it's me. Jane's still on the warpath and my mom's wanting us all to be together every last minute leading up to the funeral. Aaron's a time bomb and Megan's playing peacemaker. Same old story."

Jake pulled out of the parking lot and headed west on Mitchell.

"Where do you live?"

"Harbor Pointe, out in Harbor Springs."

Ellen raised an eyebrow. "I know the area. Why didn't you tell me you lived in the estates?"

"They're not really estates. Just large subdivision homes."

"I can't believe you live in Harbor Pointe," she said absently. She stared out the windshield and ran her fingers through her hair. "Guards at the gate, tennis courts, the bay in your backyard. Who'd have thought it? I mean, weren't you the guy who was out to live life up and avoid commitment at all costs?"

Jake grinned sheepishly and his eyes twinkled with laughter.

"You couldn't be serious about anything back then, Jake. Now look at you."

He grew pensive and remained silent.

"You're happy about it, aren't you? The success I mean?"

"Sometimes. The house is nice, the cars and boat and hot tub. They're all fine. But sometimes I think my life was richer when I was twenty-one and lived paycheck to paycheck."

"Hmm." Ellen nodded slowly. "I think that way, too, sometimes. Between Mike and me we do pretty well. We live in a nice, gated community with a two-story house a few blocks from the ocean. Nice cars, nice clothes, good jobs."

"Doesn't really help you sleep at night, does it?" He glanced at her and she shook her head, shifting so she could watch him drive.

She studied him, remembering him as he was and wondering what would have happened if, like his mother once hoped, she had waited for him to grow up. She saw that his eyes were distant. He seemed a million miles away, lost in some long ago memory.

"What're you thinking about?"

"Choices. Passages. Moments that make a difference for a lifetime."

She considered his words and smiled. Choices. Passages. Moments that make a difference for a lifetime. This was the Jake she remembered, the one she had shared her heart with, the one she could talk to for hours without growing tired. For an instant she saw him as he used to be—a tan, fresh-faced boy who could see directly into her soul. She held the image and allowed herself to miss him as she hadn't in years.

She turned away then and tried to remember the flip side. The strange phone calls from other girls at odd hours, unfamiliar notes left on his doorstep or under his windshield wipers. The impatient blond in his bathrobe. Ellen sighed. As good as things had been when they were together, it hadn't been good enough.

She gazed out the side window, her back to Jake. Leslie hadn't been the only one to warn her about him. Her father had seen it coming, too.

"He's a fine boy, Ellen," he'd said once. "I love him like a son. But I see how he is, the way he looks at other girls. He has 'em dropping like flies." He touched her cheek gently, a gesture he'd done since she was a little girl. "You deserve better than that."

"Okay," Jake interrupted her thoughts. "Now it's my turn. What're you thinking?"

She turned toward him and answered quickly, "My dad."

Jake was sympathetic. "You miss him?"

"I haven't really had time. I keep thinking I'll go back to my parents' house and he'll be in his easy chair watching a golf tournament or a baseball game or something."

"Is there a viewing? At the mortuary?"

Ellen wrinkled her nose. "Yes. Tomorrow night. I'm dreading it."

Jake nodded. "I bet. But his death will be more real after that, Ellen. You'll be able to accept it better."

Ellen thought about seeing her father's body in the cold, satin-lined casket. "Yes," she conceded. "I suppose so."

They drove around the bay and continued along the water, through the town of Bay Harbor. In less than fifteen minutes they arrived at the gate. Jake waved to the man in the booth, turned left, and drove further out onto the peninsula. As the strip of land narrowed, he slowed the truck and turned left again into an impressive stone driveway.

"This is it? This is your house?" Ellen raised her eyebrows appreciatively.

Jake nodded and shrugged. Ellen studied Jake's house. Some of the places they had driven past had been pretentious. This house was very different. An inviting Victorian, Jake's home looked warm and filled with light. It seemed cared for and lived in, the type of house she might have picked for herself. Soft slate gray siding accented with white trim and an old-fashioned, white wraparound porch. It was a two-story home with dozens of white-rimmed French windows. The roof was the color of caramel. Heavily shingled, it peaked over a handful of smaller windows.

For all its homey warmth, Jake's house was stunning, surrounded by a lush landscape and delicate petunias that bordered the home. There were panoramic views of the bay on one side and Lake Michigan on the other. The porch wrapped around the front of the house and from where Jake was parked, Ellen could barely see a redwood deck stretched out across the back. The bay was literally in his backyard and Ellen felt like she was surrounded by sandy beach.

"Jake—" she clasped her hands in delight—"it's breathtaking."

"Thanks." He moved around the truck and opened her door. "I'm glad you like it."

She followed him to the front door.

"Hungry?" He turned the key.

"Starved." She hadn't realized it until he asked, but she hadn't eaten since late that morning and she was famished. They walked inside and she stopped to take in the beauty of the place. The numerous French windows allowed the room to bask in sunlight, bathing the white walls and walnut trim in warmth. The ceilings were vaulted, accented with skylights and plant shelves. His leather living room set looked warm and inviting.

"You did this?" She moved into the room and began wandering through the house.

"The doors and windows are mine." She could see the pride in his eyes. "I hired a decorator for the rest."

"Job well done. You could have Home and Garden here tomorrow and they'd do a centerfold on the place."

Jake grinned and headed for the kitchen. "Want me to order pizza or something?"

She followed him, sliding onto a bar stool and leaning across an expanse of granite countertop. "I have a better idea."

"Okay, what?" He opened the refrigerator door and twisted around to look at her.

"Omelettes. Filled with cheese and alfalfa sprouts, tomatoes and olives. Sour cream and salsa."

Jake laughed and his eyes danced at the idea. "I haven't made one of those in years."

"Remember? We'd get home from the beach and be starved and we'd raid your mother's fridge. You made the best omelettes, Jake. I mean it."

He bent over and riffled through the icebox looking for ingredients. "Let's see. Lots of eggs. Sprouts. Cheese." He straightened, his arms filled with the ingredients. "You got it. Two omelettes coming up."

She stood up and moved into the kitchen, pulling open several drawers until she found a knife. "Hand me the tomatoes. I'll help chop."

He backed away in mock fear. "Be careful with that thing. You never were much good in the kitchen."

She wielded the small carving knife back and forth through the air, pretending to be dangerous.

"No, you don't." He grabbed her wrist with one hand and tickled her side with his other hand.

"Stop or you'll be sorry." She laughed, squirming to break free from his grasp. He let go and pretended to give up, but as she turned toward the cutting board he poked her once more in the ribs.

"Unless you want me to get the ice cubes and start an all-out war, you better stop, Jake Sadler." She was flushed from laughing, breathless from the feel of his hand on her wrist.

"All right, all right. Get busy chopping."

"Thank you!" she huffed. She caught three tomatoes as he tossed them her way.

They worked for twenty minutes preparing ingredients, and then Jake set to work. When he was finished he had two plate-sized omelettes, each oozing with vegetables, cheese, and sour cream.

"Mmmmm, smells like a restaurant."

"Remember, I was going to open my own omelette shop on the beach somewhere."

"That's right." She set two place mats side by side on the counter and filled two glasses with ice water. He joined her with the food and they sat down. "The way these things look you still could."

"Nah. You'd be my best customer and you live a million miles away."

"Eighteen hundred miles, to be exact."

"Like I said," his voice was suddenly serious, "a million miles away." He glanced at her and their eyes held for a moment too long.

He grinned, trying to break the tension. "So since you can't be around, the shop would probably go bust in a week. You're the only one who ever liked my omelettes."

She opened her mouth, teasingly astonished. "Jake! You mean you cooked omelettes for someone other than me? Shame on you!"

"I know." He grinned. "The ultimate betrayal."

"That's right. Don't forget it, either."

They laughed, and Ellen savored how comfortable they were together. He excused himself and slipped a Christopher Cross CD into the player. Music filled the house through an intricate sound system, and Ellen smiled. They had both enjoyed Christopher Cross years ago and she remembered listening to his songs between movies at the drive-in theater. The atmosphere was soothing and she felt herself relax.

Ellen ate her omelette slowly, remembering dozens of times when she and Jake had done this before. It was a simple thing, really. Eating omelettes in the waning afternoon sunlight, sitting side by side alone in his house, listening to Christopher Cross. But it took her back, made her keenly aware of him and the fact that they were alone.

What did you expect? she chastised herself. She didn't even try to answer that. She was afraid to do so. When they were finished they washed dishes together and put away food. Their conversation was light and when their elbows touched on occasion as they worked, they pretended not to notice.

"I'm stuffed." Jake stretched.

"Me too." She focused her attention on the pan she was drying. "You forget how filling an omelette can be. Especially if it's been created by the master omelette maker himself." She grinned at him.

When the kitchen was clean they went out back onto the partially covered wooden deck. The sun would set in a few hours and Ellen gazed thoughtfully across the bay toward Petoskey. A gentle breeze flowed across the water and the sky was free of clouds, a vast expanse of vivid blue.

Ellen walked to the edge of the deck and leaned against the railing, studying the sandy beach below. "You're right on the sand."

Jake moved up beside her and leaned against the railing. "Hmm. I guess I always did have a thing for the beach."

Ellen smiled, enjoying the easy sense of camaraderie they shared. It used to be like this with Mike. They used to share long, lovely days just being together, enjoying each other. She stared across the water and studied the distant shoreline. She could make out Petoskey State Park and Magnus Park. She could even see the pier at Bayfront with its dozens of sailboats and yachts, the flags that flew year round, and the beautifully kept softball fields. After a while she wandered toward a porch swing and sat down.

She looked at Jake and patted the empty spot beside her. He sauntered in her direction and sat down, careful not to brush his legs against hers. She was silently thankful. Her resolve was vanishing at an alarming rate and any contact with him was bound to make things worse. As if he could sense her feelings, he moved casually toward the outside of the swing, allowing a comfortable distance between them.

"Dad always wanted a house like this," Ellen said. She set the swing gently in motion. "On weekends we'd come look at these houses, and he'd talk about starting a business with his computer." She looked at Jake. "There was always a reason why that business never got started, always something in the way."

Jake sat there, watching her, listening.

"When I was little I thought my dad was the best man in the world, the most fun, the strongest. He could do anything he set his mind to. The whole nine yards."

Jake looked intently into her eyes. "And now?"

"I'm not sure."

He looked puzzled and she shook her head quickly.

"Don't get me wrong. No one could ever take his place. But when I grew up I saw a clearer picture of him. I don't know, maybe it's only gotten clearer since his death. I think about his dreams and intentions, the times he was going to stop smoking, start a diet."

Her eyes narrowed, seeing a thousand missed opportunities, and suddenly she felt the tears building. "You know what he said when he came out of heart surgery last year? He said he was through making excuses. Through procrastinating. He was going to be a new man, whatever it took."

Jake's face filled with compassion. "It didn't happen."

"No." She shook her head sadly, a single tear spilling from each eye onto her cheeks. "He wasn't strong enough."

"That bothers you?"

"Yes." She raised her voice. "I thought the world of him, Jake. But in reality he was just like anyone else. Just a man struggling to follow through with his intentions and failing in the end."

The swing had slowed and she set it in motion again.

"Are you mad at him?" Jake's voice was barely a whisper.

"That's hard." Ellen gazed thoughtfully at the sky. The sun was beginning to set, blazing a brilliant trail of pinks and oranges as it disappeared. She looked at Jake again. "I guess I am, in some ways. He could have had a house like this, a yard like this. He could have started the business and made it fly, and when he had to go through emergency bypass surgery it could have been a turning point in his life. He had the chances, Jake, but he didn't take them. He wasn't strong enough. That's what kills me."

She spread her fingers on her chest. "In here, where the little girl I used to be still lives, I know he could have done it. I guess a part of me thinks he didn't try. He gave up and sold us short." Her voice cracked and she stopped swinging. Then slowly, she dropped her elbows to her knees and buried her face in her hands.

"Why, Jake? Why didn't he at least try?"

Jake reached over and rested his hand on her shoulder. His fingers made soothing circles just beneath her neck. "I'm sure he tried. At least give him that."

"Not hard enough." She looked up, knowing she must look blotchy and tearstained and not caring. "What's a pack of cigarettes compared to us? What's a cheeseburger or a bag of fries compared to your family? I mean, how hard could it be to give up that stuff when the alternative meant dying young, leaving us alone?"

"Ellen, come on. You're not being fair. If it was that easy, heart disease wouldn't be the killer it is today. You know that."

She slumped over her knees, her face in her hands again. "I know."

Taking deep breaths, she worked to calm herself down. She wiped her eyes with her fingertips. Jake's arm was still on her shoulder, but when she sat up he removed it.

"Was he always like that?" Her voice was tired. "Weak, unable to follow through with things?"

"You tell me, Ellen."

She thought a moment. "He worked three jobs to keep food on the table when we were little. And every Christmas there were so many toys under our tree it looked like something out of a fairy tale."

Jake nodded. "He put you through college, didn't he?"

"I paid for my books with tips from the restaurant. But he paid for everything else." Ellen grew quiet. "And he sent me to Canada for a vacation after I graduated."

"He wasn't weak, Ellen. He just had some nasty habits, habits that were too hard to break."

"Habits that killed him." Ellen wiped at several fresh tears forging a new trail down her cheeks. "I loved him so much, Jake. Now that he's gone nothing makes sense. My whole world is falling apart."

She began to sob again, squeezing her eyes tight as if she could shut out the pain. She felt his arm go around her.

"I know." His voice was deep and filled with understanding.

Ellen opened her eyes and gazed at the sky, but her tears kept coming. The blurred pinks and oranges were fading to dark now and the moon appeared in the distance, a shiny sliver in the sky. Time passed and still they sat that way, Jake with his arm around her while she cried for her father. Gradually her tears slowed and then finally stopped. She lifted her head and remained silent, allowing the breeze to dry her face and clear her eyes.

"You okay?" Jake broke the silence first. He took his arm off her shoulder and turned to face her.

She gulped, searching for her voice and nodded. "I have to let him go. I guess this is just the beginning."

Jake smiled tenderly. "It wouldn't hurt so much if he hadn't been such a great man. Do you see that now?"

"I never doubted that." She stared at him thoughtfully. "I only wondered if the man I admired wasn't perhaps some wonderful figment of my imagination, someone who never really existed at all."

"He existed, Ellen. I can see him in your sorrow, in my own memories. Believe me. He existed."

Ellen smiled self-consciously and released a short laugh as she pushed her hair back from her face. "I must look awful."

Jake wiped his thumb just below her right eye where her mascara must have run. "No, Ellen. You've never looked more beautiful."

Ellen laughed again and sniffed. "Right."

Jake studied her a moment longer, then his face lit up. "Hey, you haven't seen the hot tub."

Ellen rose slowly from the swing, stretching her back and taking a deep breath. "Lead the way."

He moved easily down a circular redwood stairway off one end of the deck. At the bottom of the stairs, toward the left side of his house, there was a neatly manicured lawn that butted up against the sand. The hot tub was centered on a grassy knoll in the middle of the lawn. It had a spectacular view of the bay. Ellen saw that it was easily large enough for six people. Three sides were covered with redwood lattice that lent intimate privacy but did not block the view.

Jake lifted the edge of the tub's cover and steam released into the cool night air.

Ellen whistled appreciatively. "Looks good."

Jake raised an eyebrow. "Wanna go in?"

She shouldn't. She knew she shouldn't. Not alone with Jake, not as vulnerable as she was feeling right now. Instead she should ask Jake to take her home before she forgot why it was important to do so.

Jake was waiting. She shook her head. "I don't have a suit."

"Ah, come on, Ellen. I have a spare lying around somewhere."

Ellen tilted her head and gave Jake a sad, knowing look. She thought about her conversation with Leslie, her argument with Mike. And about her father's Bible. She saw his words in her mind again: "Hold fast to your faith. Temptation is a given; look for the way out! It is possible to fall!"

When she spoke, her words were little more than a choked whisper. "I can't, Jake."

Ellen watched him and knew he understood. He reached for her hand. "Okay. No hot tub. Let's go back up and watch the lights." He smiled softly at her. "There's one spot along the deck that has the most incredible view."

Ellen exhaled softly and allowed Jake to lead her back up the stairs. As they walked, she thought about sitting beside Jake, watching the dazzling lights of Petoskey across Little Traverse Bay while hot water swirled around them. She shivered. That was close. Thank you, Lord.

When they reached the top of the stairs, Jake directed her to an alcove with a cozy wooden bench. The railing dipped along that part of the deck so that the view of the bay was unobstructed. They sat down together, gazing out at the water.

"Beautiful." Ellen's eyes narrowed as she took in the distant lights and the bay as it shimmered under the glow of the moon. They sat there in comfortable silence, eventually leaning back and taking in the stars as well. Ellen closed her eyes and felt the tension melt away.

She grew vaguely aware of something…something that bothered her. A strange *buzzing* sound. Opening her eyes, she looked down to see a bumble bee making its way up her shoulder, toward her back. She screamed and batted at the insect, knocking it off her arm—but not before it stung her.

"Owww!" She jumped to her feet, glancing about, making sure the insect was gone.

Jake was up and at her side instantly. He took her arm gently and examined the red welt that had already appeared. He frowned, concerned. "Looks like he got you."

Ellen winced. "I know. I can feel it." She furrowed her brow and strained to see the sting. "Can you see a stinger?"

Jake moved closer and examined the raised area. They stood toe-to-toe, a breeze from the bay swaying about them, separated only by a thin veil of night air. "It's hard to see in this light." He ran a finger over the sting. "Wait. I think I feel it." His face was inches from hers. He gently pulled the tiny stinger loose and examined it. "There. I think I got it all."

"Ooo. It hurts." Ellen strained once more to see the welt.

"Sometimes if you rub it real good it doesn't hurt so bad." He still held her arm with one hand, and with the other he rubbed his fingers firmly over the sore area. "Is that better?" He looked up and their eyes locked.

The mood changed instantly and the air around them seemed suddenly charged with electricity. The familiarity of the moment, the impossibility of it, enveloped them. Almost of its own accord, Ellen's arm went up and around Jake's neck and he pulled her imperceptibly closer.

They were twenty years old again, crazy in love and aware of no one but each other. Their gazes locked, their faces inches apart. Then even that distance disappeared until it seemed to Ellen that the only thing she'd ever wanted to do was give in to the desire that had grown between them that week.

Ellen's breath rasped in her throat; her pulse pounded so she was sure Jake could hear it. *Just once. I'll kiss him and then let him go. Just once.*

But even as she tried to justify her intentions she knew she was lying to herself. If she kissed him now, it wouldn't stop there. If she became involved with Jake Sadler after so many years, there would be no turning back. No marriage to go back to. No faith to restore.

Once again, a verse drifted into her thoughts: "The wise woman builds her house, but with her own hands the foolish one tears hers down."

Ellen felt as though she'd been hit in the chest. Hard. She struggled to breathe, to move, but she couldn't.

It was Jake who came to his senses first.

His cheek brushed hers as he drew close, pausing with his mouth near her lips, taking her breath away. Then, ever so tenderly, he kissed her forehead instead.

"I don't know why," he whispered. "But I can't."

Slowly, Ellen lowered her head and let it rest on his chest. She was trembling from both desire and shame. She knew why Jake couldn't kiss her. After Leslie's prayer, God simply wouldn't let him. And, as though a voice was speaking in her head, in her heart, she heard: "He will not let you be tempted beyond what you can bear, but when tempted he will also provide a way out." She closed her eyes, feeling desperate. *What if I don't want a way out, Lord? Please, please show me. I can't do this on my own. I can't walk away from this—*

Jake's voice interrupted her thoughts. "If you weren't married…" Each word was an effort and she could see he was fighting with himself. "I'd do everything I could to make you mine, Ellen."

He pulled her close, resting his chin on the top of her head. Then he pulled away, his eyes filled with regret. "But not like this. "

Only when she exhaled did she realize she'd been holding her breath, waiting, afraid of what would—or wouldn't—happen. She remembered a hundred times when they had given in to these very feelings. But not now. Not when it could only bring them pain. All of them.

"I was thinking no one would know but us," she whispered, ashamed but needing to be honest with him.

His hold on her tightened. "No one else would need to know." He drew a shaky breath. "Because we would never, ever forget."

She nodded then, knowing what he meant. "A day wouldn't go by when I wouldn't remember. Wonder. Want you."

"Me, too." He took one hand away and tenderly brushed a lock of wispy hair off her face. "I couldn't live like that, Ellen. And neither could you."

He let her go and framed her face with his fingertips, studying her intently, as though memorizing her features. "I love you. I loved you before Mike, and I love you still. But you belong to him; he was better for you than I was. He treated you like I only wish I'd treated you when I had the right. But I lost that right. And you still love him. You told me so yourself."

She nodded, savoring the feel of his fingers against her face and remembering the first time he had done that on a park bench near his parents' home, the first time he had kissed her. She knew she should pull away, but there was one more thing she needed to ask him. She covered his hands with hers.

"What if I had waited for you? If Mike and I had never met?"

Jake's eyes grew moist. "I've asked myself the same question dozens of times, and I always come up with the same answer." He shook his head. "I don't think it would have worked, Ellen." He looked as though his heart might break. "I think maybe it took losing you for me to see what kind of man I was becoming, for me to change."

She nodded and lowered her hands slowly, staring down so he wouldn't see her cry. He pulled her head to his chest again and stroked her hair as her tears spilled onto his canvas tennis shoes.

Jesus, I wish I was stronger. I wish I could just walk away. But it's so hard! It hurts so much. All I want is to be loved, Lord. Like Mike used to love me, like Jake loves me now.… Is that so wrong?

This time the answer was swift, and it pierced her to the depths of her heart: "I have loved you with an everlasting love. I have drawn you with loving-kindness. I will build you up again and you will be rebuilt.... I will lead you beside streams of water, on a level path where you will not stumble, because I am your father."

The tears started afresh then, and she felt as though her heart was breaking. She'd been looking to Mike to love her.

And her father. And, yes, to Jake. But the only one who could fill the void inside her was the very one she'd been turning away from.

Forgive me...forgive me...

After a while Ellen's sobs lessened, and she sniffed, wiping her eyes and raising her gaze to Jake's. "So, Bucko, where do we go from here?" She already knew the answer to that, but she needed to hear it from him.

"We do the only thing we can," he said. Gently he pulled himself away, separating their bodies. He let his arms drop to his side and he took a step back.

"I'm listening."

"We see each other in a few days at your dad's funeral, and then we go our separate ways."

There was silence for a long moment.

"You mean we say good-bye." The idea of losing Jake now after finding him again and seeing how he had changed, cut deep. But she knew he was right. She wondered how much pain a person could take in a single week.

Jake moved further away and stared across the bay at the glittering carpet of lights in Petoskey. "Yes," he said, looking at her once more. "We say good-bye."

The tears came again and neither of them could talk. When she could trust her voice, she searched his eyes.

"I'm not sorry I called you."

Jake didn't say anything. He didn't have to. His eyes said it all.

She went on. "No one else understood what I was going through this week. Not even Mike."

"I'll never be sorry you called."

"When I remember the happy times, the years when my father was well and the rest of my family got along together, I see you, too, Jake. Being with you this week, talking with you, brought those memories back. Made them alive again. Made Dad alive again."

"For me, too."

She paused and stared out at the bay. Then slowly, she lowered herself back onto the bench. Jake watched and joined her, allowing a distance between them.

"Don't forget me, huh, Jake?" She tilted her head back toward him, took his hand in hers and allowed herself to be lost in his eyes once more.

"Ellen." Her name seemed like it was born on his lips and she could see he was still struggling to maintain his distance. "I never have," he whispered, his tears brimming, ready to spill. "I never could."

Ellen nodded and the impossibilities hung in the air a moment longer. Then she sniffed and released his hand. "Take me home, okay?"

Without saying a word they stood and returned to the house. Twenty minutes later they pulled up in front of Ellen's parents' house.

"I guess this is it." She stared at her hands folded tightly in her lap.

"No, I'll be at the service. I promised you and I'll be there."

She nodded quickly and gulped back a sob. "But it'll be different."

He leaned over and pulled her to him, hugging her one final time before letting her go. "I do love you, Ellen. Now go home and make the best of things between you and Mike. Don't cheat yourself of that because of what happened between us this week."

She nodded and, summoning every ounce of resolve, pulled away from him. "Good-bye, Jake," she whispered. She touched his face once more and then slid out of his truck. She closed the door and without looking back she walked away.

In that instant she knew with all her heart that God was still there for her, still listening. That night he had answered a prayer she had whispered nine years earlier. Because now, after seeing Jake again and knowing how he felt about her, only an act of God could have kept her from giving up everything and staying here in Petoskey with Jake Sadler.

26

$\mathcal{F}$amily members began arriving at the Barrett home early Friday morning, and the long week leading up to the funeral came to a sudden end. There were Mom's three sisters and one brother and their families, and Dad's sister from California with her children and grandchildren. Dad's parents had died years earlier, but Mom's aging parents arrived with one of her sisters. After that there were other cousins, aunts, uncles, all arriving, all talking.

Family members flowed through the house, many of them with tearstained eyes. The house was full of living reminders, of testimonies to how much John Barrett was loved, how much he'd be missed.

As planned, Ellen and her siblings were dressed and gathered at their parents' house by ten that morning, prepared to greet out-of-town relatives and help their mother with last-minute details. There were casserole dishes to receive, flowers to arrange, and conversations to take part in.

Uncle Jess, Mom's only brother, arrived with his wife, Betsy, and their six children. They lived in Grand Rapids, four hours south, and would spend the night at a local motel. They planned to be at the viewing later that night but had stopped at the Barrett home as soon as they got into town.

Dressed in a straight gray dress and gray pumps, Ellen watched the relatives arrive, but it all seemed unreal. She still ached from the night before, feeling almost as bad as she had nine years earlier when she and Jake had broken up that last time. But now that Friday had finally come, Jake was no longer first on her mind. Somehow, with the arrival of relatives, her father's death was indeed more real. They were gathered for one reason alone. John Barrett had died and it was time to say good-bye.

Ellen looked around the room, thankful that Troy had arrived from his convention in time to distract Jane. The two sat together at the dining room table, and for the first time that week Ellen didn't feel under attack. The children were quiet, watching a Disney video in the den and enjoying the company of Uncle Jess's little ones.

Across the room, Aaron filled up the living room chair, assuming John Barrett's place in the family's unspoken seating schematic. He was dressed in slacks and a slick white shirt with a subdued silk tie. He wore the dark sunglasses again and sat motionless, his arms crossed in front of him. Well-meaning relatives stayed clear of him, and Ellen knew that was what Aaron intended. The glasses hid his eyes but not the fact that he, too, was hurting.

Megan looked stunning in a navy skirt and sleeveless jacket, her hair pulled back conservatively. She sat on the couch beside Ellen, with Amy and Frank on her other side. They were somber, lost in their private worlds of grief and the inevitability of the approaching funeral.

Mom remained standing, greeting her siblings. She wore a black wraparound with pearl accents. It was a dress she had worn for her and Dad's thirtieth wedding anniversary and Ellen wondered if anyone would remember.

"Diane, how are you? Really?" Uncle Jess hovered over her. He was a large man with lumberjack hands and he had always reminded Ellen of Aaron. Her uncle spoke in hushed tones. His eyes were damp as he took their mother in his arms.

"It all happened so fast," she said.

"I know, I know." He rubbed her shoulder. "What was it? Just last month we were up for that beach party at Petoskey State Park?"

Mom nodded, too emotional to speak. All week she'd held up so well, but now, looking into the eyes of her relatives, the sorrow seemed about to consume her.

"Ellen, Megan." Uncle Jess turned and nodded his greeting to the girls. He looked at the others then, one at a time. "I'm sorry about your father. He was a great man, one of a kind." His voice rang with sincerity. "One thing I'll always remember about your family—" he looked from Jane to Aaron and around the room to the others—"you really loved each other. Not because you had to, but because you liked each other. That was really special. Somehow I think your dad had a lot to do with that."

For a brief instant Jane's eyes met Ellen's, but both turned away. Uncle Jess looked to Mom again and hooked arms with her. He led her out of the room as they continued talking.

The air was heavy as Uncle Jess's words rattled around the room.

"He doesn't know us very well, does he?" Megan muttered. She crossed her arms in front of her and stared at the floor.

Jane sighed and pretended to doodle invisible designs on the tablecloth. Ellen clucked her tongue softly and fiddled with her fingernails. Amy and Aaron stared into space, apparently intent on ignoring the uncomfortable currents in the room.

The doorbell rang, and it was Aunt Betsy and her family from California. Their plane had arrived the day before at Detroit Metropolitan Airport and they had rented a car. They planned to stay several nights after the funeral so that Mom would not be alone once the others left.

Aunt Betsy was crying as Megan welcomed them inside.

"I'm so sorry about your dad." She hugged Megan and turned to the others. "It's hard to believe he's gone. He was so…" She searched for the right word, struggling with her emotions. "I don't know, so full of life."

Aunt Betsy sat down, joining the circle of siblings. Amy asked her about her flight.

"It was fine, not that I noticed." She wiped her tears daintily with her fingers. "I thought about your family the whole time. The trips to the lake, the ice-skating and football games. You kids have always been so close, such a great family." She paused a minute. "Me and your uncle, we divorced years ago, you know. The two kids went their own way and well, I guess we never were much of a family really. But you guys—" she looked at them—"you guys had something really special. Whenever I think of how a family is supposed to be, how the kids should be close and the parents should love each other, I think of you." She wiped her eyes again and pulled a tissue from her purse.

"My brother must have been awfully proud of the family he raised. I'm so sorry he's gone." She looked at them, her eyes making a circle around the room. "At least you still have each other. No one can take that away from you."

She stood up then, dabbing at her face as she went to search for their mother.

Ellen squirmed uncomfortably in her chair, as did Jane and Megan. Was that really how others saw them? A close-knit, loving family? Apparently so, for that same sentiment was expressed continually for the next two hours as people stopped to visit and then returned to their various motel rooms to prepare for the viewing.

How fortunate Ellen and the others were, they would say, raised in a family where love had no limits. How close their relationships with one another were compared with other families…how blessed they were to have each other.

Silently, Ellen was struck by the irony. She exchanged furtive glances with her siblings and saw by their faces they were feeling the same thing. *When did we change so much, Lord? Or were we ever really the family everyone else remembers?*

Finally it was two o'clock and the house cleared as relatives left to ready themselves for the evening viewing. Diane Barrett waited until only her children and their spouses remained before addressing them.

"I'm going to the mortuary now so that I'll have a few minutes alone," she said. She only hoped she had the strength to endure what was coming.

"Are you sure you should go by yourself?" Megan looked concerned.

"Yes. I'll be fine. I'd like you children to join me in a little while." She looked at Jane. "The kids are taken care of for the evening, right?"

Jane nodded. "A friend of mine is keeping them until late tonight."

"Good. Well, I'm sure I'll see you there within the hour. I'll take the small car. Ellen, why don't you drive the van."

Diane looked at the stiff way her children sat together and she was struck, again, by the fact that they were clearly not the family they had once been.

"I know you haven't gotten along this week and I think that's to be expected. We're all under a great deal of stress." She searched their faces, pleading with them.

"But please, for your father's sake, try to be a family tonight and tomorrow. It would have made him so sad to see you like this."

Her request met with utter silence and finally, with tears welling up in her eyes, Diane picked up her purse and left.

27

Well, that was nice. You guys are really something," Aaron sneered at his sisters. "All Mom wants is a little reassurance that everyone can get along these next few days and no one says a word."

Ellen raised an eyebrow. "Don't look at me, Aaron. I've done everything possible to get along this week."

"Oh, so I guess that makes me the bad guy," Jane piped in. Troy put his hand over hers and squeezed gently. They exchanged a knowing look and Jane seemed to lose interest in the argument.

"Why'd you have to start a fight, Aaron?" Amy's eyebrows creased in frustration. "Everything was fine until you opened your mouth."

"Look, you little witch…" Aaron rose from his chair and towered over Amy. Ellen watched as Frank pretended to read a magazine, but she saw how he sat a little straighter, moving closer to his wife and keeping an eye on her brother.

"You girls are the ones fighting this week," Aaron shouted. "I haven't said a word."

"Well, you also haven't done a thing to help Mom. So don't blame us for getting her upset." Obviously Amy was not in the mood to back down. "I guess you think the girls will do everything just like we always have, right?"

"You want me to do something, Amy?" Aaron's voice boomed as he took giant strides toward the kitchen. "Fine!" He picked up a dish and threw it into the sink, shattering it into a hundred pieces. "I'll do the dishes."

Ellen cringed.

"Here's another one." He smashed a second dish against the sink.

Then suddenly he stopped his tantrum and stormed out of the kitchen. He grabbed his truck keys and slammed the front door behind him.

"Same old Aaron," Ellen mumbled.

"You know, Ellen, why don't you lighten up?" Jane glared at her sister. "All week you've been feeling sorry for yourself, wishing you didn't have to be around the rest of us." She stood up, ignoring Troy's efforts to stop her. "Things start to seem a little tense around here and what do you do? Run off and spend time with your *friends*."

Megan raised an eyebrow and stared at Ellen accusingly.

"Did you ever stop and think that maybe there's a reason why the rest of us are so edgy? Maybe Aaron's life isn't as good and golden as yours. And maybe my memories of Dad aren't straight from a storybook like the ones you have. Did you ever think of that?"

Ellen crossed her arms tightly and stared back at Jane. "I don't need to listen to this." She started to get up but Jane blocked her way.

"No. Don't leave. Not this time." Jane put her hands on her hips, her face flushed with the intensity of her anger. "Did you ever think that maybe there's a reason why Amy's so quiet and Megan's so sentimental? Did it occur to you that maybe there's a reason why Dad's funeral has me so edgy? Or that there just might be an explanation for Aaron's anger?"

Ellen stood staring at her sister, waiting impatiently for her to finish her tirade.

"Let me say this, Ellen. If there was a reason, you sure wouldn't know it. Because all you care about is yourself. Is Ellen having a good time? Is everyone being nice to Ellen? Is Mike doing what Ellen wants him to do?"

Ellen sucked in her breath at the mention of Mike. She hoped Megan didn't notice. "That's not true. I care about everyone here and you know it."

"You care about us if everything's going good and we're all happy-go-lucky. But when there's a problem, you split. That's what you've been doing all week."

Amy shifted uneasily and reached for Frank's hand. Jane's anger seemed to fade suddenly, and Ellen was surprised to see her eyes fill with tears.

"We're here for one week together, Ellen, and I'm sorry if I haven't been very nice. But you're so caught up in yourself you can't even see the way the rest of us are hurting."

Ellen's eyes stung with tears at the accusation. "That's not fair. I'm hurting, too, you know. I don't remember anyone asking me how I was doing."

"I asked you," Megan said quietly.

Jane's tears came harder now and she looked from Megan back to Ellen. "When we were younger we were like best friends. I still think of you that way. But what kind of friend are you when you don't even ask me what's wrong? I have things I'm dealing with this week that you know nothing about."

"Is it my fault you don't tell me what's wrong?" Ellen cried.

"Yes! I thought you were my friend, Ellen. I know I haven't been very nice to you, but did you even once think that something might be bothering me?"

Ellen released a burst of air, frustrated by Jane's summation of the week-long struggle between them. "If you want me to be interested in your feelings then think of mine for a change." Ellen maneuvered past Jane and found her bag. "You've been hateful toward me since we got here. Now you expect me to pretend that didn't happen, paste a sympathetic smile on my face, and ask you how you've been? Well, you can forget it, Jane." She looked at the others. "I'll be at the mortuary." Then she stormed out the front door.

⌾

The room fell suddenly silent as Jane stared at the door Ellen had just slammed. She'd tried. She really had. And look where it had gotten her.

She swore under her breath. But instead of sounding angry, it just sounded desperate. She felt a hand on her arm and turned to see Troy standing there, his eyes filled with understanding.

She turned to him and buried her head in his chest, finally sobbing as she hadn't all week.

28

Ellen drove to the mortuary like a woman on a mission. She was determined not to let Jane's outburst affect her. She cared about Jane; the others had to see that. But it was impossible to be interested in the problems of a person who spent so much time on the attack. Ellen thought about Jane's statement and wondered vaguely what had been troubling her that week. But she refused to play games. If Jane wanted to talk then she would have to make the first move.

As she drove, images from the past week demanded her attention and suddenly she could no longer shut them out—she and Jake making omelettes…she and Jake at the beach, on the swing. She could feel his fingers entwined with hers.

She slammed her fist onto the steering wheel and the images disappeared. Five minutes later she was at the mortuary. The public parking lot was empty except for her mother's car and Ellen parked alongside it, cutting the engine.

The truth hit her then. In a moment she would come face-to-face with her dead father's body. How many times had she walked into her parents' home, rounded the corner toward the den, and seen him sitting in his easy chair? How many times had he looked up, noticed her, and burst into a smile, stretching his left hand toward her?

"Hi, honey," he'd say. "Come sit down."

She would walk toward him, tucking her hand in his warm one and bending to kiss him on his cheek. Somewhere through the passing of the days, he had greeted her that way for the last time. And she hadn't even known it.

She leaned back in the van, sitting in the seat that had been his alone, and closed her eyes. If only she could remember the last time he had done that so she could savor the moment forever. She wanted something real and alive to remember him by. Otherwise the lifeless body she was about to see would be her final memory of him. She drew in a deep breath and steadied herself. Then she climbed out of the van and headed for the mortuary.

It was quiet inside; the lights reverently dim. Ellen moved through the lobby and entered a narrow doorway leading to the front of a small chapel. Twelve wooden pews lined the room on either side of a center aisle. Ellen glanced to her right and saw the oak casket they had chosen the day before. It was propped open, and her mother knelt before it on a padded kneeler, her head bowed, lips moving in silent prayer.

Ellen headed soundlessly toward her mother. She refused to look at her father's body until the last possible minute.

"Hi, Mom." She put her arm around the older woman and knelt beside her. Then she turned toward the casket and felt her breath catch in her throat.

There he was. Hands folded peacefully over his considerable abdomen, graying blond hair neatly combed. His suit was pressed and starched, the shoes shined. She stared at him and felt herself about to collapse.

Her mother looked up then and studied him, too.

"He's at peace now," she said. Her voice was calm but tears spilled down her face and her eyes searched her husband's still face.

Ellen nodded, unsure what to say. She was horrified by the sight of her father like that and needed a moment to grasp what she was seeing.

Her mom struggled to her feet. "I'm going to go make a few phone calls," she whispered. "Will you be all right?"

Ellen nodded quickly, thankful for the chance to be alone. When her mother was gone she tentatively reached toward her father's hand and touched him.

He was cold and stiff, and she recoiled as if she'd pricked her finger on a needle. She narrowed her eyes, studying the face, the body that once housed her father.

His skin was pale, dusty from the makeup they'd used. It wasn't how she remembered him, and she thought how different a body looked when there was someone living inside.

She studied his eyes, closed for all time.

If only he could open them once more, smile at her the way he had all his life. She had the urge to nudge him, to wake him up and help him out of the satin-lined box so that everyone could see he was all right. Her eyes moved slowly up the lid of the casket and she shuddered thinking of the moment when they would close it, shutting him in darkness for eternity.

Get up, Dad.

But he remained motionless, nothing but a shell of the man he had been. She wanted to talk to him, to say something she might have said if he were alive and only sleeping.

"Dad," she whispered as tears sprang to her eyes. "I love you."

She had brought something for this moment. Reaching into her purse she wrapped her fingers around them, familiar with the way they felt. She opened her hands and tried to make out the items through eyes blurred with tears. There they were… she could see them clearly now. A worn white handkerchief and a plain black comb.

She had visited her parents a year earlier when her father was hospitalized with chest pain. Deeply concerned, she accompanied her mother to the operating room where doctors performed the final test to determine the cause of his discomfort.

When they saw the gravity of his condition, they quickly decided to perform emergency triple-bypass surgery.

Ellen had been devastated, certain he wouldn't survive the surgery. But the urgency of the situation left them no time for lengthy good-byes. Instead, just before they wheeled him into surgery, he took his handkerchief and black comb from his hospital table and folded them into the palm of her hand.

"Hold these for me, Ellen." His lower lip quivered slightly and his voice was choked with emotion. "I'll be back for them. I promise."

She had nodded and clutched them purposefully. For three hours, while doctors searched for the perfect vein in his leg with which to replace the arteries leading to his heart, she kept his handkerchief and comb in her hand, praying he would survive.

Three months later she was going through the nightstand next to her bed when she found the comb tucked inside the neatly folded handkerchief. After that she looked at them now and then, running her fingers over the threadbare cloth and remembering how thankful she had been when he had come out of the operation alive.

They were the first items she packed as she prepared to come to Petoskey to bury him.

Gradually, relentlessly, sorrow welled up in her chest as she held the handkerchief to her cheek and closed her eyes. Tears spilled onto her face and she surrendered as deep, gut-wrenching sobs exploded from the center of her being.

She cried for every single distant memory, moments she would have given anything to have again. Scenes from the past flashed through her mind and she grieved for each of them, crying for the little girl she had left behind and the father who would never again take her hand or swing her around the backyard.

She stared at him, thinking of the football games when he patiently taught her the difference between the quarterback and defensive back. And the times when he had listened to her read her game stories over the telephone so he could catch her mistakes before her editors did.

She sobbed harder and reached toward him once more. She knew what to expect this time and she didn't pull away. Instead, she ran her fingers gently over his hands, remembering the way those same hands had loved her and her sisters and brother through the years. The hugs and hand-holds, the ball-tossing and shoe-tying…hands that had been loving and warm, gentle and strong.

"Dad, I wish we had more time," she whispered. The sobbing finally slowed but the tears continued, as did the empty ache in the depth of her heart.

Suddenly she couldn't stand to see him that way a moment longer and she closed her eyes. Why was she doing this to herself, participating in a ritual that meant nothing? He wasn't there, resting in a casket. He had moved on to a better place, the place for people who have loved God and done his work on earth. She knew the Lord was watching over her that very moment, wishing he could comfort her, willing her to know that her father was all right.

She opened her eyes and looked into the coffin again. Dad's body would be buried there, but not his soul, his heart. No one could bury that.

She clutched the handkerchief and comb tightly, holding them to her face a final time. Then she gently tucked them under his hands.

"Dad," her voice was choked with tears. "I have to give them back now. I...I can't hold them anymore."

She hung her head and cried again, knowing that Jake had been right. For the first time, her dad's death seemed real. She looked at him once more, still, lifeless.

"Daddy," she cried softly. "You were the best. You believed in me...encouraged me, cheered me on. You were always there for me. Even when I was wrong you never let me down." She was quiet a moment, tears streaming down her face. "I love you so much."

She gazed toward the heavens then, her voice barely a whisper. "I love you, Daddy."

The sadness was like a lead weight as she stood up and moved to the back of the chapel. She had said good-bye. She found a seat near the back of the chapel and sat down to wait for the others.

The remaining adult Barrett children arrived within five minutes of each other and met in the parking lot. Aaron did not say where he had disappeared to earlier, but he was outspoken as they gathered near their parked cars and prepared to enter the mortuary.

"I don't know what problems you all have between you," he said waving his hand at Megan, Jane, and Amy. He stared at Jane, who stood quietly by Troy. "I know there's something going on between you and Ellen, but I don't want to hear the details or whose fault it is. Right now it's time to put our differences behind us. All of us. Dad would never have wanted us fighting right up until the moment of his funeral."

He looked at each of them slowly. "I want you to listen because I don't say a lot, and this is the way it's got to be. If you have a problem, hide it. In two days we'll all go our separate ways and you can think whatever bad things you want about this family. Right now, though, we're in this together."

Jane looked stunned. "Fine," she mumbled. "It's just two days. I can pretend with the best of them."

"Fine." Aaron was satisfied. "Now let's get in there. Mom's waiting."

Ellen watched in silence as her brother and sisters came into the room. She continued watching as, for the next two hours, they took turns kneeling by their father's casket, staring at his body, and reckoning with the fact that he no longer lived there. When Megan took her turn bidding their father good-bye, she cried much the way Ellen had. *Probably regretting the lost years with Mohammed,* Ellen reasoned.

Amy's grieving was quieter, more reserved. She seemed awestruck by her father in death, much as she had been when he was alive. She didn't fully give way to her grief until she had risen from the spot near the casket and returned to the pew where Frank sat. He stood, holding his hands out toward her, and she collapsed against him, sobbing.

Ellen remained at the back of the chapel where Megan and Amy approached her at different times to see if she was all right. For a time, her mother came and sat next to her, but then as the others seemed to take turns grieving she tried to make herself available for them, too.

Jane never even looked Ellen's way. She did spend a short time kneeling near Dad's casket before returning to sit with Troy for the remainder of the viewing. As the evening went on, Ellen couldn't help but notice that Jane appeared neither concerned for the others nor anxious for their comfort. She was the only one who did not cry.

Aaron was the last to approach the casket and he did so reluctantly. He wore his sunglasses and his tall frame looked uncomfortable as he knelt before his father's body.

Ellen watched from a distance, and although Aaron neither moved a muscle nor spoke a word, she knew his pain. Not because of anything obvious about the way he grieved for his father. But because of the angle at which she was sitting. He had his back to the others, but she could see his face, the dark glasses. And the steady stream of tears that ran from beneath them the entire time he remained on his knees.

At five-thirty the first of the relatives began to arrive and the Barrett siblings found their separate places in the chapel from which to watch and remember. It was a quiet time and within two hours everyone but Ellen, her siblings, and her mother had left for the night.

"Mrs. Barrett, it's time to seal the casket." It was the director, Mr. Whitson.

Mom had been talking quietly to Amy and Frank and she seemed startled by his statement. "Oh. Of course." She stood up and looked at the others.

"You can join me if you want," she said in a voice loud enough for them all to hear. She positioned herself close to the casket and stared a final time at her husband's face. Ellen watched Megan rise and move to their mother's side. She placed an arm around Mom's waist for support. Aaron joined her, too, bracing Mom on her opposite side, while Amy and Frank joined hands and stood nearby. Ellen and Jane remained in their seats on different sides of the chapel.

"Good-bye, John." Mom's smile was tender through her tears. "You made me so happy."

Ellen rested her arms on the back of the pew in front of her and let her head drop. She couldn't watch, couldn't bear to see him disappear behind the closing lid of a coffin.

She heard them unhook the coffin lid and lower it. Then there was the sound of someone moving around the casket as they tightened a series of latches so that it was sealed.

There was nothing left to do but go home. They did so, each in a separate car, returning to the house to discuss the logistics for the following day, who would drive which vehicle, when they needed to be where.

Ellen found a quiet spot in the den where she studied the eulogy she had written earlier in the week. The others milled about the living room where they finished plans and shared a late snack. There was little conversation, and even from the next room Ellen could feel the cool way in which her siblings regarded each other.

She read her eulogy again and sighed. It still wasn't exactly what she wanted to say. She'd been inserting words and crossing out others for what seemed like hours. Finally, she set her pen aside.

Closing her eyes, she leaned her head back. She just couldn't handle this right now. The image of her father's lifeless face came to mind, and she pushed it aside. *Think of something else. Anything…*

Jake's laughing face came to her, and she felt the familiar pang. What was it about him that captured her so? She couldn't let him go no matter how she tried.

Help me, Lord, she prayed desperately as she considered the memories of her times with Jake over the last week. *Am I going to be haunted by him for the rest of my life?*

"This is a shadow of the things that are to come; the reality, however, is found in Christ."

Ellen frowned. Why had that verse come to her now of all times? What could it possibly mean? Jake? A shadow?

Dimly she heard the doorbell ring. Someone opened the front door and in the distance Ellen heard muffled conversation. She pushed the distraction away as she focused again on the images in her mind.

Jake on the beach…Jake holding her…Jake, Jake—

"Ellen." Megan poked her head around the corner and peered into the den.

"What?" Ellen looked up, startled. She felt completely drained.

"You have a visitor."

Ellen's throat constricted and sudden fear assailed her. Jake? Had he come to talk with her again? *Oh no, no, Lord. I won't be able to send him away again. Please—*

"Who?"

That's when she saw him. A man, standing there in the doorway to the room, looking rumpled and tired and still dressed in his work clothes.

For a moment she was sure it was Jake, and then the image faded, and Ellen stared, her face going hot, and then cold. Quick tears flooded her eyes.

"Mike."

29

Ellen stared at her husband in disbelief. He had come. He had found a way to be with her, and her heart soared.

Their eyes met and spoke volumes. She studied the unrestrained love in his eyes, the hope and apprehension on his face, and suddenly the Scripture was utterly clear. "This is a shadow of the things that are to come...." That was what Jake had been. A shadow. An image of something Ellen had convinced herself she wanted. Yes, he was real, but their relationship wasn't. Not the way she'd been thinking about it. All she and Jake had was a shadow.

She took in Mike's appearance, the dark circles under his eyes, the rumpled suit, the wedding band...he was the reality. The reality Ellen had found through Christ. For that's who had joined them. Forever. She remembered her anger of a week ago and felt ashamed. She had been wrong about Mike. Yes, he had botched things up, he had left her alone too many times to count and he seemed to have grown cold to all that mattered. But she, too, had let her faith go by the wayside.

Now, if only they could cling to the Lord as they had in their early days, perhaps the love they once shared would return. Perhaps they could survive after all. Ellen felt a peace come over her as she considered her husband. At least their life together was real. Not an idea or a dream or a shadow. They would have to talk about the future, the expectations on both sides. As in the early days of their marriage, they would need to pray together, find a church family where they could grow. But looking at her husband now she believed they would find a way to work it out.

Tears filled her eyes as she smiled at him, and in his face she saw the young sportscaster with whom she'd fallen in love. Mike had always been faithful beyond anything she'd ever dreamed. But in those early days there had been so much more love. Mike had supported her decisions and encouraged her writing career. He had taken time for walks on the beach and candlelit dinners at little-known restaurants. Back then he had written poetry for her and rubbed her back when she ached with tension from a day of deadlines. He never let her go alone to anything.

She saw him now and remembered their early days as if they were only weeks ago. She had never doubted back then that Mike was the man she belonged with. Theirs had been a wonderful relationship—intimate, satisfying, deeply rooted. It was a life she knew they could have again. And one she never would have had with Jake. Now, at last, she understood that.

At the thought of Jake a wave of guilt washed over her and she hoped Mike couldn't see in her eyes how close she'd come only twenty-four hours earlier to breaking her wedding vows. She refused to think about that now. Leslie had prayed for her, and although the bond between Ellen and Mike had been tested that week, it had survived. Thank God it had survived. Even before Mike made the decision to be there for her.

Megan discreetly left the room, and Ellen moved toward Mike. His arms opened, and she went into them, sliding her hands along his back, pulling him to her, overwhelmed with gratitude.

"You came."

He pulled back slightly so he could look into her eyes. "You needed me."

She sighed and hugged him tightly. "Oh, Mike. It's been such a long week."

"I know. For me, too. Do you still hate me?"

She shook her head against his chest. With him here now, solid and reassuring, things were so much clearer. What she and Mike had once shared—what she knew they would share again—was so different than what she'd shared with Jake all those years ago. With Mike, love was steady and real, without the uncertainty Jake had brought to her life. Mike was here and he was real. He was today and tomorrow—and that meant more than all her yesterdays combined.

She leaned up and kissed him tenderly on the lips. "Thank you…for coming."

He reached down and cupped her face in his hands, holding her gently but firmly. His eyes held hers. "I love you, Ellen. I'd go to the moon to prove it to you."

"Not always." She smiled sadly.

Mike's face fell. His hands moved down her shoulders, brushing her arms, until he took her hands in his. "I know. I've done a lot of thinking. Praying. I spent most of yesterday reading the Bible and begging God to make things right between us again. It was like the Spirit literally picked me up and set me at the Lord's feet."

Ellen thought about Leslie again and knew that since their phone call her dear friend had probably not stopped praying for them.

"How could we drift so far from everything we believe?" Ellen's voice cracked. *Jesus, forgive us.* Her heart felt as though it would break with regret.

"I know. I feel the same way. I've been selfish and faithless. You deserve better than that. Things are going to be different, Ellen." He met her gaze. "Forgive me. Please."

Ellen nodded and rested her cheek against his chest. She squeezed her eyes shut and felt tears fall onto her face once more. "I forgive you, Mike. Is everything okay between us then?"

He pulled back a few inches so he could study her eyes. "I don't know. Is it?"

She thought of Jake again and nodded. "A lot has happened this week. I was having my doubts about us, but God helped me work through a few things while I've been here. I do love you, Mike. I don't ever want to lose you. God gave you to me, and he wants us together."

"Then get your things." He smiled and patted her on the behind. "We've got a hotel room waiting for us."

The morning dawned chilly and overcast, unusually cool for July. The clouds would probably dissipate by noon but Ellen thought the weather seemed appropriate, as if the sky were mourning her father's death as well.

Still, the Baywinds Inn was perfectly tranquil that morning. The room she and Mike shared had a balcony with a distant view of the bay.

Ellen crept outside and sat down, letting the cool morning air wash over her as she stared across the water. In two days she would be gone and everything about the week would be behind her.

The night before, she had told Mike about the problems between her and Jane and the others, and he had kindly refrained from making cutting remarks about her siblings. Instead he assured her the week was nearly through. She would be going home the next day and could put the entire ordeal behind her. Then they talked for hours about their past mistakes. When Ellen finally told him how seriously she had considered leaving him, Mike cried.

He'd reached out for her, gathering her close and holding her tightly. He buried his face in her hair, and she stroked his back as he cried. When he could speak again, he pulled back and met her eyes. "I was a fool, Ellen. I took you for granted. I took everything I believe about the Lord for granted. In the process I let our marriage grow cold."

His words filled Ellen with joy—and gratitude to God, who had kept her faithful at her weakest moment. What she saw reflected in Mike's eyes moved her more deeply than anything she had ever experienced. They talked some more after that and then they did something they hadn't done in years. They prayed together. Finally, in the early morning hours, they fell asleep in each other's arms.

But still she said nothing about Jake. Not yet.

Mike had a game to cover Sunday morning, so he would leave later that evening on a flight back to Miami. Their hotel room was quiet as he dressed in a sleek Armani suit, and Ellen wondered how Jake would react when he saw them together that morning at the funeral. The two men had never met. She forced herself not to think about it as she slipped into the navy rayon dress she had worn from Miami a week earlier.

They arrived at the Barrett house by eight that morning. Everyone was there except Megan and Jane's family.

"Good morning, dear." Ellen's mother smiled sadly, greeting Ellen at the door and kissing her on the cheek. "You look pretty."

"Thanks, Mom. You, too."

"Hello, Mike. We're glad you could make it."

Mike nodded in response and straightened his tie, clearly unsure what to say.

Ellen's mother wore an elegant black dress with dark hose, but her makeup wasn't done yet and she was slightly breathless with the rush to get ready on time.

"Your Aunt Betsy put together a breakfast tray for us, pastries and fruit, that kind of thing." She pointed them toward the dining room table. "I still have to do my face and hair. I'll be back out in a while."

Ellen watched her disappear down the hall and in the distance she heard Aaron's voice boom through the house.

"Mom, where's the blow dryer? I can't find it anywhere."

Amy and Frank were dressed, sitting at the dining room table eating. Ellen nodded to them as she fixed a plate of food.

"How's it going, Frank?" Mike asked. He took his plate and found a seat next to Ellen.

"Good. You?"

"Fine."

They heard Aaron's voice again.

"Mom, where's the hair spray? It's always in this cabinet."

"I've got it. Just a minute, Aaron," Mom yelled in response.

Ellen nibbled at a pastry and thought how familiar the scene felt. It had been this way a handful of times before, when the Barrett family had been up early in the morning preparing for a big event. They had done this from a motel room in Ann Arbor before her graduation from the university, and again before her wedding. Later the same scene played out in this very house before Jane's wedding and then Amy's.

There was that same anticipation, the readying for an event that would mark a milestone in a lifetime of everyday occurrences. It seemed strange—almost twisted somehow. Every other time the event had been a celebration. Ellen thought something should be different about preparing for a funeral.

She excused herself and went out back to read her eulogy once more. She'd worked on it late into the night, getting up again after Mike was asleep, and she felt satisfied with what she had written. Now she wanted to be familiar with it so she could read it despite her emotions.

Jane and Troy and the children piled into Troy's rented car at eight-thirty on the morning of the funeral. Jane was particularly quiet, and Troy allowed her enough space to deal with her feelings.

"Here we go," she muttered as they pulled out of the parking lot.

Troy looked over at her, and she caught his curious glance. "You okay?" he asked.

"No, I'm not." She rubbed at a spot on her dress where Kala had spilled oatmeal. "How am I supposed to do this today, Troy? I mean, the whole week's been a disaster. Ellen and I aren't speaking to each other, and now I have to pretend to be broken up by my father's death."

Troy sighed loudly and slammed his foot on the brake. He pulled over and brought the car to a stop on the side of the road. "Something isn't right here, Jane."

She looked at him, startled. He sounded as though his patience was waning. "What do you mean?"

"First of all, you've been snapping at everyone in your family since I got here yesterday. You act as if they should understand what happened to you the night your father left. Second, last night at the viewing you were working a little too hard to convince yourself that your dad's death doesn't matter to you."

He gripped the steering wheel with both hands and stared out the window for a moment. "I think you're kidding yourself, Jane." He turned back toward her. "I think you're hurting as much, maybe even more than the rest of your family. You wrote him off years ago, and now you have to live with that. Nothing you say or do can give you those years back." Jane couldn't respond.

He paused a moment, and the children grew restless in the backseat. "Jane, it's time you let down your defenses and stop trying to fight the world because of what happened that night. The Bible says not to let the sun go down on your anger, but you've been doing that for more than a decade. No wonder you're miserable. Your bitterness has all but strangled you."

"I thought at least you'd understand," she cried. "You know why I feel this way."

"I do understand, Jane." He reached over and touched her face. "But you need to let it go, hon. Put it behind you. As long as you blame Ellen and your father, you're never going to be free of the past. You'll never be at peace with God or anyone in your family."

"It's not like I've been this way forever, Troy. It's just this funeral thing. I don't know how to deal with it."

He shook his head. "That's not true. You've been upset with Ellen for years. Sure, there are times when you two get along better than you have this week. But you blame her for what happened, just like you blame your father."

Jane hung her head, the fight gone.

"Ellen doesn't have any idea what's eating you, what's been eating you for the past decade. Neither did your father."

"I wanted her to ask," Jane said weakly.

"That's not fair, Jane. No one could guess something that terrible had happened to you. Not even Ellen."

Jane sniffed and raised her eyes meekly. "Have I been that bad?"

"Quite honestly, yes."

Jane sighed and stared at her hands, absorbing the truth in his words. "I'll talk to her."

"What about your dad? You have to deal with it, Jane. After today you might never have another chance."

"I know." She drew in a shaky breath. "I'll take care of it."

He reached out and pulled her close, hugging her. "Okay. Now we're getting somewhere."

Silent tears fell onto her lap, but she said nothing.

"Honey," his voice was gentle. "I'll be pulling for you."

Megan was pacing her apartment, frantic about what she had written for the funeral. She had not expected to have any trouble with the eulogy, but all week none of the words had fallen into place. She had memories of her father from when she was a little girl and memories from the past two years. But she had been gone so much of the time in between that she hadn't found a way to bridge the gap on paper. She had something else planned, something no one knew about. But she still hadn't pieced together the eulogy.

She stopped suddenly and remembered something she had forgotten until that instant. Years ago she had been in counseling after breaking up with Mohammed, and she had successfully survived a month without calling him or returning his phone calls. To celebrate the victory, her father had taken her to a fancy steak house for dinner. He told the waitress they were celebrating his daughter's special anniversary, but the woman misunderstood and thought it was Megan's birthday. When the meal was over a dozen food servers brought her a piece of cake with a candle. They sang her a birthday song and their waitress snapped a picture of her father with his arm around her.

For a long time she had kept that Polaroid snapshot on her dresser as a reminder of her father's unending support, an encouragement for the days when she felt like calling Mohammed. Later, when Mohammed was no longer a temptation and the picture began to collect dust, she tucked it away in a scrapbook. In the past week she had been too busy worrying about her sisters to remember the photo until now.

She disappeared into her closet, rummaging through a box of belongings until she came across the scrapbook. Flipping through the pages she searched frantically until she found it. There she was, side by side with her dad, silly expressions on their faces as they celebrated her independence.

That picture said more about her relationship with her father than anything she could have put on paper. She tucked it in her purse, grabbed her keys and an envelope that contained a single cassette tape. She was at her mother's house in five minutes.

Diane breathed a sigh of relief. All the kids were there now, and all but Aaron were ready to go. He was showered and dressed but he remained in his room, and Diane looked nervous. It was nine-fifteen and the service started at ten. They needed to leave in ten minutes according to her schedule.

"Aaron." She knocked gently on his bedroom door.

"What?" he barked.

"Are you almost ready? We need to leave in a few minutes."

"You go ahead. Go without me. I'll be there later."

Diane sighed softly. "Son, I want us all to arrive at the same time. Is there something I can help you with?"

Silence.

"Aaron?"

"I said go!"

"Can you open the door a minute so I can talk with you, please?"

There was a brief pause and then she heard the click of a lock turning as he opened the door.

"What?"

He had his dark glasses off, and she could see he'd been crying. "What's taking so long, son?" She kept her voice tender and calm. "I'd be happy to help you."

"Here—" He thrust a wrinkled piece of paper into her hand. "That's the problem."

Diane stared at the paper and read over the first few handwritten lines. "Is this what you're going to read at the funeral?"

"It's all I have, but I can't read it. It stinks. I've worked on it every day this week, and it just doesn't sound right."

She took a moment and read the opening lines of what he had written. It was jerky and not quite beautiful, but it came from his heart. She handed it slowly back to him.

"Son, this is what you remember, the way you remember him. It'll be perfect."

"You don't understand..." He began crying, and Diane watched him, deeply moved. This was the first time since he was a little boy that he had let her see his tears. "Dad deserved more than what I've written there. It's not enough."

Suddenly her tall, strong, strapping son was reduced to an oversized little boy crying for his daddy, and Diane's heart broke at the sight of him. She took his large, calloused hand in hers and squeezed it tenderly. "You, all by yourself, are enough, Aaron."

He looked up at her, questioning, clearly wanting to believe her. "What if I mess it up?"

She shook her head. "Your heart will speak for you, son. Believe me."

He sniffed loudly and wiped his face with the back of his hand. Then he reached for his dark glasses on his bedside table and put them firmly in place.

"All right, then," he said, his voice shaking. "I'll do this one last thing for Dad, even if it isn't perfect." He took his mother's arm in his. "Let's get going."

30

$\mathcal{S}$t. Francis Xavier Catholic Church stood tall and proud amidst the rows of gift shops and ice-cream parlors, novelty booths, and boutiques that filled Petoskey's Gaslight District. Jane's family drove in caravan toward the towering gray steeple that marked the church. The building was one of the oldest in Petoskey, and its brick-and-stone exterior made it appear stately and strong.

The hearse was there, across the street near the side doors. Jane and her siblings piled out of their cars and moved separately toward the black vehicle. They kept their distance from each other, aware of the tension that remained. The rear doors of the hearse were open, and two attendants prepared to place the casket on a rolling gurney.

An elderly woman appeared at the church's side entrance. "You're the family, is that right?" She wore a badge that identified her as the funeral coordinator. "And you must be Mrs. Barrett." She extended her hand. "I'd like you all to come in and have a seat about ten minutes before the guests begin to arrive."

"My son is a pallbearer," Mom said. "Can he sit with his sisters or does he need to sit with the other pallbearers?"

"Oh, no, dear," she said quickly. "He can sit wherever he'd like."

"Good. Thank you."

The woman nodded and disappeared back inside the church. The organist arrived and began practicing with the soloist, filling the air with dark, somber music.

Jane and Troy held hands and kept the children from running around. When Ellen and Mike approached and continued past them, Troy raised an eye at his wife.

"When, Jane?" he whispered.

"Later." She looked away. "I'll talk to her after the funeral."

Megan was standing next to their mother, and Jane saw her sister was shivering despite the fact that the sun was breaking through the clouds. Several feet away Aaron stood closest to the hearse, arms crossed, feet spread apart as he stared at the casket through his dark glasses.

Nearby, Frank put his arm around Amy as she leaned on him for support. She looked nervous and Jane wondered whether her youngest sister would hold up.

"Okay, everyone. Why don't you come in and take a seat," the coordinator said as she appeared momentarily at the door of the church and then vanished again.

Their mother motioned for the others to follow her. When they were huddled together inside the front of the church, she looked intently at their faces.

"I'd like you five to sit together in the front row with me." She pointed to a wooden pew that was easily long enough for ten people.

Jane started to roll her eyes, then caught herself. She stared at the ground instead.

"You mean I can't sit with Frank?" Amy sounded frightened.

"The men can sit in the row behind us with the children."

Amy looked at Frank, and he nodded slightly. She turned to her mother. "All right. That's fine."

"Is everyone okay with that?" Their mother glanced at each of them.

Jane and the others nodded and began moving stiffly into the front pew. Their mother sat on the far right with Aaron at the opposite side near the center aisle. Megan, Jane, Amy, and Ellen sat in the middle, spread out along the pew so that several feet separated them.

Let this day be over quickly, Jane prayed. *Please.*

Diane leaned slightly forward and studied her children, taking in the uncomfortable looks on their faces. They were sitting together, but they were still worlds apart. She bowed her head and whispered a silent prayer.

People were arriving and Ellen sat at an angle so she could watch for Jake. She had told Mike that she and Jake had spoken and that he might be at the funeral. Details beyond that could wait until they were back in Miami.

It was nearly ten and the church was more than half full when Ellen saw him. He was by himself and he entered the building through the back doors. Ellen watched him and saw him hesitate, searching the church for her. She stood up and moved toward the back of the church.

Jake had seen her stand up, and he remained in the back of the church, waiting for her. He was wearing a tie and Ellen thought it didn't quite look right on him. She would always see him in swim shorts and a tank top, the way he had been when they were dating...the way he had been that past week.

She motioned for him to follow her into the foyer.

"You okay?" he whispered when they could talk. He took her hand in his and squeezed it quickly.

"I'm nervous," she said. "I think my stomach's been in knots since last night."

"The viewing?"

She nodded. "Hardest thing I've ever done." She paused. "Thanks for coming, Jake."

"I cared about him, Ellen. And you."

"Jake, there's something you should know."

He waited, studying her silently.

"Mike's here. He came late last night."

Something subtle changed in Jake's expression, but he said nothing, only nodded.

"I had no idea he was coming, but I'm really glad he's here. I thought you'd want to know."

He straightened a bit and smiled at her tenderly. "It doesn't change anything. I still want to be here, if it's okay with you."

"Of course." She nodded. "Jake, I took your advice. Mike and I stayed up late last night and talked about things. We even prayed together, which is something we hadn't done in years."

When he said nothing she continued. "I want you to meet him after the service. I—" she smiled gently—"I really think you'll like him."

Jake looked at his watch and Ellen stared at him closely, wondering what he was thinking.

"You better go, Ellen. The service will be starting any minute."

"Jake…"

He leaned toward her and hugged her, a friendly platonic hug that could never have been mistaken as anything more than a show of comfort for an old friend grieving the loss of her father. "Go," he whispered as he pulled away. "We'll talk later."

"Okay." She looked at him, trying to read his expression. "Bye."

"Bye."

She moved along the side aisle and found her seat in the front row once again.

Suddenly, the music began. People who had been rustling through their programs or looking for a seat settled in, and a heavy silence fell over the church. Ellen glanced once more over her shoulder and saw that Jake had taken a seat in the back row. She looked at her siblings then and saw that they each were holding a folded piece of paper. She opened her purse and took out her memorial. Aaron was missing and Ellen figured he had gone to join the pallbearers on the side of the church. She closed her eyes and waited.

Suddenly the music changed, and Ellen opened her eyes. The wooden casket, covered with a brilliant spray of red roses, was rolled into the church. It sat atop an aluminum gurney and was flanked by Aaron and five other men. Aaron was stoic as he helped guide the coffin to the front of the church. When it was in its proper place, all the men except Aaron returned to their seats. The church was silent as everyone watched Aaron retrieve a large, framed photograph of his father and stand it gently on top of the casket. Aaron looked at it for a moment and then returned to his seat.

Father Joe, the priest who had never really known John, moved to the pulpit and welcomed those gathered there.

"We are here," he said, his voice hopeful, "to pay our respects to a man who touched the lives of many, a man who will certainly live on in the lives and love of his family." He paused and nodded toward the Barretts. "It is at times like this that we must remember the way our dear Lord viewed death, not as an ending, but a beginning. A glorious beginning. We will certainly grieve, but we grieve for ourselves because in this life we are without John Barrett. We must not, however, grieve for the man who left our presence in the prime of his life. For he is in a better place now, a place with no pain, no tears."

The church echoed with the sound of rustling tissues and an occasional sniffle.

"And so, dear friends, this is not a time to mourn, but a time to celebrate. This morning you will hear songs John Barrett sang, Scripture he often quoted, and personal eulogies from each of his five children. This service is more than a mourning of his death. Rather, it is a celebration of his life."

The priest stepped down and Megan took the cue. She went to the pulpit. Glancing at the picture of her father on the casket, she stared at her notes. Then in a shaky voice she read the Twenty-third Psalm.

"'The LORD is my shepherd, I shall not be in want....'"

In the front row, Ellen squirmed. Glancing at her sisters and brother, she saw they were doing the same. She glanced toward the casket and the picture. When Megan finished she made her way gracefully back to her seat.

Ellen stood up then and approached the pulpit slowly. She spoke of how her father had loved the Serenity Prayer and then she proceeded to recite it. Afterward she returned to her seat and the church filled with music.

The mourners listened as the soloist sang the haunting strains of "The Old Rugged Cross." Ellen closed her eyes, silently mouthing the words to her father's favorite hymn. The music stopped and the crowd waited, aware that it was time for John Barrett's children to speak. The order had already been decided.

Amy stood, turned once to look at Frank, and then walked carefully to a microphone set up in front of the church, a few feet from the casket. She unfolded her notes and cleared her throat. For a moment she said nothing, only stared at the page before her. When she looked up there were tears in her eyes. She struggled to find her voice and then, staring at the paper in her hand, she began to speak.

"My father was a wonderful man and I'd like to share some things about him for those of you who didn't know him." She coughed, as though struggling to keep her throat from choking up.

"I will always remember the way my father took us on adventures each weekend. He was always laughing, he was bigger than life. Sometimes when the others would run off to play, I'd stay back with my parents and Dad would swing me around until I couldn't stop laughing."

She opened the paper a bit more and kept reading. "I also remember that whenever I needed help he was there."

In the front row Jane hung her head and closed her eyes. "I was the youngest of John Barrett's daughters. The quietest in the crowd." She smiled tenderly at her siblings. "I may not have as many memories as the others, but Dad made a difference in my life all the same. If it weren't for him, I would have been too serious about life. But he taught me how to laugh. I remember him playing water volleyball with us at Petoskey State Park and inviting our friends to stay for barbecues. He was generous and kind to others."

She looked up from the paper. "If you know me, you know that I don't say a lot. But I see a lot. I hear a lot. I hear his laughter even now." Her voice cracked, but she went on. "He was my hero and I'll miss him."

A sob caught in her throat and she turned to face her father's picture. "Good-bye, Daddy. I love you." She folded her paper and returned to her seat, dropping her head in her hands. There, she quietly gave way to her tears.

Megan wiped her eyes and slid close to Amy, circling an arm over her shoulder and hugging her tight. Aaron, too, moved next to her. He and Amy had not gotten along for years, and it moved Ellen to see him take her hand and squeeze it gently.

Mom saw, too, and smiled through her tears.

God was doing something. Ellen was sure of it. Not just for her, but for her whole family.

Aaron sat with his arm around Amy, talking to her quietly. His heart had broken listening to her, watching her up there. When he was sure she was all right, he clutched his letter and stood up. All eyes followed him as he lumbered toward the microphone and unfolded the paper. For a moment he stared silently at the notes he'd written, his eyes hidden behind the dark glasses.

"I was John Barrett's only son," he began. It was hard to talk through the emotions choking him, but he was determined to continue. "I want to talk about the way my father loved people." He paused. "Before I was born my father worked three jobs all at the same time so that we'd have enough food on the table. Later, when we moved to Petoskey, he bought a house with a big, porched…fenced yard because he…where he…he bought a house with a porch and a big yard so we could…"

He felt the frustration growing, building inside of him as he struggled to make sense of what he had written. He tried the sentence again. "Later, when we moved to Petoskey we bought a house…he bought a house with a large porch for people…a porch where everyone could meet and…"

He stared at the paper in his hands and then suddenly, swiftly he crumpled it and stuffed it deep into his pocket. Friends and family members throughout the church remained silent. Aaron glanced at the front pew and his eyes locked with Ellen's. She looked as though she wished desperately that she could somehow help him through the awkward moment.

"Forget it," he mumbled into the microphone. He took one step toward his seat, then his eyes locked onto his father's, staring at him from the photograph atop the casket. Aaron's shoulders slumped and he froze in place. *You can do it, son,* those eyes said.

Slowly, he returned to the microphone, took a deep breath, and leaned forward. Then he began to speak.

"I can't tell you about my dad's love by reading a handful of sentences from a piece of paper. His love lives here—" he put a hand over his heart and his voice cracked— "not on some written page."

He paused, shaking his head. "I have not always been an easy person to love. I know that. But my father loved me. I have no doubts. He cheered me on in Little League and took me fishing when I was a little boy. He took my scout troop camping on Mackinac Island and helped me build a Pinewood Derby car for my junior-high class project.

"But that is not where I learned how much my father loved me. I learned that on the golf course. People thought he and I went golfing because we loved the game." He looked at his siblings. "They were wrong. We went golfing because we loved each other. The golf course was our private world, a place of fairways and tall trees where we talked about things only a father and son can share."

Aaron paused, fighting the tears that threatened to choke him. "I always knew he loved me, but it was on the golf course that he told me so. I would tell him what was bothering me and he'd put his arm—"

He hung his head and drew a shaky breath. He stayed that way for a moment, then almost abruptly he straightened again. He had missed one opportunity. He wouldn't miss this one. He brought his hand to his face and pinched the bridge of his nose with his thumb and forefinger. He was fighting the tears with all his might. He let his hand fall back by his side, then he looked up and continued.

"He'd put his arm around me and tell me, 'Son, whatever it is we can work it out together.' Then he'd smile at me and tell me he loved me. He would always tell me he loved me."

Aaron crossed his arms in front of him and stared at his feet, silent for several seconds as the tears finally broke free and began sliding down his face. Around the church people dabbed at their eyes and in the front row he could hear his sisters crying.

"But there was a problem with that," he continued. "Even though he would always tell me he loved me, I never—" A sob escaped from deep in his throat. He swallowed hard and pushed on. "I never said the words to him. Never said them to anyone."

He drew a breath, finding strength he hadn't known he had. "But I do love. I love my sisters." He removed the dark glasses and looked at each of them slowly. "And my mother. And I loved my Dad. He taught me how to love."

Aaron wiped his face with the back of one hand. "So today I promised myself I would tell him how I feel. In front of you. For everyone to hear." He took two steps and faced his father's picture once more. The eyes that smiled at him were alive, and Aaron could see him preparing to tee off on the ninth hole at the Bay View Country Club.

"Dad," he sobbed, no longer ashamed of his tears, the crowd forgotten. "I'm sorry

I never told you before…I love you, Dad. Wherever you are, I hope you know that. I love you."

He clenched his teeth and then returned to his seat.

It was done. He'd said it. And for the first time in his life, he felt free.

Ellen watched through her tears as her brother slumped into the pew. He rested his head in his hands and silently sobbed, his back heaving. Amy motioned to Megan, and the girls moved next to him. Ever so gently, Amy took their brother's large calloused hand in hers.

Ellen watched and felt the sorrow build in her chest. Her memories were filled with times when she and the other girls had gotten along with Aaron. She had always believed there were more good times than bad. And now Aaron had confirmed that. She moved toward her three youngest siblings and put her hand on Aaron's knee. He had allowed them to see him for who he was. Finally. They knew the truth now. Deep inside, he loved them after all.

Only Jane remained aloof, apart from the others, dabbing discreetly at her eyes. After a moment, she rose from her seat and released a heavy sigh as she made her way to the microphone. Her hands were unsteady as she opened a piece of paper.

"I'm not going to share a list of memories with you," she said. There was a tinge of defiance in her voice, and Ellen held her breath. She prayed Jane wouldn't do anything to spoil the service.

"Instead I want to use this time to read a letter I wrote to my father." She held up the piece of paper and cleared her throat.

Ellen frowned. A letter? What was this about?

Somewhat fearfully, she settled back against the pew and listened.

Jane stared at the paper in her hands. Then, with a quick glance at Troy, she began reading.

"'Dear Dad'—" That was as far as she got. She was suddenly seized by an unexpected wave of emotion. Several moments passed before she took another breath and tried again. "'Dear Dad, I know you can hear me, wherever you are, and you're probably wondering why I became a stranger to you. When I was a little girl I craved your attention, but for some reason I never thought I was good enough for you. You had other daughters with better talents and character traits than me'—" she glanced sadly at Ellen, then back to the letter—"'and I thought you loved me less because of it.'"

People were silent, waiting.

"'I was wrong and I want to explain myself. See, something happened twelve years ago that changed my life forever. It was something that I thought made me unlovable.'" Jane was seized by sudden fear, and she shifted nervously, unsure if she should continue. *I can't. I just can't.*

She looked at Troy and his eyes told her to go on.

Swallowing her fear, she started reading again. "'Ever since then I have blamed you and told myself that you never cared for me. I blamed you and I blamed my sisters for not asking me what happened. I have become an angry, hateful person, and…I never thought they were interested in why.'" She caught Ellen's attention, and suddenly tears filled her eyes. "'Especially Ellen. I have been so hard on her over the years.'"

Tears made their way down Ellen's face.

Jane's voice grew raspy. "'But I have learned something this week. What happened to me was not your fault, Dad. I put myself in the situation and it was up to me to tell you about it. I could have allowed you to comfort me, but I kept the pain inside. I was wrong, Dad. And now it's too late. My stubborn heart refused to let you in and'—" A solitary sob escaped and the letter slipped from her hand onto the floor. Jane hung her head then, crying soundlessly, unable to speak, the pain so intense she wished she could die.

Watching her sister, Ellen finally understood. Jane wasn't angry at her, she was angry with herself. But there was something else, too. Something that Jane had said earlier in the week rang painfully true: Ellen had been too concerned about herself to worry about what was tearing her sister apart. She hadn't even tried to find out what was at the root of Jane's behavior. She'd been too busy taking the attacks personally and complaining about Jane to everyone who would listen.

Regret, piercing and heavy, seized Ellen, and she wondered for the first time what terrible thing her sister was referring to. What had happened twelve years ago?

Pulling a tissue from her purse, Ellen stood up. She moved across the front of the church, bent to pick up the letter, and then stood at Jane's side. She handed her sister the tissue and took her hand, squeezing it tightly, willing Jane to continue.

A small, sad smile came across Jane's face as she stared at Ellen for a moment. She blinked back her tears and then looked at the letter once more, struggling to find her voice.

"'And so…you had to leave this life wondering why I had changed, why I didn't love you like I had before.'" She paused again and moved closer to Ellen, leaning on her. "'I find comfort knowing, believing, that you are in heaven now and that somehow you can hear me. Dad, I never meant to hurt you…I love you, really I do. Please forgive me.'" She closed her eyes, then tilted her head heavenward.

"I'm sorry, Dad," she said so softly people had to lean forward in their seats to hear her. "I never stopped loving you. I always have."

Then she turned to Ellen and hugged her for a long moment, sobbing in her arms. Ellen's tear-filled eyes met her mother's tender gaze, then moved to Mike. His smile was proud and encouraging. Finally, Ellen sought out Jake, and she saw that he was crying too. She knew he was sharing her joy— that he was as thankful as she that the two sisters he had watched grow up together had once again found common ground.

Ellen took Jane's hand, and together they moved back to their seats, the distance between them finally dissolved.

Ellen closed her eyes for a moment, still holding Jane's hand in hers. *You are so good, God. Thank you…for Mike, for Jane. For all of this.*

Megan wiped her cheeks with a tissue and sniffled softly as she stood up and moved to the microphone.

She closed her eyes for a moment, steadying herself. Then she studied the Polaroid snapshot taken at the restaurant so long ago. She had no notes.

"My dad was not the kind of person who loved you based on what you did or how well you performed." She smiled sadly at Jane and then at each of her siblings. "I know there have been times when one or more of us thought that way about Dad, but it wasn't true. With so many children in one family we tended to think he loved those of us who excelled. Those of us who stayed out of trouble."

She stared at the floor, her shame apparent. When she looked up there were tears on her cheeks, but she continued, her voice strong. "For a long time I strayed away from my father, my family. I missed countless family outings and vacations and chances to be together. But during that time my dad never stopped loving me. Even after I had given up on myself, he believed in me." She looked at the photo again and smiled through her tears. "He knew I would find my way home…even when I was so lost I couldn't see the path."

She studied the individual faces in the crowd. "I could stand here and tell you that John Barrett was born in Battle Creek, Michigan. That he studied math and logistics and became a brilliant computer analyst. That he made a difference at every company he worked for and left a legacy at computerized offices in a dozen major cities. That he went on to share that knowledge with hundreds of students.

"I could tell you that he was a family man who liked to take a drive to the beach and who, after leaving Detroit, never grew tired of Petoskey and the breathtaking views of Little Traverse Bay. I could tell you he liked classical music and Michigan football and a hot juicy hamburger straight off the grill."

She smiled, unashamed of the tears that streamed down her face. "But that is not what I will remember about my dad. It is not what I want you to remember." She held up the photograph now, showing it to the crowd. "When you think of John Barrett, think of the way he loved us. Even when we weren't very lovable. The way he celebrated our victories with us, no matter how small."

She lowered the photo and smiled at it once more. Then she turned and smiled at her siblings. "But most of all, when you think of him think of the love he left behind." Her smile faded then, her voice cracked. "Because now that he's gone, it's all we have left."

There was silence for a moment, and Megan nodded to someone unseen in the choir loft. Suddenly music filled the church and she saw the surprised look on the faces of her family. The song was one sung by country-western singer Collin Raye, a ballad called "Love Remains." Despite her tears, Megan's voice rang clear and sweet.

For three minutes she sang about the passing of time, of growing up and growing old, of living and dying. The last verse specifically dealt with relying on each other in times of sadness. The song's message was clear: people die, but there was still hope, still love. That love was her father's legacy.

When she finished singing, Megan clutched the snapshot to her chest and hesitated for a moment, thankful she had found the courage to sing for her father one last time. She returned to her seat then and took her mother's hand as her siblings surrounded her. Aaron took her other hand protectively in his.

There was brief rustling throughout the church as people reached for fresh tissues. They had witnessed something special and no one was left untouched. In the front row, Megan's mother squeezed her hand and leaned close to her.

"That was beautiful, dear," she whispered. "Thank you."

A hush fell over the crowd once more as people waited. It was Ellen's turn.

Ellen took a deep breath and stood up. She moved slowly to the microphone, lost in thought.

When she was in place, she considered her siblings, clustered at the end of the pew holding hands and crying. She stared at the eulogy she had written and knew that it was both eloquent and emotional. But somehow, in light of what was happening between them, it was not enough.

She folded it gently and wrapped her fingers around it. Her knees shook and she felt suddenly faint. She leaned forward and willed herself to speak.

"I have listened to my brother and sisters talk about our father and—" she crossed her arms in front of her, overwhelmed by the moment—"I have realized how little I knew him."

She looked into the crowd and for an instant her gaze met Mike's. Tears spilled onto his cheeks and his eyes silently encouraged her. She made herself turn away and look at the other faces in the church.

"I did not know until now that he was Amy's hero. Or that he and Aaron shared secrets on the golf course." She looked at Amy and then Aaron, pain twisting her face, fresh tears blurring her vision. "I didn't know that he had given Megan hope when she felt worthless or that—" She began to cry in earnest and she paused.

"I'm sorry," she said. People waited for her to compose herself. She drew a shaky breath and continued. "I didn't know about Jane." She twisted her hands, unsure of what to say next. "My dad was exactly who he needed to be for each of us, and until today I only saw him the way I knew him. He was someone who believed in me and pushed me to succeed, someone who was excited about everything I did until his final week." She thought of Leslie's words then. "And his faith will be an example for me all my life." She sniffed. "That was the John Barrett I knew. And I loved him with all my heart."

She looked at her siblings. "But I know so much more about him now...and—"

A sob welled in her throat as she directed her words toward her family. "I want to thank you for sharing him with me. Because I know him better now than I ever did when he was alive. I know all of you better, too."

She closed her eyes and when she opened them, she stared at her father's photograph. "You were the best. I'll always love you, Daddy." She moved toward the casket and paused for a single moment, gripping the polished wood corner, not wanting to let him go. She lowered her head and sobbed once, too softly for anyone to hear. Then, with the determination that he had taught her, she returned to her seat.

For a long while no one said anything. The muted sound of people crying filled the church, and Ellen and her siblings and mother held hands in the front row, their heads bowed. Finally, Father Joe stood up and walked to the pulpit.

He cleared his throat and waited until he had the crowd's attention.

"I believe you understand now the reason we must view this service as a celebration. John Barrett was a man who truly made a difference in the lives of his family and friends. A man who lived life to the full. We would do well when we leave here today to follow John's example. And when you think of his passing, smile through your tears." He looked tenderly at Ellen and her family. "Because his life touched yours, and in that you have been truly blessed."

The priest looked once more at those gathered in the church and nodded his head. "You are dismissed. There will be a procession of vehicles to St. Francis Cemetery on Charlevoix Road just west of town. Maps are available near the doors." He paused a moment. "Let's pray."

Throughout the church people bowed their heads.

"Dear Lord, bless us today with the insight to understand death, to know that it is a necessary passage, a door to a better place. And let us, in our hearts, never forget John Barrett. Let us keep him alive in the love he left behind. And let us always smile when we remember him. In Jesus' name. Amen."

31

No words were needed as Ellen and her family formed an exclusive circle, exchanging hugs, unaware for the moment of the people milling about them.

"What was it, Jane?" Aaron asked. His glasses were in his suit pocket. "Can you tell us what happened?"

Jane glanced around, then pulled her mother and her siblings into a huddle, away from the milling crowd. She tried to speak and couldn't. She clasped her throat, as though willing her voice to work.

When the words finally came out, they stunned Ellen. "I…I was raped," Jane said simply. Her gaze fell to the floor and she allowed the tears once again.

Ellen's heart sank and Aaron's face filled with anger. For a moment they were silent as each of them absorbed the blow. Mom closed her eyes, and Ellen wondered if she was imagining her daughter being attacked and grieving that she hadn't been there to help her.

"Who was it?" Aaron demanded "Do you remember his name, Jane? He should be in jail."

She shook her head. "I didn't know him. It was the weekend Dad left. After he lost his job."

"You went to a party in Charlevoix," Ellen remembered. "When I asked you about it you wouldn't say anything."

Jane nodded. "I met some guy and took a walk with him. He…" She began sobbing and her family closed in tighter around her.

"It's okay, Jane, you don't have to tell us if you don't want to," Megan said softly. The others nodded.

"No. You don't need to know the details, but I have to tell you what happened. Otherwise I might never have another chance. Besides," she sniffed, "if I tell you what happened I won't have any reason to hold on to it anymore."

"Go ahead, dear," their mother encouraged.

"He—he raped me on a private beach at the end of the street." She paused, composing herself. "I screamed for Dad, but he was gone. He had left the day before."

"And you blamed him for not being there when you needed him," Amy finished and Ellen understood now. As far back as she could remember, their father had always been there for her. But not for Jane. Not that night in Charlevoix.

Jane nodded, her eyes glistening with tears. "I blamed him. But it wasn't his fault. If I'd told him what happened he would have found the guy and dragged him to the police station himself. I know he would have. But I kept it inside. I didn't tell anyone until this week, right before I came here. Troy wanted to know why I seemed so..."

There was raw pain in her eyes and she cried unashamedly. "I was so indifferent. Like I didn't care. And finally I told him what had happened."

Ellen closed her eyes. She imagined how it would have hurt their father to know Jane was raped the weekend he disappeared.

Jane looked up through her tears at her family. "I'm sorry. I never meant to hurt any of you."

They surrounded her, hugging and holding her, murmuring words of forgiveness and comfort, proclamations of love. They cried because of life and its sometimes cruel hand and because they felt like a family again. Before they were ready to let go, Aaron spoke up.

"I think Dad would have wanted us to pray," he said. Then, without waiting for a response, he did something none of the others had ever seen him do. He prayed.

"Dear God, thank you for bringing us back together today. Thank you for making us a family." He paused, his voice choked. "Be with our sister, Jane, and heal her from the scars of what happened...of that terrible night. Help us to follow our father's example, to love you and each other, even when it isn't easy. Amen."

When he finished, Ellen saw that people had gathered some distance away and were waiting for a chance to offer words of condolence. Her mother saw, too.

"Thank you." Mom looked into the eyes of her children, her face was tearstained but peaceful, as if a great burden had been lifted. "There is no greater gift you could have given your father or me today than to let the barriers between you fall. To finally love each other like you did when you were younger. I know things are different for us all. You're grown up and you have your own lives. It may be years before we are all together again like this. But after today I will always know that you still love each other. That your father's love really does live on."

She smiled then and motioned toward the people waiting for them. "Let's greet the others. We need to get over to the cemetery."

They pulled away from one another and turned to acknowledge the family and friends waiting to comfort them. Ellen glanced toward the back of the church and then scanned the rest of the building. Jake was gone.

She sought out Mike then and hugged him tightly. "Everything okay?" He smoothed her hair away from her face and studied her eyes.

Ellen nodded and smiled; she was sure her face was red and swollen from crying. "Yes. It's going to be just fine." Later, when they were alone, she would tell him about Jane and together they could pray for her sister.

Mike looked around. "So where's Jake?"

Ellen shrugged as she searched the church once more. She was disappointed that he had left without saying good-bye. "I guess he's gone on to the cemetery. I'll introduce you later."

For ten minutes Ellen and the others mingled with the group of mourners, comforting and being comforted. Two attendants from the mortuary moved the casket back into the hearse and signaled the funeral coordinator. It was time to leave for the cemetery.

A procession of forty-seven cars made its way to St. Francis Cemetery, winding through town toward Spring Street and then turning right on Charlevoix Road. The park was a mile down the road just past the Knights of Columbus Hall where Ellen's parents had played bingo occasionally on Wednesday nights.

The cars proceeded into the park and pulled up near a yellow canopy. Clouds still covered the sky but they were breaking up and the sun was peeking through. A fresh breeze drifted off the bay and rustled the leaves of the sturdy maples that lined the cemetery.

The pallbearers gathered at the back of the hearse and carried the casket onto a device that would eventually lower it into the earth. There were six chairs set up before the flower-lined grave and the Barretts each took a seat.

The crowd grew quiet as the priest stepped forward.

"Dear God," he began, and around him people lowered their heads. "Help us to remember that our bodies are but dust and that to dust we must return. May the soul of John Barrett rest forever in your loving care. Amen."

Ellen looked across the bay and smiled through eyes damp with tears. She was glad her father's body would rest in a place overlooking the bay he loved so dearly. She could hear him even now. *"Behold, the beautiful bay."*

The priest was speaking tenderly to the crowd. "John Barrett, the John Barrett you know and remember, is not in that casket." He motioned gracefully with his hand. "Nor will he be buried in this piece of earth. We must remember that this is the resting place for his earthly body only."

He paused. "When you come here, when you bring flowers and remember him, do not look for him among the dead. Look out across the water and up to the heavens above. He lives in heaven as surely as our dear Lord lives there. And he will always live in the memories you cherish. You are dismissed."

Everyone except Ellen, her siblings, and their mother stepped away, quietly returning to their cars so they could drive back to the Barrett house. Ellen and the others remained in place, holding hands while their mother lay a single red rose atop the spray of flowers already covering the casket.

"Good-bye, John," Mom whispered. She touched the casket lightly and then stepped back, returning to her seat.

The priest took Mom's hand and squeezed it gently. "Call me if you need anything," he said.

"I will. Thank you." She smiled, and he turned and left them alone.

The mortuary attendants stood some distance away, discreetly waiting for the family to leave before lowering the casket into the earth.

No one moved for a moment. Ellen stared at the casket, knowing that in some ways, despite the priest's comforting words, it was her last opportunity to be with her father.

At least in this life.

Finally they stood and without saying a word returned to their cars where Mike and Frank and Troy and the children waited. Only then did Ellen look around and notice that Jake had not followed them to the cemetery.

She wanted to say good-bye to him one last time. But she understood his reason for leaving quietly without her knowledge and she thought again how much he had changed. She stepped over tree roots and onto the sidewalk, walking slowly, remembering. There had been a time when Jake would have gone to any lengths to keep her from loving another man. Now, though he knew she still had feelings for him, he had let her go. He had sent her back into the arms of the man she had married. The man she truly loved with all her heart. It was, in some ways, his final act of love for her. She glanced once more across the bay toward Harbor Pointe. Somewhere along the distant shore stood a gray-and-white Victorian house and a man she could never again go back to. A part of her heart grieved at the thought.

Mike took her hand then, and she smiled up at him, knowing she had made the right choice. As they left the cemetery she was struck by a comforting thought. That week she had visited the people of her past—Jane and the others. Her father. Jake. Leslie. Even God. She had made peace with them all.

Now it was time to go home.

32

Ellen drove Mike to Petoskey's Pellston Regional Airport where he would take a prop plane to Detroit and catch a jet home. The conversation between them was pleasant, and for the first time since her father's death, Ellen's mind was clear and focused on the future.

"I wonder how things are at the paper?" she said absently.

"I'm sure they're struggling without their ace reporter," Mike teased. "It's a wonder they could get by at all without the dirt you dig up for the front page."

"Stop!" She jabbed him playfully. "Hey, what's the deal with the rental car again?"

"You and Jane take it back to the airport tomorrow when you fly out. Makes things easier on everyone."

Ellen nodded. She was quiet for a moment, studying the light traffic and looking for the tiny airport on their right.

"I guess Jake must have left early," Mike ventured, glancing at her.

"Hmm. Guess so."

"You haven't said much about him, Ellen." Mike's voice was curious but without accusation. "Did you see him this week?"

Ellen remained focused on the road ahead of her. "Yes. A few times."

Mike waited.

She wanted to brush it off, to tell Mike it was no big deal. But she couldn't. She wasn't going to hide anything from him. Not now. *Okay, Lord. Help me say this right.* "I spent time with him, Mike. In some ways it helped me, because he was my sounding board, an old friend for me to lean on. But in other ways…" Her voice trailed off. She glanced at him, and the patience and trust she saw on his face encouraged her. "In other ways, I felt very confused. Jake listened to me. He showed me he cared in very tangible ways. And that felt good."

"What are you saying, Ellen?" Mike studied her but there was no accusation in his voice. "Are you in love with him?"

The question stunned her, but not nearly so much as the answer that resonated within her. "No." She smiled then and met his gaze. "No, Mike, not at all. There's only one man I'm in love with, and he's in this car." She focused on the road again. "Jake knows that, too. I told him."

He reached out to take her hand. "That's all I need to know for now, Ellen," he said, and her love for him grew even deeper.

"There's more I need to tell you—"

He smiled. "Don't worry about it for now. You have other things to think about. When you get home, we'll talk." He squeezed her hand. "We'll pray then. And we'll be okay."

Ellen nodded and a peace that could only be described as divine filled her heart. They had been the most difficult seven days of her life, but in the end the past week had made her and Mike love each other again. More than that, it had restored their faith. Suddenly their future seemed alive with hope.

She spotted the airport then and pulled off the highway. In two minutes they were at the front entrance. She leaned over and gave him a lingering kiss good-bye.

"Tomorrow evening, five-thirty, right?" he asked.

"Right. I'm anxious to be home."

Mike caressed her face. "I know it's been a hard week for you, Ellen. I'll be glad when you're home."

She paused. "I really love you, Mike."

"I love you, too. See you tomorrow."

He kissed her again and then disappeared into the airport.

Casseroles and sliced meat, breads and salads, desserts and a dozen different dishes were spread out along the Barrett family dining room table when Ellen returned.

As she entered the house she realized that something had changed. The somber gloom that had hung over them at the funeral and later at the cemetery had disappeared. Instead there was laughter and conversation as people swapped fun-filled stories about John Barrett, remembering the good times.

Ellen realized then that there would always be sadness over her father's death, but there would also be times of celebration in remembering his life.

She smiled and joined in the conversation. This was one of those times.

Ellen and her family were about to share a final breakfast together before everyone went their separate ways. Conversation was pleasant among them and the tension that had plagued them all week had disappeared. Ellen guessed she had five minutes before it was time to eat and she disappeared to her parents' bedroom.

Thumbing through her purse she found what she was looking for and dialed the long-distance number.

"Hello?"

"Leslie, it's me, Ellen."

"Ellen, how are you? I've been thinking about you constantly. How was the funeral?"

"Amazing. I'll call you when I get home and tell you all about it. Listen, I only have a minute, but I wanted to tell you about Jake. Everything worked out okay, Leslie." She paused as a lump formed in her throat at the thought of her long-lost friend praying for her on the phone earlier that week. "Thanks for praying."

"I'm not surprised," Leslie said, a smile in her tone. "God wasn't going to let you go, no matter how confused you felt. What about Mike?"

"He came. It was…amazing. We talked and prayed together and worked things out. Or we started to. We need the Lord in our marriage, Leslie, just like you said. We're going to start going to church again as soon as I get home."

"Oh, Ellen, I'm so glad. Hey, let's not let so much time pass before we talk again. Okay?"

"Okay. And thanks again. For praying, I mean. I think I know what would have happened otherwise. Remember that Scripture in 1 Corinthians, you know, the one about temptation?"

"'God will not let you be tempted beyond what you can stand, but when tempted he will also provide a way out.'"

"That's the one. It was sure true this week. You prayed and God showed me a way out."

"It's a battle, Ellen. Prayer is our most powerful weapon. Don't forget that."

"Never again. Listen, I gotta go. I'll call you next week."

The conversation ended and Ellen returned to the table to join the others for breakfast.

"I'm stuffed," Ellen said thirty minutes later. She wiped her mouth with a napkin, glanced at her watch, and turned to Jane. "I think we'd better get going. Our planes leave in six hours and we'll need time to check in."

Their bags were already packed, lined up near the door, and Troy began loading them into the rental car. When he finished he buckled the children into the backseat and stood by the car waiting for Jane and Ellen.

Megan approached her sisters and smiled, her eyes brimming with tears. "I told myself I wasn't going to cry today and I'm not." She hugged each of her sisters. "I love you guys. Write, okay?"

Ellen and Jane nodded, their eyes damp.

"And you come out and visit sometime," Jane told her. "The kids would love to spend a week with their Aunt Megan."

"Hey, Megan, it was too crazy yesterday to tell you, but thanks for that song," Ellen said. "Dad would have loved it."

Amy left Frank at the table and moved to join her sisters. "I feel like we should have another week together now that everyone's getting along." She smiled sadly, hugging Ellen and Jane.

"Now, let's not push our luck," Jane said. The others realized she was joking and they formed a circle then, laughing because it was easier than giving in to the flood of tears they each held back.

"Remember how we used to be when we'd leave some city and move across the country?" Ellen asked. They remained in a tight cluster, thinking back. "The four of us girls. I thought we'd be like that forever."

"Me, too," Megan added.

"Inside here—" Jane spread her fingers over her heart— "we're still those little girls." She looked at each of her sisters. "Let's stay in touch, huh?"

"We have to," Amy said. "It's too much work to be strangers."

They all laughed again and gently pulled away. Aaron approached them and hugged Jane first, then Ellen. "I can say it now." His voice was gentle and warm and it seemed that the dense layer of ice that once covered his heart had finally melted. "I love you guys. Take care."

They hugged him and repeated his sentiment.

"I was proud of what you did at the funeral, Aaron," Ellen said.

He nodded. "I should have done it sooner."

"Well, take care of yourself."

His eyes grew watery. "I'll miss you. Really."

"Hey, none of that now. We'll be together again sometime," Ellen's voice was thick with emotion. She looked at the faces around her. "We'll have to have a reunion or something, right?"

Everyone nodded and moved about uncomfortably, not wanting the moment to end. Finally their mother cleared her throat and stepped forward.

"You girls have a safe flight. And call me tonight so I know you got in safely."

Ellen and Jane looked at each other and laughed.

"You thinking what I'm thinking?" Ellen asked.

"Some things never change, right?"

"Right."

"Now, girls, I'm only concerned for your safety," Mom defended herself, grinning at them.

"I know." Ellen smiled at their mother and hugged her. "I'll call."

They pulled Jane into the embrace then, and Jane's voice was raspy. "Me too."

"Love you," Mom said, holding on to them a bit longer.

"Love you, too," they replied.

Then waving once more at their brother and sisters, Ellen and Jane turned and walked toward the car. As they had done so many times when their father was alive, the remaining Barrett siblings filed onto the sidewalk and waved good-bye until the car bearing their older sisters had disappeared from sight.

33

The airport was busy and by the time they arrived inside the terminal, Ellen and Jane were running late. Ellen's gate was five minutes away from the one where Jane and her family were flying out, and the two sisters suddenly found themselves forced into a hurried good-bye. Troy and the children stood several feet away giving them a few moments of privacy as a constant stream of travelers flowed around them.

Jane looked at her sister, her face filled with regret. "Ellen, I wanted to say something to you yesterday but there were always so many people around that I—"

Ellen held up a finger. "Don't," she said gently. "You've already said it. Besides, you were right. I should have asked you what was wrong a long time ago."

"But I treated you so badly. How can you forgive me?"

"Jane, do you really think I could ever hate you?"

Jane looked down, staring at the bag in her hands. "I could understand if you did."

"I don't. I never have hated you."

"Well, now, there were a few times there…" Jane's voice trailed off and she grinned.

Ellen smiled, glad to see her sister's sense of humor again. She'd really missed it. "I don't know when we'll see each other again."

Jane nodded and tears glittered in her eyes. "You and Mike'll have to come spend some time with us."

"Or vice versa. There's always room for your family at our house if you need some time at the beach."

"You know, Ellen, despite all the mean things I said…you'd make a great mom." Jane took Ellen's hand in hers. "I'll pray for you…that next time there won't be a miscarriage."

Ellen nodded, too choked up to speak.

There was an awkward silence then, and Jane looked at her watch. "Well, I'd better get going. The plane leaves in twenty minutes."

Ellen nodded, blinking away her tears so she could see clearly.

"Jane, remember when we were little, what we used to say to each other every night?"

"Sure," Jane smiled, her eyes distant. "I remember. Why?"

"I don't know. I just wondered if you remembered."

Jane's smile faded then and she rushed into her sister's arms. She held her for several moments, unaware of the people around her. Her voice cracked when she was finally able to speak. "Good-bye, Ellen, I love you. See you around."

It wasn't exactly what they had said to each other all those years ago but it was as close as they would come. Ellen smiled, her tears falling onto Jane's shoulder.

"Good-bye, Jane," she mumbled. "I love you, too. See you around."

They pulled away then and studied each other one last time before turning, and without looking back, going their separate ways.

The plane took off smoothly over the Detroit area, circling gently around lower Lake Michigan and heading back across land toward the Atlantic coast. Ellen sat next to the window watching Detroit disappear behind them. She wore her sunglasses again, her back turned slightly to the passengers beside her. She wanted the next three hours to herself so she could remember all that had happened that week, to try to make sense of it.

She had made peace with everyone, it seemed. Her father, her sisters, her brother, Mike. Even her Savior. But she hadn't really made peace with Jake. There were things she would have told him if she'd had a chance at the funeral.

She stared at the tree-covered land below, thinking. Suddenly, she knew what she had to do.

She opened her bag and found the pad of lined paper and a black ink pen. Gazing into the endless blue sky, she pictured him sitting beside her in his truck, splashing in the waves with her at the beach, letting go of her on his redwood deck. Perhaps things would have been different if she'd met Jake later in life. Or if she had never married and run into him again. But that wasn't the way it had been...and everything about Jake Sadler was borrowed from a place where yesterday lived.

She began to write.

"Dear Jake..." The pen moved effortlessly across the page and Ellen paused, drifting back. With a sigh, she continued.

I wanted so badly to talk to you at the funeral but you left before I could say good-bye. I think I understand. Mike was there and you wanted the two of us to be alone together. Like we should be.

I'm in the air as I write this, suspended between your world and my world with Mike, and I feel compelled to talk to you one last time. I cannot put into words what seeing you this week meant to me. It was as if all the years between us disappeared in an instant. And yes, it made me wonder.

I think of your question on the beach, when you asked me if I still had feelings for you, and I can tell you honestly that I do. You were my first love and my heart has not forgotten. It never will. I needed you this week and I will always be glad I called.

But you were right to let me go, to send me back to Mike. Because what you and I shared has come and gone, and I believe you understand that even better than I. As you said, if we had stayed together it would never have worked. Right now we'd still be fighting over some different girl in a different bathrobe standing on your grand front porch. And I'd still have a broken heart.

I guess I'm trying to thank you for loving me enough to leave what we shared in the past. You have grown into quite a kind man, Jake Sadler.

You should know I'm doing all right about my dad. The sadness has faded somewhat, and when I think of him now I see him where I will always see him: sitting with us five kids at a Michigan football game, his cheeks red from the cold, his fist raised in the air and that smile stretched across his face.

I keep finding myself thinking about what you said that night when we were on the way to your house. "Choices. Passages. Moments that make a difference for a lifetime." Seeing my dad that way is one of those moments.

So were you, Jake. You must know that a part of me will always love you, always remember what we shared. And every once in a while I will think of you, as I know you will think of me.

By the way, about that omelette shop, I really think it'd be a winner. And I'm never wrong, you know. Except once when I was a kid and I thought I'd grow up to marry my best friend. I was wrong about that.

You have changed so much since then. You've made a wonderful life for yourself, and I know one day you'll find the right person to share it with. When you do, I pray you'll place God at the center of your home. He alone can make the difference when troubled times come. That much I know from experience. I never told you, but I gave my life to Christ after we broke up. And even though I'm still growing, Jesus has never given up on me. His peace and love truly do surpass all understanding. It might sound like a cliché, but my life really would be nothing without the Lord.

Anyway, I wish only the best for you, Jake. I guess that's all. I don't expect you to write back or call me when you receive this. It wouldn't be right. Just know that I enjoyed this past week, being with you again, remembering a thousand memories of the way we were. The way everything was. It was a passage of sorts, another moment. But most of all this past week gave me a few precious days in the place where yesterday lives.

Thanks, Jake. I won't forget you.

Love always, Ellen

❧

That same moment, in a small country kitchen in Maplewood, Pennsylvania, Imogene Spencer placed a telephone call to Erma Brockmeier.

"Erma, I've just got word from the church office. That young woman we were praying for? You know, Ellen Barrett?"

"Yes, how is she?"

"Everything worked out just fine, dear. You can take her off the prayer line."

"Oh, that's wonderful. Praise the Lord. I'll be sure to tell the other ladies."

"Yes. Now about that other couple, the one in Ohio whose son is in the hospital? Here's what I think we need to pray..."

Dear Reader,

Thank you for traveling with me through the hallways of Ellen Barrett's past. My guess is that the journey will have taken you back to your own yesterdays as well.

Scripture says, "Forget the former things; do not dwell on the past" (Isaiah 43:18). Certainly there can be no growth for today and tomorrow by remaining where yesterday lives. Still, the Lord gave us our ability to remember. He provided us with the ability to capture scenes and log them in a storehouse to be brought out and played again when the occasion allows. I hope *Where Yesterday Lives* provided such an occasion.

If so, it is my prayer that by remembering, by visiting once more that place where faith and family and love are born, you were convicted again of the truth that Jesus Christ is our only hope. Unless the foundation is built on him, it is merely shifting sand.

However, if Ellen's journey led you on one that was painful, filled with memories of a life devoid of Christ's love, then there is no time like the present to begin the greatest journey of all. By putting your faith in Christ today, you will start a trail of yesterdays that will one day conjure up beautiful memories.

Faithfully yours in Christ,

Karen Kingsbury

DISCUSSION QUESTIONS

1. Dealing with death is difficult for most of us and often brings up unresolved conflict—with others, with God, and with ourselves. Have you had an experience like the Barrett's? If so, how did you handle it? Which character did you identify with the most?

2. Our view of God is often a reflection of our view of our earthly father. How has your view of your father affected your view of God?

3. Ellen and Mike let the busyness of their jobs crowd out their spiritual life. How did that affect their relationship? Has that ever happened to you? How were you able to get back on track spiritually?

4. Jane's pain, which resulted in anger toward her siblings, was tearing the family apart and making everyone miserable. Do you have a "Jane" in your family? Have you ever tried to discuss this person's actions with him or her to discover the reason for the pain?

5. Ellen stated that the "key to peace is to stop talking." Do you agree or disagree, and why?

6. What was your reaction to Diane, who always tried to smooth things over and see that no one was offended?

7. Reread 1 Corinthians 10:12–13. This would be a good verse to memorize and quote during times of temptation. Can you remember a time when you almost gave in to temptation but found a way to escape?

8. Have you ever felt the nudge of the Holy Spirit to pray for someone, and you found out later that he or she was in some kind of crisis at that exact moment? How did that feel?

9. We are commanded to confess our sins to one another. Have you developed relationships with those who would risk confronting you when you're wrong or whom you would risk confronting when they are wrong? Why is this important?

10. Dealing with death often causes a person to examine his or her own life. What emotions and memories did this story stir in your heart and mind? Are there areas of your life that you've tried to block out with busyness or other things so you don't have to deal with them? Are there people with whom you are angry? Are there people you hold a grudge against? How is your relationship with the Lord?

[Book Two]

WHEN JOY CAME TO STAY

DEDICATED TO...

Donald, who is and has been my very best friend regardless of the storms of life. Thank you for believing in me, loving me, and praying for me as if your life depended on it. Persecution is a promise in the kingdom of God, but with you by my side the lessons we have learned this past year are both vivid and welcomed. My greatest joy is knowing you are by my side, now and forever.

Kelsey, caught somewhere between the oh-so-cute little girl and the tenderly precious young woman whose image grows clearer with each passing season. Whether kicking a soccer ball, mastering a math test, or seeking God's heart on the daily dilemmas of growing up, you are proving yourself to be intensely committed, deeply devoted, sincere, genuine, and true. I am the most blessed mom in the world to have the privilege of calling you my daughter, my little Norm, my song.

Tyler, tall, strong, and handsome—in the days of becoming, it is clear the type of man you'll be. And yet now, for a short while, you're still a little boy, remembering to pick a dandelion for me on family walks. Kind and compassionate, always ready to share, thinking of others. When I look at you, so often I see your daddy. And on many wonderful moments I see your Father, too. If I could bottle your zest for life, your sincerity, and share them with others, the world would be a different place.

Keep your eyes on the goal, son; God has great plans for you. I love you always.

Austin, no longer making baby steps but running through our house and our hearts. It's marvelous to see the way God has made you focused—gifted with the ability to master an action regardless of the time and energy involved. Even more amazing are the glimpses of a tender heart beneath the toughness—"Daddy, I'm going to kiss your wife…"

Mingled with your three-year-old laughter are words that will ring through the decades. I remain always in awe of the miracle of your life.

And to my loving Lord and Savior, who has, for now, blessed me with these.

ACKNOWLEDGMENTS

As with all my books, this one was written with the help of many friends and professionals who made it ring true literally and sing true spiritually. Writing about depression is not something I've done before; although I've wrestled with testing and persecutions, battling depression has never been one of my trials. For that reason I did extensive research on what I came to understand as an illness and drew heavily from the results God brought my way.

In this light I especially want to thank my dear friend, Sylvia Wallgren—a Christian counselor and licensed psychiatrist—for giving me understanding. In a way that was both miraculous and timely, the Lord ordained that Sylvia and I meet. She also is a prayer warrior and lifted me up to heaven's throne daily as I wrote this book. I strongly suspect Sylvia will be a treasured friend—part of my close, close circle—throughout our journey here and on into eternity. Sylvia, I can't tell you strongly enough how much your daily encouragement and e-mailed prayers meant to me, still mean to me. I thank God for you.

Again, thanks go to my amazing editor, Karen Ball, who takes my work and fine-tunes it so that the music you hear is truly a thing of beauty. Karen, you're a gifted editor, and I am blessed for knowing you, working with you.

To the Multnomah family, from my dear friends in sales to those in publicity, marketing, editorial, management, cover design, endorsements, and everyone in between—you are the most amazing people to work for. Every now and then, in the quiet moments before dawn, I find myself in awe that this is my job and you are my coworkers. I believe God is taking our books someplace we've never imagined before! Thank you, a million times over.

Like last year, thanks to Kristy and Jeff Blake for taking care of my precious angel child during those hours when I absolutely needed a moment to write.

Also a special thanks to my niece Shannon Kane, to Jan Adams, and to Joan Westfall for always being the first in line to read my books and give me valuable feedback. Also to my other family and friends for your love, support, and encouragement in every aspect of my writing. Especially my mom and dad, who have been there since my first stapled, colored-in book at age five.

With every book I write there are people who pray for me and lend an ear while I talk plots and character traits. These are my special, oh-so-close friends and sisters in Christ, the golden ones who will never change or leave regardless of the passing of days. You know who you are and how precious each of you are to me and my family. May God continue to richly bless our friendships.

There are nights in the midst of writing a book when leftovers are the best thing going at dinnertime and the laundry is piled to the ceiling. For those times and any others when I might have been just a tad preoccupied, I thank my incredible husband and sweethearted children—I couldn't do this without the combined efforts from each of you.

And thanks to the Skyview basketball team, for always giving me a reason to cheer, even on deadline.

THE DESCENT

Weeping may endure for a night,
but joy comes in the morning.
PSALM 30:5, NKJV

PROLOGUE

❧❦❧

$\mathscr{S}$ix days had passed since Laura Thompson's job as a mother had officially ended.

The wedding had gone off without a hitch, and the last of Laura's four babies was out of the house, ready—like his siblings—to build a life of his own. She would always be their mom, of course, and in time she and Larry would welcome grandbabies and opportunities to visit with their grown children.

But for all intents and purposes, Laura was out of a job— and that was the primary reason for today's meeting.

She let her gaze fall on the circle of women gathered that Friday morning at Cleveland Community Church—women she'd known most of her life—and she was struck by the realization that they'd arrived at this place together. Houses quiet, children gone, grandchildren still years away…

Only their Friday morning Bible study remained the same.

The chattering among the women diminished and Emma Lou, women's president for the past year cast a tender smile their way. "Pastor gave me the names this morning."

A hush of expectancy settled over the group, and several of the women crossed their legs or tilted their heads, shifting their attention to the bowl in Emma Lou's hand. Inside were the names of younger women, women who felt the need for prayer, women who were diapering babies and solving multiplication problems over dinner dishes and wondering how to make laughter and love last even in a Christian marriage.

Laura swallowed hard, surprised to feel tears in her eyes. Women like she and her friends once had been.

"Before we open our Bibles, let's everyone draw a name. And remember, these are women who want your prayer and support, possibly even your mentoring. We may be finished raising our families, but these young gals are just starting out." Emma Lou's eyes shone with the memories of days gone by. "Draw a name, keep it confidential, and take the responsibility of praying for that one as seriously as you once took the job of mothering. I believe the Lord would find our work in this task every bit as important."

Laura dabbed at a tear and sucked in a quick breath. She wouldn't cry, not here, not now. She had a wonderful family and a million happy memories. There was nothing she could do to change the fact that her family was grown. But this—this role of praying for a young mother in their church fellowship—was something she could do today. Something that would give her life purpose, meaning, and direction.

Laura intended to carry out the assignment with all her heart.

The bowl was passed around the circle, and when it came to her she reached in, moving her fingers through the papers. *Who, Lord? Who would You have me pray for?*

She clasped a small slip and plucked it from the others. Would it be a mother overwrought with financial challenges? One burdened with the daily demands of mothering? Or perhaps a sweet daughter of the Lord whose husband didn't share her faith? Whoever she was, Laura knew the power of lifting a sister directly to the throne room of God. She could hardly imagine the results of praying for such a one over time.

Laura waited until Emma Lou asked them to read the names they had drawn, then her eyes fell to her hands as she unfolded the piece of paper and saw the bold writing inside. For a moment, a sharp pang of disappointment stabbed at her. *What's this? I must have grabbed the wrong slip.*

Maggie Stovall?

Of all the women in the church, God wanted her to pray for Maggie Stovall? What special needs could an exemplary woman like Maggie possibly have? How could she require daily prayer? Surely there was someone who needed her support more than Maggie Stovall.

Laura settled back in her chair, surprised Maggie had even gone to the trouble of requesting prayer. The young woman was a regular at church. Each week without exception, she and her husband volunteered in the Sunday school wing to lead the children in song. As far as Laura knew, Maggie was a successful newspaper columnist, her husband an established attorney. For the past few years, they'd even opened their home to foster children.

In need of prayer? The Stovalls were part of the blessed crowd—popular, well-liked people who cast a favorable impression on the entire church body, people the pastor and elders were proud to have in their midst.

Never, not even once, had Laura seen Maggie Stovall look anything but radiantly happy and perfectly put together.

Maggie Stovall? Am I hearing you right, Lord?

The answer was clear and quick: ***Pray, dear one. Maggie needs prayer.***

Immediately an image filled Laura's mind. The image of a woman wearing a mask.

Laura couldn't make out the woman's features, nor were the details of the mask clear. Still the image remained, and though Laura had no idea what to make of the mental picture she was instantly seized with remorse. *I'm sorry, Lord. Really. I'll pray...maybe there's something I don't know about Maggie.*

Laura ran her finger gently over the young woman's name, then folded the slip of paper and tucked it inside her Bible.

The vision of the masked woman came to mind again, and a sadness covered Laura's heart. Was it Maggie? Was there something she was hiding? *What is it, Lord? Tell me?*

Silence.

Laura sighed and her resolve grew. She might no longer be needed in the daily tasks of mothering, but clearly she was needed in this. God had spoken that much to her months ago when she had first suggested the idea of praying for the young women in their midst. And if this woman was the one she was to pray for, so be it.

She would pray for Maggie Stovall as though it were the most important job in the world.

And maybe one day God would let her understand.

I

The moments of lucidity were few and far between anymore. Thankfully, this was one of them. Aware of the fact, Maggie Stovall worked her fingers over the computer keyboard as though they might somehow propel her ahead of the darkness, keep her inches in front of whatever it was that hungered after her mind, her sanity.

Despite all that was uncertain that fall, Maggie was absolutely sure of one thing: She was losing it. And the little blond girl—whoever she might be—was only partly to blame.

Maggie's desk in the newsroom of the *Cleveland Gazette* was one of the remaining places where, most of the time, she still felt normal. The twenty or forty minutes a day she spent there were an oasis of peace and clarity bordered by a desert of hours, all dark, barren, and borderline crazy. The newsroom deadlines and demands left no room for fear and trembling, no time for worrying whether the darkness was about to consume her.

Maggie drew a steadying breath, glanced around the newsroom, and saw that the office was full of more reporters than usual for a Wednesday. *Slow news day. Great.* When news was slow her column got front-page billing, and the one she was writing for tomorrow's paper was bound to gain attention: "The Real Abuse of Abused Children." She let her eyes run down the page. This column would be clipped out of papers round the city, tacked to office walls, and mailed to the Social Services department by irate citizens. She would receive dozens of letters, and the paper would receive more, but none of that bothered Maggie.

She'd gotten the job at the *Gazette* more than two years earlier and she'd been churning out her column, "Maggie's Mind," five days a week since. She'd developed a reputation, a persona, that a segment of the public hated and a greater segment couldn't seem to get enough of. People said she put words to the thoughts and conversations that took place in a majority of homes in their area and around the country. The conservative homes. The people who voted against tax hikes and partial-birth abortions; people who wanted tougher prisons and longer sentences, and prayer in public schools. The segment of the population who wanted a return to family-friendly governing.

For those people, she was a welcome voice. The voice of morality in a time and place where few in the paper, or anywhere in the media for that matter, seemed committed to speaking on their behalf. Most *Gazette* readers loved Maggie. From the beginning they had applauded her, and a few months after starting at the paper the editorial staff had been forced to hire an assistant simply to weed through the mail generated by Maggie's efforts.

"You know, Maggie girl, I think you've really got something with that column of yours," her editor had told her more than once. "It's disconcerting, really. Like the rest of us are writing for some small special interest group, but you…ah, Maggie, you're writing for them. The moral majority."

Maggie knew the paper's editorial board was glad to have her on staff, even if many of her peers disagreed with her political views. But no one was more proud than her husband, Ben, an assistant district attorney who was also president of the Cleveland Chamber of Commerce. After nearly seven years of marriage, Ben was still in love with her; she had no doubts. Even now, when they had to search awkwardly for things to talk about and her attitude toward him was vastly different than a year ago, he would still walk over burning coals to prove his love.

Because he doesn't know the truth.

No. Not now, Maggie thought. *Not with a column to finish.*

Among the silent voices that taunted her these days was her own, and at times like this she was her worst enemy. If Ben knew the truth about her past, if he knew the real person he'd married, he would do what Joseph set out to do to Mary two thousand years ago: divorce her quietly and leave town on the first passing donkey.

"How's it coming, Mag?" It was Ron Kendall, managing editor, and he shouted the question from twenty feet away where the editors' desks formed an imposing island in the middle of the newsroom.

"Fine. I'll file in ten minutes."

"I might need it for page one. Give me a liner." Ron leaned back in his chair for a clearer view of Maggie's face.

She glanced at her screen and summed up her column. "Woman's lawsuit demands changes in the way abused children are handled by Social Services."

"Good. Got it." Ron returned to the task at hand—planning the paper's front page.

There were those at the paper who disliked Ron, but Maggie wasn't among them. Built like a linebacker with a mass of unkempt white hair and a perpetual two-day beard, the man's voice rang through the newsroom whenever a deadline was missed or an untruth reported in print. But deep down, beneath his work face, Ron Kendall was the last of a dying breed of editors, a churchgoing conservative who cherished his role in shaping and reporting the news of Cleveland.

Once Maggie ran into Ron at a dinner raising money for the city's rescue mission. Near the end of the evening, he pulled her aside.

"Someday you're going to get offers to leave us." The flint was missing from his eyes and in its place was a sparkle that couldn't be contrived. "Just remember this: Losing you would be like losing one of my arms." He patted her shoulder. "Don't ever leave us, Maggie. We need you."

That was a year ago, and Maggie was surprised to find Ron had been right. Offers had come from Los Angeles, Dallas, even New York. Editors might have enjoyed staffing their papers with liberal-minded news seekers, but nothing met the readers' appetite like a conservative columnist—and those who were well liked were in high demand.

Maggie had done what Ron asked and stayed. She liked Cleveland and their church friends at Cleveland Community. Besides, Ben's job was there.

If they knew the truth about me… Maggie closed her eyes. *They'd fire me in a heartbeat. I'd have no marriage, no column…*

Stop it! Stay focused! That was seven years ago, Maggie.

But Maggie knew it didn't matter how many years had slipped by. She would never get past the truth. And there would never be any way she could tell Ben.

Let no falsehood come from your mouth, but only that which is…

There it was again. The familiar calm, still voice…and with it a strange feeling of impending doom so great Maggie had to fight the urge to take cover. Her eyes flew open and she moved her hands into position at her keyboard. "Let's get this thing done," she hissed through clenched teeth. This was no time for strange, scriptural warnings about lie telling. She had a deadline to meet.

What was done was done.

Help me concentrate, God. Help me forget about what's behind; help me look ahead without this…whatever it is that wants to consume me.

Her head cleared, and she studied her computer screen once more.

Her column that day was based on a lawsuit filed against the city's Social Services department by a Cleveland woman contesting that the department was to blame for destroying her son. She'd adopted the boy when he was five years old. Over the next four years he'd been diagnosed with a host of disorders all attesting to the fact that he was unmanageable, unable to attach emotionally, and inappropriately aggressive toward her other children. Finally, the woman felt forced to turn the then nine-year-old back over to Social Services.

The lawsuit shone a flashlight of concern on the Social Services department, which still held to the notion that children should be raised by their parents whenever possible, regardless of the situation in the home. The woman contended that if Social Services had removed the boy from his birth mother sooner, he wouldn't have been so badly scarred emotionally.

Maggie's heart ached with understanding.

She and Ben were foster parents, currently of seven-year-old twin boys. Their mother was an alcoholic, their father dangerously violent. Still, Maggie knew that one day, long after the boys had bonded with her and Ben, they would be returned to their birth mother. Stories like the one she was writing about were tragically common, and Maggie hoped her words might touch a nerve across the city. Perhaps if enough people demanded change...

She scanned what she'd just written.

The way the department operates today, a child may be kept hostage in closets while Mom sells herself for drugs; he can be beaten, mocked, and left to sleep in urine-soaked rags, yet that type of home life is deemed best for the child. The solution is obvious. We must fight to see the system changed and demand that such children be removed from the home the first time harmful circumstances come to light—while the child is still young enough to find an adoption placement.

The statistics tell the story. With each passing year, the odds of a troubled child finding an adoptive home diminish by 20 percent. In the first year, the chances of adoption are brilliantly high. Even at age two most children will find permanent, loving homes. But many children removed from abusive homes are not released for adoption until age five, and often much later. What happens to these children?

Too often they are left to squander their baby years in abusive situations and temporary foster homes, moving every few months while Mom and Dad dry out or serve jail time. In the process, they become emotionally "damaged goods": children too old and too jaded ever to fit into a loving, adoptive family. In cases like these, we have only one place to point the finger for the tragic consequences: The archaic rules of the Social Services department.

I thank God for people like Mrs. Werdemeir, whose lawsuit finally exposes the type of tragedy that has gone on far too long. The tragedy of thinking that no matter the situation, a child belongs with his mother.

Tonight when you kneel beside the bed of your little one, remember those babies out there sleeping in closets. And pray that God will change the minds of those who might make a difference.

Suddenly Maggie's mind drifted, and her eyes jumped back a sentence: *Your little ones...little ones...little ones...kneel beside the bed of your little ones...*

Her eyes grew wet and the words faded. *What about us, Lord? Where are the little ones we've prayed for? Haven't we tried? Haven't we?* She remembered the testing, the experimental procedures they'd participated in, the drug therapy and nutrition programs that were supposed to help her get pregnant. A single tear slid down her cheek into her mouth. It tasted bitter, like it had come from some place deep and forbidden in her soul, and she wiped at it in frustration.

Nothing had worked.

Even now her arms ached for the children they didn't have. Foster kids, yes...but no babies to pray over, no little ones to be thankful for. *Why, Lord? It's been seven years...*

You had your chance. You don't deserve a child of your own.

The truth hit hard, and her breath caught in her throat.

Maggie blinked twice, and the taunting voice faded. She quickly included a footnote at the bottom of her column advising readers that there would be more information in the coming weeks and months on the issue of abused and forgotten children in the Social Services system. She saved her changes and sent the file to Ron's computer.

"It's in." She spoke loudly, and when she saw her editor nod, she turned her attention back to the now blank computer screen. Seconds passed, and a face began taking shape. The newsroom noise faded as the picture on the screen grew clearer, and suddenly Maggie could make out the girl's features...her pretty, innocent face; her lovely, questioning eyes.

Do you know where my mama is? the girl seemed to ask.

Maggie wanted to shout at the image, but she blinked twice and before her mind could give her mouth permission to speak, the girl disappeared.

It was her of course—the same girl every time, every day. She saw the child everywhere, even in her dreams.

The girl's presence had been a constant for nearly a year, making it difficult for Maggie to think of anything else. As a result, the days were no longer consumed with her work as a columnist, her role as a foster mother, or her duties as the wife of an important lawyer and civic leader. No, each day had become consumed with the idea that one day—perhaps not too far off—the little girl would not fade into air.

One day, the girl would be real.

The visions of the blond child had pushed Maggie to the edge of insanity. And with them came something else that filled Maggie's mind even now, a darkness that threatened to destroy her, to leave her locked in a padded cell, wrapped in a straight jacket. Or worse.

The problem wasn't so much that she was misplacing her car keys more often than usual or forgetting dentist appointments or leaving cold milk in the pantry by mistake or seeing imaginary little girls every time she turned around. It was all of that, yes, but it was something more that made her truly question her sanity. It was the certain feeling that something hideously dark and possibly deadly—something that now seemed closely linked to her secret—was closing in on her.

Something from which she couldn't escape.

A chill ran down Maggie's spine; the secret was no longer something she could ignore, something she might pretend had never happened. It didn't matter whether she acknowledged it or opened it and laid it on the floor for everyone to look at.

It simply was.

Indeed, its presence had become a living, breathing entity. It was the embodiment of darkness that lay beside her at night and followed her through the making of beds and breakfast and daily appointments in the morning. It sat next to her in the car, breathing threats of destruction should anyone find out the truth—

Stop this! You're making yourself crazy!

Maggie pushed away from her desk and gathered her things. Fresh air, that's what she needed. Maybe a walk through the park. She glanced at a stack of magazines on her desk and did a double take. There she was again! Gracing the cover, looking directly at Maggie...the same little girl.

Then in an instant, she was gone.

Air released from Maggie's lungs like a withering party balloon.

Yes, she was losing it—free-falling over the canyon's edge—and there was nothing she could do to prevent the coming crash. She wanted help, truly she did, but there wasn't anywhere she could turn, no one to talk to.

No one who would believe that Maggie Stovall was having a problem she couldn't handle by herself.

Finally, desperate, she'd placed her name in the offering bucket when the pastor had asked which women would like prayer from an older, senior Christian. Maggie didn't know if it would help, but it couldn't hurt. And it was better than facing someone with the truth.

She headed for her car.

How had things gotten so bad? Years ago she would have had two or three days a month like this and called it depression. Not that she told anyone how she was feeling, even back then. She was a Christian after all, and Christians—good Christians like her and Ben—did not suffer from depression. At least not as far as Maggie could tell. But this...this *thing* that haunted her now was beyond depression.

Far beyond it.

This was the kind of thing that sent people packing to psychiatric wards.

*A*manda Joy sat huddled on a narrow bed, leaning against the chilly wall of the third house she'd lived in that month. The silence was scary, like in the movies before something bad happened…but then she was only seven, and lots of things seemed scary. Especially since coming to the Graystone house.

Footsteps echoed in the distance, and Amanda gulped. Mrs. Graystone was awake, and that meant she'd be coming to check on her. Pushing herself off the bed, Amanda yanked on the covers and straightened the sheets. Beds had to be neat or…

Amanda didn't want to think about it.

Maybe there was another place she could go, some other foster family who wanted a little girl for a while. She tugged on the bedspread as she remembered the house she'd stayed at just after summer. Her social worker had called it a mistake, a bad placement. Five days later Amanda was packed and sent to a home five miles south, a working farm with three teenage boys.

She shuddered at the memory.

The boys' parents wanted a foster girl to give the missus a hand with laundry and indoor chores. But while she did up dishes or folded laundry the boys teased her until she was afraid to get dressed or take a shower. Two weeks later the mister found her in the barn, hands tied behind her back with baling twine. Her shirt lay in a rumpled heap on the ground, and the boys were taking turns poking at her, threatening to do terrible things to her if she screamed.

The boys received a whipping from their pa, and she escaped with her social worker before dinnertime.

She didn't know what she would have done without her social worker. For a moment, Amanda forgot about the chores and sat slowly on the corner of her bed. Kathy Garrett.

In some ways Kathy was more like a mother than anyone she'd ever known. Anyone except the Brownells.

The Brownells had been Amanda's only real parents. They adopted her as a baby and gave her a wonderful life for five short years.

The house was quiet again, and Amanda wondered if Mrs. Graystone had fallen back asleep. There had been an empty liquor bottle on the table when Amanda got home from school. Alcohol made Mrs. Graystone very tired, so maybe she would sleep for a long time.

Amanda slipped off the mattress and lifted the plain, gray bedskirt, poking her head under the bed. There it was. Gently she pulled out a brown paper bag, opened it, and sat cross-legged on the floor, staring at the contents inside. A photograph of her with the Brownells, three folded-up awards she'd won in school, a bracelet she'd found in the lunchroom the year before. She plucked out the picture and stared hard at it. The checkered dress she'd worn that year was a hand-me-down from the neighbors. All the girls in kindergarten had laughed at it, but Amanda figured out how to make them stop. She prayed for them.

She'd knelt beside her bed at the Brownells and prayed. "Dear Jesus, help those girls in my class be nice. Because they don't have happy hearts, at least I don't think so."

Neither did Mrs. Graystone. Which was why Amanda had been praying for her, too. She sighed and set the photograph back in the sack. As she peered inside, her eyes fell on the yellowish newspaper article.

Amanda pulled it out and opened it carefully.

She couldn't read very well, but she'd read the article often enough to know what it said. It was a news report of the accident that killed the Brownells.

"Icy tree limb lands on car, kills Woodland couple," the big words on top yelled out.

Amanda felt tears stinging her eyes. The smaller letters said how the Brownells had a five-year-old daughter. But they didn't say there was no one for her to live with once the Brownells were gone.

She remembered meeting Kathy Garrett for the first time at school that afternoon—the day of the accident. Kathy told Amanda that she had known her as a little baby and that she had helped the Brownells with the adoption. At first it had been nice, sitting in the office talking with the pretty lady. But then Kathy told her about the accident and after that her tummy had felt sick inside.

Sick and scared.

"You can stay with us tonight, sweetheart," Kathy said. "But after that we'll find you a foster home. A place where you can stay until another family adopts you."

They'd found a home. A foster home, like Kathy had talked about. And then another one. And another one. But the best times of all were when Amanda was between foster parents and got to spend a night or two with Kathy and her family.

Amanda closed her eyes and pictured Kathy Garrett's home. Warm, with lots of light and laughter and good smells from the kitchen. Someone was always talking or telling a story or singing or dancing. When Amanda was there she didn't feel like her name was Brownell at all. She felt like it was Garrett. Like she belonged there. Like she was one of them. She even had her own chair at the kitchen table.

At times like this she wondered if they left her empty chair at the table when she wasn't there, if the Garretts missed her as much as she missed them.

She opened her eyes again, folded the article, and slipped it back inside the bag. It was the same bag she'd had for two years, and she was careful not to rip it as she folded the top down and slid it back under the bed.

Kathy Garrett was married to a happy man named Bill. He would lay on the floor and wrestle with the kids until they were laughing so hard they couldn't breathe. He always laughed. But one time…

One time Bill didn't laugh. When he brought everyone together in a circle once to pray for Amanda. During the prayer, when he thought she wasn't looking, Amanda caught him crying. Not loud tears like kids cry, but quiet ones that rolled off his face and didn't make his nose sound stuffy.

Amanda stared at the barren walls in the chilly room, but in her mind she could see Bill and Kathy, laughing, playing with their children. Lots and lots of children. The Garretts had more kids than anyone Amanda knew. Seven altogether, all squeezed into three happy bedrooms. Kathy liked to say it wasn't the size of the house that mattered, it was what the house was made of. After living in a dozen different houses in two years Amanda was sure of one thing: Kathy wasn't talking about bricks and carpet and stuff.

She was talking about feelings. So as far as Amanda was concerned, the Garrett house was made of all love and sunshine.

There were footsteps again and Amanda's heart quickened. Mrs. Graystone had four other foster children living with her, all of them crammed into two small bedrooms. Her husband drove a truck for a living and was hardly ever home. The other kids liked to tell secrets about Mrs. Graystone, and the first day Amanda arrived they told her what they thought of their foster mother.

"Old Graystone uses all our money to buy her smelly cigarettes," one of the kids told her that first day.

Amanda frowned. "What money?"

An older girl laughed out loud. "The gov'ment money, goofball. She's supposed to use it to buy us food and clothes and stuff."

"Yeah, but she never does," the first boy poked Amanda on the shoulder. "You'll see soon enough. Two meals a day if you're lucky. And if you're hungry at night then too bad for you."

The kids had been right; Mrs. Graystone's house was made of scary sounds and hungry nights. Lots of hunger.

There was a sharp knock at the bedroom door, and Mrs. Graystone burst inside. She was a big woman with an angry mouth and rolls of stomach pushing against her flowered dress. Amanda jumped to her feet and backed up against the farthest wall as Mrs. Graystone waddled toward her.

"Why aren't you cleaning your room?"

Amanda looked about and saw nothing out of place. "I made the bed and picked up the clothes like you said."

"Anyone could do that." She came closer and shook a finger at her. "Do you think

I brought you here so you could live like a princess?" The woman's voice rattled like windows in an old house when the wind blew hard outside.

"What else do you want me—"

"Don't be impertinent with me, young lady." Mrs. Graystone's face was red, and Amanda was scared. The woman had never hit her, but that didn't mean she wouldn't. Other foster parents had done it. Not all of them, of course. Some of Amanda's foster placements had been wonderful homes like Kathy's. But her stay at those homes was never permanent. They were something called short-term or crisis-care stays. Something like that. After a little while in those places, Amanda always got packed up and sent to the next foster home.

Since she was not sure what *impertinent* meant she squirmed toward the corner of her bed and remained silent.

Mrs. Graystone lowered herself over Amanda and glared at her. "I don't need no insolent brat living with me. I can make the same money with someone who'll do as I say. Do you hear me?"

"Yes, ma'am."

The woman raised her hand, and before Amanda could take cover it came crashing down across her cheek. The blow made her fall to her knees, and she gasped for breath. *I'm scared, God, help me!*

Amanda covered her face with her hands and felt her body shaking with fear. *Don't let her hit me again, please...*

"Don't you 'yes, ma'am,' me, missy. Now get up and get to work."

Amanda separated her fingers so she could see Mrs. Graystone again.

"Move your hands from your face!"

Amanda's cheek felt hot and sore but she did as she was told. The woman pointed to a broom that stood in the corner of the room. "I want that hardwood floor swept and polished. And when you're finished you can take a rag to those awful walls. I swear the last brat who had this room didn't do any better than you."

She was still on her knees, afraid to move. *Kathy's coming today. It won't be long. Just a few more hours and I can leave. Kathy won't let me—*

"Move it!" Mrs. Graystone grabbed Amanda's arm and yanked her to her feet. Then she pulled a rag and a bottle of floor polish from her apron and tossed it on the floor. "I want this place clean in an hour or you can forget dinner."

The woman took slow steps toward the hallway, then slammed the door shut as she left.

Why does she hate me? Are You there, God? Don't You hear me? All I want is a mom and a dad. I'll clean my room perfect every day, I promise. But please, God, please give me a mom and dad. Someone like Bill and Kathy.

Tears stung at the girl's eyes as she took the broom and worked it across the floor in long strokes. She would be eight in six months and though she was small for her age, she'd been sweeping floors for as long as she could remember, so she had the task finished in a few minutes. Her mind began to drift back to when she was little, before her adoptive parents were killed. As she took the rag and began working polish into the floor, she started to cry harder.

Even if she were going to see Kathy later, it wouldn't solve anything. She'd still be a ward of the court, a foster child looking for a family. She wandered tentatively over to the brown sack and the photograph of her with her adoptive parents, the Brownells. They had been wonderful people, but they hadn't been like real family.

She closed her eyes and she could hear herself asking the familiar question:

"If you adopted me, how come I can't call you Momma and Daddy?"

Mrs. Brownell's answer was as clear now as it had been that spring day all those years ago. "Child, we will always think of you as our daughter, but Mr. Brownell and I never planned to have children and we don't think it proper for a child to call us by so familiar a term. Mr. and Mrs. Brownell suits us better. But it doesn't mean we love you any less."

Even back when she was five the answer had felt uncomfortable, like a shrunken sweater. She studied the picture once more and as she went back to work on the floor she thought of her mother. Her real mother.

The Brownells had told her about a young woman who had been unable to care for her new baby and so, out of love, had given her to them to raise. But ever since God had taken the Brownells home, Amanda had kept a secret wish that somewhere out in the big world her real Momma was missing her.

And that one day God would bring them back together again.

3

*M*aggie stood in the parking lot outside the newspaper building, pulled her running shoes from the trunk of her car, and slipped them on. Just then her cell phone rang, and she exhaled in frustration. *What now? I only have an hour to finish my run and get the boys.* If she didn't burn off some of the anxiety coursing through her she wouldn't make it through the day. She grabbed her purse and yanked the phone from inside.

"Hello?"

There was a hesitation on the other end that almost made Maggie hang up. Then the voice of an older woman cut the silence. "Maggie Stovall?"

"Yes?" *Great. Now I'm getting sales calls on my—*

"Maggie, this is Laura Thompson. From church. I'm sorry to bother you…"

As the woman's voice trailed off, Maggie pictured her: late sixties, gray hair, soft face, always involved in one committee or another. Concern transcended Laura Thompson's voice, and Maggie felt herself tense up. What would Laura Thompson want with her? "No, that's fine. What's going on?"

The woman cleared her throat. "Well, dear…we picked names last week, and I wanted you to know I got yours."

Maggie's mind was blank. *Names?* What was Laura talking about? "I'm not sure I'm following you."

"The prayer team, remember? You put your name in the basket so one of us would pray for you."

Maggie's concentration was waning and without reason her heart began to race. "Prayer?" Then it hit her. Laura was right; she'd written her name on a slip of paper requesting one of the older women in the church to pray for her. She'd never expected a phone call from one of them. Silent, anonymous prayer was one thing, but this… She felt her cheeks grow hot. "I remember now. So, uh, thanks for letting me know."

"Yes, I'll be praying. And I'm here for you, dear. If you need anything, anytime. You can call me. We'll pray on the phone, or I can meet with you. Whatever you'd like. Whatever's on your heart."

Pray with Laura Thompson about what was on her heart? The idea was so terrifying it was ludicrous. Impossible. If Laura knew her secret everyone at Cleveland Community would know, too. And they would never look at her the same. Maggie's heart beat faster still, and she managed a polite laugh. *Control, Maggie. Show her you're in control.* "Thanks for the offer, Laura. But really, everything's fine. I only asked for prayer because…well, you know…it can't hurt." She laughed again, forcing her voice to sound upbeat.

Silence.

She knows. Oh no, it can't be. How did she find out about me, Lord? Maggie closed her eyes and forced her trembling knees together. "Laura?"

"Yes, dear, I'm here. It's just—"

Maggie cut her off. "Don't get me wrong. I'd still like you to pray. But there's no crisis or anything, that's all."

"Okay." Laura didn't seem convinced. "I'll let you go, dear. But I'll be praying all the same. My number's in the church directory."

She knows. I know she knows. Maggie hung up and slipped the phone back in her purse. Who had told her? Why else would she have called? Wasn't the prayer team supposed to do things in private, secretly?

Her hands were shaking, and perspiration ran down her arms and neck. She glanced at the running shoes. Why did she have them on? Oh yes, her run. She frowned, glancing about the parking lot and across the street to the park. *Think, Maggie, come on.* Had she finished her run already? So quickly? She barely remembered a moment of it.

Remembering to breathe, she slipped her shoes off and froze. She felt the breath of something evil on the back of her neck, something close enough to touch. Tossing her shoes back in the trunk she hurried into the driver's seat, slammed the door shut and hit the lock.

It was no use.

The invisible darkness had followed her into the car and now was locked inside with her. *How did I finish my run so fast?* She looked across the street once more at the familiar park and its asphalt jogging trail that ran the circumference. *I did run, didn't I?* Her body was sweaty, her heart beating hard. She must have run.

Maggie started the car and again felt the presence of evil beside her. "Get out!" Despite her shouted command, the feeling didn't ease. *All I want is peace, Lord, what's it going to take?*

Confess your sins and you will be clean.… The prayers of a righteous person are powerful and effective.…

Maggie shook her head. No. She wouldn't confess to anyone. Not after years of building the life she had, her marriage with Ben, the career she loved. She wouldn't throw it all away now by admitting the truth.

Not even to one whose prayers might be powerful and effective.

One like Laura Thompson.

Maggie pulled out of the parking lot and realized she had never been so tired in all her life. *I must have overdone it on the run.* She needed to pick up groceries and stop at the post office before getting the boys, but in that moment every breath required a conscious effort.

As she drove, the darkness closed in around her. If only there were a hole she could crawl into, a place where she could sleep for ten years or twenty, she would have gone there without hesitating. She forced herself to regain control, summoning the strength to keep the car on the road. Things began to look familiar, and she knew she'd be home in a few minutes. *Maybe I'll take a nap.*

Other drivers were passing her, and Maggie wondered why they were speeding. She let her eyes fall to her speedometer. *What? Twenty miles an hour?* How long had she been driving that slowly? She stared at the road ahead of her, concentrating, frowning. *I need to pick up something…buy something…*

Up ahead, a store sign caught her eye, and she made a sudden turn into the parking lot. That was it; she needed food. They were out of milk and eggs and cheddar cheese. But she was so tired. The idea of climbing out of her car and grocery shopping right now felt as impossible as attempting the Boston Marathon on two hours' sleep. *You can do it, Maggie. It's not that hard.*

She parked, climbed out of the car, and pulled herself across the parking lot. For what seemed like an hour she wandered through the produce section, staring at row after row of vegetables, fruits…round, even, orderly rows…

What food did she have back at home? Ben liked apples, green apples mostly. Or was it red apples? She ripped a plastic bag from the roll, opened it, and began placing apples inside. *Five, six, seven apples, that ought to do it. One a day.*

She dropped the bag into her cart and made her way deeper into the store. Vegetables. Canned vegetables. She had a casserole to make for the weekend. A church function. What was it? A potluck? A reception? Maggie stopped walking and pulled her cell phone from her purse. She scanned the numbers programmed into the directory and pushed connect when she saw "C.C. Church."

"Hello, Cleveland Community Church, can I help you?" Maggie started at the voice, then froze in place. *Why am I standing in the middle of the grocery store calling church?*

"Uh…never mind. Wrong number."

She put the cell phone back and stared at the shelves. What did she need here, anyway? Why couldn't she remember what she was doing and how come she was so tired? If it wouldn't seem a little crazy, she would just as soon lie down right where she was standing—smack in the middle of the canned vegetable aisle—and take a nap. An hour of sleep, that was all she needed. Maybe then she'd feel better. But of course people would notice if she took a nap in the middle of the grocery store, wouldn't they?

They would, Maggie was fairly sure. She'd have to wait and sleep at home. What was it she needed? Tomato sauce. That was it. She pulled four cans from the shelf and moved on to the next row of food products.

At that moment a woman entered the aisle from the other direction and beside her was—

Maggie gasped and her hand flew to her mouth. It was her! The blond girl. She was six, maybe seven, and her blue eyes took up most of her face. Cascades of curls spilled over her shoulders, and she had that questioning look in her eyes, the same one she always had, like she wanted Maggie to help her find her mama.

Other times Maggie knew she'd imagined the little girl, but not this time. This time it was really her. Maggie dropped all four cans of tomato sauce on the floor and pushed her cart straight for the child. When she got close enough, she left her food and knelt in front of the girl. Moving slowly so as not to frighten the child, Maggie took her small, warm hand—but before she could speak she heard someone talking above her.

"Excuse me, ma'am? Do I know you?"

Maggie blinked. An Hispanic woman in a tailored business suit was peering down at her, and though the woman's tone was polite, her face was lined with concern.

Where did she come from? Maggie blinked again. "Yes…I mean, I thought your little girl…" She glanced back at the child and inhaled sharply. The girl whose hand she held had short brown hair and brown-skinned features.

The little blond girl was gone.

Maggie dropped the child's hand and uttered a nervous laugh as she stood and faced the girl's mother. "I'm sorry. I thought she was someone…" Maggie's mind raced. "Someone I knew from church. Sunday school, actually."

The woman smiled coolly and reached for her daughter's hand. "I don't think so." She pointed to the other end of the aisle. "I think you forgot your tomato sauce."

Tomato sauce? Maggie saw the cans lying on the floor and forced another laugh. "Right. Thanks."

She pushed her cart back down the aisle, retrieved the cans, and dropped them in the cart. *Why did I need tomato sauce?* She stared at the bottom of her cart and squinted in confusion. There was a bag of onions where her apples had been. Did she have the wrong cart? Had someone taken her apples and replaced them with onions?

The girl and her mother had moved to a different aisle, and Maggie hoped they didn't think she was crazy. She wasn't, after all. Tired maybe, worn out. But not crazy. It wasn't her fault the little blond girl followed her everywhere she went.

Maggie wandered the aisles. Later on she would look back and know that the breakdown truly began in frozen foods, somewhere between the boxed pizzas and bagged tropical fruit. But now…now she didn't know what was happening, only that tears were coming quickly, filling Maggie's eyes and making her mind a jumble of thoughts. Why had she married Ben in the first place? How had she survived so many years living a lie? Why was she so tired and what was she doing with tears streaming down her face and a cart full of tomato sauce and an overstuffed bag of onions, paralyzed by something she couldn't see or understand?

A white-haired man with a cardigan sweater and a concerned look tapped her gently on the shoulder. "Are you all right, ma'am?" He waited for an answer.

Maggie dried her eyes. *I'll be lucky if he doesn't call a doctor and have me committed.* "I'm fine." She nodded tersely at the man. "Just...it's been a long day. I'm tired."

"Okay." The older gentleman hesitated a moment longer, then continued shopping.

Collect yourself, Maggie. Get it together. You're bigger than this; you've been bigger than it for years. Why should things be any different now? She thought of the little girl and how sure she'd been that this time—finally—it was really her and...

Help me, Lord... Please.

I'm here, daughter. Come into the light.

But there was no way out, no light to come toward.

Maggie began to tremble again. She was on the edge of the darkest, deepest canyon that had ever bordered her path, and the only thing stopping her from tumbling over was a threadbare rope of memories. Even that was fraying badly.

She forced herself to take deep breaths and suddenly she was at the checkstand, falling asleep on her feet. The ground seemed to shift as her eyes flew open and her head jerked back into an alert position. What was that in her cart? Onions? Tomato sauce? Where were the apples? The milk? She had forgotten every item she'd come for.

She stared over her shoulder into the store. The thought of turning around and heading back for milk was overwhelming. Too many aisles and food displays stacked high above her. Too many colors and people and sales signs fought for her attention. Suddenly the store seemed like a sinister maze, one from which she might never come out alive if she ventured back inside. She exhaled slowly. *Help me, God. I need You.* The words felt empty, much as they had often felt lately. Maggie waited for an answer. Silence. *Okay, Maggie, concentrate. You can do this on your own.*

Over the next thirty minutes she forced herself back through the store where she painstakingly collected the three necessities and several canned goods and packaged food that would help get her family through the week.

As she pushed her cart out of the store toward her Chevy Tahoe, she congratulated herself on having survived. Whatever it was that wanted so badly to consume her, she would simply have to be tougher, think things through, and gather her determination. It was merely a matter of trying harder.

The darkness isn't going to get me. Not ever again. I don't need to wait for an answer to prayer; I need to believe in myself. I'm stronger than I think.

She unloaded her groceries, slipped the cart back into the nearby rack, and climbed into her vehicle. Only then, as she glanced into the rearview mirror and saw her face in the reflection, did she realize things were worse than she'd thought.

How long had she looked like this? Why hadn't anyone said something more to her?

If the mirror was right, she was weeping without her knowing it; tears streaming down her face. Minutes passed, and suddenly she was jolted awake by the honking of a horn behind her. Two cars vying for a parking space.

I've been sleeping...

The realization shook her. *The boys! What time is it?* She glanced at her watch and her heart sank. She'd lost almost an hour. She was still tired, but she forced herself to stay awake.

Casey and Cameron needed her.

4

aggie slipped on a pair of dark glasses, then raced to get the boys. Since her eyes seemed bent on shedding tears, she kept her glasses on even after she and the boys got home, wearing them during snack time and while she made dinner. Everything inside her cried out for the warmth of her bed. Now, before the sun sank and the nighttime demons refused to let her sleep.

She searched the cupboards. *Macaroni and cheese, that'll work. It's been months since we've had that.*

Maggie opened a box of noodles and poured it into a cold pan of water. She began slowly stirring the mixture. Ten minutes passed…twenty…and suddenly one of the boys was at her side, tugging on her sleeve.

"Aren't you going to cook it, Maggie?" He dipped his finger into the water and Maggie pushed him back.

"Don't! It's hot…can't you see it's boil—" She blinked twice. The water was not boiling; the macaroni inside was no closer to being ready to eat than it had been half an hour earlier.

She dropped the spoon on the countertop and pulled Cameron into a hug. "I'm sorry, honey. I didn't mean to push you. I thought—"

There was fear in his face. Her strange behavior was probably worrying both boys even though they'd only been living with her and Ben for a month.

"Right, honey. Maggie has a lot on her mind, that's all."

"I like macaroni and cheese. We had it last night, too."

Last night? Maggie thought hard, but she had no memory whatsoever of the night before. She watched Cameron return to the table and then she switched on the burner beneath the pan. At the same time she heard the door swing open.

"Hey, Maggie, I'm home."

It was Ben. Maybe he could cook dinner and she could get some sleep. That was all this was, this darkness and desperation. A simple lack of sleep. Ben tossed his briefcase and overcoat onto a living room chair and came up behind her.

"Hi." Maggie knew she didn't sound very enthusiastic, but she could no longer force herself. Everything about their marriage, about who she was when she was with him, all of it was a lie. What was the point of making small talk?

Ben kissed her neck tenderly and glanced over her shoulder. "Good thing we all like macaroni and cheese."

She could hear the teasing in his tone, but she bristled anyway. "You don't like it, *you* cook for once."

He stepped back, his expression changing. "We had it last night, Maggie. I'm fine with that, but don't get defensive with me. I'm only trying to make you laugh."

His eyes searched hers. "How was your day?"

Maggie thought about the desperate feeling of doom that had followed her from the keyboard at work, to her jogging, to the frozen food section of the grocery store. She thought about how—without knowing it—she had wept while paying for her groceries and how she had stirred a pan of cold water and hard macaroni noodles for thirty minutes before realizing she'd forgotten to turn on the burner.

She looked at Ben and forced a smile. "My day was fine. You?"

He walked toward the boys, keeping his eyes trained on her. "Things are coming along with the Jenson murder trial. The evidence is in, and I think we'll get a conviction." Leaning over, he studied the boys' homework sheets and smiled broadly. "You boys are going to be scientists one day, mark my words."

He looked back at Maggie. "Brightest boys in Cleveland, Mag, wouldn't you say?"

Why am I here? Why are we going through the motions when it's all a big lie? "Yep," she mumbled.

Dinner was uneventful, and Maggie maneuvered her fork through the pile of cheese-covered macaroni trying to figure out how she'd made the same meal two nights in a row without remembering it.

When they were finished eating, the boys went upstairs to their room to get ready for baths. Maggie dropped her fork on top of the now cold noodles and stared at her husband. "I'm not hungry." Her voice was flat as she stood and moved toward the kitchen, aware that Ben's eyes followed her.

"Sit down, Maggie."

His voice was not angry, but neither did it leave room for negotiation. Maggie set her plate in the sink and returned to face her husband. There was nothing she could think to say, so she waited.

"What's wrong with you, Mag?"

She sighed and studied her fingernails for a moment. "Nothing."

Ben shook his head. "There's something wrong. Either something with you or something with me or something with both of us. But I'm tired of walking around here acting like everything's okay."

Why didn't I tell him the truth from the beginning? Then he never would have married me, and we wouldn't be in this mess. "Okay." She leveled her gaze at him. Her voice sounded tired as she continued. "You want to know what's wrong with me, I'll tell you."

Ben waited expectantly. There was love in his eyes, so much so it pained Maggie to know she was hurting him. But sooner or later he would have to know that she wasn't the sweet, Christian girl he thought he'd married. Maybe if she told him now, at least part of the truth…

Not too much, Maggie. Don't tell him too much.

She drew a deep breath. "I'm tired of pretending."

Ben couldn't have looked more dazed if she had just announced she might like to dye her hair pink. "Pretending?"

"Yes." Maggie crossed her arms. "All day long I pretend. I pretend to be this wonderful Christian woman worthy of handing out advice to half the people in Cleveland, then I pretend that managing foster children is a satisfying substitute for having babies of my own. And when *you* get home…" Her voice trailed off and she saw his eyes fill with fresh pain.

"What, Mag? When I get home, what?"

The walls of the dining room began to close in on her. *Why, God? What's happening to me? How come I can't leave it alone and let it go?* She gripped the edges of her chair.

Come on, tell him. He's waiting. Tell him the truth about how you feel. At least give him that. This isn't someone you love, remember? He's hurt you; he's the enemy.

"Ben, it's just—" Her voice was barely a whisper and this time she could feel the tears gathering in her eyes. "What I'm trying to say is, well…I pretend with you, too."

He hesitated, and a flash of fear skittered across his eyes. "Come on, Maggie. You're overreacting, having a bad day or something. I mean, there's nothing here that can't—"

"No! You're wrong." She was trembling now, crying openly and raising her voice. "I'm telling you how I *feel*. Don't you understand?"

Ben was silent, and Maggie saw his eyes were wet, too. *Tell him, Maggie. You've lied to protect him long enough. It's your turn to hurt him for a change.*

She closed her eyes for a moment and when she opened them she felt stronger than before. He had done this to her, after all. Forced her to live a lie, to pretend she was the perfect Christian girl, and then later, the ideal wife. What choice had she ever had but to lie to him?

Maggie exhaled and steadied her voice. "The truth is…you don't know me, Ben." She leveled her gaze at him and held it there. "You never have."

His face grew pale, then flushed—all in a matter of seconds. He stood and turned away. Maggie gazed out the window where the sun had not quite settled beyond the nearly bare tree line. *I hate this; all of it.* Her arms ached, and she recognized the feeling as familiar. Aching, empty arms. The same way they'd been that May morning so many years ago…

Stop! The order echoed in her heart and stopped all other thoughts. She shifted her gaze to Ben and then, without saying another word, without stopping and doing up the dinner dishes or looking in on Casey and Cameron, she stood and dragged her feet up the stairs. It took the rest of her energy to tear back the comforter that lay twisted on her unmade bed and bury herself beneath.

There, still wearing her clothes and shoes, with visions of the little blond girl filling her mind and the sun not quite set in the evening sky, Maggie Stovall willed herself to sleep.

5

The column was fairly scathing, at least that's what Kathy Garrett's coworkers at the Social Services department were saying. Kathy found that hard to believe. Now, after going nonstop through lunch, she finally had a moment to read it for herself.

"Okay, where is it?" she muttered as she pulled the paper out of its plastic sleeve and spread it on the table. Kathy was a fan of "Maggie's Mind" and figured that if the columnist had taken on the department there was probably some merit to her argument. She opened the paper and saw the headline at the top right side of the front page: "Maggie's Mind: The Real Abuse of Abused Children." Kathy studied the columnist's picture that accompanied the article and was struck by a familiar thought. Something about the reporter's eyes was more than a little familiar.

She dismissed the idea and delved into the article, immediately swept up by the picture Maggie painted. Children shuffled from one home to another, experiencing enough trauma to destroy their psyches and change them forever into societal misfits. Maggie's view was simple: Social Services was a system desperately understaffed and far too quick to place kids back in a dangerous environment because of some noble idea that children are better off with their birth parents.

Kathy closed her eyes and pictured the children she'd seen pass through the system in just that manner. Maggie was right. Many times the department's good intentions to keep children with their biological families only made matters worse. And there was nothing anyone at Social Services could do to prevent it from happening again, not until laws governing parental rights were changed.

Kathy could see why the column upset the staff at the department, but she silently applauded Maggie for having the courage to take on a federal agency and illuminate an issue that was every bit as troubling as the columnist had described it.

Of course there was the other problem with the system—one Kathy was sure Maggie would inevitably tackle in future columns: the lack of quality foster homes. Sometimes, it seemed, the need for foster homes throughout the state was so great only a cursory safety check was done on the applicants. Motives certainly could not be checked, and since Social Services provided foster parents with a stipend to provide for the child's food and clothing, there would always be those who provided substandard care as a way to make money.

She thought of her appointment later that night—pictured the lonely little girl—and her eyes burned with the beginning of tears. Amanda Joy Brownell. The child had been in the system so long she had only a very slim chance of ever being adopted. Foster care was also difficult. The better foster homes tended to take young children; not seven-year-old girls with a history of removals.

It isn't her fault, Lord. Kathy hung her head as two tears splashed onto the newsprint and worked their way into the layers of paper beneath. Kathy remembered the day she was called to the hospital to talk with the girl's biological mother, a wide-eyed twenty-three-year-old who had been convinced that being a single mom would ruin her life. At least before the delivery. But that day at the hospital the young mother had broken down and wept, so distraught over giving up her baby that Kathy had asked her to reconsider. Instead the girl had been adamant, repeating over and over that giving up the baby was something she had to do.

Kathy stared out her window across the tree-lined parking lot. The sky was slate gray, and most of the leaves had fallen from the maples. Thanksgiving was coming, and Christmas. Another year gone by, and still Amanda Joy had no place to call home. The situation—like so many others Kathy worked with—was enough to break her heart.

Where's her birth mother today, Lord? Kathy released a slow breath and wondered like she had a dozen times before about the girl's young mother. Did she regret her choice to give the baby up for adoption? Kathy still remembered her hesitation as she'd signed the paperwork that day at the hospital, and again as she took the newborn girl from the trembling arms of her mother and whisked her into the waiting arms of Stan and Tammy Brownell. Most babies were placed through private adoption agencies housed in decorated suites on the fifteenth floor of a corporate high-rise in downtown Cleveland. Kathy remembered thinking it unusual that the young mother chose to come to Cincinnati's Social Services Department to give the baby up.

At first Kathy had been happy for the Brownells—a couple without the means to adopt privately but with a great desire to have a child. Her opinion changed after she met with them. The couple seemed so serious and somber… Kathy had a very real feeling that although their home study was complete, the placement wasn't right for the baby girl. Either way—as with most of her cases—there was nothing Kathy could do but pray about the situation.

She hadn't expected to see the little girl again.

Kathy cringed like she always did when she thought of the accident, the frozen tree limb that had fallen on the Brownells' car, killing them both instantly. Since the Brownells had no extended family, Amanda Joy was made a ward of the court and again Kathy was called in to help. She had met the child at her kindergarten class that day and escorted her to the office, where together with the school counselor they revealed the awful news.

Amanda's reaction had confirmed Kathy's fears from years earlier. The child had stared at her nailbitten fingers and scuffled her feet nervously. "Will I still be living at their house?"

Kathy had been confused. "Whose house, honey?"

"Mr. and Mrs. Brownell's." The girl's eyes were dry.

The words had hung in the air a few moments. "You mean your house, your mom and dad's house?"

Amanda shook her head. "I'm not allowed to call them Mom and Dad. They said it wasn't formal."

Looking back Kathy wasn't sure which realization hurt more, the fact that Amanda Joy was once again without parents or the fact that she'd been little more than a favorite guest in her home for all of her five years. Since then Amanda had spoken kindly of the Brownells, so Kathy knew they had not been harmful in any way. They just hadn't given her the love and acceptance a child deserves.

Kathy noticed a squirrel scurrying down the trunk of a tree just outside the office window. *Even he has a home, Lord…*

Her eyes welled up again. *The Brownells were better than anything she's been dealt since then. We'd take her in a minute if we could, God. You know that.* She and Bill had brainstormed several times ideas for buying a bigger house. They knew no judge in the county would award them another child until they had more room. They'd already petitioned for an exception, and been denied. *Dear God, there has to be someone for her…somewhere out there. Please…* Another tear fell. *She's a good girl, Lord, but every month, every year that goes by…it'll take a miracle to find her a family now.*

Amanda had been shy before the death of her adoptive parents. Now she had slight learning disabilities and trouble attaching to people. When she was scared or anxious she stuttered, so in addition to weekly counseling and special education courses, the child was mandated to receive speech therapy.

Kathy closed her eyes and loosed two more tears. It wasn't fair. The child's file was full of "problem areas," tarnished judgments that in all likelihood would scare off potential adoptive parents and send them hurrying to private agencies for younger children without the baggage Amanda carried.

She wiped her tears and gazed out the dining room window once more. *I'm not a miracle worker, God. But You are. Please…please help me find someone who'll give her a home.*

Then because she knew too well the department's statistics, she added one more thing. *And hurry, Lord.* She thought of the children who started out sweet and anxious for love only to become jaded and antisocial after too many transfers to different foster homes, too many years waiting for a family that never came. Despite her file, Amanda Joy was not yet one of those. But she could be if something didn't change soon.

Kathy sighed softly and folded up the newspaper. Yes, God would have to speed things up if He was going to work a miracle this time. The child needed a home and parents who loved her, and she needed it now.

Before it was too late.

6

$\mathcal{B}$en Stovall stared out the window of his fourth-story office and wondered exactly when his life had started falling apart.

Days like this it was difficult to concentrate on establishing motives or gathering depositions. A death penalty case couldn't have mattered less to him now that it seemed clear his marriage was crumbling. And no matter how long or hard he thought about it, he couldn't come up with a single reason why.

Everything about his life with Maggie had seemed literally plucked from a story-book. They were married young, both strong believers bent on putting God first in their relationship. And though there hadn't been any children, Ben believed there would be one day. Whenever God deemed it right. And if not, then he believed it was because the Lord had a different plan. Adoption, maybe. Or more years of foster children.

Ben loved the idea of affecting the lives of a different set of children every year or so. Besides, things were going well at work and he figured the coming spring might be a great time to initiate a private adoption. Live right and experience the rewards. That had always been his motto.

For that reason, Ben knew there'd be children one day. After all, he and Maggie had done everything right in their relationship. They had been pure when they came together on their wedding night and had remained faithful to each other since. They tithed at church, prayed daily, and read their Bibles—usually cover to cover in any given year.

Ben thought about that for a moment. Well, maybe not daily. But for the most part he and Maggie lived a godly life. Even at work they did whatever they could to please the Lord, and He had always rewarded their efforts. After all, blessings didn't come any bigger than Maggie having her own column. Not in the newspaper business, anyway.

Between her job and his, they pulled in a steady six-figure salary, and because they were in their early thirties they had plenty of time for children.

Outside his window a sparrow appeared from nowhere and began attacking a much larger crow. *Probably protecting his nest.* Ben watched them for a few minutes, thinking.

What was it Maggie had said? *"You don't know me...you never have."* He could see her face, the way it was cloaked in discouragement, as though she were holding back a very deep, dark secret. What did she mean he didn't know her? Of *course* he knew her.

Didn't he?

Now, alone in his office, he wasn't so sure.

He remembered the first time he saw Maggie, when their churches had joined a handful of others in Cleveland for a statewide prayer rally. The event had lasted all weekend and had included numerous activities. It was during the tug-of-war competition, when his church's college group was about to beat the group on the other end of the rope, that Ben spotted her.

She was without a doubt the most gorgeous woman he'd ever seen. He would never forget the way she'd made him feel that day, all tingly inside as if something magical had happened. Both hands securely on his team's end of the rope, Ben had leaned to the side for a better view of her. In the process, the rope slipped and he fell to the ground. He could still close his eyes and see Maggie grinning at him as she and her team doubled their efforts and won the event before Ben could get up.

His attraction for her increased daily after that, despite the fact that he was dating someone else at the time. Ben sighed. Those first years for he and Maggie were rough. They wrote and talked on the phone, and in his heart he knew there was no one else he could spend the rest of his life with. But the girl he was dating came from a family that his parents had known all their lives. There was no easy way to break things off—especially after the accident.

If I could do one thing over again...

Ben let the thought hang there. When he had been unable to end things with his girlfriend, he and Maggie agreed to go on with their separate lives. Of course after only eighteen months apart, they had found each other again and began dating exclusively. But somehow Maggie had seemed different than before, older than her years, less willing to share...

He frowned. Was it possible she could have held that time against him? Harbored anger because he had chosen another girl for that period in his life?

Ben shook his head. *Ridiculous.* Whatever was happening to Maggie now it was a phase, nothing more. All that had ever mattered was how he felt about her when they found each other again. How he'd felt about her ever since. If he could do anything over again he would have broken things off with the other girl immediately. Maggie had to know that. But he'd been so young, so confused. After the accident it seemed that staying with his old girlfriend was the right thing to do.

Ben turned his attention toward the work on his desk. *Impossible.* Whatever was troubling Maggie couldn't be rooted in something that had happened so long ago.

Still, as he set about dealing with the tasks at hand, trying to put Maggie's hurtful words out of his heart and head, Ben was troubled by one very serious suspicion: *What if...*

What if, despite living a pure life and being devoted to God, Maggie had turned into someone else, someone who had hidden her real feelings from him for months or years. Ben hated himself for even entertaining the thought, but it was possible that Maggie was right. Maybe she *was* pretending around him. And maybe somehow, no matter how much he had always loved her, Maggie had changed, become someone Ben didn't even know.

He glanced at his watch and saw that it was four o'clock. One more hour and he would wrap things up. He picked up the telephone receiver and dialed a number he'd long since memorized. "Hi, this is Ben Stovall."

A woman answered on the third ring. "Hello, Ben." He could hear the smile in her voice. "What can I help you with today?"

He grinned, sure this was the answer he was looking for. "I need a dozen long-stemmed red roses for this evening."

"Very good, and a white ribbon like usual?"

"Yes, like usual."

Ben felt better when he hung up the receiver. Maggie was wrong; of course he knew her. She was his soul mate, his best friend. And whatever was troubling her yesterday, why it was nothing that couldn't be made better with a bouquet of flowers. She loved red roses, especially when there wasn't any special occasion.

"It's a celebration of our love," Ben liked to tell her. And it was. She was the perfect woman, handpicked for him by God above. He loved her more than life itself.

He thought of the roses again and grinned. He could hardly wait to see the expression on her face when he brought them home.

Maggie had the strangest feeling…

It was as if she were single again.

As if by being even somewhat honest she had severed ties to Ben, to the man she married, the man to whom she had been lying for nearly eight years.

For that reason—or maybe because the little blond girl hadn't yet made her daily appearance—Maggie was looking forward to her run in the park. For months it had been her favorite way to spend the hour between finishing up at work and picking up the boys at their bus stop. The first lap was effortless, and as she ran Maggie thought about her columns, how they might help children caught in the foster system. They were a good influence on society, good for her career. Even if her personal life was falling apart, even if there were times when the darkness seemed overwhelming, she was still doing something useful. Helping in some small way.

Maggie picked up her pace and as she rounded the corner of the trail, she saw a blur of motion near the playground, a hundred yards away. From this distance it was hard to make her out, but then…

Maggie pushed herself faster, her eyes trained on the child. Her view was better now. The child was swinging, while a teenager—a baby-sitter or older sister—sat with a teenage boy at a nearby picnic table. *Closer, Maggie. Get closer.* With only fifty yards between them she spotted the hair.

Long blond curls. It was her! This time it wasn't a mirage or a figment of her imagination or any other such thing. It was a living, breathing child, and Maggie was almost certain it was the same girl she'd been seeing. *Who is she, God? Why is she here?*

Maggie was sprinting now. She wouldn't approach the girl, not yet. Not until she was absolutely sure it was her. Even then she didn't want to scare the girl. Maggie kept running until she was parallel with the child. Glancing over her left shoulder she saw the girl's face. Yes! It was her; there was no doubt in Maggie's mind.

Not sure what to do next, Maggie kept moving. Whatever terrible force desired her, it wouldn't catch her here—not with the little girl so close. *If only I could talk to the child, ask her who her mother is, learn more about her. Then maybe I'd understand why my thoughts are so filled with her image...* Especially now, nearly eight years after—

Run, Maggie! Faster...faster!

Three laps around the park equaled a mile, and usually Maggie did no more than six laps. But as long as the little girl stayed on the swing, moving back and forth, smiling and unaware of her presence, Maggie kept running. Twelve laps, fourteen...sixteen...

Finally, on the eighteenth lap, Maggie realized her heart was pounding erratically, and her vision was blurred. She clutched her side, dropped her pace to an unsteady walk, and headed for the little girl.

Without saying a word, Maggie dropped into the swing beside the child and smiled at her. "Hi. My name's Maggie."

Before the girl could respond, Maggie felt a hand take hold of her upper arm and she spun around, jerking free from the grip. Fear sliced through her gut like a hacksaw. *God, please, no...*

The man standing beside her wore a police uniform and a badge that glistened in the midafternoon sun. "Ma'am, I'd like to have a word with you, please." He motioned toward a grassy area several feet away.

"Nicky! Nicky!"

At the sound of the child's cries, Maggie turned back to her at once. The girl had jumped from the swing and was running toward an older boy and girl seated at a nearby table. Then the child glanced back at Maggie...and Maggie's whole body went cold.

This wasn't a blond little girl. Instead, the child running away from the swings had red hair and a freckled face. *But...where did she go? Why is this happening again? What's wrong with my eyes? Am I that far gone, Lord?* Maggie stared at the child and then directed her attention back to the officer. She was sweaty and rumpled and desperately in need of a water fountain. She had never run six miles in her life, and now she was about to be interrogated by a policeman.

"I think I'm going to faint." Maggie slipped her head between her knees and urged herself to breathe slowly. After several seconds, she raised her head and looked over her shoulder. The officer was waiting.

"I'm serious, ma'am. Get up. I need to talk to you."

"Sorry, I just...I don't feel very well." Maggie rose up off the swing and followed him, terrified that she would collapse and be taken away in an ambulance or worse, be arrested in the park adjacent to the office where she worked. If her peers got hold of the story...

Help me, God...please!

When they were a distance away from the playground the policeman turned and faced her. "I'm Officer Andrew Starmer. Got a call from one of the neighbors in the condominiums across the street that a female jogger was stalking a child on the playground."

Maggie saw black spots dance before her eyes. *Breathe. Breathe, Maggie. Don't faint now.* "A female jogger?"

The officer glanced at her sweatsuit and nodded. "Did you know that child, ma'am?"

"Child?"

Officer Starmer sighed. "Yes, the one you were talking to."

"Oh, her. I, uh...I thought she was my niece. My niece lives near here and plays at the park all the time."

The officer raised an eyebrow. "Tell you what, why don't you follow me to the car, and I'll make a report. Just to be sure."

Panic coursed through Maggie's veins. "An arrest report?" She did her best to sound indignant. *What have I done, Lord? Help me.*

"No. Just informational. Take down your name, that kind of thing."

Maggie wiped her hands on her pants legs and released a laugh that said there must have been a mistake. "Officer, I work across the street. I jog at this park every day at this time. I thought the girl was my niece. Isn't that enough information?"

Officer Starmer eyed her for a long moment. *Let him believe me, please...* "You work at the newspaper?"

"Yes. My car's parked there right now."

His eyes narrowed. "Okay. Just be aware that people are sensitive about strangers getting too close to kids. You read your paper, right?"

"Sure." *Oh, thank You, God. He doesn't recognize me, doesn't know I'm a columnist.* "Right. Definitely. I'll keep that in mind."

The officer glanced once more at the redheaded girl then back to Maggie. "If you've finished your jog, why don't you make your way back to the office."

"I'm on my way." Maggie smiled at him and nodded as she and the officer headed in different directions. She was ten steps away before she remembered to exhale.

That was too close. What if he'd taken my name? What if he'd arrested me or taken me in for questioning? What was I doing there anyway? And why does the child keep disappearing? Who is she?

Come into the light, child.

What light? Maggie argued with the still, silent whisper. *There hasn't been light for years.*

She had the strangest feeling she was forgetting something but she could hardly stop and think about it. Not with the officer watching her from his squad car across the park. She opened her car door just as her cell phone began to ring inside her purse on the front seat. Instantly her eyes flew to the watch on her wrist.

The boys! That was it! She had forgotten the boys.

Maggie tore open her purse and grabbed the phone, speaking in a voice that sounded half-crazed even to her. "Hello?" Her heart raced and she was assaulted by a wave of nausea.

"Mrs. Stovall?"

"Yes, I'm late to get the boys. Are they okay?" Her words spilled out in a panicky blur.

"Uh…yes. They're back at school. They waited at the bus stop for thirty minutes, and apparently one of your neighbors verified you weren't home. She contacted the school, and we sent the bus back out."

This was crazy. She was losing her mind. Everything she was doing proved that. She needed to be honest, ask for help. Maggie's mind raced.

"I…my car…" She cast a frustrated glance upward, grasping at anything that might sound logical. "It…my car broke down and I…I was just going to call and see…make sure they were okay."

The school secretary hesitated. "I had to contact Social Services, Mrs. Stovall. These children are wards of the state and anytime something like this happens…"

What was she insinuating? That Maggie was an abusive foster mother? That she and Ben were no better than the foster parents she referred to in her column? Maggie thought of how she'd failed even to tuck the boys in the night before, and a murky cloud of fear suffocated her. *Get a grip, Maggie. Come on.* Her racing pulse was causing her body to tremble, making it difficult for her to speak.

How could I have forgotten the boys?

"What did…what did Social Services say?"

"They said these kinds of things happen and they made a note of it." The woman paused again, and Maggie could hear disapproval in her tone, almost see the indignation on her face. And if the officer had taken her name… She couldn't bring herself to think about it.

"I'll be there in ten minutes. Please tell them I'm coming." Maggie hung up the phone and steadied herself. *How could I forget them? I love those boys. They may not be worth much in the eyes of society, but right now I'm all they have. And I let them down.*

You're a wretch! Worthless. The voice in her head had changed from doubt and discouragement to a devilish hiss. **No one would notice if you drove off a cliff, Maggie Stovall.**

Forget about it, Maggie. Think about something else.

Images shot through her mind—the blond girl, the onions in her shopping cart, the policeman—as Maggie pulled into the school parking lot, she was horrifyingly aware that the sense of approaching doom was worse. It clawed at her with every step, making it nearly impossible for her to breathe as she found her way inside the school, comforted the crying twin boys, and led them back to the car.

When they were buckled in, Maggie rested her head on the steering wheel and began to cry, too. At first the sobs were muffled, but within a few minutes she was wailing, terrified by the despair that seemed to be sucking the life from her.

Where am I? Why am I weeping in the school parking lot and why can't I think clearly?

"Mrs. Stovall, what's wrong?" It was Casey and he'd stopped his own crying.

Oh no…I've scared him.

She straightened in her seat and quickly wiped her eyes. The child's question cleared the fog and brought everything into focus again. She was crying because she'd been so busy looking for a little girl that didn't exist she'd forgotten her foster boys at the bus stop. She was crying because thirty minutes ago she'd been on the verge of being arrested and losing everything she had ever worked for over the past seven years.

And she couldn't think clearly because she was going crazy. What other explanation could there be?

"I'm fine, honey." Her voice was still trembling, but she glanced in the rearview mirror and saw a relieved look cross the twins' faces. *They believe me. Good. Now we can go home and have a normal night.*

Maggie pulled out of the parking lot and headed east toward their neighborhood, fighting off another bout of tears. Normal? It had been months since she had felt anything close to normal. Most likely, she'd spend the evening barely tolerating her husband's probing glances and tidying a house that never seemed to be clean. Then she would stumble into bed and lie awake under the watchful eyes of whatever demons had taken up residence in her home.

The thought of it made her want to turn around and drive west, maybe until she reached California or the ocean. Maybe drive the car into the ocean until it swallowed her up—along with whatever was trying to destroy her. However far it took to get away from it all. The tears came again, and though Maggie willed herself to drive home, forced herself to battle the desperation, she couldn't still the one thought screaming through her mind …

Maybe it really was time to check herself into a mental hospital.

7

Maggie remained an emotional hurricane through a long night of ignoring Ben and his roses and on into the next morning as she tapped out a column decrying the standards in many foster homes. She could barely concentrate for the voices waging war in her head.

She focused on the computer screen and the task at hand. *Come on, Maggie. You can do this.* She began typing.

> Something is terribly wrong with our system when we place the abused children of our state in homes where, at least on occasion, they'll be abused again. What type of safety net is that for a child who's falling through the cracks? The time has come to toughen the standard by which we judge people worthy of taking in foster children.

Her fingers refused to move, and she pictured the boys, alone and scared at the bus stop.

Hypocrite. Hypocrite, hypocrite. You're the worst foster mother of all. Leaving those boys out at the bus stop while you...

"Lots of good feedback on the Social Services column, Mag." Ron Kendall leaned against her desk so he could face her. "This the final one in the series?"

Maggie gulped. She was having trouble understanding him. Something about Social Services and a series. "Yeah...it's a series, Ron."

His face reflected his confusion.

What? Why's he looking like that? What did I say? Everything about who she was seemed to be disconnecting. As if nothing she was thinking or hearing or doing made any sense at all. Ron frowned. "Hey, Mag, you feeling all right?"

The way his eyes narrowed told Maggie he was genuinely concerned, and she felt a rush of panic. If Ron was worried, then maybe she really was losing her mind; maybe it wasn't only a couple of bad days or the fallout from having forgotten her foster boys and nearly having been arrested the day before. "I...I feel fine, if that's what you mean." Maggie stared back at the computer screen, hoping Ron would get the hint and leave her alone. She had just thirty minutes before deadline.

"Okay." Ron angled his head and waited until he had her attention again. "You just haven't seemed like yourself lately." He chewed on his lip and gazed at the ceiling, and she had the strong sense he was searching for the right words to say. "I'm here for you, Maggie. That's all. If something's wrong let me know, okay?"

She forced a smile. "Thanks, Ron. I'm fine. Really."

He walked away, and she stared at her column. *Everyone knows.* It might as well be written on my forehead: *"Maggie Stovall is going crazy."*

Over the next fifteen minutes she finished her column and for the first time since working for a newspaper, she didn't bother to read it through again. Instead she filed it, pulled her things together, and headed home.

It was time to get to the bus stop. She would not forget again.

Five after three.

That's when the bus arrived. Five minutes after three. 3:05 P.M. 3:05 in the afternoon.

The number sounded in her mind like the words to an unforgettable song: *3:05, 3:05, 3:05. The boys' bus comes at 3:05.*

Maggie had rushed through every activity since early that morning, everything from getting dressed to writing her column. She would not be late this time.

It was 1:45 when Maggie shut the door of her home behind her and set out on the five-minute walk to the bus stop.

The walk involved crossing a very busy street, one that gave mothers nightmares about children getting knocked under the wheels of a speeding car or being struck by a menacing tractor-trailer. The twins—like other foster children Maggie and Ben had cared for—were absolutely forbidden to cross it alone.

Maggie moved quickly, doing her best to ignore the haunting feeling that something was chasing her, closing in on her. When she arrived at the stop she checked her watch again: 1:50. Her shoulders eased downward, and she allowed herself to exhale. She didn't mind the wait; her feet could take it. They would have to. She could never be like those foster parents she'd written about earlier, the type who gave a child more trouble, more pain and heartbreak. More insecurity. No, Maggie would never do that again. Even if she had to stand in place for an hour or more, she would be there when the boys got off the bus.

The temperature was dropping, and a cloud layer had taken its position in the sky above her. Maggie couldn't help herself. She kept looking over her shoulder, sure someone was there, waiting with a hunting knife poised above her head.

Help me, God. Clear my mind so I can think again. Please.

She rocked back and forth…back and forth, licking her lips nervously as the minutes trickled by…3:05, 3:05, 3:05. It became a rhythm that surrounded her, kept her company.

At one point she thought she saw the bus and she straightened. Yes, it was the bus all right. But...

Maggie inhaled sharply. Every face beyond the bus driver's was that of the little girl! Ten or twenty girls with curly blond hair filled the bus, and Maggie didn't know whether to run away or flag the vehicle down before it could get away. She moved further into the road, her eyes locked onto the busload of little blond—

The sound of a blaring car horn jarred her from her thoughts, and she reeled backwards, tripping over the curb and falling onto the sidewalk behind her. Her head smacked the concrete, and for a moment she lay there unmoving. She heard a car slow down and someone shout, "Hey, lady, you all right?"

Instantly she sat up and was assaulted by the urge to vomit. She waved weakly at the man in the car and smiled. "I'm fine."

He looked doubtful but drove off anyway. When he was out of sight, Maggie ran her hand over the bump that was forming on the back of her head; something warm and wet met her probing fingers. *Dear God, help me! I'm bleeding...*

How far out in the road had she been when the car honked at her? She had thought it was a bus full of little girls, blond girls...all with the same face...

Where had the speeding car come from, anyway? There ought to be a law against driving so fast on a residential street! It was downright dangerous. Maggie fixed her hair over the wound so that the blood wouldn't drip onto her white jacket. Did she need stitches, or would her hair be enough to stop the bleeding?

While she was trying to decide if her headache was from the fall or the anxiety that consumed her, the bus pulled up. Immediately Maggie saw the shocked look on the face of the bus driver and she realized she was still sprawled on the sidewalk. The driver opened the door and shouted above the sound of the engine. "Mrs. Stovall? You okay?"

She was on her feet, brushing off her jeans and fixing her hair again so that the driver couldn't see any signs of blood. "Fine. I tripped."

His expression grew slightly less concerned. "I was afraid you'd been hit by a car."

The children were making their way out of the bus, and Maggie choked out a laugh. "No...nothing like that. Weak ankles. Happens all the time."

How long have I been rambling? Five minutes? Ten? Where are the little girls who were on the bus a few minutes ago? Or was that a different bus?

The bus driver was still staring at her.

"I'm okay, really. Just clumsy, I guess. Don't know why I wasn't more care—"

Cameron and Casey appeared at the top of the stairs. *Thank, God...* The boys were all right and she was there, on time. They made their way to her. "Mrs. Stovall!" Their voices rang as one as they ran the remaining few feet and threw their arms around her.

"We were scared you might not be here." Cameron flung his backpack over his shoulder and grinned at her.

"I told him you'd come." Casey cast her a confident smile. "You never missed us before."

Maggie put her arms around the boys and hugged them close. *If only they were my own children…*

You don't deserve children of your own. Not after what you—

"Boys, let's go home and have some hot chocolate. Sound good?" She forced herself to be clear minded. If the darkness wanted to hound her it would have to take a backseat. This was her time with the boys, and there was no room for delusional voices. She'd waited all day to hold the twins in her arms and reassure them that she would never, never again forget them.

The bus pulled away, and Maggie looked at the boys with a frown. *What are they doing? Why aren't they sitting down?* Maybe they wanted to talk first, before she made them their snack. She plopped herself down and sat cross-legged on the hard surface. "Come on, sit down at the table. I want to hear about your day."

The boys stared at her, an odd fear and uncertainty clouding their eyes.

"What?" Maggie felt a stabbing sense of terror. Had they seen her bloody head? Her fingers poked at her hair once more, and she made a mental note to turn up the heater. The house had never felt so drafty. "Come on, boys, sit down. I'll get your snack as soon as you tell me about your day."

Other children who had been let off at the stop had already walked home, and Casey and Cameron looked at each other. "Mrs. Stovall, why are we gonna sit here in the middle of the sidewalk?"

Maggie's eyes widened, and she shot furtive glances about her surroundings. *What am I doing?* Cameron was right. A moment ago she had been certain she was back home at the dining room table. She hadn't heard the passing traffic or realized that she was sitting cross-legged on the cold cement.

I'm crazy, God. What's wrong with me?

She said nothing, only rose slowly and took the boys' hands in hers. She was suddenly so tired she didn't know if she could make it across the street.

Just go, Maggie. The boys are hungry. Squaring her shoulders and tightening her grip on the boys' hands, she stepped off the curb.

It was Casey's screams that caught her attention first, and then the horrifying realization that they were in the middle of the road, with cars coming at them from every angle. Seeing no way out, Maggie clutched the boys to herself and shielded them with her arms.

The sound of the crash was so deafening Maggie was certain they were all going to die. *Please, God, take me but not the boys…*

And in that moment—believing her death was imminent and knowing she wouldn't have to battle the demons another day—Maggie finally felt at peace.

The blow never came.

Maggie didn't know how much time passed before she realized it, how long it had been since the screams of brakes and grinding metal and breaking glass all came to a stop. She just knew, for whatever reason, it was strangely silent around her.

Was this death? This silence and stillness?

She opened her eyes. She and the boys were fine, but two cars had collided head on—Maggie guessed in an effort to avoid hitting them. From where she stood, frozen in place, she could see that both vehicles' airbags had inflated.

Let them be okay, God. I didn't mean to...

There was a wailing coming from the wreckage, and Maggie wondered which car contained people who were crying. Then she looked down and saw that it was Cameron and Casey. The boys were shaking badly, crying and clinging to her in desperate fear.

My God, what have I done? I could have killed us all! What's wrong with me?

She knelt between the boys and stroked their backs, keeping her eyes trained on the damaged vehicles and the host of people running toward them to help. "I'm sorry..." She whispered the words over and over until in the distance she heard sirens, then not long afterward, a man's voice behind her.

"Ma'am, I'm Officer Boe. You and the boys all right?"

Maggie looked over her shoulder and saw a policeman. "It was...it was an accident."

The man's face was filled with kindness. "We know that, ma'am. There were several witnesses who saw it happen. Looked like you and the boys were talking and accidentally walked into traffic."

Maggie's entire body was vibrating and she thought for a moment she might be sick. *No, not here.* She swallowed hard. "I'm so sorry."

The officer came closer and put his hand on the top of her head, moving it so he could get a better look. "You're bleeding."

At this news another flash of fear tore across the twins' still-stricken faces, and Maggie tightened her grip on them. "It's okay, boys." She turned to the officer once more. "I banged my head earlier. Twisted my ankle and took a fall."

A knowing look filled the officer's eyes. "Ma'am, I think you might have a concussion. Could be why you walked into traffic."

Maggie ignored him and stared at the broken vehicles. "Are the people...is everyone okay?"

The officer nodded. "Only one person in each car. Both had airbags, so it looks like they'll be fine." He ran his finger over her skull and around the tender area, making her wince slightly. "Right now we need to take care of you."

Officer Derek Boe stayed with the woman until paramedics lifted her onto a stretcher. He'd worked accident scenes for more than ten years and he knew a concussion when he saw one. Whatever else might be wrong with the woman's ankle, one thing was sure: Her brains had been scrambled in the fall.

She had the dress and demeanor of a gentle suburban housewife, but when he ordered paramedics to load her on the stretcher, she was almost combative.

"No! Let me go! I'm okay, really, I don't want to go to the hospital. The boys need a snack...hot chocolate..."

The officer took the boys' hands in his and directed his words at the woman. "Now, don't worry about a thing. The boys and I will be right behind you. We'll just get you in and have you checked out, then you can go home and have hot chocolate, okay?"

The woman shook her head and for a moment she looked like some of the drug overdose victims they found on the streets of downtown Cleveland. Wide-eyed and frantic, shaking from head to toe. Almost crazed. "Ma'am, you need to relax. Everything's going to be fine. We just want to get you checked out."

The paramedics were ready to roll when the officer realized he didn't have her name. "Ma'am." He raised his voice so she could hear him above the commotion and traffic. "Could you tell us your name?"

The woman stopped shaking and stared at him blankly without blinking. "My name?"

Seconds passed, and Officer Boe tried to conceal his concern as one of the paramedics jotted something down on his notepad. "Never mind, ma'am. We'll get it later."

Loss of memory was further proof of a concussion.

"It's Mrs. Stovall." One of the twin boys tugged on Derek's arm so he would be heard. "Her name's Mrs. Stovall."

The officer looked down at the boy. "But I thought she was your mom?"

The woman tried to sit up, but the paramedics eased her back down. "I'm...I'm their foster mother," she managed.

The officer sighed. That would complicate things. Whenever victims in an accident were wards of the state, the Social Services department had to be notified. He looked back to the woman. "What's your first name, Mrs. Stovall?"

Again the woman hesitated. And then as if someone flicked on a light switch in her brain, she said, "Maggie. Maggie Stovall."

She rattled off her phone number, and Officer Boe wrote it down quickly as the paramedics whisked her into the ambulance. "Wait!" she screamed. "I don't want to go to the hospital. What about the boys? Wait! Isn't anyone listening to me? Isn't anyone—"

Her voice echoed in the roadway as they slammed the doors shut and sped off.

Officer Boe shook his head and walked back to his car, the young boys still at his side. There he telephoned Social Services and reported that two of their charges had very nearly been killed in a traffic accident.

Ben arrived at the hospital and rushed to Maggie's side just as the doctor was explaining to her the severity of her head injury. Her heart soared at the sound of his voice.

"Doctor...I'm sorry, I couldn't get here until now. I'm her husband. What hap-

pened? How bad is it?" Ben was breathless and looked several shades paler than he had
that morning. He stood next to Maggie's bed and intertwined his fingers with hers.

Warmth washed over her, surprising in its strength. *I still love him, Lord…really.
Help me understand what's happening, why I'm acting so strangely.*

For the first time in days, Maggie felt safe. Ben was with her, his hand warm and
big enough to cover hers.

**But nothing is big enough to cover the way you lied to him all those years ago.
You're a liar, a hypocrite. A sickening excuse for a wife.**

Maggie closed her eyes. Nothing could make her shake the feeling of dark desperation that seemed to be tightening its grip on her with each passing hour.

The doctor nodded at Ben and turned his attention back to Maggie. "It isn't as
bad as we first thought." He seemed to be choosing his words carefully, and Maggie
forced herself to listen. If it wasn't bad, then there was no reasonable explanation for
her behavior. She had sat down with the boys in the middle of the sidewalk thinking
that they were at the dining room table. Then she had taken hold of the twin boys
who had been trusted to her care and walked directly into oncoming traffic.

"Do I have a concussion?"

The doctor glanced down at the X rays in his hands. "No. Doesn't appear so." He
approached her and ran his hand over a bandage on the back of her head. "The bleeding's stopped, no stitches needed."

Ben's sigh rattled around the examining room. "Thank God."

The doctor shifted his weight and stared first at Maggie, then at Ben. He obviously had something important to say, but instead he slid his hands into the pockets
of his white coat and studied Maggie once more. "Officer Boe will be in to see you
both in a minute."

When they were alone in the examining room, Ben leaned over the bed and
kissed Maggie's forehead. "Honey, I was so afraid…I got the call as soon as I walked
in the door. All they said was you'd been in an accident and you had a head injury. I
thought…"

Maggie saw tears form in his eyes, felt his love, his relief, his fear…

How can I love him so completely and hate him all at the same time?

"I thought…I was worried that if something happened to your head you might
never be the same." His voice fell to a whisper. "I thought I might have lost you."

Maggie stared at him, not sure what she felt. *It's all your fault. You wanted perfection, and I gave it to you…*

Ben bent over and put his face against hers. "I couldn't bear it if I lost you,
Maggie."

She waited until he straightened up. "You never had me." As soon as the bleak,
flat words escaped, she chided herself. Ben didn't need to hear that. He had no idea
what she was talking about.

His eyes clouded and he set his jaw, but before he could speak, Officer Boe
entered the room. There was something foreboding in his expression and he waited

until he had both their attention. "Mr. and Mrs. Stovall, I need to talk with you about something serious."

"Where are the boys?" Maggie's voice was suddenly shrill with concern. "I thought they were with you." How could she be a foster mother if she couldn't even keep track of two well-behaved boys? *Weren't we just about to have hot chocolate?*

The officer nodded toward the hallway. "They're safe; they're just outside."

Ben crossed his arms and leveled his gaze at the officer. "Go ahead."

"It's about the boys. Social Services is sending someone over to pick them up."

Ben cocked his head, his face a mask of confusion. "That won't be necessary, Officer. I'll be driving my wife and the boys home as soon as they discharge her."

The officer frowned. "Well, that's just it. The caseworker is concerned, what with Mrs. Stovall's accident and, well, apparently there've been several incidents lately…"

"What incidents?" Ben turned his focus on Maggie. "What're you talking about? The boys are fine at our house, right, Maggie?"

She felt herself breaking into a sweat and she wanted desperately to escape, to run out of the hospital and keep running until she dropped. Keep running until she died from exhaustion. Anything to avoid the scene that was unfolding before her.

Officer Boe glanced at his notes. "Apparently the school reported that the boys were sent to school without lunches three times last week. Then yesterday the boys were left at the bus stop. Someone, a neighbor most likely, called the school, and the boys were picked up again and brought to the principal's office where—" he looked up at Ben—"your wife picked them up nearly an hour late."

Ben's eyes grew wide and he stared at her. "Maggie?"

She had the unnerving feeling that something was crawling on her face and she realized it was her perspiration forming drops and rolling off her forehead. Ben was waiting for an answer, but she had no idea what to say. The conversation was headed someplace that terrified her. *They can't take the boys, God, no. Please, no!* She closed her eyes and nodded.

"Yes? You forgot the boys at the bus stop?"

Opening her eyes, she nodded again. Officer Boe closed his notebook and stared at them, making eye contact only occasionally, as though he were uncomfortable with the awkwardness of the moment.

Maggie realized with surprise that her eyes were dry. What had happened to her ability to cry? Didn't she care about this? Wasn't she upset that the boys weren't coming home with her? She noticed her legs stretched out on the hospital bed and she bit her lip. *What am I doing here?*

When the officer saw that neither of them was going to speak, he continued. "Either way…" He paused and appeared to be searching for the right words. "Either way someone from the department is coming to take the boys." He looked at Ben. "If you could go home and collect their things, that'd make the transition a lot easier for the children."

"No!" Maggie screamed the word and threw the hospital sheets off her body. Before anyone could stop her, she was out in the hallway. "Casey! Cameron!" Everything seemed to be tilting. "Where are my children?" She turned on the nurses who had stopped working and were now staring at her. "What have you done with them?"

Officer Boe was there almost instantly. He shot the nurses an apologetic look and forcefully took Maggie's arm. "Mrs. Stovall, if you don't come with me I'm going to have to place you under arrest."

Ben appeared at her other side, and together the men led her back to the hospital bed. A minute later, a nurse gave her a shot and she felt herself losing consciousness.

They've killed me. Good. I don't want to live anyway. I want my boys. "Casey... Cameron..." Her voice was weak, and she could no longer open her eyelids.

Then there was nothing but all-consuming silence and deep, utter darkness.

When Maggie woke up she was in her own bed, and Ben was asleep beside her. Images flashed in her mind. She had banged her head on the sidewalk and walked into traffic with the boys and gone to the hospital and someone had taken the boys and...

She sat straight up in bed. The boys! Were they really gone or had the entire ordeal been a crazy nightmare? She moved slowly out of bed and crept down the hallway until she reached the boys' room. *They're here; of course they're here.* She looked inside and let her eyes adjust to the darkness. The bunkbeds were empty; everything that had belonged to Cameron and Casey was gone.

Maggie collapsed slowly onto the floor outside their room. So it was true, all of it. They were gone; her boys were gone. She felt her shoulders hunch forward with the weight of the truth. The nightmare was real, and it wasn't her dreams that were crazy.

It was her.

Minutes passed until she formed a plan. Moving quietly she made her way back to bed and crawled in next to Ben, where she pretended to sleep until he left for work. When she was sure he was gone, she got up, packed a suitcase, and wrote her husband a letter.

Then, at eleven o'clock that morning she did something she never in all her life thought she'd do. Something she was sure her Christian friends would consider shameful, a sure sign that perhaps she wasn't a believer after all. Or if she was, the sin in her life was so severe that God had abandoned her.

Maggie drove to Orchards Psychiatric Hospital.

Refusing to think or feel or do anything more than survive moment by moment, Maggie stared at the building. It was over now: her life with Ben, her dreams of being a mother. No need to run from the darkness anymore. She went over her game plan and refused to give in to her desire to flee. It was this or...

She shook off the thought. No, she would not flee. She would check herself in, and when the admitting nurse asked her to describe her current mental status, Maggie Stovall, popular columnist and formerly sane person, would have just one word:

Suicidal.

8

$\mathcal{O}$rchards Psychiatric Hospital was a privately run facility supported almost entirely by donations and money paid out by insurance companies. The building was set back from the road and was difficult to see because of an imposing brick wall and a row of elm trees that lined the front of the property. The arch that ran over the paved roadway leading into the facility said only Orchards. As though the grounds might house a stately bed-and-breakfast or perhaps a fine dining establishment.

Red brick made up much of the exterior of the three-story structure, and a covered walkway led to heavy French doors and an impressive foyer filled with old English furnishings and, in one corner, a Steinway baby grand piano. Only the white uniformed nurse stationed behind the admitting desk gave visitors any indication that the nature of business conducted at Orchards might somehow pertain to the field of medicine.

Maggie waited for the woman to complete her paperwork and a sense of devastating shame washed over her. How had things gotten so bad? Why had it come to this?

"What religious preference are you, Mrs. Stovall?" The nurse's voice was soothing, like honey melting into hot lemon tea.

"Does it matter?" Maggie knew the nurse meant well, but she was terrified of making this decision. What would the people at the *Gazette* say? What would her readers think? She couldn't *do* this!

She started to stand up.

"Sit down, Mrs. Stovall."

Maggie did as she was told.

"Orchards is a Christian-based hospital. We need to know for the records if that is something you're okay with."

"What? I thought it was for anyone…" She had to force herself to stay in her seat. A Christian facility? They would kick her out as soon as they learned the truth. How could she bare her soul to a hospital full of Christian counselors and expect to get any real answers?

The nurse smiled patiently. "Orchards is for anyone. We can make a note that you don't want any Christian counseling if that's the case—"

"No!" Maggie's heart was pounding again. *And He shall be called Wonderful Counselor...* "I mean, yes. Christian counseling is okay. I just...that's not what I expected here."

"Are you a Christian, Mrs. Stovall?"

Somehow Maggie knew in that moment that the nurse was a believer.

"Yes...but not a very good one." She muttered the last part, and the nurse put a comforting hand over hers.

"That's okay. None of us is, really."

Another nurse appeared and smiled down at Maggie. "Ready?"

Run! Get out of here before they lock you up and throw away the key...

My peace I give you, My peace I leave you...do not let your heart be troubled, daughter. Do not be afraid.

Run! Leave now before—

The warring voices echoed loudly in her mind, and Maggie gulped, not sure what to say. Not sure even what the nurse had asked her.

The admitting nurse patted Maggie's hand again. "My name is Tani, and I can answer any questions you have now or later." She hesitated. "Do you have any questions, Mrs. Stovall?"

Maggie shook her head and looked from Tani to the new nurse, still waiting expectantly beside her. "What's going to happen to me?" Her voice sounded different, like a lost child's, and Maggie felt the now familiar confusion clouding her thinking. The new nurse leaned down and gently took her arm.

Don't arrest me, please! Maggie flinched at the woman's touch and then realized it was time to go.

"We've got your room ready, Mrs. Stovall. Everything's going to be okay."

Everything's going to be okay, everything's going to be okay, everything's going to be...

Maggie repeated the words to herself as she allowed the nurse to lead her down the hallway. In her free hand, Maggie carried her suitcase, which was stuffed with all that she had left of the life she once lived.

The life that was over now.

The nurse escorted Maggie down a series of halls and into a room. "This is where you'll stay. We'll be notifying your insurance carrier later today and seeking approval. Generally, we get permission for a two-month inpatient stay if that much time is required.

Panic pulsed through Maggie's veins. *What if I need three months? What if I can never live on my own again?* The questions assaulted her like so many hand grenades but she nodded helplessly at the nurse.

"Here..." She handed Maggie a glass of water and two capsules.

Maggie took tiny steps backwards, shaking her head at the nurse. "No. I don't want to sleep." *The nightmares will be too much tonight.*

"They're not sleeping pills, Mrs. Stovall. They're relaxants. To help ease your anxiety."

What's wrong with me, God? What happened to the days when Your Word was all I needed to feel peace? She took stock of her trembling legs and clammy hands and the way her heart bounced about in irregular patterns. Then without another word she reached out and took the water and pills. She swallowed them quickly before she could change her mind.

"Very good, you should feel better in no time." The nurse glanced at Maggie's belongings on the bed. "Why don't you open your suitcase? We like to check the belongings when a patient is first admitted. Certain items are not allowed in the private rooms."

Maggie stepped back and watched in horror as the nurse removed a blow-dryer and a leather belt from her things. "Very well." The nurse's tone was cheerful, as if there were nothing out of the ordinary about sifting through someone's suitcase and taking away various personal items. "Go ahead and put the other things away. After that you can take a nap for an hour or so. Your first session will be an evaluation with Dr. Camas at two o'clock."

The nurse left, and Maggie felt the darkness close in around her like a shroud. She was dead, wrapped in grave clothes made up of the very blackest doom, and there was no way out. She was no longer the proud Maggie Stovall, author of "Maggie's Mind," conservative columnist and local celebrity.

She was just another mental patient.

Maggie stared at what was left of her things and it dawned on her why the nurse had taken the blow-dryer and belt. Both items could be used to kill herself.

Two o'clock came quickly, and a nurse appeared to escort Maggie to her appointment with Dr. Camas. Maggie sat up and stretched. For a moment she wasn't sure whether she was at a hotel or in the hospital. Then she remembered. It was the middle of the day, the first day of the rest of her life. And she had an appointment with a psychiatrist.

She moved slowly down the hallway to Dr. Camas's office. The moment she stepped inside Maggie knew she was going to like him. He had a warm glow about his face, short white hair, and a neatly trimmed beard. He smiled with his eyes when she walked in and sat down.

"Mrs. Stovall?" He rose and held his hand out to her. His handshake was firm and something about it made her feel safe. Maggie relished the feeling. How long had it been since she'd felt that way? *Not long, really. She'd felt safe in the hospital, with Ben at her side, holding her hand…*

"Dr. Camas, I'm…it's just…I'm sorry to bother you…" Maggie stumbled over her words, apologetic and relieved at the same time. At least she wasn't like the typical patient at a hospital like this. Whatever was wrong with her probably didn't require a lobotomy or a straight jacket, and Maggie didn't want the doctor to think she was wasting his time. After all, she wasn't really crazy.

Her mind filled with the image of herself sitting on the sidewalk by the bus stop. Who was she kidding? The doctor had probably never counseled anyone as crazy as she was.

"No apology needed." He paused, and Maggie relaxed into her chair. *The pills must still be working.* Dr. Camas looked calm and unhurried. "Now why don't you tell me what's been going on?"

She closed her eyes and drew a deep breath. When she opened them, she saw the unmistakable look of Christ in Dr. Camas's eyes. "It's sort of a long story."

He leaned back and folded his fingers over his waist. "I've got time, Mrs. Stovall. Go ahead."

Where to begin? Yesterday? The day before? Eight years ago? Her eyes grew wet and her vision blurred with unshed tears. She blinked, and several tumbled onto her cheeks. Maggie studied Dr. Camas and somehow knew she could trust him. "One thing first…"

"Very well."

"I don't want my husband to see me. I…he isn't welcome here."

A troubled look crossed Dr. Camas's face. "Are you in danger, Mrs. Stovall? Has he hurt you or threatened you?"

Maggie shook her head, remembering again the warmth of Ben's hand the day before. "Nothing like that. It's just…our marriage is finished and I need to go forward. Seeing him would only make matters worse."

Dr. Camas jotted something down on a pad of paper. "Very well, I'll inform the desk of your wishes. We can intercept phone calls and personal visits, but I'm afraid there's nothing we can do about written correspondence. Perhaps you can tell him yourself if he writes."

Maggie nodded and imagined Ben's reaction when he got home from work later that day and found her letter. She winced, and her heart felt gripped by pain for what he would suffer when he found out. The air was beginning to feel stuffy, and Maggie drew a deep breath. Their marriage was over—she had no choice in the matter. If she were going to survive, it was time for both of them to let go and move forward. *I still love him, though. I'll always love him…*

"Mrs. Stovall, you were about to tell me what's been happening in your life…"

Maggie snapped to attention and suddenly knew there was only one place to start, only one that made any sense at all. She would start where it all began: nine years ago at the Cleveland Community Church Annual Prayer and Picnic.

The first time she ever laid eyes on Ben Stovall and knew she would never—as long as she lived—love anyone else. It was as true then as it was now. And even though her marriage was over, it would be true until the day she died.

Maggie drew a steadying breath and allowed herself to remember.

Deep in the heart of the city, Ben spent the afternoon meeting with three different judges and a host of attorneys establishing court dates for coming trials. It was the type of work that didn't require much concentration but made the time pass quickly all the same. Ben was thankful. There was no way he could have done anything more taxing; there hadn't been a spare moment all day that he wasn't thinking about Maggie.

He'd considered staying home and talking it out, insisting that she tell him what was wrong. But the doctor had said she might sleep most of the day, and Ben wanted her to get rest.

Of course, that wasn't all the doctor had said. He'd confided in Ben that he suspected Maggie had suffered a nervous breakdown. There was medicine she could take for a while, pills that would stabilize her anxiety and help her cope. But there would not likely be improvement in her outlook until she got real help.

Psychiatric help.

Just the sound of the word—*psychiatric*—sent shivers of fear down Ben's spine. Psychiatrists were for people who battled emotional problems, weren't they? Medical doctors helped people fight illness. But psych doctors—everyone knew *their* role. They worked with people who were crazy, people for whom life held no hope. Non-Christians, basically.

Ben had pondered these thoughts continuously throughout his day and now that it was finally almost time to go home, he could hardly wait to talk to Maggie. He had called her several times but she hadn't answered. That was understandable, especially if she were tired. But tiredness was not a sign of mental breakdown. Surely the doctors were wrong. His faith-filled wife had not suffered a nervous breakdown and she was not in need of psychiatric help. He had been her covering, after all, the one who prayed for her and took his role as spiritual leader of their home as seriously as he took his need for a Savior.

She had to be okay, didn't she?

What have I done to her, Lord? Wasn't I good enough? Didn't I pray for her as often as I should have?

He left the office half an hour early and a feeling of peace came over him as he pulled into the driveway. He had done all those things; of course she would be okay. As hard as she worked, wasn't it normal for her to have some kind of letdown now and then? Maybe her column was getting to her; maybe writing about children was making the fact that she didn't have any of her own more painful than usual.

Of course! That must be the problem. Maggie was desperate for a child. Ben allowed the relief to wash over him as he made his way into the house. He would sit down with her tonight and they would make a plan, figure out a time when they could try the in vitro fertilization again. Or if Maggie wasn't up for that, they could discuss adoption. If she wanted a baby, then by God's grace they would find her one. Whatever it took to bring back the smile that had all but disappeared from her face over the last two years.

"Maggie, honey, I'm home."

He had decided the best way to handle her was to downplay the events of the day before. She was bound to feel terrible now that Cameron and Casey had been taken from her. There was no reason to make her feel worse. He thought about yesterday's accident and thanked God again that no one had been seriously hurt. Maggie would have been devastated if her carelessness had caused anyone to be injured or…

He couldn't bring himself to think about it.

And we know that in all things God works for the good of those who love him, who have been called according to his purpose.

The verse from Romans flashed in his mind, and he allowed it to bathe him in peace. Of course they did. All things, even this. The fact that Cameron and Casey were gone was sad, but perhaps that meant it was time to have a baby of their own. He would share that with Maggie and help her believe it was so.

"Maggie?" Ben tossed his coat and briefcase on the stairs and bounded up. *Those must have been some drugs. Maggie's never slept all day long before.* He rounded the corner into their bedroom and jerked to a stop. The bed was made, and Maggie was nowhere to be seen. On his pillow lay a white envelope with his name scrawled across the front.

"Maggie, honey?" He moved quickly toward their bathroom, then glanced inside the closet. No one. He made his way to the different rooms of the house, one by one, until he was sure she wasn't there. Panic began building deep in his gut. Where had she gone? Was it safe for her to be out on the streets if she really was having a breakdown?

He dashed back up to their bedroom and snatched the envelope from his pillow. Sitting on the edge of the bed, he tore it open and pulled out the letter inside. His heart pounded loud and erratically as he unfolded it and began reading:

Dear Ben,

I'm sorry you have to learn the truth this way. But things are what they are and I can't run from them any longer. I don't know what's happening to me, why I'm so confused and tired and forgetting things. Yesterday I couldn't remember where I was or even who I was half the time. I really think I might be losing my mind.

Because of that I have packed some things and moved out…

Ben felt his insides tighten and he closed his eyes for a moment. *No, God! This isn't happening. Everything has always been perfect between us. Why? Why would she leave me?*

As though in response, another Scripture banged about inside his head: *In this world you will have trouble, but be of good cheer…I have overcome the—*

No. He couldn't handle this type of trouble, not now. Not with his wife packed and gone to who-knew-where. He opened his eyes and continued reading.

I'm checking myself into Orchards Psychiatric Hospital but I don't want you to come looking for me. You need to understand that no matter what help I can find for myself, things are over between us. When I am able to think more clearly, I will hire a divorce attorney who will contact you at that time.

Until then, please pray for me. I feel like I'm suffocating in darkness and I know for certain this is my last hope. I love you, Ben. I'm sorry I lied to you about everything. I'm sorry it's brought us to this. I hope you'll move on and meet someone else so that one day you can have the life you always dreamed of. And I hope in time you will forgive me.

Love, Maggie

The shock was more than Ben could imagine. A strange tingling sensation made its way down his spine and over the tops of his arms. *This can't be happening; it's a bad dream, a joke.* He felt as though he'd fallen into some sort of strange dream world. There was no way Maggie would leave him and ask him not to follow her! She was a woman of faith, and never in a million nervous breakdowns would she hire an attorney and sue him for divorce. It wasn't happening.

He moved toward the telephone, working to convince himself the news wasn't real. Then he called information. "The number for Orchards Psychiatric Hospital, please?" It felt strange hearing himself speak the words. *Psychiatric Hospital.* When was he going to wake up? Surely Maggie would laugh at him for having such a strange dream.

He dialed the number and waited.

"Orchards, may I help you?"

With his free hand, Ben rubbed his temple and tried to concentrate. "Uh, I'm looking for a patient. Maggie Stovall…was she admitted today?"

There was a pause. "Who's calling, please? Our patient information is highly confidential."

Ben felt himself beginning to shake. "This is…I'm her husband. I'm trying to find her."

The nurse's tone changed and she seemed almost apologetic when she spoke. "Your wife is a patient here, yes."

He took two steps backward from the blow, his mind reeling. *It was true.* His wife was in a psychiatric hospital. Ben paced the bedroom floor, desperately searching for a solution. "What kind of place is Orchards, anyway?" He was buying time, trying to think of a way to get Maggie home where she belonged.

"We're a private Christian hospital for patients suffering with mental illness."

Mental illness? Maggie? It wasn't possible. "All right, when will she be released? This evening? Tomorrow morning?"

The nurse hesitated. "Sir, the inpatient program can last up to two or even three months."

Ben couldn't breathe; pain wracked his body as though someone had sucker punched him in the gut. The blow forced him to sit down on the edge of the bed. "Three months?"

"Yes, sir."

"Can you put me through to her, please?"

"Your wife is very ill, and I hope you understand what I'm about to say." She paused again. "I'm afraid she's requested no contact with you, Mr. Stovall."

This time the shock of her words sent him to his knees. *"What?"*

"She has advised us that she will not accept your phone calls, letters, or visits."

Ben struggled to breathe. *God...help me.* "She said that?"

"Yes. But understand that her feelings could change once she's had time to talk with the doctor."

"Does she...is she in a private room?"

The nurse seemed to consider whether this was information she should share. "Yes, but we have her in a special unit."

Ben's head was pounding, and he didn't know what to say, how to respond. "Special unit? What...what special unit?"

"Suicide watch, Mr. Stovall. I'm sorry."

Ben hung up the phone and, still on the floor, hunched over his knees.

It couldn't be true. It couldn't...but it was. In the last twenty-four hours his wife had caused an accident that could have killed herself and their two foster boys. She'd been hospitalized for a fall that still didn't make sense. She had lost custody of Casey and Cameron and written him a letter stating in no uncertain terms that she was finished with him and would divorce him soon. She had admitted that somewhere along the course of their life she had lied to him about something, apparently something crucial. And then she'd checked herself into a mental hospital where she was under—of all things—a suicide watch.

It was too much to bear.

"No! Help me, God...please!" He screamed the words, and they ricocheted against the textured walls of his empty home. When he didn't hear anything back from the Lord, he buried his head in his hands and did something he hadn't done since he was a little boy.

He wept.

What was Maggie doing? Did she intend to sever their vows, forget about him, push him aside? Why hadn't she shared any of this with him? *I'm your best friend, remember, Maggie? How could you do this? God, help me understand.* He remained unmoving, pain tearing through his body until slowly, carefully, he was able to accept one part of his new reality: Whatever her motivation, Maggie was very, very sick.

An hour later he still had no answers, no explanations. But he did have a single goal. Maggie was his partner, his confidante, his wife. He was closer to her than to anyone, anywhere. She was his Maggie girl. Whatever the problem was, he would help her. Even if he spent the rest of his life trying. Ben exhaled, pushing the pain from his lungs and realized it was the same way he'd felt back in 1991, the day he met her.

And just as he'd decided then, he would win Maggie over and prove his love, whatever it took.

Ben pulled himself to his feet and sat on the edge of the bed. He forced himself to think. Who would know Maggie well enough to shed light on the situation at hand? She had no siblings, no close friends since Tammy left the neighborhood the year before. Her father had died of a heart attack five years earlier, and that left...

A thought dawned on him.

Maybe his mother-in-law would be able to explain Maggie's behavior. Ben leaned back against the headboard. No, it wasn't possible. The old woman wouldn't know anything. Maggie and her mother had never been close, not really. Too different, Maggie always said. Her mother lived in Santa Maria, California, and was an upstanding, private person who wore her faith like a medal of honor.

Once every few years Ben and Maggie flew to the West Coast for a visit, and Ben would inevitably wonder how this woman could possibly be related to his wife. The older woman was wiry thin, with a rope of gray hair that she kept tightly knotted near the nape of her neck. Proud, private, and pinched. That was the feeling one got after spending ten minutes with Madeline Johnson. She was not a woman who hugged or cried easily, and from all Ben could tell she had struggled to understand her only child since Maggie was old enough to talk.

She said little and cared less, by Maggie's assessment, and Ben doubted she'd be any help.

Still, if this breakdown were somehow tied to something in Maggie's past, her mother was the only link Ben had, the only person who might help him understand whatever mistruth Maggie was talking about.

Lead me, Lord, that I might understand her. His vision grew blurred by tears again. I can't live without her, God.

The next morning Ben called his office and requested a two-week emergency leave. He'd rarely taken a sick day and he'd built up three months' time if he needed it. Four hours later, he was on a plane headed for Southern California.

The entire flight he prayed for one thing—that Maggie's mother could somehow provide Ben with what he desperately needed: A key to unlock the secrets of Maggie Johnson's past.

9

The first session with Dr. Camas went better than Maggie had expected. She stumbled over her words and hadn't gotten far in her story. She had the uncomfortable feeling that the things she said rarely made sense. But at least she'd kept her focus. And though the blanket of dark desperation still lay draped around her shoulders, she could somehow sense an occasional ray of light as she spoke. More than once during that initial conversation, Maggie was sure the light was coming from Dr. Camas's eyes.

If her life were an oversized ball of secret tangled knots, Maggie believed after one meeting that Dr. Camas was someone who had the patience to untie them. At the end of the session, Maggie felt more hope than she'd known in years. And though she battled unseen demons long into the night, she had a sense of urgency and excitement about meeting the doctor again.

Maggie spent her second day at Orchards, in the hours before her appointment with Dr. Camas, getting familiar with hospital layout and studying other patients as though she were going to write a column on the place. She had expected to see people with catatonic expressions head-butting walls or chanting single-syllable words for hours at a time. Instead, Orchards was filled with quiet people.

Quietly desperate people. People just like her.

Maggie wondered about their lives and what secrets they'd kept that caused them to break down and wind up in a psychiatric hospital. Was she the only one whose crisis was brought about by telling lies?

I haven't only told lies, I've lived them.

Breakfast and lunch could be eaten in the cafeteria, but the strange sense of not knowing what she was doing or who she was still hovered nearby, so Maggie thought she'd be safer eating in the chair near her bed. There was a sign on the wall of her room just above the desk that said Orchards Psychiatric Hospital. Maggie figured it was there for people like her. People who were inclined to forget even the most basic information.

When her mind was tempted to imagine Ben and the warmth of his smile, the security of his embrace, the pain he might be feeling, she forced herself to think of something else. Ben would get over it; after all, he had never really known her. If he had, he never would have married her. He deserved someone real, someone better. Someone holier. He would be better off without her.

The concentration it required to think correctly and only about certain things left Maggie exhausted by noon. She slept without ever touching her lunch tray.

The wake-up call came at five minutes before two, and Maggie jumped to her feet. She wasn't sure where she was or why she was there or what had caused her to sleep, but one thought was clear: Dr. Camas was waiting for her.

Moving through what felt like a fog, she ran a wet cloth over her face and tried to remember how she had gotten to the hospital. What had happened to her foster boys? Who was caring for them while she was here? The trip through the halls to Dr. Camas's office felt like it took an hour. When she took her seat across from him, her hands were sweaty and she was breathless, desperate for even a moment of fresh air.

"You feeling okay, Maggie?"

The calm in Dr. Camas's voice worked warmth through her and she settled back into the cushioned chair. "Not really."

Silence.

He must think I'm crazy. I am crazy...why am I here? Where are the boys? Where's Ben? She started to get up. "I think I better go since I'm supposed to—"

"Maggie." The doctor's voice halted her, and she fell back into the chair, her eyes locked on his.

"Yes?"

"This is our time. Remember?"

Our time? Our time...our time. That's right. They'd planned this meeting. She gritted her teeth and forced the clouds from her mind. "Our session, you mean?" Her voice was quiet and weak, nothing like she remembered herself sounding.

"Right. Our session. You were going to tell me more about your past...about what's happened to upset you."

Yes, that was it. She was upset. Very upset. She dug her fingertips into her temples and rubbed in small, tight circles. Then suddenly, almost as though she were seeing it played on a motion picture screen, her past began to appear right before her eyes.

As it did, she shared every detail with Dr. Camas.

It was the summer of 1991, the summer before Maggie's senior year in college, a season when she was standing on the edge of everything pure and good and hope-filled about the future, a time when the plans God had for her life seemed firmly in reach.

It was the summer she met Ben Stovall.

Maggie had grown up in Akron; Ben, in Cleveland. Once a year the church Ben attended staged an annual Prayer and Picnic. It was a time when neighboring churches from various denominations could gather and agree on two things: the sovereignty of Christ and the necessity of prayer. Over time, the celebration grew until by the late 1980s the event lasted through the weekend and was sometimes attended by thousands of people from more than a dozen churches. Games were held for various age groups, and revival-style preaching echoed across the grounds each evening.

The summer of '91 was the first time Maggie's church had joined in. She was twenty-one and studying journalism at Akron University. There'd been nothing else going on that day so when her parents suggested the Cleveland picnic, Maggie agreed to go.

"Maybe I was trying to earn points with them," Maggie told the doctor. "I never…"

Dr. Camas waited. "Yes?"

"I never knew if my mother was proud of me or not. She was quiet, I guess."

Maggie drifted back again and explained that if one thing mattered to her parents, it was the importance of church family. After all, Maggie's family was very involved in their small congregation. If the elders had planned an event for the weekend, the Johnson family would be there. It was that simple.

Flyers were handed out to people as they parked their cars and headed for the open field where the event was set up, and Maggie's mother looked the information over carefully. "There seem to be events for young people too, dear. Why don't you run along and see if there's anyone you know? That way you won't be stuck with us."

Even now Maggie could hear the frown in her mother's voice, feel her cool, impersonal touch as she turned Maggie in the right direction and sent her off to find her peers. She took the flyer and found the sports events at the east end of the field, and as she arrived at the location she saw a dozen friends from her church in Akron.

"You came!" Susie Fouts ran up and pulled Maggie into a hug.

"Nothing better to do." Maggie linked arms with Susie and took in the scene. There were at least two hundred college kids milling about while a handful tried to organize games.

"They're doing a tug-of-war, but it has to be teams. Come on…" Susie grabbed Maggie's hand and pulled her into a full run. "We're next."

Maggie paused in her storytelling and stared at her hands.

"What is it?" Dr. Camas's words did not come out in a hurry; clearly they weren't demanding an explanation for her pause. Instead, they were gentle, carefully prodding, as though he were looking for the bruised area in an injury.

Tears flooded Maggie's eyes and she blinked them back, struggling to speak. "Susie…Susie…" She couldn't finish, and a sense of panic welled up in her. What if she started sounding crazy again? What if she couldn't force herself to remember? What if Susie hadn't gotten sick…

Dr. Camas folded his hands comfortably and waited. "Whenever you're ready, Maggie."

She had the feeling the doctor would be content to wait that way into the evening if necessary. After all, neither of them was going anywhere. She exhaled slowly. "Susie was my best friend growing up." She gulped and wiped a tear that had broken loose and tumbled down her cheek. "I...miss her."

"Yes."

Maggie looked up and again she saw that strange, comforting light in Dr. Camas's eyes. *Is that You, Lord? Beckoning me to Yourself?*

No one wants you, Maggie. You're not a Christian, you're an imposter.

She shifted her gaze back to her hands. "She died in childbirth a year after Ben and I were married." Maggie met the doctor's eyes once more and saw them fill with compassion.

"I'm sorry." His voice was warm, comforting.

"I...never told Ben."

Dr. Camas said nothing, but Maggie thought he wanted her to continue. "He would have asked too many questions."

Her mind drifted back again and the images returned. Susie running up to her, taking her hand. The two of them joining the group breathless and giggling. Maggie continued recounting the story.

Maggie's church youth group lined up on one side of the rope opposite Cleveland Community. Since the Cleveland group was hosting the Prayer and Picnic weekend, they had matching shirts and boastful attitudes.

"They think they're king of the tuggers, but not this time!" Susie shouted. "Come on everybody. Grab the rope and get ready."

Both teams took their places, and at the last possible moment a young man on the opposing team stuck his head out of line and made eye contact with Maggie. Something in his smile made her heart skip a beat, and Maggie couldn't help but grin at him.

"Pull!" A voice instructed loudly. The young man was still staring at her, and as the rope went taut, he lost his grip and was yanked forward where he fell face first in the dirt. Without his help, his team's momentum shifted badly, and Maggie and her teammates surged backward, landing on the ground in what was an unquestionable victory.

"We did it!" Susie had one fist in the air and the other around Maggie's neck. "I think it was the spinach I ate last night for dinner. Had to be good for something."

Maggie stood up and dusted off her jeans, her eyes still focused on the guy from Cleveland Community. Susie followed her gaze. "Whatcha looking at, Mag?"

"Nothing." Maggie turned away but it was too late.

"Don't lie to me. You're looking at that guy. The one who let go." She looked from

Maggie to the young man and back. "Hey, I think he likes you, Mag..." She lowered her voice and took another look at him, and both girls saw that he was standing up, brushing himself off, and taking a fair amount of ribbing from his friends. Later Susie had told her that every few seconds he was glancing in Maggie's direction.

"Is he still looking at me?"

Susie nodded, her eyes wide. "He's gorgeous, Mag. I'm serious."

Maggie held her head high and kept her back to her apparent admirer. She hissed in a whisper barely loud enough for Susie to hear. "Stop staring at him. You'll scare him off."

Yanking Susie by the sleeve, the girls started to leave when the young man ran up. "Hey, wait!"

Maggie and Susie whirled around at the same time. Susie recovered first. "Did you want our autograph? We did just beat the host team, after all."

"No..." His gaze connected with Maggie's, and she felt an attraction that went to her very core, far beyond anything she'd ever known. "I'm Ben...Ben Stovall."

The girls nodded, and Susie looked from Ben to Maggie and back again. "Well, I'll be right back. My little sister's at the picnic tables and I promised her a snow cone.

"Yeah." Ben tore his eyes away from Maggie for a moment and glanced at Susie. "Nice to meet you."

Maggie tried to suppress a smile as Susie left. "You didn't even get her name."

A dimpled grin spread across his face. "I wasn't trying to get *her* name..." Maggie felt something inside her begin to melt under his unshakable gaze. "I was trying to get yours."

Susie's family had to leave early that day, so Maggie and Ben spent the rest of the afternoon and evening playing Frisbee and water balloon toss and sitting side by side as they waited for the prayer meeting to begin.

He was the son of missionaries and had spent the first fourteen years of his life in and out of Africa. His parents worked for the church now, helping with outreach programs in downtown Cleveland.

"Why'd you come back?"

"Sports. I'm the oldest, and my parents knew I wanted to go to high school in the States."

Over the next hour she learned that Ben had been quarterback of the Cleveland State University football team until he graduated the year before. Now he was about to begin his second year in the college's law school. Maggie felt like she'd fallen into a marvelous dream until he said the words she'd been fearing all day.

"You seeing anyone?" His eyes sparkled in the waning sunlight and Maggie felt her heart quicken.

"No. You?"

"Actually..." His gaze fell and he poked his toe at a chunk of Bermuda grass. "Yes. But it isn't serious."

Eventually he filled in the details and admitted that her name was Deirdre. Her parents and his had been family friends forever and now she worked as a loan officer at a bank in Cleveland.

"But you aren't…you know, serious?" Why was he paying her so much attention if he already had a girlfriend?

Ben shrugged. "Deirdre's a nice girl. We're definitely not serious physically, if that's what you mean." He caught Maggie's gaze. "I'm waiting 'till marriage for that. You too?"

Maggie remembered the hot feeling that had worked its way up her cheeks. She was completely taken by Ben, by everything about him—even his knack for being completely direct. "Yeah, I'm waiting."

He smiled at her, meeting her eyes in a way that made her insides melt like butter on hot bread. "Good." His voice was smooth and measured as his gaze lingered. "I like a girl who waits."

Her cheeks grew hotter still, and she fingered the ring on her right hand.

Ben noticed and took her fingers carefully in his, examining the silver band. "Pretty. Who's it from?"

Maggie's senses were entirely focused on the way their fingers felt together. *What is this? I barely know him.* No one had ever made her feel the way this man, this stranger, was making her feel. "A faith promise ring. My dad gave it to me."

Ben withdrew his hand and grinned at her again. "That's great, Maggie. Making a promise to wait until you're married to have sex, and knowing your father's praying for you. Not many girls around like you, you know that?"

"What about Deirdre?" Maggie was enjoying his attention, but if he had a girlfriend…

"I guess the trouble is I've never really felt any spark with her." Something about his tone of voice left Maggie no doubt that he was feeling sparks now. His smile faded, but his eyes welled with admiration for her. "Know what I mean?"

She swallowed and glanced down at her hands as they twisted nervously. "I think so."

The evening music and sermon were getting ready to start and Ben took her hand. "Come on, let's find somewhere to sit."

Maggie looked around. "Is she here?"

"Deirdre? No. Her cousin invited her to Detroit for the week."

Maggie silently blessed the girl's cousin and felt herself relax. If it wasn't serious and Ben wasn't in love with this other girl, then what was the harm of enjoying his company for one night?

Their conversation continued, and Ben told her about his plans to be a district attorney. He seemed intently interested when Maggie told him her dream of writing for a newspaper one day.

"This country needs people like you out there reporting the news, Mag." It was the first time he'd called her that, and Maggie felt her heart lurch. Somehow it seemed like the most natural thing in the world, sitting next to him, pretending he was her boyfriend and not some other girl's, hearing him call her *Mag*. A summer breeze danced over the dry field grass, and a praise band warmed up in the distance.

Maggie studied him while he talked. His words came out slow and deliberately, honey leaving a jar, and confidence was as much a part of his facial features as his chiseled chin and dancing blue eyes. In all the hundreds of college age guys at the picnic, clearly Ben was the most desirable.

With a sigh at the memory, Maggie stared sadly at Dr. Camas. "About that time I began having this, I don't know…a strange feeling, I guess. It made me remember something that happened when I was in seventh grade."

Dr. Camas shifted slightly, his eyes locked on hers. "Why don't you tell me about it, if you're comfortable."

Maggie nodded. "I was at Camp Kiloka, at a church retreat the fall I was thirteen. The first night of camp I stayed up late into the night talking to my counselor…"

The moment took shape in Maggie's mind, and she told the story, capturing every detail.

"Do you ever pray about the man you'll marry one day?" The older girl had asked. She was a college student, a volunteer who'd come along as a chaperone.

Maggie had shrugged. "Not really. I guess I'm too young to think about it."

The college girl looked surprised. "Your parents are Christians, right?"

"Right."

"I thought all Christian kids prayed about their spouses."

Loneliness stabbed at her. "My mom and dad are busy. We don't…pray together much."

Maggie and the girl were inseparable the rest of the weekend, and when Maggie came home she had a changed attitude toward prayer. From that point on she had done as the girl suggested and prayed for her future husband, that he would stay strong in the Lord and that she'd recognize him when she saw him.

Maggie was quiet.

"Did you feel that way then, when you met Ben?" Dr. Camas folded his hands together and angled his head thoughtfully.

Tears stung at Maggie's eyes. "Sitting beside Ben Stovall that warm summer night in 1991, listening to him talk about his faith and feeling him so strong beside me, I could almost hear God telling me he was the one."

Without further prompting from the doctor, Maggie continued her story.

As the evening wore on their conversation grew more personal. She told him how strict her parents had been and that she had never had a serious boyfriend.

"Come on, Mag, there must be a string of guys pounding down your door." The sky was growing darker, and the moonlight shone in his eyes, making a picture Maggie knew even back then she'd never forget.

She considered his statement. Boys had always been interested. But her parents hadn't allowed her to date until she was sixteen. And now that she was in college she was often too busy with her studies for serious boyfriends. Most of her social life was spent in group settings with friends from church. A gentle smile filled her face and she angled her head so their eyes met again. "No one special."

Ben grinned at her, and Maggie felt another rush of heat in her cheeks. "You know something? I knew from the beginning you were different." She felt herself grow shy under his unwavering stare. "Do you know how many girls call themselves Christians but act like everyone else? Most of the girls I know have already given in."

Maggie raised her eyebrows. "Deirdre?" *Was that why they weren't more serious?*

Ben's face filled with sadness and disappointment as he nodded. "She regrets it, but that doesn't change the fact. She gave in and now she'll never have that part of her back again."

"Is that why…" Maggie was afraid to ask the question that welled in her heart, but she could tell by Ben's expression he understood.

"I don't know. Maybe." He stared up at the stars for a beat. "I care about her a lot. I just can't picture marrying her."

Though his statement sounded harsh, Maggie couldn't say she disagreed with him. There was nothing arrogant in his tone, but his words made her thankful she was a virgin. Thankful she would never be considered damaged goods by Ben or any other man. For a moment she imagined how she might feel if she had already had sex—and she couldn't help but wince. Ben's words would have felt like stones cast directly at her heart.

"You know what I mean?" He was waiting for her reaction.

"Definitely." Maggie nodded and thought of the friends she knew—some of whom attended various church college groups—who were having sex with their boyfriends. Since her junior high retreat she had believed what the college chaperone told her: *"God has a plan for you, Maggie, if only you'll follow His ways. Remember how special you are; God wouldn't want you to give yourself away to anyone but your husband."*

Maggie wasn't sure she had understood the words then, but she understood them that evening at the picnic, with Ben inches from her. In that moment she felt sure she'd achieved something great and honorable by staying pure.

The praise music was drawing to a close, the prayer meeting about to begin when Ben looked intently at her. "Maggie, do you believe in love at first sight, the kind of love that's meant to be?"

Maggie had felt her heart dissolving and she was thankful for the cover of night so that Ben couldn't see the way her hands trembled. "I guess I believe God's going to work things out for me. One day He'll introduce me to the right guy."

"Can I tell you something?" Ben lowered his head so that there was no way anyone but Maggie could hear him.

"Uh-huh." Maggie kept her eyes focused on his. She wanted to shout out loud that yes, she believed in love at first sight, because she'd just experienced it. And that she would love him until the day she died. But all she said was, "I'm listening."

Ben hesitated, and Maggie could see how serious he'd become. "I feel something different with you, Mag. It's like I knew you the moment I saw you."

Maggie drew back a few inches and glanced around. Her parents would not think kindly of her sitting so close to a guy she'd only met that day—even if she was a junior in college. "What about your girlfriend?"

"I told you...she's not my girlfriend. It's nothing serious." For a moment she wondered if he might actually kiss her. Instead he sat straighter, and in his eyes she saw the attraction he felt for her. "Maggie, would you mind if I called you sometime?"

Even before she answered yes she knew that if she started dating Ben Stovall there would be no turning back. Her heart was drawn to him in every way that mattered, and whoever else she might meet in years to come would forever pale in comparison. The sermon lesson that night had been on fighting the good fight and persevering, on believing that God had a plan for His people, if they would only seek Him in love and truth.

Maggie felt like he was speaking directly to Ben and her.

Then why do you want to divorce him?

The voice came out of nowhere, breaking through her memories, and Maggie jerked backward, closing her eyes. She wasn't ready to return to reality, to psychiatric hospitals, and to seven long years of lies and a marriage that was supposed to last forever but was about to end.

She wanted to stay in that distant place for as long as possible, live again in that time when everything about the two of them was exactly what it should be, when plans God had for them were clearer than the evening summer sky over Cleveland.

There was silence in the doctor's office for a moment, and Dr. Camas finally cleared his throat. "Is this a stopping point for you, Maggie, or do you want to keep on? I have time."

If only that were where the story ended...

"No, that's enough."

Her heart was racing, and she gripped the edges of her seat so she wouldn't run out of the office, tear down the hallways, and burst out the doors to freedom. She didn't want to deal with the truth, the fact that she had done more than lie to Ben over the years. Sadly, she had lied to herself, too. Tears came hard and fast, making it difficult to breathe without sobbing.

Help me, God. Give me strength.

Weeping may remain for the night, but joy will come in the morning...

She caught her breath. *What was that last part? Joy?* In the surprisingly comfortable silence Maggie pondered the thought and realized something she hadn't before.

That's what had been missing: joy. A sinking feeling lodged itself in her stomach. *It won't come in the morning, not for me. I'm stuck forever in the weeping night.*

Dr. Camas leaned over and slid a box of tissues closer to her. "There you go. It's okay to cry, Maggie. Crying is good. It means you're getting ready to deal with the issues at hand."

Crying? Had she been crying all this time? She ran her fingertips over her cheeks and found them dripping with tears. This was the second time she'd cried without knowing it. Even here, under the care of a kind and gentle psychiatrist and with antianxiety medicine coursing through her veins, Maggie was losing it.

The thought was discouraging and frightening, particularly because somehow she knew it meant she was closer to the truth than before. Terrifyingly close. Maggie took two tissues and dabbed at her face. "I can't do this anymore, doctor. I'm sorry."

"Nothing to be sorry about. It was a good session. I think we're headed in the right direction."

Maggie feared the direction they were headed, the direction of honesty. She had kept herself miles from the truth since the day she and Ben married—since before that even. And now here she was walking backward in time, hurtling toward the place where she would have to reckon with her past. And with it, every demon and monster and vestige of blackness that had tormented her over the years.

In that moment, it was all much more than Maggie was ready to take.

10

The drive from Los Angeles International Airport to Santa Maria was beautiful, oak trees draped in mild fall colors, foot-high grass blowing gently over the rolling hills. For most of the way, the Pacific Ocean lay sprawled on Ben's left and more than once he was tempted to pull over, to find a place alone on a rock and stare out to sea. He needed to talk with God but since he wanted to get to Santa Maria before nine o'clock, he held his conversation in the car.

Where had he gone wrong? He asked God over and over, and each time he felt the same thoughts fill his head: *Love deeply. Love covers a multitude of sins.*

Ben tried, but he could not make sense of the Scripture in light of what was happening. Who had sinned? Had Maggie done something crazy? Was she seeing someone else on the side? Ben almost laughed out loud. It was impossible. She was a committed Christian, a woman who had saved herself and been a virgin bride. A woman who had loved him the way he loved her—completely—since the day they first met.

Ben remembered that meeting and felt tears sting his eyes. He blinked hard and forced them back. He needed to concentrate, not fall apart. Of course Maggie wasn't having an affair. *So what is it, Lord? Why that Scripture?*

Love covers a multitude of sins, My son. Love deeply.

Ben stared ahead in the distance and barely noticed the way the sun shimmered on the ocean. It would be twilight soon, and again he was drawn to pull over and get out. Maybe rail at God for letting this happen or cry out loud at the top of his lungs. He *did* love deeply, and look where it got him! His wife was losing her mind, locked up in a mental hospital and refusing his phone calls and visits. What good had loving deeply ever done for him?

Love as I have loved you...

A twinge of something that resembled fear struck a chord on the keyboard of Ben's mind. Why did it feel like God had something against him? This was Maggie's fault, the whole mess. He would be patient, of course. If there were secrets, he was willing to uncover them and then forgive her, whatever it was. So what did God mean by implying he hadn't really loved Maggie?

He shifted uncomfortably in his seat, wrestling with the still small voice through Cambria and Lompoc and finally into Santa Maria. It was quarter to nine when Ben pulled up in front of the Johnson house.

Maggie's mother must have heard his car because she appeared at the door wearing wool slacks and a sweater, her hair pulled back severely in the familiar bun. Ben climbed out of the rented car and made his way up the walkway. The Johnson home was modest and the result of good planning on the part of Maggie's father. Since his death, Madeline Johnson had lived here alone with her memories, connected not to people but to a host of charitable organizations and busy work. Ben hadn't told her what was happening with Maggie, only that there was a problem and he needed to see her immediately.

"Good evening, Ben." She nodded curtly, making no effort to hug him. Instead she stepped back and gestured for him to come inside. When they were seated in the living room, she sat stiffly, her hands folded, and sighed. "I'm not sure I understand why you're here. But whatever it is it must be important." She hesitated, almost as if she did not want to ask the next question. "Is everything okay with Maggie?"

For the first time since meeting Maggie's mother, Ben wished they had a closer relationship. His parents had gone back to Africa after he and his brothers were grown, so they had little contact. It would have been comforting if only this one time he could break down in front of this woman and know he would have her care and support. But since that wasn't the case, he drew a deep breath and pondered how best to explain the situation. "Maggie's had a breakdown."

Madeline angled her head sharply and frowned. "A what? What type of breakdown?"

Weakness, perceived or otherwise, was something Maggie's mother hated. She wore the look of someone who had caught a whiff of week-old trash.

Help me here, Lord. I need to make her understand how important this is.

"What I mean is, Maggie's taken some time off work…she's at a facility…a place where they help people figure out what's wrong. Do you understand what I'm saying, Mrs. Johnson?"

Madeline's face lost some of its color, but otherwise there was not a flicker of emotion. "Maggie's at a psychiatric hospital? Is that what you mean?"

Ben nodded. "She's not been well. Things…they've been getting worse over the last few years."

"She never mentioned a word to me…" Madeline huffed softly, clearly indignant that her only child wouldn't have trusted her with such information.

"Well, Mrs. Johnson, she didn't say much to me about it either. A few days ago the state took the twin foster boys out of our home, and then yesterday Maggie checked herself into the hospital."

Ben thought about telling her how Maggie was refusing contact with him, but he decided against it. He didn't want to give her any reason to be less than honest with him about the questions he needed to ask.

"Is that why you've come?" Madeline leaned slightly back into the sofa as though it pained her to relax even a little.

"No…I mean, yes. The truth is Maggie keeps alluding to the fact that I don't really know her."

Ben was studying her closely, watching for signs that Maggie's mother might understand more about her daughter than she'd ever let on to him—and for a fraction of an instant there was a flicker in her eyes. A knowing look, as though Maggie's comment hadn't come as a surprise at all. Ben felt a surge of hope.

She knows something. Come on, Madeline, clue me in here.

"I'm sorry, Ben." Madeline's face softened some. "This must be very hard for both of you. I wish Maggie's father were still alive. He…he always knew how to talk to her."

They were veering off track. "Listen, I'm here because I think you can help me make sense of what Maggie's saying. She wrote me a letter, too…before she went to the hospital." A lump appeared in Ben's throat and he had to swallow hard before he could continue. "She said something about having lied to me."

Madeline Johnson sat perfectly still.

"So…I'm trying to find out the truth, whatever it is."

Madeline stood in a rush of motion and waved one hand in Ben's direction. "Well, young man, I'm afraid you've wasted your time. I don't have the slightest idea what Maggie's talking about." She made her way into the kitchen and returned with two cups of coffee. She handed one to Ben, black like he drank it. "Have you and Maggie prayed about this issue, whatever it is?"

Ben sighed and let his head fall gently into his hands. He rubbed his temples searching for the right words. "I think we're past that at this point."

"Past prayer?" Madeline shot him a disapproving look. "I didn't think there was such a thing."

Help me, Lord… "Of course not…not in that sense. It's just that Maggie's really hurting right now, and I have to find out what she means. What did she lie about?" He paused. "My guess is it's something relatively minor, like maybe she hasn't wanted to live in Cleveland all these years…or she doesn't want to work for the paper anymore…something like that." *Liar!* A voice in his mind taunted. *You think she's seeing another man. Admit it.* "Whatever it is, it's eating her up. It's destroying her, Mrs. Johnson, and if you can help me at all…"

The older woman set down her coffee cup, and again Ben thought he caught a hint of fear in her eyes. "It's destroying her?"

"Yes. To be perfectly honest, I think the hospital is worried she might kill herself."

This time Maggie's mother felt the blow. Her eyes filled with tears, and though she remained utterly still and dignified, Ben could see her heart breaking.

"Things have changed since I was a girl…"

Ben waited. Wherever she was headed, he had a feeling he was close…close to getting the information he so desperately needed.

"In my day, a young woman would never have allowed herself to become so self-absorbed. After all, God's given her a—" she motioned toward him and glanced his direction—"an upstanding Christian husband. In my day that would have been enough. A woman would have known to let dead dogs lay, not dredge up the past for strangers to sift through and analyze looking for answers. My goodness!" Madeline raised her voice a level. "Maggie has everything a girl could possibly hope for. And I'm sure one of these days God was planning to give her the babies she wants. Why can't she leave well enough alone?"

Ben didn't do or say anything to stop the woman. *Keep talking, Madeline. Keep talking.* "Maybe whatever it is seems too big to leave alone."

Madeline shook her head and stared into her coffee cup. "Times have changed."

"Mrs. Johnson, remember when Maggie and I fell out of touch there for a year or so? Before we were married?"

The expression on Madeline's face changed again, and Ben had the oddest feeling the older woman was steeling herself against something inevitable. She stared hard at him. "Yes…she was devastated."

Ben felt the dig. *Is this it, Lord? Did something happen while we were apart?* A ripple of fear skittered down his spine, and he felt almost sure they were treading on a hidden layer of information that would lend insight to Maggie's madness. After all, it had been the darkest year of his life, too.

"Maggie never said much about that time." Ben searched for the right words. "Do you know if—"

"His name was John." Her words spilled out, pouring forth information as if she couldn't bear to hold it in another minute. "John McFadden."

Ben felt his world tilt crazily. *"What?"*

At his whispered exclamation, Madeline lifted her coffee cup once more and took a long sip, leveling her gaze at Ben. "Maggie dated John quite seriously for several months that year. She didn't tell you?"

What is she talking about? Maggie hadn't dated anyone else, ever. Was this the lie? Had it been that easy to discover her secret?

"No…she never mentioned him."

Whoever he was it couldn't have been serious. Maggie had been in love with Ben before meeting this John McFadden, and after Ben was finally able to work his life out, Maggie had married him, not the other man. Whoever John McFadden was, Maggie couldn't possibly have cared much for him. *But then why did she lie to me, Lord?*

Madeline seemed anxious to take control of the conversation. "Ben, you broke Maggie's heart when you stopped calling. John had been pursuing her for months and that summer the two of them spent…" She paused, clearly searching for the right words. "They spent a lot of time together. Her father and I did not approve."

Ben's head was still spinning. He could understand Maggie dating someone else, but someone her parents didn't approve of? "Was he a Christian?"

"Definitely not. He was popular and handsome, and in some ways he reminded us of you. Except that he made a mockery of Maggie's faith."

The truth settled heavily on Ben's heart. "I don't understand. Maggie would never have been attracted to someone who wasn't..." He let his voice drift.

"She wasn't exactly herself after you disappeared. Like I said, she was very hurt."

Obviously Maggie's mother blamed him. It had been Ben's fault back then, therefore it was Ben's fault now. He had made one bad decision in the spring of 1992 and as a result he had lost touch with Maggie for more than a year. Now, eight years later, he was supposed to believe Maggie's choice to date this John McFadden was the reason she had suffered a nervous breakdown?

The pieces didn't add up.

"Is that all? Did anything bad happen between them? I mean..." Ben couldn't bear to ask the questions that poked at his mind, but he had to know. "He didn't hurt her or do anything against her will, did he?" He knew Maggie well enough to know she would never have allowed John McFadden or any man to touch her before her wedding night.

But that didn't mean she hadn't been...

"She was not raped, if that's what you mean." Ben was shocked that Maggie's mother would speak so bluntly, but he was thankful all the same.

He exhaled slowly and realized he'd been holding his breath. "I guess I'm still a little confused."

Madeline crossed her legs and glanced nervously at her hands. "I'm not sure I should tell you this...but if Maggie is really that bad..." She folded her fingers together on her lap and Ben could see they were shaking. "Maybe you have a right to the information."

Not more lies. Lord, give me strength. "Go ahead, Mrs. Johnson, please."

"John McFadden still lives in Cleveland. Your area, actually. I believe he runs a bar on the south side. Topper's...something like that."

Ben struggled to make sense of all Madeline had told him. "Why would you still know that?"

"I could be wrong. But last time I was in Cleveland I saw an ad someplace and noticed his name. He's been there quite a while."

"Is there something else, anything you're not telling me?" Ben had the feeling there was. *Come on, Lord, make her talk to me.*

"I've told you all I know. Anything else you'd need to get from John. But I'm warning you...he's not a nice man. I think he's into some very nasty things, illegal things. Be careful."

Ben's mind raced. "How would you know that unless Maggie had told you?" Had she kept in touch with the man? And why hadn't she ever mentioned him? The whole thing was crazy.

"Maggie's father kept tabs on him. He threatened Maggie more than once, and Mr. Johnson liked to know where he was, what he was doing. Just in case."

"Just in case what?"

"I'm not sure. Maggie's father had a bad feeling about the man."

Ben wished there were some way he could blink and wind up back in Cleveland. He wanted to visit Maggie's old boyfriend before another fifteen minutes passed.

Patience, My son. Love covers a multitude of sins...

The voice that spoke to his heart calmed his trembling and helped him deal with the situation at hand. "That's all, then?"

Madeline drew a lengthy breath. "Yes. This thing Maggie's dealing with, I have a feeling it might be connected to John McFadden."

It had gotten late, and Ben accepted Madeline's offer of the guestroom and a full breakfast in the morning. Before he left, she studied his face. "Tell Maggie I'm praying for her. And whatever you find out, Ben...try to understand. Maggie would never have given John McFadden a second glance if you hadn't left her."

Ben bore the burden of the woman's comment every minute of the four-hour drive to the airport and on into his six-hour flight home. All the while his emotions took him in a dozen different directions—anger at Maggie for lying to him, guilt and regret for having broken up with her, anticipation and expectation for the moment when he could meet John McFadden and ask him about Maggie.

And, of course, overriding fear.

Because more than anything else, Ben was afraid of the meeting he was about to arrange. Afraid of what he might learn about the wife he loved more than life itself.

Terrified that the information might change his life forever.

II

Laura Thompson took her seat in the fourth row at Cleveland Community Church and reached for her husband's hand. He winked warmly at her, and she leaned close, whispering even though the service hadn't started yet. "Have you seen Maggie Stovall?"

Larry frowned and glanced over his shoulder, scanning the congregation. "No. Whaddya want with the Stovall woman?"

Laura hesitated. She'd told him about the prayer mission her Bible study had taken on, but not the name of the woman she was praying for. Eventually she would tell him, when it became clearer why God had asked her to pray for Maggie Stovall in the first place. "Nothing. Just wondered if you'd seen her."

Laura settled back against the cold, wooden pew, occasionally checking over one shoulder or the other in search of the woman. Maggie hadn't missed a Sunday as far back as Laura could remember. She was always there, second row, middle of the aisle, smiling and greeting visitors as though she hadn't a care in the world.

Where is she, Lord? Is something happening to her? Is Maggie in trouble?

Pray, daughter. Pray diligently.

Laura was overcome by the gravity in the silent voice that resonated throughout her heart. It was true, then. Maggie must be having some kind of problem, and now Laura's prayers were needed quickly and desperately.

Without hesitating another moment or letting Larry in on the urgency that accompanied her thoughts, she closed her eyes, bowed her head only an inch or two, and prayed for Maggie Stovall as though her life depended on it.

On Maggie's third day at Orchards, Dr. Camas decided she needed to be on more medication. She had continued to take the antianxiety drugs, which seemed to help her heart beat normally, but now the doctor was bringing out the big guns. Along with breakfast that morning there were two additional pills on a small plate, and Maggie rang for the nurse.

She pointed to the pills when the nurse appeared. "What are these?"

"Oh, I'm sorry, Mrs. Stovall. I thought the doctor explained those. I guess he'll be in later to talk to you about it. You've heard of Prozac?"

Maggie's heart sank and she squeezed her eyes shut. Prozac? Christians didn't go on Prozac. *Lord, what am I doing here? Why did You let me build my whole life on a lie? I hate myself, God. Please...just take me now. I don't want to live...*

"Mrs. Stovall? Are you all right?" The nurse sat down on the edge of the bed and placed a hand on Maggie's arm. "It's okay, he didn't give you a high dosage. Just something to help you think more clearly."

None of it made any sense. She kept her eyes closed, ignoring the nurse's attempts at comfort. A week ago she'd been jogging around the park, enjoying Casey and Cameron, and writing a successful column for a major metropolitan newspaper. Now she was under watch and supervision by a staff of doctors and nurses at a psychiatric hospital. What had gone wrong?

"Does it bother you, having to take this type of drug?" The nurse's voice was gentle, but Maggie felt her anger rising to the surface. Her eyes flew open.

"Yes! It bothers me very much. I'm not a lunatic or something! I should be able to control my moods, my personality, the way I think...without taking some...some sort of *psych* medication."

A tender smile filled the nurse's face. "That isn't always so, Mrs. Stovall. There are many reasons why a person might need these types of medications. Here at Orchards we believe that God has allowed the development of drugs like this to help medical professionals restore us to the place we were before we were sick. Would it help you to think of it that way?"

Maggie sighed, then started when she realized there were tears streaming down her face. *Are You even there, God? Or did You check out at the door?*

It was possible. After all, God had a lot better things to do than baby-sit Christians who couldn't keep from falling apart, let alone live a joyful life. And other than the fact that it was based on a foundation of lies, Maggie knew her life should have been joyful.

"Fine." Maggie gulped down the pills with a single swallow of water. "What other drugs does he want me to take? Is there a happiness drug and a rational drug and a drug that'll make things right between me and my husband? Because I'm a candidate for those, too."

The nurse rose and headed toward the door. She still wore the trace of a smile, but Maggie could see she'd pushed her too far. "I'm sorry this is so hard for you, Mrs. Stovall. I'll be out at the nurse's station if you need anything."

Maggie crossed her arms furiously and pushed away her breakfast. She hated it here; hated being locked up and treated like a child. There was no point to it. The darkness still hung over her very being, lurking in the shadows of her room and following her down the hall to every meeting, every appointment. She still dreamed of the beautiful blond girl and still woke with arms aching from their emptiness.

That morning there were three physical examinations and two appointments with therapists who asked questions about how Maggie was feeling now that she was at Orchards.

"Honest." Maggie said the word with all the defiance she felt. She had never intended to be honest about any of this. She was being forced into it. She didn't want to revisit her past, to face the lifetime of hurt that lay ready to be discovered...but the medical staff at Orchards was leaving her no choice.

There was only one place where the feeling of impending doom seemed to lift, and that was in the quiet calm of Dr. Camas's office. Maggie took her lunch in her room again and dozed off and on until her two o'clock meeting. It was strange that she felt any peace at all heading toward the meeting with Dr. Camas. Especially since it was in his office that she was likely to come face to face with a past she'd been running from all her married life.

When she was situated in her chair, he gently recapped the things she had told him the day before. "Seems like you had very special feelings for Ben back then, is that right?"

Maggie thought for a moment and uttered a brief laugh. "Yes. I wanted to marry him from the moment I saw him."

The doctor nodded his understanding. When Maggie said nothing, he ventured forward. "Something happened to change that?"

Maggie felt a chill pass over her, the feeling of pure, cold, terror. The light in Dr. Camas's eyes caught her attention, and she felt compelled to tell the story, the complete story in all its frighteningly painful details.

She drew a deep breath and began to speak.

Ben placed the call to Topper's Pop Bar at just after noon that same day and immediately knew he had the right place. "I'm looking for John McFadden."

"Whaddya need?" The man on the other end was gruff, unwilling to share any more information than was absolutely necessary.

"I'm a friend of his from a few years ago. He owns the place, right?" Ben was guessing, and his heart sounded loudly as he waited for an answer.

"Yeah, okay, I guess so." His voice bore a thick New York accent, and Ben wondered if Maggie's mother was right. Maybe John McFadden was into more than selling whiskey to the people who found their way to his bar. "Johnny's in after six. Call then."

Six hours. Ben thanked the man and hung up. No way was he going to wait six hours to call the man on the phone. If this was the same John McFadden who had dated Maggie that year, Ben wanted to see him. Now. In person.

He roamed aimlessly around the house wondering how he was going to pass the time. As he scanned the rooms, he realized their home had taken on a disheveled look. Maggie had always kept everything so neat. Laundry cleaned, clothes hung up, dinners on the table every evening. Of course, that was before things changed. In the past two years the house had been messy more often than not, and sometimes when she didn't have a column to write, he'd come home at six o'clock to find Maggie still in her pajamas.

Whatever it was that was eating at her, it had been a long time coming. *Why didn't I see it before?* Ben didn't like any of the answers that came to mind.

He made his way upstairs and started a load of towels. He guessed on the amount of laundry soap and hoped three scoops were enough. Then he grabbed his Bible off the nightstand near his bed. Everywhere he turned the message seemed the same…

Know the truth…the truth will set you free…worship in truth…

What are You trying to tell me, God? That You're glad I'm doing this, that You want me to find the truth out about Maggie? He finished reading and worked some more on the laundry, but still time passed slowly. Two-thirty, then three o'clock. Three hours before he would get in his car and head for a bar, three hours until he would come face to face with a man Maggie had cared for.

A man Ben hadn't known existed.

Maggie let her mind drift. She remembered the phone call like it was yesterday.

After meeting that summer, she and Ben talked to each other often, sometimes writing letters and making promises to be together. Maggie was busy with her school year, involved with her friends at church and working part time for the *Akron Beacon-Journal*. Ben was preoccupied with his toughest year of studies yet, in addition to studying for the bar exam and still, on occasion, seeing Deirdre.

One night, Ben invited Maggie to a party with some of his buddies from school. Before the night was over, Deirdre and a friend showed up, and Ben introduced them.

The girl barely spoke to Maggie, and though Ben seemed unaware of the tension, Maggie was certain of one thing from that moment on. No matter what Ben thought, Deirdre considered him more than just a friend. It couldn't have been any clearer if she'd written it in ink across her face. She was in love with Ben, and that gave Maggie an immediate feeling of insecurity.

"We'll be together more soon," Ben had promised Maggie a few weeks later. "Even this spring, after exams. That'll give us plenty of time to do stuff."

"What about Deirdre? I saw how she looked at you and I think you're wrong about her." Maggie wasn't sure if her words were meant as a warning to Ben or to herself. She knew only that he held the power to break both her heart and Deirdre's.

"Maggie, how many times do I have to tell you?" Ben's voice was kind and compassionate, filled with all the emotion she'd seen in his eyes that first time they met. "It's nothing serious." She tried to feel comforted, but something in the distant places of her heart warned her of danger where Ben was concerned.

Still, he would tell her the same thing over and over. "She's a friend. Kind of like she's always been there. I don't know…it's hard to explain."

No matter what Ben said, Maggie didn't understand. As far as she could see, there was no reason to spend any time with Deirdre if he felt so strongly about his budding relationship with Maggie.

Twice when she had a free weekend, Maggie drove up to Cleveland and spent the day with Ben, watching him play touch football with his law school buddies. He was a gifted athlete, hanging back in the pocket long enough to let his receivers find their right places on the field and then flinging the ball to them with uncanny accuracy. Maggie was proud of him and wished she'd seen him play for CSU. Even there, though, on the intramural field, she felt her heart nearly bursting with pride.

On one of her visits he took her to another party. Most of the people there had been part of the Cleveland Community College youth group and Maggie had the uncomfortable feeling she was being compared to Deirdre. About an hour later— once again—Deirdre and a friend arrived and made their way toward Ben and Maggie.

"Deirdre's here," Ben whispered, nodding toward the blond *on the right*.

"Hi, Ben." Deirdre put her arm comfortably on Ben's shoulder, leaned toward him, and kissed him squarely on the mouth. Although the kiss didn't last long, Ben's expression grew strained; he seemed to stumble over his words. When Deirdre and her friend wandered off to find something to eat, Maggie turned to face him.

"I thought it was only a friendship thing?" She was furious at him for lying to her and she had to fight the urge to walk out and never look back. If Deirdre was his girlfriend, she wasn't interested. "Good-bye, Ben. Call me when you're free."

Ben came after her. "Maggie, really. She never acts like that…that kiss thing. We aren't like that. Can't you believe me?"

Maggie stopped to face him again. "I'm not blind, Ben." She whirled around and continued toward the door.

"What's that supposed to mean?" Ben moved in front of her and blocked

"It means that Deirdre is in love with you. And as long as you two are seeing each other, I'm bowing out." In the distance she could see Deirdre watching them, whispering to her friends. Maggie leaned dramatically around Ben and made eye contact with the other girl. Then she smiled and waved with all the sweet, sticky sarcasm she could muster. When she was sure she had the girl's attention, Maggie leaned over and kissed Ben the same way Deirdre had. Only Maggie made sure her kiss lasted longer.

It was their first kiss, and even now, all these years later, Maggie felt a stab of regret that she had used it as a weapon of revenge.

Especially because it was a kiss she'd dreamed about for months.

Ben's face was layered in confusion and desire. "Hey, Mag…what was that all—"

Maggie interrupted him with a brief wave and an artificially sweet smile. "See ya, Ben." Then she turned and left.

There were phone calls after that, but Maggie kept them short. "Still seeing Deirdre?"

Ben would sigh in frustration. "You can't expect me to cut her out of my life overnight. We've known each other since we were kids."

"It's been nice talking with you, Ben. Gotta run." And she'd hang up.

By February, when Ben began studying more intensely for the bar exam, he had finally stopped seeing Deirdre except at college church functions. He called Maggie constantly, swearing his love and asking to see her more often. She took her time before accepting his offers, and finally they agreed that he would accompany Maggie to a dance at her university later that spring. They began dating every other weekend and often their good night kisses lingered for several minutes before Maggie would pull herself away.

"I love you, Mag…" Ben would tell her as she left.

"You, too." It was true. Maggie trusted Ben and believed that Deirdre was no longer an issue in their lives. Ben Stovall was the man God had chosen for her and she could see nothing but happy days ahead for both of them.

But that was before the phone call.

The news that would change her life forever, the words she would never forget, came one Monday in late March, four days before the big dance. Maggie was working on a term paper for investigative journalism when the phone rang.

"Hello?"

"Maggie…oh, Maggie, something awful's happened."

Even now she remembered how his tone had shot adrenaline racing through her body. She could see herself, the way she had dropped her pencil and leaned back in her chair. "What is it?"

On the other end, Ben drew a deep breath, and Maggie thought she could hear him crying. "Deirdre's mother was killed in a boating accident. They were out on Lake Michigan and…I don't know, something happened…a storm came up. I guess it was hard to see and another boat hit theirs head on. Deirdre broke her arm and fractured her hip. Everyone else was okay, but Deirdre's mother hit her head…"

"I'm sorry." An array of emotions assaulted her, and she had a sick feeling about where the conversation was headed.

"They radioed the Coast Guard and got Deirdre's mom to a local hospital…but it was too late. She was bleeding internally and…there was nothing anyone could do for her."

Maggie was silent for a moment, not sure what she should say. She remembered the party where Deirdre had gone out of her way to mark Ben as her own, and how Maggie had made sure to pay her back. "Deirdre must be devastated."

"Everyone is." She heard him stifle a sob. "Maggie… Deirdre's mother was my mom's best friend. She was like a second mom to me. I can't believe this is happening."

"Is Deirdre…" Maggie didn't want to sound jealous. Not at a time like this. "Is she at home or what?"

"She's in the hospital in traction. They transported her to Cleveland General this morning. They're going to operate on her hip first thing tomorrow and hopefully they'll let her out for the funeral."

"When is it?" Maggie knew the answer before she asked.

"Saturday. Same day as your dance." Ben hesitated, and Maggie squeezed her eyes shut. She was sorry for Deirdre, but something deep inside her heart desperately feared where all this could lead. Ben cleared his throat. "Maggie…you understand, don't you? Deirdre needs me with her at the service."

Maggie's hesitation lasted only a moment. "Absolutely, Ben. Definitely. It's just a dance." With all her heart she wanted to believe the words that so easily flowed from her mouth, wanted to trust Ben and not feel threatened by Deirdre's mother's death. But jealousy swelled deep inside her, leaving a lump in her throat and making it difficult to talk.

"I'm sorry, Mag, but I knew you'd understand." Ben sounded so relieved and deeply troubled at the same time that Maggie hated herself for being worried. She pictured Deirdre…and somehow the image of Ben comforting the blond in her greatest hour of need troubled Maggie to the point of tears.

"Hey, I gotta run, Maggie. I want to be there when Deirdre comes out of surgery. She needs me."

Maggie was silent, Ben's last words ringing through her head: *She needs me, she needs me, she needs me.*

Ben cut in quickly on her thoughts. "You know what I mean, right, Mag? She doesn't need me in that way. It's just that…well, she's lost so much." He paused as if he was searching for the right words. "And I'm still probably her best friend. You understand, right?"

Maggie stifled the tears that threatened to break loose at any moment. What choice did she have but to understand? "Sure, Ben. Call me later."

"Pray for her, okay?" She could hear in his voice that he was anxious to go.

"Sure."

When they hung up, Maggie dropped her head into her hands and muttered a sincere prayer that God show mercy to Deirdre in the days to come. Then she wept for Deirdre and the death of her mother and the sad fact that tragic things happen even to godly, Christian people. But most of all she wept for herself and the strange feeling that had come over her.

The feeling that she had just lost Ben Stovall forever.

Maggie fell silent and Dr. Camas shifted his position. "Is that all for today?"

The room was quiet except for the gentle whirring of heat circulating from a ceiling vent. That phone call from Ben had been the beginning of the darkest days in Maggie's life, the culmination of which made it hard for Maggie to think clearly eight years later.

Confess to one another…live in the light, daughter…

At that moment, the whispering of God did not seem intertwined with doom and desperation. Instead His words seemed the very seeds of hope. Her eyes met the doctor's and again she saw a wealth of warmth and light and somehow she knew she had to continue. Only by going back would she ever move forward toward the place of sunshine and hope that Dr. Camas—and God, Himself—were calling her to.

Fresh tears spilled from Maggie's eyes and she shook her head. "No, there's more."

"I've got time, Mrs. Stovall." His slight smile bathed the room in kindness. "Why don't you go ahead."

Maggie nodded and again allowed herself to drift back in time, back to the place where Ben began spending every spare moment with Deirdre.

At first it had been out of necessity. There were details for Deirdre's father to handle, matters to be taken care of, and with Deirdre in the hospital, Ben was often the only person available to sit by her side. Maggie went to the dance by herself that weekend and spent the evening with a host of friends, including John McFadden, local baseball sensation and easily the most popular boy on campus.

"Hey, Maggie. I know you're one of those Christian girls, but what about you and me going out sometime, huh?"

Maggie felt herself blush. He was so good looking. In fact, in some ways he reminded her of Ben, with the exception of his eyes. Ben's eyes were filled with a love for God; John's were filled with something else…something dark and a little bit dangerous.

Though Maggie enjoyed every moment with John that evening, she knew about the rumors, how John used a girl and left her for another conquest. There was a significant trail of broken hearts lining the hallways of Akron University and a few guys even attested to the fact that John McFadden kept lists of the girls he'd been with.

So she looked at him that night and laughed lightly. "John, you and I are far better off as friends."

After the week of the funeral service, Deirdre had doctor appointments and physical therapy sessions, and much of the time Ben drove her around town or spent afternoons encouraging her to work her damaged hip so that she would get better. When she broke down, missing her mother and terrified of the future, Ben was the one who comforted her.

He explained all of it to Maggie, and though his reasons were good, Maggie could sense him pulling away from her. "She's a wreck, Mag," he told her once a few weeks after the accident. "Deirdre's never been like this before. It's like I'm all she has. She doesn't want me to leave her side."

His words seemed to imply something, but Maggie didn't question him. She was too busy comforting herself. Her gut told her clearly that her relationship with Ben was on shaky ground, and one month after Deirdre's mother's death, he called and confirmed her worst fears.

"Mag, I don't know how to say this…"

She closed her eyes and leaned against the hallway wall. *Say it, Ben. Tell me it's over.*

When she didn't say anything, Ben continued. "Deirdre needs me…"

"More doctor appointments?" Maggie hated the fact that she sounded bitter. It wasn't Deirdre's fault her mother had died, and Ben couldn't help the fact that he'd been friends with Deirdre all her life. Still the anger that boiled in Maggie's heart seeped out in her words, and there seemed nothing Maggie could do to stop it.

"No…I mean, yes, she has more doctor appointments, but that's not it." He sighed loud enough for her to hear. "I'm so confused right now, Mag. I think it'd be best if…"

The tears started then. They flooded her eyes and streamed down her face as though her heart had sprung a leak too severe for anyone to repair.

"Maggie? Are you okay?" He knew she was crying and she hated that fact. "Maggie girl, talk to me."

She swallowed and did her best to sound normal. "I'm fine."

"No, you're not. Listen, Maggie, I didn't plan any of this and neither did Deirdre. It happened. And now…"

"Now you're in love with her." It was a statement, not a question, and though the tears continued to pour from her eyes, her sinuses had not yet swollen so she sounded almost unaffected.

Ben moaned in frustration. "No, I'm not in love with her…I mean, well…I don't know *what* I am."

"Ben, don't be afraid to admit the truth. You've spent a lot of time with her lately; it's only normal that you two would become closer."

"I don't want to lose you, Maggie. I love you. But…"

Here it came, the part where he would ask for time away and promise that maybe someday things would work out. From the beginning Maggie had done her best to avoid this. But here she was: completely in love with him, plans made in her mind to spend the rest of her life with him…and now he was pulling the plug. That was more than Maggie could bear.

She grabbed a tissue and wiped at her eyes as Ben mumbled the very things Maggie had known he would say. She caught the key words. *Time apart. Maybe later. Deirdre needs me.* None of it was important. The relationship she and Ben had started—the one she had believed God had brought about as an answer to years of prayer—was over before it had ever really begun.

Dr. Camas eyed Maggie thoughtfully. "You're married to him now; is that correct?"

"Not for long. I want a divorce."

There was no obvious change of expression on Dr. Camas's face. "Really?"

Maggie remembered the admitting nurse's information that Orchards was a

Christian facility. She hadn't seen many overt signs of this, but there was a sense of God's Spirit everywhere. The doctor's question only added to that.

"There's more to the story. When Ben left, I figured God didn't have someone special for me, after all. I did—" Her voice broke and tears came harder. "I did some terrible things, Doctor. Things Ben doesn't know about."

Again there was no look of shock or condemnation. Instead, Dr. Camas gently patted Maggie's hand. "I think we've gotten through enough for today. Maybe you'd like to tell me about that time in your life when we meet tomorrow?"

A chill passed over Maggie and she forced back a sense of panic that suddenly threatened to overtake her. The session was over; nightfall was near. And the monsters that tortured her in the darkest hours were more tenacious than ever, reminding her exactly how worthless she was.

"Yes, that's fine." She wiped her eyes once more and stood to leave.

Outside Dr. Camas's office the desperation was waiting for her. *Help me, Lord…is this depression? What's wrong with me?* She'd heard a few of the nurses mention that she was being treated for depression and the thought appalled her. What did she have to be depressed about? She had a husband and a God who loved her. She should be filled with joy at all times, in all situations. Wasn't that what the Bible said?

She was halfway back to her room when she saw the little girl. The same one, with long, curly blond hair and questioning blue eyes. She was holding hands with a woman near the front desk, and Maggie stopped in her tracks. Resisting the impulse to run and take hold of the child, Maggie fell against the wall and froze in place.

Blink, Maggie. Blink until she disappears. It isn't her…it can't be.

The advice seemed simple enough, and she followed it willingly. Her eyes snapped shut once, twice, and on the third time the child became a dark-haired little boy. Maggie pulled in quick, short gulps of air and stared wide-eyed down the hallway toward her room. Despite the medicine and counseling and safety of Orchards Hospital, she was still out of her mind. Why else would the little girl have followed her here?

Her entire body trembled and she felt lightheaded as she forced herself to move. *You can do it, Maggie. One foot forward, another…another.* As she walked back to her bedroom, the place where the nightly battle with the forces of desperation would take place, she wondered for the hundredth time since coming to Orchards if there was anything anyone could do to help her escape the darkness. But even as the question came to mind she knew the answer.

It was as clear as the image of the little girl had been moments ago.

The feeling of doom had already consumed her, and the light—whatever light there had ever been—had been snuffed out long ago.

12

It was a full moon that night and Ben figured he could find Topper's Pop Bar without a map. It was in a rough part of Cleveland, where graffiti marked the vacant office buildings, and convenience stores were operated by gun-toting clerks. A neighborhood where more than the usual number of homeless people milled about or lay on bus stop benches.

Ben spotted a used car lot that boasted, "All our cars run!" and he kept driving. Down another block he saw a cheap, 1970s-style neon sign blinking the words "Booze" and "Buds."

Ben took a steadying breath and pulled his car into the lot. He paused for a minute and hung his head. *It's now or never, God.* He climbed out, set his car alarm, and crossed the parking lot. Inside, the bar was nearly black with only a haze of light and swirling cigarette smoke, through which the silhouettes of people could be seen. Ben waited while his eyes adjusted, then made his way to the bar.

"Whaddya want?" The bartender was a short man with an attitude twice his size.

Ben figured the man must have failed the customer service aspect of his job training. *How does a dive like this stay open?*

"Yeah. How 'bout a soda water with a squeeze of lemon." With his eyes adjusted to the light, Ben could clearly see the man's incredulous expression.

The bartender poked his coworker, who was also pouring drinks. "Get a load of this…rich guy here wants a *soda water with lemon.* Do you buy that? Soda water with lemon?" The short man turned his attention back to Ben. "What are ya, Mormon or something, pal? Need a break from the wifey—"

"Wifies," the second bartender interrupted. He leaned over the bar and sized up Ben as though he were an alien. "Those Mormon boys have lots of wives."

"Listen, buddy," the short one said. "If you've got lots of wives you better have a double at least."

Ben was not afraid of the men, but he was growing tired of their noise. He stared at the short one first and then the one who had joined him. "Listen, I said I want a soda water with lemon. If that doesn't work for you, I'll take my business somewhere else." He thought he'd dressed down for the occasion but he could see that his tailor-made trousers and knit pullover still made him stand out among the patrons.

The taller bartender stuck out his hand and angled it back and forth. "Scare me, rich boy."

Ben was tempted to go behind the bar and get the drink himself when the bartenders suddenly stopped hassling him and returned to serving customers.

"Hey, sorry 'bout that..." A man in a pinstriped suit appeared at Ben's elbow. He was dark and handsome, and something told Ben he'd found the man he was looking for. "The boys think they're funny, but they get a little carried away sometimes. Did you, uh, come for anything else?"

Madeline Johnson's words flashed in Ben's mind. *He's into some nasty things, Ben...be careful.* Ben frowned. Wasn't there an article that appeared in the *Cleveland Gazette* not long ago? It had said that bars often were sites of heavy-duty drug smuggling. The sale of beer and other alcohol only helped the success of the cover-up. Shady characters frequented bars all the time, so if one showed up and left with a case of something, most people would assume it was alcohol.

Ben cleared his throat. He wouldn't be surprised at all to find out this was such a place.

"Actually, I'm looking for John McFadden."

"That's me. Did Bobby send you?"

"No...I'm here on my own." His soda water arrived and Ben took a sip. He noticed that the man in the suit was built like an athlete. Odd, but he even thought they resembled each other. *So this is the man, huh, Maggie? The one you hid from me all these years, the one who—*

"Good...good. What can I get for you?"

Again Ben had the sense that McFadden was offering more than alcoholic beverages, but none of that mattered now. He was here because of Maggie, not to uncover a drug smuggling ring. "This is going to seem a little strange, Mr. McFadden, but I need to ask you a few questions about Maggie Johnson."

Ben prided himself on being able to read people, and the moment he mentioned Maggie's name any doubts that he had the right man dissolved instantly. A look of recognition came across McFadden's dark face, followed quickly by deep suspicion. "What about her?"

"I'm married to her." He hesitated. "Maggie's...well, lately she's been having some trouble. Her mother told me the two of you used to see each other."

John held up his hands in mock surrender. "Hey, man, I don't have AIDS or nothing, if that's what you want to know. Me and Maggie only dated for a little while. Not like we were lovers for a year or none of that..."

Everything about Topper's Pop and John McFadden and the atmosphere in the bar felt like an assault on Ben's spirit. A dozen unspoken warnings told Ben to turn around and leave, but he was sure this man held part of the secret to Maggie's past. *Give me strength, God. Please.*

"I'm not here to get a health report on you." Ben paused and slid his hand into his pocket. "I need to know if there's anything you can tell me about Maggie, anything that happened during the time you two were together that she might still be troubled by now, eight years later."

McFadden leaned casually against the bar and sized up Ben much the way the bartenders had earlier. "What's it to you?"

Ben was confused at first. "She's my wife. I need to know."

"No…what I mean is what's it to you; how much you willing to pay?"

Anger flared through Ben, burning his chest and throat. He straightened to face the man, squaring his legs and crossing his arms. "I didn't come here to bribe you. I came here to find out about my wife."

John shrugged and a slow grin spread across his face. "Those are the kinds of things that sometimes go together." He held out his hands, palm up, raising and lowering them as if weighing something. "Information on Maggie, money; information on Maggie, money."

"All right, look. I'll give you a hundred dollars. It's here in my pocket. All you need to do is tell me what happened that year. Anything, any details you remember about Maggie."

Now it was the man's turn to stand straight and as he did he took a step closer so that he was only inches from Ben's face. "No deal, friend. Why don't you take your questions and your lousy hundred dollars and get lost." He spun around, shouted several orders to the bartenders, and disappeared into a back room.

Ben watched him go, fighting the urge to chase the man down, tackle him to the floor and…

Instead, he pulled out a business card and set it on the bar with a five-dollar bill. "Here. For the soda." The short man took the five and started to get change but Ben stopped him. "Keep it. And give my card to your boss, will you?"

The bartender looked pleased with the tip and took the card gladly. "Hey, rich boy, you come on back anytime you want. We'll serve you up the best soda water in town."

There was a chorus of laughter behind the bar but Ben didn't bother to acknowledge it. *Cretins.* He left and headed back to the parking lot. *How do people have fun in places like that?* Outside, he spotted three or four men unloading a crate full of boxes from the back of an unmarked blue van. Ben recognized John McFadden as one of them, and at that instant their eyes met. McFadden whispered something to the other men and then vanished into the storage facility.

God, this place gives me the creeps. He knows something about Maggie and he won't tell me. Help me, Lord. At the last second, before reaching his car, Ben changed directions and headed toward the blue van and the men still working with the boxes.

"Get lost, buddy!" one of the men shouted as Ben approached. "This is private property."

"I'm looking for Mr. McFadden. We weren't finished talking." Ben continued toward the man but before he could ask another question something came crashing down on his head. His knees buckled and he fell to the ground, his body screaming, writhing in pain. Instinctively he reached for his head and felt a pulsating, warm, wetness in his hair.

Blood! I'm bleeding. Help me, God; I don't want to die here.

He covered his head protectively with his hands. "What do you want?" He shouted the question, but there was no answer. He couldn't move, couldn't see clearly. He thought of Maggie and how if he bled to death here in the parking lot of this bar she would never know why, never realize that he was only here because he loved her. At that instant a second blow connected with his skull and one of his hands, and he felt the searing pain of his fingers breaking. "Stop! I'll give you whatever you want…"

Ben had considered bringing his handgun with him tonight but he figured John McFadden wouldn't be antagonistic—certainly not to the point of harming him. Now as he lay there, two sets of feet walked past him. One foot kicked him in the head, and then the feet all walked toward the van and inside the warehouse.

In the distance he heard another set of footsteps, this time growing closer. *They're going to kill me. Lord, take me quickly. And please, God, let Maggie know I love her. Whatever it was she did or lied about I love her.*

His head was pounding and he felt himself losing consciousness. How much blood had he lost anyway? And how much longer would it be? The steps were closer now, and he could make out the shoes. They stopped inches from his face. "Give me the hundred dollars."

Ben struggled to make sense of the words and realized they were coming from John McFadden. Apparently he had ordered the beating. Ben's reflexes were slow, and pain seemed to assault him from every part of his body. But he managed to slip his good hand into his pocket and retrieve the hundred-dollar bill. There was almost no strength left in his arms, but he held it out for him anyway.

"What…what do you want from me?"

"I want you to leave me alone and never come back." McFadden's words were more of a hiss and they held a threat Ben knew was worth taking seriously. If he lived long enough to worry about it. "Are you getting this, Ben Stovall, *attorney* at law?"

The man had Ben's business card. Whatever McFadden's staff was involved in, they communicated directly to the man leaning over Ben, and apparently he didn't take kindly to curious lawyers. Ben struggled to stay conscious.

"Now listen and listen good." McFadden jerked Ben to his feet and walked him across the parking lot to his car. The pain came in white-hot waves, and Ben was sure he'd lose consciousness soon. "You will get in your car and drive yourself to the hospital. You will report the news that you took a bad fall and you will never, ever set foot on my property again. Is that understood?"

Ben nodded. "Yes...let me go." He was woozy and his eyesight alternated between blurred and double vision. Something dangerous and secretive was going on at Topper's Pop Bar. Something much more secretive than whatever John McFadden knew about Maggie. Half expecting to be shot or beaten again, Ben pulled free of the man's grip. Was it possible? Was McFadden going to let him drive off the lot with his body still functioning?

Help me, God; get me to the hospital before I lose too much blood. I can't die without seeing Maggie one more time, without telling her I love her no matter what she's done...

The man shoved Ben into his car and hunched down so that Ben could see him as he spoke. "Oh yeah. Your information...I almost forgot." He smiled wickedly as if whatever he was about to tell Ben was going to bring him a great deal of satisfaction. "Maggie and I had a kid." He chuckled. "But you probably already knew that."

Ben's heart dropped, and his body was hit by a wave of pain far greater than any he'd received so far. His eyes grew wide and he stared at John McFadden in disbelief. "You...*what?*" It was impossible. Maggie was a virgin when they married...she couldn't have slept with...with this man. There couldn't have been a baby...not with his Maggie.

The man tossed his head back and laughed. "You mean she didn't tell you? Sweet little church girl like Maggie, and she didn't tell you she gave a kid away? Imagine that."

Someone called McFadden's name and he was suddenly on alert again. "Now get out of here. You come back, and I'll finish you off myself." He slammed the driver's door and kicked it hard with the heel of his boot before turning and walking away.

Ben did not hesitate. He started the engine, peeled out of the parking lot and headed immediately for Cleveland General. His head was still bleeding badly and his body was racked with pain. There were moments when he felt himself drifting, but still he drove on.

In the depth of his heart, he wasn't sure he was going to make it.

Not because of the beating he'd received, but because of the other blow. If John McFadden was telling the truth—and Ben had the unnerving sense he was—then Maggie truly had lied to him from the beginning.

Determined to hang on, Ben raised his eyelids and forced himself to remain conscious. As he drove, he changed his mind. It wasn't possible. If Maggie had given a child up for adoption, certainly her mother would have known about it. The woman had said nothing about any of that. Ben felt himself growing calmer.

It was a lie. Of course it was a lie. That creep McFadden knew Maggie was a Christian and a virgin. She had probably refused to sleep with him, and he was using this false information as a way of further punishing him for spying on whatever clandestine operation was taking place in the parking lot.

He pulled into the hospital parking lot and veered his car toward the front door. Halfway to the emergency room entrance, he collapsed.

"Maggie!" He shouted her name as loud as he could, and all around him he heard people responding, hurrying toward him, trying to help. Blood covered his face and hands now and he felt himself slipping away.

"Sir, sir, what happened? Can you talk to us, sir?" Someone in a white jacket bent over him as he was placed onto a stretcher and hurried into the emergency room. But the sounds and sights were growing dimmer, and Ben couldn't make his mouth work. *Tell Maggie I love her. Please tell her. Oh, God, please.*

Then everything disappeared and there was nothing but darkness.

13

Despite the chill in the air that late September afternoon, Amanda Joy walked home from the bus stop slower than usual. Things had gotten worse at the Graystone house; two of the foster kids had even talked about running away. It wasn't that the old lady was always mean. But when chores weren't done just so, Mrs. Graystone would change into…well, a monster.

And then the beatings would begin.

Amanda pushed the thought away. She didn't want to think about that; she just knew she didn't want to be anywhere near the woman. Chores had been assigned that morning—fold a load of laundry, make her bed, clean her windows, and wash the walls in her bedroom—but Amanda's second-grade teacher had assigned a science project and much of her morning had gone toward finishing it.

Surely Mrs. Graystone wanted her to get her homework done, didn't she? She wouldn't punish Amanda this time, would she?

She slowed her pace even more, kicking up fallen leaves and stopping briefly to stare into the cloudy sky. *Are You there, God? Isn't there somewhere else I can live?* She waited, but the only sound was the rustling of leaves in the trees overhead. *I don't really need a mother, God. I'd be happy to live with Kathy and her family. Or just someone who liked me a little.*

There were no booming answers, no voices from heaven, but Amanda had the distinct feeling someone had hugged her close. The only one who hugged her now was Kathy, and Kathy hadn't seen her all week. So this hug, this feeling of being warm and safe in the arms of someone who loved her, must have come from God. She glanced once more toward the sky. *Thanks, God. I know You're working on it.*

By the time she walked through the door at the Graystone house, the other children were busy doing homework or cleaning. With her arrival, they stopped and stared at her, and the mixture of fear and warning she saw in their eyes made her heart pound.

"Hi." Amanda set her things down and heard heavy footsteps coming closer. Mrs. Graystone marched into the room and headed straight for her.

"I'm sorry about my chores…" Amanda took two steps backward until she was up against the wall. Her eyes were wide; her breathing was fast; and her arms and legs began to shake.

"You're a good for nothing, *brat!*"

"I'm s-s-sorry, I had to f-f-finish—"

"Shut up! You sound like an idiot when you stutter." Mrs. Graystone was upon her, yanking her by the hair and dragging her from the room. Amanda Joy knew better than to fight the old woman and she moved her feet in quick shuffling steps so the pain in her scalp would be less severe. Mrs. Graystone's breath was strong, sickening…like it sometimes was late at night, when her words didn't make sense. What was happening? Was Mrs. Graystone sick?

In the background Amanda Joy heard one of her foster sisters begin to cry. Chores had gone undone before, but Mrs. Graystone had never acted like this. Why did the other kids look so scared?

Mrs. Graystone flung her into her bedroom and closed the door behind them. Amanda regained her balance and then stood still, head down, waiting for her punishment.

"When I tell you to do something, I want you to *do* it, do you understand me?"

Before the girl could raise her head, the woman yanked her hair so she could see her face. *"Look* at me when I talk to you!"

Amanda winced. Mrs. Graystone seemed fine but her breath had that strong, funny smell. "Yes, m-m-ma'am." Amanda shook from head to toe. Whatever was wrong, it scared her to death.

"Oh, so you're gonna play scaredy-cat around me, is that it, missy? Well, I'll give you somethin' to be scared about."

Before Amanda could think or cover her face, Mrs. Graystone's palm hit her hard across the cheek.

"Stop!" Amanda froze, terror seizing her. She knew the moment she'd let the scream out that her punishment would—

A second slap hit her face so hard it knocked her to the ground. Mrs. Graystone looked furious—and crazy. She yanked Amanda's hair and pulled her to her feet.

"I will not have a brat under my roof who can't carry her own weight, am I making myself clear?"

Amanda felt dizzy, and her vision was fuzzy around the edges. She wanted to answer, but the words seemed stuck in her throat somewhere. Before she could make herself respond, she heard a hissing sound and felt a terrible burning sensation in her eyes. She screamed. "M-m-my eyes! Oh, my eyes…!"

At the same moment she smelled the fumes and realized that Mrs. Graystone had sprayed cleaner at her face. "Help m-m-me!"

The words came out loud and shrill, and Amanda prayed someone would come take her away before—

"You're a filthy excuse for a girl!" the woman shouted at her. "I'll clean you up and maybe you'll be worth something someday."

"No, p-p-please! Stop!"

Another cloud of cleaner came at Amanda; the liquid and fumes filled her nose and throat and made her gag. "I can't b-bbreathe..."

"Shut up!" Amanda heard the bottle hit the wall, but before she could be grateful the cleaner was gone Mrs. Graystone slapped her across the face even harder than before. Amanda fell flat on the floor. There was something wet running from her nose and mouth, and she ran her fingers over it. Forcing her burning eyes open, she saw blood.

God, help...I'm bleeding.

"I hope you're ready!" Mrs. Graystone jerked her up from the floor by her hair again, and Amanda's entire head flamed in searing pain. She scrambled to her feet and realized she was crying. Big, gulping sobs. Her blood mixed with tears and bright red drops began to fall on the floor.

"Please, s-s-stop!" She continued to shout, terrified now that the only way out of the room alive was if someone heard her. "Help me!"

Mrs. Graystone's face grew hard and hateful, and her eyes blazed with something scary and evil. Amanda closed her eyes. Her entire body hurt and she was sick from the cleaner, struggling for every breath. The blows just kept coming, making her feel dizzy.

She was going to die.

Mrs. Graystone paused and glared at Amanda where she was huddled on the floor now. This time her voice was barely more than a whisper. "You better be ready, little girl, because it's time for your punishment to begin."

Carol Jenson stared out her window to the house next door.

Many times she had wondered about the goings-on there. Too many children under one roof for one thing. But she almost never saw them playing outside. She'd heard from other neighbors that the Graystones were foster parents. Well, what kind of parents kept their children indoors every day, even when the sun was shining?

And there was something else, a feeling or sense of some kind that she couldn't put her finger on. The children were sometimes bruised and withdrawn...

Carol was almost sure they'd been beaten, but she'd never said anything. After all, bruises could be caused by a fall on the playground, a fight at school.

Still, whatever was happening at the Graystones, it had kept Carol up at nights on many occasions praying for the children who lived there.

Sometimes she would bring Mrs. Graystone baked goods or stop by with a piece of misdirected mail, hoping to catch her in the act if there was indeed abuse going on. That way she could report the situation and rest assured that the children would be taken care of.

If Carol had been concerned before, she was doubly worried now after reading the series of "Maggie's Mind" columns in the *Gazette*. Carol and her husband had one child, an infant, who at the moment was sleeping soundly in her crib. They were churchgoing folk, who lived a quiet, clean life and enjoyed the weekly wisdom in "Maggie's Mind." When Carol had caught the words "Children Sometimes Abused in Foster Homes" in a recent column headline, she had read it twice through. Foster homes, the article said, were often every bit as abusive as the homes children were taken from.

It was for that reason Carol was particularly sensitive to noises or actions or anything out of the ordinary coming from the Graystone house of late. Earlier, just after putting her baby down, Carol noticed a sad little girl making her way slowly to the house next door. She was fairly new, but Carol had seen her before.

This time something about the girl's walk caught Carol's eye. In that moment she'd had the desperate desire to intercept the sweet-faced little thing and ask her point-blank if there was someone hurting her or making her afraid of going home. But then Carol had to remind herself that it was none of her business—at least until she had more than suspicion to go on. Maybe the children didn't like playing outside. Maybe they were little couch potatoes who preferred video games and television programs to outdoor play.

With a sigh, Carol went to finish folding a load of laundry. But no sooner had she pulled a towel from the basket than she heard a sound that sent chills through her. It was a scream. She was sure of it. A muffled scream, coming from next door.

She dropped the towel in her hands and hurried to the nearest window. Unlatching the lock, she raised the glass pane and listened.

A woman was yelling, probably Mrs. Graystone. Carol couldn't hear everything but she was able to understand key words. "Shut up!" and "brat" sounded loud and clear. And in between the angry words Carol was sure she could hear the faint screams of a child. As she listened, the exchange grew more heated, the child's cries more desperate.

Should I call, Lord? Is this really what I think it is?

The response came with a sense of urgency unlike anything Carol had experienced.

Call now, daughter. Call!

Without hesitation or worrying about the ramifications if she were somehow mistaken, Carol grabbed her cordless telephone and dialed 911.

Officer Willy Parsons and his partner arrived at the home less than five minutes later. He had been investigating a nearby breaking-and-entering when the call came in: Suspected child abuse.

Parsons gritted his teeth, yelled to his partner, and ran for the patrol car. The idea that anyone would be deranged enough to harm a child was almost more than he could stomach. When he'd joined the police force ten years earlier it had been because of an article he'd read in the paper stating that child abuse was on the rise.

The two officers parked and ran to the front door. Parsons knocked sharply. "Police! Open up!"

A woman answered the door looking disheveled and overexerted. "Whaddya want?" She ran her tongue nervously over her bottom lip, and Parsons noticed a layer of perspiration on her face and arms—and the strong smell of alcohol on her breath.

"We have a report from one of your neighbors of domestic violence, ma'am. We'd like to come in and take a look around."

Anger flashed in the woman's eyes, then faded as she laughed lightly. "It's just me and the children." She motioned to the dining room table, where four children sat quietly doing homework.

"Ma'am, our records show this is a foster home, is that right?"

The woman attempted a smile. "Why, yes. I like to help out whatever way I can. All my children are from the foster system."

Officer Parsons squeezed his way past her. "Then since you have wards of the state in your care, I'm sure you know the rules. We're able to check out your home environment whenever any concerns arise."

"Well, yes, but..." Her voice faded. "The children are all here."

At that moment, from the back of the house, there was a strange noise. Parsons cocked his head. What was it? The sound was a moan or a cry, like something from an animal. One that was wounded...

Or dying.

Chills passed over him and took up residence deep in his soul. There it was again. The sound echoed through the hallway, and suddenly Officer Parsons was propelled by a terrifying thought. He pushed past the woman and ran down the hallway, shoving bedroom doors open until he saw her.

"Dear God..."

At first glance, it looked like a bundle of red-stained rags lying in a heap on the floor, but then the bundle moved. And moaned. In that instant it became horrifyingly clear that what the officer was looking at was a child...a small, frail child in torn, blood-covered clothes.

He hurried to the little girl's side and looked intently into her eyes. "Hang on, little one. Everything's going to be okay." Then he turned around and yelled for his partner. "Get an ambulance here quick! And cuff the suspect! I don't want her to run."

He turned his attention back to the girl. She was six, maybe seven years old, and she lay in a pool of blood and vomit. Her face was swollen and cut beyond recognition, and grotesque, hand-shaped bruises covered her arms and upper torso. Wads of the girl's hair lay on the floor nearby, and the room reeked of household cleaner.

Parsons knelt over the girl, feeling for a pulse. It was rapid and shallow. She was in shock; each breath was labored. The child's left eye was swollen shut, but Parsons thought she could see something through her right eye. "How are you doing, sweetheart? Can you hear me?"

The girl groaned softly and muttered something about her head. She struggled for every breath.

"Your head hurts?" Parsons wanted to go back in the other room and tear the woman limb from limb. But right now the battered girl needed him, and he tried to keep his thoughts focused on her.

She moved her head slowly up and down, and Parsons could see fresh tears falling from her eyes. "Help me…" This time the girl's words were clearer. "I can't…breathe."

Parsons ran his fingers gently over her hair and leaned his face closer. "It's okay, honey, we're going to get you help real quick here." His eyes searched the room and spotted a bottle of cleaner on the floor near the bed. "Did someone spray cleaner at you, sweetheart?"

The girl coughed and winced in pain. "My head hurts."

"I know…it'll be better soon, I promise."

She moaned again, her breathing dangerously strained. "She sprayed it…in my eyes…and mouth."

Parsons felt his heart constrict. *How could anyone…?* He couldn't finish the thought. There was no telling what horrific things the woman had done to this girl. She looked like she was suffering from a concussion, possibly several broken bones. Stitches would be needed to close the gashes on her cheek, forehead, and arm. On top of everything else, she was in dire need of oxygen, suffocating from the effects of being forced to inhale the cleaner.

Officer Parsons did not consider himself a religious man, but he liked to think God listened to him anyway. And now, as the sirens closed in and paramedics scrambled through the house with their equipment, he begged God to let the girl live. And to somehow help her find a real home.

"Sweetie, the medics are here now. They'll take care of you, okay?" He took her small hand in his and stroked her knuckles tenderly. "Hang in there for me, okay, honey?"

The girl was breathing too hard to answer him, but from somewhere in her battered body she summoned the strength to squeeze his hand. Parsons had to wipe tears off his cheeks as he left the bedroom and searched for his partner.

Now that the woman had been caught, she was belligerent as they led her to the patrol car. His partner informed him that the girl's social worker—a woman named Kathy Garrett—had been told of the girl's condition and would meet them at the hospital. If the girl lived, she would be placed in Kathy's home indefinitely.

Parsons helped his partner squeeze the woman into the patrol car, and then he stuck his face inches from hers. "You're lucky you get a trial in this country…" He spat the words, and she struggled to put distance between the two of them.

He studied her, this creature that was more beast than woman. "If I had my way, I'd—" He choked back the rest of what he wanted to say. His anger was getting the better of him. With a ragged draw of breath he shot her a final glare. "God have mercy on your rotten soul, lady."

They were loading the girl into the ambulance, and Officer Parsons left the patrol car to check on her.

In whispered tones, the lead medic told him the news. "She's in bad shape, but we're hopeful. If we can keep her heart rate steady and if she doesn't have too much bleeding in the brain she might make it."

A woman walked up, and Officer Parsons saw that she was crying.

"I'm Carol. I live next door."

"Are you the one who made the call?" Parsons stepped aside so they could talk.

"Yes...I feel awful. I should have called days ago, weeks ago. I always knew things weren't right here and that something bad was—"

He shook his head, placing a gentle hand on her arm. "You can't do that to yourself, ma'am. You called today; that's all that matters."

The woman nodded and looked wide-eyed into the ambulance, where the medics were still working to stabilize the girl. "Is she...will she be okay?"

There were tears in his eyes as he answered. Like most officers he did his best to stay detached from the crime scenes he worked. But this was more than a crime scene. It was a little girl clinging to life because of circumstances completely out of her control. He blinked back his tears and stared kindly at the woman. "If she lives, it'll be because of you."

A moaning sound came from the ambulance, and Officer Parsons was at the girl's side in an instant.

"Kathy...want Kathy..." The tiny voice quivered.

The medics shrugged and looked at Parsons as he nodded his understanding. The girl wanted her social worker. "Kathy Garrett? Is that who you want, honey?"

The girl moved her head up and down a few inches. "Listen, sweetheart. Kathy's going to meet you at the hospital. She's there now, waiting for you, okay?"

Through the blood and bruises and swollen tissue, Parsons thought he saw the girl smile. There wasn't a reason in the world for this child to be happy, and yet she was smiling. Again she struggled to speak. "I'm okay...I know it." Her words were slow and deliberate, punctuated with pain and raspy breaths, but she continued to speak anyway, and the team of professionals around her listened intently. "I prayed to leave here...and so..." She took a deep breath and flinched from the pain. "Everything's okay...because now..." She moved her fingers to her face and lightly touched the broken areas. "I get to be with Kathy..."

There were tears streaming down the faces of the three men as they huddled around the child, the medics working furiously to hook up an intravenous line while Parsons did his best to keep her calm. She was trying to finish her thought when Parsons saw it again—a hint of a smile on the girl's broken face.

"I don't have a mommy. I have Kathy. If I can be with her...then God must have heard my prayers..." Fresh tears flowed from the girl's swollen eyes, and Parsons had the feeling they were almost tears of joy. "And if He heard my prayers, then maybe...maybe He loves me."

The three men were speechless.

Parsons squeezed the girl's hand in his. What could he say to a girl who'd been beaten to within a breath of her life, a girl who could still find it within her to smile—and beyond that...to feel loved by God? His throat was too thick to speak so he clung tightly to her small fingers—his tears falling softly on the girl's long blond hair—while the medics completed their work.

Less than a minute later, they were ready to transport her and one of them checked her vitals. "We're losing her," he whispered to his partner. "Let's get this thing out of here."

Parsons released the hold he had on the child's hand and pulled himself out of the ambulance, praying that the beaten little girl without a home or a mother or a chance in the world was somehow right.

That maybe God really did love her, after all.

14

That night, for the first time in a long time, Maggie wasn't tortured by demons spewing taunts of condemnation and blackest darkness. The doom and fear were gone, and in their place was a meadow with endless acres of summer grass and wildflowers. In the distance a child was frolicking about, chasing a butterfly or dandelion dust in the breeze.

Who are you, little girl?

Maggie squinted in the sunlight, and though her feet were not moving, her body was suddenly propelled to within feet of the girl. It was her! Of course it was! *Sweet child, why are you here? How can I help you?*

The little girl stopped what she was doing and turned. Her cotton dress danced on the gentle stir of wind in the air and she smiled at Maggie. "Hi."

Maggie wanted to get closer but her feet were stuck and she looked down. *What in the—? Who put shackles on my feet?* Thick, heavy iron cuffs held her legs in place and prevented her from getting closer. "Who are you, honey?"

The girl tilted her head, and Maggie was struck by her face, innocent and so much like… No, it couldn't be!

The girl opened her small mouth and said something, but Maggie couldn't hear her. "What, sweetheart? I can't hear you. I want to help…what can I do?" Maggie strained against the chains until she felt the skin on her shins shredding.

Again the girl spoke and though she couldn't hear her, Maggie could read her mouth. "I want my mommy…my mommy…my mommy." Then the girl began to cry.

Suddenly, Maggie was sure that the child's mother, or maybe even—*It can't be…it's impossible.* "Don't cry, honey. I'm here…"

She shouted the words but they were lost on the breeze, and the image of the girl began to fade. *No…don't go. Not yet…I have to talk to you. I still don't know who you are…Wait!*

Then the scene changed.

She was in a hospital room and the air was filled with quiet strains of lullaby music. *Jesus loves me this I know, for the Bible tells me so…* Maggie cradled the infant girl tenderly, and around her the entire room was painted in soft pastels. Gently, quietly nuzzling the baby's cheek, Maggie rocked her back and forth, back and forth.

Then the music changed and became suspenseful, faster and faster giving Maggie the feeling something was about to overtake her and the infant, both. About that time someone burst into the room dressed in a black hooded gown. A quick glance told Maggie it was John McFadden, hidden by a cloak and carrying a hatchet in his hands. The music grew faster, more intense, more frightening as he moved closer.

In the dream, Maggie held the baby tighter and heard herself screaming. "I have to save her! Get away from me. Please! Someone help me!" But the figure moved closer still and raised the hatchet over his head. Maggie knew if it came down it would be on the baby in Maggie's arms.

Suddenly another figure entered from the other side of the room, and Maggie spun around to see a nurse. She stared at Maggie with vacant eyes, her face utterly expressionless. Then, in a slow, robotic manner, she made her way toward Maggie.

Again the music grew louder, and suddenly the baby began to speak. "Mommy, don't do it. Don't leave me, Mommy. I need you."

Her words were perfect and articulate, and Maggie felt herself flooded with confusion. The dark figure still loomed at her side while the nurse moved steadily closer, only now the face on the dark man beside her was not John's, but Ben's. Robed in midnight, her husband Ben held the hatchet over Maggie and the baby, but instead of John's sinister expression, Ben's face was filled with godliness, his eyes glowing with the light of the Lord.

"It's time to break the ties. For me, Maggie. It's time. Decide who you love more. Come on, it's time…"

Then she looked and saw a thick piece of twine tying her hand to the baby's. "Somebody stop that awful music!" But no one was listening to her. Before she could stop him, Ben brought the hatchet down on the center of the cord so that the baby and Maggie were no longer tied together. With that, the hatchet became a white dove that flew through an opening in the window.

The nurse tapped her on the shoulder. "Give her to me. Give her to me. Give her to me…"

That's when Maggie saw it wasn't a nurse at all, but a machine—an unfeeling, uncaring, cold-blooded machine with glowing electric eyes and a hinged mouth.

"Don't do it, Mommy, please!" The infant was speaking again, crying for Maggie to hold on, and she did so with all her strength. But Ben took her arm and began pulling her away.

"It's for the best, Maggie. Let her go." Without waiting for Maggie's response, he pulled harder. At the same time, the nurse grabbed the baby from her arms and spun in the other direction, moving mechanically toward a narrow door.

"Wait! Don't take her from me…" Maggie began sobbing hysterically, desperate for the feel of the baby in her arms once more. "Bring her back…please!"

But Ben was relentless. His eyes still glowing with faith and hope and love, his clothing black as the terrors of night, he tightened his grip on her arm and moved her from the room.

When they walked out the door, there was no longer a floor to step onto, but a sharp cliff leading to a deep, dark, deadly canyon. The music was almost deafening now, and in that instant she and Ben began to fall—

Maggie awoke with a start, sitting straight up in bed. The sheets were drenched in perspiration and she was trembling violently from the inside out. Where was she? Her eyes darted about the room and her breathing came fast and hard. Where was the baby? The little girl? Ben?

The fog began to clear and she forced herself to exhale.

Calm down. It was only a dream. "Dear God, why?" The words escaped from her like the cry of a wounded animal. How could she have done it? Handed her baby over to the state's foster system all so she could...

Maggie climbed out of bed as her eyes darted around the room. The red glowing numbers on the clock told her it was five in the morning. Sweat continued to drip from her forehead, and she realized she was in the middle of a panic attack. She needed something, another pill or a doctor. Something.

Her eyes fell on the Bible sitting in the center of her bedside table. She had noticed it before but had never felt the need to open it. She could talk to God if she needed help. What more could His Word do for her at this point? After all, it hadn't brought her peace and joy and it hadn't prevented her from falling apart and being admitted to a mental hospital. No, she didn't need the Bible. She needed medication.

Her eyes searched the room again, focusing on a meal tray from last night. It lay on the floor, near her bed. Maggie rushed to it, rifling through the dirty items. Maybe she'd forgotten to take her antianxiety pill. She knocked over a glass of water in her haste and huffed in frustration. There were no pills on the tray. She pushed the nurse's call button.

After a beat, Maggie heard the nurse's voice. "Mrs. Stovall, can I help you?"

"Yes! I'm...uh, not doing very well here. I think I need...maybe you can get me one of those pills, okay?" Her voice shook from the fear raging through her.

"Mrs. Stovall, I'm afraid it's not time for that medication yet. It's very important that you don't take too much. Remember, the goal is to help you live without the medication if at all possible."

"It isn't possible!" she screamed. *What am I doing? Why can't I get a grip here, God?*

Joy will come in the morning. My word is a lamp unto your feet and a light unto your path...

The Bible. God wants me to read the Bible. Maggie's heart rate slowed considerably, and she stared at the intercom in her hand. "Never mind. I think I'll just...I'm sorry. Never mind."

Maggie dropped the device and moved slowly around the bed to the portable table. Was it still true, even after all the ways in which she'd failed everyone who mattered in her life? Could God's Word still light her path?

She remembered her father saying if people really wanted a friend in Jesus, they needed to get friendly with the Gospels. Flipping the pages gingerly, Maggie allowed herself to remember the thin, crinkly feel of them between her fingers—and the peace that spending time within them had once brought. She stopped at the book of Matthew and skimmed past the genealogy of Christ. Then she began to read in earnest.

Her sweating stopped and her trembling body stilled as she drew in the wonder of God's truth for the first time in months.

Nine hours later when she sat in Dr. Camas's office she was convinced there was still power in God's Word.

"I'm ready to finish the story." She sat straighter in the chair and though she had barely been at Orchards a week, Maggie had the faintest feeling that something inside her was learning to cope. If lies were like a wound to the soul, Maggie's had been festering for more than seven years. Only by exposing them to the light of day could the raw place inside her ever begin to heal.

Dr. Camas leaned back in his chair and his eyes offered encouragement. "Go ahead, Mrs. Stovall."

"Maggie. You can call me Maggie."

The corners of his mouth lifted slightly. "Very well. Go ahead, Maggie. Tell me the rest."

She closed her eyes, begging God for strength. Then she did what she hadn't ever wanted to do again. She allowed herself to drift back in time to the spring of 1992, to a place of reckless abandon.

To the season she dated John McFadden.

The worst part about dating John was that she'd known from the beginning what he was about, what he stood for. Her mother always said rumors were like smoke, and where there was smoke there was usually a fire or two; and that if it looked like a duck and walked like a duck and quacked like a duck, well, it probably *was* a duck.

After the dance—the one Ben couldn't go to because of Deirdre—John called Maggie several times a week and flirted mercilessly, doing his best to get her out on a date. Maggie enjoyed his attention but refused to take him seriously. Guys like John scared her. They were experienced and worldly and would want from her the one thing she intended to keep intact: her virginity.

But by the end of the third week, Maggie felt her defenses weakening. Ben hadn't contacted her once since his devastating phone call, and she figured he and Deirdre were probably spending much of their time together. *Forget him,* Maggie thought. *Let him go; I don't have to wait around until he's engaged to have fun. Besides, I'll be careful...*

Thoughts like that consumed her and they were dangerous, Maggie knew. But she no longer cared. Ben had broken up with her; how could she believe God had a plan for her life?

With that mind-set, she found herself giggling and blushing whenever John called; and finally, four weeks after the dance when he suggested they see a movie together she agreed to go.

Maggie remembered her father's reaction like it was yesterday.

"I've heard about him, Margaret." Her father only used her given name whenever he was deeply troubled by her actions. "He's a womanizer...not the kind of young man suitable for a girl like yourself."

He was talking about Maggie's purity, but his upbringing wouldn't allow him to spell it out for her.

"Daddy, he's fun..." She couldn't think of anything else to say.

Instead of outlining the reasons John might be bad for her, Maggie's father raised his voice to a level he rarely used. "You will *not* date John McFadden!" He stood tall and stern, his posture symbolic of the way he felt on the issue. Maggie's mother waited quietly in the background, her head bowed. Clearly she was disgraced that Maggie had even considered dating such a one. "Hear me clearly on this, Margaret. You will not date him. I absolutely forbid it."

Maggie ran to her room and cried herself to sleep and for the first time since she could remember, she refused to pray. There no longer seemed any reason. If God had taken Ben from her, then obviously He didn't mind whom she dated. There wasn't one special person for her after all. And the gift she'd once held as precious and worthy only of her husband began to feel more like a burden.

On June 12 that year Maggie turned twenty-two, and the next week she used all her savings to buy an old Honda. Despite feelings of uncertainty she moved into an apartment with two girlfriends from college. She had secretly hoped her parents might try to stop her, maybe explain to her that God still had a plan for her life and that if only she would wait on Him things would fall into place. But they did nothing of the sort.

Instead, while Maggie packed her belongings into a borrowed van, her mother mended a pile of clothes and refused even to make eye contact with her. That day, her mother's single bit of advice to Maggie had been this: "If you must go, do it quickly. And be aware that you're breaking your father's heart."

Her father clearly disapproved also, but he helped her pack her things and hugged her before she left. "I am letting you go in the grace of God, trusting that by His mercy He will one day bring you safely home."

Maggie had always wondered how much her father loved her. He was so analytical in his thinking, so devoted to things of God. Often she figured he couldn't possibly have time for thoughts of her. But that afternoon, under clear, blue summer skies, she saw tears in her father's eyes—and every question she'd ever had about his love was answered in a single moment. Her father loved her, and he was willing to let her go so that she might find out for herself the weighty importance of one's choices in life.

After that, she and John began dating in earnest. At first it seemed to Maggie that she'd made a wonderful choice. John doted on her, bringing her jewelry and flowers for no reason other than to declare his love for her. Concerns about his character and intentions vanished like fog in the morning sun. But by the end of July, their relationship grew more physical.

They'd be sitting in the front seat of his car kissing and he'd move his mouth along her neck up toward her ear, begging in raspy whispers to come up to her room for a while, promising her it would be all right. "If you really love me, you'd trust me. I'll only stay an hour…come on, Maggie."

Twice she told him no, but on the third time, Maggie thought about her roommates and knew they wouldn't mind. They had been casual friends of Maggie's at Akron University, girls who hung out at beer keg parties while Maggie attended her church's college group and weekly Bible studies. They were thrilled to see Maggie "loosening up," as they called it, and Maggie knew they wouldn't pass judgment if she had John up to her room. Besides, guys had actually spent the night in their rooms several times since Maggie had moved in.

It was the first week of August and the air was hot and heavy. As she returned John's kisses in the stuffy car, Maggie finally caught her breath and smiled at him. "All right, come up. But you have to behave yourself."

Maggie had a television in her bedroom, and that first night John kept his promise. They talked and laughed and watched late night sports on TV. But two days later the scenario was wildly different. She and John had been talking about her plans for after college when he moved closer and began kissing her. The physical sensation of being close to John, kissing him, was something she had never experienced with Ben. She felt truly alive for the first time.

That night as their kisses grew more urgent she allowed him to ease her down onto the bed. At first she convinced herself they could stop if they wanted to. But his kisses built a fire in her that grew with each passing minute.

"Trust me, Maggie. It's okay…" His whispered words of reassurance convinced her that she had nothing to lose—nothing of any real value. Instead she might actually gain something: a closer relationship with John, a better understanding of what real love was about.

And so, with those thoughts in mind, she did the one thing she had promised since junior high never to do.

The changes in John did not happen overnight as she once had feared they would if she ever gave in to him. Instead, he seemed to love her more than ever. When they spent time together in her room at night, they no longer pretended to be interested in television. Instead they did the thing that made Maggie feel better with John than she'd ever felt with anyone in her life.

Including Ben.

Her feelings for John were never the intense longings she had felt for Ben, never the love she had imagined sharing with her husband one day. Rather it was a thrilling sort of sensation, as though she were flying above the masses of regular people and had been let in on a high only a privileged few might ever experience. Later she would remember a pastor telling his congregation that the fruit Eve took from the snake must have been delicious beyond belief because the lure of it was enough to make Eve turn her back on God.

It had been the same way with John, even if Maggie didn't recognize it at the time. She thought only about how complete and whole she felt being desired by someone like him, someone who could have had his pick of girls. John filled her senses until she was satisfied beyond anything she'd ever felt, and she hoped her days with him would never end.

As time passed, Maggie had done such a good job of convincing herself what she and John were doing was okay that she rarely suffered twinges of guilt while she lay in his arms. But in the light of day…that was another story. She often had moments of gut-wrenching conviction. From nine to five, Maggie worked at a nearby clothing store so she could pay her share of the rent. Sometimes the voices that haunted her during her shift were so distracting she could barely help the customers.

Flee immorality…be pure, daughter, as I am pure…

The memory of those holy warnings snapped Maggie back to the present.

"Are you okay?" There was concern in Dr. Camas's voice and he leaned slightly forward, resting his elbows on his oak desk. "Should we take a break, perhaps?"

Maggie shook her head. "No. I was just remembering something that happened before I came here. I almost…I was nearly arrested for talking to a little girl I didn't even know. She was…she was blond, and I've been seeing her everywhere…at the market, at the park, on my computer screen at work…" She stared at him and wondered what kind of terrible person he must think her. "It was part of what led up to this, to my coming here, I guess."

Dr. Camas cocked his head and frowned, but contrary to Maggie's fears, there was no contempt in his eyes. "You can't change the past, Maggie. It happened."

"But I lied. I'm the worst possible wife ever!" She choked the words off, aware she was yelling. Taking a breath, she went on, but more calmly. "And what about my column?" Maggie felt tears stinging at her eyes again. "Like I have any room to comment on society…"

He waited and after a beat Maggie lifted her head. "Now you see why my marriage is over."

"We can talk about that later."

"I hate him for making me—"

"Maggie, try not to blame when you're talking about yourself." It was the first time Dr. Camas had given any guidelines to their discussions.

His comment stung. *It is Ben's fault, all of it.* Maggie closed her eyes angrily, and two tears trickled down her cheeks even as the truth trickled into her heart, her mind.

Much of it may well be Ben's fault, but her behavior certainly wasn't. She sucked in a slow breath and stared at the doctor. "You're right. I have my reasons for hating Ben, but I hate myself more."

"Do you want to continue the story?"

Maggie sighed. "Eventually things changed between me and John…pretty fast, actually."

"It usually does."

Dr. Camas might not say much, but Maggie had found that what he did say was generally profound.

Two weeks after Maggie had given in to John, he called her and told her he'd be gone for a few days. "I've got things to do, love."

An alarm sounded in Maggie's gut, but she took him at his word. Five days later he called again. "Hey, Maggie…I've been thinking a lot…about us and…well…"

Fear coursed through her, and she told herself it wasn't happening. He wasn't doing to her what he'd most certainly done to so many other girls. Not when she had trusted him implicitly. "What are you saying?"

"I guess I'm saying we need time apart. I'm not ready to settle down with just one person yet." He waited a beat. "I'm sorry, Maggie."

She and John spoke just once after that, when Maggie called to tell him she was pregnant. "What do you want me to do about it?" His voice no longer held any pretense. Instead he sounded like a stranger. An angry, agitated stranger.

"It's your baby, too." She held the results of the pregnancy test in her hand, terrified of what they meant to her life and her future. Desperate to think it all a mistake.

"Can you *prove* it's my baby?" His voice was mean, full of disregard for her and the child she carried.

"Of *course* it's your baby. When did I have time to be with anyone else?"

"Come on, Maggie. You gave up the goods too easy. What's to say you weren't doing some other guy at the same time?"

A flash of terror pierced her heart. Everything her parents had warned her about was true. She'd gone against God's Word and now she was left holding the apple core of sin. She remained silent, absorbing his callous tone, sorting through her options. Abortion was out of the question. There was no way she could take the tiny life inside her for the mistakes she herself had made. She could have the baby, maybe move into a less expensive apartment somewhere and try to raise the child on her own. That thought caused another flash of terror.

Maggie closed her eyes and resolved that however she might handle the situation, she would do so without his help. "Never mind, John. Forget I ever called."

In the days that followed, she halfway expected him to call and at least promise his support. But there were no phone calls, no promises.

She had done the math and figured she'd gotten pregnant sometime that second week of August. Her last phone call with John took place in late October, and now she was nearly five months pregnant and still not showing. By that time, although much of what she would do in the future was still undecided, she had arrived at one conclusion.

She loved her baby.

Ben may have turned his back on her, and John might have seen her as little more than a conquest, but the life growing inside her was one she could love with all her heart. And she knew with absolute certainty she would be loved in return. It didn't matter that her parents would be disappointed or that she might have to walk a lonely road as a single parent. At least she and her baby would have each other.

But even the strongest love couldn't dispel the increasing doubts that nagged Maggie as the days wore on. Doubts about how she would care for her child, what means of support she would have. Time and again she found herself wondering what would have happened if she and Ben had stayed together, if this were his baby she was expecting under the marital umbrella of God's favor.

Although she still hadn't heard from Ben, her mind was consumed by memories of their conversations, the way he'd looked at her that first night at the picnic, his reaction when she'd kissed him that night at the party while Deirdre looked on.

Eventually Maggie made a plan. One of her roommates had family in Cincinnati. When Maggie confided her situation, the friend contacted her parents and made arrangements.

"You can live with them until you have the baby and stay there while you find a way to live on your own." The girl leveled her gaze at Maggie. "You know, you could always give the baby up for adoption."

Maggie's heart sank. She'd thought of that option and knew it was impossible. Not when she already felt the way she did for the child. "I...I couldn't."

Her friend took her hand and squeezed it gently. "You really want this baby, don't you?"

The question rattled around her empty heart. *If only Ben and I had...* "Yes," she finally answered. "With all my heart."

"Okay then, my parents' door is open."

After that it was just a matter of telling Maggie's parents. The holidays had come and gone by then and her parents were relieved about Maggie's apparent breakup with John McFadden. Of course, they had no idea how serious things had gotten.

"I always knew God would bring you back to your senses, Maggie," her father had told her when first she admitted they were no longer an item. "You're a very special girl, a girl who will save herself for her husband."

Between her father's sureness that Maggie was still a virgin and her mother's quiet disapproval of Maggie's recent choices, she could not bring herself to tell either of them the truth. Not yet. Maybe not until after the baby was born. They both were upset with her decision to move to Cincinnati; she could only imagine how they'd react if they knew she was pregnant.

"What's in Cincinnati?" her mother said, spewing the word as though it were an infectious disease.

Maggie sighed impatiently. "I'm tired of Akron, Mother. I need to get out and see the world and right now Cincinnati is the best I can do."

Her father watched from a distant chair and said nothing. Maggie had the unnerving sense he somehow knew she was in trouble, but she never revealed any details to him and he never asked.

The month before her move to Cincinnati she left her apartment and returned home to save money. She was searching her closet for pants with elastic waistbands one afternoon when the phone rang. She lifted the receiver.

"Hello?"

Silence. Maggie almost hung up, but then someone spoke. "Hi, Maggie girl."

It was Ben, and her heart swelled at the sound of his voice, the voice her heart had longed for every day since their last conversation. She was speechless.

"Maggie...it's so good to hear your voice."

For a while neither of them said anything. Maggie collapsed cross-legged on a pile of clothes, her hand firmly on her slightly rounded abdomen as tears streamed down her cheeks.

Why now? When it's too late?

In the wake of her silence, Ben rushed ahead. "Maggie, I'm sorry...so sorry. I won't blame you if you hang up and never speak to me again. Really...but I had to call you, had to tell you...Maggie, I can't stop thinking about you. I never have."

Maggie swallowed several times, composing herself so that he wouldn't know she was crying. "Why, Ben? After all this time?" Whatever they might have had was lost forever now. She had thrown away the most precious gift God had given her, and in a few months she would be a single mother. She and Ben stood on separate continents now with no way to bridge the ocean between them.

He sighed and launched into an explanation of his choices that past spring. "Deirdre needed me...I don't know." He paused. "We thought...she thought if we were together maybe everything would be right with her world."

Maggie waited. Clearly Ben had felt the same way or he wouldn't have broken things off with her. Not that it mattered. The conversation was pointless. Everything about her life had changed, and if Ben knew the truth he'd hang up and never give her a second thought. He saw her as a precious virgin, the pure and wholly faithful girl she'd been back before their separation.

He released a rush of air. "Whew...this is harder than I thought it'd be."

"I guess I don't understand. You must have wanted to be with her, too."

"I loved her mother, Maggie. It seemed like the right thing to do—like I owed it to her...to stay with her through that whole mess. I figured if we were supposed to be together, the way everyone always thought we would, then I'd know if we spent a few months with just us. With no distractions."

Maybe she should tell him the truth outright and stop the silly charade. But she couldn't. Instead she continued to listen.

"At first it seemed like maybe we'd made the right decision, but after a few months—when things settled down and Deirdre's hip healed—we both came to the same conclusion. What we have between us is more like a brother-sister thing. She started dating someone else two months ago."

Maggie closed her eyes, struggling to take a deep breath. If only he had called her sooner! Given her some hint that things weren't going well with Deirdre, that in fact his heart resided with her…

"I've thought about calling you every day, but I didn't want you to think I wasn't sure. So I waited. Maggie, I've never been more sure of anything in my life."

Her mind raced, searching for some way to make it all work out after all. "I've got plans now, Ben." She threw the comment out there, not sure what she was going to say next or what lie she might be willing to say to back it up.

"Plans?" He sounded nervous. "Have you…have you met someone?" When she was silent, he moaned out loud. "I should have called you sooner. Who is he? Where did you meet him?"

Suddenly a story appeared in Maggie's mind so tight and true she felt compelled to tell it. Maybe…just maybe… "I didn't meet anyone, Ben. I'm going away for a semester. I leave next week to get set up."

"Where?" Ben sounded crushed.

"Israel." Maggie spouted the word before she could stop herself. "As an exchange student."

"*What?*" Ben's shock was evident. "Maggie, why would you do that?" She nestled both hands protectively over her belly and felt her anger rise. "Listen, Ben, until ten minutes ago I thought we'd never speak to each other again. Now you're asking me why I'm going to spend a semester abroad? I'll tell you why. Because you turned my world upside down when you left, and I had no choice but to make a way for myself without you."

He was silent, and her voice grew softer. "Maybe being out of the country for a month will give us both time to think."

"Okay…I'll give you that. You can take a semester or a year. Take whatever time you want. But when you're ready to give me a chance, I'll be here, Maggie. I'll wait as long as it takes—until you can look me in the eyes and tell me you don't love me."

Maggie wished she *could* tell him that, wished she could call him over to her parents' house and be honest about the past six months, then do just what he'd said—look him in the eyes and tell him she had no feelings left for him whatsoever. But it wasn't true. Her heart was pounding with the sound of his voice, and hope soared within her in a way it hadn't for far too long.

And yet, even as she celebrated inwardly, a small voice of concern sounded in her conscience: *What about the baby, Maggie? What about the baby?*

"Pray about us, will ya, Mag? I believe God will help you know what you want. And then…when you come back, let's get together and talk, okay?"

Her mind raced, trying to match the dates correctly. The baby was due in May. She'd have to figure out a way to leave the area until then and…

And then what? Ben would have to know about the baby sometime. Unless…
"You could always give the baby up for adoption…give the baby up for adoption…"
"I'll pray."
"Good."
Her mind was racing weeks and months ahead. Why couldn't she give the baby up? There would be others with Ben, wouldn't there? Children who would be born into a loving home with both parents happily married. And what about the child she carried? If she really loved her baby, she would consider its future. No father, a mother who might have to work multiple jobs to keep them off the streets… What kind of life was that for a little one?

The idea began to take root, and she imagined holding the baby, giving her over to someone else…

She closed her eyes. *Don't think about it now.* If Ben was willing to have her, then giving her baby up might be the price she had to pay. A price that would bring about the best future for her *and* her child. Fresh tears formed in Maggie's eyes as raw pain settled over her heart.

Ben's voice interrupted her. "When do you get back?"

Maggie swallowed another sob. "I'll call you."

"Maggie, you're crying! What's wrong?"

Don't give it away, not now. "Nothing. I'm just…I wasn't expecting this, Ben. I thought you were gone forever."

"What about while you're gone? Will you write…just so I know what you're thinking?"

The threads of deceit worked their way around Maggie's throat, making it difficult to speak. "No…no, that won't be possible. I've got a lot planned and… Ben, I have a lot to think about."

"Your parents are okay with you leaving the country like that?"

"Of course." The threads tightened with every lie. "It's the Holy Land, after all."

"True…how are they, your parents, I mean?" Ben seemed suddenly desperate to catch up on all he'd missed over the past months.

"Fine."

"And what about you…what've you been doing since spring?"

Maggie exhaled slowly and forced herself to sound natural. Why did she still love him, still picture him as clearly as if he were standing before her? How could she lie to keep him even after he had chosen Deirdre over her? Then it occurred to her that what he'd done for Deirdre was actually quite noble. Very Ben-like. And if Maggie hadn't been so personally involved she might even have thought it the right thing to do.

"Maggie?"

She answered quickly this time. Too much silence was bound to make him wonder. And the lies were too fresh, too newly thought up for him to start questioning her now. "I got a job at the mall, put some money away, and spent a lot of time thinking."

Ben considered that for a moment. "I'm sorry, Maggie. It's all my fault. I wish—"

"Don't!" Maggie's grip on her abdomen tightened, and she could no longer stop the tears from flowing freely. "Don't, Ben. The past is behind us."

She was suddenly desperate to finish the phone call. They had five months before they would see each other again, and in that time she had a million details to work out.

Most of all she had to find a way to let go of the only one she had loved these past months: her unborn child.

The memories faded, and Maggie was suddenly back in the doctor's office, trying to make sense of the nightmare that was her life. Inhaling, she filled her lungs with a deep, cleansing breath. She had told Dr. Camas the truth and still her heart was beating. The darkness had not completely consumed her; if anything, she felt somewhat lighter than before.

"So you moved to Cincinnati…is that right?" Dr. Camas crossed his legs casually, and Maggie felt nothing but empathy from him.

She nodded and wrung her hands nervously together. Then she forced herself to go back to the small farming town of Woodland, Ohio, fifteen minutes out of Cincinnati. Back to Nancy and Dan Taylor and a four-bedroom house full of love and laughter and everything Maggie had never felt growing up as an only child with a busy salesman for a father.

Maggie moved out just before her seventh month, when the right clothing was still able to hide her pregnancy. Not wanting to alienate her parents again, she told them she'd be staying with a Christian family and that she'd be back sometime that summer. Maybe for good.

Maggie's parents were busy and, with John out of the picture, they trusted that what she said was true. They kept in touch by telephone once a week and never for a moment suspected that Maggie had gone away to give birth to a baby.

As the due date neared, Maggie began to have second thoughts.

The child inside her kicked and moved and had become so much a part of her she couldn't bear the thought of giving her up. A doctor in Woodland had discovered by ultrasound that the baby was a girl and that everything else about Maggie's pregnancy was proceeding normally.

Everything except the fact that upon birth, Maggie intended to give her daughter away.

She spent hours thinking about her own mother and how desperately she wished for a closer relationship with her. Sometimes whole days would pass while Maggie fantasized that she was keeping the baby and that she would certainly not be cold and militant as her mother had been. This daughter would be her heart's mirror image.

They would sing silly songs together and hold sleepovers on the living room floor, complete with popcorn and root beer; they would giggle late into the night. Maggie would shop with her little girl and pray with her, and together they would share the very secrets of their hearts

Then reality would hit her, and she would remember the truth: Someone else was going to have the joy of this child. She had chosen Ben over the tiny baby within her, and her decision would stand. How could she or the baby have any real life otherwise?

Because Maggie knew no other way, she made plans with Cincinnati Social Services office to give the baby up for adoption immediately upon birth. She signed a stack of paperwork and felt as if she were tearing away pieces of her daughter's heart with each stroke of the pen.

Once a social worker found Maggie going through the document that asked the birth mother's opinion on the type of family she would like to have adopt her baby. Tears were streaming down Maggie's face, and the concerned social worker put a hand on her shoulder. "Dear, are you sure this is the right decision for you?"

Maggie smiled through her tears. "Yes. I'm sure." But inside she wondered how she could spend her life with a man like Ben Stovall if she couldn't be honest with him. The mere thought of him—his strength and confidence, the presence he brought when he entered a room, the way he hungered after things of God—still made her heart soar, but what kind of man would demand absolute perfection of her? Worse, what kind of mother was she, willing to give her daughter away to strangers in an effort to appear perfect?

There were no answers, and tears flowed easily, especially in the final days before her due date. In some ways it was like the last part of a wonderful vacation with someone she could never see again, someone she'd come to love deeply.

Given the choice of dozens of home studies, families ready and waiting for the opportunity to adopt, Maggie chose a well-off couple in their late thirties with no other children and definite plans to stay in Woodland. Maggie thought them a perfect match and that Woodland—with all the conveniences of Cincinnati and all the charm of a small town—was the ideal place for a little girl to grow up. Since the couple planned to adopt other children, Maggie's daughter would be the oldest. A princess, of sorts.

Of course there was one other benefit of giving the baby to a couple who planned on staying in Woodland. If Maggie ever wanted to find her... *At least I'll know where she is.* The fact was the only comforting thought as each day brought her closer to delivering.

It was almost time to say good-bye, and the prospect nearly broke Maggie's heart.

Finally, three days after her due date, her water broke. Twelve hours later, just as the sun set on May 10, 1993, she gave birth to the most beautiful little girl she'd ever seen. The advice from Social Services was clear. Allow the baby to be taken by the nurses, sign the paperwork giving up rights to the child, and don't look back.

Don't ever look back.

Instead, Maggie watched every move the nurses made, allowing her eyes to follow her newborn daughter around the delivery room as a crew of people worked to clean her skin, check her heart rate, and cut her umbilical cord. *The first step toward taking her away from me forever.*

For the next fifteen hours Maggie held her daughter to her bosom, ignoring all requests by nurses to set the baby down or make a trip to the restroom or have a bite to eat. If this was all the time she would have with her daughter, she wasn't wasting a moment of it. She cooed at the infant, whispering words of love and praying a blessing over her that would have to last a lifetime. When the baby stirred, blinked, and made eye contact with Maggie, she felt a rush of emotion unlike anything she'd ever experienced.

Is this what joy feels like, little one?

She nuzzled and whispered to her daughter, and sometimes for hours at a stretch she bathed her infant with tears of guilt and regret and self-hatred. How could she call herself a Christian and give away her own precious daughter? What kind of person was she to choose Ben Stovall and his expectations of purity over the bundle of love and hope and joy in her arms?

Maggie had no answers.

Finally, at just after nine the next morning, a pretty young woman from Social Services came to take the baby away. Maggie refused to look up as the woman entered the room. She kept her eyes on her baby's face, memorizing every feature, every detail in her cheeks and lips and chin because there would never be another chance.

"Mrs. Taylor?" The woman came closer and stood inches away at Maggie's bedside. At first Maggie thought they must have the wrong patient, but then she remembered. She'd used Nancy and Dan's last name so that no one could come back years later and find out that Maggie Johnson had given a baby away in Woodland.

The social worker put her hand gently on Maggie's shoulder. "The nurses said you're...having a hard time."

Maggie stared deeply into her baby's eyes and spoke without ever looking at the woman. "Please whisper...my daughter frightens easily."

The woman was speechless for a moment. When it seemed the room might burst from tension, she pulled up a chair, sat down, and softly stroked Maggie's arm. "Mrs. Taylor, if this isn't the right decision for you, we need to talk about it."

If only the woman had grabbed the baby and run! Then Maggie could blame someone else and not be forced to live with the fact that she alone was responsible for the decision. Maggie's tears landed erratically on the infant's face, and she gently lowered her head and kissed them off the silky, newborn cheek. "It's okay, sweetheart, Mommy's here."

The social worker crossed her legs and seemed to be waiting. "Mrs. Taylor, should I tell them you've changed your mind?" Images of Ben swept her mind. He was the only man she'd ever loved, ever dreamed of marrying. Surely God would bless them with other babies. But if she kept this child now, there would be no future with Ben, no house full of babies raised in the loving light of godly parents. She would live her life as a single mother, and the baby would grow up most likely troubled and lonely. Probably repeating the very mistakes Maggie had made.

No, that was no life for the sweet angel in her arms, not when giving her away meant a secure future and two loving parents. Maggie snuggled the infant closer and squeezed her eyes shut. She had no choice.

The baby began to cry, and Maggie opened her eyes, turning to the social worker. "No, I haven't changed my mind." The words were so strained, so filled with desperation she barely recognized her own voice.

"Very well. I'll take her when you're ready. The adoption won't be official until the baby's adoptive parents complete the proper paperwork. But you should know, Mrs. Taylor: once you sign the papers, it's only forty-eight hours until your rights are severed."

Maggie nodded and her stomach began to tighten. Not the postpartum contractions the doctor had warned her about, but a terrible ache, like something inside her had slowly begun to die. *I can't do this, little girl. I'll remember you forever... God, help me know what to do...*

She nuzzled the baby close to her face and allowed herself to think the unthinkable. There would be no dresses bought for this tiny girl, no quiet moments to braid her hair or read her bedtime stories. Not for Maggie. *Maybe I'll die from the pain...then I won't have to spend a lifetime wondering.* She knew with utter certainty that the bond she felt in that moment would stay with her until the day she died. Giving her daughter up now felt almost as if she were about to drop the child off the edge of a cliff—it went against all the surprising maternal urges that had welled up in her over the past seven months.

Help me, God. There must be another way... But there simply were no other choices; not if she wanted to give them both a better life.

Maggie whispered into the infant's ear. "No matter where you go, little one...whatever you do...I will always be your mommy. And I will always—"

Her body was suddenly racked with a landslide of sobs so great she could only clutch the child in grief-stricken desperation and speak softly over and over, "I love you, honey...I'll always love you."

When it was more than she could bear, when she knew that if she waited one more minute she would change her mind and forget Ben Stovall entirely, she gave the baby a final kiss and handed her over to the social worker.

The woman—who had watched the scene quietly—had tears in her eyes as she took the infant. For a moment she held the baby and said nothing, only stared sadly at Maggie. When finally she could bring herself to speak, she said, "It's the right thing, Mrs. Taylor. I've met the couple...your daughter will have a wonderful life."

Maggie nodded, consumed by a feeling of longing for her baby, a feeling that was wild and desperate. *What could be more wonderful than being raised by your own mother?* How could the baby have a good life knowing that Maggie had given her away, hadn't wanted her?

She averted her gaze so that she wouldn't be tempted to let her eyes fall on the blanketed bundle in the social worker's arms. *She belongs to someone else now. Let her go. Let her go. Let her go.*

"I'll have someone bring in the paperwork." The social worker stood, and she and the baby left the room. It was the last time Maggie had ever seen her daughter.

Dr. Camas shifted positions. "And you never told your husband about the child?"

Maggie shook her head. "How could I? He thought I was a virgin. Once I got back home, Ben and I started seeing each other right away. He asked me if I'd dated anyone, and I told him there'd been nothing serious. He assumed…well, that things hadn't changed."

"And physically he never doubted you?" Dr. Camas's voice held no accusation, only a desire to understand.

"Ben was a virgin. If there would have been a sign or something that might have told him I hadn't been sexually pure, he wouldn't have known it." She thought for a moment. "If he'd doubted me, I'm sure he would have said something."

Dr. Camas leaned back in his chair and looked at Maggie for a long moment. "So then, you've kept this a secret for eight years?"

Tears stung at Maggie's eyes, and the cloak of darkness was as heavy and threatening as if it had never lifted. "Yes."

Christ is light, and in Him is no darkness…

The Scripture came from nowhere and for several seconds the darkness eased. *Come back, God! Don't leave me now.*

Christ is light, and in Him—

"How do you feel about that?"

The holy whispers faded. Caught off guard, Maggie blinked and tried to remember what the conversation had been. "About what?"

There was not even a flicker of impatience on Dr. Camas's face. "Having lied about the baby for the past eight years. How do you feel?"

For an instant, Maggie wanted to scream at the doctor. How did she *feel* about it? Couldn't he see for himself? It had driven a wedge between her and Ben almost from the beginning of their marriage. Not a day passed when she didn't think about the daughter she had given away. And when they had been unable to have children, she was certain God was punishing her for trading a precious baby for a life of lies.

Adoption in and of itself was a good thing, Maggie knew. For many women it was a beautiful choice indeed. But not for her. Her reasons had been entirely self-centered, rooted in the soil of desire for a man who would not have wanted to share his life with her if he'd known the truth. So she lied and lost her daughter in the process.

All for selfish reasons.

How did she feel about it? "It's making me crazy. I hate Ben. I hate myself. I don't know what to think anymore."

Dr. Camas jotted something down on the clipboard in front of him and smiled softly at Maggie. "I think you're ready for the next step."

"Next step?" Maggie didn't want a next step. She wanted to keep meeting with Dr. Camas and going over her life. Searching for some reasonable explanation that would shed light on the choices she'd made and the desperate darkness attempting to consume her.

"Yes. Starting tomorrow we'll be adding group therapy to your daily program. You'll still meet with me; this will be in addition. Group therapy generally is where the most healing takes place. You'll be meeting with a group of people who have situations similar to yours."

Maggie's heart rate doubled. "Meaning what?"

Dr. Camas rested his forearms on his desk and angled his head in a gesture that reminded Maggie of her father. "Everyone in your group is here because of anger issues and severe depression."

He had to be kidding. "I'm not ready for that. I can't sit in a group and—"

"Maggie..." His voice was quiet, calm. He reached out and clasped his hand around hers, and although a great deal of fear and darkness remained, she felt the fight leave her. "Maggie, you're ready."

Her shoulders slumped forward, and she let her head fall as tears formed and spilled onto her lap. She didn't want to share her life with anyone else, especially with people who had troubles of their own. What if they recognized her? What if she forgot who she was or what she was saying and what if everyone in the group suddenly became blond, blue-eyed little girls looking for their mamas? "I can't..."

Dr. Camas waited until Maggie dried her eyes and met his gaze. "You can. Here's what will happen..."

They spoke several more minutes, Maggie asking questions about the group while she tried to calm her pounding heart. What if it wasn't time yet? There would be nowhere for her to run in a group setting. If he forced her to attend, she would refuse to speak, acting only as a silent observer. Nothing more.

By the time she stood to leave, she was so filled with panic her knees were knocking. She made her way to the door and as she set off down the hallway for her bedroom, she was filled with an overwhelming sense of doom.

Dr. Camas was wrong.

She would never be ready to bare her soul to a group of strangers. Much less tell them the truth. Even if her fight against the demons of depression or darkness or whatever it was lasted a lifetime.

The Depths

Trust in the LORD with all your heart
and lean not on your own understanding;
in all your ways acknowledge him,
and he will make your paths straight.

PROVERBS 3:5

15

*W*hen Ben Stovall regained consciousness in a hospital bed at Cleveland General, his head swathed in gauze wrap, his entire body pulsating with a pain already dulled by medication, he was overwhelmed by two realizations—both of which rocked the foundations of his world.

First, he was alive. He was breathing; he could move each of his limbs; and he was thinking clearly enough to recognize both facts. Without a doubt he had been spared by God Almighty Himself.

The second realization was even stronger.

The events that had put Maggie in a psychiatric hospital and landed him near death in this one had come together in his head to form an undeniable sense, a deep and unfathomable longing that defied description. He was swept up in a protective feeling, one that made him want to swim oceans or leap mountains, whatever it took to get to Maggie.

He was in love.

Back when everything about his marriage came easily he had expected her devotion as absolutely as he expected morning. Now, with Maggie refusing his visits and phone calls—with their marriage hanging in the balance—he was madly, undeniably, head-over-heels in love with his wife. And determined to find a way to reach her.

What John McFadden had said wasn't true; it couldn't be. Maggie never would have slept with that…that man. She'd never gotten pregnant. And if she *had* been pregnant—if McFadden had raped her or forced her in some way—Maggie would have kept the baby. Ben was sure of that. Children were priceless by Maggie's standards. Certainly she would have felt comfortable enough at that age—what, twenty-two, twenty-three?—to tell Ben the truth. Rape was an awful thing, but it wouldn't have been Maggie's fault. Why would she have lied about such a thing?

The whole notion was ridiculous. She was a virgin when they were married; she had to be. Maggie was one of the most fine, upstanding women he knew. True, she was suffering from something terrible, something bigger than angry fan mail or failed attempts at pregnancy, something larger than anything she'd come up against before.

But Maggie would never have given herself to a man like McFadden.

Still, in those first waking moments he realized that whatever was bothering Maggie it had to be worse than anything he'd previously guessed. He pictured her lifeless eyes and empty voice that last day, the day before she went to Orchards.

Whatever it is, honey, we'll work it out. I'll take some time off work, spend more time letting you talk, hearing you.

He sighed.

Why had it taken all of this for him to realize the depth of feelings he held for Maggie? His love for her was greater than life itself; he needed her more than the air he breathed. Without a doubt, if he hadn't been in the hospital—if somehow he could have walked out on his own volition, hailed a cab, and made his way to Orchards Psychiatric Hospital—he would have done so. He would have sought Maggie out, found her, and held her close so she would never again feel the need to lie to him about anything. So she would know exactly how he felt about her.

He gritted his teeth and tried to lift his arm over his head, but after a moment he let it drop again. Pain worked its way through every muscle in his body, seizing him in a vise grip. On his second try he found the strength to reach the telephone receiver. After getting the number from the operator again, he dialed the psychiatric hospital.

"Orchards, may I help you?"

This isn't going to work. Hope leaked from Ben like air from a damaged tire. *How can I get her to talk to me?* "Uh, yes, Maggie Stovall please."

The receptionist paused. "Who may I say is calling?"

Ben forced himself to think quickly. "Jay. From the *Gazette.*" Seconds passed, and a phone began to ring. "Nurse's desk, just a moment. Maggie will be here in a minute."

Be here in a minute? She didn't even have a phone in her room? *How bad are you, Maggie? What happened to make you like this?*

"Hello?"

Maggie's voice took him by surprise. It had been over a week since he'd heard it. He basked in the sound.

"Maggie...it's me."

In the seconds that followed, Ben prayed she wouldn't hang up. Her anger was the first thing he heard. "That's a lousy thing to do, Ben."

He hesitated. "Maggie, we need to talk."

She drew several quick breaths, and Ben was struck by the nervousness in her voice. "No! There's nothing to say. We're finished. I told you in the note. I'll call you when I'm out of here." More quick breaths. "Now don't call back. Please. I...I can't take it, Ben."

She hung up before he could respond.

Stunned, Ben remained motionless, the receiver still in his hand. The woman he had just spoken to sounded like a stranger. *What's happened to you, Maggie?* He fought the urge to bolt from the room, the desperation to find a way to reach her and convince her she was wrong. Again only the intravenous tubing sewn into his arms held him in place.

Ben held his breath. The reality of the situation was becoming clear.

Whatever had happened in Maggie's past, whatever parts of McFadden's story were true or false, one thing was certain: Maggie wanted nothing to do with Ben. She wanted to be left alone. And in the coming months she planned—unbelievably—to divorce him and move on with her life. Alone.

Ben felt tears stinging at his eyes, and he blinked them back. *Help me, Lord, there's got to be a way to reach her.*

You were saved for a purpose, My son. Follow Me.

Ben struggled to sit higher up in bed and allowed the reassuring holy whispers to wash over him. Somehow, even though his entire life had fallen apart in the past few weeks, God had a plan. God always had a plan for those who loved Him.

Ben tried to assess his injuries, but it wasn't until the doctor came in an hour later that he understood how grave his condition had been.

The emergency team had infused him with two units of blood and by the time they got him on an operating table his heart had all but given up. In addition, his skull had been fractured, and they were even now watching for signs of a blood clot in his brain.

"You're a lucky man, Mr. Stovall." The doctor was wrapping a fresh piece of gauze around his head injury. "A few minutes later, and you wouldn't have survived."

Ben was barely listening. He had the overpowering sense that God wanted him to continue searching. That somewhere—even if it had nothing to do with the lies McFadden told—there was truth where Maggie was concerned.

Love in wisdom and truth...love covers a multitude of sins.

The thoughts were enough to make Ben jump out of bed. His doctor was rambling on about resting and taking it easy, but when the man got to the part about filing police charges, Ben began to listen again.

"Police charges?"

"Yes. Do you know for certain who beat you up?"

He nodded. He could see as clearly as if he were watching it again the strange activity taking place near the van, the dozens of boxes being loaded from it into the bar storeroom. "I know everything. His name, where he works. All of it."

The doctor nodded. "How do you feel about filing charges?"

Love in wisdom and truth...

Ben frowned. How in the world did that Scripture fit his current situation? He inhaled slowly, grimacing at the pain in his ribs when he did so. He had no choice in this situation. Regardless of McFadden's threats, Ben would pursue charges because it was the right thing to do. "I'll do it. Whenever the officers are ready."

"Very good. Now, why don't you see if you can get some sleep."

Alone in his room, Ben stared hesitantly at the phone. Should he call Madeline Johnson again? Did Maggie's mother know more about her daughter's past than she let on? Reaching out, he rummaged through his bedside table and found his wallet. In it was Madeline's number and a calling card. In three minutes he had the woman on the line.

"You're calling me from work?" Maggie's mother sounded worried, and Ben was glad he'd left out the fact that he was in the hospital. "What sort of trouble is she in now?"

"Nothing new." Ben glanced at his bandaged shoulder and cleared his throat. "I talked to John McFadden."

A moment passed. "Was I right?"

Ben tried to shift positions and he winced. "Yes. He's not a very nice guy."

"He never was."

A dozen questions fought for position. *Why did Maggie date him if he was so rotten?* "He said something...I'm sure it's a lie. Still, I thought maybe there was something you might have missed—something that would help me understand Maggie's situation better."

There was a pause. "What did he say?" At the nervous edge to the woman's voice, Ben shifted, suddenly uncomfortable. "He told me..." Ben sighed. "He said Maggie got pregnant and that...that she gave the baby up for adoption."

The silence on the other end was enough to make Ben's heart skip a beat. "Mrs. Johnson?"

The shaky sound of shallow breathing filled the phone line. "That's absolutely false. Maggie would never have...they broke up after only a few months."

"So other than her semester in Israel, she was with you that whole year. I mean, she never left for a few months, nothing like that?" Ben was angry with himself for asking. Of course Maggie hadn't left. Why would she? The conversation was pointless because everything John McFadden had said was a lie, and the fact that Ben even toyed with the idea was—

"Israel?"

Ben's world tilted crazily. "Yeah, Israel...you know, Maggie's exchange program. Through the university?"

Another beat. "This isn't making sense."

His mind reeled, racing to understand the conversation. "What?"

Maggie's mother inhaled sharply. "Why would she have told you that?" Her voice sounded tired, as though it were all too much for a woman her age. "Maggie didn't study in Israel. She never spent a day outside the country."

Ben's head was spinning now. *Was this the lie? Why on earth would she have told me she was leaving the country if she wasn't?*

It was as though the foundations upon which he'd built his life were crumbling, as though he were scrambling to stay on solid ground....

He tried to swallow. He almost knew the answer to his next question before he asked it. "She was home the whole time, is that what you're saying?"

Madeline Johnson exhaled slowly. "No." The air eased out again. "Maybe this is the lie Maggie's running from."

Ben felt his head begin to spin. What was she talking about? "I'm listening." His heart stopped while he waited for her to continue.

"It was right after Maggie moved out of that apartment, the one she was sharing with those girls from—"

"Wait a minute." His heart thudded into a nervous rhythm.

Help me, God. What is this? "What apartment? How come I didn't know about this?" Ben's insides felt like a ball of yarn that was free-falling, unraveling too fast to do anything but stand helplessly by and watch. How had they lived all their lives together and never discussed this? Why hadn't it come up sometime at a gathering with her family?

"Well...she did, Ben. She lived in an apartment with two friends from college. Girls that were wilder than she; girls her father and I didn't approve of. She dated John during that time." She sounded almost angry, and he wondered if it were because she didn't want to be saying these things, didn't want to think about it all...

As if she wanted to run from this as badly as he did.

"She and John broke things off sometime that fall. A few months later—early spring maybe—Maggie went to stay with some friends near Cincinnati."

A wave of nausea washed over Ben. Cincinnati? Why there? And more important, why hadn't she ever told him about it? "I ...I didn't know."

"Her father and I thought it would be a good thing. Maggie was still broken up about you and that girl you were seeing. We wanted distance between her and John..." The woman paused, her implied accusation hitting its mark. "She was gone three months or so, I'm not sure. She came back the beginning of summer. About the same time you began calling again."

Ben's mind raced, and he tried to ignore the pounding in his temples, the tearing pain behind one eye...was he getting a migraine headache? "Did you see her during that time? Visit her?"

"We were busy, involved in the lay leadership of our church. Maggie's father was very much in demand, and I spent much of my time helping him."

Ben wanted to reach through the phone lines and shake her. They hadn't seen Maggie *once* during that time? Not even one time? "Did you talk to her?"

"Of course." Madeline Johnson snapped her answer. "We were in touch every week. She was living with her friend's family and she seemed to be doing very well." She sighed loudly. "Remember, she wouldn't have been there at all if you hadn't walked out on her the year before."

Anger surged through Ben like volcanic lava. He forced it down beneath the surface. "We can't go back now. The only thing that matters anymore is Maggie, and whatever she went through that spring."

Maggie's mother seemed to concede that much because when she spoke again her voice was less defensive. "Are you thinking it's possible...I mean, do you think it could be true?"

Ben closed his eyes and loosed the possibility that lay coiled like a deadly snake on the pathway of his mind. "Do I think she went to Cincinnati to have a baby?" Ben massaged his temples and blinked his eyes open once more. "I don't know. I can't believe it, but…well, nothing's adding up like it should."

Madeline Johnson's tone became lighter. "Wait a minute…" Ben could hear her rifling through something. "I may still have the phone number and address."

Ben held his breath. *Help her find it, Lord. This may be our only chance to learn the truth.* "Here it is. Get a pencil."

A pencil? That's right, I'm supposed to be at work. Ben felt a stab of pain as he yanked on a drawer in the bureau next to him and found a hospital pen. Writing on a scrap of paper from his wallet, he jotted down the number Madeline Johnson read off.

"Their names are Nancy and Dan Taylor. Of course, they might have changed the number or moved by now."

Ben exhaled slowly and reminded himself to breathe. He thanked Maggie's mother and promised to call if he learned anything. Then he hung up and tried to get a grip on his emotions. He hated where this seemed to be going. After all, it wasn't even possible. Maggie was a good girl from a strong family. The idea of her having her own apartment and dating John McFadden, possibly even sleeping with a man like that and getting pregnant, was as foreign as if he'd seen his wife's face on the FBI's most wanted list.

Maggie simply wasn't that kind of girl. He wouldn't have married her if she…

As I have loved you, so you must love…love covers a multitude of sins, My son.

The Lord's words pierced the terrified place in his soul and he was engulfed by a different sort of anxiety. *Whose sins, Lord? What other lies has Maggie told?*

There was no shout from heaven in response, but the feeling—and the command to love unconditionally—remained. *I have loved Maggie that way, Lord. I'm still in love with her.*

But was he? Would he love her if her lies were as great as McFadden had said? Doubt, like the first pebble in a landslide, bounced down the rock wall of certainty in his mind.

Ben stared at the number he'd written and decided to call. He had to know if it was the same home, the same family who had once housed Maggie. He reached for the phone.

A mature-sounding woman answered on the third ring. "Yes, Taylors."

Taylors. That was the same name Madeline Johnson had given him. Nancy Taylor. "Yes, is Nancy or Stu there?" He threw the second name in to give himself an out. If it was the right number, he had no intention of having a conversation with them over the phone.

The woman sounded puzzled. "This is Nancy, but there's no Stu here."

Ben felt his heart thudding loudly in his chest. "Oh, never mind then. I must have the wrong number."

He hung up the phone and stared at his battered body again, willing it to heal. The moment he was well enough to walk out of the hospital and drive a car, he would set out for the place where he could find the next piece of the puzzle. Pieces he had not known existed…pieces that had been a part of Maggie all along.

Yes, he would go to Woodland, Ohio—just outside Cincinnati—to the home of Nancy and Dan Taylor.

What will you do if it's true, Ben?

For a fraction of an instant, he thought about how he might spend the rest of his life if what John McFadden had said about Maggie were true. Alone. Or possibly remarried. Because lying in the hospital bed, wrapped in layers of bandages and uncertainty, Ben couldn't imagine how their marriage might survive if McFadden had told the truth.

If the worst were true, then Maggie had kept crucial parts of her past from him for nearly eight years.

There's no way.

A nurse entered the room and gave him additional pain medication. When she was gone, he slid back down on the bed and closed his eyes, much of his body still throbbing from the beating.

He thought about their wedding—a beautiful ceremony in her home church— and later how they'd danced for hours at the reception, then taken off for their honeymoon. The week in Mexico's coastal Tenacatita Bay had been better than Ben had dared imagine. Maggie had been shy at first, tentative, very much the virgin, he thought. But in little time the two of them shared a bond that was only heightened by their physical intimacy.

McFadden's claims were ludicrous.

He closed his eyes, begging God to make sense of Maggie's struggles, to reveal what information might be missing from her past. Then he put all the questions about why she'd lied and gone to Cincinnati instead of Israel out of his mind, anchored himself to what he still believed to be true, and fell asleep.

16

The meeting between Kathy Garrett and Dr. Skyler Wilson took place in a visiting lounge outside the girl's hospital room. Normally it was the type of meeting that would be conducted with a child's parents, but in this case Kathy was all the girl had.

In the days since Amanda had been beaten nearly to death, Kathy had visited the hospital each night, after her own children were fed and bathed. Now, with her husband at home putting them to bed, Kathy faced the doctor who had cared for Amanda.

"How is she? Really?"

Dr. Wilson wore a dark expression, his eyebrows knit together in concern. He flipped through the pages of Amanda's medical file and then glanced at Kathy. "Physically? She's healing. I don't expect any permanent damage. But the rest..."

Kathy looked down at her hands and nodded. Amanda might heal from her beating, but she would never be the same again. Her eyes rose to meet the doctor's once more. "Can she recover from it?"

"She's a very troubled little girl, Mrs. Garrett." Dr. Wilson sighed and opened the medical file. "Here. Take a look."

Kathy reached for the file and her eyes scanned the page. The notations were frightening: "Withdrawn and anxious... Severely depressed... Possibly suicidal... This child has little will to live and talks incessantly about her mother." Tears welled in Kathy's eyes and she passed the file back to the doctor. "Her mother isn't in the picture."

Dr. Wilson clutched the file and tilted his head. "Is there any effort being made to find her?"

"No. Amanda was given up at birth, Doctor. Even if there were a way to find the mother, I'm sure she's gone on with her life."

"What about a foster family?"

A soft rush of air escaped from Kathy's throat. "She was at a foster home when this happened."

Dr. Wilson's eyes narrowed and the muscles in his jaws flexed. "Are police pressing charges?"

"Oh, sure." Kathy's heart constricted at the mention of Mrs. Graystone. How had a woman like that slipped through the system and earned a license to provide foster care? Even if she spent the rest of her days in prison it wouldn't make up for what she'd done. What had happened to this precious child was enough to make Kathy plead with the Lord for His immediate return. "The woman will serve time, but it doesn't change what happened to Amanda."

The doctor held her gaze a moment longer. "She asks about you, also. Nearly every day. Sometimes I'm not sure if it's her mother she's wanting or you."

The tears that had been building spilled onto Kathy's face. "I love her like one of my own, but we can't take her. We have seven children, doctor. The state says any time she spends with us has to be temporary."

The doctor sighed. "I hate these situations." He glanced back at the open door to Amanda's room. "She's so...I don't know, vulnerable, I guess. She needs a home. Isn't there something the system can do?"

Kathy pulled a tissue from her purse and dried her tears. "I've been spending the past two years trying to answer that question. She's slipping through the cracks, and there doesn't seem to be anything any of us can do about it."

He shook his head and opened Amanda's file, discussing her physical injuries. Many of her bruises had begun to fade. Her young body was resilient and though she'd suffered a collapsed lung, three broken ribs, and multiple stitches from the beating, Amanda would heal.

"I expect she can go home with you in a few days, if that's all right." The doctor stood and held out his hand to Kathy. "Thank you for being here. It...well, I don't know if she'd have made it without you."

Kathy nodded. "Just give me a call. I'll be here the moment she's released."

When the doctor was gone, she headed for Amanda's room.

"Kathy! Hi!"

The girl's face lit up and Kathy felt her heart lurch. *This is the girl who's depressed? Suicidal?*

If only they could buy a bigger house, build on an additional room. *I love her, Lord. Isn't there anything I can do?* She stooped over the child and ran a hand along her small forehead. "Hi, honey. How're you feeling?"

The light faded from her young eyes. "I might have to stay two more days."

"Yeah..." Kathy wrinkled her nose. "But you have to get those ribs healed up."

"I'm going home with you, right?" There was such hope in the child's face. Kathy wanted to crawl in bed beside her, hold her close, and soothe away the pain like she would for her own children. *It isn't right, Lord, that this little one should be all alone. Help her, Father. Give her a miracle.*

That's what it would take at this point. People were not looking to adopt seven-year-old girls—especially those who had been abused almost to the point of death. Children like Amanda were marked with the failings of the system, considered damaged goods marred permanently by the very government agency designed to help them.

The newspaper column, "Maggie's Mind," had certainly been a true assessment in this child's case.

"Right, Kathy? I get to go home with you, right?" Amanda was waiting for an answer.

Kathy sat beside the girl, bent down, and gently kissed her cheek, careful not to touch the area above her eye where the stitches remained. "For a little while, sweetie. We can take you in, but only until they find another foster family."

The child sighed and a lonely teardrop meandered down her cheek. "Kathy, do you think maybe it will happen soon?"

Kathy cocked her head and studied the child. "What, honey?"

"My mom. Do you think she'll find me soon? This year, maybe?"

"Oh, sweetie, I hope so." A weight settled in around Kathy's heart, and she leaned over, hugging Amanda. *God, please…hear her cries, Lord. I'm at the end of my abilities, Father.*

The girl was crying now, and Kathy could feel her small back shaking from the sobs that welled up inside her. "I…I just want to find my mommy. I know she's…she's somewhere."

"Ah, honey, it'll be all right. God loves you; I love you. He has a plan for you, even if it doesn't feel like it."

"So—" the child whimpered into Kathy's hair and she struggled to understand her—"do you think maybe this is the year?"

Kathy felt her own tears making their way down her cheeks. "Sweetie, I hope so. I really hope so."

Long after Kathy was gone, Amanda sat wide-eyed in bed, staring at shadows on the ceiling…wondering about her mother.

She had to be somewhere, didn't she? And wherever she was, she had to remember she'd given a little baby girl up for adoption, didn't she?

Amanda studied the shadows, trying hard to imagine her mother's face, her eyes. She would be beautiful and kind and gentle, just like Kathy.

Amanda smiled. Just wait! When her mother found out about her and what had happened to her and how much she needed a family, she would come for her. She would take her home and love her forever. Amanda was sure of it.

Then, like they did every night since the beating, the shadows changed and began moving on the ceiling. Suddenly they became terrifying shapes, looming figures with pointed teeth and claws and horns. And in the midst of them was Mrs. Graystone's face. The woman was moving in closer, coming after her, trying to kill her.

"No!" Amanda clasped her hand over her mouth. She didn't want a pill or a shot like she'd gotten the other nights. She bit her lip and lay still, as quiet as she could. But she kept her eyes wide open, and felt her arms and legs tremble as the Graystone shadows came closer.

Please, God, make her go away! Suddenly the shadows were still again.

In the silent darkness, other thoughts began to take shape in her mind. She was seven years old, and no one wanted her. No one at all. Oh, Kathy loved her. She believed that with all her heart. But Kathy didn't have room for her.

Sometimes on nights like this she thought about all the people in the world—or just in Ohio—and how many families could take in a seven-year-old girl. There were lots of families. Lots of them! But no one had come forward to claim her.

Because no one wanted her.

There must be something in me that people hate. Especially people like Mrs. Graystone. It had been different when Amanda was little, when she lived with Mr. and Mrs. Brownell, before they went to heaven. But now that she was older, there must have been something in her smile or her eyes, something she couldn't see when she looked in the mirror, but something other people saw. Something that made people turn away from her.

Otherwise why had she spent time in so many different foster homes? People traded her in like a doll no one wanted to play with anymore. When they didn't get tired of her, they hurt her. Like the farmhouse boys and that awful Mrs. Graystone.

The girl squeezed her arms around her ribs and winced in pain. It still hurt, and that made her mad. She had something wrong with her for sure. Something other people wanted to beat out of her.

The girl thought about it long and hard. It was probably something deep inside her, maybe something that came from her heart. The longer she thought about it the more the shadows began to move again, taunting, threatening...

Mrs. Graystone was in the hospital somewhere. Amanda didn't know where—hiding in the corner, maybe—but she was sure the woman was there. Wherever she was, it was close. She was probably just waiting for the nurses to take a break so she could sneak into the room and finish Amanda off.

The shadows moved more quickly now, and Amanda put her hand over her mouth so no one would hear her scream. Screaming never stopped the shadows anyway. As the tears came stronger and harder, it dawned on her the reason people hated her. It all started back when she was born. Because if her own mother had been willing to leave her alone in the world, how could anyone else ever love her?

As quietly as she could, without being heard by the nurses or Mrs. Graystone—wherever she was hiding—the girl began to call for the one who could make a difference, the woman who could make everything right.

"Mommy, where are you? I need you, Mommy. I'm here. I love you. I'm not mad at you for giving me away. I just want to be with you. Please come and find me, Mommy. Please. Mommy...Mommy...I need you..."

Her whispered pleas continued until sometime in the early morning hours when, despite her tears, she fell asleep still afraid and drifted to a place where shadows prevailed and Mrs. Graystone ruled.

The place of Amanda's very existence.

∾◌∽

Three hundred miles away, from inside an unmarked police car, two Cleveland officers watched a strange transaction taking place in the back of Topper's Pop Bar. A blue
van had backed up to a storage unit, and now four men worked quickly to unload
what seemed to be more than thirty boxes.

The officers were there for one reason: to arrest John McFadden for attempted
murder in the beating of Ben Stovall the week before. But they had taken the
unmarked squad car because of something the department had suspected for more
than a year. Drugs had been infiltrating the south side of Cleveland for months—
large quantities of marijuana and cocaine that were making their way into the hands
of dozens of small-time dealers. On more than one occasion the bar had come up
during questioning. But police never gained enough information to make a bust or
even be granted a search warrant.

Officers routinely drove by the bar looking for suspicious activity. And though
plenty of obvious criminal actions took place—public drunkenness, assault and bat-
tery, drunken driving—none of them had anything to do with drug smuggling.

But now, late on this dark Thursday evening in September, the officers were
nearly certain they were witnessing a drug operation, and that raised an interesting
dilemma. Should they carry out the arrest as planned and risk frightening away the
proof of their longtime suspicions? Or would it be better to approach the men working around the van, guns raised, and then call for backup for what might amount to
half a dozen arrests?

In minutes they both came to the same decision. Take care of the business at hand
and bring the other information back to the office. If the men were drug dealers, then
they were most likely armed. Heavily and to a man. By the time the officers might
call for backup, the men would be finished unloading their cargo and long gone.

"Let's go get McFadden." The senior officer motioned to his partner, and a
moment later they were inside the bar.

John McFadden was leaning against the counter, making small talk with two of the
patrons when the officers approached him.

"What the—?" McFadden straightened. He hated cops. Why'd they have to
come around at all? Especially tonight when the guys were delivering a shipment of—

"John McFadden?"

He scowled at the uniformed men. "Yeah, what's it to you?"

"We have a warrant for your arrest." The officer stepped forward and snapped
handcuffs onto McFadden's wrist.

He jerked away, but the officer caught his loose hand and cuffed it, too. What
was this? And what was happening outside? Had there been a bust, and now he was
going down with his guys? Whatever it was, he would post bail before anyone would

make him spend an hour in jail. He pulled his cuffed hands away from the officers and glared at them. "Isn't there a law against coming into someone's workplace and arresting them for no reason?"

"We're arresting you for the attempted murder of Ben Stovall. You have the right to remain silent. Anything you say or do can and will be…"

McFadden stopped listening. His mind was consumed with two all-invasive thoughts: Ben Stovall had lived, and more important, he'd been crazy enough to tell the cops what had happened. McFadden scowled. Stovall had seen his boys unload a shipment of marijuana. If the lawyer filed a police report on the beating, he probably mentioned the drugs, too. John gritted his teeth and allowed himself to be led away. Whatever the outcome of all of this, he had no intention of staying in jail. He would post bail and then take care of the business he'd failed to finish the first time.

Eliminating Ben Stovall from the face of the earth.

17

Of all the hours in a day, Laura Thompson loved the early morning. Back when her children had flooded her home with noise and activity and constant conversation she had savored the predawn hour as the only time she and God could meet without interruption. How often had the Lord used those morning meetings to speak understanding to her heart or impart life-changing perspective from His Word? This fall morning was no different, and though her house was quieter now Laura couldn't imagine welcoming her day any other way.

For years she had enjoyed starting her quiet time with a psalm; today she was in chapter 30. Nearly every line seemed vibrantly alive and relevant to all that consumed Laura lately.

> O LORD my God, I called to you for help and you healed me.... You brought me up from the grave; you spared me from going down into the pit. Sing to the LORD...praise his holy name. For his anger lasts only a moment, but his favor lasts for a lifetime; weeping may remain for a night, but rejoicing comes in the morning.... You turned my wailing into dancing; you removed my sackcloth and clothed me with joy.

It was Maggie, of course. On the surface she looked bright and put together, but inside she was falling apart. Just like in the image she'd seen that first day, the image of a woman wearing a mask.

Pray, daughter. Maggie's in trouble...

Laura blinked back tears. Weeks had passed since Maggie had been to church, and though Laura had called the Stovall home twice since their initial conversation, no one had ever answered and she'd been forced to leave a message.

Help her, God...whatever she's going through. I can't reach her, but You can, Father.

Coffee brewed in the kitchen nearby and, as the words of prayer came, Laura's mind was filled with another picture. That of a little girl, alone and frightened.

What's this, Lord? Who is this little one?

Pray for her…trust Me; trust My Word. Anything you ask in My name will be given to you…

The words filled her heart with peace and Laura continued to pray for Maggie and the little girl and whatever secret lay behind the mask. Throughout the morning she held fast to the promise in the psalm: *Weeping may remain for the night, but rejoicing comes in the morning.*

She prayed the Scripture throughout her morning coffee and well past the folding of laundry and making of bread for dinner that night. By midday the urgency in Laura's soul was replaced with a deep-seated, peace-filled assurance. Somehow Laura knew the words to the psalm belonged especially to Maggie Stovall for this time in her life. And whatever dark place she was in, however the little girl fit into the picture, one day very soon there would come something from God Himself.

Great, abundant, overwhelming joy.

Only five minutes remained before Maggie's first group session, and she was trembling badly. Other patients filed in and took their places in the circle as Maggie gripped the edge of her chair and forced herself to stay put. She wanted desperately to flee the room, to sneak down the hospital corridor and climb back into bed.

Maggie wasn't sure if it was the medicine she was taking or the fact that in talking to Dr. Camas she'd finally told the truth about her life, but for some reason sleep no longer eluded her. Instead it had become an escape, a way of numbing the pain that assaulted her when she stood in the glaring, harsh light of truthfulness.

The chairs were full except one, and Maggie remained motionless but for her eyes, which darted about the circle taking in something about each of the patients. There was a balding man whose polyester pants hung loosely on his skeletal frame. He leaned forward in his seat and studied the tops of his shoes rather than make eye contact with anyone. Across the circle a pretty girl of no more than twenty with fading bruises on her cheek bit her lower lip and rocked nervously.

Maggie wondered about the bruises as her gaze moved around the circle to a heavyset, middle-aged woman in an elegant cashmere sweater and wool pants. The woman's soft, leather shoes bore testimony to the fact that she had money, but the circles under her eyes proved that wealth had done little to ease her pain.

As far as Maggie could tell, the others were inconspicuously doing the same as she: checking out the circle and trying to decide what paths in life had led them here, as patients in a psychiatric hospital.

Maggie took in the group as a whole and noticed only a few that whispered casually among themselves. For the most part those seated in the circle were quiet, each person lost in his or her own ocean of stormy darkness. In some strange way, there was comfort in a roomful of people who were suffering like she was. Dr. Camas had said the others in the group had been meeting daily for the past week and that all of them were suffering from various stages of depression.

"You're not alone, Maggie," he'd told her at the end of their last session. "Many people hurt the way you have, but most do not seek help until it's too late. You're here. That tells me that deep inside you believe God will use this time to help you get better."

She would have loved nothing more than to walk away from the group and find Dr. Camas now. He could make sense of her racing heart and shaking hands.

Peace I leave you, My peace I give you...

Maggie started to argue with the Scripture as it flashed across her mind, but she stopped as the words played again and again.

My peace I give you...My peace I give you...

Not me, Lord, I don't deserve peace. Not after what I did.

My peace I give you...

It wasn't a promise Maggie felt worthy of claiming, but for reasons she couldn't understand, her heart rate slowed, and she was able to draw a slow, deep breath. Before she could analyze her feelings further, a woman with a radiant complexion and twinkling eyes took her place in a nearby chair. On her pale blue sweater she wore a simple name badge, and once she was seated, she introduced herself as Dr. Lynn Baker.

"Welcome, everyone." Dr. Baker crossed her legs and smiled at the group. A glow of sincerity in her eyes put Maggie at ease, and she felt the muscles in her neck relax. "We have someone new with us today." She motioned to Maggie. "Why don't you introduce yourself to the group."

Instantly her muscles seized. What was she doing here, about to bare her soul to a group of perfect strangers? And what if they found out about her column? *I'll have no credibility at all once I'm finished here.* She cleared her throat hesitantly. "I'm Maggie."

Dr. Baker waited as though Maggie might want to expound on her introduction. When Maggie remained silent, the doctor continued. "Let's start with revelation." She looked at Maggie. "Revelation is a time early in group session when each of you has the opportunity to share something about your past, something about the reason you're here. It's an optional time."

The doctor looked around the room slowly, and there was an uncomfortable silence. The young girl in her twenties began twisting her hands together and shifting restlessly in her chair. There were no sounds coming from her, but tears fell onto her jeans. Maggie guessed she was fighting some type of inner war, wanting to share with the group and terrified at the same time. Maggie could relate. She had no intentions of talking in front of these people. Not now or ever.

The group had focused its complete attention on the girl, and Dr. Baker took the initiative. "Sarah, do you have something to share?"

Sarah looked at Dr. Baker, and there was a well of deep desperation in her eyes.

The girl opened her mouth and ran a hand self-consciously over her bruised cheek. "Y-y-yes. I think it's t-t-time." She glanced down at her hands again and Maggie saw that her fingernails were bitten down past the point of pain. The picture of Sarah sitting there, searching for a way to begin the journey into her darkest place, was so pitiful, Maggie forgot about her own fear.

Help her, God. Give her the words to speak her heart…

"C-c-can you tell them m-m-my name and stuff, you know, why I'm here?"

Dr. Baker smiled kindly and drew an easy breath. "Okay, everyone, this is Sarah. She's here by choice because she suffered a breakdown. Her parents have recently become part of her life again and are very supportive of the therapy she's receiving at Orchards." Dr. Baker looked at Sarah and waited until the girl nodded, apparently giving the doctor permission to continue. "Sarah's struggles come from having had three abortions." Dr. Baker paused. "Sarah, you want to tell them what you're feeling?"

Everyone in the group seemed to settle back in their chairs, and Maggie wondered if it was out of interest or because they were relieved to have the spotlight on Sarah.

Sarah ran the bony fingers of her right hand over her left forearm and kept her eyes trained on the floor. Seconds passed and her shoulders began to tremble as tears spilled onto her dime-store canvas tennis shoes.

"If you're not quite ready to share, we'll move—"

"No." Sarah looked up and wiped her shaking hand across her wet cheek. "It's time. If I don't talk about it now, I never will."

Maggie took in everything about Sarah and felt the unfamiliar stirrings of compassion in her heart. *Have I been so caught up in myself that I've forgotten how to feel for someone else?* Maggie didn't want to think about the answer. Not now, with Sarah about to bare her very soul.

"I never meant to get pregnant." Sarah exhaled loudly and tilted her head up so that her eyes fell on a Victorian print of a woman and child that hung on the wall. Fresh tears filled her eyes, but when she continued speaking, her voice was steadier than before. "I never meant to sleep with the guys I dated."

"Are you saying you wish you hadn't been sexually active with them?" Dr. Baker's question was soft, gentle.

Sarah nodded. "I was raised in a Christian home but, well, I didn't think it was what I wanted. All my friends were going to parties and drinking, sleeping with their boyfriends. I didn't want to be different. You know, Miss Goody Two-shoes." Sarah hung her head. "I stopped going to church and talking to my mom. She asked me stuff like always, but I wouldn't answer her. Just told her I was fine and to leave me alone. I deserved a life of my own."

Sarah stopped talking and wiped at her cheeks. Maggie's heart ached for the girl. How many others like Sarah were out there, suffering from a similar rebellion, with no one to talk to, to help them? No wonder there were so many hurting women in the church. Women like Sarah.

And like me, Maggie realized with a start. She'd been the same, hiding, in rebellion, not talking about her baby until…

"After that I ran with a wilder crowd. It was like I could do whatever I wanted for the first time. I broke curfew and snuck out my bedroom window in the middle of the night. The first time I got pregnant I was only fifteen."

Dr. Baker shifted her position. "Could you tell us how you felt when you found out?"

Sarah crossed her ankles and clenched her hands as the weight of tormenting regret filled her face. "At first I was a little excited. My aunt had a new baby at that time and I used to love to—"

She gave way to two quick sobs. The middle-aged woman beside her put an arm over Sarah's shoulders and hugged her close.

"Whenever you're ready, Sarah." Dr. Baker's voice was barely audible, more a verbal embrace than an urging to continue.

Sarah steadied herself, drew a deep breath, and leaned into the middle-aged woman's arm. "I love babies. I always have. So at first I dreamed about having it and what it would look like and what names I would choose. But after a few weeks my boyfriend broke up with me and all of a sudden I was terrified. He paid for the abortion and a year later I was pregnant again—this time by another guy."

"Sarah, help us understand something. Why did you choose to sleep with your next boyfriend after all the pain it caused you the first time around?"

Sarah's forehead creased. "That wasn't something I thought about much." Her eyes met Dr. Baker's. "I guess I figured I wasn't worth anything anymore. And that was the only way I could please the guy I was with. But since I've been here I've thought about it a lot and I think maybe…well, maybe I wasn't willing to be honest with myself."

"What do you mean?"

"Well, like I bought the lie."

"The lie about abortion."

Sarah nodded. "Right. I told myself everything the people at the clinic said was true. It wasn't really a baby, it was my choice. It was legal. There was nothing wrong with what I did. Those kinds of things."

"And you kept telling yourself those things after your second abortion?"

"Even after my third. The dreams didn't start 'till last year." Dr. Baker nodded as if she was familiar with Sarah's dreams. "Are you comfortable talking about that?"

Sarah nodded and her face grew pale as she bit her lip. *I've been there, Sarah,* Maggie thought. "About a year ago, I started dreaming about my babies. All three of them. And there, in my hours of sleep, I began to really know them. There were two girls and a boy."

Silence echoed through the room for a moment, and Maggie felt a unified concern for this girl who had so clearly suffered for her choices. This time Sarah clenched her hands so tightly her knuckles turned white. "Of course I don't know if my babies really would have been two girls and a boy. But in my dreams they're the same each time. Three babies, each in a crib, and me in the middle. One by one I would take them in my arms and love them, snuggle them the way I never...never got to—" Sarah hung her head and wept.

Several group members went to her then, each placing a hand of support on Sarah's knees or shoulders.

Maggie wanted to join them, but she remained frozen in place.

"Do you want to stop, Sarah?"

The girl sniffed loudly and shook her head. "No, I've come this far. I want to finish if that's okay."

"Of course. Go ahead, whenever you're ready."

Sarah sat up straighter, and those who had surrounded her eased back to give her space. "The dream always changes then. After loving each of my babies, the room gets dark and a strong wind begins to blow. Then one at a time I'd take my little babies and walk them to the edge of a cliff. And...and throw them over the edge. I would look over and w-w-watch them until they disappeared. And I would know I was the most awful person in the world."

Sarah's body convulsed from the silent sobs that assaulted her. Maggie imagined living through such a dream, over and over and over again, and tears filled her own eyes. How had the girl survived such torment?

"Sarah, you know you don't have anything to fear anymore, right?" Dr. Baker leaned over her knees bringing her that much closer to Sarah.

"I know. The dreams stopped as soon as I confessed everything to Christ. He forgives me, and in my head I know I can go on without the guilt. But..." She swallowed thickly. "I can still hear their cries as they fall into the canyon. And somewhere in heaven there are three little babies that should be—" a single sob escaped—"five, four, and two years old."

Maggie felt her own tears turning into deep, desperate sobs. She wasn't alone. There were other mothers who had turned their backs on their babies to make their own lives easier. But there was one difference. She had actually held her baby and then tossed her over a canyon's edge. Or she might as well have done so. She had wanted to keep her little girl, but had instead given her away for the love of Ben Stovall. The wave of tears continued to wash over her.

The group uttered its support to Sarah, looking furtively at Maggie and the avalanche of pain that had been released. Dr. Baker took control. "Sarah, why don't you and the others take a ten-minute break, and then we'll meet back here. I think we've shared enough for this session, and I'd still like to spend some time looking at Scripture and talking about honesty."

Maggie remained in her seat, her head down, tears still flowing, as the others quietly filed out of the room. Dr. Baker moved to the chair next to Maggie's and placed a hand on her knee. "Touched a nerve?"

Maggie's head was spinning and she tried to remember what Dr. Camas had said.

Would Dr. Baker know her entire history? Had he shared it with her before assigning Maggie to the woman doctor's group session? Maggie was, after all, a well-known personality. Dr. Baker would certainly know that much. The woman behind the "Maggie's Mind" column shouldn't be falling apart like this, in public, in group therapy, while a patient at a psychiatric hospital.

Let no deceit come from your lips…

No deceit? Maggie feared the thought. No deceit meant being transparent with people she'd never met. Her heart raced and a thin layer of perspiration broke out on her forehead. She couldn't tell the truth, could she?

"Maggie…do you want to talk before the others come back?" Dr. Baker's voice was patient, and suddenly Maggie knew the murmurs about avoiding deceit could only have come from a holy God. For the first time in longer than she could remember, Maggie chose to heed the counsel God had given her.

"Yes."

Dr. Baker crossed one leg over the other and Maggie silently thanked her for not seeming in a rush. She wasn't even sure she knew what to say. "How did it make you feel?"

Maggie thought about that for a moment. How did it make her feel? *Guilty, of course. And like an awful wretch.* "I…I guess I did the same thing she did. Only mine wasn't in a dream."

"I'm not sure I understand."

Maggie wiped her tears and tried to compose herself, but still the sobbing continued. "No. I…I gave my baby girl up for adoption and then lived as if I'd never…never had her. Like she'd never existed."

"Oh, Maggie." Dr. Baker stroked Maggie's back the way her mother had done when she was a child, before Maggie grew too old to warrant her attention. "Maggie, giving your baby up for adoption isn't the same as tossing her into a canyon. Many times it's the very kindest choice of all."

Maggie's tears came harder. *How could this stranger understand? Help me, God…the darkness is closing in quickly.* "I can't talk about it now." The others were returning without a word, careful not to interrupt her discussion with Dr. Baker.

"Very well. We can talk about it later. Perhaps you could come to group twenty minutes early tomorrow?"

Maggie nodded and sat up straighter in her chair. She controlled her tears for the remaining hour of group time and barely registered the things Dr. Baker was saying about honesty and God's love. Something about a fictitious town named Grace where everyone lived in the sunshine and transparency of truth. A place completely motivated by the love of God.

Many of the others shared their thoughts on such a place, but Maggie kept silent. Every now and then a tear would slither down her cheek. Even later when she was in her room she couldn't shake the mantle of desperation that had settled over her.

There was a reason for feeling this way, and Maggie didn't believe any amount of counseling or talking to God could ever make it go away. The reason was a living, breathing child who was being raised by someone else. All because she was afraid of telling the truth to Ben Stovall.

As Maggie fell asleep, she couldn't decide which emotion burned stronger inside her: the aching loss for the child she'd never known or her hatred for the man who had demanded nothing less than perfection from her. The man for whom she'd lived a lie for the past eight years.

The man who had by his standards forced her to throw her tiny daughter over the edge of a canyon, then watch in agony until she disappeared forever.

18

Nancy Taylor paced the living room floor of her modest ranch home and wished for the tenth time that hour that Dan were still alive. His lungs had never been strong, not really. So when he caught pneumonia three years back during one of the coldest weeks that winter, doctors said there wasn't much they could do. His body stopped working, pure and simple, and in two weeks time the illness claimed his life.

At first all there'd been were the memories—fond scrapbook pages that filled her mind and helped her pass the time. Nancy and Dan had been married a month shy of forty years, after all. But eventually time had a way of bringing to light the tasks at hand. Seasons changed, children and grandchildren filtered through the house, until one weekend the previous year Nancy woke up and realized she'd actually done it. She'd learned how to live life without her beloved Dan.

All that changed last night when she got the call.

Ben Stovall was his name, and Nancy had the uncanny feeling he was not some wacko from the big city, not some traveling salesman looking to sell a big-time insurance policy or a Kirby vacuum system. He'd said he was married to Maggie and really that was all he needed to say.

Though Nancy couldn't be sure of the young man's last name, back when Maggie lived with her and Dan she definitely was smitten by a boy named Ben. That much was certain. And thinking about Maggie brought every memory of Dan and the kids and that time in their lives back to mind.

Maggie Johnson.

Taking her in had been the Christian thing to do. Nancy and Dan had only discussed the idea for a few minutes before bowing in prayer and agreeing together that however crowded they might be, there was room for Maggie.

At first, the pale young woman hadn't opened up much. She'd been helpful and quiet and kept to herself. But as her due date neared she gravitated to Nancy, sharing the feelings in her heart and finally talking about Ben, the boy who made her blush at the mention of his name, the boy she loved so desperately.

Nancy stopped pacing and closed her eyes. For a moment she could see Maggie, lovely and radiant in her ninth month of pregnancy despite the emotional battle waging war in her heart. "Mrs. Taylor, this is the right thing, isn't it? Giving the baby up for adoption?"

Back then Nancy had been so certain of her answer. "Yes, dear. Of course it is. You have a lifetime of babies and marriage ahead of you. If this weren't the right thing, you wouldn't be here now, would you?"

In fact it was Dan who had first expressed doubts on the subject. Late one night while Maggie was sleeping he had pulled Nancy aside and frowned sadly. "I'm worried about her."

"Maggie?"

"Yes. I think she's getting herself too attached to that baby she's carrying." Dan struggled for a moment and doodled a design on the hardwood floor with the toe of his boot. "Ah, I don't know, Nancy. You and me understand how it is with babies. They're for keeps. Not something you can give away lightly."

"Dan, it's different with Maggie. She's not married, and she's not ready to be a mother. She said so herself. Adoption is a beautiful thing when the—"

"I know all that. For goodness sake, Nancy, my own two sisters were adopted. Adoption is wonderful for most people, but maybe not for Maggie. Watch her sometime. See how she holds her belly just so and strokes it when she thinks we ain't looking. She's getting attached, I tell you, and I think she might be making the mistake of her lifetime to give that baby up."

Nancy remembered the evening as though it were yesterday. She had considered her husband's words back then, but written them off. Besides, a woman knew more about these things than a man. Yes, Maggie was confused and anxious, but that was to be expected. Adoption still was the best possible choice. How could Maggie be ready for motherhood when she hadn't been willing to discuss her pregnancy with any of the people who mattered to her? Besides, there were so many childless couples desperate to have a baby. Certainly Maggie's child would be cared for and loved, nurtured in a way that Maggie never could have done at her age.

Nancy sighed. Eventually the baby was born, and Maggie had given her up. But far from the relief Nancy had expected, almost overnight a light burned out in Maggie's eyes. For the next month—until she returned home to Akron—Maggie would cry herself to sleep. Even now Nancy could hear the muffled sound of that sweet girl weeping for her baby.

Why didn't I do something back then? Nancy gazed out the window, watching for the car Ben had described. In the years since Maggie left she hadn't stayed in touch…but Nancy had come to believe that Dan's whispered words late that night so long ago had been right all along.

It had been a mistake for Maggie to give up her baby.

The awful truth about the whole thing was that there'd been nothing any of them could do about it after the fact. Dan never brought it up again the way he had that night in the kitchen. But every now and then, when a television program would end and they'd turn off the set and make their way up the stairs to bed, he'd pause at the landing and mutter out loud, "I wonder how Maggie's doing..."

It was a statement that hadn't demanded an answer, and Nancy generally said nothing in response. Still the image hung in their home—and in their hearts—a moment. As it always would. And that was when Nancy would wonder why she hadn't seen it the way Dan had back when Maggie was nine months pregnant.

Why hadn't she asked more questions? Made Maggie call her parents and come clean about her pregnancy, or tell Ben— whoever he was—that there was a baby in the picture? She could have encouraged Maggie to keep the baby, but she had done nothing of the sort. Why?

Nancy had no answers for herself. Not years ago when Dan was alive, and not now.

She opened her eyes, glanced out the window, and searched for the navy blue Pathfinder. Nothing yet. It was 2:45 and, according to Ben's call, he'd arrive sometime in the next fifteen minutes. Her feet propelled her from one side of the room to the other as she considered the situation.

She still couldn't imagine why he'd contacted her.

The man had been polite. He'd introduced himself as Ben Stovall and asked permission to visit the following day. How in the world had he found their number? Nancy stopped pacing and thought about that for a moment. There was only one answer. Somehow Maggie's mother must have held onto it all these years and now Maggie was in trouble. If that were the case, then Ben Stovall—the same Ben, Nancy guessed, that had caused Maggie to blush eight years ago—needed help.

Nancy began moving again, and this time she paced herself into the kitchen where two envelopes lay on the freshly wiped Formica countertop. The first held a slip of paper on which she'd written the name of the social worker who had handled Maggie's adoption case. Though Nancy hadn't doubted Maggie's choice those long years ago, she had always felt it wise to tuck away that information. After all, if Maggie hadn't held onto it—and Nancy doubted that she had, as confused and distraught as she had been after her baby's birth—there might be no one else who would know how to link Maggie with the baby she'd given up.

The second envelope was sealed, and inside was a letter for Maggie. Nancy had written it a few months after Dan's death, on a sunny morning with the house absolutely silent...that was the moment she first realized Dan had been right.

In part the handwritten letter was an apology from Nancy for not encouraging Maggie to follow her heart. But it was also a prayer to almighty God. For though Nancy had not kept in touch with Maggie, and though she might never know what happened to Maggie's baby, God knew. He knew as surely as He knew the number of hairs on her head.

And so the letter was part prayer, asking God to keep special watch over Maggie's little one and begging Him to reunite them one day, should His will warrant such a meeting.

Nancy wasn't sure what Ben Stovall wanted to talk about or what could be so important that he would drive straight from Cleveland to meet with her in person. But whatever it was, he would leave her house with the two envelopes.

After so many years of doubting her actions during Maggie's pregnancy, this one act was the least she could do for the girl who'd been so dear to Dan and her. The only thing she could do.

19

By his estimation, Ben Stovall was ten minutes from Nancy Taylor's house and he pushed the accelerator as far down as he safely could.

Why, Maggie? Why are you doing this to us? Did you really have to lie to me about Israel?

He asked the questions countless times on the five-hour drive from Cleveland to Woodland, and still he had no answers. There were other questions, too…horrible concerns about the things McFadden had said, but Ben refused to think those things through. He couldn't stand doing so.

Besides, after today he would probably have more answers than he wanted.

He felt the familiar thickening in his throat and blinked back tears. *Why, God? What did I ever do to make her lie to me? We did everything right, didn't we? Followed Your plan, sought You at every turn? Why has it come to this?* Ben was baffled at what had become of his life. Two weeks ago he and Maggie were happily married, their foster boys were flourishing in their care, and he had never had a run-in with the law in any way, from any angle. Now…

He gave a humorless laugh. Now his wife was in a mental hospital refusing to see him, while her former boyfriend—a drug-dealing street thug, no less—had told who knew how many lies about his relationship with Maggie. A relationship that happened the year before she and Ben had married.

On top of that, the man had very nearly beaten him to death, and now Ben had signed a criminal complaint in a case that would likely drag through court for two years. The foster boys were gone, his job at the office was on hold, and he had driven three hundred miles south on a crazy search for a woman he'd never heard of before to see if she knew whether his wife had ever had a baby out of wedlock.

It sounded like a soap opera, not the kind of life a man of faith should be living. *How did we end up here? What terrible thing did my Maggie girl do when she dated—*

Judge not, or you, too, will be judged…

The advice filtered through his mind, and Ben dismissed it. He wasn't judging anyone. He was defending Maggie's honor. He knew her better than that…that *criminal* ever had. Nothing could have forced Maggie to give a baby up for adoption. And if that part of what John McFadden had said was false, Ben guessed the rest was false, too.

Whatever time and energy he might spend on his trip to Woodland, it was worth every minute. He would defend his wife and perhaps, in the process, help her come to her senses so that when she did, they could resume their lives.

Ben followed the directions Nancy Taylor had given him and turned a corner, which put him in the heart of a middle-class neighborhood with 1970s-style ranch homes. He drove past four houses, then pulled over in front of the largest one on the block. Ben turned off the car and studied the house for a moment.

So this was where Maggie had lived. *Definitely not Israel.*

He paused. Maybe Maggie had lied because she was trying to impress him. Maybe the whole story about Israel was designed to make her look well traveled and educated. The truth—that she'd spent the semester in Woodland with the Taylor family—wasn't nearly as appealing. But would such a lie cause Maggie to reject him completely, to look him in the eyes and tell him he had never really known her?

Ben doubted it and for a moment he was pierced with fear of the unknown.

What if Maggie—

He shook his head and climbed out of the car, slipping on a pullover sweater. He wouldn't consider the idea. It was impossible.

He walked up a brick pathway to the front door and rang the buzzer.

A woman in her midsixties answered the door and offered him a smile that never quite reached her eyes. *Help me here, God. Please.*

"Hello, I'm Nancy Taylor. You must be Ben?"

"Yes, thanks for letting me come."

The woman opened the door wider and extended her hand. "Come in. Have a seat, and I'll be there in a minute."

Ben followed her into a front room and sat down while Mrs. Taylor disappeared into the kitchen. The smell of fresh-baked bread filled the air. At the far end of the sitting area a cheery blaze danced in the fireplace beneath a mantle lined with framed photographs of smiling teenagers. Ben had the feeling he'd come home somehow, and he felt himself relax.

No wonder Maggie wanted to spend a semester here.

The place was as warm and inviting as anywhere Ben had ever been. Mrs. Taylor brought him a mug of coffee and a plate of cookies and then settled down across from him. She was weathered and white-haired, but she had an amazing energy and a light in her eyes that seemed to come straight from her soul.

"One question first…" Nancy set her cup down and leveled her gaze at Ben. "Are you the Ben Maggie talked about when she stayed with us?"

Ben thought back to that summer those eight years earlier and his fears faded almost completely. Maggie had talked about him to the Taylors, even though they hadn't officially gotten back together at that point. "Yes. Maggie and I talked before she moved here. She knew I was waiting for her back in Cleveland."

Nancy nodded thoughtfully and stared at the cast on Ben's arm. "Were you in an accident?"

Ben knew the visible bruises had faded now so he didn't feel the need to explain. "Nothing serious."

Relief filled Nancy's eyes. "I thought…I was worried Maggie might have been in an accident…"

Ben understood the woman's concerns. "No, nothing like that."

Situating herself more comfortably, Nancy cocked her head. "Okay, I'm ready. Tell me what's happening with Maggie."

Ben sighed and combed his fingers along the length of his cast and noticed that the pain was not as intense as before. "She's not doing very well, Mrs. Taylor."

"Nancy. Call me Nancy."

"Okay. She's in a psychiatric hospital and…well, she doesn't want to talk to me."

This was harder than he'd thought. How did he tell a woman he didn't even know that his life was suddenly in disarray? Ben studied Nancy Taylor's face and felt encompassed by her quiet spirit. "I guess I need to start at the beginning."

He took a fortifying swig of coffee and set the mug down while Nancy waited. He was no longer afraid of what he might find out. Maggie wouldn't have spent the semester talking about him if she'd been hiding a pregnancy by McFadden.

"For the past few months she's been saying strange things to me, telling me I never knew her and acting weird, out of character. I guess it was part of the buildup. Then one day she forgot our foster boys at the—"

"Foster boys?" Nancy sat up straighter. For some reason she seemed concerned by this bit of information.

Ben hesitated. "Yes. We've tried but…well, we can't seem to have children of our own. We were actually considering adoption when Maggie had her breakdown."

Nancy sighed and shifted positions. He couldn't tell for sure, but it looked like the weight of the world had just taken up residence on the woman's shoulders.

"No children?" The question was low, heavy.

"No, ma'am."

"Maggie very badly wanted babies. But, of course, you know that, I'm sure."

Ben felt like a man waiting for the other shoe to fall. Why was the woman stuck on this subject? "Yes. She still feels that way, I'm sure. But since she accused me of not knowing her, I decided to do some research into her background. Figure out what she's been hiding."

"Maybe her breakdown has nothing to do with not knowing you…"

Ben decided to let Nancy continue.

"Maybe this is about the baby."

Ben felt the blood leave his face. *Baby? No, God, it can't be true…* If there had been a rewind function on the tape player of life, Ben would have hit it immediately, excused himself from the room, and never returned to the Taylor house. Instead, he remained glued to his seat, motionless but for his heart, which had skidded into a wild, unrecognizable rhythm.

"Ben? Are you okay?" Nancy leaned forward in her seat, her face etched with grave concern. "I'm assuming you never connected the two?"

Ben swallowed hard and tried to keep his mind from spinning. "I'm not sure I follow you. What baby?"

A look of realization came over Nancy's face and a shadow of guilt filled her eyes, as if she'd accidentally done or said something that she only now understood to be taboo. "Why, Maggie's baby of course. The baby she had when she was staying with us."

Ben couldn't have felt worse if someone had walked up and sent a hammer deep into his gut. So, it was true. The horrible things John McFadden had said about Maggie had actually happened. And the foundation of everything she'd ever told him was a lie.

The realization was more than Ben could bear.

He stood and moved across the room to the front window. There, turning his back on Nancy Taylor, Ben stared at the cloudless sky and tried to absorb the pain. *Say something, do something! Scream or cry or run back to the car.* But he was completely paralyzed by the truth.

Maggie had lied to him for eight years.

The woman he had married was none of the things she had pretended to be.

From behind him, Ben heard Nancy set her coffee cup down on the saucer. "Ben, I'm so sorry. I always thought you knew. Maggie told us you were…"

Ben spun around, hot anger coursing through his veins. "The *father?*" He turned back toward the window. "Don't believe it, Nancy. That was a lie, like a lot of other things Maggie said back then."

"So…the baby wasn't yours? You're sure?"

Ben clenched his fists and faced the older woman once more. This time he returned to the overstuffed chair and sat perched on the edge, his gaze leveled at her. "Maggie and I waited until we were married to become…intimate. There is no way on earth that baby was mine."

Shock settled over Nancy's features and then sorrow. "It all makes sense, then."

Ben was too angry to care. He dug his elbows into his knees and planted his head in his hands. "How could she lie about that? Make me believe she was a virgin? Keep me in the dark about this for *eight years?*" His voice was seething with rage and when he fell silent, Nancy cleared her throat.

"I don't know the answers to your questions, Ben, and maybe this is none of my business. But you're here, and I believe the Lord would have me say this. Maggie agonized over giving that baby up for adoption. When we talked about it, the only thing she would say was that the two of you weren't ready for children yet. She loved that baby, but clearly she loved you more."

What was this now? Was Nancy fighting Maggie's cause for her?

How could anyone calling herself a Christian defend Maggie's decision to sleep with a man like John McFadden, to lie about the fact, and then to give her child up for adoption all to marry another man. And all under the guise of false virginity?

It was an indefensible crime.

For all have sinned and fall short of the glory of God…forgive, My son, forgive.

Ben squeezed his eyes shut. This was no time for Scripture. He'd just been dealt the most devastating blow of his life. Everything about the past eight years, the woman he'd married and all she'd represented, had been a lie. All might have fallen short, but what Maggie had done crossed a line, and Ben wasn't about to forgive her. His heart filled with the image of Maggie in her wedding dress, her eyes aglow.

How could she have…?

His emotions warred within him, and he knew that the undying love he'd felt for her the day before was now rivaled only by the intensity of his hatred.

When Ben remained silent, Nancy continued. "Do you blame her?"

For an instant he started to raise his voice, then he remembered that Nancy wasn't his enemy. Maggie was. "Of course, I blame her. This is all about her."

Nancy settled back into the sofa and leveled a curious gaze at him. "Listen to you, Ben. You're furious with her. If this is how you react now—with your wife suffering a breakdown at a psychiatric hospital—perhaps she felt she had no choice but to lie to you back then."

Ben glared at Nancy. "With all due respect, Nancy, you don't know the whole story. Maggie did more than tell a simple lie. She slept with an awful man, got pregnant, gave the baby up for adoption, and never told me a word of it."

Nancy was silent, but there was a maddening calm and compassion in her eyes—feelings Ben was certain were not derived from any pity for him. The woman was sympathizing with Maggie!

Why couldn't she understand Maggie's fault in this? "Oh, never mind. You don't understand." Ben stood to leave. "Listen, I gotta get out of here and do some thinking, get a hotel or something."

The woman remained seated and said nothing.

"Thanks for your time."

Ben moved quickly across the room and was halfway out the front door, when she spoke up. "Ben?"

He paused, tempted to ignore her, to leave and never look back, to forget everything she'd said…or that he was ever married to a woman named Maggie in the first place.

His insides seemed to be deflating and his sense of balance was off. *How could she? All those years of marriage and never, not once, did she tell me the truth! And then her boyfriend nearly killed me—*

He turned and stepped backward into the Taylors' front room. With his back to Nancy, he braced himself against the door frame. "Why?" He shouted the word and it hung in the air. Struggling to find his composure once more, he turned abruptly and found Nancy still on the sofa, her watery eyes locked on his.

"Listen carefully to what I'm going to tell you, Ben. I don't know if it'll make a difference between you and Maggie, but maybe it'll help you understand."

Ben didn't know what to do, what to feel. *I don't want to listen; I need to think, Lord. Get me as far away from this as…as…it can't be true, Lord. No…not my Maggie!*

His blood was hot with the intensity of his anger. The muscles in his hand twitched and he craved the relief of crashing his fist through a wall. Anything to relieve the rage and sorrow that warred in his heart. Helpless to act on any of these feelings, he stood motionless, his shoulders slumped, utter defeat washing over him.

Nancy continued. "In this world there is no shortage of phonies, of people who come at you with one line or another never intending to make good on their word. Maggie wasn't one of those. She never could have been. Maggie Johnson was a scared young woman desperately in love with you. And in the midst of the most terrifying time in her life, she made a decision to give her baby up for adoption—from the sounds of it, the only baby Maggie's ever had—all because of her love for you."

Nancy wiped an errant tear off her cheek and cleared her throat. "But Maggie couldn't live a lie like that forever. So gradually, year after year, the truth must have been eating away at her. Not only the truth about the lies she told you, but the truth about her baby, that she gave that child up when everything in her screamed not to do so."

Ben closed his eyes and crossed his arms; the woman was romanticizing the entire situation. There was nothing sentimental about what Maggie had done. She had lied, plain and simple, and then lived that lie every day for too many years. She was no longer someone Ben could—

"I don't know what thoughts are rambling through that self-righteous head of yours, Ben, and forgive me for being so forward. But in a world full of people who say what they want, when they want, and never look back, Maggie is genuine. The fact that she's lived these past years never knowing her child's love, never certain of that baby's welfare, never telling you the truth about her past—those facts have obviously become more than she can bear."

Ben raised his head and stared at Nancy. "The whole thing could have been solved up front—" he pushed the words out through clenched teeth—"if only she'd been honest with me. Don't you see that? Maggie's right. We have no marriage now because I can't be married to someone I don't know. And this…this Maggie who would do these things…is someone I don't know at all."

Nancy sat back into the sofa and cocked her head thoughtfully. "Is that right? A Maggie who would go to whatever extremes necessary to win your love? You don't recognize that woman?"

Ben sighed. Nancy was twisting everything around. It wasn't only the lies Maggie had told. It was the reality. The fact that she'd been with another man—a man like John McFadden—before they were married. It was something Ben couldn't stomach even if he—

"Ask yourself this, Ben. Would you have married Maggie if she'd told you the truth? Would you have married her if she'd confessed she wasn't a virgin on your wedding night?"

Ben twisted his face in confusion. "I don't know...I'd saved myself for Maggie, and she was supposed to do the same thing. *I always thought I'd marry a—*"

"A virgin." Nancy finished his sentence. "Exactly." She paused a moment and studied Ben through disappointed eyes. When she spoke again her voice was barely more than a whisper. "And you wonder why she lied?"

Forgive, My son, as I have forgiven you...

No, Lord, I don't want to. None of this was how I planned it and now my whole life is ruined, changed forever—

For I know the plans I have for you...plans to give you a hope and a future and not to harm you.

Ben pushed out the quiet whisperings in his soul so that he could think about his next step. Where in the world did he go from here? Should he call Maggie and tell her he knew the truth? Tell her he was in agreement with her plans for a quick divorce? Maybe initiate the proceedings himself before—

"I'll be right back." Nancy stood and slipped into the kitchen. When she returned she handed Ben two white envelopes. One looked slightly yellowed, as though it had been sealed years earlier. The other was bright and new. "I think you should have these before you go, in case I never see you again."

His anger subsided briefly as he studied the envelopes. "What's this?"

Nancy pointed to the older envelope. "That's a letter I wrote Maggie years ago when my husband died. I didn't know where to send it so I held on to it."

Ben was confused. What was he supposed to do with it? Especially now, with Maggie refusing his visits. Was he supposed to wait until they were in divorce court and then hand them to her? In Nancy's presence he felt like the villain, as though she unconditionally accepted Maggie and her choices and somehow blamed *him* in the process. It was easy for her to stand in judgment of him, assuming he had driven Maggie not only to lie but also to give up her child.

She doesn't know me, Lord. What's happened isn't my fault.

Nancy reached out and ran her finger over the yellowed envelope, then brought her eyes up to Ben's. "After my husband died, I realized Maggie never should have given that baby up for adoption. She loved that little girl more than life itself. But somehow she was bent on making you happy."

Ben's head reeled once more. *Girl? Maggie's baby had been a girl?* "Did you say the baby was a..."

Ben checked his heart and wondered at the strange sensations coursing through him. He chided himself for his reaction. It didn't matter whether Maggie's baby was a girl or boy. The child belonged to another man. Besides, she was adopted more than seven years ago. She might live in another country by now for all he knew.

So why was the knowledge of her existence, and the fact that she'd just been made more real by the identification of her gender, causing a lump in his throat?

"Yes, Maggie had a girl. Which brings me to the information in the second envelope. The name of Maggie's social worker in Cincinnati. I don't know what your intentions are, Ben, but while you're here it wouldn't hurt to look that woman up."

Ben clutched the envelopes tightly and jammed them inside his jacket. For a moment he hung his head, not sure what more he could say.

Forgive…as I have forgiven you, so you must forgive…

This time the quiet whispering sparked a twinge of compassion in his soul. He was still angry, but somehow the image of Maggie all those years ago, missing her little girl…not knowing where she was… *Poor Maggie, hiding the truth all these years…giving up a baby girl…all because she loved me.*

His anger sounded loudly once more. *No matter what happened, she didn't have to lie. Year after year after—*

He met Nancy's gaze once more wishing only for the solitude to sort through his feelings. "I'm sorry about my reaction. I guess I…I thought Maggie was…I believed her. It makes me feel like I really don't know her."

Nancy leaned toward Ben and patted him firmly on the shoulder, her eyes wet with tears. "Maggie's a good girl, Ben. She loves you more than you know. But you're going to need to pray hard this time, because if she's set on divorcing you…well…if I know Maggie, it's going to take a miracle to change her mind."

Maybe I don't want her to change it. Maybe it'd be best to let it… Ben pushed his thoughts back, thanked the woman again, and left.

He walked in a haze, feeling as though his life had been decimated by an atom bomb. Everything he knew to be right and real and true had been obliterated in the time it took Nancy to say four words: *"Maybe it's the baby."*

Shuffling, Ben made it to the car, slid inside, and pulled the newer envelope from his pocket. The one with the information on Maggie's social worker…the information that could lead him to Maggie's illegitimate daughter. He stared at it for a minute, then tossed it on the seat beside him. As he started his car, Nancy's words came back to him, taking up residence in his mind and taunting him as he drove across town to the local motel, checked in, and climbed wearily into bed.

Through every action, the woman's words remained:

"I don't know what your intentions are, Ben, but while you're here it wouldn't hurt to look that woman up…look her up…look her up. It wouldn't hurt to look her up.

Ben had no intention of contacting the social worker. He wanted only to get home, return to work and sign whatever divorce papers Maggie was having prepared from the hospital.

It wasn't until three o'clock that morning—while Nancy's words rattled around in his head refusing him any sleep—that he realized maybe the woman was right. After all, his office wasn't expecting him back for another week. Why not do some checking?

He flipped on the bedside light, climbed out of bed, and found the crisp, white envelope where he'd set it on the table. Fine. He'd open it and find out what was inside. Working his finger under the seal, he ripped the flap and pulled out a single slip from inside. Scrawled neatly across the middle it said: "Social worker Kathy Garrett handled the adoption of Maggie's baby girl. Kathy works out of the Cincinnati County Courthouse."

Ben let his eyes linger on the words. *Maggie's baby girl. Maggie's baby girl? How could it be possible?* The whole ordeal was unimaginable, like something from a terrible nightmare. He rubbed his eyes and stared once more at the slip of paper.

Nancy Taylor was right. If he didn't want to lie awake all night tossing and turning while her words haunted him, he'd take the next day and do some research. What could it possibly hurt?

Ben leaned back with a sigh. How many times over the years had he wanted a little girl of his own? A child who was part Maggie, part princess…one who would look to him with adoring eyes knowing he would protect her, cherish her to the end of time.

A little girl. Maggie's daughter. I can't believe it, Lord.

He tried to imagine what Maggie's little girl might look like. Blond hair, probably, like Maggie's when she was a child. Big, cornflower blue eyes in a face that—

He sat up with a jerk. *Forget about it! She's McFadden's daughter, too. Besides, she probably has a wonderful life with her adoptive parents. His interference now would do nothing but harm her.* His emotions warring within him, he lay back down and sometime later that night fell asleep, dreaming about little girls who looked like Maggie and a social worker named Kathy Garrett.

20

In the week since John McFadden had posted bail he'd had plenty of time to reconsider his earlier vow and decide that killing Ben Stovall might not be necessary. The guy should have died from the beating, but since he hadn't, John had come up with an alternative plan. One that involved the kid.

Of course, killing Stovall would be the most satisfying solution. And the easiest. No one to testify against him in court, nobody pressing charges for assault. No witnesses to the drug trafficking taking place at the bar. But after thinking it through, John recognized several drawbacks.

The worst was the chance of getting caught. If John acted alone, he'd get the death penalty should the police catch him. And more often these days, police seemed to do just that. Not more than a month ago a regular at the bar had been nailed for knocking off an…associate. Took the guy out nice and clean with a simple car bomb. The bum deserved it. If he'd tampered with one of John's laundering operations, he'd have gotten the same thing. Dead. The guy who did the killing had been careful. No fingerprints, nothing. But the police still figured it out.

No, the chance of being caught where murder was concerned was very real. As real as the gas chamber.

The whole idea of the death penalty had forced John to examine his reasons for wanting Stovall dead in the first place. Yeah, the guy had seen them handling drugs, and being a lawyer, he was sure to blow the whistle on them. John gritted his teeth. His whole operation could come down around his ears if Stovall talked. Still, time in prison for drug smuggling—however long that might be—beat a death penalty conviction.

Then there was the chance that Stovall didn't know what he'd seen. Could be the upright, uptight lawyer-man didn't know John and his boys were unloading drugs. If he did Stovall, took him out like he itched to, it was a sure bet the cops would be on his doorstep. He'd be a suspect, no doubt. And a murder investigation would have blue uniforms swarming around the bar looking for any information they could find. And that would also kill his operation.

He uttered a curse and went to pour himself a drink. Why did the guy have to show up anyway? Why didn't he have the sense to die from the beating?

John took a slow sip of his drink. Maggie's husband, huh? Figures she'd marry a straight-and-narrow like that. He sneered at his reflection in the bar mirror. Yeah, it would feel good to kill Stovall…problem was, there was really no clean way to kill the guy. If there was one thing John couldn't stand it was a messy crime scene. Bloody fingerprints and murder weapons and signs of struggle…any of it could lead police to his front door. And then it would be all over but the switch pulling.

Which meant he needed another plan. He thought of the little girl again, and his face twisted into a satisfied smile.

No, he wouldn't kill Ben Stovall, he'd drive him crazy instead.

And if the kid got hurt in the process, so be it.

21

Late that night, Amanda rolled onto her side and inhaled sharply. It still hurt. She'd looked in the mirror before going to bed—the bruises were starting to go away. Ugly, yellow-brown streaks still showed on her face and arms and ribs. And her eyes were still that icky red, even after two weeks. Broken capill…capill…

What was that word? She couldn't remember. Broken something.

She gently touched the place over her eyebrow where she'd been cut, and traced the scar across her forehead to the place where her hair began. Forty-two stitches, the doctor said. And it still hurt to take a deep breath, but the doctor said broken ribs were like that. Sometimes it took months before you could breathe without pain.

But the happiest thing was that none of it mattered. Not the pain or the scars or the scary memory of Mrs. Graystone.

The only thing that made any difference at all was that she was back with the Garrett family. And as long as they couldn't find a foster home for her, she'd stay right there, sleeping on the couch and doing her best not to be a nuisance.

Sometimes on nights like this, she would lie awake and thank God over and over and over again for letting her live with the Garretts.

"You love me, don't you, God? I can tell." The whispered words slipped out into the empty room, and Amanda smiled at the darkness. The Garretts were sleeping, and she didn't want to wake them even if she wasn't the slightest bit tired. Wonderful thoughts danced in her head. Maybe they'd never find another foster home for her. Maybe the Garretts would build that thing, whatever it was called, so that there'd be an extra bedroom and she could live with them forever.

She thought of Kathy Garrett, so kind and gentle and loving. Even when Kathy was busy with the other children she would draw Amanda close, stroking her hair and arms and promising her everything would turn out okay. When Amanda's ribs hurt and she couldn't help crying, Kathy would lie next to her and rub her back, asking Jesus to find the right home for Amanda and help her heal up real quick.

But most of all, the thought that kept Amanda awake at nights was one she hadn't shared with anyone else. It was a crazy thought, maybe, but it was so wonderful it was worth thinking about for hours and hours. Even if it meant lying awake on the couch under a pile of blankets while everyone else was sleeping…

Amanda smiled. What if, somehow, just maybe, Kathy was actually her real mother? Amanda hugged herself and let out a soft giggle. She bet it was true. She bet, maybe, a long time ago, Kathy gave up a little girl and maybe she'd been looking secretly all these years trying to find her. Maybe she hadn't said anything about her missing little girl because she had given up any hope of finding her.

It was possible. Maybe that's why Kathy took in foster kids and even adopted some of them. Because she had given up Amanda and didn't know where to find her, didn't know that living right there on her very own sofa was the little girl she'd been searching for. After all, Kathy had said she'd known Amanda all her life. So maybe…just maybe…

"Amanda?" She heard the soft padding of Kathy's slippered feet and watched as she came around the corner in her bathrobe, a worried look on her face.

"Hi." Amanda remembered to whisper. It was a lot of work for Kathy when the other kids woke up too soon.

Kathy sat down on the edge of the sofa and smoothed back Amanda's bangs. Amanda loved the way Kathy's hand felt on her skin…cool and gentle.

"Sweetie, why're you still awake? You went to bed five hours ago. Are you feeling okay?"

"Mmm-hmm." Should she tell her?

Kathy ran her fingers over Amanda's cheek. "Then what is it, honey? You need your rest, just like the other kids."

Tell her. Go on, tell her and maybe it'll be true after all.

Amanda squirmed under the covers and rolled partially on her side so she could see Kathy better. "I got a thought the other day and it won't go away."

"A thought?"

"Mmm-hmm."

"You wanna tell me?"

Kathy wasn't mad at her for still being awake. It seemed to Amanda like she never got angry, not when you spilled your milk or asked too many questions or waited until morning to do your homework. Amanda wasn't worried that her secret thoughts would make Kathy mad, just that…well, what if she said them out loud and they weren't true?

"Amanda?" Kathy eyes got that soft look, like they did whenever she had a question. "What is it, sweetie?"

"I'm not sure I can tell you."

Kathy smiled that favorite smile. The one that made Amanda sure she was safe and warm and loved. The one that made her think that somehow, Kathy might be her real—

"Honey, you can tell me anything. You know that. We've had some great talks since you've been here."

Amanda bit her lower lip. *Why not? If it was true, it would be the happiest day of her life.* "Well, okay." She waited, trying to think of the best words to explain. "You know how me and you have known each other ever since I was a baby?"

"Yes. Ever since you were placed with the Brownells."

"Well, I was wondering… Kathy, did *you* ever give a baby up for adoption?"

Kathy's face clouded. "Why, no, honey, I never did. What makes you ask that?"

Amanda felt her smile fade. Maybe Kathy had trouble remembering…maybe it was something she'd tried to forget, like the months Amanda had spent with Mrs. Graystone. "Think real hard, Kathy. Don't you remember?"

"Sweetheart, why do you ask?" Kathy was sitting up straighter and now she wore that confused look.

Amanda sighed. "I was thinking maybe you gave a baby up, you know, maybe seven years ago, and maybe you work with adoptions 'cause you wanted to help kids. So you wouldn't feel so bad about the little girl you gave up. And I was thinking maybe if you did give a little girl up, then maybe that's why God let you be in my life."

Kathy's eyebrows moved closer together, and her mouth opened and closed a few times. "God let me be in your life because I had a little girl I'd given up? That's what you thought?"

Amanda shook her head. "No." Her voice got quiet, and there was a deep aching in her chest that had nothing to do with her broken ribs. "I thought if you gave up a little girl, maybe I was her. And maybe all these years you'd been searching for your own little girl and the whole time it's been me. Right here." Amanda felt two tears trickling down her cheeks and she wiped them with her pajama sleeve.

"Oh, honey, I'm so sorry." Kathy leaned over her and pulled her into a hug that lasted a long, long time. "I love you like you're my own little girl. That much will always be true."

Amanda's tears were coming faster now, and her body trembled with sadness. "S-s-so…you never gave a little girl up for adoption?"

Kathy's arms tightened around her. "No, sweetie. But that doesn't mean I don't love you. I couldn't love you more even if you were my own little girl."

"But you'd let me live with you forever if I was, right?"

Kathy was quiet, and Amanda pulled back enough to see that she was crying.

"Oh, Amanda, of course. I'd let you live with us now, but it isn't up to me. You know that. The state says our house is too small for another child."

Amanda knew. She didn't understand, but she knew. It wasn't like she was that big, like she took up that much space…

They both were quiet for a long time while they dried their tears and remained locked in a hug. "I have a mother somewhere, don't I, Kathy?"

"Yes, dear."

"Tell me about her again. Please." Amanda lay back down on the sofa as Kathy sat up once more and sniffed back her tears.

"Your mother was very young when you were born, Amanda. Too young to take care of you or give you a nice home. So instead, because she loved you very much, she decided to give you to the Brownells. The Brownells couldn't have their own children, so you were their little princess. They were wonderful people and would have been your forever family if it hadn't been for the accident."

Amanda squeezed her eyes shut. She had loved the Brownells, but they were gone and she didn't want to talk about them. Not now, when there was nothing they could do to help her. "What about my mother? What happened to her?"

Kathy angled her head thoughtfully. "I imagine she returned home, wherever that was, and grew up. Probably got married, that sort of thing."

"Do you think she misses me?"

"Sweetheart—" Kathy swallowed hard and her voice sounded funny—"I'll bet there isn't a day that goes by when she doesn't think of you."

Amanda thought about that. Her mother was out there somewhere, and wherever she was, she spent time each day thinking about the little girl she gave away. If that was true, then there was a chance her mother might actually try to find her. And if she did, then it was possible that one day—maybe even one day soon—her mother would show up and take her home forever.

The ache in her chest faded a bit. "Really, Kathy? You really think she remembers me like that?"

Kathy bent down and kissed Amanda's cheek. "Really and honestly and truly. For all we know, she might be thinking about you right now."

With a soft good night Kathy stood and left Amanda to fall asleep. And as Kathy—who wasn't her real mother after all— padded up the stairs, Amanda prayed harder than she'd ever prayed before that God might move mountains or send angels or do whatever He needed to do.

As long as He helped her find her mommy.

22

It was time to tell the group. After that first session the previous week, Maggie had taken to coming twenty minutes early every day. Combined with her time with Dr. Camas, Maggie was finally able to move beyond the past and begin unraveling her current thoughts and emotions. The conversations with Dr. Baker had helped Maggie feel more comfortable with the group as a whole.

In the past week she had learned all of their names. She had listened while—one at a time—they each had bared their hearts to the others. There was the bone-thin man who had trouble making eye contact. Howard was his name, and six months ago his wife and daughter were killed in a car accident. He had stopped eating. That was his way of checking out, of expressing his lack of will to live. In group discussion he realized that his depression centered around a very real feeling of abandonment. Not only by his family, but by God, as well.

The well-dressed woman in her late forties was Betty, a homemaker whose husband had left her ten years earlier. Now her children were raised and gone and she was desperately afraid of being alone. Her fears had built over the previous year so that now she was battling anxiety so great she was terrified of leaving her house. Being homebound had left her with little to do but eat and now, in addition to her fears, she was fifty pounds overweight and suffering from clinical depression. After much discussion it seemed clear both to Betty and the others that she had developed a dependence on everything but the Lord she claimed to serve. First her husband, then her children, and now her fleeting image.

Sarah, the sweet young girl who had been through three abortions, began to recognize the consequences of living for self, with no regard for others. Although her missing babies still left a deep ache in her heart, her depression seemed to have lifted.

And there were others who Maggie thought were smiling more, talking more easily, making eye contact where once they could only hang their heads. The solution seemed to have everything to do with honesty. As they each were able to share more of their heart, the desperation faded. In fact, the darkness that initially seemed to cloak all of them seemed to be lifting for almost everyone.

Everyone, Maggie thought, but her.

She considered this as she made her way to the group session room. *Is it my pride, Lord? Is that the problem? Is it because I haven't been honest with them?* The group was still unaware of Maggie's professional identity, but was that the only reason she'd kept silent every day while one group member or another bared his or her soul?

Maggie had no answers, only a realization: If she was going to get better, she needed to talk about what was in her heart. And that meant finding the strength—somehow—to tell the group about her past. She rounded a corner and opened the first door on the left.

"Hi, Maggie." Dr. Baker smiled up from a small stack of papers.

"Hi." She made her way across the room and sat down next to the doctor. "Today's the day."

Dr. Baker raised an eyebrow. "Revelation time?"

Maggie nodded. "I've waited long enough."

There was silence. That was something Maggie had grown to enjoy about Orchards Psychiatric Hospital. The silence. None of the people who worked here seemed to feel the need to fill holes in the conversation with meaningless chatter. Instead it was almost as though they encouraged moments of reflection.

"I see they've decreased your medication again."

"Yes, but…"

"That worries you?"

Maggie nodded. "I…I'm still having the nightmares, still feel the darkness dragging me down at different times throughout the day."

Dr. Baker flipped through a few sheets of paper and paused as she studied what was written there. "Dr. Camas hasn't reduced the Prozac, Maggie. Just the antianxiety medication." She looked up. "Are you still feeling anxiety?"

Maggie sighed. "I'm a believer trapped in a fog of darkness, Dr. Baker. I'm a conservative, God-fearing woman about to divorce my husband after seven years of lying to him about a child he knows nothing about. On top of that, I'm a columnist who writes about the need for morality and returning to godly standards in our world." Maggie planted her elbows into her knees and let her head fall into her hands. "Yes. I still feel anxious."

"Try to understand, Maggie. The medication you were on was very strong. And now that you're not—"

She raised her head and stared sadly at the doctor. "Now that I'm not suicidal? Is that what you mean?" Her gaze fell to the floor. "Maybe I still am."

Dr. Baker leaned back in her chair and set her clipboard and paperwork down beside her. "Okay, Maggie. Tell me the truth then. Do you still want to die?"

Maggie closed her eyes and there, standing before her, was the little girl. Seven, almost eight years old, dressed in blue jeans and a sweatshirt, her blond hair pulled into a simple ponytail. She was waving sweetly, mouthing the same words she mouthed every time she appeared this way: *Mommy? Where's my mommy? Do you know where my mommy is?*

Maggie reached out for the girl but suddenly, in her place, there was nothing but a wisp of fog that evaporated without a trace.

"I have to find her." Maggie's voice sounded desperately sad, even to her.

"Your daughter?"

Maggie nodded. "I can see her, hear her, imagine her in my arms. But when I reach out for her, she…"

"She isn't there, is that right? Like it always happens?"

"Yes."

"Then I guess your answer is simple, isn't it?"

Maggie looked up and saw a holy glow in Dr. Baker's eyes. "What do you mean?"

"I mean you can't possibly be suicidal. You don't want your life to end, Maggie. You just want to find your daughter."

Tears spilled from Maggie's eyes onto her cheeks and she nodded again and again. "She already has a home, of course. A mother and father and people who love her. But…"

Dr. Baker waited until Maggie could find her voice and the strength to continue.

She sniffled loudly and reached for the tissue box at the center of the circle. Blowing her nose, she turned once more to Dr. Baker. "No matter who has her, she's still my baby and nothing will be right, nothing…until I can see for myself that she's okay. Maybe then I can tell her I'm so—" Maggie's voice halted.

No, Lord, don't take me down that path. It isn't my fault. I never would have given her up if it weren't for Ben. It's his fault, God. Don't make me tell her I'm sorry…

"Tell her what, Maggie?"

"Nothing."

Dr. Baker hesitated, but when the silence remained, she stood and stretched. "The group will be here any minute. I'll let you decide if you're ready to talk. If you are, I'll do whatever I can to help."

"Okay." A heavy feeling settled over her shoulders and Maggie moved them up and down, trying to rid herself of the oppressive weight. When it would not leave, she went to pour herself a cup of herbal tea, found her regular seat, and nervously waited for the others.

Sarah opened up revelation time by announcing that she had received her discharge orders.

"Next Monday I'll be going home with my parents." She smiled, and Maggie noticed that the bruises on her cheeks were gone now. Sarah had explained to the group several sessions ago that her last boyfriend had beaten her regularly. Her breakdown had come when she feared she was pregnant for a fourth time and had suffered the worst blows of all when she'd told him the news. She had been considering suicide, but went home instead and shared everything with her parents. With their help, she'd gotten through her time at Orchards more quickly than many people. She would be expected to continue treatment on an outpatient basis for the next three months.

"How do you feel?" Dr. Baker leaned back in her seat and focused her attention on Sarah.

"Most of the time great, like a truck has been lifted off my shoulders."

"Most of the time?"

Sarah's face clouded. "There're still times when I think of my babies, Dr. Baker. But I've learned something here at Orchards." She looked at the others and for a moment her eyes caught Maggie's and held them. There was compassion there, and Maggie wished she had taken the time to get to know Sarah better. "I've learned there's nothing I can do to change the past, but I can take responsibility for today. By doing so, I can grasp onto tomorrow, too. My babies are safe in the arms of Jesus. When I think of them now, I think of them that way. And I look forward to the day—in God's timing—when I'll join them there."

Dr. Baker smiled at Sarah and looked around the room. Maggie had the uncomfortable feeling that everyone was looking at her, that they were all thinking how she was the only one in their midst who hadn't shared yet. "Anyone else?"

Say something, Maggie. It's time you talked it through. She gritted her teeth…and suddenly the words were out before she could stop them. "I hate my husband."

Every member in the group was suddenly focused on Maggie. Dr. Baker cleared her throat. "Do you want to talk about it, Maggie?"

Normally this was when the doctor would step in—especially if it was a person's first time to share in front of the other group members. But Maggie didn't want someone else summarizing her situation. *She* wanted to tell them. They had shared their hearts with her, their lives and losses. Now it was her turn. She nodded to Dr. Baker, then turned to face the group.

"I'm here because I had a…well, a breakdown, I guess. All because of something that happened nearly eight years ago."

Maggie glanced from face to face and saw she had their undivided attention—and more than that, their empathy. They had each journeyed back in time at one point or another and found it almost unbearably painful. Now Maggie could see that they were there for her, ready to hold her up or hug her close or cry with her should her journey backwards become too difficult.

She drew a deep breath and told them about falling in love with Ben, and how young and pure and ideal her intentions had been. How Ben had—for a time—chosen Deidre over her, and how she had taken up with John McFadden. She shared with them the fact that she'd gotten pregnant and how, for a brief while, she had considered keeping the baby.

"I dreamed about her even then." Maggie had come this far without tears, but now her eyes filled quickly. "I imagined what she'd wear, and how she'd look, and how it would feel to hold her in my arms. I was her mommy and even if everything else was falling apart I knew I'd be the best mother in the world. I l-l-loved her so much."

Sarah fell to her knees, shuffled across the circle, and took Maggie's hand in hers.

Dear God, how could I choose Ben over my very own baby? She closed her eyes tight, clinging to Sarah's hand, and allowed the sobs to wash over her.

After several minutes, Howard handed her a tissue and patted her back. "We're here for you, Maggie. Whenever you're ready."

Maggie blew her nose again and forced herself to continue her story. She told them about hiding the pregnancy from her parents while she thought about her options, how just when she was going to tell them the truth, she received the call from Ben.

"He was a perfect man, at least I thought he was." Maggie sniffled, and Sarah squeezed her hand. "When he told me he still loved me, I knew there was only one thing to do."

Dr. Baker had been quiet through most of the story, but she interrupted now. "Can you explain yourself, Maggie?"

She nodded. "I lied to him. Told him I was going to Israel for a semester as an exchange student. Instead I went to Woodland, Ohio, moved in with a wonderful family, and finished my pregnancy."

More tears fell onto Maggie's cheeks. "She had this tiny, perfect face. The most beautiful little girl I'd ever seen. And…" Sarah leaned her head on Maggie's knees.

"Oh, God, how *could* I?"

Dr. Baker waited while Maggie's sobs subsided again. "You gave your baby up for adoption, is that right, Maggie?"

"Everyone said adoption was the best choice…"

"It's a wonderful choice for a vast number of women, young and old."

"But not for me! I loved her so much it killed me…handing her over to the social worker and watching her disappear from my life." She sniffed loudly. "I gave her away for one reason only—so I could convince Ben I was the sweet, young virgin he'd always wanted to marry."

The room had grown quiet. "Is that why you feel so strongly about him now?"

"Yes!" Maggie could hear the anger in her voice. *Where's this rage coming from, Lord? What's happening to me?* She drew a steadying breath. "I don't ever want to see him again."

"So you blame him for having to give up your daughter, is that right?" Dr. Baker's voice was calm, without accusation or judgment. Still Maggie felt a piercing sense of conviction.

What? It is his fault. I would never have given her up, never have lied if it hadn't been for him.

"Definitely. He forced me to lie and made me give up my baby girl. I hate him." Maggie's voice rose. "I'll hate him till the day I die. And when I'm out of here, the first thing I'm doing is filing for divorce."

Sarah made her way back to her seat and an uncomfortable quiet echoed through the room in the wake of Maggie's statement.

What was everyone's problem? Wasn't this where they were supposed to circle her

and cry with her and help her get through it? Weren't they supposed to agree with her
and empathize with her? The familiar fog of darkness began to settle once more over
Maggie's mind and soul, and she fought the urge to dart from the room.

Make them understand, God. Come on. I need Your help here.

"Maggie? Can I say something?" It was Howard, and although Maggie had always
seen him as floundering and pathetic, today he was sitting straight in his chair and
his eyes held a serenity that Maggie hadn't known since before her daughter's birth.

All eyes were on Howard, and Maggie nodded in his direction. "Sure."

Although he'd filled out somewhat during his stay at Orchards, Howard was still
painfully thin, and he shoved the sleeves of his sweater up past his elbows as he prepared to speak. "Don't take this wrong, Maggie. But after losing my family I've
become certain of one thing—" he glanced at the others and Maggie saw them giving him silent encouragement to continue—"God wants families to last forever. Or
until He takes one of you home. Have you—you know—have you ever explained
any of this to your husband?"

Suddenly, as though someone had thrown up a window blind, Maggie had a
glimpse of the situation from Ben's perspective. It was the first time since coming to
Orchards that she'd even considered his side. Obviously he knew by now that she
wasn't receiving his calls or visits. But otherwise he knew nothing. Not about the lies
she'd told or the baby she'd given up. Not even about how she blamed him for all that
had gone wrong in the past eight years.

She could picture him, see the worry on his face, in his eyes…the care and concern for her. She closed her eyes and pictured him, still loving her even as he struggled
to figure out what had happened to them, to her. The image caused her burning
hatred to cool some. For a moment.

Then she blinked hard, and the images of Ben disappeared.

She didn't owe him an explanation! He didn't love her, not really. He loved an
image, someone he'd created in his mind—the perfect godly wife; the chosen virgin
bride. But that wasn't Maggie.

No, she wouldn't feel sorry for him. All of this was Ben's fault.

"That's ridiculous, Howard." The anger in Maggie's voice was gone, but she felt
the tension between her and the rest of the group.

Dr. Baker looked at her watch. "Well, Maggie, maybe you can finish tomorrow.
For now we better move on. I've got a passage in the book of Romans I'd like us all
to take a look at…" Bile was rising in Maggie's stomach, and she was suddenly
engulfed in a closet of anxiety. *I can't breathe in here, Lord. Get me out.*

Repent, My daughter. Come into the light of honesty and repentance.

No! It's not my fault! None of this would have happened if only—

Everyone else had their Bibles open, but Maggie could no longer understand
what they were saying. The darkness that had pursued her for so long was back and
it was demanding something of her—something Maggie couldn't understand. No,

wait. This was different. This time it wasn't really darkness at all. It was ominous, but not in an evil way…

It was like the hand of God.

Maggie tried to breathe but couldn't, and in that moment she knew she had mere seconds before her entire breakfast would be on the floor. She stood quickly and grabbed her things. "I have to go now…"

Her words jumbled together and she couldn't decide whether to run to the nearest bathroom or down the hall and out into the courtyard for the air she so desperately craved.

As she ran out of the room she felt her stomach heave, and she barely made it to the bathroom before the first wave of vomit shot from her body. She remained there, huddled on the floor, her face hanging over the edge of the toilet, while her stomach convulsed again and again. She might have stayed there longer, but when she was finally finished, she felt a gentle hand on her shoulder.

"Maggie, are you okay?" She looked up and saw Dr. Baker.

"I need air."

"Come on, let's get you cleaned up. Dr. Camas wants to see you."

Something about the doctor's tone made Maggie feel like a naughty child. She struggled to her feet and once more felt the familiar heaviness on her shoulders and back. She should never have talked to the group. Now she'd blown it for sure. They'd probably kick her out and tell her to find help somewhere else. Anger singed the edges of her heart.

"Oh, I get it!" Maggie snatched a paper towel and wiped her face. "This is a *Christian* hospital, and I made the mistake of mentioning the fact that I hate my husband and can't wait to divorce him." She stared at herself in the mirror, then turned around slowly to face Dr. Baker. "They're going to kick me out, right?"

"Not at all." Dr. Baker's face broke into the most genuine smile Maggie had ever seen. "Dr. Camas heard about our session. He thinks you've reached a breakthrough."

23

After wrestling with his decision most of the night, Ben chose to sleep in. Whoever Kathy Garrett was and whatever information she might hold, it would simply have to wait. By the time he showered and made his way across the street to Hap's Diner for the Wednesday morning omelette special, Ben began doubting his decision to visit the Cincinnati courthouse at all.

Ben set down his fork and from his seat along the counter he stared out the window through a layer of greasy residue, the same residue that seemed to cover nearly everything in the diner.

So this was where Maggie went? Not Israel, but Woodland, Ohio.

He let his eyes fall on a horse and rider making their way down Main Street. Woodland was little more than a glorified farm town, too close to Cincinnati to warrant any industry of its own and too far away for most commuters.

Still, there was a sort of old-fashioned charm about it. Ben sighed, picked up his fork, and poked around the omelette again. The melted cheese had grown cold, and grease had begun to harden along the edges of the egg, turning Ben's stomach. Was it possible that somewhere between this sleepy little place and downtown Cincinnati there lived a seven-year-old child who was Maggie's very own daughter?

He shoved his plate back and clenched his jaw. What did it matter? Even if the girl did live here, she was probably part of some wonderful family, happily getting on with her life. Possibly even unaware that she had been adopted. What good could come from digging up a situation that had been sealed and buried so long ago?

A grisly old man sat down on the stool beside Ben and took off a threadbare baseball cap. The man's plaid lumber jacket smelled faintly of old motor oil and cow manure and as he leaned onto the counter, Ben caught an offensive stench of body odor. Wringing his hands together nervously, the old guy turned to slap Ben on the back so hard Ben had to use his feet to stop from falling off the stool.

"Mornin'! Y'must be new around here."

For a moment, Ben wondered if he was the brunt of some kind of practical joke. He glanced over his shoulder but throughout the diner people were minding their own business. Looking back at the man, Ben snorted softly. *Just my luck...*

"See ya ate the special." He laughed out loud, and Ben felt suddenly self-conscious. The guy was probably homeless—a bum or something—and now he was going to attract the attention of everyone in the diner. He tossed the old man a sideways glance and figured him to be in his late eighties. At least. *Probably half deaf, too.*

"Uh—" Ben looked down at his plate—"Yeah. The special. Sure." He signaled the girl behind the counter and asked for his bill. Quaint or not, he'd had enough of Woodland. It was time to go home and face Maggie, time to hire a divorce attorney so both of them could get past this nightmare and go on with their lives. A flash of gnawing emptiness filled his heart at the thought of losing Maggie. She was his best friend, his…well, his everything. Wasn't she the one—other than God—who made his life complete? Or had he never really known her? Had the woman he'd loved only existed in his imagination?

Either way, this was no time to be sentimental. After all, Maggie was the one who wanted the div—

"You remind me of me at your age."

Ben faced the old man, trying to find a balance between being polite and discouraging the conversation. He'd spent enough time in Woodland; it was time to get home. "Do I know you?"

"Nope." The man stroked his whiskered face. "But I've seen your type. All sure 'o yourself, thinking you're better 'n everyone else."

Ben clenched his jaw. Where was the old man going with this? If only he'd skipped breakfast; he'd be halfway back to Cleveland by now. "Listen, I have to get—"

"Just finished up a mighty fine Bible study, I did." The man's interruption forced Ben back into his seat. Maybe he needed a handout. In that case Ben was more than willing to pick up the old guy's breakfast tab or help him out some. As long as Ben could get back to his car in the next five minutes.

"Look, do you need something. Money for breakfast, a few—"

He waved a gnarled hand in Ben's direction. "Got everything I need in the Good Book. Yes, siree."

The man rubbed his eyebrows and his smile disappeared. "I was young once, too. Had me a pretty wife, children." He gazed straight ahead and Ben saw that there were tears in the man's eyes. "They wouldn't recognize me now."

Ben glanced at his watch. *What would Maggie's little girl look like? How was life in her adoptive home?*

Ridiculous, he silently chided himself. *Forget about her.* Better to listen to the old man's story and be on his way. It was getting too late to see the social worker anyway. He angled his head at the old man. "Did they move away; your family, I mean?"

The man stared down at his weathered hands and shook his head. "Nope. Died in a car wreck back in the fifties. Started drinking a week later and, well…here I am." He locked his hands together. "Know something?" He brought his gaze up again and this time his tears were unmistakable. "I miss 'em like it was yesterday." He kept his eyes on Ben's. "You got a family, young man?"

Ben thought of Maggie locked in a psychiatric hospital across the state, and of her little girl…whatever her name was…

He swallowed hard. "I…uh…yeah. I have a family."

The man took a swig of coffee and put a hand on Ben's shoulders. "Do something for me, will you?"

In light of the old guy's sad story, Ben no longer cared about the other customers in the diner or how it might look if he was fraternizing with a homeless man. He resisted the urge to pull away. "Sure you don't need some money or a meal or something?"

The man shook his head. "Nah, I get by." He aimed his gaze at Ben, and a single tear navigated its way down the creases and crevices of his worn face. "I want you to love that family of yours, you hear?" The man brushed at the tear and tightened his grip on Ben. "Don't let even a minute go by without loving 'em and telling 'em so. Not a minute, understand?"

A strange sense of knowing came across Ben's entire being, as though God Himself had sent the man. *Don't let a minute go by…a minute go by…a minute go by.* The old man's wisdom rattled around in Ben's broken heart, and suddenly his throat was thick with sorrow and longing for the only woman he'd ever loved. He stared hard at the old guy and nodded. *Maggie girl, where are you? I love you, I do…if only I could tell you.* He pictured the child, Maggie's little daughter, and felt an overwhelming desire to see the social worker. Wherever it might lead, he would do at least that.

The man dropped his hand and his expression softened. "You won't be young forever…and take it from me, you can't go back. Not ever."

With that, the man finished his coffee, took two quarters from his pocket and laid them on the counter, then stood to leave. Before heading for the door he cast a final glance at Ben. "Do it now, you hear? Make every minute count."

Ben tipped his head at the man. They were the exact words he'd needed to hear. *God, did You send him to talk to me?* The question hung in the rafters of his mind. "Thanks." Then the man took off down the street before Ben could give more thought as to how he might help the man or how grateful he was for the unexpected insight.

As Ben climbed into his car he had no idea what the future held, but one thing seemed clear. Whatever else he didn't understand about his meeting with the old man, however dismal the situation between he and Maggie, the old guy was right. Time really was fleeting; every moment did matter. Because of that he would not leave town without doing a very important task, one that was quite possibly an errand sent from heaven.

Looking up Kathy Garrett.

24

It was one of those days at the department of Social Services, a time when it was difficult even for someone like Kathy Garrett to see the good in what she was doing. There were children needing foster homes, foster parents needing relief, and an hour ago a judge had ordered a two-year-old crack baby—born addicted to heroin—back into her mother's house because the woman was finally out of prison.

Kathy huffed out loud as she sifted through a mountain of case folders, all of which needed her attention in one way or another. If only she weren't so tired. Poor Amanda, up half the night wondering if maybe by some God-ordained miracle Kathy might actually be her real mother. Tears welled up in Kathy's eyes again and she dabbed at them angrily. *Why, God? Why isn't there someone for her?*

There was a knock at the door, and she sighed. She needed time alone, a chance to sort through the foster home files and maybe find a placement for Amanda that would last longer than a few months. One where she would fit in, maybe even find some happiness.

Kathy moved easily across her office and opened the door to find a man standing there, a man she'd never seen before. He was young—early thirties, maybe—dressed in expensive slacks and a slightly rumpled, button-down shirt. "May I help you?"

The man shifted his position awkwardly and glanced back at the front door. Then he met her eyes and forced a smile. "Uh…yeah, I guess. I'm looking for Kathy Garrett."

If this was a potential foster applicant, Kathy wished one of the clerks had helped him. *Make me more patient, Lord.* "That's me. What can I do for you?"

The man squirmed again, and Kathy had the distinct feeling that this wasn't about a foster application. He was nice looking, a little over six feet tall, good build. But his eyes were shadowy and they seemed to bear a reservoir of pain or anger, some deeply intense emotion that Kathy couldn't quite read.

"I…my name is Ben Stovall. I'm from Cleveland, visiting for the day." He ran his fingers through his hair. "I need to talk to you. In private, if possible."

Kathy thought about the myriad of cases that needed her attention. "I'm sorry, I'm very—"

Talk to him, daughter.

The voice was so clear she wondered if the man had heard it, too. *Fine, God. I'll talk to him.* She opened the door and motioned to a chair near her desk. "I have a few minutes. Come in."

"Thanks." The man didn't hesitate. "I'll keep it brief. I know you're busy."

She glanced at her desk and smiled, the weary feeling lifting a bit. "Just a little."

When they were both seated, the man ran his hands along his pant legs and drew a deep breath. "Seven years ago my wife moved to Woodland and had a baby." The man must have seen her puzzled expression because he hurried to explain. "We weren't married at the time. I thought she was out of the country on an exchange student program." He stared at his hands a moment, then his eyes met hers again. "I didn't know about the baby until…until recently."

"Mr. Stovall, I'd like to help you, but if your wife had an open adoption, the paperwork can be found by filing a request at the county courthouse. If it was closed—"

"It was." There was desperation in his eyes now, as if she held information that he absolutely had to have. "I already checked."

"Well, then I'm sorry. I'm afraid there's nothing I can do." Except get back to work so some of these kids have a safe house to sleep in tonight. *Please, Lord, make him leave so I can get on with my day.*

"Actually, I think there is something." He bit his lower lip and leaned over his knees. "I spoke yesterday with Nancy Taylor; she was the woman my wife lived with before the baby was born…"

Nancy Taylor. Nancy Taylor… The name ran through Kathy's mind a handful of times. She recognized it from somewhere, but with the number of cases she saw each day the connection might have been any one of a hundred possibilities. "The name sounds familiar, but I can't place it. I'm sorry, I—"

"Wait!" He held up his hand. "Forgive me for interrupting you, Ms. Garrett, but my wife's name was Maggie Johnson at the time. According to Nancy, you were the one who arranged the adoption. She said she thought you…"

"I what?"

"You were a believer."

Listen to him, Kathy.

The holy request came gentler this time, and Kathy leaned back in her chair. Where was this going? "Yes…I'm a Christian."

The man exhaled as though he'd been holding his breath. "See…my wife and I are believers, too. And right now she's…" He let his head fall a few inches and for a moment he seemed too overwhelmed to speak. His focus remained on his hands as he cleared his throat. "She's in a psychiatric hospital. They're treating her for depression."

The pieces were still not coming together. "Does she regret the adoption, Mr. Stovall? Is that what you're saying?"

The man rested his elbows on his knees and clasped his hands. "I don't know; we haven't talked since she was admitted. But Mrs. Taylor seems to think I need to find out about the baby—the girl, actually, since she'd be seven now—and make sure she's okay. At least then I could tell Maggie she'd made the right decision."

A wave of compassion came over Kathy, and she resisted the urge to walk around her desk and take the man's hands in hers. He was here for that? To give his hurting wife some small ray of hope? Something to assure her that her unknown child was doing well and that adoption had been the kindest thing she could have done at the time?

Kathy pushed aside her emotions. Rules were not meant to be played with. It was a state-run agency after all, and adoption files could not be pulled without her having to account for her reason in doing so.

She sighed softly. "Sir, I'm very sorry about your wife. But I'm not at liberty to check the files of closed adoptions."

The man drew a deep breath and stood to leave. "Okay, then. I guess I did everything I could."

He shook Kathy's hand and left the office without any further request. Kathy watched him go, sitting motionless in her chair, her eyes glued to the door. Something about the man's request didn't sit right.

Seven years ago...seven years ago...

Kathy had the unnerving feeling that she'd just missed a God-given opportunity. Her mind raced backward in time, trying to make sense of her overwhelming desire to catch the man before he left the building.

Seven years...

Then it hit her. Kathy caught her breath sharply. Seven years ago...there was only one little girl she could clearly remember having been given up for adoption at about that time. But it couldn't be...

Kathy worked thousands of cases from Cincinnati and the surrounding suburbs. There might have been a dozen baby girls given up for adoption that year. Still...what if it *was* her? What if this Maggie Johnson, Maggie Stovall, now receiving treatment for depression was actually...

Kathy was on her feet, pushing around her desk and tearing down the hallway, then out into the parking lot. Frantically she looked around and she saw him, about to climb into a Pathfinder. "Mr. Stovall!"

Her feet carried her quickly to where he stood. Breathless, she met his questioning gaze and smiled. "If you can come back in for a minute, there's something I'd like to look into."

Minutes later they were both seated at her desk again, Mr. Stovall staring strangely at her, waiting for her to explain.

"Sorry about that, but I just thought of something, and I didn't want you to leave before I could check it out." *Be calm, Kathy. Oh dear Lord, could it be that these are the people? Could it possibly be that this man sitting here is the answer to my prayers?*

Suddenly she wanted to know more about him, his wife, and everything that made up their lives. "Do you have other children, Mr. Stovall?"

The man angled his head and his eyes bore an expression that was just short of hope. "No. We…we haven't been able to."

A vision filled Kathy's mind, images of this man and his wife healed and whole taking Amanda into their home and loving her for a lifetime. Just as quickly, Kathy chided herself for romanticizing the situation. The woman was in a mental hospital, after all, and probably wasn't even Amanda's mother. Still, it was worth pursuing if only she could justify looking up the file. She pictured Amanda's teary eyes last night, heard again her small voice hoping and praying that somewhere her real mom was thinking about her.

A child's life was at stake here. That was justification enough.

"Mr. Stovall, I'm going to see if there's a way to check the file. Wait here a minute, will you?"

The man's eyes implored her again. "Listen, you don't know me, but I wouldn't be here right now if I didn't believe God Himself had sent me. Please…" He swallowed hard, again nearly overcome by emotion. "Please look it up for me. Tell me she's well adjusted and enjoying life, tell me she has a wonderful family here or somewhere else. Just tell me something, so I can finally understand all the missing pieces."

Kathy frowned. "Missing pieces?"

"It's a long story. Just please, please look it up."

She refused to promise him anything. "I'll be back in a few minutes."

Adoption records were all in computerized files now, so Kathy knew it wouldn't take long to find what she was looking for. Alone in the dimly lit archives room she found the correct screen. Under "birth mother" she typed in, Maggie Johnson; date: 1991. Then she clicked the search button, and three seconds later she had her answer: *No matches for that search.* Disappointment rocked her back in her chair and brought tears to her eyes.

Lord, I wanted her to be the one.

Keep searching, My daughter…

The prompting made no sense. Maggie Johnson—whoever she was—obviously hadn't given her baby up for adoption in Cincinnati. Kathy thought of how disappointed the man in her office would be. Maybe he had his facts wrong or maybe his wife hadn't given a baby away. Or if she had…

Kathy let out a shout and her hand flew to her mouth. That was it! Of course! There was no reason Maggie had to use her real name. Kathy frowned, trying to remember. What was the name of the woman Ben Stovall had mentioned, the woman his wife had stayed with?

Tanner…Trumbell…*Taylor!* There it was. This Maggie woman had been living with a family named Taylor.

Without hesitating, Kathy typed in two words: M-a-g-g-i-e T-a-y-l-o-r. Maggie

Taylor. The name was suddenly very familiar. An hourglass appeared indicating the search was underway. Seconds passed.

Come on, give me something. Please, God…

Suddenly a file appeared. As Kathy scanned the information she felt herself sliding off the chair, falling to her knees on the cold linoleum flooring.

It was her; it had to be. The woman Amanda had been praying about for years. It was all coming back now, the frightened girl living with the Taylors, saying all the right words, making them believe she wanted nothing more than to give her baby up for adoption. Kathy remembered a scene from seven years ago and it hit her as strongly as if she'd been slapped in the face.

The young mother had not wanted to let go of her baby.

It had been at the hospital, the day Maggie delivered. She'd been sad, despondent even. Kathy choked back her tears and closed her eyes as the memory grew clearer. She could see the images clearly in her mind…

Kathy had approached the girl and asked her if she was sure. "You don't have to do this, Maggie," she remembered saying. "Adoption isn't for everyone." But the girl had gritted her teeth with determination and promised that this was the choice she needed to make.

Kathy's tears fell freely now and she wondered why she hadn't pushed the girl for more answers. Certainly if she interviewed a birth mother now and found her ambivalent, she would ask a host of questions. If only she'd had it to do over again, she would ask Maggie why she hadn't felt up to keeping the baby herself.

God, I've made a terrible mistake. Everything that's happened to Amanda…all of it could have been avoided if only I'd been more aware, more thorough with her mother. A thick sob worked its way up from her heart and echoed against the particleboard in the archives room. *What have I done, Lord? How different Amanda's life would have been if only I'd talked her mother out of the adoption. And what of Maggie, Lord? Is she beyond caring? Does she even wonder about her little girl?*

Kathy remembered the well-dressed, clearly distraught man waiting in her office. They were childless, after all. Was he the baby's father? If so, then Amanda was their only child. A child who had nearly died from abuse while waiting year after year for someone to give her a home.

Trust with all your heart and lean not on your own understanding.

A rush of peace passed over Kathy, and she felt physically comforted by the Holy Spirit. Amanda's life had been miserable, but maybe…

Trust Me, daughter.

Kathy exhaled. She wiped her eyes with her sweater sleeve and worked herself back to a sitting position. Closing out the computer screen, it was all she could do to stop the accusations that threatened to consume her. *If only…*

Trust Me.

Kathy closed her eyes. *Lord, I want to trust You. Really, I do. But all these years. What if—*

Trust.

Okay, give me wisdom then, God. Wisdom and strength to go back in there and face that man with the truth about Amanda Joy.

Fifteen minutes had passed, and Ben was getting restless. Maybe it was a crazy idea. First Nancy Taylor, then the old man at the diner. How could they possibly know what God wanted from him? Here he sat, in some tiny social services office, wasting the time of an obviously busy woman over an adoption that was sealed from the public. Ms. Garrett had been clear on the matter: The records were not available.

He scanned her desk for a piece of paper. He'd just write her a note, explain that he'd left town, and thank her for her help. He spotted a notepad, but as he reached out, she returned. The tearstained look on her face made Ben's breath catch in his throat.

"I found her, Mr. Stovall."

Ben's heart pounded in his chest. *What? She'd found her? The child? Maggie's daughter?*

The social worker sat back in her desk chair and faced him squarely. She opened her mouth to say something but no words came out. She paused, then tried again. "She lives very near here."

Until that moment it had been easy for Ben to blame Maggie, to find fault with her for sleeping with John McFadden and giving a baby up for adoption without ever saying anything about it. Ben's attention had been mainly on the way Maggie had betrayed him. But now...now there was a living, breathing child involved, and not just any child. This little girl was the daughter of the woman who still meant more to him than he could admit or understand. Maggie's flesh and blood.

His eyes were wet, and Ben hung his head, unable to speak.

Maggie girl, you have a child. A daughter. After all these years... If only she were here beside him, holding his hand, hearing this news with him. *I've found your little girl, Maggie...* He closed his eyes for a moment. *Dear God, what does it all mean?*

He swallowed, trying to squeeze words through a throat thick with emotion. "She's...she's okay, then? Adopted by a family somewhere nearby?"

Kathy Garrett shook her head and brought her clasped hands up to her chin. "Her name is Amanda...she's living with me, Mr. Stovall."

Ben's thoughts were instantly jumbled. *Amanda...Amanda...* The name seemed to work its way into his heart. So it was true. Maggie's daughter was alive and well and growing up. Her name was Amanda.

"You mean, you adopted her? I thought...Nancy Taylor told me you were the social worker, not the adoptive—"

"No." The social worker closed her eyes, and Ben wondered if perhaps she were praying. "I've been Amanda's social worker from the beginning." She hesitated. "Mr. Stovall, normally it is not ethical to give out information about a private adoption.

But I've prayed about this situation for years and I believe with all my heart that God would have me tell you about Amanda."

Ben sat up, suddenly alert. *What was there to tell? Had something happened to the girl?* Feelings of love—amazingly strong and protective—assaulted Ben until his heart seemed to lodge tightly in his throat. "What about her?"

Ms. Garrett sighed. "It's a long story. To begin with, Amanda was adopted by a childless couple—the Brownells. They were not well off, but they were kind and loving and good parents for Amanda."

Ben couldn't stop himself. "Were? They were? Isn't she with them anymore?"

The sadness in Ms. Garrett's eyes pierced Ben with deep concern. "They died, Mr. Stovall. When Amanda was five. It was an awful ice storm, and best we can tell they were headed to the school to find Amanda. A branch fell on their car moments after they left home." She paused. "They were both killed."

Ben settled heavily back into his seat, his heart breaking for Maggie's little girl. What an awful thing for her to have suffered through. The death of her adoptive parents, and at an age when they would have been everything in the world to her. He crossed his arms against the pit that had formed in his stomach. "Amanda went to live with you then, is that it?"

"No." Ms. Garrett's expression grew dark. "The Brownells had no extended family. Amanda was made a ward of the state and put back into the Social Services system."

Ben frowned, trying to sort through it all. "But she's with you now…"

Fresh tears filled Ms. Garrett's eyes. "She's lived with us off and on since her adoptive parents' deaths. She's been in several foster homes for the most part. The last one…"

Her voice trailed off and she covered her eyes with her fingers. As she did, panic rose in Ben. What happened to Amanda? "Was there trouble?" Maybe the girl was violent or given to tantrums. Or worse.

Ben couldn't bring himself to imagine anything worse. *Please…no…* Not Maggie's little girl.

The social worker lowered her fingers and the pain in her eyes was almost more than Ben could bear. "Amanda was beaten, Mr. Stovall. She nearly died."

The words hit his heart squarely, but that impact was nothing compared to the rage that suddenly pulsed through his body. The state had assigned Maggie's seven-year-old daughter to a foster parent, to be cared for and nurtured, and that monster had nearly beaten the girl to death?

Ms. Garrett sighed. "Amanda's been with us since being released from the hospital."

No, God, it can't be true. He hung his head and imagined a child so young and helpless hurt to the point of…

In that heartbeat, Ben knew with every fiber in his being that he had to see this child, had to hold her in his arms if only one time, and love her the way Maggie surely would have loved her if she'd ever had the chance. She was Maggie's daughter.

Maggie. The thought of his wife caused him to close his eyes. His feelings for her seemed to change daily. Before her breakdown—if that's what it was—Ben had loved her in a way he thought was unconditional. Then he'd learned the truth and before this meeting with Kathy Garrett he knew he'd have willingly accepted a divorce from her. Now he wanted nothing more than to sit down beside her and hold her, rock away the pain and pretense and…and what? Ben wasn't sure how to feel anymore.

Was he supposed to forgive her and act like none of it had ever happened? Like she hadn't spent their lifetime together lying to him? Like she hadn't refused his calls and visits and threatened divorce from the moment she left their home?

His heart was so heavy it nearly forced him to the floor. With his eyes still closed, Ben willed his racing heart to slow down. Whatever the future held for him and Maggie, dwelling on it would have to wait. There was something more important at hand now. "I'd like to meet her, Ms. Garrett. Is that possible?"

"I assume you're her biological father? Is that right?"

Here it was. The question of the hour. How many more times in his life would he have to address the fact that his wife had gotten pregnant by another man the year before they were married? He sighed and tugged on his chin, running his thumb and forefinger over his day-old beard. "No. I didn't know about the baby until recently."

There was a pause. "I thought—"

"She…Maggie saw someone else before we got engaged."

The woman's eyes widened a fraction, and she seemed at a loss for words. Ben inhaled deeply. He no longer cared what Maggie had done or about any of the lies she'd told. He cared only for this little girl, battered and without a home, the daughter of his wife.

And of a man who nearly killed you…

He shook his head. Even that didn't matter. He could hardly contain the sudden, inexplicable love he felt for the child, love that had no reason except that it was. "Does it matter? Can I see her anyway, for a few minutes?"

The woman's eyes twinkled. "If you only knew her, Mr. Stovall; she's the sweetest child I've ever worked with."

Again his heart swelled. "Well, then…"

Ms. Garrett shifted uneasily in her chair and her face fell. "I don't think it's possible, not legally anyway. Now, if you were a licensed foster parent interested in an interview so that—"

"Wait a minute!" Ben's heart was instantly light in a way it hadn't been since he'd found Maggie's note in their bedroom. "I *am* a licensed foster parent. Since we couldn't have our own kids, Maggie and I have been taking in foster kids for the past two years."

"In Ohio?"

"Yes, in Cleveland." Maybe he would get to meet the girl after all. And then maybe… He forced his thoughts not to race ahead. This wasn't the time to be planning the girl's future. She might not even want to meet him or care to know the whereabouts of her real mother. It was all so overwhelming, yet the thought of meeting her—holding her the way he had dreamed of holding his own children one day—filled him with hope. Kathy Garrett's grin worked its way across her entire face. "Are you serious?"

"Check the computer." He pulled out his wallet, ripped his driver's license from inside, and tossed it to the social worker. As he did so he remembered the old guy at the breakfast bar an hour earlier. *"Make every moment count…every moment…"*

He was trying. God help him, he was trying.

Another smile flashed across Kathy's face. "You're in!"

Hope washed over Ben. Not that it made any sense. Not that the situation with Maggie was any less real or true or devastating now. But he welcomed the hope all the same. "Well?"

Ms. Garrett rested her forearms on her desk and turned to face him with a mock businesslike expression. "All right then, Mr. Stovall…about that foster child you'd like to meet." She grinned again. "How about this afternoon?"

25

ess than two hours after Ben Stovall walked into the Cincinnati County Courthouse, the phone rang in John McFadden's suburban, middle-class home.

"He's here, just like you said."

It was Alfie; John recognized his buddy's voice immediately and felt a surge of vengeful relief. He could always count on the boys; anytime he needed a favor they came through.

"You sure it's him?"

"You bet, boss. Everything lines up. Signed his name on the information request form and everything."

So, Stovall wanted the kid after all. John chuckled softly; his plan was taking shape nicely. "Who talked? The curvaceous redhead?"

Alfie chuckled long and hard. "Is that what Mikey told you?" His laugh grew until he sounded like an excited donkey. "She was curvaceous all right. Sixty extra pounds curvaceous."

John enjoyed these lighter moments with the boys. Dealing was so tense sometimes, what with worrying about authorities, guarding the stash so no one took more than the right amount along the way, making sure the goods were as pure as promised. Too many details. But this was more enjoyable than John had expected. "What'd you do, promise her a date?"

"Nah, Mike went in a few days ago and flashed a hundred. Dame about wet her pants. Got all secretive, looking both ways, making sure no one was watching. Mikey slipped her his cell phone number, told her to call if a Ben Stovall came to the courthouse for any reason at all." Alfie stopped laughing and struggled to catch his breath. "I think she liked the attention, boss, know what I mean? I bet she'da done it for ten bucks, you know?"

John smiled. If Ben Stovall intended to shut down his operation, the bribe was money well spent. He'd reimburse the boys with cash from the next shipment. "She took the money?"

"Right. Mikey promised another hundred if she delivered the information. We got the call just after noon today."

"Nice work. Tell Mikey there'll be two loads for him, free, in the next shipment and—"

Alfie hooted loudly. *"Two* loads, boss? Free? Hey, Mike'll like that. We thought we was doin' this just for the—"

"I'm not finished." John paused. He liked the boys, but sometimes they tested his patience—especially Alfie, who had never been the sharpest knife in the drawer. "I was about to say all I need from you boys is a little surveillance work. Grab a pen and write this down."

"Surveillance?" Alfie's tone went blank.

"Yeah, you know, follow the social worker—Kathy Garrett's her name. Find out who she is; watch the parking lot and follow her home. And look out for Ben Stovall. You writing this down, Alfie?"

"Sure boss, yeah. I'm writing. How'm I gonna know what Stovall looks like?"

"He's dark-haired, tall, good build, I guess. Looks like Mr. Corporate America. Clean cut, harmless face. My guess is he'll be with the social worker."

"Social worker…" Alfie hesitated. "Oh, right. Kathy Garrett. Okay, I got it."

"Pass the information on to Mikey, will ya?"

"Sure, boss, we're on it."

McFadden's heart pounded as he calculated how little time he had to face the judge and make a plea as the child's long-lost father. "Call me when you find Stovall and then update me every time they go anywhere."

"Like driving, you mean?"

John sighed. "Right, Alfie. In the car, on foot. Anytime they go anywhere let me know." His mind raced ahead. "Oh, and one more thing. They might have a little girl with them. Seven or eight years old, something like that."

There was a pause, but Alfie didn't ask for any details. That was one of the things John liked best about Alfie and Mike: They never asked questions when they shouldn't. "Okay, boss. A little girl. What's she look like?"

John thought a moment and again a chuckle sifted up from his gut. "Like me, Alfie, okay? Watch for a kid that looks like me."

Alfie thought that was even funnier than the bit about the redhead. He guffawed so loudly John had to move the receiver away from his ear.

"Hey, boss. Really, now. What's she look like?"

"She looks like a little girl, Alfie. Never mind. Just call me, will ya?"

"Cell phone, right?"

"Right. I'm leaving in an hour, and I'll check into a room somewhere in town when I get there."

John moved to open the suitcase on his bed and began tossing in socks and underwear and T-shirts. Enough to last a week, at least. If it took longer than that, something definitely would have gone wrong. In that case, he didn't want to think about what clothes he'd be wearing, since they'd probably be issued by the local jail.

"Understand?"

"Right o, boss. Got it all down on paper right in front of me. Uh, hey boss…two loads? You sure about that?"

"Absolutely. You and Mike just make sure you get hold of Kathy Garrett before she takes off early and we miss her altogether. I want her followed today, got it?"

"Got it."

McFadden hung up the phone and made a mental list of the things he would need. At least one nice pair of pants and a dressy shirt—one of the silk deals he'd picked up in Vegas last year would work. Just right for showing the judge he was the fatherly type.

He'd get to town, request an emergency hearing, and explain the situation to the judge. The suitcase already held the results of a quick but pricey DNA test done the previous week. Of course, the results would match those on the adoption papers—there was no doubt he was the kid's father. He'd present the test and give the court a teary-eyed report on how he'd looked high and low for the girl with no luck until now.

Oh, yeah, and that he'd absolutely begged Maggie Johnson to keep the child, but Maggie had tricked him, moved to another part of the state and handed off the baby without his having any say in the matter. All he'd ever wanted was to claim his rightful spot as the baby's father.

And now here he was, prepared to do just that.

Yes, that's exactly what he'd tell the judge. And with the kid stuck in Social Services, what better timing?

Another chuckle slithered to the surface as John shut his suitcase. He figured he'd get a meeting with the judge by tomorrow. Matters involving children tended to get precedence. At least that's what the redhead had told Mikey. Then it'd be just a matter of hours before John and Ben Stovall met again. The do-good lawyer could have the brat for all he cared, but first he'd have to pay up.

McFadden ambled across his expansive bedroom, pulled open the top drawer of a mahogany chest, and grabbed the loaded revolver. If Plan A worked, he wouldn't need it. Stovall would give him the cash and make the call to Cleveland police withdrawing the assault charges. That done, John would happily make his way back home.

If Plan A failed, though, he was prepared.

One way or another, Stovall was going to cooperate. Even if it meant taking the kid by force.

26

In the ten minutes Maggie had to clean up before meeting with Dr. Camas, she went to her private room and locked herself in the bathroom. She brushed her teeth to rid her mouth of the stale smell of vomit, and when she was finished, she leaned forward against the countertop and stared at her face in the mirror.

Nothing.

Not a single thing about her face or her eyes resembled the tenderhearted young girl who had attended that picnic so many years ago, when she first fell in love with Ben Stovall. Back then her dark blond hair and lithe, attractive figure were only added benefits. Her real beauty had come from somewhere deep within. It was something that burst through her smile and radiated from her eyes, something that made her face alive with the vibrancy of hope and the expectant promise of her future.

Maggie studied herself. How different would she look now if she'd told Ben the truth? Okay, so she'd made a mistake. She'd done the one thing a good Christian girl is never supposed to do: She'd had sex. But wasn't Ben supposed to forgive her?

She let the question dangle in her mind for a moment, and the answer was clear. They'd only been friends back then. Ben might have forgiven her, but he wouldn't have had any obligation to marry her. He very simply would have offered his condolences and moved on with his life. Without Maggie. He'd made it clear: He was looking to marry a woman of virtue, a virgin, plain and simple. Girls who gave up their purity were a dime a dozen, and Ben planned to hold out for someone like himself.

Someone with a modicum of self-control when it came to things of the flesh.

She drew back from the mirror, taking in her lifeless lip-line and the hardness around her eyes. She was still pretty, she knew. Fit, polished, store-bought. But no amount of money could undo the years of lies and the poison they'd bled into her system. No, the light that once burned inside her, the flame of youth and faith and hope and promise, had been extinguished long ago.

And it was all Ben's fault.

I hate him, God… He never loved me, not a single moment. Not for me, anyway.

Let no deceit come from you.

Maggie squeezed her eyes shut, and the Scripture faded. Just as well. She didn't have time to think about it. She needed to be in Dr. Camas's office in two minutes.

He was waiting as usual when she entered the room, calmly, coolly, so that the peace and confidence than ran through him fairly filled the air. Being in his presence made Maggie feel safe and warm, and as she sat down she exhaled slowly.

"You wanted to see me?"

Dr. Camas smiled, and Maggie knew this conversation would be slow and meaningful, like all her discussions with him. "Yes." He shifted his position so that he faced her squarely, crossing one leg over the other knee, clearly relaxed. "It was something you said in group."

"I figured."

The doctor cocked his head curiously. "Figured what?"

"The part about wanting a divorce. I figured that'd get a rise out of somebody in a Christian hospital like Orchards."

Doctor Camas's expression remained the same. "Actually it wasn't that at all. You should know by now, Maggie, we aren't here to force morality on you. That's a choice you have to make, something between you and God. We're here to help you unravel your feelings because the knot you brought into this place was making you sick, remember?"

She felt like a petulant junior high student, and her cheeks grew hot under his gaze. "Yes. I'm sorry."

Dr. Camas picked up a pencil and tapped the eraser a few times on his desk, his gaze still on Maggie. "No need to apologize. I just want to make sure you're clear on our roles."

If they aren't pushing me to do the right thing, then what was I feeling in the bathroom before I was sick? Maggie struggled with the question, but realized Dr. Camas was waiting for her response. "Okay. I'm clear. So what'd I tell group that made you think I was making progress?"

He caught his chin in his forefinger and thumb in a gesture that had become strangely comforting to Maggie. "You said you hate your husband."

Maggie's defenses rose and anger burned in her gut. "Don't I have a right? After all he expected of me and all it's caused me in my life, don't I have a—"

"Maggie…" He waited until he had her attention. "Did I put a judgment on your statement?"

She thought back a moment. It had to be wrong, making a statement like that about her husband. Didn't it? "No. I guess not. But it isn't exactly godly, telling a group of strangers that you hate your husband."

A faint smile turned the corners of the doctor's lips upward. "No, it isn't. But it means you're willing to talk about more than what happened."

Her heart filled with uncertainty, and she blinked twice, waiting for the doctor to continue. "Meaning?"

"Meaning in the past you've talked about what happened between you and Ben. You talked about your pregnancy and how it felt to give your daughter up for adoption." Dr. Camas paused, and Maggie dropped her gaze to her hands and felt the familiar pit in her stomach. *Where are you, precious baby girl?* She couldn't take much discussion about the adoption now, not when she was dying to get out of Orchards and begin taking steps to find the child.

The doctor cleared his throat and she looked up again. "What you seldom talked about was how you felt about Ben. Until now." He leveled his gaze at her. "Okay, Maggie, go along with me for a minute here, will you?"

She nodded.

"Why do you hate your husband?"

"Because he expected me to be perfect." There was anger in her voice again, but she didn't care. There would never be a better time or place to talk about this.

"He thought you were a virgin."

"No, he *expected* me to be one. There's a difference." Maggie could feel her cheeks growing hot again.

"And since you weren't, you lied to him."

"I *loved* him! I had no choice."

The room filled with the ticking sound of Dr. Camas's wristwatch. "What if you'd told him the truth?" The question was calm and measured and unquestionably reasonable.

Maggie huffed and crossed her legs in a blur of motion. "He'd have moved on to someone else."

"Are you sure?"

"Of course." Who did Dr. Camas think he was, second-guessing her and acting like he knew Ben better than she did? "He was going to marry a virgin, no matter what."

Dr. Camas leaned back in his chair. "Let's try something for a minute."

A sigh escaped and Maggie resisted the urge to roll her eyes. This entire line of questioning was pointless. What was done was done. She hated Ben for forcing her hand, forcing her to give up her baby girl and to live nearly eight years of lies in order to appease his appetite for perfection.

The doctor was waiting and Maggie knew she had no choice but to go along. "Fine."

"Think back, Maggie. What was it about Ben that first made you love him?"

She didn't like the question. At this point in her life and treatment, she was finally getting over Ben, feeling strong enough to stand up to him, preparing for the day when she would face him with the truth and hand him the divorce papers. This was no time to muddle her emotions with a trip back to where and when and why she first loved her husband. She crossed her arms in front of her and clenched her jaw. "I think we're past that, doctor."

"Perhaps. But humor me, will you? What was it? Come on, Maggie, think."

"Oh, okay." She cast her gaze upward and studied the pattern of tiles on the ceiling. This was pointless, but…well, he was the doctor. She thought back to the picnic, to the way so many of her friends had been there that day. "He was different."

"What do you mean? Go deeper, Maggie."

She squirmed in her seat. "He knew what he wanted in life. When he talked about his faith it was like…a real thing, a real relationship. Stronger than mine, even; stronger than my parents'. And they'd been Christians all their lives."

Dr. Camas nodded slowly. "But he said he wouldn't marry a girl unless she was a virgin, is that right?"

Wasn't it? Hadn't he said it that way? Maggie thought hard …

She could feel the humid, night air on her skin, hear the worship band playing in the background. And suddenly it was as though Ben were sitting beside her again, the way he had been that night on the grass at the picnic. She closed her eyes and she could almost hear his voice…

She shook her head. "I don't think he mentioned it that night, honestly. He said he knew God had a plan for his life and he…he wanted to obey so the plan would happen one day. Something like that."

"Okay, so sometime in the next few weeks, then. He must have told you he wouldn't marry a girl who wasn't a virgin, right? Think back, Maggie."

She sighed and her vision blurred as tears filled her eyes. He had said that several times. At least, that's how she'd always remembered it. She shut her eyes again, squeezing out several tears that fell onto her cheeks. "He…we didn't see each other that much, but we talked on the phone…"

Memories flooded her mind. Ben sharing his heart with her, and she with him. Snapshots of laughter and innocence and promises that lay ahead. But none of the memories was the one she'd hung onto these past years. Her eyes flew open as frustration swept her. "I can't remember. Can we be done with this?"

Dr. Camas remained still, his eyes connected with hers. "I think you remember more than you're willing to admit. Try harder, Maggie. Let's lay it out so we can take it apart and figure out where the hate comes from."

A gnawing feeling ate at Maggie's gut, and she wondered if she'd be sick again before this session was finished. She did hate Ben, she had every right. But until she finished this…this *game* or whatever it was, she couldn't move on. Gritting her teeth, she thought back once more—and this time she could hear her voice.

"How come you always talk about God's plans for your life, Ben? How do you know He has plans for you?" She'd been playing with him, baiting him to see what he was really made of.

"It's true, Maggie. The Bible says so right in Jeremiah and probably a dozen other places, too. That's why I've never wanted to get too serious with anyone."

"I don't get it."

Maggie could hear her response as clearly as if she had tape-recorded the conversation years ago and now had the opportunity to play it back over loud speakers.

She remembered the words...heard them again...and froze. *No*...no! *That's not how it was.* Maggie squeezed her eyes shut. Her heart and mind went blank...and cold. "I'm finished, Dr. Camas." She rose, wringing her hands and biting fiercely on her lower lip. "I need some air."

Before Dr. Camas could speak, Maggie rushed out of the room, slamming the door behind her, certain that if she'd stayed in the office another moment she would have suffocated and died.

27

Alfie and Mike were in a panel van looking very much like repairmen resting between calls. It was the perfect cover. Earlier, Mike had gone into the office asking for Kathy Garrett, just like the boss wanted. When the clerk returned with a gentle-looking woman in her forties, Mike stood and approached her. "My name's Harry Bedford. We have a four o'clock appointment."

The Garrett woman had looked at him strangely. "Bedford? There's nothing on my calendar about it. Are you sure you made it with me?"

Mike forced a grimace. "I thought so. Wife and I are interested in adopting a child from the inner city. That's your specialty, right?"

A knowing look filled the woman's face. "No, I handle foster children. I think you're probably looking for the downtown office." She scribbled something on a slip of paper. "Do you know that area?"

Mike took the piece of paper and began backing away. "Like the back of my hand. Thanks a lot."

Now he was sitting in the parking lot with Alfie, frustrated that the job was taking longer than he thought. They had business to do back at the warehouse and women lined up for later that night.

"I'm hungry." Alfie had finished off a bag of chips and two sodas.

"You're always hun—"

"Hey," Alfie cut him off. "Is that her?" He nodded toward a woman leaving the building. She was alone and headed for a blue sedan.

"Bingo." Mike started the engine. *Good. We'll follow her home, get the news to the boss, and be home in time for the party.*

In the seat next to him, Alfie picked up the cell phone and tapped in a series of numbers. There was a pause. "Boss, we got her." Alfie gazed through the windshield at the woman as she climbed into the sedan. "Yep. She's getting in her car right now. We'll let you know where she lives as soon as we get there."

Kathy Garrett made her way home more quickly than usual. So much had happened, she could hardly wait to tell Amanda.

God, You are faithful beyond anything, beyond anyone.

The fact that she had just located Amanda's mother by means of a man who stopped in her office on a whim was nothing less than an answer to the child's prayer. Kathy was sure of it. She pulled into her driveway minutes later and bounded lightly up the steps. "Kids, I'm home."

A chorus of voices greeted her from various parts of the house. The older children were always so good with the younger ones, and Amanda was no exception. She was probably caught up in a checkers match with Jenika, their oldest.

Kathy hung up her coat and unwrapped her scarf. It wasn't quite Thanksgiving and already it felt cold enough to snow, but no chill could dispel the warmth that radiated through Kathy at that moment. She made her way into the den and found the girls. For the first time her heart ached at the news she was about to share…it might mean saying good-bye to Amanda for good. She swallowed a lump in her throat and smiled at the child, sitting cross-legged on the floor with Jenika. "You girls have a good day at school?"

"I need help with my math." Jenika made the announcement and then looked up and grinned. "Other than that it was great."

"Betsy didn't sit by me today because she said she's going to Elle's sleepover on Friday and I can't come." Amanda's eyes looked sad.

"Did you work it out?" Kathy was impatient to get past the small talk. *None of it's going to matter in a minute, Amanda. Your prayers have been answered! I've found your mommy!*

Amanda shrugged and the corners of her lips turned slightly upward. "We played together at second recess, so I guess so."

"That's good." She paused. *Give me the right words, Lord. Please…* What she was about to tell Amanda would change her life forever. The smallest part of her wanted to wait and keep Amanda to herself a little longer. But that wouldn't have been fair. Besides, Amanda had been waiting too long already. "Amanda, may I talk to you for a minute?"

Jenika was five years older, but Amanda was far more intuitive in matters dealing with Social Services. Her eyes fell and she cast a knowing look at Jenika. Kathy understood the exchange. Whenever she came home from work and needed to talk to Amanda it usually meant one thing: They'd found a foster home for her. And it was painfully obvious that Amanda hated the thought of ever leaving the Garrett home.

But this was different. So different Kathy could hardly wait to talk to the child. She took Amanda's hand, helping her to her feet. "Come on, honey. It's good news. Really."

The two moved into the dining room and sat side by side at the kitchen table, their chairs angled slightly so that they could see each other. "I met someone very interesting today."

Concern creased the corners of Amanda's eyes and she reached instinctively for Kathy's fingers. The child's gaze fell and she seemed to study the way her hand fit in

Kathy's. After a moment a small tear splashed on her pant leg and when she spoke, her voice was barely audible. "I don't wanna leave."

"Oh, sweetie, I know." Kathy stared sadly at the child. If only Maggie Stovall had kept Amanda from the beginning. And if Kathy had listened to her heart all those years—

"Can't I stay with you, Kathy, please?" Amanda's eyes begged through a pool of tears as she reached out and placed her other hand in Kathy's, so that they both nestled in Kathy's palms.

"Come here, honey." Kathy felt tears in her own eyes as she pulled the child into her arms, stroking her hair and whispering, "It's okay, baby. Everything's going to be all right."

Amanda paused, then pulled back, studying Kathy's eyes. "It's true then? You found me a foster home?"

A single tear spilled onto Kathy's face, and she wiped it quickly with the back of her hand. "Well, actually..." She forced herself to sound upbeat. "Actually, it's good news."

"Good news?" Again Amanda tilted her head. She was such a darling girl, peachy skin with only the faintest smattering of freckles across the bridge of her nose, and long hair that looked spun by the hands of angels. For all that Amanda had gone through, something innocent still sparkled in her eyes, and the effect only made her more beautiful.

Looking at her now, it was hard to believe that scant weeks ago she was in the hospital fighting for her life. Kathy let out a single, soft chuckle at the lovely picture Amanda made.

All right, here goes, sweetheart. "Yes, good news. A man came into the office today very interested in you. He said he thinks he and his wife would like to be your foster parents and..." Kathy tried to read Amanda's reaction, and since she saw nothing that resembled excitement, she gently took the girl's shoulders in her hands and stared deeply into her eyes. "And one day they might even want to adopt you. Forever, Amanda."

Panic worked its way across Amanda's face. "B-b-b..." She exhaled in a huff. "B-b-but..." Amanda crossed her arms, and focused her attention on her feet. "Kathy, I c-c-can't make my words right."

Kathy's heart melted. "Oh, sweetie, it's okay. Lots of people have trouble making words when they're upset. Just take your time." She ran a hand down the back of Amanda's head.

When Amanda's eyes lifted they were filled with tears. "I d-d-don't even know him..."

Kathy swallowed back a lump in her throat. *Poor little darling, Lord. Help me say the right thing.* "Honey, I know that. But he's a very nice man. He said you were exactly the type of child he and his wife were looking for." Kathy hated keeping the facts from her, but Ben Stovall had asked that she do so. Besides, Kathy wasn't at all sure it would be wise to tell Amanda she'd been found by her birth mother.

Not when the woman was in a psychiatric hospital being treated for depression, unaware that her husband had even located the child.

Momentary worry washed over Kathy. What if Maggie Stovall refused contact with Amanda, let alone a foster or adoption arrangement? That would be too great a heartbreak for Amanda to take. It was better to keep the details simple, at least for now.

"W-w-why would he w-w-want an old girl like me? Most p-p-people want little kids…b-b-babies."

Kathy felt the girl's shoulders trembling and she moved her hands slowly down the thin arms to take hold of Amanda's small fingers again. "That's true." She lowered herself so that she could see directly into Amanda's eyes. "But this man is different. He said they were looking for a girl like *you*. They don't want a baby who cries all night or a toddler who hasn't learned to read. They want a girl just exactly like you, Amanda."

She shook her head and fresh tears filled her eyes. "I don't wanna go, Kathy. P-p-please. Don't m-m-make me."

"Baby, we've been through this before. The state won't let me keep you. Not unless there's no foster homes available."

"Yeah, but I…l-l-love you guys. I don't wanna leave."

"Oh, Amanda…" Kathy pulled the girl to her and held her close. The enthusiasm she'd felt earlier was all but gone. *How am I ever going to let her go, Lord? She doesn't even know these people. They could be awful for all any of us know. How can I—*

Trust Me, daughter.

But…

Trust Me.

There it was again, the soothing reassurance Kathy knew came from the Lord. She exhaled slowly, forcing herself not to get caught up in her selfish feelings. If God had brought Amanda's mother back into her life there had to be a reason. Besides, Amanda was pretty well out of options in the Social Services system.

Kathy just needed to do all she could to help make the transition as smooth as possible. Amanda remained nestled in her arms, her head against Kathy's chest. What was she thinking? How does it feel to know your life could change at any moment, that you have no control over where you might be sleeping on any given night? *Help her, God. Please shut the door on this if it isn't from You. And give me wisdom to know what's best for Amanda.*

The girl pulled back and studied Kathy's eyes nervously. "Am I going with him tonight?"

Kathy smiled. "No, silly. Of course not. You need to meet him first."

Another look of terror flashed in Amanda's eyes. "By m-m-myself?"

"No, sweetie, I'll be with you." Kathy reached out and smoothed her hand over Amanda's hair. "How 'bout we all meet at Party Pizza tomorrow for lunch?"

The fear was gone for the moment, but in its place was resignation. Amanda had been this route before; she knew the protocol. "So I leave tomorrow night?"

Kathy shook her head. "The man's wife is in the hospital right now. We'll have to see what happens, but I think it could take a few days to get everything lined up." She hesitated. "Are we on then? For tomorrow, I mean?"

"Okay." The girl's eyes glistened with unshed tears, and Kathy was struck again by how tender yet tough this child was. Tender to all that was good and right with God and the world, yet tough enough not to break down sobbing when her very existence was being turned upside down.

Kathy hugged her close. "I wish you could stay. You know that, right?"

Then Amanda did something she'd never done before. She reached out a single finger and softly traced a heart on the back of Kathy's hand. "Know what that means?"

Kathy fought back tears. "No, honey, what?"

"It means that even if I go, you'll always have my heart."

Amanda tried to sleep, but it was hard. She wasn't sure what to feel. Kathy had said the man's name was Mr. Stovall and that he was good and kind and that he and his wife were probably an answer to prayer. Amanda turned onto her side and tried to keep her eyes shut. It was possible, wasn't it? That God had heard her prayers for a forever family and brought the Stovalls as an answer?

But why hadn't God given Kathy a bigger house instead? That would have been the best answer.

She didn't want to meet this man tomorrow. Because if things went well, she'd be leaving Kathy's house very, very soon. She blinked and stared about the shadowy room. What if Mr. Stovall really was a nice man? The kind of friendly-looking man that Amanda had seen on television shows. Maybe he went off to work in the morning and came home at night, and he'd play with his kids—with her—on the living room floor like Mr. Garrett. Maybe he and his wife were sent by God to take her home and love her forever.

Amanda closed her eyes again. Of course she'd thought that about Mrs. Graystone, too.

No, there could only ever be one, true answer to prayer where her life was concerned. If God wasn't going to give Kathy a bigger home so Amanda could stay with her, there was only one person who would qualify as an answer to prayer. And it wasn't Mr. Stovall.

It was her mother. Her *real* mother. The one who somewhere, somehow must still remember the baby she gave away. The one who surely one day would do whatever it took to find her.

28

Judge Caleb "Hutch" Hutchison hated emergency hearings and he rarely granted them. Especially first thing in the morning. But that brisk November day a week before Thanksgiving, he had examined the circumstances and decided there was no other choice.

The situation seemed on its surface an open-and-shut case. Long-lost father shows up to claim a child caught in the Social Services system. Judge Hutch's job was merely to make sure the facts matched up and send the father and daughter on their way. Still, something about the man and the little girl he claimed to want for his own troubled Hutch. Deeply.

Alone in his chambers, five minutes before the meeting was to take place, the judge reviewed the situation for the fifth time. One John McFadden waltzes into the courthouse, fills out an emergency request form saying he only recently learned he had a child in Cincinnati, and then produces enough information to convince the clerk he's the real father. The child is a girl named Amanda Joy Brownell, a ward of the Social Services system who's been wasting away in a series of foster homes for the past three years.

Judge Hutchison had worked as a jurist in that same courthouse for more than twenty years. He knew his peers considered him both brilliant and tough—a judge criminals feared, whose sentences brought a sense of justice to the people of Cincinnati and the surrounding area. But criminals weren't the only group Hutch detested. There was one other group of citizens he was loathe to waste time on: dead-beat dads.

Therefore, his decision to meet with the man today had nothing to do with any generosity of spirit. If this McFadden had truly been concerned with the welfare of his daughter, why hadn't he come forward before now? The possibilities as to what had motivated him—after so many years—to seek custody of the child now were less than encouraging.

So the only reason Judge Hutchison was giving the man five minutes of his time was pure and simple: Hutch loved children. He had five grandchildren of his own and often found himself fighting back tears when the victims in his cases were kids too young to help themselves. Amanda Brownell's file had made his eyes watery after only the first page.

If there was even a remote chance that this McFadden character really was an upstanding citizen who only recently realized he'd fathered a child and who truly wanted to give this hapless little child a permanent, loving home, Judge Hutchison did not want anything to stand in the way.

He checked his watch. The man should be there by now, sitting in his courtroom waiting the judge's decision, which could go one of two ways: a temporary grant of custody rights—one day, for instance, so the two could become acquainted—or a refusal until the situation could be further examined.

Judge Hutchison had long ago learned to trust his instincts, and they were telling him that McFadden was almost certainly not the type of father who would give little Amanda a happy, loving home.

The man was in too great a hurry.

No, McFadden was more the kind of man Hutch would subject to intense scrutiny; the kind that might not only be false, but perhaps even dangerous.

He opened the door and walked from his chambers into the courtroom. A dark-haired man with a falsely humble expression rose to his feet. "Your honor, my name is John McFadden, and I'm—"

"Sit down, Mr. McFadden." Hutch glowered at the man, more certain than ever that something wasn't right. Something about the flashy cheap suit and the depth of darkness in McFadden's eyes made him look more like a Las Vegas pit boss than a loving father who had only recently stumbled onto his long-lost daughter.

Hutch took his seat and sorted through his docket. Several minutes passed before he looked up and rapped his gavel twice. He nodded to a court reporter sitting nearby. "I will now hear the emergency matter of John McFadden regarding his request to be granted custody of his seven-year-old daughter, Amanda Brownell, who is currently a ward of this court." He peered down and found the man watching him with great expectancy. "You may present your information, Mr. McFadden."

As he stood, the man glanced behind him, then side to side. *Nervous sort,* Judge Hutch thought. McFadden took a handful of documents and presented them to the judge. "Here. I believe this is everything you need."

The judge sifted through the papers. A notarized DNA test, a request form asking the judge to check McFadden's DNA against that of the child's, a request form for temporary custody, and another request form for a hearing that would give him permanent custody. Everything was in order...but the gnawing feeling that something was wrong remained.

"All right, Mr. McFadden, why don't you give me your driver's license, and I'll go back to my chambers, make a copy of it, and check out the DNA with the child's birth certificate. It shouldn't take long to pull up the information on the computer."

McFadden's shoulders relaxed and his face seemed to sag with relief. "Thanks, Judge, you don't know what this means to me. I can't wait to see her. I mean, after all these years and such, you know how it is. This is really amazing…"

The man was still rambling as Hutch took his identification and slipped back into his chambers. Before he checked the computers for matching DNA; before he contacted Kathy Garrett, the social worker listed on the girl's file; before he did anything else for that matter, he was going to run the man's information by someone else. Just in case.

He picked up the phone and was immediately connected with the court clerk.

"Yes, your honor?"

"Get me the police department, please."

John McFadden tapped his foot, anxiously awaiting Judge Hutchison's return. With each passing minute, his heart rate increased. Finally, when the eighth minute passed, John clenched his teeth, cursing under his breath. No DNA match should take this long. That judge must have discovered more than whether or not John was the kid's father.

He stood and took three quick steps toward the court reporter. "Tell the judge…uh, I had to use the restroom."

The court reporter looked up briefly. "Sure."

In three minutes, McFadden was in his gold Acura, pulling out of the courthouse parking lot. He steered into the first alley he saw and dialed Alfie's cell phone.

"Yah, buddy." Alfie's words were muffled; the lug was probably eating again. Alfie was always stuffing his face.

"It's me."

"Oh…hey, boss, what's up?"

John gritted his teeth. They'd forced his hand. He had no choice now but to—

"You follow the girl this morning?"

"Sure thing, boss. Walked to a bus stop a block from her house. Waited, oh, maybe five minutes." He paused. "We didn't follow the bus. Was we supposed to?"

"Nah, you did good. What was the name on the bus?"

"Wood-something."

This guy was the limit. "Ask Mike, will ya?" John tried not to get impatient with Alfie, but there were times…

In the background he heard Mike's voice. "Woodland Elementary, I wrote it down."

"Hey, boss, he wrote it down. It was—"

"I heard him. Never mind. Do me a favor and put Mike on. I need to know exactly where the bus stop is."

When John had the directions, he hung up and called the operator. "Yeah, I need the number for Woodland Elementary."

A minute later he was on the phone to the school secretary. "Hi, my son told me school's out at 2:15 today, is that right?"

"No, sir, 3:10, like usual."

"I thought so. I tell ya, that boy has an active imagination. Thanks."

He looked at his watch as he hung up the phone. 10:15. Smiling, he started the engine and headed for his motel. As he drove he fingered the loaded handgun beside him, running over the plan again in his mind. In less than six hours he would meet his daughter for the first time.

Then he would take care of business his way.

The demons were still taunting her, hissing at her, reminding her of the doubts that had first taken shape in Dr. Camas's office the day before.

Had Ben really been to blame?

Maggie rolled over, caught in the layer of reality somewhere between sleep and consciousness.

It's your fault, Maggie. Everything that's happened. Your fault. The hissing became louder until it became a ringing that grew more and more persistent.

The alarm clock! Maggie shot up in bed and hit the buzzer on the machine beside her. It was 9:30 in the morning, and though Dr. Camas had honored her request for solitude the day before, he had insisted on today's early appointment. She had thirty minutes until their meeting, and she flipped onto her back, staring at the ceiling.

Ben must have been to blame, God. Tell me I'm right.

Silence.

I can't think about it, won't. Then, moving like a woman late for the last bus out of town, Maggie showered, dressed, and ate a blueberry muffin from her breakfast tray. Through the routine, a thought occurred to her.

For the first time since entering Orchards, she had awakened filled with energy. By ten o'clock she was sitting across from Dr. Camas.

"I've talked with Dr. Baker. We're excited for you, Maggie."

Her heart pounded. How could there be anything exciting about the confusion she was feeling? She was awful, sick in the head, the worst wife anyone could possibly—

"Maggie…you okay?"

She twisted in her chair and struggled to maintain eye contact with the doctor. "I, well…I keep thinking about our talk yesterday."

"Yes, me too." He smiled gently and reached out, patting her hand the way her father used to do when she was a little girl. "It's all right, Maggie. You can finish the story whenever you're ready. We were talking about what Ben said to you back in your early days together."

Maggie nodded and forced her fingertips into her temples.

Go back, Maggie…remember it right this time.

Be truthful, Maggie…come into the light. My grace is sufficient for you, daughter.

Maggie felt herself relax. Wherever it went, whatever happened afterward, she had to remember the truth about her past. The truth about Ben.

"I'm trying to remember what he said…" She let her hands drop to her lap, and this time she caught Dr. Camas's gaze and held it. "And I'm…not sure he ever really demanded that I be—"

She stopped short as Ben's long-ago words came back in a rush: *"I wanna be pure, Maggie. My wife—whoever she is—deserves that. I wanna be pure…I wanna be pure…"*

Dear God, was it true? The reality nearly knocked her to the floor. The idea of purity hadn't come as a directive from him, but rather a promise. He had wanted to offer himself pure, as a precious gift. The notion that she—in turn—could be nothing less than a virgin had come from—

"No! It can't be…" Her voice was a hoarse whisper; a piece of her heart felt as though it had been ripped open.

Dr. Camas leaned slightly forward. "Go on, Maggie. What do you remember?"

Sobs welled up in her chest. There had to be other conversations! Times when he had pompously demanded perfection from anyone who might grace his arm down the aisle of a church, anyone who would wear his ring and take his name…

She was weeping now, and still the doctor waited. She knew there was no choice but to tell him what she remembered. "I…I think he said he wanted to…be pure. S-S-something like, h-h-his wife deserved that." She gulped and her shoulders shook from the sobs that washed over her. She didn't know how long it took to compose herself enough to speak. "Then I asked him…" She squeezed her eyes shut, horrified she hadn't remembered things correctly until now. "I asked him if that meant he wouldn't marry a girl who wasn't a virgin."

The only sound in the room was that of Maggie crying as she forced herself to remember the rest of the conversation. How could she have hung on to a memory that had never existed? How fair had that been?

The questions weighed on her heart as she found her voice. "He told me he thought God had a girl for him, someone like him…someone who loved the Lord and had s-s-saved herself the way he had. H-H-e told me he thought she had hair like mine, and a smile like mine, and a laugh like…"

The memory of her husband and all he'd been back then lay in front of her, like an innocent child about to receive a punishment for something he hadn't done. Ben hadn't demanded perfection from her after all. He had merely been teasing, baring his heart and telling her in his own, shy way that he could picture the two of them marrying one day. Somehow…sometime, she had twisted the truth, convincing herself Ben had started the conversation, that he'd stated his expectations up front: He'd only marry a girl who was as pure and wholesome as he was.

"I convinced myself it was something he demanded, a requirement." She grabbed a tissue and blew her nose. Trembling from her fingers to her knees, Maggie stared at Dr. Camas, desperate for answers. "Why did I do that?"

The doctor considered her for a long moment. "You tell me."

The answer danced on the tip of her tongue, but it was so bitter she hated to speak it. Her voice grew quiet, and she felt regret like a millstone around her neck.

"So I wouldn't have to…" She drew two quick breaths and stifled another wave of sobs. "So I'd have someone to blame…someone whose fault it was that I gave my baby away." Maggie covered her face with her hands and sobbed.

She had been running from the truth all this time, refusing her part in what happened. By blaming Ben every time she thought of her baby, her little girl growing up somewhere else, with some other mother, she had eventually…

She looked up, her sight blurred from the tears. "I taught myself to hate him, didn't I?"

"What do you think?" Dr. Camas's tone and gaze were filled with compassion.

"Yes. I did. So I wouldn't have to blame myself."

"Maggie, depression often comes from lies we tell ourselves. When we're willing to lie to those we love—the way you did when you married Ben—then it's quite normal to lie to ourselves, as well. That's at least part of why you're here, wouldn't you agree?"

Maggie nodded, feeling as though she were falling into a dark hole. *What have I done, God? Help me, please…help me find a way back out.*

"How do you feel, Maggie?" The doctor wasn't pushing, but his question stabbed at her all the same. How was she feeling? Like she was suffocating under the weight of her bad decisions. Like there would never again be hope for her. Like she was the worst mother, the worst wife in the world…

"Like I made a lot of mistakes."

"And…"

Suddenly it dawned on her. All she'd ever wanted from God was deep, genuine joy. The kind that would remind her in the darkest days how close and real God was, and that somehow hope was at hand. But every bit of joy she'd ever felt had vanished that terrible day, the morning she gave her daughter up for adoption. She had always thought it was because she'd been forced into it. Backed into an emotional corner.

Now she knew different.

Not only had she walked away from her child, she'd walked away from God as well. Hadn't she heard His quietly urging voice that day telling her not to let go, to hold tight to her tiny daughter whatever the cost? It had taken every ounce of strength to fight against the screaming inside her soul, her desperate longing to stop the social worker from taking her baby. Back then she'd thought she was fighting against herself, her selfish desires. But the situation was clearer now. She'd gone against the prompting of the Holy Spirit, choosing to take matters into her own hands—and every day since then she'd blamed Ben for having expected perfection from her.

But no one had forced her to give her baby up for adoption or to lie about it all these years. The lies were hers and hers alone.

And never, not once since then, had she ever repented. Maggie fought back the sobs that caught in her throat.

I'm here, daughter, turn to Me…

Slowly, finally—after all this time, all her pain, the quiet prodding of the Holy Spirit felt like balm to her soul. She exhaled and forced herself to remain steady, for her entire being ached to do the thing God had always wanted of her.

Okay, Lord, I will…I'll repent. She made the promise silently, but she meant it as much as if she'd broadcast it throughout the hospital.

"What're you feeling, Maggie?" Dr. Camas waited patiently.

She drew a deep breath and allowed herself to be comforted by the kindness in his eyes. *Where do I start, Lord?* "I need to make things right with a lot of people."

"Such as?"

"Well, Ben most of all." How cold she'd been to him, how unbending and hard-hearted. Could he ever forgive her for all she'd done? Even if he could, would he still want her?

The questions were staggering; Maggie would have to deal with most of them later.

"Are you ready to talk about it in group?"

Maggie nodded. "In some ways I've never felt worse than I feel right now." She wrung her hands together and blinked back fresh tears. "But I also feel hope; it doesn't make sense."

A warm smile filled the doctor's face. "God promises us joy in the morning, Maggie, and I believe for you the darkness is beginning to lift." He paused. "It's all about being honest. First, with God; second, with ourselves."

The words washed over Maggie, easing the anxiety within her. He was right, and even in the fading darkness it felt wonderful to finally be truthful with the Lord and herself.

Now it was time to be honest with everyone else. The group, her parents, her daughter. And of course Ben.

Him more than anyone.

Early the next morning as she slept, Maggie dreamed of a hospital in Woodland, Ohio, and a beautiful baby girl sleeping in her arms. A nurse entered the room and made an announcement. "Liars can never be suitable mothers." Then the woman walked up to Maggie's bed, snatched the baby from her arms, turned, and disappeared through the door.

Maggie screamed for the nurse to stop. "I won't lie. I'll tell the truth, I promise. I love my baby. Please, bring her back. Please!"

But the nurse was gone, and a strange aching developed and grew stronger until finally it woke Maggie at four o'clock in the morning. Drenched in sweat, tears running down her face, she realized the aching was the emptiness she felt without her baby.

"Where is she, God?" Maggie whispered the question through her tears. "I only want to know that she's okay."

Is that all?

The startling question seemed to come from the Lord Himself, and it echoed quietly in her heart.

Yes, God, that's all. Even as she thought it, Maggie knew she was lying again. She wanted more. Much more. She wanted her daughter back, wanted a chance to undo what she'd done that day at Woodland Hospital, wanted to hold her daughter close and take her home and raise her the way she'd imagined in those early days of her pregnancy.

"Why can't I stop lying, Lord?"

Repent, My daughter. Now. While your heart is right. My grace is sufficient for you…

Maggie's breath caught. She had realized her need to repent, but she'd never actually done it. The day had slipped by, and still she hadn't met with the Lord, asked His forgiveness. Quietly, reverently, she slipped out of bed and landed on the cold, linoleum hospital floor. There was no time to wait.

Forgive me, Father. Forgive me…

She hung her head, pouring her heart out to the Lord, begging His forgiveness and promising to be honest with Him and herself and everyone else as long as she drew breath.

Then, one at a time, she confessed the lies she'd told—lies to herself, lies to Ben, and lies to the Lord—until finally she repented of the one she'd just told. And then, just before breakfast, she did something else…something she'd been wanting to do since she checked herself in at Orchards.

She pulled a small phone book from her purse and turned to the T section. There it was. Laura Thompson. Wrapping her robe tightly around her waist, Maggie carried the book into the hall, toward the community phone, and made the call.

"Hello?"

Maggie closed her eyes, squeezing back tears. *Help me find the words, Lord.* "Laura…this is Maggie Stovall. I should have called you sooner…"

"Maggie, dear! I've been praying." The woman's voice was pure and filled with such love that Maggie almost went to her knees again.

She's been praying for me all along, hasn't she, Lord? His love, His provision, overwhelmed her. "If you have a minute, Laura, I have some things to tell you…things I'd like you to pray about…"

"I'm listening, honey. Tell me whatever's on your heart."

Maggie poured out the entire story, amazed that there was cleansing in every word she spoke. Laura listened and Maggie could feel her concern and understanding through the phone lines.

"So that's why I needed prayer." Maggie was grateful for the older woman, certain that along with everything else God had done, He'd blessed her with a lifelong friend in Laura Thompson.

"Well, I finally understand the mask."

"The mask?"

"Yes, dear." There was no condemnation in Laura's voice. "The Lord gave me a picture that first day, the day I drew your name. A woman in a mask."

Goose bumps rose on Maggie's arms. "Me?"

"Yes. And the image of a little girl, too. Your little girl, I'm guessing. When I pray for you, I pray for her, too."

"Oh, Laura…I don't know what to say…" Maggie closed her eyes briefly. *It's all coming together, Lord.* Was the arm of God that far-reaching? His love that persistent? Had He cared so much that He'd put Maggie's deepest needs in the heart of Laura Thompson? *I stand in awe, Father.*

Maggie made plans to talk with Laura again soon. And after she hung up, Maggie was engulfed by a peace so vivid she could almost feel it wiping away what remained of the darkness. The older woman's words of hope and encouragement rang clear in her mind.

I'm sorry, Lord…so sorry. I want to be close to You again, clean and right and ready to do Your will.

Daughter, I have loved you with an everlasting love…I will remember your sins no more.

"Oh, Lord, you're so faithful." Maggie hung her head as the words flooded her heart with peace—and with the beginning of what Maggie knew was joy. Joy of knowing she was a daughter of the King of kings, joy of being saved by His precious blood, joy of being certain that one day she would live with Him in heaven, eternally. Deep, abiding, genuine joy. And once it had taken root in her heart, Maggie knew it would continue growing until the darkness was gone forever.

Forgiveness, wholeness, restoration…they all were hers. Even if she ached a lifetime for the daughter she would almost certainly never know.

29

It was noon, and the commotion at Party Pizza was at a fever pitch. Picnic tables lined the dining room where mothers, preschoolers, and the occasional older child gathered for lunch.

Ben ordered a large Hawaiian pizza as he took in the scene and tried not to be nervous. Kathy was picking Amanda up at school fifteen minutes before lunch, so the two would be there any moment.

He'd been thinking about Amanda Joy since the moment he'd learned of her existence. Would she look like Maggie? Would her eyes twinkle when she laughed? What would her personality be like? *Probably jaded from years in the Social Services system...*

For what had to be the hundredth time in the past twenty hours, he wondered how different all of their lives might have been if only Maggie had been honest.

Judge not, lest you be judged.... Love covers a multitude of sins.

The sting of conviction came, as it always did lately, every time he tried to blame Maggie for what happened. He planted his forearms on the table and exhaled slowly. The Lord was right. Back then he would never have understood. He would have written Maggie off, broken up with her without looking back. There would have been no getting together again, no engagement, no marriage.

But even if he and Maggie had parted ways, at least one little girl might have been spared a beating, one child might have known a lifetime of love rather than sorrow.

Ben pushed the thoughts from his head. *It wasn't my fault she got together with John McFadden.*

Love covers a multitude of sins...

A sigh escaped him, and Ben massaged his eyebrows with his thumb and forefinger. That same Scripture had haunted him for days now. Weeks, even. Ever since Maggie left, it seemed. *What does it mean, Lord? I loved Maggie; I treated her right.*

Silence.

Fine. Leave me wondering. But one of these days, Lord, I'm going to need You to make it clear to me.

A blur of motion near the front door caught his eye, and he turned and stared. It was Kathy. And clutching her hand tightly was a beautiful, wide-eyed, blond-haired child, whose face...

Ben sucked in his breath. *Oh, man...she looks just like Maggie.*

He watched them weave their way closer until they were standing before him. If the girl had come by herself and stood among a throng of children, Ben would have recognized her without any trouble. He'd have known her anywhere. The shape of her eyes, the way she held herself—stiffly, wanting him to think she was tough even though her eyes showed her fear—she was the image of her mother.

Maggie, if you could only see her. Ben had an overwhelming desire to take the child in his arms and soothe away a lifetime of pain and hurt and abandonment. Instead he held out his hand. "Hi, I'm Ben."

Amanda nodded curtly and gave him a polite smile. "I'm Amanda." The child still held tightly to the hand of her social worker and after several seconds, Ben pulled his back. It hit him then. Amanda loved this woman, this social worker. In a world of uncertainty, Kathy Garrett had always been there for Maggie's little girl. Now the child would see him as the intruder, the man who wanted to take her away, maybe forever.

What am I doing, Lord? She's got a life already. Give me wisdom, please; the child's been hurt enough.

Kathy had been watching the brief exchange between Ben and Amanda, and now she opened her purse. "Well, you two sit here and get acquainted. I'm going to order pizzas and—"

"No, sit down." Ben motioned to her. "I ordered a few minutes ago. It'll be up any minute."

Amanda and Kathy took their seats beside each other, across from Ben. He noticed how the girl snuggled close to Kathy, how her small eyes had softened just a bit. She looked at Ben with a gaze that didn't waver. "I like pizza."

He was taken aback at how her comment made him feel. His heart soared at the small concession—it seemed a white flag of sorts, her way of saying she was going to try to like him. He smiled at her. "Me too."

Kathy slipped an arm around Amanda's shoulders and squeezed once. "Listen, I have to use the ladies' room."

"Me too! I—"

"Amanda..." Kathy's tone was part warning, part reminder. Ben wondered if the two had talked about the child needing time alone with him.

Amanda's face fell and she nodded a slight smile in Kathy's direction. "Okay. I'll go later."

Great. Kathy's leaving. What am I supposed to say? What do seven-year-old girls like to talk about? He studied her face, and the image of Maggie was so vivid he had to blink to focus his thoughts. "So, tell me about school."

"It's fine." Amanda's gaze followed Kathy until she was out of sight. Then she turned to him, her eyes veiled in uncertainty.

Off to a good start... Fine. If she wasn't in the mood to talk, he'd make up for both of them. And maybe, just maybe... "Okay, so tell me about the class pet. I mean, everyone in second grade has a class pet, right?" Before Amanda could answer, Ben cocked his head. "Let's see, I think our class had a monkey when I was in school. No, wait. That was the teacher. She just looked like a monkey..."

Amanda giggled and a twinkle—Maggie's twinkle—brought a spark of life to her eyes. "We have a goldfish."

"A *goldfish?*" Ben's voice was filled with mock indignation, and Amanda giggled again. "That's not the right kind of pet for second grade. You need something like a muskrat or a house of rabbits or a giant python. Something the boys can let out of the cage to scare the class half to death, isn't that right?"

"We have a lizard, too, named Frank."

"Frank the lizard? Sounds like a very old lizard to me; does he do tricks? Read newspapers, work the computers, that kind of thing?" Ben made his eyes wide, as though he actually suspected Amanda might say yes. This time she let her head fall back and the laughter that spilled from her throat sounded so like Maggie a lump formed in his throat and a wave of sadness washed over Ben. It was Maggie back in the days when they first met...back when she still had something to laugh at. He worked hard to keep his face from reflecting what he was feeling.

"Are you always this goofy?" Amanda leaned forward, resting her thin arms on the table and meeting his gaze.

"What day is it?"

"Wednesday."

"Yes. On Wednesdays I'm always this goofy. Now Thursdays are my days to sleep a lot, and on Fridays I'm serious nearly all the time. But on the weekend...well, then I'm actually extra-goofy. Sometimes I tell knock-knock jokes for an hour straight. Especially on Saturday."

Amanda's eyes danced with laughter. "Tell me one."

"A knock-knock joke?" Ben made his eyes wide again. "On Wednesday?"

"Yes!" Amanda's laughter made him smile. "Please..."

"Well, since we just met and you've never been with me for a Saturday knock-knock joke hour, I guess just this one time..." He thought a moment. "Knock-knock."

"Who's there?"

"Boo. "

"Boo who?"

The silliness faded from Ben's voice. "Ah, that's okay, Amanda. Don't cry." He paused, hoping with all his heart that she could see he was no longer joking. "Everything's going to be okay, Amanda Joy. I promise you."

Her eyes clouded, and her expression grew serious. "Why do you want me, Mr. Stovall?"

She wasn't afraid to ask the big questions, that much was certain. But then, there wasn't enough time to make small talk, really. Not if he was going to take over as her foster parent in the next day or so. Ben sighed. How best to answer her? He didn't want to tell her about Maggie, not yet...not when he had no idea how that news would affect her. *Lord...help me.*

"Kathy showed me your file and...well, I knew I was going to love you." That was true, anyway. "I guess it felt like my wife and I have known you all our lives."

Amanda's eyes softened again and the hint of a smile played on her lips. "Really?"

"Yep. Kind of like there was always a missing piece before. And now it seems like..." Ben felt his eyes grow watery and he blinked. This was no time to be emotional; Amanda would not understand the significance of the moment. "It seems like we've waited all our lives for you."

The child thought about that for a moment, her small face pensive and earnest. "But you don't even know me."

Ben looked into her eyes and saw Maggie looking back at him. His heart swelled with love for this child he'd known only ten minutes, and a smile covered his face. "I know you, Amanda Joy. Better than you think."

Concern flashed across her face as if she were recalling an awful memory. "I d-d-don't clean my room very w-w-well, though. Sometimes that gets me in trouble. P-p-people send me back when that happens."

Ben ached to climb around the booth and take her in his arms. The poor child. What had she suffered over the years? Unable to resist any longer, he reached across the table and wrapped his fingers around hers. Suddenly he knew with everything in him that he could never, ever let this child go. He wanted to promise her that nothing could make him send her back, but he still needed to talk to Maggie.

He drew a deep breath. How could he help her understand his feelings for her? "Amanda, love—the kind of love God wants us to have—doesn't change because of a messy room. Do you believe me?"

Amanda nodded. "Kathy loves me that way."

"Did I hear my name?" Kathy walked up, a pizza in one hand and a pitcher of root beer in the other. She grinned as she set both in the center of the table, next to three plastic cups and plates. "Didn't either of you talkers hear the order come up?"

Ben and Amanda shared a conspiratorial glance, and then the threesome dug into the food. Amanda chattered about different pizzas and knock-knock jokes and classroom pets, while Ben and Kathy exchanged occasional smiles. When the girl was finished eating, she pointed toward the video games and gasped. "Hey, I can't believe it. Kristen's here! She must be on lunch break, too." Amanda flashed a questioning look at Kathy. "Please? Can I go play with her? Just for a few minutes?"

"Well—" Kathy looked at the child's plate—"I guess so. But hurry. You have to get back to school soon."

When Amanda was out of earshot, Ben leaned back in the booth and shook his head. "She looks exactly like her mother." He watched the child talking animatedly with her friend across the dining hall. "I mean, exactly. Nearly took my breath away."

Kathy folded her hands neatly on the tabletop and studied him. "She likes you."

"Yeah." He met Kathy's gaze again. "The feeling's mutual. She's…after all she's been through, she's something else."

"I know." The social worker's eyes fell for a moment, then found Ben's again. "Believe me."

Ben angled his head. "She loves you very much."

Kathy looked away and took a sip of her drink.

Something had bothered Ben since he first recognized the attachment Kathy had for Amanda and he figured it was time to ask. "How come you never…"

"How come I didn't adopt her a long time ago?" Kathy's smile didn't reach her eyes. "We have seven children living with us—five by birth, two by adoption. I've tried to take Amanda in as a foster child, but every time I petition for her, the court says I'm at my limit. No more children unless we get a bigger house. My husband is in construction, so money isn't always regular. Moving is out of the question. Anytime Amanda is with us is strictly temporary according to court records until a more suitable arrangement can be made."

The irony of Amanda's predicament hit him hard. The only reason he and Maggie had a chance to make the girl their own was because the state was unwilling to let Kathy Garrett have her—even after Kathy had invested so much in her. "I'd like to bring Amanda home, short term, anyway. For the weekend, say. That way she wouldn't miss any school."

Kathy looked at him thoughtfully. "Will you tell her? About her mother, I mean?"

"I'd like to. In fact, I'd like to introduce them this weekend, if everything works out." His voice softened. "It's a long shot, I'm afraid."

"I know it's none of my business, Mr. Stovall, but what happened?"

"With Maggie?" Ben braced his arms on the bench beside him and took a deep breath. It was such a hard story, especially when he had only learned the details so recently himself. "There's a lot to it. Basically, back before we were married, we were apart for a year or so, and she got pregnant. By the time we got back together, she'd already given Amanda up. She told me she was a virgin, and until a month ago I didn't know anything about the baby."

"How'd you find out?" Kathy asked.

"When Maggie checked herself into the hospital she left me a note saying we were finished, that she wanted a divorce. She…they were worried she might be suicidal." He clenched his teeth, not sure if he was saying too much. Her eyes caught his and the compassion there encouraged him to continue. "She told me I never really knew her. Since then she's refused my letters, phone calls. Everything."

Kathy's eyebrows lowered in concern. "A psychiatric hospital?"

Ben sighed. "Doesn't sound very Christian, does it?"

He caught a momentary flash of concern in her eyes. When she spoke, her tone was firm. "Do you know how many Christians suffer from depression, Mr.…Ben?

We've all convinced ourselves that believers aren't supposed to wrestle with darkness or hard times. And nothing—absolutely nothing—could be further from the truth."

Ben leaned back, frowning. *Is it true, God? Are there other women like Maggie? Women in the church?* "No one ever knew…she didn't…she always seemed so happy."

The expression on Kathy's face softened. "They all do, especially when they know the rejection they'd face otherwise." She stirred the straw in her soft drink. "You'd be surprised how many people wear masks to church."

What was she saying? "So you mean it's a good thing, this hospital stay?"

Kathy smiled. "I know it's hard to understand, but many times depression comes from a chemical imbalance. Stress, other factors in life become too hard to handle and the body's chemistry is thrown off. When that happens, nothing but medication will set things right again. Even if it's only temporary."

Medication? Ben hadn't thought of that—his Maggie being on drugs to get through life. "It seems so…I don't know, worldly, I guess. Shouldn't prayer be enough?"

Kathy's shoulders lifted in a gentle shrug. "Lots of people would say the medicine available today is an *answer* to prayer." She paused. "It seems your Maggie is where she needs to be. The bigger question is whether she'll want to see Amanda."

Ben made a fist and gripped it with his other hand. Before all this happened he would have known the answer—of *course* Maggie would want her daughter. But now…now he had no idea what might be going on in his wife's mind, what her reaction to Amanda would be. "You're right." He stared across the room at Amanda and her friend. "That's why I'm afraid of telling her anything yet."

He sighed. The question had haunted him since the moment he laid eyes on the child. Now that he'd found her, there was something deep within him that couldn't imagine ever letting her go. "I haven't worked through all the details and, well, I know Amanda needs a mother figure." His feelings for Amanda were greater than he'd thought possible. And if Maggie wasn't interested…

Does it matter, God…what Maggie decides about this? Aren't children sometimes raised by single fathers?

He searched for the right words. "What I'm trying to say is, I want to give her a home, Ms. Garrett. No matter what Maggie decides."

Kathy studied him and an understanding smile worked its way across her face. "I hoped you might feel that way." Kathy glanced at her watch. "We can talk about it later. Let's get Amanda back to school, then head back to the office so we can file the right paperwork."

He hesitated. "I've been a foster parent but…I can't believe it's this easy to take custody of a child in the foster system." The idea worried Ben. What if he'd been the type of foster parent Amanda had had before?

"The moment a licensed foster parent breaks the law or is arrested, that type of thing, a red flag shows up in the computer and the license is automatically revoked. But…" Her shoulders settled forward a bit, as though the weight of the matter were almost more than she could bear. "Obviously it's not a foolproof system."

She looked at him intently. "I've prayed about you, Mr. Stovall. I know you're a licensed foster parent in the state of Ohio; and I believe you're married to Amanda's birth mother. I also believe you know the same Lord I do. Because of that, I'm ready, if you are, to arrange a short-term agreement. I trust God to make the other details fall into place later." She smiled, even as her eyes filled with fresh tears. "Much as I'll miss her, you should know one thing, Mr. Stovall."

"What's that?"

"I'll be praying that your wife will get the help she needs…so she can see the chance God's giving her. And that one day very soon—" Kathy's eyes sparkled with hope—"the three of you will be a family."

The paperwork was easier than Ben was used to. Short-term care—especially for a foster parent already licensed by the state—was by nature designed to be an expeditious process, so that the child could be transported as soon as possible into the foster home. In this case, he and Kathy had talked to Amanda before taking her back to class. They'd agreed Amanda would go with him after school tomorrow. She could miss Friday and spend a three-day weekend with him.

Now it was just after two o'clock, and Ben lay on his bed, sorting through the feelings assaulting him. Sometime tomorrow he and Amanda would drive the five hours back to Cleveland. Then, on Friday morning he would call and—by the grace of God—get a report on Maggie. As long as she was making progress and nearing the end of her treatment, he would do what some might consider the craziest thing of all: He would take Amanda to Orchards Hospital, where he wouldn't leave unless Maggie refused not just him, but her daughter as well.

How should I feel about Maggie, God? Part of me still can't believe it, can't imagine that she lied to me all those years, that she hid something as serious as this. But part of me feels guilty, Lord.

For the life of him, Ben couldn't understand why. What had he done to drive Maggie into John McFadden's arms? How had he pressured her to give up her daughter and lie to him all these years?

Love covers a multitude of sins, My son.

Ben flipped onto his stomach and breathed in the sterile scent of hotel bedding. "What's that mean? Tell me, God. Please." He voiced the request through clenched teeth.

Nothing came to him, and he closed his eyes. But as the minutes passed he drifted back in time through a series of memories, times that until then, he had completely forgotten.

The first one took shape…he and Maggie were fishing on the edge of a dock along a small lake, hidden away from the main road. It was seven, maybe eight years ago. They heard something and turned to see a teenage couple walking hand in hand, heading into the woods. The girl looked nervous; she checked over her shoulder more than once. The boy had a thick blanket under his arm, and his steps were sure and steady.

"Looks like trouble," Maggie had whispered.

He could see the concern on her face as clearly as he had seen it that day.

Ben snorted softly. "She doesn't look too worried."

Maggie's eyes had widened, her eyebrows set in frustration. "What's that supposed to mean?"

Ben remembered being taken aback. "It means whatever happens out there in the woods today, she asked for it."

He could still see the indignation that had flashed in Maggie's eyes. "That girl isn't asking for anything."

"Look, Maggie, when a girl sneaks off into the woods with a guy and a blanket, she's asking for it." He placed an arm around her and smoothed his thumb over her troubled brow. "Look at you and me. We didn't get in trouble because we held ourselves to a higher standard, a godly standard. I'm not saying it's easy to stay pure, Maggie. But we did it, didn't we?"

In the memory, Maggie's response was something Ben hadn't recognized before: A shadow crossed her face and she let her gaze fall to the water without answering him. Ask her what's bothering her! He screamed silently at the image of himself in the memory, but it did no good. Years had passed since then, and the moment was obviously gone. Instead there was only the same verse that had plagued him too often.

Love covers a multitude of sins...love covers a multitude of...

Another image took shape. He and Maggie were sitting across from each other in a restaurant just after church one Sunday a handful of years earlier. It was a day when one of the elders had shared news of his fifteen-year-old daughter's unplanned pregnancy.

"Maybe I'll give her a call," Maggie had said. She was staring out the window.

"I guess, if you want to." Ben kept his eyes trained on the menu, but in the memory he could see the hurt expression on Maggie's face.

"What's that supposed to mean?"

Ben looked up. "Nothing against you, Maggie. But she made her choice when she slept with the guy. I mean, don't get me wrong. I feel badly for her, but she never should have let herself get in that situation."

Like with the previous memory, Ben saw the veil of shame cover Maggie's face. But at the time he'd been too involved in whether to order grilled swordfish or chicken alfredo. He hadn't really thought much about her silence, her expression.

Maggie, I'm so sorry, honey. The signs were all there. How could I have been so blind? The questions tore at him, making him wish for a way back in time so he could look deep into her soul and gently pull the truth from her, talk with her so he wouldn't have to wait until now to understand her pain.

Love covers a multitude of sins...love covers a multitude...

Memory after memory filled his mind. Each time the conversation was about immorality or fleshly weakness. And each time, as Maggie expressed compassion, Ben had silenced her with righteous indignation. Finally at the end of the last conversation Maggie had tears streaming down her face—and again Ben had missed the opportunity to connect with her.

Love covers a multitude of sins.

Ben lay in bed wrestling with himself and with the Scripture that refused to let him sleep. He rolled onto one side, then flipped onto the other until finally he lay on his back, his heart pounding, his eyes wide open. "I might have been kinder back then, God…but I loved her. This isn't about me; it's about Maggie. It's her fault she…"

A new image took shape in his mind. The image of a man, nailed to a cross that was anchored on a hill and surrounded by a throng of people. But rather than weep for the crucified man, the people mocked and jeered and held their heads high. "You brought it on Yourself! You asked for it!" Suddenly Ben heard himself gasp out loud. Among the faces in the crowd, he had spotted his own. Then at the same moment, he caught the eyes of the one on the cross. Jesus' eyes, calm and merciful and full of lovingkindness.

Forgive them, for they know not what they do.

Jesus' words washed over him, and he blinked back the image. "Oh, God, what have I done?" Tears gave way to gut-wrenching sobs that tore at his heart and threatened to consume him. "What have I *done?*"

He had asked for a sign, hadn't he? Well, the Lord Himself had given one. He could deny the truth no longer. The same way the crowd had mocked Jesus, Ben had mocked those around him who were in pain. By believing himself somehow superior or invincible to the destructive reality of sin and temptation, he had missed dozens of opportunities to get to know Maggie, to really love her.

Suddenly Ben knew with certainty that had he seen her back then the way he'd seen her tonight, in his memories, he would have pulled her close and asked her what was wrong. Had he seen her that way even a few years ago…a few *weeks* ago, maybe they could have unraveled the ball of lies that had become their life and prevented Maggie's breakdown.

Maybe Amanda would never have been forced into a foster home where people hurt her.

And maybe the Lord wouldn't have had to show Ben's face among the crowd of people mocking Jesus.

"Forgive me, God. Please, forgive me." Ben wept, and as tear after tear coursed down his face, his heart grew softer than it had been in years. A hundred times over he apologized to Jesus, begging Him to prepare Maggie's heart for the moment when he could finally tell her how sorry he was. When he was finished, he felt drained of every wrong emotion he'd ever experienced. What's more, he no longer even considered Maggie's role in all they'd been through. He forgave her completely and wanted only for her to be able to say the same about him.

"Let her love me again, Lord. Make her believe me." Ben did love Maggie. He knew that now more than ever, more than at any point since their first meeting on that long-ago summer's night. Maggie was the only woman he would ever love, and Ben wanted nothing more than to take her in his arms and soothe away the years of hurt and lies and anger. The years when she must have thought daily about her child, yet was unable to share those feelings with him because of her desire to meet his standards.

And now where were they?

The reality of their situation hit him harder than ever before. Maggie wanted a divorce. Having kept her feelings locked away for so long, she was no longer willing even to consider working things out with him. The thought terrified him until he realized something else. He loved Maggie's child. If Maggie refused to come home, if she no longer wanted anything to do with her daughter, he would continue to pursue Amanda's adoption.

"I love that little girl, God," he whispered into the still, night air. "Like she was my own flesh and blood."

As his tears eased, he begged God to work a miracle in the situation...pleaded that somehow, when this nightmare was over, the three of them could be something none of them had ever been before.

A family.

30

The time had finally come.

Now that it was here, Maggie noticed something that made her heart soar. It happened while she sat stiffly in a padded folding chair with the members of the group forming a protective circle around her. There, in the midst of them, she realized the darkness was gone.

She closed her eyes and they filled with tears of gratitude.

"Most of you know why we're here." Dr. Baker stood in the center of the circle, her hand on Maggie's shoulder. Maggie felt the presence of the Holy Spirit as tangibly as if God Himself were standing there beside her. "Maggie has had a significant change of heart, and this afternoon she asked if we could meet here and pray for her." Dr. Baker turned to Maggie. "Do you want to say anything to the group?"

She nodded and wiped the tears from her face with the back of her hand. "I want to thank you for…for being honest with me." She sniffed once and then took a tissue from Sarah, who knelt at her side. "Sarah and Betty and…" Maggie looked at Howard and smiled, "and you, Howard, for being bold enough to be honest with me even when you knew it might make me too mad to ever come back."

Her watery eyes made their way around the group until she had connected with each of them. "You've taught me that depression isn't something strange or unusual, that people who love God very much can suffer in the pit of darkness and still be believers."

There were gentle smiles from the group members; Sarah wiped at the tears that were now running down her face. Maggie knew she might not have another chance to say all that was on her heart, so she continued. "I used to think believers couldn't be depressed. Or shouldn't be. If a person trusted God and prayed and read the Bible and really had faith, then there was no room for things like depression, right? Christians who were depressed must have something wrong with them, or they didn't trust God enough. That sort of thing."

Maggie couldn't stop the small, sad laugh that escaped her. "Then I found *myself* fighting depression…and losing. So I was sure there was something wrong with me, that I just needed to trust more." She firmed her shoulders. "But I know now that was all wrong. The problem is something else entirely. Too many of us have been afraid to be honest, afraid that by being honest, our spouse or daughter or sister wouldn't love us. God wouldn't love us. We haven't felt able to walk and live and love in the abundant sunshine of God's honesty and grace. I know *I* didn't feel able…until now."

Dr. Baker squeezed Maggie's shoulder, encouraging her. "So, I wanted to ask you to come here, to pray for me. Pray I'll find a way to be honest with the people who matter in my life." Her throat tightened with emotion, and she looked down at her hands. "It'll take a miracle to save my marriage…"

She looked up, met the eyes watching her again, and went on in a whisper. "But then, God's done far greater things. I only have to look at the cross to remember that." She hesitated as a fresh wave of tears slid down her face. "I know you'll be okay when you leave here. We all will be so long as we remember how very big our God is, and how unconditional His love is. Even if we never see each other after this, I know we'll meet again. Because I believe God will see us through. Thank you, each of you."

Maggie's words faded into silence, but she didn't mind. It was true…she would survive. God had brought her, as He'd brought so many others, out of the darkness into the sunlight of His grace and joy.

Before they started to pray, Maggie remembered something else. "You know some of the specifics of my situation, but I need you to pray for something else."

"Whatever it is, just tell us, Maggie." Sarah handed her another tissue and waited expectantly. "We'll pray daily, you know we will."

Maggie nodded. "Somewhere out there, outside the safe walls of Orchards, I have a daughter I've never met. She's probably doing fine, living with her adoptive family. But when I'm finished here, if I feel it's really what God wants, I'll do whatever I can to find her. I'm not sure I can have peace about that part of my life until I know she's okay."

Then the group of downtrodden, desperate people, many of whom had only recently escaped the throes of desperation and found hope again, formed a chorus of voices and lifted Maggie and her needs straight to the hallways of heaven.

31

At 2:55 that afternoon, Kathy Garrett was working as diligently as possible on the stack of files that had gone unattended that day. She knew with everything in her that the decision to let Amanda go with Ben Stovall for the long weekend was a good one. And, true to her word, she prayed that he would be successful in meeting with his wife and introducing her for the first time to her daughter.

Kathy had no doubt that Amanda had made a connection with Mr. Stovall at their lunch. The child had an uncanny ability to recognize a genuine person, and from everything Amanda had said, she was hopeful things would work out with the Stovalls.

Amanda was good that way, not given to long bouts of sadness when she had to leave the Garrett family. It had happened often, and she understood.

But this time—if things worked out—Amanda's absence would be for more than a few days…and the idea of saying good-bye to the child caused Kathy's mind to wander, making it nearly impossible to concentrate on the files in front of her.

Kathy took a sip of lukewarm coffee and reached for the top folder on the stack. As she did, the phone rang.

She sighed. *It never stops, does it?* "Hello?"

"Ms. Garrett?"

Kathy didn't recognize the voice. "Yes, this is she." Something in the man's firm tone sent an unexplainable ripple of alarm through Kathy's veins.

"This is Judge Hutchison. I'm worried about one of your charges, Amanda Joy Brownell. Earlier today I heard an emergency session for a man by the name of John McFadden. He appeared with documentation proving he was Amanda's biological father. Before he got much—"

Kathy's heart skipped a beat. Amanda's biological father? What was the judge talking about? "Wait a minute…why didn't you call me?"

"It never got that far. I doubted the man from the beginning—something about his eyes or his look…I couldn't put my finger on it. Anyway, I went into my chambers and ran a rap on him." The judge hesitated. "DNA matches. He's the girl's father, all right. But he's a bad man, Ms. Garrett. I've left you a few messages since then."

Kathy hadn't had time to check her answering machine since lunch. Her mind raced in a dozen directions. "What'd you tell him?"

"That's just it. He left the courtroom before I could make my decision."

Kathy's heart rate doubled. "You aren't worried, are you?"

"Actually, I am. He wanted custody of Amanda immediately. He knew she was a ward of the court and that she was between foster homes. He hadn't found out about her until recently, but he wanted full custody."

A pit formed in Kathy's stomach. What could this mean? What could the man possibly want with Amanda? "So, where is he now?"

"He could be anywhere, I guess. But if he wants the child..."

"What do you mean?" Panic rose and Kathy's hands began to tremble. Who was this John McFadden and why was he here in town now? Was he somehow connected with Ben Stovall? Kathy glanced at her watch. Three P.M. Amanda would be getting out of school in ten minutes.

"It took a little while to run the check on him. My guess is he panicked and ran before I could call the police."

Kathy worked her fingers through her hair and tried to calm her pounding heart. "What's his rap sheet say?" She closed her eyes, not wanting to hear the judge's answer.

"Officers are investigating him for drug trafficking, and he's currently facing charges on attempted murder of a man in Cleveland. A Ben Stovall."

The room began to spin, and Kathy fought to maintain her balance. "Ben...Stovall?"

Judge Hutchison hesitated. "Stovall pressed charges. The report says the beating nearly killed him."

"Oh no!" Kathy forced herself to concentrate. "This can't be happening. Judge, listen, thanks for the information. I've got to go meet Amanda at the bus."

"If you see anything out of the ordinary, I want you to call the police immediately. I already notified them that McFadden's in town. I hate to say it, Ms. Garrett, but my instincts tell me the guy could be dangerous."

Seconds after hanging up, Kathy called the motel where Ben Stovall was staying. When he answered, she didn't mince words. "I don't have much time here, Ben. There's a man in town by the name of John McFadden. He came before the judge today and wanted immediate custody of Amanda. What do you know about him?"

"He *what?*"

"I'm serious. We don't have much time. What do you know?"

"The guy's dangerous. He's Amanda's father, but there's no good reason why he'd be here unless it's somehow about me."

"You remember where I live?"

"Sure, I'm a mile away."

"Amanda's bus stop is a block up the street. Meet me there." Kathy hung up and raced out of her office, praying desperately that she had nothing to worry about.

And if she did, that she would reach the bus stop in time.

32

John McFadden hunkered down in the front seat of his car and watched as the weathered, yellow school bus screeched to a stop.

Deciding which child was his would be the trickiest part. Of course, it would get trickier when police got wind the kid was missing. By then, though, he would have made contact with Stovall and presented his demands. If things went right, he could be done with the kid in an hour or so.

But then, things hadn't gone great so far.

He fingered his gun and tapped his thumb on the steering wheel. Maybe this wasn't the best plan, after all. If the police arrested him, he'd have to prove the girl was his daughter. They couldn't arrest him for kidnapping his own kid, could they? A gnawing pain ate at the pit of his stomach, and he tried not to think about it.

The bus pulled away, leaving two boys and a girl, who immediately began walking in different directions. John squinted through his sunglasses. *So that's her.* He stared at the girl, surprised to feel a twinge of regret. What if he'd stayed with Maggie, worked things out? What would his life be like today if they'd moved in together and raised the kid? Whatever it would have been like, it probably wouldn't involve him running from the police.

You're weak, McFadden! Forget the brat! This was no time to be thinking fatherly thoughts. The girl was moving quickly along the shaded, residential street, and he had to get her. He looked around—no signs of cars coming in any direction. It was now or never. He started the engine and moved the car slowly toward the girl. "Let's get it done with…"

As his car pulled up alongside the kid, she glanced at him over her shoulder and picked up her pace. John was struck by how pretty she was. Just like Maggie had been that summer…

He hit the automatic button and rolled down the passenger window. "Hi, Amanda." She started, but kept walking, holding her books more tightly to her body. Great. She probably knew about not talking to strangers. He gave the car just enough gas to keep even with her. "I'm a friend of Ben Stovall's. He asked me to meet you at the bus stop and drive you to the park."

Hurry, kid. It was only a matter of minutes before she reached that social worker's house or a car drove up and thought something suspicious was happening. "Ben and Kathy Garrett are going to meet you there. At the park."

The girl stopped and turned to face him. Fear showed clearly in her eyes, and the feeling in his gut intensified. She bit her lip. "Kathy sent you?"

Thatta girl. Come on, get in the car. "She wanted you to come with me." He'd have to thank Mike and Alfie later for giving him the right details.

Amanda moved closer to the car. "I'm not supposed to go with strangers."

That was it; he couldn't wait another moment. He drove up a few feet ahead of her, slammed on the brakes, and pushed open the passenger door. Before she could get past him, he pointed the gun at her. "Don't make me shoot you, Amanda." His friendly tone was gone. "Get in the car. Now!"

She looked ready to run, so John pulled out his final card. "You leave now, and I'll kill Kathy Garrett. I know where she lives *and* when she gets home." Amanda froze, her eyes wide. "I'll do it, Amanda. Now get in the car."

The girl clenched her jaw and hesitated only a moment before walking briskly toward the car and climbing inside. She barely had the door shut when he jerked the vehicle away from the curb and sped out of the neighborhood.

He had expected her to cry or scream or carry on. Instead she sat there, staring out the windshield. Then she broke the silence by humming something. It was the same tune over and over and over again.

"Don't you wanna know where I'm takin' you, Amanda?" The girl kept her eyes straight ahead.

"How do you know Mr. Stovall?"

Her voice was a strange combination of jaded maturity and tender innocence. Again he wondered why he was doing this. To blackmail Stovall into dropping the charges against him? It didn't even make sense anymore. Not when he was driving his own daughter at gunpoint back to his hotel. What if he really did want to have custody rights at some point? She was his kid, after all.

Maybe so, he mocked himself, *but no judge in his right mind would grant you a stinkin' thing after this. Not even visitation.*

The girl's question about Stovall hung in the air. Stovall. This was all *his* fault. "Well, Amanda, your old daddy knows a lot of things."

At that she stopped humming and spun around, eyes wide, mouth open. "You're not my daddy."

He grinned at her. Sassy little thing…just like he'd been as a kid. "Well, actually, I *am* your daddy. No time like the present to get acquainted, eh?"

She turned to stare out the windshield, and the dratted humming started up again.

Fine.

If she wasn't interested in getting to know him, forget her. He ran his finger over the gun in his hand. She wasn't his daughter. She was just a kid with DNA that matched his. And if she pulled anything funny or caused too much trouble, he'd waste her and hide her body. He wouldn't have any trouble getting away with it. After all, she was just a lonely Social Services brat; the system wouldn't even miss her.

The humming was getting on his nerves. "Would you shut up, already! I hate that song."

"'Jesus Loves Me'?" There was no fear, no anger in her soft voice. It was weird. Like she was in some kind of safe place, all by herself. She started humming again.

"Listen, kid, you're with me now. Jesus ain't exactly in the picture."

She just smiled. "Jesus loves me and whoever you are, He loves you, too."

Of all the—

"You're crazy, kid. I could shoot you right now, and no one would know the difference. And all you can do is sit there humming some stupid song about Jesus?"

She turned and leveled her gaze at him. "That's not all I'm doing."

Why wasn't she scared? The uncanny calm in her eyes was enough to make his skin crawl. If he hadn't regretted his decision to take her before, he sure did now. Of course, she *was* his daughter—so it made sense that she was tough even in the face of a gun. He turned onto a busier street. "Okay, smart mouth, what else are you doing besides staring out the window humming some stupid song about Jesus and getting on my nerves?"

She bit her lip and studied him. "I'm praying for you."

Ben had a sick feeling in his stomach.

He and Kathy arrived at Amanda's bus stop at almost exactly the same moment, and there was no sign of Amanda. Ever since receiving the call from Kathy he'd been in a panic, but now he was hit with genuine terror.

He pulled his car up alongside Kathy's and motioned for her to roll her window down. "Where *is* she?"

"The bus should have come by now." Kathy's face was ashen, and though Ben had only met her that week, he was sure she was feeling the same jolts of raw fear he was.

"So she's at your house, right? Wouldn't that make sense?"

Kathy nodded, and the stiff way she held her mouth made Ben think she couldn't talk if she'd wanted to.

Ben looked around and spotted an older woman across the street. She was hanging a Thanksgiving wreath on her front door, then she turned and stared at them. Ben motioned to Kathy to follow him as he jumped from his car. "Excuse me, has the school bus come already?"

The woman walked the few steps to meet them and her face knit into a mass of wrinkled concern as she considered the question. "A while ago."

Kathy smiled politely, but Ben noticed her hands were trembling at her sides. "I'm Kathy Garrett. I live down the street; I don't think we've met."

"Polly. Polly Russell. Me and Grandpa been living here thirty years now. Watch the school bus come by same time every day."

Ben jumped in. "Mrs. Russell, there's a little blond girl that gets off at this stop…did you see her today?"

Again concern filled the older woman's eyes. "I always notice the girl. Reminds me of my own sweet babies; same hair, eyes, and coloring. That kind of thing."

Kathy shifted anxiously, speaking in quick, choppy sentences. "The girl lives with me and my family. She's waiting for a foster home. Did you see her? Maybe talking to someone when she got off the bus?"

"Matter of fact, I did. A man pulled up in a big ol' car and talked to her while she was walking. After a minute or so, she climbed in with him." The woman looked from Ben to Kathy and back to Ben. "I figured he was her daddy, since she went so willingly."

"Thanks…thank you, Mrs…" Kathy's face was white, and Ben thought she might pass out.

"The child's okay, isn't she?" Alarm filled the woman's features at the thought that something may have happened to the little blond girl. Ben knew how she felt.

"It's fine. We'll take care of it. Thanks." He nodded at the woman and led Kathy by the arm back to his car. "Pray. Start and don't stop."

"That's all I've been doing." Kathy's voice was shaky.

Father, how can this be happening? I've just found Amanda, Maggie's very own daughter, and now she's been kidnapped by…by… He remembered McFadden's blows as he lay on the pavement, the merciless kicks to the—

No. Ben couldn't bring himself to think of Amanda with that man. It was too horrible to imagine. She'd already been through so much…

Dear God, let her be home by now. Protect her. Please!

He helped Kathy into his car and—leaving her car parked at the bus stop—they sped down the street to the Garrett home.

"What if…?" Kathy's question hung in the air as he parked the car.

"Don't! That woman might be wrong. Maybe Amanda's already here." He followed Kathy as she raced inside, but she stood frozen in the entry and hugged herself tightly. "Hey, kids, I'm home." Each word was an effort. "Is…is Amanda here?"

"Not yet, Mom. How was your day?" It was the voice of a teenager from a room across the house.

Ben forced himself to breathe as the hurried exchange went on. *No, God. No! Let her be okay. Please…*

Amanda wasn't there. Kathy sat down on the sofa and leaned over her knees, rocking slightly. "He took her. McFadden took her. I feel it in my heart." A sob caught in her throat and she pointed to the phone. "Hurry, please. You make the call."

Without hesitating another moment, Ben picked up the phone and dialed 911. The dispatcher barely got two words out before he blurted, "My daughter's been kidnapped."

Officers Aaron Hisel and Buddy Reed deeply enjoyed their work as Cincinnati police officers. As partners they had seen each other through ten years of arrests and criminal investigations—not to mention the births of their combined seven children. They were family men, dedicated to keeping the streets safe.

It was just before four o'clock, when the two would normally have been making their way back to the office and checking out for the day. But they were working on a case they were close to breaking, a case that put them squarely in the heart of Woodland, a suburb just east of the city.

They had spent much of the day interviewing witnesses and were making more progress than they'd hoped when the call came in. An APB to be on the lookout for a white male suspect named John McFadden, driving a gold Acura. McFadden was already facing charges of assault and attempted murder and now he was running from the law.

Hisel glanced at Reed. "Didn't we get that call a few hours ago?"

Reed nodded as he turned the wheel. "I thought so, too. Check with dispatch, will you?"

Hisel picked up the radio and called headquarters. "This McFadden APB, is that an old call? We got word about him earlier. Something about him leaving the courthouse in the middle of a meeting with Judge Hutch. Hutch ran the rap and found an attempted murder charge. Are we talking about the same call?"

The radio crackled as dispatch answered. "Negative. You must have missed the first part of the call."

"What else do you have on him?" Hisel grabbed a pen and a pad of paper from where it was clipped on the dashboard.

"He just kidnapped a seven-year-old girl. She's got long blond hair, blue eyes. Took her from her bus stop approximately thirty minutes ago. There's reason to believe he's armed and dangerous." The dispatch provided the location of the bus stop and repeated the license plate number of the Acura McFadden was driving.

Hisel's stomach clenched and he exchanged a glance with Reed just as his partner flipped the squad car around and headed toward the address.

"Let's go get him." Hisel thought of his own children, safe at home with their mother. Then he thought of all the unspeakable things a child might suffer in the course of a kidnapping.

He and Reed had discussed it a hundred times over the years and each time their consensus was the same. High on the list of crimes that were the worst, most atrocious, horrific actions a person could commit were those that caused the blood of both officers to boil.

Crimes against children.

33

The mean man was driving very fast. Deep inside it made Amanda nervous, but she wouldn't let him see that.

She wondered where he was taking her. Would he really kill her when they got there? *Jesus, help me be safe, please.*

She knew God would answer. After all, He'd saved her from the boys and their baling twine; He'd rescued her from Mrs. Graystone. No matter what happened to her, God always brought her through okay, and Amanda knew there was a reason. The Lord had a forever home for her and somehow He would find a way to get her there.

She glanced at the man. His face was all sweaty. Shivers ran down her arms and she was glad he wasn't her father. What a terrible lie. She turned to stare straight ahead. *Help that man know about You, God. He needs to change and love You more.*

The few times the man had talked to her, he'd been grouchy and scary, but Amanda wasn't frightened. God wouldn't let him hurt her.

"Whatcha looking at, brat?" The man's face twisted up in an angry look.

"I'm p-p-praying for you."

"Praying? What're you doing *that* for?" The man's voice was growly and hard.

"It's what I always d-d-do when someone's mean."

She could hear Mrs. Brownell's kind, caring voice: "That's a good girl, Amanda. You pray for them. And make sure to tell them you're praying, just so they know."

Most of the time when she told someone mean she was praying, he stopped being mean and walked away. Mrs. Brownell had said being nice and praying for someone made it hard for them to be mean anymore. Something about putting coals on their heads.

Amanda had never noticed coals on the heads of the mean kids at school. And they hadn't shown up on the boys' heads in the barn, either, or on Mrs. Graystone's head. She glanced again at the man beside her. There were no coals on his head, either. Maybe the coals thing meant something else. Like about how hearing something nice can make you hurt all over. Especially if all you've been is mean.

Praying was the right thing to do, though, because it was the only thing that absolutely worked every time. God wouldn't let her down. He would see that she stayed safe and found a way back to Kathy Garrett and that nice Mr. Stovall. Maybe he would be her forever dad and take her to live in an always, ever-after family.

Dear God, help the police find us so I can go home with Mr. Stovall. Please let them catch this mean man and take him to jail.

The car turned suddenly, and Amanda struggled to keep her balance.

"I prayed that the police would c-c-catch you."

The man squinted his eyes at her. "If they catch us, I'll tell them you're my kid." He laughed at her, and his loud voice hurt her ears. "Or maybe I'll just shoot you and them, too. You don't want that do you?"

"I'll k-k-keep praying for you. Did you know that Jesus loves you, mister?"

A strange, sad look came across the man's face…maybe he was feeling the burning coals after all. *Make him change, Lord, please.*

She didn't know where they were driving. Where was he taking her? She sank back in the seat. Maybe he really would shoot her. Maybe that was God's plan for her. She considered that and realized she was not afraid. If he killed her, she'd be with Jesus right away. And then she'd have the best forever home of all.

The only sad part was that if she went to be with Jesus, she'd never find her real mom, never hug her or touch her face or ask her if she'd been looking all her life for the little girl she gave up.

And Amanda still wanted to do all that. Very, very much.

Hisel and Reed were cruising Broadway, checking side streets and scanning the horizon for any hint of a gold Acura. Ten minutes had passed since the APB went out, and both men were feeling a sense of urgency. Statistically, the odds of finding her alive decreased with each passing minute.

"I'm worried about her." Hisel clenched his jaw and kept searching the road.

His partner cocked his head to the left and pressed his foot down on the gas pedal. "Wait! I think I see him."

Almost two city blocks ahead of them was a gold car! Within seconds, Reed maneuvered their police car directly behind it. "Gold Acura, all right. Run the plates."

Hope surged through Hisel as he grabbed the radio and checked the number with the one scribbled on his notepad. "It matches!"

"Notify dispatch; request multiple backup units." Reed kept his eyes trained straight ahead. "I'm afraid the guy's going to take off if he sees us."

Hisel picked up the radio and made the request. "I can't believe he hasn't noticed us yet." The man was driving the speed limit and seemed almost oblivious to his surroundings.

"Looks like he's talking to the little girl."

"Come on, let's get this thing over with. Hit the siren."

Reed shook his head. "No. Not yet. I'd rather have backup, just in case. We'll follow him until he sees us or until other units show up. I don't want him panicking and hurting the child. A few more squad cars and he'll know he doesn't have a chance. Just stay on the radio and let dispatch know which way we're headed."

The strange feeling that everything was falling apart had taken root the moment John laid eyes on the child. And now the feeling was so strong it was making his chest hurt. His face was cool and clammy and his left arm ached.

Probably a heart attack.

He kept driving. Something about the girl's quiet calm, the serenity in her eyes, and the way she insisted on talking about Jesus was making him crazy.

Look at me. I'm a loser! After this I'll spend most of my life in jail. I must have been nuts to take the kid and think it could make things better. He stroked his chin. Now what do I do? Kill her? Leave her in an alley somewhere? Go back to the warehouse and pick up business where I left off?

The pain in his arm intensified. None of it made sense anymore. No wonder the kid doesn't want me as her father. Look at me. Drug dealer, wanted by the police. Yes, sir, a real Mr. Good Guy.

He thought about his home and the three used sports cars parked in his garage and he felt...dirty. Go figure! Almost like someone had walked up and plastered him with layer after layer of pure crud. His language, his friendships, his business dealings—everything he was had been bought with dirty money.

And now it had come to this.

He and his very own daughter were outrunning police so that he could blackmail an attorney into dropping charges against him. The whole situation was so rotten it stunk. And it was all for nothing. John had the unnerving feeling that the foundation of his reputation and his drug empire were crumbling as quickly as it had taken Amanda to say, "I'm praying for you."

He tapped the steering wheel and glanced in his rear and side mirrors. *No cops; not yet.* If he heard another word about prayer or God or Jesus loving him, he would explode! It was stupid. No God would ever love him now. He'd made his choice long ago, sealed his fate. All he could do was find ways to make the path he'd chosen stretch out as long as possible, because one day...

John shut the thoughts out of his mind. Death wasn't something he had to think about for decades, so why was it on his mind now? He shifted positions to ease the discomfort in his chest. If only he could forget his kid's innocent eyes or her words about Jesus...

Let her go...turn to Me and let her go.

The voice was almost audible, and John spun his head around and checked the backseat. No one. He wiped the sweat from his forehead. His heart pounded through the wall of his chest. *I'm losing it. Five days off work, and already I'm going crazy. That's all this is. Stress. Too much going on back at the warehouse for me to be driving around Cincinnati with some wise-mouth brat.*

Let the child go...

He gripped the steering wheel tightly to prevent his hands from shaking. It wasn't a real voice, not one that sounded through the car. It was more like a silent echo in his mind, his soul—

The girl's prayers! Maybe this was some kind of answer to Amanda's prayers. The thought sent chills down John's arms, and suddenly the pain in his heart eased. He had to let her go; it was that simple. Otherwise that God of hers would make his heart explode inside him, and he'd be left with nothing. No estate, no cars, no dirty money...

No life.

"You still praying?" He heard the fear in his voice as he let the gun drop to the floor of the car.

Amanda turned to him and nodded. "Yes, very hard."

There was a gas station up ahead, and John jerked the wheel of his car, turned into the lot and pulled to an abrupt stop. He stared straight ahead. "Get outta here, kid. Go on, get!" But just as Amanda was opening her car door, a siren sounded behind them, and in his rearview mirror John saw the flashing lights of a police car.

Kathy's confession came as soon as Ben Stovall hung up the phone after calling the police: She had a terrible feeling in her gut that she was about to lose Amanda. The woman's tears came slowly at first, and then as the minutes passed they came in silent torrents. Ben positioned himself beside her as if by doing so he could stop her body from shaking.

"It's okay, everything's going to be fine. The police will find them." He heard how his voice lacked confidence, and he knew he was trying to convince himself as much as her.

"What if I lose her? She's the sweetest, most trusting child I know. After all she's been through, I couldn't bear it if—"

"Shhh. Don't!" She was scaring him, making him picture terrifying scenarios where Amanda was being hurt or worse. The love that gripped his very soul was so strong it stunned him. He had only met the girl once, but he loved her like his own daughter. And now she might be gone forever.

No, he couldn't think that way. Without saying another word, he closed his eyes and reached for Kathy's hands. "Come on now, let's pray. God knows where she is; He'll get her back safely."

Kathy's quiet weeping continued while Ben begged God for mercy, asking that the police find McFadden and Amanda, that no harm be done to the child. "God, we know that where two or more are gathered, there You are also. Please, Lord, save Amanda from harm. Bring her back safely. We beg You. In Jesus' name, amen."

"I'm so afraid..." Kathy collapsed against Ben, seeming too distraught to do anything more. They remained that way as Ben's eyes fell onto a framed picture on the wall of Amanda and Kathy, smiling and holding hands. Suddenly he was struck by the realization that Kathy had been the closest thing to a mother Amanda had ever known. Even if the police were able to rescue the girl from McFadden, and if somehow Maggie was willing to meet her daughter and take them both back...no matter what happened, Kathy Garrett would come out the loser.

She remained in his arms, crying for several minutes until finally she pulled away and reached for a tissue. "We have to hear something soon. This is driving me—"

The phone rang. Immediately she lunged for it. "Hello?"

Ben waited breathlessly. *Please, God, let it be good news. Please.*

"Yes. Okay." Kathy's swollen, tearstained face lit up, and her smile made Ben's heart soar with relief. "We'll be right there."

Then she pulled him into a tight hug, exhaling as if she hadn't done so all afternoon. "She's okay."

Ben drove, and along the way Kathy cleared her throat and turned to face him. "I think you should tell Amanda the truth about your wife."

His heart skipped a beat. "Don't you think I should wait? Until I've talked with Maggie? I mean, what if she—"

"It doesn't matter." Kathy's voice was sure and strong, as though she'd given this careful consideration. "Amanda is seven, almost eight. That's old enough to know the truth, and the truth is she's been praying that she'd find her real mother for as many years as I've known her. No matter what Maggie does, Amanda deserves to know the truth."

There was something so final about telling Amanda. And what if Maggie didn't take him back, didn't want to meet her daughter?

Lean not on your own understanding, but in all your ways acknowledge Me and I will make your paths straight.

The verse from Proverbs stopped him cold. That was it. He needed to trust God, because once he told Amanda the truth, he'd be in way too deep to find any other way out.

They pulled into the gas station and parked behind six police cars. McFadden was there, sitting in one of them, cuffed and looking—of all things—strangely sad. A distance away on the sidewalk, Amanda stood beside two of the officers, her eyes searching the road anxiously.

"She's looking for us." Kathy led the way, and in a moment Amanda saw her.

"Kathy!" The child ran the remaining steps that separated them and flung herself into Kathy's arms. Ben stood beside them and placed his hand protectively on Amanda's shoulder.

"I prayed and Jesus s-s-saved me."

"I know, honey. He always does." There were fresh tears in Kathy's voice, and

Amanda pulled away and kissed her on the cheek. At the same instant, she looked up and spotted Ben.

"Mr. Stovall! You're here!" She moved away from Kathy and wrapped her arms around Ben's waist—and he thought his heart would burst with joy. "I knew you'd come. I thought if God was going to let me live with you, and if maybe you and your wife were going to be my for always family, then of course He'd bring you here to find me." She leaned back and beamed at him. "And here you are."

Ben caught a look of unfathomable pain in Kathy Garrett's eyes as she took in the scene, but it only lasted a moment. Then the woman smiled and put her arms around both of them. "I have a feeling God's going to answer all your prayers, Amanda." She met Ben's gaze with a wink. "Every single one of them."

Kathy moved away and motioned to the police. "I need to check on the arrest report and make sure they've contacted Social Services. That'll give you two time to talk."

Despite all the bad that had come from Amanda's time in the Social Services system, at least she'd had Kathy Garrett. Ben watched the woman go and knew without a doubt that losing Amanda was breaking the woman's heart. He respected her deeply for the job she'd done with the girl, for allowing herself to love Amanda like one of her own, all the while knowing that someday she'd most likely have to say good-bye.

Ben pulled Amanda close and knelt down on one knee so they were eye to eye. He studied her eyes and saw the light of God there. No matter what happened, this child would always be his. Maggie might not forgive him, but, God willing, he would hold tight to Amanda as long as he lived.

Right now, though, he needed to tell this wonderful little girl about her mother. *Help me, God. I'm trusting You on this.* "Amanda, there's something I want to tell you."

Kathy Garrett checked with the officers, making sure her department had been notified of Amanda's status.

"Sweet little girl," one of the officers said, nodding toward Ben and Amanda.

Kathy followed his lead and looked at them. "Yes, she is. She's something."

For a moment her gaze lingered, and she saw that Ben was having a serious discussion with Amanda. *He's telling her the truth about her mother.* She watched Amanda nod several times, then saw how her face burst into the biggest smile Kathy had ever seen.

Her sweet Amanda knew the truth now: God had answered her prayers and brought her together with her real mother.

Kathy watched the two hug for a long while, but the happiness she felt for Amanda was no match for the pain she felt deep in her heart. The premonition she'd felt earlier had been right after all.

She was going to lose Amanda. And even though she was sure it would be good and right and the greatest answer to prayer Amanda would ever know, the thought of living life without her was enough to break Kathy's heart in half.

34

After moving from house to house in the foster system, Amanda had precious few belongings to pack. There was the photograph of her and the Brownells taken on Amanda's first day of kindergarten.

She wrapped the photograph inside a T-shirt and stuck it in her suitcase. Then she gingerly took hold of a scrapbook Kathy had made for her. The first part held pictures of Amanda as a baby and a little girl, of happy times with the Brownells. The rest of the book was pictures of her and the Garretts.

Amanda sat cross-legged on the floor and opened the book, flipping quickly to the back. She smiled at the memories in the pictures. Kathy's family gathered around, celebrating Amanda's seventh birthday; she and Kathy on the back of a horse at the stable two blocks from the Garrett house; the two of them roller-skating at the park across the street.

The foster homes she'd been forced to live in didn't matter—she had always belonged to Kathy. But now God had answered Amanda's prayer about finding her mother, and Amanda was going to have to say good-bye.

She closed the book and felt the sting of tears. For several minutes she held it close to her heart and let the tears come. Then she set the album carefully into her suitcase alongside her few clothes and things. So much had happened the last few days. Now Kathy said a whole new world was waiting for her.

Amanda wondered what that world would be like.

Mr. Stovall said that her mother was sick right now. That she was in a hospital, and that they would need to pray very hard for her. But Amanda was sure that one day very soon her mother would be well again. Then they would meet. And Amanda's life would truly begin.

But even though she knew it was all going to be okay, Amanda just couldn't imagine her life without Kathy and the Garretts.

She could hear Kathy in the other room, talking with Mr. Stovall. After today she wouldn't hear Kathy at all. Amanda closed her eyes and it was suddenly hard to swallow. She always knew God would answer her prayers.

She just didn't know it would hurt so much when He did.

ﾟꮛꙅoꙗ

The children were playing kickball in the front yard so the house was quiet as Kathy
and Ben sat at the kitchen table and talked about the coming week. Sitting across
from Ben, Kathy felt a peace that ran deep in her veins. There was something in the
way this man was so willing to rearrange his life for Amanda that made Kathy know
it was the right thing for the child to be with him.

He must love his wife very much.

Ben grew quiet, his eyebrows lowered. "Have you ever worked around people
with depression?"

Kathy thought of the number of times she'd been forced to place a child in foster care because one or more parents was paralyzed by the effects of that illness. "Yes.
But usually the people I work with have other problems, too. Drugs, alcohol addiction, criminal behavior."

"Okay." Ben set the mug down and looked at Kathy. "Tell me what you know
about depression. I know we talked about it a little at the pizza place, but how can
someone be a believer all her life, then wake up one morning and check herself into
a psychiatric hospital?"

Kathy drew a steadying breath. "I'm not an expert, but from what I know depression is pervasive. People like to think it only happens to weak individuals, those
without faith or character or inner strength. But nothing could be further from the
truth."

Ben ran his thumb around the rim of his still-warm mug. "Someone like Maggie,
for instance. I loved her all those years. We had fun, we laughed, we prayed together.
I thought our life was good. So how does it happen?" Ben braced his forearms on the
table and his eyes grew watery.

"Lots of reasons. Our faith can help us *through* the valley, but it won't always give
us a way around it."

Ben shook his head and stared at the table for a moment. When he raised his eyes,
the pain there took Kathy by surprise. "What about the Bible? 'I can do all things
through Christ who gives me strength.' Or giving your burdens to God? Why wasn't
that enough for Maggie?"

Kathy folded her hands in front of her and thought for a moment. "I don't know
your wife, Ben. But from what you've told me, my guess is Maggie never allowed herself to really believe those verses. She was too busy pretending to be someone she
wasn't. At least in her mind." Kathy leaned back in her chair. "Imagine living nearly
eight years with the kind of secret she kept from you. The pressure of that grew until
she couldn't take it anymore."

Ben let his head drop. "She couldn't take me anymore, either." He glanced up.
"I've had some long talks with God about this. He's done a good job of showing me
how I held Maggie—everyone really—to an almost unattainable standard. But
still…if only she'd told me."

"Do you think there's hope? For your marriage, I mean?" Kathy reached for her coffee and took a slow sip.

Ben rubbed the back of his neck, then sat straighter in his chair. "Realistically, I don't know. But I believe Scripture is true and that with God all things are possible, Kathy. Even this."

Amanda walked into the room carrying her tattered, beige suitcase. "I'm ready."

Kathy felt a surge of panic. *Not yet, Lord. I don't want to say good-bye.* She steadied herself and forced a smile. "Okay, honey. Come on, let's load up the car." The three of them walked outside, and Ben lifted the suitcase into the trunk as Kathy waved to her other children. "Come on, say good-bye to Amanda."

One by one they bid her good-bye, promising to see her soon and talk on the phone. This was a familiar scene for them, but only the older ones knew the finality of the situation this time. As far back as they could remember, Amanda came and went from their lives. There were no tears among them, and Kathy could tell by their faces that even the older children believed somehow she'd be back. Probably sooner than later.

Sometime in the next few days she'd have to explain that this time was different.

"We'll see you all the time, right?" Jenika was the only one who looked concerned.

"Yes, Cleveland's only five hours away." She smiled at Ben. They had discussed the different scenarios—whether Maggie would want to take custody of Amanda or whether she might prefer a trial extended foster care period—either way, they would need to work with the Cincinnati court and Kathy in order to keep the paperwork straight.

There would be visits, but Amanda's time with the Garretts would never be what it had been before.

The other children returned to their game, leaving Kathy and Ben and Amanda huddled in a small circle. "I'll be back next week, right?" Amanda peered up at Kathy and bit her lip.

"Right, sweetheart. Mr. Stovall will have to file some papers to determine what type of arrangement you'll have with their family." *Please, Lord, let me be right. Don't let them reject her after all she's been through.* The one possibility none of them had dared consider was that Maggie might be willing to take Ben back, but not Amanda. *If that happened...* Kathy refused to think about it. God was in control, and He knew there was only so much a child could take.

Ben put his hand on the girl's shoulder and smiled warmly at her. "Once things get settled we can come back and visit Kathy anytime you like, okay? We have a lot to do next week, introducing you to your mom and all of us getting to know each other. But we'll be back."

Amanda's eyes fell, and she studied her feet for a moment. Then in a burst of motion she threw her arms around Kathy. Dropping to her knees, Kathy held Amanda close and whispered into her hair, praying the child couldn't hear the tears in her voice. "This is what you've always wanted, Amanda. It's okay. It's a good thing."

"I-I-I'm going to m-m-miss you so much, Kathy. Who will t-t-tuck me in and talk to me at night when I'm s-s-scared?" Amanda rarely cried, a trait Kathy recognized all too well among children who'd survived year after year in the foster system. But the pain Amanda was feeling now was terrible, and Kathy wiped the child's tears as they streamed down her face.

"Mr. Stovall will." *Please, God, let it be true...* "And your real mother will, too, one day. I believe that with all my heart."

Those final words seemed to comfort her and she pulled back, studied Kathy for a minute, then leaned over and kissed her on the cheek. "I'll always love you, Kathy."

The lump in Kathy's throat was so big she couldn't speak. Instead she nodded and pulled Amanda to her one more time. "I'll always love you, too, honey." Her voice was hoarse with sorrow. "Now go on and don't forget to pray. God has a plan for you, Amanda." She stood up and gently presented the child to Ben. In a whispered voice intended for him alone she said, "I'll be praying for you."

He studied her for an instant and then shook his head slightly. "You're amazing, Kathy."

"Call me when you know how it's going, okay?" She could feel tears falling from her eyes and wiped at them self-consciously. "Now go on and see what God has for you."

The two of them climbed into the car.

Kathy remained on her driveway until she could no longer see the sadness in Amanda's eyes or the way she reached out her hand toward Kathy from the side window.

When the car was gone, she let the tears come. Waves and torrents of them, washing the pain from her heart and causing her to remain firmly in place, unable to walk or move or do anything but miss the ray of sunshine that had just been taken from her life.

"What is it, Mom? What's wrong?"

She looked up to find Bobby, her youngest, beside her, his eyes wide. He must have seen her crying and left his game to come to her.

She swallowed and tried to find her voice as she put her arm around his small shoulders. "Nothing, honey. Mommy's just happy, that's all. Very, very happy."

It was eight o'clock on Saturday morning, and Amanda was still sleeping. Ben's heart raced and he couldn't still his shaking hands.

Would Maggie refuse his request like every time before? Or would she understand that at some point they needed to talk? *Lord, speak to her heart. Make her understand that we need this time, and if she'll let me see her, please open her heart.*

As Ben picked up the phone, a knot formed in his stomach. *It's like a first date,* he thought. Then he dialed Orchards Psychiatric Hospital and held his breath. "This is Ben Stovall." He closed his eyes and exhaled. "My wife, Maggie, is a patient there, and I'd like to make an appointment to see her, please."

"Mr. Stovall?" The nurse sounded like she was about to end the conversation, and Ben clenched his fists.

Come on, God. I need Your help. "Yes. My wife's been there for quite some time…"

He heard the nurse sigh. "Yes, Mr. Stovall, I'm aware of that. Your wife has requested no visits, no phone—"

"Wait! I know that's how it was before. But I thought now that she's been there a while…just ask her, will you? This is…it means a lot. Please."

There was a hesitation. "All right. I'll ask her. Hold for a minute."

While the seconds passed, Ben thought of how far he and Amanda had come over the past couple of days. She was cautious about giving her heart, but they had forged a bond over Scrabble games and picnics at the park and knock-knock jokes that would make a foundation for the future. *If there is a future. Come on, Maggie. Meet with me.*

Two nerve-racking minutes passed before the woman returned to the phone. "You were right." There was apology in her voice. "Mrs. Stovall said she'll meet with you this afternoon at two o'clock."

Ben felt relief surge through his body. He had so much to tell her, so much ground to make up. To think that she'd loved him enough to let Amanda go…

"Thank you. Please tell her I'll be there."

He could barely wait to tell Amanda, but before that, before anything else might distract him, he clasped his hands, bowed his head, and thanked God. Of all the pain and discovery he'd been through in the past month, the most incredible lesson of all was this: He'd finally gotten a glimpse of the real Maggie, the woman beneath the mask…the woman he'd married. What he'd seen there was flawed and real, warm and caring.

And more beautiful than anything she had ever pretended to be.

35

The discharge papers came less than an hour before Ben's call, and Maggie wondered if Dr. Camas or Dr. Baker or one of the well-meaning Christian attendants at the hospital hadn't tipped Ben off. The doctors had agreed the day before that Maggie was ready to live life on her own again. She had come face to face with clinical depression and by God's grace she had not been consumed. Instead she had explored the darkness and analyzed the desperation until finally she was coming to understand it, willing to be honest with herself and God and everyone else.

Even Ben.

Her anger and resentment toward him had been replaced with a sorrow deeper than anything Maggie had ever known. She would apologize to him, though she knew it wouldn't make any difference. Their marriage still seemed like a pretense—a way to manage the passing of the years—rather than anything real and intimate the way God had intended.

That doesn't mean the Lord wants you to go your separate ways.

Maggie nodded at the thought. They were, after all, still legally married. Even if nothing about their marriage had ever been true.

She sighed. The point was probably moot, anyway. Once Ben learned the truth he would hire a divorce attorney quicker than she could ask for forgiveness.

Maggie, open your heart to Me, to My ways...

The call came from deep within, and tears filled Maggie's eyes as she recognized the still, small voice. *Lord, if You want me to stay with Ben You'll have to change us both. I'm willing, Lord. But he has to forgive me.* A sob escaped and bounced off the walls of her hospital room. *Oh, if only he could forgive me...*

The tears came harder until Maggie closed her eyes and forced herself to regain control. Ben would be there any moment; there would be time for tears later. Now she needed to think about what she would say, how things would go, and what she might do if he turned and walked out of her life forever.

She sat on the edge of her bed and looked around the room. It looked more like a luxury hotel accommodation than part of a hospital. After weeks of living here, the subdued, striped wallpaper was beginning to feel like home—the only home where she'd been able to be herself for too many years. Although she still had much to work out about her life outside Orchards, she would always be grateful for their intervention.

And for leading her back to a place of freedom in Christ.

She would stay through the weekend, but by Monday morning she needed a place to go, to live. Maggie looked at the clock on the wall. Ten minutes, and Ben would be there. Her heart raced, and the anxiety that had welled up within her would not go away, but the darkness was gone. There was no doubt about that.

Maggie noticed her palms were sweaty and she wiped them on her pants. A combination of God's grace, her willingness to be honest, and the medications and counseling had set Maggie free in a way she had never imagined possible.

But the questions loomed.

Where did she go from here? Would she and Ben be able to salvage their life together, to go on together in truth and honesty?

She didn't know. She could always rent an apartment until she figured out what to do.

The idea of returning to the paper ratcheted Maggie's anxiety up a notch. Did her coworkers know where she'd been? What would they think? Worse, what would her editors think? Yes, they'd told her in the beginning to take her time, that no matter what happened her job would be there when she returned. But how could she resume writing a conservative, morally minded column when she had pretended to be something she wasn't?

Trust in Me with all your heart and lean not on your own understanding.

As soon as the Scripture flashed in her mind, Maggie's heart rate slowed and she felt infused with strength. She could do this; she could face Ben and, with God's help, she could deal with whatever the outcome was. She hung her head and wove her fingers tightly together. *God, You've been so good to me. Your words are nothing less than a healing oil to my spirit.*

In all your ways acknowledge Me and I will make your paths straight.

There it was again, absolute truth, the very words that had so often provided her a safe tower—and they would do so again in the coming minutes with Ben. Those words were a road map that she could safely follow the rest of her days. And somewhere along the journey she knew she'd find the daughter she gave up. That certainty pulsed within her as strongly as her renewed desire to live. With her mind fixed on God, and thoughts of her child filling her head, Maggie was reminded that although the next hour might be one of the saddest of all, she had every reason to be excited about the future.

The only question was whether Ben wanted to travel it with her or not.

Although Thanksgiving was just four days away, the weather was unseasonably warm and sunshine filtered through a hazy layer of clouds as Ben parked his car and he and Amanda headed, hand in hand, for the front door of Orchards Psychiatric Hospital.

He'd explained to Amanda that her mother was not sick in the way some people get sick, with coughs and high fevers. But she was sick all the same—it had more to do with her heart, where feelings and thoughts can get all tangled up.

"She's been very sad, Amanda."

"Sad enough to be in the hospital for a long time?" Ben was pleased that the girl's stuttering had disappeared after the first day with him. He'd purchased a pink-flowered bedspread for the guestroom to make Amanda feel more comfortable, and she'd loved it. She talked to Kathy every night and seemed to be adjusting well.

"Yes, sad enough for that."

Amanda had smiled a little, empathy dimming the usual glow in her eyes. "Then I'll have to pray extra hard for her."

The fact that Maggie had agreed to the meeting at all proved that God was, indeed, at work answering their prayers. Ben opened the front door and he and Amanda entered the lobby.

"Looks like a rich person's house," Amanda whispered to him. Her eyes were wide as she took in the velvet upholstery and elegant curves of the carved mahogany furniture. She moved closer to him.

Ben's mouth was dry from the raw terror that ran through his veins. *What if Maggie turns me away? What if she doesn't want to meet Amanda? What if she's mad at me for finding her? What if she—*

Trust in Me with all your heart and lean not on your own understanding…

I'm trying, Lord, really I am. I can't even believe I'm here. Open her heart, God…I love her so much more than ever before. He swallowed hard before leading Amanda to a chair near the reception desk. "Stay here, sweetie. I'll talk to Maggie first and then…then you can come in and meet her."

She sat quickly in the chair, gripping the armrests firmly and keeping her eyes trained on him. Her hair looked like the palest spun gold, and she wore a new pink dress that they'd picked out together for the occasion. Ben could see how Amanda's knees trembled beneath the skirt, and for a moment he forgot his own fears at the realization of how frightened the child must be.

Meeting her mother for the first time had to be the most overwhelming moment of Amanda's life. He stooped and put his hands on her shoulders. "It's going to be okay, Amanda. God wants us to trust Him."

Her eyes were locked on his, absorbing his words and every ounce of strength they might offer. She nodded quickly. "Okay."

Ben grinned and squeezed her hand. "Thatta girl."

He checked in with the receptionist and was given directions to Maggie's room.

"Could you keep an eye on her?" He motioned to Amanda. "I don't want to bring her in just yet."

"No problem." The woman behind the counter smiled warmly at Amanda as Ben winked at the child and headed down the hall toward Maggie's room. With each step he felt more and more like a giddy, nervous schoolboy, as though he were about to find the angel of his dreams and ask her to be his steady girl. *Make her say yes, God, please.* Although his heart moved along twice as fast as his feet, he was suddenly just outside Maggie's door.

Whatever happened now Ben knew this much: The rest of his life depended on the next few minutes.

The gentle knock at the door made Maggie jump, and she stared at the handle for several seconds before standing. *Give me the right words, Lord...*

"Coming." She opened the door and there he was. Ben Stovall, the man of her childhood dreams, the one for whom she had been willing to sacrifice everything: her honesty, her heart, even her daughter.

Like the first time she saw him, she felt her breath catch in her throat. Ben's conservative, darkly handsome looks were so striking they could stop women at a busy supermarket—which they had done a number of times.

"Maggie..." His eyes were tender and filled with teary forgiveness, and she felt herself flinch. *If he knew what was coming he'd look different...*

They stood there, drinking in the sight of each other—and Maggie realized how long she'd been away and how much she'd missed the nearness of this man. Without saying another word, Ben moved to her and pulled her close. They came together the way two people do at a funeral, when someone they both love has passed on. His embrace told her everything she could ever want to know, that he loved her and missed her and wanted her home.

With all her heart she wanted to let him hold her that way forever and never tell him the things he needed to hear.

But finally she could bear it no longer and, tears pricking her eyes, she pulled away. "I need to tell you something." Her words were so heavy with sorrow Maggie expected to hear them hitting the floor.

Ben searched her eyes. "No...me first. Please, Maggie, I—"

"We both need to talk; I realize that. But there's something you need to know first. Something I should have told you years ago. Before we were married."

The weight of what she'd done to him, to their marriage, to her child was almost too much to bear. Ben sat down on the edge of her bed, and though her feet felt like they were dragging through syrup she pulled up a chair and sat across from him, her eyes trained on the floor. After a moment she looked up and spoke in what sounded like barely a whisper. "I'm not even sure where to begin."

There was an energy exuding from Ben, and suddenly his eyes flashed with realization. "Maggie, you don't have to." He looked like he wanted to close the gap between them and take her in his arms again, but was too nervous to do so. "I already know."

She stared at him numbly and her mind went blank. *What did he mean?* "I'm not talking about my breakdown; I'm talking about my past. The year before we got married."

Tears filled Ben's eyes and the subtle lines on his face smoothed into a reflection of serenity. "I know all about it, Maggie. All of it."

Her stomach was suddenly in her throat, as though she'd fallen down a forty-two-story elevator shaft. *What is he talking about? There's no way he could have found out about...* "I don't know what you mean, but there's something you don't—"

"Maggie, please, listen to me." He wiped his palms on his black jeans and held her with his gaze. "I know. About McFadden and the baby and everything that happened that summer."

A faint feeling came over her, and her cheeks felt like they were on fire. If he knew, then he probably had come with divorce papers. "How...how long have you..."

Ben reached out and slowly, tenderly took her hand in his. "A lot's happened these past few weeks, Mag."

Her arms and legs were trembling now, and she hugged herself tightly. She hadn't even had time to apologize, and already the tombstone of truth stood on the table, marking the death of their marriage. "So you want a divorce, is that it? You came here wanting my signature? Because before we talk about—"

Ben closed his eyes and shook his head, but there was not even a hint of condemnation in his expression. "Maggie, stop." He pulled an envelope from his pocket and handed it to her. "This isn't from my attorney, it's from me. Read it, will ya, Mag? Before we go any further."

Maggie tried to remember to breathe as she stared first at Ben, then at the envelope. Finally she slid her finger under the flap, pulled out the letter, and froze. "Ben, don't tell me goodbye in a letter...I want to talk face to—"

"Just read it, Mag. I'll sit right here and wait." He planted his elbows on his knees and cupped his fist with his right hand. "Go on."

Her heart was pounding so loudly she figured the patient next door could hear it. Whatever Ben had written, it was time to face it and move ahead. She opened the letter and began reading.

My precious Maggie...

She paused. *He called me his Maggie! Maybe it isn't too late, maybe...* No, it wasn't possible. Not after what she'd done. She forced her eyes to continue.

So much has happened since you checked into Orchards, I hardly know where to begin except at the beginning. You said something to me before you left, something that has stayed with me daily since then. You told me I didn't even know you, and at different times over the past month those words have taken on two very different meanings.

The letter went on to say how he had learned about John McFadden and then taken it upon himself to look the man up.

> I caught him in the middle of what looked like a drug deal, so he beat
> me up pretty good…

Maggie gasped and her eyes flew to meet Ben's. "John beat you up?"

"I lived. Keep reading." There were still pools of tears in his eyes, and for a moment Maggie wished more than anything she could forget the letter and just take him in her arms so she could love the hurt away. She let her eyes fall back to the letter.

> I learned about the baby from McFadden, and that led me to Woodland
> where I found your old friend, Nancy Taylor.

Maggie blinked hard. Ben had found Nancy Taylor? It didn't seem possible.

"You met Nancy?" She couldn't believe any of this was happening.

"Yes. That reminds me, she gave me a letter for you. I have it in the car. She said to tell you she tried to find you but couldn't. She blames herself for not telling you her real thoughts sooner."

Maggie's mind raced. What did all of this mean? "What real thoughts?"

"How she never should have encouraged you to give your daughter up for adoption, how badly she regretted not telling you so at the time. Before it was too late."

"You…you know my baby was a girl?"

Ben squeezed Maggie's knee and whispered. "Keep reading."

A wave of sorrow washed over Maggie and threatened to drown her. So Nancy knew the adoption had been a mistake. It was one more sad affirmation that she had made the wrong choice. But it was too late to change the past. What was done was done, and it hadn't been Nancy's fault, it had been Maggie's. And wherever Maggie's little girl was now, she had a life of her own, and nothing Nancy or Ben or any of them could say would ever change that.

"I can't believe you already know." Maggie's voice was heavy with regret, and she was stunned by the way Ben was handling the situation. "Why didn't you say something sooner?"

Ben said nothing, just held her gaze and smiled sadly. The answer to her question was suddenly obvious. Ben couldn't have said anything if he'd wanted to. Until that afternoon, she had refused his phone calls and visits. She returned to the pages in her hands.

> When I first learned you'd been with John McFadden, gotten pregnant by
> him, I was angry with you, Maggie. I believed you were right, that I never
> really knew you and now that I did it was probably better that we stay clear
> of each other. It seemed like you said that our marriage was over. But then
> I found Amanda.

If the first free-fall was enough to make her dizzy, this one turned Maggie's stomach and made the blood drain from her face. She was terrified to ask the question, because deep in her soul she already knew the answer. "Who…who is Amanda?" Her fingers twisted together and she couldn't still her shaking.

"She's your daughter, Mag." Ben's words were slow and steady, measured by the calm of a man controlled by the Holy Spirit. "She'll be eight in six months or so."

The tears came then, and Maggie moved into Ben's arms where she collapsed against him, sobbing, desperately trying to make sense of what he was telling her. How was it possible? Ben had learned the sordid truth about her past and instead of finding an attorney and being done with her, he had continued his search until he'd found her daughter. *Amanda. Amanda…Amanda, Amanda, Amanda.*

She ran the name over and over again in her mind.

"It's okay, Mag. She's fine and she…she looks just like you." He spoke softly, into her hair. "You should see her. She's beautiful."

"Y-y-you've *seen* her?" Maggie couldn't control her weeping.

Lord, what is all this? Why didn't You let me know this was happening? She exhaled, and when she could speak more clearly she leaned back and searched Ben's eyes. "You found her? Is she…is she okay?"

"She's wonderful." He took the letter from her hands and finished reading. "After I found Amanda, I knew what you'd told me was truer than I could ever have imagined. I never knew you. And now that I do, Maggie, now that I know how much you gave up to be my wife, I feel like I know you for the first time."

He studied her eyes. "I love you, Maggie. I just—" His voice was choked with emotion. "I think of all the times I seemed unforgiving, like I expected you and everyone else to be perfect." He sighed and shook his head. "What that must have done to you, Mag. I'm so sorry."

She was having a crazy dream. That had to be it. Or maybe someone had slipped her some psychiatric medication. Every hour since her moment of reckoning, she had dreaded facing Ben with the truth and apologizing for the sins of her past. But here he was, already aware of all she'd done—and he'd found her daughter. Now he was asking her forgiveness. None of it made sense…

Trust in Me with all your heart and lean not on your own understanding…

She closed her eyes briefly. Of course it made sense—God had been working on Ben behind the scenes at the same time He was working on her here at Orchards. There could be no other explanation. That's why Ben had come, why he was here now, of all things, apologizing to her.

Her eyes locked on his again, and she shook her head. "I'm the one who's sorry. I should have given you a chance, told you the truth from the beginning."

"It doesn't matter." Ben pulled her close again and stroked her hair. "We're here now and we have a future to figure out."

"There's still something you don't know, Ben."

He waited, his eyes only mildly curious, as though nothing she might say could change the way he felt about her. "I'm listening."

Maggie drew a deep breath. "I've ached for that child since..." Her voice cracked with emotion. "Since I gave her up. I've seen her in supermarkets and at church functions and looked for her on milk cartons. I've dreamed about her nearly every night and in the past week I decided to do whatever I could to find her." Maggie gulped back a sob. "I don't know what the future holds for us, Ben. But she's my daughter. I can't deny that another day."

He smiled at her and despite the tears in his eyes she caught a glimpse of the familiar twinkle, the one that always appeared when he was keeping a secret or about to surprise her with flowers or a night out. "I'm not *asking* you to deny it, Mag."

The questions hung around her heart like a heavy curtain, and she was terrified to ask even one, but she couldn't wait any longer. In some ways, she'd been searching for her daughter since the moment she'd let her go back in the hospital room in Woodland. And now the man she'd thought would turn his back on her had found her little girl. She had to have answers. Just knowing Ben had found her, seen her, made Maggie's arms ache from missing her. She could still remember the way her daughter felt as a swaddled newborn safe in her embrace.

God, I want to hold her again. Just one more time...

"About Amanda...is she...are her adoptive parents good people?"

Ben pulled back slowly and helped Maggie back to the bed. "Her adoptive parents died nearly three years ago, Maggie." He held both her hands and she was sure he was looking straight into her soul. "She's been in the foster system, up for adoption ever since."

Maggie gasped and her hands flew free of his to cover her mouth. Three years ago? For three years her daughter had been in the foster system? And though Maggie and Ben had been licensed foster parents they hadn't even known about her. How could that be? It was devastating. But at the same time it offered the slightest ray of hope. If she was still up for adoption...

Ben framed Maggie's face with his hands. "She's in the lobby, Mag. I didn't know if you'd want to see her today or not."

This final shock was greater than the other two combined. Every day since determining she would find her daughter, she'd prayed that God would make the way clear. And now, here was Ben, offering not only sorrow and forgiveness without reservation, but also the moment she'd dreamed of every day since letting her daughter go.

Maggie let loose a laugh that was half cry, half triumphant shout. "Are you serious?"

"She wants to meet you. She's been wanting to find you as badly as you've wanted to find her."

"But why do you have her—? I don't understand." Again she wondered if she were dreaming. *God, I can't believe this...You're so good...*

"Her social worker assigned me as her temporary foster parent. We didn't know if you'd…how you'd feel about meeting her."

Fresh tears stung at Maggie's eyes. *Was it really possible? Was her daughter actually waiting in a room just down the hall…waiting to meet her?* "Oh, Ben, please go get her." She was on her feet, hugging him as her heart filled with the greatest anticipation she had ever known. "Hurry, Ben. Please."

At first Amanda had made time go by with watching the people who passed the reception desk. But after a while her stomach grew nervous, so she closed her eyes and prayed. *Make my mama happy again, dear God. She's been here a long time because she's sad. And I know You don't want her sad anymore.*

Just then Mr. Stovall walked around the corner and smiled at her. "You ready?"

Her heart jumped inside her and she was on her feet at his side in an instant, her hand safely in his. "Yep." She grinned up at him. The butterflies weren't because she was worried; they were because she was happier than she'd ever been in her entire life. She was actually going to get to meet her mother!

Amanda could hardly wait.

36

The moment Maggie saw her, she inhaled sharply.

Lord, she's exactly the same girl… The precious, blond child I've seen so often over the past year.

And now she was suddenly standing there for real, hand in hand with Ben, looking so like Maggie at that age that she wondered again if it weren't all part of some marvelous, imaginary moment.

"Hi, honey." Maggie held her distance, not wanting to frighten her. *She's beautiful, Lord. I can't believe she's here…*

With eyes that glowed, the child smiled sweetly at Maggie and stepped forward, one hand outstretched. "Hi, I'm Amanda."

It was actually her, the daughter Maggie had held only a few hours, the child she'd loved every moment these past eight years. She reached out to shake the girl's hand, then caught herself. What was she doing? This was the daughter she'd dreamed of holding as far back as she could remember.

"Oh, Amanda! Honey, come here." Maggie felt tears in her eyes as she slid to the edge of the bed and held out her arms. Amanda ran to her, and they joined in a way that only mother and child can. Ben moved into the room but allowed them this time. Maggie's heart was nearly bursting with gratitude for him and a love that seemed to be blossoming by the moment, a love far more intense than anything they'd shared in the past.

The details about Ben and Maggie would have to wait. Right now she had Amanda, and that was all that mattered. She held onto her little girl and allowed her tears to mingle with her daughter's long blond hair. "I've wanted to find you since the day I gave you up."

Her daughter's arms were locked around her and she could feel her small body convulsing with sobs. "I've p-p-prayed for this f-f-forever."

Maggie couldn't tell which emotion was stronger: the heartache for the years they'd lost or the joy at having found her now. She pulled back a bit and gently moved Amanda's bangs out of her eyes and wiped her daughter's tears with her thumb. "So who are you, Amanda? Tell me about yourself."

Amanda looked at Ben and a grin flashed on her tearstained face. "I'm braver than the Crocodile Hunter, that's what Mr. Stovall says."

Maggie laughed. "You mean you've been watching that crazy crocodile guy on TV?"

Ben and Amanda exchanged a smile, and Amanda's laughter rang across the room. "Mr. Stovall says there's nothing like the freshwater crocodile gallop and that the Crocodile Hunter is the only guy who thinks rattlesnakes are beautiful."

"He's got that right." Maggie beamed at the girl in her arms and cupped her face tenderly in her hands. "I can't believe you're here, Amanda. And you've been in foster care how long?"

In the background, Ben shook his head and mouthed the word, "Later." A sick knot formed in Maggie's stomach, and she remembered the columns she'd written on the Social Services department before going to Orchards. She flashed him a questioning look, but he only shook his head and something pained in his eyes told her that Amanda's time in foster care had not been good.

"A l-l-long time. But I had Kathy, so it was okay."

"Kathy?"

Ben cleared his throat and cut into the conversation. "Kathy's the wonderful social worker I was telling you about."

Amanda nodded. "Kathy was going to adopt me, but the state said her house was too small. So I had to keep going to foster homes. Whenever things didn't work out there, I stayed with Kathy."

Whoever this Kathy was she had found a special place in Amanda's heart, and Maggie couldn't wait to fit the pieces together and meet the woman. Whatever had happened during her years of foster care, they could talk about it later. Now was the time to hold her and laugh with her and help her understand that even though they barely knew each other she would always be safe and loved with them.

Is this a forever thing, Lord?

She ran her hands down Amanda's arms as she studied her daughter again. It was utterly unreal that she was here—a living, breathing little girl standing before her, and that she was indeed the child she'd wondered about for so long.

She wanted to ask Amanda never to leave, to consider staying in Cleveland and live with them for always. But that, too, could wait.

Amanda hugged her again and this time when she pulled back, she looked sad. "Mr. Stovall says you're here because you're sick. And that you've been sad. Are you getting better?"

Maggie caught Ben's eye in the background and tried to convey to him the love that was bursting in her heart. "Actually, I'm not sad anymore at all. In fact, I can probably go home today if I want."

Ben's eyebrows raised and he started toward her, then stopped. She understood and again she was grateful. This was Amanda's moment not his, and he obviously wasn't going to do anything to interfere.

She grinned at Ben, then back at Amanda. "So what do you think of old Mr. Stovall?"

"He's great. We got to do all kinds of things the last couple of days. He even bought me a new bedspread—it's pink with flowers on it." Amanda cast Ben a look of trust and admiration. "Best of all, he prays with me whenever I feel like it. No one ever did that before except for Kathy."

Ben shrugged and returned a smile to Amanda.

Maggie's jaw dropped as she watched the exchange. The situation grew more amazing by the moment. Her husband had clearly been captivated by Amanda's beguiling charm and was now so smitten by her little-girl love for him that he was looking every bit the proud father.

"Can you believe it, Maggie?" Ben's eyes said the things his words didn't.

"I keep pinching myself ..."

All her life she'd feared Ben might refuse contact with her daughter if Maggie ever found her. *I didn't really know him, either.*

Trust in Me with all your heart, My daughter.

Maggie chuckled. "I guess God must be smiling pretty big right now."

Amanda clung to Maggie again, and she could feel the girl nodding in agreement. "I'm so glad you've been thinking about me, Mrs..."

She let the word hang there for a moment, and Maggie leaned back far enough to see her daughter's questioning eyes. "What's wrong, honey?"

"I guess I d-d-don't know what to call you yet." Amanda's face was a mixture of fear and anticipation, and Maggie felt a wave of protective love more powerful than she'd known could exist.

"Sweetheart, what do you want to call me?"

"Well...Mrs. Stovall seems kind of funny."

Maggie glanced at Ben and saw tears form in his eyes as he watched the scene unfold. "Yeah, it is kind of funny, isn't it? You could call me Maggie, I guess. If you want."

Amanda cocked her head and seemed to wrestle with the idea for a moment. "No...not Maggie. That's kind of like a sister or something."

I don't want to push her, Lord. "Is there something you'd like to call me?"

A single tear spilled onto Amanda's cheek, but her gaze was unwavering as she looked deeply into Maggie's eyes. "C-C-Can I call you Mommy?"

Maggie knew she wasn't dreaming now, because as she pulled Amanda close again, her heart soared with a love that couldn't be contrived even by her own imagination. "Yes, honey, yes. Call me Mommy, little girl. I've prayed for you every day, Amanda. Thought of you and wondered about you. I am your mommy, I'll always be your mommy, and it would be the greatest gift in the world to have you call me that."

Ben came closer and wrapped his arms around them both so that they were clustered in a group hug that seemed to need no words. When he straightened again

Maggie saw him nudge Amanda and send her a lopsided grin. "I think I'm the only one with no name."

Amanda laughed. "That's silly. If she's my mom, that makes you my dad." A troubled look settled over her face. "You know that mean guy, the one who took me from the school bus?"

"Yes…"

Alarm sliced through the warmth of the moment and Maggie flashed a wide-eyed look at Ben. He held up a hand and shook his head as if to tell her this, too, could wait until they had time to talk alone.

"He said he was my dad. Is that true?"

Maggie felt her heart lurch and she gulped back the questions she was frantic to ask. Then she reached for Ben's hand and pulled him close. "Honey, I think you already answered that question a minute ago when you said if I'm Mom, Mr. Stovall must be Dad."

Amanda sighed and nodded her head. "Good. That's what I thought."

Maggie smoothed a hand over Amanda's hair. "What's your middle name, Amanda?"

"Joy. Amanda Joy Brownell…unless I get adopted." She grinned at Ben again, and Maggie wondered what they'd been talking about the past few days. She had so much to catch up on; she could barely wait to hear the weeks of details she'd missed out on.

Then it hit her.

"Joy? Your middle name is Joy, honey?"

Amanda nodded. "Isn't it pretty? The Brownells told me they gave me that name because I brought so much joy to their lives."

Maggie caught her breath. Joy was what she'd been missing all these years and now, when she finally had been set free from the darkness, joy had come to stay. Homeless, full-hearted, lonely little Amanda Joy.

"Well, it's almost dinnertime…" Ben met Maggie's gaze and held it, his question clear.

She smiled at him. Dear, sweet Ben. How had she ever for a moment thought he'd turn his back on her for telling the truth? *God, You were right again…I had only to trust You and everything has fallen in place.* She directed her gaze at Amanda again. "If you guys'll help me pack, I'd like to join you for dinner. We have a lot to catch up on, don't you think?"

At the thought of Maggie coming home with them, Amanda was back in her arms, her hands clasped tightly around Maggie.

Maggie smiled. "I love you, honey. I've always loved you."

There was silence for a moment and then the muffled sound of Amanda's voice, ringing with sincerity. "I love you…Mommy."

In that moment Maggie knew she was blessed beyond anything she'd ever known or imagined, and that no matter what happened from that point on, she would be thankful for this time with Amanda as long as she lived.

৵৩৶৾

That same afternoon a hearing was wrapping up in Judge Hutchison's courtroom.

"Mr. McFadden, do you understand that you are being charged with felony kidnapping, and that the sentence for this crime—should you be found guilty—is a possible life in prison?"

John McFadden stood upright, his shoulders straight, and met the judge's gaze head on. "Yes, your honor."

"Very well then, how do you plead?"

"Not guilty, your honor."

The judge wrote something on his pad of paper and checked a thick book at his side. "This case will be handed over for judgment and will be given a preliminary trial to be scheduled the third week of January. Your attorney will inform you of the exact date as the time draws closer. Until that time you will remain in the…"

John tuned him out. The fact that he was the girl's father should get him a lighter sentence. It was what his attorney had suggested, and it sounded all right to him.

But it didn't matter, really.

All that had mattered since that day was the way his little girl's faith had been unwavering, even in the face of extreme danger. *Jesus loves you…I'm praying for you…* He might never see her again, but her words had come back to him over and over—and with them, he felt a certain…peace. They could do what they wanted with him now; his drug-dealing days were behind him for good.

Somehow he'd come to believe his daughter's words, and that belief made his heart light with a hope that was as foreign to him as the message she'd given him that day.

Jesus loves you…Jesus loves you…Jesus loves you.

It didn't make sense, not by a long shot, but John felt freed by those words. And if Jesus loved him, he was going to spend the rest of his life trying to figure out why.

37

$\mathcal{G}$radually the phone calls grew less frequent, and Kathy took that as a good sign. In fact, the letter was the first she'd heard from Amanda in two weeks.

Kathy waited until she was alone with a cup of coffee before reading it. She studied Amanda's painstakingly neat printing— Amanda must have been doing better in school, penmanship was never her strong point. On the back of the envelope, Amanda had drawn two hearts and written underneath, "Love and kisses."

Kathy slit open the envelope and took out the folded note inside. The carefully written sentences took up the top half of the page, and at the bottom was a picture of Amanda and the Stovalls with a caption underneath that read, "Mommy, Daddy, and me."

The picture spoke volumes, and Kathy smiled and shook her head. *Lord, You're amazing. Who'd have ever thought this would happen to Amanda Joy?* She moved her eyes to the top of the page and began reading.

Dear Kathy,

I just got legally adopted and I'm so happy. God has answered every one of my prayers. We went into court and Mr. Stovall told the judge he wanted to be my dad forever. Then my mommy told the judge she wanted me for always and ever. And the judge asked me what I thought and I said I wanted to be with them, too. So he made us a family. But really the truth is God did that, right? I miss you and the kids. But mostly you. I love you always.

Love, Amanda Joy Stovall.

Amanda Joy Stovall. Kathy's heart swelled with gratitude for all God had done for the child. Thousands of kids were wasting away in state-run foster systems across the country, but Amanda had found a way out because her faith had never once wavered. She read the letter again and let her eyes settle on Amanda's drawing. Kathy studied it and noticed something she hadn't before. In the past, Amanda's hand-drawn people had straight lines where the mouth should be. They weren't dark or sad or odd-looking. Just adorned with straight-line mouths. But this picture was different.

All three people were smiling.

For just a moment there was a familiar stinging in Kathy's eyes and a single teardrop landed on the picture. She would never forget Amanda, not ever. Her situation had seemed utterly hopeless to everyone—everyone but a little girl with a heart as good and big as her future had suddenly become.

And to her God—who in the end had been bigger than all of them put together.

The church service was under way and Amanda—wearing her pale pink chiffon dress—sat nestled between Maggie and Ben. It was her big day, and they had bought the new dress to mark the occasion. Maggie glanced down at Amanda and savored the way her daughter's small fingers felt linked with her own. Amanda loved to hold Maggie's hand, and although Maggie still felt deep sorrow for the years she'd missed with her daughter, she was too busy cherishing the current days to dwell long on the past.

The music that Sunday was particularly moving, and it allowed Maggie a moment to reflect on all she'd learned over the last three months. She'd worked through the feelings of shock and anger over the truth about Amanda's time in foster care, and though she was grateful her daughter had survived, a part of her would always hurt over what had happened. She tried not to play the "what if" game, but now and then she'd catch herself wondering how different things might have been if she'd followed her heart all those years ago.

Then there were the details of Ben's search for who she was; why she'd succumbed to the darkness of depression; his dangerous encounter with John McFadden; and the man's eventual kidnapping of Amanda. Never had she imagined Ben would love her like that, without standards or expectations, but just because she was his wife. His other half. He was so much more a godly man than she'd ever believed possible, and she was struck daily by how horribly different things might have been if he hadn't been devoted to God's will through it all.

The music played on, and Maggie's heart soared as she recalled the several meetings they'd had with Kathy Garrett, a woman for whom Maggie would be forever grateful. Kathy was a living example of why one could never generalize about the pitfalls of the state-run foster system. After all, without the system, Amanda never would have known the love of that one, very dedicated and devoted woman.

Maggie could still hardly believe all that had happened while she was at Orchards. She went once a week now for follow-up counseling, but the darkness was so far gone it felt as though it had happened to a different person altogether.

What she'd learned at Orchards had given her perhaps the most amazing truths of all—that in Christ there is only honesty, no matter how grave or wrong or desperate life becomes. That only in that truthful place can the sunshine of God's grace and joy and forgiveness find its way through the darkness.

The music stopped, and the worship leader opened his Bible and began to read.

Beside Maggie, Amanda looked up and smiled first at her, then at Ben. *Oh, Lord, I can't believe she's really here. Thank you…thank you.* It was a prayer that was constantly on Maggie's heart.

The worship leader was saying, "Proverbs tells us there are times when our lives take a wrong turn, for whatever reason, and when that happens there is one thing we must remember. Trust in God with all your heart and lean not on your own understanding. In all your ways acknowledge Him and He will make your paths straight."

Maggie's eyes flew open. It was the verse! The very one that had spoken to her heart whenever things seemed desperate and hopeless. Of all the days to have it read in church… Out of the corner of her eye she caught Ben motioning to her as if he had something important to say. They leaned close, forming a shelter over Amanda.

"That's the Scripture," he whispered so quietly that Maggie knew Amanda couldn't hear him. "Whenever I thought things were hopeless, that verse came to me."

Maggie felt goose bumps rise along her arms and neck. "Me too!"

Ben gave her a look of amazement. "The same verse?"

She nodded, and they exchanged a look that said they'd probably spend hours on the subject later, like they did on so many topics these days, almost as though they were newlyweds again. Only this time they had nothing to hide, and the intimacy of their hearts was greater than Maggie had ever imagined.

As they returned their focus on the worship leader, Maggie was overwhelmed by God's faithfulness. *Lord, how could it be? You were speaking the same promise to each of us? During the darkest time in our lives?* Peace washed over her at the mercy they'd both been shown. *Everything I have is because of You…my marriage, my life*—she glanced at Amanda beside her—*especially my daughter.*

The worship leader moved from the piano to center stage and interrupted Maggie's thoughts. "We have something special we'd like to do before the sermon today." He smiled, and Maggie thought there were tears in his eyes. "If the Stovall family will please come up."

Maggie and Ben rose, each taking one of Amanda's hands as they made their way up front. When they had turned to face the congregation, the worship leader explained that the couple wanted to dedicate their newly adopted daughter, Amanda Joy. While he was talking, Maggie saw someone near the back of the church that made her heart swell.

Laura Thompson.

The two women caught each other's gaze over the crowd. Maggie could still hear Laura's tearful voice. *"I've been praying for you night and day, dear…night and day…night and day…"*

God had been faithful in so many things! Laura had been down with the flu for two weeks, but here she was, well enough to be part of Amanda's dedication service. *God, You are good beyond words.*

Maggie glanced down at Amanda and caught the love in her daughter's eyes as she looked from her to Ben and back again, squeezing their hands.

Maggie focused her attention on what the minister was saying. "Is it your desire to raise this child in a Christian home, in the love and knowledge of Jesus Christ?"

I've never known any greater desire, Lord. Ben and Maggie nodded in unison. They had planned ahead that Ben would speak at this point, so the worship leader handed him the microphone.

"Some of you know what Maggie and I have been through these past few months." He scanned the people before him. "I just want to tell you that whatever you're going through, whatever thing you're up against today, give it to God. Seek Him with all your heart, because the Scripture we heard a few moments ago is a promise straight from heaven." He looked from Maggie to Amanda and smiled. "The three of us are here today as living proof."

Maggie watched him with a full heart, amazed at how totally and completely she had fallen in love with him since returning home. *I never would have believed it, Lord...* He was wonderful with Amanda, and Maggie knew he loved her unconditionally, the way she had only dreamed of being loved.

The worship leader took the microphone back. "Why don't some of you come up and surround this family as we pray for them."

Led by Laura Thompson, people—many of whom were now familiar with their story—came and circled them in a wreath of support that brought tears to Maggie's eyes. Laura laid her hand on Maggie's shoulder and bowed her head, eyes closed. While the worship leader prayed aloud, the overwhelming presence of the Holy Spirit surrounded them and Maggie was washed in the light of God's love and kindness. Suddenly she had the strangest sensation that Laura was sick, sicker than any of them knew. And that praying for her these past months had been her last earthly task.

No, Lord, don't let it be so...

Lean not on your own understanding, but in all your ways acknowledge Him...

Maggie felt her eyes sting with the beginning of tears. Whatever Laura's future, she would forever be part of the Stovall family, and if it would soon be Maggie's turn to pray for a season, she would welcome the task. *The way a family should.*

The music started again, and Maggie recognized the tune: "Great Is Thy Faithfulness."

They huddled close, with Ben's arms around Maggie and Amanda, and Laura praying beside them. Together they sang as one.

"Great is Thy faithfulness, O God my Father. There is no shadow of turning with Thee..."

Maggie felt the tears fall onto her face as she clung to her husband and daughter. This was a hymn that had brought pains of conviction in the past, conviction because she, herself, had lived in the shadows far too long, blind to the faithfulness of her God. But the conviction was gone now, and in its place was unspeakable joy. Their three voices rang together and it was the sweetest sound Maggie could remember hearing.

"Morning by morning new mercies I see. All I have needed Thy hand hath provided..."

With Amanda snuggled closely between them, Maggie and Ben looked at each other. Their eyes met and held for the remainder of the song, and what she saw there was a love she knew would last through the years. God had given her real, lasting joy and along with it, an understanding that in Christ alone there is victory over the darkness—whatever trials might come.

They held tight to each other and finished the song together as if they were the only three people on earth.

"Great is Thy faithfulness, great is Thy faithfulness, great is Thy faithfulness, Lord, unto me."

Dear Reader,

I believe with all my heart that God gave me this story for such a time as this. Around us, throughout our country, the spiritual battle is heating up in more ways than we know. Scripture tells us the enemy comes to steal, kill, and destroy. To that end, I've seen him try two common tactics: distraction and discouragement.

Distraction often happens first. We start off meaning well, reading our Bibles and viewing life with spiritual eyes. But over time complacency veils our enthusiasm until we wake up and lie down with thoughts that have nothing to do with our Savior. We opt for a cup of coffee instead of a chapter of Scripture to get us going, and we become so caught up in the here and now we forget that our focus, that our entire lives must be directed at the ever-after if we are to live free, effective, joyful godly lives.

When we are fully distracted, we no longer tap into the greatest resource given mankind—the Holy Spirit. Instead we walk by a compass of our own design, and in very little time end up lost and confused. This is when discouragement hits.

Depression, then, is the combination of the two: distraction and discouragement, multiplied to whatever degree the enemy is seeking to destroy us.

Although I have never personally dealt with clinical depression, I know what it is to be buried in discouragement. I remember driving to Northern California on a family vacation and taking in the beauty of the Lake Shasta area. The trip followed a lengthy period of warfare and spiritual attack—a season of discouragement. As my husband drove through the mountains that day, tears fell from my eyes as though a dam had broken in my heart.

The Lord, in all His lovingkindness, reminded me of some basic truths as we made our way through the pines. First, He is bigger than any problem I have. Second, everything in this life—absolutely everything—is temporary. And God's Word says we are to fix our eyes not on the temporary but the eternal. Finally, He adjusted my perspective so that I no longer hurt for things that had taken place that past year. Instead, I knew that somehow they would work to the Lord's glory. My eternal perspective was back in place.

Now I know that a season of discouragement pales in comparison to depression, but over the past year, God let me understand pain in this area. Pain that is being buried, masked by thousands, perhaps even millions of women today—both in and outside the church.

If you are one who is suffering this way, please seek professional help without shame, and know that God loves you just as you are. He is beckoning you even now to come into the sunshine of His grace and truth. Come in honesty and never look back.

Some of you have no idea what it means to have a relationship with the Lord. To you I pray that you please make a decision to accept God's gift of salvation. Tell Him you can't live any longer without Him. Buy a Bible, find a Bible-believing, Christ-centered church near your home, and get connected.

If you're already there and are silently suffering, it's time to be honest with your church family. If news of your depression isn't received well, continue to seek those who will listen with an open heart, and pray for your church. I believe the time has come for all of us to recognize the enemy's hand in this pervasive illness and come together the way Christ would have us do.

If you have never dealt with serious depression, thank God sincerely and ask Him to make you compassionate. Someone—probably someone closer than you think—may be hiding in the darkness even now. Ask Him to show you how you can help, how you can care for others and be a light in the darkness.

Thank you for journeying these pages with me. I look forward to hearing from you, especially from those of you who have faithfully read each of my novels. You can still write me at my e-mail address: rtnbykk@aol.com.

Blessings abundant to you and yours and grace as you seek to walk in His light.

Sincerely,

DISCUSSION QUESTIONS

1. Maggie thought she could walk away from her past and lead a new life, but her sin caught up with her. Numbers 32:23 talks about our sin finding us out if we do not obey the Lord. Discuss how this was manifested in Maggie's life.

2. At some point in their lives, at least 8 percent—and there are estimates as high as 17 percent—of the American population experience severe depression like Maggie's. If you have ever experienced a form of depression, discuss how you felt and how you handled it. How did others treat you?

3. Ben was unaware of Maggie's problems and was shocked when things finally unravelled and she left. Have you ever been in a relationship where your spouse or significant other was clueless to a significant emotional trial you were experiencing? How did that make you feel? How did you overcome those feelings?

4. Some believe that for Christians to seek professional counseling for emotional problems is taboo. They believe that Christians should never be depressed and just need to pray more if they are dealing with some kind of frustration. What are your feelings about this belief?

5. Why was Maggie so quick to blame Ben for what she did, while Ben was quick to blame Maggie? What was the main obstacle keeping them from accepting the responsibility for their own actions?

6. The Lord kept bringing to both Ben's and Maggie's minds Proverbs 3:5: "Trust in the LORD with all your heart and lean not on your own understanding." Why is that so important? Why is it so important to memorize Scripture and teach it to our children? What part does Scripture play in this story?

7. Emotional healing takes time and is hard work. What finally brought about Maggie's breakthrough in her healing? How will she maintain her healing?

8. Discuss ways in which you can be a support to someone exhibiting signs of depression and perhaps their family members.

9. Not all foster homes are bad, but unfortunately, there are people who take in foster children for the wrong reasons. Discuss ways in which you can be a support to a foster parent or child, a case worker, or how you can become more aware of the signs of abuse and what to do about it. You may want to invite a special speaker to address these issues.

10. The title *When Joy Came to Stay* is based on Psalm 30:5b: "Weeping may endure for a night, but joy comes in the morning." When one is dealing with depression, the length of the night often depends on the willingness of the person to deal with the issues causing the depression. If you are currently experiencing any form of depression, take some time to get away to evaluate your situation. Then seek out a confidant who can pray for you and share your burden. And if needed, make an appointment to see a professional counselor. As you have learned from Maggie's story, the way we deal with sin affects the lives of those around us, as well. Give God a chance to pour out His grace and bring peace back into your life.

[Book Three]

On
Every
Side

DEDICATED TO...

DONALD, my closest friend, my other half, the best husband always and forever. I love you more today than a hundred yesterdays, laugh more at the silliness between us, and live more with one eye on the rearview mirror, only too aware of how fast the days go. With you all of life is a series of memories and blessed magical moments, a roller coaster of thrills in which you are constantly at my side, steady and strong. Remember when you told me you loved the Lord more than me? Let's just say I'm glad it's still true. It's what makes it all so good.

KELSEY, my sweet and precious little Norm, who can boot a soccer ball like no one else and still be the prettiest girl around. I thank God that He lives within you, helping you know right from wrong, helping you understand the plans He alone has for you. Your tender heart has more discernment than most adults. As you told me the other day, you don't need a "play" boyfriend to feel good about yourself. You need the Lord. And I'm so thankful you have Him in a way that shows in everything you do…your eyes, your smile, and the joy you bring me and your dad every day of our lives.

TYLER, my strapping eight-year-old treasure, who has no idea how talented and bright and kindhearted he truly is. If only you could see the picture God is painting of you, the one your dad and I see more clearly every day. Please know that I'm glad you're not rushing the process, grateful that for a little while longer I might hear your humming, happy voice making up the music of our lives. Congratulations on winning statewide honors on your "Reflections" story, Ty. One day I'll be reading *your* dedications!

AUSTIN, who is still Michael Jordan. The marvel of you, my precious child, is not that at three years old you can slip into your No. 23 jersey and dribble a ball between your legs, watching wide-eyed when your dad coaches the big guys and taking in every bit of it. It isn't the way you can reverse dunk on your kid-size hoop, or shoot nothing-but-nets all afternoon. Rather, it's the way your eyes fill with tears when you hear a song about Jesus. We knew from the beginning that your heart was special…we're beginning to see how very special it really is.

E. J. and SEAN—As I write this I am twelve days from taking a plane to Haiti where I will pick you up and bring you home to live with us forever. My prayer for you, my chosen sons, is that God will impress upon your hearts how very special you both are, how great the plans He has for you. As surely as night follows day, He has amazing reasons why He brought you here to be a part of our family. We have prayed and planned for this moment for a very long time and are humbly awed at the privilege of being your parents. We—all of us—love you more than you could know or understand.

And to GOD ALMIGHTY, who has, for now, blessed me with these.

ACKNOWLEDGMENTS

As always, when I put together a novel there are people to thank, people without whom the entire process simply would not have been possible. On that note I thank the Lord first and foremost for allowing me the dream of writing stories straight from my heart while still being a stay-at-home mom. Also thanks to my husband and kids for not complaining when dinner is little more than a cold tuna sandwich and a sliced apple. You guys are the best family in the world.

Thanks to Kristy and Jeff Blake for continuing to take my little Austin on days when there's no other way the writing will get done. My heart is always at ease knowing my little boy is in your care. And to Sorena Wagner, the best nanny and all-around helper anyone could have. Truly, Sorena, I couldn't have gone to the next place in my writing career—the place God was calling me to go—without your help.

There are a number of people I am indebted to professionally, and top of the list is my agent, Greg Johnson. Greg, your God-given ideas and ways of making books come together are truly awe-inspiring. I thank the Lord for the day Terri Blackstock introduced us...and I look forward along with you to many, many more books and shared blessings together.

Thanks also to my amazing editor, Karen Ball. So often someone comments on a certain scene in my books or on a character's personality, and I smile proudly and tell them the truth: That came from Karen Ball! You're blessed at what you do, and I am doubly so for working with you.

The staff at Multnomah Publishers always deserves a great big thank-you for being the amazing people you are. Every one of you, from Don Jacobson to the staff of sales and marketing and editorial, is driven by God's purpose. Clearly the Lord is blessing your efforts on His behalf, and I pray He continues to do so a hundredfold in the years to come. Thank you for believing in me four years ago when I first set out to write inspirational fiction.

It may not be customary to thank the cover designer, but in our world a book truly is judged by its cover. That being the case, I attribute much of my recent success to the God-given talents of Kirk DouPonce from Uttley/DouPonce DesignWorks. You have a way of bringing all the emotion of my stories—the heartache and joy, the highs and lows—into a single illustration. And you do it better than anyone around. I am humbly grateful for your work on my books.

There are always certain friends who take my books and make them topics of conversation at their workplaces or among their social circles. In my life those faithful friends and public relations experts include my sisters Tricia, Sue, and Lynne; my parents, Anne and Ted Kingsbury; my niece, Shannon Kane; Phyllis Cummins; Betty Russell; Lisa Alexander; Joan Westfall; Debbie Kimsie; Tish Baum; the Chapman family; Christine Wessel; Pastor Mark Atteberry and his wife, Marilyn; Sylvia and Walt Wallgren; Ann Hudson; Vicki Graves; Barbara Okel; the Provo family; Sherry Heidenreich; Peggy Babbitts; Amber Santiago; the Daves family; Connie Schlonga; and dozens of friends from my Crossroads Church family, along with many others. Thank you for being my first line of encouragement and constant prayer support. Especially the handful of you who literally pray for my writing ministry and me every day. How can I ever thank you for your love and prayers other than to say please, please keep praying. It's only by His power that any of this ever comes together in a way that might change lives for His glory.

A special thanks goes to the hundreds of readers who have written me at my e-mail address, which is listed in the back of my books. I feel as though I'm friends with so many of you and I continue to look forward to your occasional updates and letters of encouragement regarding my books. You know who you are. You're the best group of readers an author could ever hope to have!

Finally, to the Skyview basketball team, who this year went from being a new school with one league win to a second-place league finish under the best coach (and husband) in the state. Thanks for giving me a reason to cheer—even on deadline. Go, Storm!

I

*J*oshua Nunn shuffled between a closet full of file cabinets and the boxes lining his office floor. He hadn't expected it to be this hard—packing up his dead partner's things and facing whatever was left of his own future. There was a heaviness in the air, a somber silence as though even the walls grieved the loss of the charismatic man whose presence had once consumed the place.

Joshua sighed. He had never felt so alone in all his life.

Bob Moses, senior attorney and Joshua's lifelong friend, opened the Religious Freedom Institute in Bethany, Pennsylvania, for one reason only: To take back ground lost to the enemy. "Join me," Bob had said when he presented the idea to Joshua three years earlier. "The promised land awaits!"

And so it had. They'd won two local Pennsylvania cases in the past six months—one in which a group opposed to religious freedom sued a school district to prevent students from praying before football games. The case threatened to capture national attention—much like the one in Texas a few years back. But this time, when the opposition faced Bob and Joshua, they backed off.

"God has His hand on this office," Bob would say. "I can feel it, Joshua. He's taking us somewhere big."

There were dreams of hiring more attorneys, buying a bigger office building, and finding a place on America's legal center stage where they could join similar organizations in the national fight for religious freedom.

But every one of those dreams seemed to die the day Bob Moses slumped over his office desk, dead of a heart attack at age fifty-seven.

Now there were bills to pay, office expenses to maintain, and not a single viable case on the horizon. With Bob gone, clients apparently assumed the firm was closed, and now, after just three weeks of Joshua working on his own, the phone calls were few and far between.

He grabbed another stack of files, carried them across the office, and dropped them in a box. When he was finished clearing out his partner's things, he would deliver them to Bob's widow. The woman was taking it well, but many nights since

Bob's death Joshua had come home to find his partner's wife sitting with his own dear Helen at the dining room table, tears in their eyes.

Poor Betty.

I know he's in a better place, Lord, but why? He still had so much to do...

Be strong, Joshua.

Be strong? It was the answer he seemed to be getting from the Lord more and more these days and it seemed an odd bit of advice. He *was* being strong, wasn't he? He hadn't broken down or refused to get out of bed. No, he'd been at the office every day since the funeral, and still not a call or case had come his way. He'd researched potential lawsuits, made phone calls, written letters—but still nothing.

The facts were simple. If he didn't start bringing in cases soon, he would have to close up shop and face the reality that at fifty-six years he was as desperately in need of a job as he'd been his first month out of college. A shallow laugh made its way to the surface, and Joshua shook his head.

Be strong?

He and Bob had worked as trial lawyers with Jones, Garner, and Schmidt for thirty years before joining forces in this religious freedom venture. In addition to their lofty goals for the Institute, there were other benefits. No more commutes to the big city, extra time for evening card games and barbecues when any of their kids were home, more time in the town they loved. Joshua felt the sting of tears in his eyes and he blinked hard as he remembered how his partner seemed to have a bounce in his step at the idea of spending more time with his wife.

And with Faith.

There was a lump in Joshua's throat and he coughed so it would ease up. Much as he missed his friend and partner, young Faith missed the man more. Especially now, when it was supposed to be—

He couldn't bear to think of Faith, of how difficult her father's death had been on her. Instead he drifted back to the beginning, back to the early 1970s where it had all begun. The year he was hired by the big city firm, he and Helen and their two girls moved to Bethany—the most beautiful place in all the world. Bob, Betty, and their daughters followed suit two years later, and the families had been practically related ever since. Joshua and Bob would tease each other about being surrounded by women.

"Not a son among us, can you believe it?" Bob would throw his hands in the air.

The memories faded. Joshua carried a stack of books across the room and finished filling the box. As he did he glanced at the portraits on the wall. Bob Moses and Joshua Nunn, attorneys at law. *We were the luckiest guys in all of Bethany, Bob.*

These days everything was different. Bob was gone. Joshua's kids were both married and lived a few hours' drive away, and Bob's oldest daughter lived in Chicago. All that remained was Bob's youngest—Faith—still single at twenty-nine and trying to find her way in a world that offered little assistance, especially when the chips were down. Faith lived in Bethany and commuted fifteen minutes to Philadelphia's

WKZN affiliate station where she anchored the nightly news. Joshua pictured her as she had been a few weeks back at her father's funeral: Long, blond hair and far-off, pale blue eyes. Beautiful girl; a celebrity really.

And very close to her father.

Bob hadn't talked about it much, but Joshua knew Faith was part of the reason he wanted to work in Bethany. "I worry about her," Bob would say now and then. "She's had a rough go of it."

The plan to open a law office in Bethany seemed like a winner from every angle. They could leave the high-powered, high-pressured firm and would work from a leased office anchored in the center of the city's quaint downtown district, just minutes from their homes in Maple Heights. They would spend hours building cases and strategizing trial appearances and swapping stories of the good old days—back when they ran cross-country for rival Philadelphia high schools and squared off more than once on opposing debate teams.

Bob was so sure of himself, so full of energy and desire, convinced beyond discussion that God's hand was in this venture. And from the get-go God blessed their intentions in a way that made it look as though Bob had been right.

Joshua knelt down and yanked packing tape across the flaps of the full box.

"Retirement is for old people." Joshua could still hear Bob's voice as it rang loudly through the office. "We could run this law office another twenty years." A smile would fill his face. "Remember, Joshua...where God guides, God provides."

The memory faded on a wave of doubt. Joshua stopped for a moment, gazing outside at the late summer green in the leaves that lined Main Street. *Why would You guide us here...take us from our steady jobs...just to leave me all alone? How will I provide stability for Helen now? For Faith?*

Joshua, hear me, son. You are not alone...

The voice was as strong and certain as ever, a constant reminder that Joshua's relationship with a mighty God was intact, the single guiding force in his life. He opened another box and struggled to his feet. Once Bob's things were gone, maybe he could advertise for a partner. Someone who didn't need to make money up-front. Joshua huffed at the thought. How likely was that? The situation was hopeless.

There was something else, too.

With Bob gone, Joshua wondered whether he was actually up to the task of fighting religious freedom cases. Bob was the outgoing one, the lawyer with flair and style and conviction. Joshua? He was merely a simple man who loved God above everything and everyone else; a man whose arguments in court were succinct and heartfelt rather than memorable. Bob had said more profound things at lunch over a cheeseburger and fries than Joshua had ever said in court. Joshua had figured he'd enjoy fighting nearly any cause at Bob Moses' side. But without him?

His doubts were rampant as barn mice.

Joshua pulled himself into a nearby chair and hung his head. What was he supposed to do now? The firm wouldn't hire him back... His retirement fund was intact, so it wasn't a financial concern. But with Bob gone Joshua felt as though he'd lost his sense of direction, his focus as a man. He looked up and studied the office, taking in the way Helen and Betty had arranged the plants just so, how the windows on three sides allowed the light to fill the room. Joshua closed his eyes. *This was Bob's dream, God…tell me if I'm supposed to let it go. Please…*

As I was with Bob Moses so I will be with you. I will never leave you nor forsake you.

Joshua let the silent thought settle on his heart. It was true of course; God would be with him. But what about the law office? What of the dream to fight tyrannical forces bent on destroying religious freedom?

Joshua was suddenly more tired than he'd been in weeks. He rested his head on his desk and closed his eyes. *As I was with Bob Moses… As I was with Bob Moses… As I was with Bob Moses…* Joshua remembered the two cases he and Bob had battled together, how God had indeed been with them, bringing both victory and visibility, a presence in the Philadelphia area that had caused certain political groups to take notice. *But that was then, God…I'm all alone now. I can't do it on my own.*

Be strong and courageous…you will lead the people of this town to inherit the land…

Joshua closed his eyes tighter. *Are You talking to* me, *God? Lead the people of the town to inherit* what *land?* He shook his head slightly to clear the strange words. He probably needed more sleep. He might even be coming down with something. That could explain this heavy, tired feeling…

Inherit the land? He couldn't scrounge up a single case, let alone inherit the land.

Before he could pull himself up from his desk he heard a voice. Not the kind of inner knowing that comes when God whispers…but an audible voice.

"Be strong and very courageous, Joshua. Be careful to follow all the ways My servant Bob Moses showed you; do not turn from them to the right or to the left, that you may be successful wherever you go."

Joshua sat straight up, eyes wide. A clamminess came over his hands and neck, and he glanced about the room. The boxes were no longer scattered over the floor, but stacked neatly by the door. And one of the photos on the wall looked different. In place of Bob's picture hung one of a younger man—a man with angry eyes and a handsome, chiseled face. *What in the…?*

"If…if that's You talking, God…I want to be strong for You." Joshua's eyes darted about the room, but the windows offered none of the familiar views—only golden light almost too brilliant to take in. His heart began to race. "I…I can't do it alone…"

"Have I not commanded you?"

Joshua sat stone still in his chair as the voice rang out again. It was booming, yet it warmed the room the way Joshua's heater warmed his car on winter days.

"Be strong and courageous. Do not be terrified; do not be discouraged, for the Lord your God will be with you wherever you go. Remember the command that Bob Moses, servant of the Lord, gave you. The Lord your God is giving you rest and has

granted you this land. You will cross My Jordan, and take possession of the land the Lord your God is giving you for your own."

Joshua banged his head twice against the palm of his hand. Was he having a stroke? No, maybe it was an inner ear infection, something that made sounds form into sentences when he was the only one in the room. There was a flash of light— and then he saw it.

In the corner of the room, there in front of Bob's old bookcase, stood a man wearing the finest armor, a man whose eyes blazed with shining light. A golden man unlike anyone Joshua had ever seen before. His breath caught in his throat and his jaw dropped as the man drew his sword. Joshua's teeth and even the tips of his fingers trembled, but something deep in his gut told him he was not in danger. He could trust this man.

He stood, his knees knocking, and made his way closer to the soldier. "Are you…are you friend or foe?" Joshua forced his voice to cooperate and then waited stiffly, as though his feet were planted in cement.

"Neither. I have come as commander of the army of the Lord."

Joshua felt his eyes fly open even wider than before. *Commander of the army of the Lord?* That meant the man was an…an *angel?* It was impossible…but what other explanation was there? Joshua fell facedown to the ground, managing in a muffled voice, "What message does my Lord have for me?"

The strangely peaceful soldier studied Joshua for a moment. "Take off your shoes, Joshua, for you stand on holy ground."

Immediately Joshua fumbled with his laces, loosened their grip on his feet, and slid his shoes off, arranging them neatly so they faced Bob's bookcase. Who was this man and where had he come from? If he was an angel did he know about Bob? Had he spoken with him? Was this God's way of getting Joshua's attention? And what of the strange light outside and the odd picture on the wall?

But before he could ask any of the hundreds of questions pelting the roof of his heart, the phone rang. Joshua groped about, but nothing was where it should have been.

Again and again the phone rang, until Joshua sat bolt upright and opened his eyes, his mouth dry, heart pounding. He was breathing fast and he glanced around the room, stunned at the sight that met him.

The man was gone. In his place were all the boxes and piles of papers and books that had been there minutes earlier. His eyes darted to the photographs on the wall and he exhaled his relief. Bob's picture was back, and there was no sign of the angry young man whose picture had been there a moment ago.

Joshua remembered the voice and what had been said. What land? How could he be crossing the Lord's Jordan when the Holy Land was thousands of miles away?

None of it made sense.

The phone rang once more and the sound of it startled Joshua, jerking him further back to reality. There was wetness at the corner of his mouth, and he wiped it with the back of his hand as everything became utterly clear. He hadn't heard a voice or been visited by a commander in the Lord's army. Of course not.

He had fallen asleep and it had all been a dream.

He reached for the receiver and snapped it to his ear. "Religious Freedom Institute, Joshua Nunn."

"Good. You're in." It was Frank Furlong the town's mayor. Joshua eased back into his chair and willed his heart to slow down. He and Frank had been friends for twenty years.

"Yeah…sorry, I was busy. What's up, Frank?"

There was a pause. "I got wind of something today. Could be big, could be nothing, but I'd like to talk about it. How about over lunch tomorrow?"

Images of the golden soldier and the sound of a booming voice like none he'd ever heard before still clamored for Joshua's attention. "Tomorrow's Saturday. Can't it wait?" He and Helen had plans to drive to the lake and take in an afternoon of fishing. Joshua figured they'd talk about his work plans—especially now that it seemed clear the law office wasn't going to survive.

Again the mayor hesitated. "This is very big, Joshua. If it happens, it'll come down on Monday, and we'll need your help. In fact, you'll be the primary counsel." There was a beat. "Tomorrow at noon, okay? Alvins on Walnut."

The fog was still clearing from Joshua's head, but he heard the urgency in Frank's voice. He and Helen could fish Sunday after church. "I'll be there."

He hung up the phone, staring at it, pondering. What could possibly be so urgent? Whatever it was, it involved the city of Bethany, and Frank wanted him as primary counsel. A surge of hope wound its way through Joshua's being. Was this the answer he'd been praying for? Was God going to let him keep the office after all? He considered the idea when a draft from the air conditioning sifted between his toes.

Frowning, he glanced down. He had only socks on his feet. *What's this about?* In the dream there'd been something about taking off his shoes because the place was holy, but that had only been a dream, right? So where were his shoes? He looked around the room and finally spotted them several feet away.

Sitting neatly, side by side, facing Bob's old bookcase.

2

*J*ordan Riley paced confidently in front of the judge like a caged and hungry animal, feeding off the fact that every eye in the room was on him. These were his closing arguments, and in the New York courtroom where the drama was taking place he had already claimed victory more times than he could remember.

He was certain this case would end in similar fashion.

"Finally, Your Honor, Mr. Campbell completely disregarded school policy by praying with a child during school hours." Jordan reached for a document from the plaintiff's table and found the highlighted section. "Page four, section thirteen, states clearly that if a teacher ignores the existing separation between church and state he or she shall be terminated immediately."

Jordan set the paper down and stared hard at the simple man across the courtroom. Flanked by frustrated attorneys from the local branch of the teacher's union, the man looked calm, almost serene. As though he didn't understand the ramifications of what was about to take place. Or perhaps he believed, thanks to some misguided faith in God Almighty, that the battle might end miraculously in his favor.

A bitter feeling as familiar as his own name oozed from the crevices of Jordan's heart and seeped into the core of his being. *We'll see where your God gets you this time.*

He faced the judge again and motioned toward the defendant. "The religious right threaten to take over this country every day, Your Honor. Their agenda is clear: to evangelize all those around them to their way of thinking." Jordan took several steps toward the peaceful teacher and gestured in his direction. "Your Honor, the danger here is clear. If we allow people such as Mr. Campbell to control the minds of our youth, we lose the free society our forefathers fought to give us. In its place we will have a culture of robots controlled by some mystical belief in a God that doesn't exist. Human robots without compassion for people different from themselves. Robots who teach hatred toward people with alternative lifestyles or differing religions. All of this under the guise of public education?" Jordan waited a beat. "It's a travesty of the most frightening kind, Your Honor."

Mr. Campbell's attorneys shifted, glancing furtively at their notes and avoiding eye contact with their client. Jordan resisted a smile. Even Campbell's counsel could tell which way the case was going. It was all over but the celebrating.

"For that reason, it is my recommendation that Mr. Campbell be fired by the school district for violating this country's separation of church and state. In doing so, this court will send a message to other teachers, other school districts that prayer of any sort simply will not be tolerated on public school grounds." He nodded. "Thank you, Your Honor."

He took his seat and watched one of Campbell's attorney's weakly take the floor. The man adjusted his glasses and cleared his throat. "Our stance in this matter, Your Honor, is of course the matter of freedom." He checked his notes. "Freedom of speech and religious freedom."

Jordan was up immediately. "Objection, Your Honor." He smiled in a practiced way that fell just short of condescending. "Mr. Campbell's right to religious freedom has never been the issue. No one told him he couldn't pray. He just can't pray with a student in a public school setting."

The judge—an icy woman in her late forties whose patience for the religious right was limited at best—nodded her chin pointedly. "Sustained." She tossed a disdainful look at Campbell's counsel. "You will stick to the issue at hand."

The man looked lost. "Yes, Your Honor." His eyes fell again to the file in his hand, and Jordan shifted his gaze back to the teacher, still seated peacefully at the table. *Where's your God now, Campbell? You're going down in flames.* Jordan relished the thought. One less do-gooder trying to change the landscape of American culture on a belief that was no more substantiated than Santa Claus.

Without warning, a picture flashed through Jordan's mind of himself at age thirteen, kneeling in prayer, tears streaming down his face and—

For a single moment, Jordan's heart ached for the child he'd been. He blinked and the image disappeared.

Campbell's attorney finally gathered himself together enough to speak. "Uh…very well, Your Honor, our stance will focus entirely on Mr. Campbell's freedom of speech."

The man looked at his partner, and Jordan almost felt sorry for him. None of the attorneys he knew working for a national teacher's union would want the job of defending an instructor in a religious freedom case. Obviously the legal team was ill-prepared, and the way they glanced at their watches every few minutes confirmed the fact that they were merely marking time until they could get back to the office.

"Your Honor, you'll remember that the student Mr. Campbell was praying with had lost her best friend in a car accident the day before."

Jordan refrained from wincing, but he couldn't stop his heart from remembering a sorrow that could never be resolved. Praying in the wake of a friend's death did more harm than good. After all, how would the girl in question face life now, knowing that God—assuming there was a God—had chosen not to help her friend?

Campbell's attorney was droning on, and Jordan glanced again at the teacher. Much as he disliked what the man had done, what he stood for, Jordan had to admit there was something likable about the guy. Besides that, something about Campbell's eyes looked familiar. Where had he seen eyes like that before?

Another image filled Jordan's mind, and he flinched as he remembered. Long, long ago...the eyes had belonged to a man he'd trusted...a man he'd loved like a father...a man who'd lied to him.

Jordan brought himself back to the present and made a mental note to stay in tune with the proceedings. This was no time to be drifting back to the hardest days of his life. Back when people's prayers had been for him...back when his mother—

"And so, Your Honor, we'd like you to consider the spirit of the law in this case." Campbell's attorney actually sounded as though he meant it. "The defendant was not leading his class in prayer, nor was he teaching on prayer in the classroom. Rather he was doing what comes naturally for someone of his religion. He was praying with a student who looked as if she needed prayer." The counsel shuffled his notes into a different order and cast a last glance at the judge. "Thank you, Your Honor."

Without missing a beat the judge slid back her chair and leaned into the microphone. "There will be a ten-minute break while I evaluate the information. After that time I will return with my decision." She rapped her gavel on the desk and left through a door behind her chair.

Joshua caught himself watching Campbell's attorneys, how they whispered to their client and shook their heads, their eyes narrow and dark. Jordan looked back at the file on the table in front of him. Why was he so drawn to Campbell, anyway? The man deserved to lose his job; indeed, whatever punishment the court might decide would not be enough to undo the damage done to that student. She would have trusted Campbell. He was an adult—a *teacher*, no less—and clearly the girl was suffering through one of the hardest times of her life. Now she had only two choices: Buy into the faith lie or be scarred for life knowing God had failed to help her friend—and in the process probably doubting whether He even existed. Jordan knew where that went. He never wanted to go there again.

"Great job, Riley." The hand on his shoulder belonged to Peter T. Hawkins, president of Humanity Organized and United in Responsibility, better known as HOUR. The legal group ranked up there with any other civil liberties organization fighting against the religious right. Jordan had been working with HOUR for nearly six years and was considered young and brilliant, talented in a way that made his superiors salivate over the cases they might win at his hand.

"Thanks, sir." Jordan grinned. "Looks pretty good."

"Another slam dunk." Hawkins crossed his arms and smiled hard at Jordan. The senior lawyer had been a brilliant litigator in his day and now made only occasional appearances for closing arguments in the cases of his attorneys. It was considered an honor when he showed up, and he showed up often at Jordan's cases.

Hawkins shook his head. "Lady Luck was smiling on us the day we hired you, my friend. By the time you're done with this country's Jesus freaks, they'll be meeting in barns at night and prayer will be little more than a state of mind. I'm telling you, Riley, you've got the gift. We have big things planned for you, real big."

The long ago memory of the man's face—of eyes filled with compassion, a voice lowered in prayer—came to mind again, and Jordan willed it away. This was no time to be sucked into the past, not with his career taking off before his eyes. "Right, thanks."

The judge entered the courtroom and resumed her place at the bench, rapping her gavel until the crowd quieted. Hawkins smile faded into an appropriately somber expression as he took a seat next to Jordan. "Here we go," he whispered.

"Order. I have a decision in the case of Humanity Organized and United in Responsibility versus The New York School District." The judge sifted through several pieces of paper and looked at Campbell. "This case is not about emotions, Mr. Campbell. It is not about car accidents or grieving high school students. It is about following the rules as they are spelled out." She sighed and Jordan could taste the victory at hand. "You are a state employee, paid by the state to impart education to the children of this state. The rules—as Mr. Riley pointed out—are very clear in this case: A teacher may not pray with a student because to do so would be a violation of the separation of church and state." She sat back in her chair and angled her head. "The consequences are also clearly spelled out. And since you chose to ignore them, I have no choice but to do as Mr. Riley has recommended and order the New York School District to terminate your contract immediately."

The thrill of notching another win filled Jordan's senses, but rather than revel in the victory he glanced over his shoulder at Campbell. The man lowered his head for the briefest moment—and Jordan had the disconcerting feeling that the disappointment was a mere speed bump on whatever private journey Campbell was a part of. Then Campbell looked up and smiled at the judge, his eyes still full of that strangely disquieting peace.

Doesn't he get it? No one'll hire him now. Jordan wanted to shake the man, make him renounce the faith that had gotten him into this mess in the first place. Instead Campbell looked surer of himself than ever.

It was often the way his opponents looked in defeat, and that baffled Jordan beyond understanding.

The proceedings were over and Hawkins was pumping his hand, patting him on the arm and telling him he was a god among men. Even as he did so, a handful of local reporters circled around Jordan hungry for quotes and sound bites. He paid no attention to any of it. His eyes were glued on Campbell, watching as the man stood and shook the hands of his two attorneys. That done, he moved toward the spectator section of the courtroom and embraced a pretty woman whose eyes were filled with unshed tears. Campbell placed his hand alongside the woman's face and stroked her cheek with his thumb, his face lowered close to hers. Whatever he was saying to her, she smiled and nodded in response, circling her arms around his neck and holding him tight.

Seems like a nice couple…

They stayed together longer than any standard hug, and Jordan felt a knot form deep in his gut. They were praying. Anger worked its way into his bloodstream, quickening his heart and turning his stomach. Here, in the aftermath of what had to be the greatest blow of their lives, they were praying. Talking to the same God who had let them down and asking…for what? Another job to replace the one Campbell had just lost? Money to fall from the sky? What possible good could it do to pray now, when praying had already cost him everything?

"Mr. Riley…Mr. Riley…" Jordan faced the reporters with an easy smile he knew would make the next day's *New York Times*. Hawkins had told him from the beginning that image was everything and Jordan prided himself on doing his part to keep the firm in a good light. "Mr. Riley, what message do you think this sends to teachers across the state?"

Jordan opened his mouth to answer and for an instant caught a peripheral view of Campbell and the woman walking out of the courtroom, their arms around each other. *I refuse to feel bad.* He faced the cameras squarely. "This case sends a message to every instructor in America: We will not allow teachers to use a public classroom to impose religion on innocent children."

The questions went on for thirty minutes, long after Hawkins winked at him and left through the double doors. When it was over, Jordan loaded a stack of papers into his briefcase and made his way to the parking lot and his shiny, white Lexus. It was quarter after four and he had a date that night with Ashley Janes. Beautiful, plastic-coated Ashley, the well-known model he'd met at a corporate dinner the year before. She was a welcome distraction, but too caught up in the jet-set crowd and her own popularity for anything long-term.

"You're fun, Jordan," Ashley had told him after they'd gone out a few times. "Just as good-looking on my arm as I am on yours."

At the time her words had felt like a slap in the face and he'd regretted his attraction to her. But since then he'd come to understand what she meant. Their looks were just one of the aspects they enjoyed about each other, and since neither of them was looking for a commitment, their relationship was ideal.

Jordan tossed his briefcase in the backseat and headed toward his apartment in the heart of the city, where a forest of dirty buildings made up the landscape and the hum and screech of traffic was constant. Jordan wouldn't have it any other way. The distractions of city life kept him from thinking about the ghosts of his past—ghosts he'd spent a lifetime outrunning.

He smiled to himself. After Monday he'd have one less memory to run from.

He'd already shared his thoughts with Hawkins, and again more recently at a general meeting with the firm's three partners and twenty-one attorneys. To a man the group was excited about Jordan's plan, and why not? Suing a conservative little town such as Bethany, Pennsylvania, over something that should have been taken care of decades ago was right up their alley. Since it was Jordan's idea, he was given the go-ahead to spend a few days in Bethany, where he would file the suit, then round up the city officials and see if they were interested in complying without going to trial.

If not, the suit would inevitably make headlines across the country. Victorious headlines. And a victory in Bethany would go a long way toward helping him forget the past and the things that had gone wrong in that town so many years ago.

Jordan took the elevator to the twelfth floor and made his way into his apartment. The building was nice, security guards and a workout room that Jordan used every morning at five. He grabbed a glass of ice water, took it into the living room, and kicked back in a white, leather recliner. The view from his front window was standard city fare: No sky, only the angular walls and windows of a handful of buildings.

Jordan loosened his tie. No, there was nothing homey about his apartment. Professional decorators had appointed it with leather, chrome, and glass, but there were no personal details, no photographs or sentimental knickknacks. Just a place to unwind at the end of the day and sometimes—when he couldn't help himself—a place to wonder what if…

What if his mother hadn't died that awful summer in 1985? What if she'd lived long enough to see him and his sister through school, to be a part of their lives, to make them a family? What if God had seen fit to let her live instead of…

He shook his head. What if the state hadn't placed him and Heidi in separate foster homes? What if—wherever his little sister was, whoever she'd grown up to be—she still remembered him? And what if he hadn't lost track of his childhood friend, a beautiful girl with blond hair and blue eyes as innocent as a baby's?

Most of all what if there really was a God who had loved him?

Jordan took a sip of ice water, and the questions ceased. If there was a God then He was unreliable and inept. Or perhaps sinister and judgmental—striking people down at random. Because that summer in Bethany, Pennsylvania, Jordan had prayed his heart out, begging God to spare his mother and believing all the while He would. But Evelyn Riley died anyway. At first Jordan figured there was nothing God could have done to help his mother's sickness. Later he realized the truth: Either God didn't exist or He didn't care about a young boy's prayers. And so Jordan had turned to the courtroom, determined to push what remained of society's religious deceptions into hiding or expose them for the lies they were.

That was why he needed to go back to Bethany—to even the score. With God.

He stood up and set the glass in the kitchen. There were places in his heart that he was sure weren't ready to visit his hometown again, to walk the streets where the old Jordan—the naive, trusting Jordan—had died alongside his mother. Where the person he was today had been birthed in bitterness. The place where he'd lost the three women who had ever really mattered to him.

His mother, his sister…and a girl he had never quite been able to forget.

A girl named Faith.

3

Faith Evans checked her look in the mirror and made certain every strand of her long, blond hair was tucked neatly into the knot at the back of her head. Dick Baker, the station manager at the WKZN affiliate where she worked, had frowned on her hair from the beginning, giving her two options: cut it or wear it up. "Makes you look too young," he'd grumbled. "Don't make me work to justify having you on the air, Evans."

Faith had seen other anchors with hair similar to hers—halfway to their waists—but the issue wasn't worth arguing about. Besides, she was under enough scrutiny already.

She made her way back to the soundstage, but before taking her place she saw one of the associate producers. "It's Wednesday...are we running the special?"

The man stopped what he was doing and stared at her, unblinking. "Special?"

"*Wednesday's Child.* Remember?" Faith held her breath. This segment was especially important. He had to include it in the lineup.

She'd started the *Wednesday's Child* program six months earlier and used her own time to put together the two-minute segments. Each one highlighted a special-needs child who was up for adoption through the state's social services department. So far more than half the children featured had been adopted, and more than once her boss had said the program was a success. But without her constant reminders, the station executives tended to forget the segment altogether.

"So what're we talking?" A tired look crossed the man's face. "One minute, two?"

Faith kept her frustration in check. "Two."

He checked his chart. "Okay, immediately after sports."

"Thanks." Faith felt the familiar surge of hope. There were reasons for her attachment to the state's homeless children. Reasons that went far beyond good citizenship or Christian character. Faith headed back across the soundstage and eased herself onto the stool opposite the one where Ron Leonard already sat studying his notes. *Okay, Lord, these next thirty minutes are for You...help me make You proud.* "You ready?" She smiled the question at her coanchor.

Ron was fifteen years older and his position anchoring for the Philadelphia station had clearly been a demotion for him. Generally his mood reflected that truth and tonight was no exception. Rather than answer, he bunched his eyebrows together and looked hard at his watch. "When the producer says 10:45, he means 10:45. Not 10:47."

Faith swallowed. "Thank you, Ron. I'll try to keep that in mind." Her voice held not a trace of sarcasm. She respected Ron and knew he was right. Every minute counted. "I had to check on the *Wednesday's Child* segment."

Ron's shoulders dropped several inches. "It's not on the schedule."

"I guess we should write it in. Two minutes, right after sports."

A heavy sigh escaped through Ron's clenched teeth. "We're a news station, not a church."

Faith ignored his comment and studied her notes. In many ways she was marked by her beliefs and the fact that she was Bob Moses' daughter. It was why she'd agreed to use her middle name at work. Faith Evans. Bob Moses was well known locally and by using Faith's middle name, her boss hoped viewers wouldn't identify her as religious or one-sided.

It was something he had worried about since the day he hired her.

Before that first newscast Dick pulled her aside and gave her a warning she remembered to this day: "The viewers may not know who you are, but I do. Bob Moses is a visible person with extreme religious views." He'd tapped his pencil on his desk. "I like your work, Evans, but the executives expect me to keep my anchors in line. This station is not a pulpit for you to preach your doctrine, do you hear me?"

Faith had been shocked by his warning. After four years at Penn State and five years working her way up the ladder as a sports reporter, Faith had still believed there was fairness in reporting. But in the two years since taking the position as nighttime news anchor, there were many times when she'd seen otherwise. Too often stories that favored a conservative, Christian worldview were cut or changed or balanced with opposing interviews that lasted longer and sounded more professional. It was as though the executives had mandated a certain politically correct response for most news topics, and the station manager's role was to see that response carried out.

Occasionally a child's outstanding achievement or the way a family survived a personal tragedy might be worthy of a news story, but not without heavy editing. Stories along those lines tended to feature Christians who attributed their success or survival to God, but rarely did their statements of belief make the final televised piece.

There wasn't much Faith could do about it. It was an industry rule that anchors and reporters be unbiased in their work. It was written that way in her contract. If she used her visible position in any way other than to report the news without opinion, it was grounds for dismissal. She knew the rules and she had no intention of breaking them. Not with all that had happened over the last few years.

"Three minutes…" The off-stage warning caused Faith to sit straighter in her seat as she memorized the story order. Ron had the first segment: Gunman takes a hostage. She had the next one: budget cuts at the city hospital. Two more follow-up segments, including cutaways to taped interviews, and they'd have their first commercial break. One more eight-minute news segment with additional footage, another commercial break, weather, and then sports.

"Three, two, one...and...go!" The voice stopped abruptly as intense, upbeat music filled the soundstage. Faith and Ron adjusted themselves on their seats and sorted briefly through their individual stacks of paper as they faced the camera, serious expressions in place.

"A gunman takes three hostages in a shootout today that left one local man dead and another critically injured..." Ron's voice was crisp and upbeat with the polish that comes from years of working the cameras.

"And good news for the city hospital. Budget woes may be over but at whose expense...?" On cue Faith glanced at Ron.

"Good evening everyone, I'm Ron Leonard."

Back at the camera. "And I'm Faith Evans. Welcome to tonight's edition of *WKZN News.*"

Faith angled her head toward Ron and he kicked in with precision timing. "A burst of gunfire ripped through a family home in the two-thousand block of Westchester Avenue this morning as an escaped convict broke in and took three people hostage. We have more on that from Alicia Rodriguez who was there at the scene." A thirty-second segment filled the screen with live reports and statements from family members. Faith and Ron checked the story order again and prepared once more to go live.

The newscast continued without a hitch, and Faith prayed between stories for the little girl in tonight's *Wednesday's Child* segment. Rosa Lee, a six-year-old biracial Asian sweetheart abandoned by her parents at birth and shuffled through five foster homes since then. She was legally free for adoption but she had a problem: She had been born with just two fingers and a thumb on her left hand.

Faith had spent an afternoon with Rosa and her social worker over the weekend, amazed at how well the child worked to compensate for her handicap. Even so, the missing fingers were another strike against her. Chances were Rosa might never be adopted, unless God used the news segment to touch someone's heart.

Ben Bloom, the weatherman, was wrapping up.

Lord, prepare the right person's heart even now... Faith loved talking to God even in the middle of a newscast. It was something her dad had taught her when she was only a child. *Father, please...find a home for little Rosa, please.*

A brief commercial break ended and the sports segment began. Chase Wilson was a former college athlete with model-like looks, a beautiful wife, and three children. He was in his early thirties, and rumor was the network had plans to move him into the national spotlight sometime soon. Women viewers often wrote to the station saying Chase was the reason they tuned in at all. He smiled and began talking into the camera.

"We've got baseball scores from around the league and stories from NFL camps, but before we get to that we have breaking news on a player out of Dallas. Tight end Mike Dillan's name is back in court tonight after two women—longtime friends—filed paternity suits claiming he was the father of both their children."

Faith felt the blood drain from her face. Mike Dillan? Not tonight...she couldn't think about him now. But images of the rugged athlete filled her mind as Chase continued.

"The women claim he impregnated both of them at a party three years ago..."

Three years ago? That was when she and Mike...

Faith forced herself to remain in position and prayed that she didn't look as shaken as she felt.

The monitor showed taped footage of Coach Graves at a press conference admonishing Mike Dillan and any other player who continued to act irresponsibly.

Faith struggled to focus while Chase finished and looked first at her and then at Ron, a casual smile draped across his face. "Exciting time of year in sports..."

Ron straightened a stack of papers and tapped them on his desk as he grinned at Chase. "Days of October right around the corner."

Faith lowered her chin and raised her eyebrows in a manner intended to be teasing and lighthearted. She doubted she was fooling anyone, including the viewers. Everyone in Philadelphia probably knew about her and Mike. "Doesn't look like my Mets'll be anywhere near a field by then."

Chase chuckled and flashed a handsome smile in her direction. "That's the nice thing about August. Everybody has a chance. Even your Mets, Faith."

A round of easy laughter died out, and Faith took the cue as the camera zoomed in on her. *Focus, Faith, focus.* "Each week for the past six months we've been bringing you a segment called *Wednesday's Child,* highlighting special-needs children who are up for adoption in Philadelphia's social services system. Tonight we take a look at six-year-old Rosa Lee."

Saxophones led the way as the haunting strains of a child's lullaby filled the station and faded into the laughter of children playing at Jericho Park. Rosa was living with a foster family in Bethany, and the park was her favorite place to play. Faith noticed that the cameraman had avoided the hundred-year-old Jesus statue, anchored just to the right of the play area.

Throughout the piece, a phone number remained on the screen for viewers interested in adopting Rosa. Faith watched the monitor as the camera panned in past the other children and settled on the dark-haired little beauty. Mike Dillan forgotten, Faith again savored the child's giggles as she'd done over the weekend when they'd been together for the interview. From the moment she met Rosa, Faith had felt captured by her, desperate to find her a family. Faith heard her own voice begin to sound over the footage.

"Rosa Lee's life has never been easy. Not since the morning her mother abandoned her on the steps of a Philadelphia hospital days after her birth." The camera zoomed out from Faith strolling the park grounds, her face serious, eyes on the camera, to Rosa running alongside three other children, chasing butterflies across the park's grassy hillside. An edit showed the same children eating a picnic lunch and a close-in shot gave the television audience a first glimpse of Rosa's deformed hand. "Rosa was born with just two fingers and a thumb on her left hand, making her one of thousands of special-needs children up for adoption across the United States."

The monitor showed Rosa brushing the crumbs from her play clothes and running back to the swings and slides. "Rosa will always have special needs, but don't tell her that. When it comes to using her hands, she's more determined than most kids twice her age."

The footage showed Rosa using a pencil, catching a ball, and playing tennis at the city courts. The segment finally cut to Rosa, her head tilted, long silky eyelashes batting shyly at Faith as they sat together on a park bench. "...A mommy who'll stay with me forever. That's what I want."

What?

From where Faith sat staring at her monitor she felt the piercing sting of betrayal. Someone had gotten to the segment and edited out the first part of Rosa's statement. She remembered how the girl's words had pierced her heart when she'd smiled and said, "I'm praying for a mommy who'll stay with me forever. That's what I want."

God, I can't fight this battle anymore...

Be strong and courageous, daughter. I will go before you in the battle you are about to fight.

What battle? The muscles in her stomach tightened at the thought. Had she correctly heard the still small voice she knew so well? *I can't fight the system, Lord...You must be thinking of someone else.*

Be strong, daughter. The battle belongs to Me.

Faith felt the reassuring presence of the Lord and her anger eased. *It's so unfair, Father...*

How could the station allow references to everything but a person's faith in God? And how could that be considered unbiased reporting when it was nothing *but* biased. Bias and censorship, pure and simple, and though Faith was not a fighter, it made her tempted to take a more vocal stand for her beliefs.

The footage of Rosa faded to a still shot of the child swinging high in the air against a deep blue sky, her eyes sparkling with love and hope and light. The camera angled back in on Faith live in the studio.

"Rosa is an Asian biracial child who is currently available for adoption to anyone with a valid home study. If you're interested in adopting this precious little one call the number at the bottom of your screen and someone will help you through the process." She glanced at her prompt and looked pleasantly at her partner. "Ron?"

"We'll take a break for a moment, but when we come back, a look at Julia Roberts's box-office hit, *Where Yesterday Lives.*"

Faith nodded. "Bring a *box* of tissues for this one..."

The break played out, and in five minutes the newscast was over.

"That's a wrap," a director yelled from behind the camera. "See ya tomorrow. Same bat time, same bat channel."

A technician flipped a series of switches to cut the studio bright lights and stop the whir of the cameras just as Ron's smile faded. *Right on cue.* Faith watched, somewhat amazed. It was almost as though her partner's facial expressions were on the same electrical current as the camera equipment.

Faith studied him as he turned to leave. "See ya, Ron."

He held a hand up in her direction, not even looking back. *At least he's a good actor.* She turned and was headed for her purse and car keys when Dick Baker caught her attention. "Come here, Faith. I need a word with you."

She felt the familiar knot in her stomach. What had she done now? Had he read her mind and known she was praying just to survive the half hour? Could he see on her face the way Mike Dillan's name had made her feel? She approached him and felt the corner of her lips raise a fraction of an inch. "Yes?"

Mr. Baker was in his sixties, a gruff, hardcore veteran of television news determined to gain the favor of the network executives. For the most part Faith thought he was her ally, a professional who appreciated the quality of her work. But there were times when whatever pressure he must have been getting from the higher-ups took its toll and turned him into a tyrant.

Faith had a feeling this was about to be one of those times.

She had only seen his soft side once—after her father's heart attack the month before. The station covered the story, portraying her father in a flattering light, stating that he died chasing after his life's passion: maintaining rights for the people of Pennsylvania and the United States. Mr. Baker himself had helped edit the story, making sure it included the fact that Bob Moses was survived by a wife, Betty, and two daughters—one of which was their very own Faith Evans.

The man standing before her now looked far less compassionate. "Haven't we warned you about references to prayer?" His words sounded as if they were leaking from a pressure cooker.

Faith was tempted to look ignorant, but instead she folded her arms and maintained eye contact with her boss. "Yes. But that wasn't *my* reference, it was—"

"Let me finish!" Mr. Baker's face was a mass of angry knots. "If I hadn't checked that *Wednesday's Child* segment first it would have aired that way, with that girl sharing her private prayers for all the world to hear."

Faith felt her face grow hot. "It's what she wanted to—"

Mr. Baker raised his hand. "Don't speak. I'm not done." His head was nearly bald, and in his frustration it had grown damp with sweat. "We've been over this before, Evans. It's bad enough that our Bethany *viewers* know your religious stance. But surely you understand the network execs know about it, too. 'Watch her, Baker,' they tell me." He shook his head and a choked, sarcastic huff escaped him. "And to tell you the truth I try, Evans, honest I do. You know why I had to fix that segment?"

"No, sir, it didn't need fixing if you'd—"

Her boss gave a quick shake of his head and glared at her. "I'm not finished! If I hadn't made that cut that would have been five God stories in two weeks. Five, for cryin' out loud, Evans. Your stories include mentions of God and prayer ten times more than the stories from other reporters. If that doesn't change, you and I both know the executives will talk." He leveled his gaze at her. "You remember that contract you signed?" He paused, but not long enough for her to answer. "You start giving biased reports, and if I don't fire you the network executives will fire me. It's that simple."

His voice was louder than before, and Faith noticed various cameramen and technical staff members scurrying off the soundstage. "Do I make myself clear?"

Faith had to fight back tears.

Go forth, daughter. Be gentle and take up the fight...

Not now, Lord, I can't... Her knees began to tremble.

Her boss's face grew still darker. "I said, do I make myself clear?"

Be strong and courageous. I will go before you...

Send someone else, Father. I'm not strong enough.

Daughter, nothing is impossible with Me...

But it was no use. Her knees were already weak; if she stood up to Dick Baker now she was likely to faint flat across the man's feet. "Yes, sir."

At Faith's compliant answer, her boss's scowl eased. "You're a darn good reporter. Don't get me wrong. We've..." He paused as though he didn't want to share this information with her. "Well, we've had calls about you and Chase. There's talk about moving you up." He pointed at her, his finger inches from the bridge of her nose. "The network's watching, Faith. Don't do anything to ruin it for yourself."

Her heart felt as though it had been shredded by competing emotions. The network? Was it possible? Were they really interested in her for a potential national spot? Hope surged through her, then dimmed as her boss's words rang in her mind again: *Don't do anything to mess it up...to mess it up...to mess it up.*

In other words, don't be a fanatic. Don't wear your beliefs on your sleeve. Don't be sold out to God.

Faith sighed. "I won't, sir."

Her boss smiled. "Thatta girl. When you look good, we all look good. Remember that." He started to turn, but paused. "Don't let me see that prayer thing again, Faith. I mean it."

She caught herself nodding, and the sensation made her picture Peter two thousand years ago sitting around the fire outside the room where his friend, Jesus, was being interrogated. *I swear, I don't know the man...* She could almost hear the ancient words of the apostle's betrayal, feel the way his heart must have sank as he met the eyes of Jesus at that very moment.

Faith walked slowly to her car. Was she any different from Peter? Drawn and pulled and tempted to give up pieces of her soul—bit by bit—in a proud climb toward a position of power. The feeling clung to her like a damp blanket in summertime, and she couldn't will it away no matter how hard she tried. *What's this feeling, Lord? As if trouble's brewing and I'm not hearing Your will for me. And my enemies are rallying against me on every side.*

Be strong and courageous…the days ahead will bring testing.

Testing? Great. *Haven't I been tested enough, Father?*

She climbed into her Jeep and headed back to Bethany, wishing her father were still alive. Mom always turned in just after nine o'clock when she wasn't out at a fundraiser or charity event. Once a week she'd tape the news and the next morning she and Faith would watch it over coffee. Her mother always said the same thing. *You look lovely, dear…your father and I have always been so proud of you.* Faith loved that time with her mother, but Dad…he was something else. He'd stay up until the news was over waiting for Faith's call. She would never forget those conversations as long as she lived.

She'd call him from her cell phone the minute she climbed in her Jeep. "Dad, it's me. What'd you think?"

"Sweetheart, you were more beautiful than ever. One of these days the network suits are gonna give you a call, and then everyone'll know what a wonderful reporter you are!"

The memories dissipated and Faith drove home in silence. What would her father think of Rosa's words being edited? Or of the way Dick Baker had practically threatened to fire her if she used stories that mentioned prayer or God? The worst part of it all was that Baker was right—Faith *had* signed the contract knowing the rules upfront.

The heaviness grew worse. She knew what her father would think. He'd tell her the same thing the famous Jim Elliott said before he was killed on the mission field: "He is no fool who gives what he cannot keep to gain what he cannot lose."

It was her father's favorite quote outside of Scripture.

Fifteen minutes later she pulled into her driveway, climbed out, and headed straight for her bedroom. How strange it had been to hear Mike Dillan's name after so many years. Strange to think that she had survived not only the breakup with him, but also the accident that followed. No one had ever broken her heart the way Mike had. At least not since she was thirteen, the year she lost Jordan. Her heart drifted still further downstream. Jordan Riley. The boy she'd grown up with, the one she thought she'd marry some day.

As she walked back through the milestones of the past, she realized that at every turn her father had been there. Always it was Dad who held her close and convinced her that through prayer and trust in the Lord her losses would turn into something beautiful. It was only months after she'd taken the Philadelphia job that he quit working for the big city law firm and opened an office with his best friend.

"That way I can help keep an eye on you, sweetheart."

She could hear his voice even now as she lay in bed and uttered one last prayer before falling asleep. "Thank You, Lord, for all You've brought me through. And please tell my dad—wherever he is up there and whatever he's doing—tell him I said hi." She paused.

"And tell him I miss him."

4

The meeting took place at Alvin's because, other than the Jesus statue in Jericho Park, it was the most well-known landmark in all of Bethany. Despite the smattering of fast food places that had sprung up along Highway 40, Alvin's had continued to thrive. It was the only place in town where you could still get a burger, fries, and Coke for less than three dollars and not go away hungry.

At a quiet table for six in the back corner of the diner, Joshua met Mayor Frank, three of the city councilmen, and an attorney who handled general matters for the people of Bethany. The men exchanged pleasantries, talked about how big the trout were this time of year and the number of weeks until football season started. Then a silence fell over the table, and Frank cleared his throat.

"I'd like to explain the situation to Joshua." Frank's face was a mask of somber lines, and Joshua felt his heartbeat quicken. *What could be this serious?*

"Go ahead, Frank." One of the councilmen nodded, and the others moved their heads in agreement.

Frank sighed. "You've heard of the HOUR group, right?"

Joshua's mind raced, trying to remember. "They're opposed to religious freedom…I'm trying to remember." This was Bob's expertise, not his. He felt a sense of panic as the others waited for him to place the group. "Wait a minute, I know. Humanity Organized and United in Responsibility."

Frank nodded. "Exactly."

A waitress appeared and took their order. When she was gone, Frank continued. "I have a connection in New York who called me yesterday. He told me on Monday morning someone from HOUR is planning to file suit against the town of Bethany."

Joshua's heartbeat accelerated. He looked from Frank to the other men and back again. File a lawsuit against Bethany? The town was too quiet, too small to ruffle the political feathers of a group such as HOUR. "Why would they do that?"

The men at the table exchanged glances, and just when Joshua thought he couldn't take the suspense any longer, Frank spoke up. "They want the Jesus statue."

For a moment Joshua was confused. The Jesus statue? What would a group such as HOUR want with Bethany's Jesus statue? "I'm not sure I understand."

Frank leaned closer. "They want it down, Joshua. Removed from the park. It's a Christian symbol standing on public property, exactly the kind of thing HOUR loves to go after."

A tingling sensation began in Joshua's fingers and made its way up through his arms and down his spine. HOUR wanted to remove the Jesus statue? Immediately his mind kicked into gear. "This is big…"

Frank sat back in his chair. "Exactly." He looked at the others. "Joshua, we've had a meeting and this is a battle we don't want to lose. We need more than general attorney wisdom this time." The general attorney in the group raised his eyebrows and took a sip of orange juice. Frank obviously was not worried about hurting the man's pride. "We'll have to wait until they file suit, but if they do…we've all agreed we want you to be our primary counsel on the case."

HOUR wanted to remove a monument that had stood as the single, most well-loved landmark in town for more than a hundred years? The story was bound to gain statewide attention—even nationwide. Joshua had a sudden sense of panic.

This was too big for him. He needed Bob for this kind of thing.

As I was with Bob Moses so I will be with you.

But this is serious, Lord. It'll take more than me—

Joshua, I will never leave you nor forsake you.

Frank was looking at him. "I'm assuming you want the job." He paused, his gaze leveled at Joshua. "It'll be the biggest case you've handled since you and Bob opened shop."

"Right, I know." *Be strong and courageous…* "Of course…I'd be honored. The statue has to stay, it's that simple."

"Off the cuff, could you…I mean, you know, if you had to make a guess at it now…do you think they could force us to take it down?" Frank's usual eloquence had fled in light of all that was at stake.

Joshua swallowed hard. "Depends on how much precedent they pull."

"Precedent?" Frank's eyes narrowed. "Isn't the law clear-cut?"

"Not usually." This from the general attorney, who cast a look at Joshua. "My understanding is that case precedent works against us this time, am I right?"

Joshua nodded. "Right. HOUR prides itself on eliminating the aspects of American culture they feel violate the separation of church and state. The Jesus statue is the perfect target."

There was silence as Frank crossed his arms, his teeth clenched. "That statue's part of this town. They don't have the right to come in here and—"

"We'll have to find a loophole, a way to outsmart them." Joshua hung his head for a moment and then looked at the others again. "I have to be honest, with Bob gone it won't be easy."

"You'll have our support, whatever we can do." The general attorney tapped his pencil. "It isn't a matter of the religious right or separation of church and state. That statue belongs to the people of Bethany, and my guess is there's not a person within a hundred miles offended by it."

"Save that." Joshua smiled. "We might need it for closing arguments—"

Frank broke in. "None of it matters unless they actually file suit. And we won't know that until Monday."

The men agreed to keep the issue to themselves unless it became a reality. In that case, they'd need all the favorable media contacts they could get. Joshua thought of Faith Evans and hoped it wouldn't have to involve her. She'd been through enough without adding this.

The meeting was over, and the men went their own ways—all but Frank and Joshua. They talked about the possibilities as they wandered toward the parking lot. "I'll do whatever I can to help you." Frank shoved his hands in his pockets. "Be ready."

Be ready...be ready... The same words he'd felt God laying on his heart the day before. *Be strong...be ready...I'll go before you.* Yes, though the situation might seem impossible, the Lord had His hand in it.

Frank drove away and Joshua followed. But instead of heading home to Helen, he turned right and then right again on Main Street...half a block down to Jericho Park. It was a small place, really. Not like those built by newer communities, with tennis courts and indoor swimming pools and play equipment stretching half an acre. On the left stood a double swing set and two slides—set in sand. Also in the play area were two teeter-totters and an old metal merry-go-round, the kind kids powered by running alongside. Ancient maple trees edged the park on both sides, and a cement walkway meandered along the entire perimeter. Across from the play yard was less than two acres of neatly manicured mature grass.

And standing proudly in the center of the grass was the Jesus statue.

Joshua climbed out of his car and walked toward it, remembering all the times he'd worked or played or loved or laughed in the shadow of that chiseled, ten-foot piece of stone. A few years ago the Bethany *Chronicle* ran a story about the statue, detailing the history of the piece. Created by a local artist, it was donated to the city before the turn of the twentieth century. Of course, back then Bible lessons were taught in public schools and the Ten Commandments hung in every classroom. The townsfolk received the statue gratefully, in awe of the artist's ability to capture Christ's expression of compassion.

Over the decades stories had risen and become part of the town's folklore—stories of people passing through town, spotting the Jesus statue, and being so moved they gave their lives to the Lord then and there. Or of people who'd been to the park a hundred times suddenly seeing something about the eyes of the sculpture that caused them to come clean with God and pray for a fresh start.

Joshua moved closer to the statue. It was no surprise.

The statue depicted Jesus, arms outstretched, palms up, beckoning those with hurts or fears or pain to come to Him. There was something about the eyes...something steeped in love and peace and grace and forgiveness. Something that showed the way Christ would always yearn for the return of His people.

Joshua was at the foot of the statue now and he read the placard engraved at its base: "Come to me, all you who are weary and heavy burdened, and I will give you rest... Take my yoke upon you and learn from me, for I am gentle and humble in heart, and you will find rest for your souls. Jesus."

That was it. A person could actually feel his soul resting in the presence of Christ's words, in the shadow of His image. Not that the statue itself held any power, it simply directed one to consider the greatness of God, the peace one might experience if only he took Jesus up on His offer.

Certainly in light of the political climate and in light of the persecution promised in Scripture, it was understandable that some might find the statue offensive. But remove it from the park? Joshua thought about other public places he'd visited, parks with statues of famous generals, influential Native American leaders, or great men and women in the Civil Rights movement. If those statues were allowed, what right did HOUR have to remove one that depicted Jesus Christ?

Regardless of whether people took Him at His word, Christ was real. He lived and died and made a tremendous impact on people, both in His day and in the present. That alone should be justification for keeping the statue up. Christ was an historical figure.

But Jesus was so much more than that. And Joshua was willing to bet the people at HOUR knew this. Certainly they were aware that no other man in history had affected mankind as much as Christ. No other had demonstrated the power to instill such deep emotions and widely varying reactions from people. His presence was life-changing for some while it filled others with violent hate. There was no one else who evoked such a dramatic response from all who came to know of Him.

But then no other man was the Son of God.

Joshua sighed, studying the statue's eyes. They seemed so lifelike. So full of love, of compassion.

Joshua closed his eyes. *Don't let them file suit against us, God. What if we lose? What of the cost to the people of Bethany if the statue is forced to go?*

Joshua blinked and turned his back to the statue. Gazing into the blue sky over Bethany he begged God again to keep HOUR from filing, painfully aware that the law was on their side, not his.

Be strong and courageous, Joshua. I will go before you.

The holy whispers resonated in Joshua's soul, bringing a sense of peace he hadn't felt since Bob died. Somehow he knew that whatever might happen Monday, God would see him through. He rested in that thought for a moment. *Okay, Lord...I'll trust You.*

After all, what choice did he have? Outside of God's intervention, if HOUR filed suit against Bethany on Monday the situation would be hopeless.

Whether Joshua was strong and courageous or not.

5

*J*ordan drove to Bethany Sunday afternoon and by ten o'clock that night had checked into a local motel. Normally, seven hours in the car would give him time to review his caseload, strategize about upcoming lawsuits, and work on closing arguments for those in progress. This time, though, he'd been plagued by unwanted images, memories that had propelled him into an exhausting inner battle. Every few moments he was drawn to remember the past, to walk through it and touch it and savor life the way it had been. But just as quickly would come his determination to keep such thoughts at bay. He was a survivor, not a sentimentalist. He refused to live in yesterday's time zone.

If that wasn't enough, he was burdened by the uncomfortable feeling that his life's work was somehow flawed. His opponents were defenseless types, such as the New York schoolteacher or pastors or youth group leaders. Was there really victory in winning cases against such people? People who certainly had never intended to cause harm? Shouldn't he have been using his legal talent to rid the streets of real criminals?

Of course, anyone who encouraged public expression of religion was a criminal in Jordan's mind. But still the feeling remained.

In the end he blamed his confusing thoughts on overwork and a lack of sleep. When he reached the hotel, he put away his things, brushed his teeth, and dropped into bed, where he immediately fell asleep.

When he awoke Monday he fairly sprang out of bed, showered, shaved, and had a cup of coffee two hours before he needed to be up. He had three very special visits to make. How they went would determine his final decision about filing suit against Bethany. His boss would agree with him either way. If Jordan called and said he'd changed his mind, that the statue was not as offensive as he remembered it to be, Hawkins would never mention it again.

Fifteen minutes later, he drove up in front of the Bethany courthouse and found a parking space. As he made his way up the steps, Jordan caught his reflection in the mirror. He prided himself on looking nice and today was no exception. A professional wardrobe should make a statement and his consisted of Armani suits, starched buttoned-downs, and soft leather dress shoes.

He cursed himself for not driving to Bethany and doing this sooner. Five years sooner. Back when the clerks at the courthouse had first refused to find his sister's file. He'd made more than twenty calls in the months and years since then, but always the answer was the same: "The records are sealed, sir. No one can get that information."

Jordan's heart beat hard in anticipation. He'd learned a few tricks since 1995. The only way past the fortress of red tape was to show up in person. He walked up to a counter labeled Records and waited his turn. Would this be it? In the next few minutes would he actually find out where they'd sent his sister?

"Next." A stout woman barked the word and cast an impatient glance at Jordan. He clutched his briefcase to his side as he moved up against the counter and smiled at the woman. Her name tag read Olivia.

Often women were moved to do what Jordan wanted simply because of his looks. Olivia scowled at him, waiting for him to speak. Somehow he feared this was not one of those times. "Hi. I'm an attorney working on a local case." He smiled as though that were all the explanation he needed to provide. "I need to check out a file."

She scrutinized him, her face a twist of wrinkles and bad attitude. "You new around here?"

Jordan tried to look unaffected by her frigid tone. "Actually, I'm from New York. One of your citizens in Bethany asked me to consult on a matter. Can I give you the file name?"

Olivia shifted her weight, her lips a single line of distrust. "What local citizen?"

There was a beat while Jordan's mind raced for an answer. "He asked me not to mention his name. The lawsuit is highly confidential."

"You got ID?"

Jordan pulled out his wallet and flashed her several pieces, including his Bar Association membership card. Finally he tossed her a business card. Jordan Riley, attorney at law. *Come on, lady, what d'ya want?* When he could think of nothing else to hand her, he smiled again and waited.

Olivia released a heavy sigh. "All right, what file do you need?"

Did all the clerks at the courthouse have Olivia's charming demeanor or was he just lucky? He cleared his throat. "It's a Social Services file. Mother died, two kids were sent to different foster homes. Should be two files, actually. I need the one under the daughter's name—Heidi Riley. No relation."

He hadn't spoken his sister's name for years. The pounding of his heart was so loud within him he figured everyone in the room could easily hear it. He watched Olivia write down the information and waited for her to turn around and head into the archives room for the file.

Instead she shook her head and set down her pen, like a judge rapping his gavel on the bench. "Social Services cases are closed to the public."

Jordan forced a chuckle to cover up his frustration. "I told you, I'm an attorney. I need the file for a case I'm working on."

Olivia planted her hands on her hips. "I don't care who you are, or what high-falutin' big city you're from. You're not getting a Social Services file. Cases where children are placed with foster families are of the utmost privacy in the state of Pennsylvania."

Panic replaced frustration as Jordan saw his opportunity slipping away. "Listen, I can see the file if I want to. But all I really need is one piece of information. Maybe you could check it yourself and give me that detail."

Olivia stared at him, not answering one way or another.

"I need to know where the girl, Heidi, was placed. Who she was placed with." *Give me a break, here, lady…*

Olivia's eyes grew wide and she laughed out loud. "That's exactly what the state wants kept private." She thought a moment. "How old did you say the case was?"

Jordan's shoulders fell. "Sixteen years." Would he never find Heidi? Was there no way to see the file?

A deep chuckle rang from behind the counter again as Olivia shook her head. "A case that old wouldn't be at this courthouse anyway. Those files are at the state's microfilm library. You'd have to petition them if you want a chance to be heard. Even then, I've never heard of opening a placement case. Only the person whose file it is has a right to see those records."

"Fine, I'll try the microfilm library." Jordan smiled, wondering if it hid the pain that racked his heart. *Heidi, don't give up on me…I'm trying to find you.*

"You know—" Olivia's expression softened, as though what she was about to say might actually help Jordan feel better about his wasted effort—"after sixteen years she wouldn't be at the same foster home anymore. She's probably married and living halfway across the country."

"Yeah." A hundred knives pierced Jordan's heart as he stared at the woman. "Thanks."

He was in his car in five minutes, driving to his second visit. As he navigated the streets of Bethany the memories came again. He and his mother and sister riding bikes through the shady roads near their home.

"I'll race you, Jordan…"

Heidi's voice echoed in the hallways of his memory, sounding as alive today as it had all those years ago.

Stop! Jordan ordered himself to remain in the present. Three more turns, and he was on Oak Street, the place where he and his family had lived for what seemed his entire childhood. He slowed the car, struck by how small and crowded the houses looked. *We thought we lived in a castle back then.* He kept driving, searching for signs of the house he still knew better than any other, the only place he'd ever felt at home.

Finally he saw it. It was beige now instead of white, with chocolate brown shutters instead of the blue his mother had painted the summer he was six or seven. It seemed to be about half the size he remembered, but otherwise it looked the same. He thought about walking up to the door and asking for a look around. Then he changed his mind. It would be one thing to walk once more through the rooms where they'd been a happy family. But there would be no avoiding his mother's room, the place where she'd spent most of her time in the months before her death.

Jordan felt tears in his eyes and blinked them back. That was years ago. He had moved on, and now there was just one reason for driving through the old neighborhood. His gaze shifted to the house next door, where the Moses family had lived. Was it possible they still lived there? That maybe—just maybe—after all the years that had passed…Faith was right here in Bethany?

He parked the car and walked up the sidewalk to the place where he had spent so many of his boyhood days. He knocked on the door, then took a step back, running a hand over his suit, smoothing the wrinkles. If Faith didn't live here, maybe the new owners remembered the Moses family.

The door opened and a man in his sixties—a man Jordan had never seen before—looked at him curiously. "Can I help you?"

His heart sank. "Yes, I'm looking for the Bob Moses family. They…uh, they used to live here."

The man smiled, but it didn't hide his guarded expression. "You a friend of the Moses family?"

Jordan nodded and remembered his small-town manners. "Yes, sir. Lived next door when I was a boy. I live in New York now, just passing through."

"You haven't heard then?"

Heard what? Had something happened to Faith? Jordan fought the urge to turn and run before his memories could be altered by whatever the man was about to share. "No, sir. Last I knew, they were still living here."

The man swept his palm over the top of his white hair. "I'm sorry to be the bearer of bad news, but Bob Moses died not too long ago. Let's see, it's been about a month now. Had a heart attack at his law office here in town."

Jordan could think of nothing to say. Bob Moses had been the only father figure he'd ever known, a man who personified everything good and honorable and trustworthy. Even if he had lied to him. And now he was gone. A thickness in Jordan's throat made it difficult for him to talk. "The…the rest of the family? They moved, I guess?"

The stranger waved his hand as though he were chasing off flies. "Oh, they moved years back, bought a nice place in the country five miles out of town."

What about Faith? The question perched on his lips ready to take wing, but Jordan contained it. He'd had enough bad news for one day. He reached out and shook the older man's hand. "I'm Jordan Riley, I should have introduced myself."

"Joe Cooper." The man's handshake was firm and strong despite his years. "Good to know you."

Jordan took another step back. "Well, I guess I'll be going. I'm…I'm sorry about Mr. Moses."

"All of us were. Whole town showed up at his funeral. Never saw two young women cry harder than those girls of his."

Faith! Maybe she did live somewhere nearby. "Girls?"

"Bob's girls. Faith and Sarah. You musta known 'em if you lived next door."

"Yes, sir, I did. Do they…are they still in the area?"

"Sarah married herself a chemist and moved a few hours away, I believe. And Faith…well, son, everyone knows about Faith."

Again Jordan fought to keep control. He loosed a quick laugh. "Like I said I've been away for a while now. Lost touch, I'm afraid."

Joe's eyebrows lifted. "Faith's a local star. Does the eleven o'clock news every weeknight. I think she married some football hero, but don't hold me to it. Not sure where she lives, either, but it must be close."

Jordan fought the urge to race for his car and drive to the news station. So what if she was married? With everything they'd shared as kids he was sure she'd want to see him now. He jingled the keys in his pocket. He had come this far…

Suddenly he wanted to find Faith so badly he could barely stand to wait another moment. "What station is she with?"

The man cocked his head back and squinted. "I believe it's WKZN." He leveled his gaze at Jordan. "Yeah, that's it. WKZN."

Jordan backed up another two steps. "Listen, I gotta run, but thanks for the tip. Maybe I can find her before I leave town."

Joe waved and let his hand hang in the air. "Nice meetin' you, Jordan. Now don't go and get yourself lost in that big city of yours."

Jordan waved one last time and climbed in his car. Maybe Faith would know what happened to Heidi. He was out of the neighborhood and on Main Street before he realized that Faith wouldn't be at the station yet. It was only ten thirty in the morning. Besides, Jordan had one more visit to pay. Even if it was the hardest one he'd make all day, he had no choice but to go. He stopped at a local florist, purchased a dozen long-stem yellow roses—his mother's favorites—and headed for the cemetery.

He had only been to the place where his mother was buried three times. Once on the day they buried her and twice after that—in the weeks before Social Services stepped in—when he had needed her strength and had ridden his bike to the cemetery to sit by her simple grave, marked by a flat, square stone supplied by the state. Jordan had promised himself he'd replace the marker with a proper tombstone when he had the money, but he hadn't been back to Bethany to take care of it. Now the idea seemed to belong to another person.

Carrying the roses, Jordan tried to remember where his mother's plot lay. His eyes fell on a grave that looked newer than the rest, with tiny blades of grass just starting to poke through a fresh mound of dirt. Jordan meandered toward it and saw a large, bronze plaque at the base of the plot. "Robert Samuel Moses, 1944–2001, Lover of Betty, Sarah, Faith, and Jesus, most of all. Religious freedom fighter."

What?

Jordan's gut recoiled at those last words. Religious freedom fighter? Bob Moses? Hadn't he worked corporate law back when their houses were next door to each other? If he was a religious freedom fighter, that meant…

Jordan hunched down near the stone and hung his head. It meant he and Bob Moses had been waging battle on opposite sides of the war. They could even have wound up in court against each other. The reality cut Jordan to the core. How disappointed would Mr. Moses be if he knew the truth about Jordan's occupation? Especially after the Moses family had done so much for Jordan, his mother, and his sister…

Jordan studied the tombstone again. *Jesus, most of all…Jesus, most of all…Jesus, most of all…*

His mind flooded with images of his dying mother, of Heidi driving off with the social worker—and Jordan's heart steeled itself again with determination. What good had Jesus done for his mother? For him or his sister? For that matter, what good had He done for the Moses family? Faith and her parents and sister had lived for God, trusted in Him, depended on Him, and where had it gotten them? Bob Moses was buried just as deep underground as Jordan's mother. Two people who loved God more than life, yet here they were. Their lives cut short by the very same God they'd spent a lifetime serving.

He stared at the roses in his hands and scanned the burial grounds. The image of a willow tree appeared in his mind and he looked over one shoulder, then the other until he saw it. There, at the back of the cemetery…the pauper's section, where they buried people with little money. People forgotten over time. Jordan clenched his teeth and strode in that direction, not stopping until he found it. The white marker was dirty, dulled by the years and neglected. Weeds—though cut back—grew around the plot.

Tears stung at Jordan's eyes. *Mom…*

He knelt and laid the flowers on the ground, noticing how they dwarfed the small stone. "Evelyn S. Riley, mother." That was it; all that was left to remember her by. Jordan ran his fingers over the rough marker and ached to have her at his side again, yearned once more to be the boy who would run home from school and share his day with her, feel the validation of her hug.

Jordan pictured her, pretty and petite, a brown-haired woman whose hardships in life he'd known nothing about because she'd never once complained about them. Jordan's father had abandoned them before he and Heidi were out of diapers. Two years later police notified his mother that Earl Riley had been killed in a head-on collision with a cement wall. Drunk and out of work, behind the wheel of a stolen car. Jordan's mother had been careful to spare him and Heidi the sordid details, but after she died—when Social Services stepped in and took them—the facts were repeated before judges and social workers a number of times.

"Jesus will take care of us, kids…don't you worry about us…"

His mother's words rang simply, sweetly through the whispering fronds of the willow tree, as though she were still speaking them now. A teardrop rolled off Jordan's cheek and landed on the grave marker and he rubbed it with his fist, cleaning off some of the dirt.

Jesus. Jordan released a short laugh. Yes, lot of good He'd done. Left Jordan's mother to raise two kids alone, then sat back and watched while she died of cancer. What kind of God would let that happen?

"I'm going home, Jordan…this isn't my home and it isn't yours, either. Cling to Jesus, son… Don't let walls grow around your heart because I'm sick…because I'm sick…because I'm sick."

His mother's words ran across his heart again and again. His poor, sweet, gullible mother. There was no God and no heaven. Only lonely, old cemeteries where people such as Evelyn Riley and Bob Moses lay rotting beneath the earth's surface.

"Jesus loves you, son."

Right. Jordan wiped his cheeks, stood up, and stared once more at his mother's tombstone. "I miss you, Mom." His voice came out in a strained whisper, which was all he could manage under the burden of his emotions. "If you can hear me, if you can see me…I miss you." A sob lodged in his throat and he swallowed it back. "I'm trying to find Heidi, but I'm not sure how. I wish…"

He couldn't finish the sentence. Couldn't bring himself to say that he wished the God she had so strongly believed in had been real after all, and that if He were real, He might have cared about them as much as his mother believed. If He were, if He had…maybe she could ask Him to help find Heidi.

But it was all a batch of fanciful stories and groundless traditions. Jordan bent down and touched the stone once more. "Good-bye, Mom. I still love you."

He turned and made his way out of the cemetery, back toward his motel…back to consider whether he would file a lawsuit against Bethany that afternoon. He would lock himself in his room, lay out the briefs he'd written, and make a decision, once and for all.

He drove back along Main Street and—

Jordan slammed on his brakes, nearly causing a pileup. Waving his apology at three drivers, he pulled to the side of the road and stared. There it was—a block from the old neighborhood—Jericho Park and the infamous Jesus statue.

He climbed out of his car, crossed the street, and found the bench he'd been so familiar with sixteen years ago. A bench just five feet from the statue. As he sat, his eyes were drawn to the lifelike expression in the carved eyes. Powerless against the pull, Jordan felt himself drifting back in time.

He could see his mother, stirring a pot of soup on the stove and smiling at him. "You know what?" The memory of his mother's voice rang in his heart. "My favorite place in town is Jericho Park and the Jesus statue."

The Jesus statue…the Jesus statue…the Jesus statue. Jordan closed his eyes and pictured himself a ruddy-cheeked teenage boy riding his bike to this spot, this very bench…night after night after night…to his mother's favorite spot.

Begging God to let his mother live.

He blinked and saw the statue the way he had as a boy, the arms beckoning him, the eyes seeming to know his pain. And suddenly it wasn't one memory or two, but a whole flood of scenes and voices all taking Jordan back in time to the days when he had actually believed they would all live happily ever after.

6

The house had belonged to Earl Riley's family. Otherwise there would have been no way Evelyn Riley and her two children could have afforded to live on Oak Street. They'd lived in a one-bedroom apartment until word came that Jordan's father was dead. Jordan was five at the time and though he didn't remember Earl or the policemen who came to the door that afternoon, he remembered what happened next.

There was a party—at least it had seemed like a party—and everyone was paying special attention to him and Heidi. A fancy lady with a feathered hat spent much of that day bawling and fussing over his mother, saying things like, "You poor dear" and "I had no idea Earl wasn't taking care of you."

Back then Jordan hadn't been sure what it all meant, but a little while later he and his mother and Heidi moved into the house on Oak Street. "It's a gift from your grandma," was all his mother would say. Often Jordan wondered why his grandma had given them a house but never came to see them or stay for dinner.

It all made sense now, of course.

Jordan blinked and felt the chill of a breeze against the back of his neck. His father had been the black sheep, the boy-gone-bad from a wealthy, upper-crust family in Philadelphia. His father's father had died in his fifties of a stroke, and Jordan guessed that his grandmother hadn't known a thing about him or Heidi or their mother until the accident. Then—so her grandchildren would always have a place to live—the old woman had paid cash for the small house on Oak Street and given it to his mother. That done, she'd washed her hands of the three of them.

"I want the lady with the pretty hat to come see us again," Heidi had said one night while they were cuddled on their mother's lap for a bedtime story.

"The pretty lady is busy, sweetheart. But I'll tell her you'd like her to come and maybe one day…"

Another memory came into focus. Jordan was eight years old—maybe nine—and he and Heidi and Faith had walked home from school. When they came inside, they found his mother at the kitchen table, her hands over her face.

He and Heidi were at her side immediately, while Faith stood close by, her pretty face shadowed with concern.

"Mom, what happened? What's wrong?"

His mother had sniffled once and wiped her eyes with her fingertips. "Nothing, kids. I'm fine." She smiled at them, her cheeks swollen from crying. "You remember the nice old lady? The one who gave us this house?"

Jordan and Heidi nodded.

Their mother sniffled again. "Someone called today and told me she...she died."

At the time Jordan remembered feeling relief. It was too bad for the old lady, but at least there wasn't something wrong with his mother. Strange, he'd thought, that she would be so upset over the death of someone she barely knew.

A flutter of action brought Jordan back to the present, and he watched a bird land on the Jesus statue. He narrowed his eyes as though trying to see into the past. His mother's tears were easier to understand now, in light of thirty years of life experience. She must have felt so alone, so abandoned. First by his father, then by the old woman. True, she had given them a house. But she had never extended her friendship, her seal of approval that Jordan and Heidi and their mother were worthy of her time and attention. That afternoon, hearing that she was dead, must have ended his mother's dreams of someday being close to the only family she had left.

It had been another reminder that all they had in the world was each other.

Jordan could see himself throwing his arms around his mother's neck and comforting her that day. "It's okay, Mom. You don't need anyone but me and Heidi."

And that was true, until the year Jordan turned ten.

Everything about his childhood seemed to crystallize that year—his relationship with Heidi, with his mother, with God Himself. That was the year Jordan knew without a doubt that everything would work out for them. And that belief started because of his growing friendship with Faith Moses.

For the first five years of living on Oak Street, Jordan saw Faith as little more than a nuisance. She was a yucky girl who happened to live next door, someone to talk to and walk home from school with, a big sister figure for Heidi, but nothing more. Faith hung around the house after school sometimes, and once in a while he and Heidi would go to her house. But the summer he turned ten, it was as though someone flipped a light switch and he could see Faith for the first time. She was beautiful, even back then, possessed of a combination of joy and grace that gave her the air of a princess. Not that she ever acted that way. It was simply who she was.

One night she and Jordan played checkers after school while Heidi stayed home with their mother. The afternoon gave way to evening and just before dark a big man with an even bigger smile burst through the door and shouted. "Hey, family, the happiest man in the world is home!"

Jordan had never been formally introduced to Faith's father until that evening. "And who do we have here?" The man wore a neatly trimmed beard and the light from his blue eyes seemed to fill the room.

Faith jumped up and ran into her father's arms. "This is Jordan from next door,

Daddy. You've seen him before." Even now Jordan could remember the pang of jealousy he'd felt seeing Faith and her father that way.

Jordan blinked back the wetness in his eyes as the image faded. What would it have been like to be hugged by his dad, to be loved that way by a father? The little boy inside still wanted the experience, but Jordan had no more understanding of that kind of love than he'd had twenty years earlier. But even twenty years hadn't dimmed the memory of the smile on Bob Moses' face when he and Jordan met.

"Jordan, welcome to our home. This is the place where Jesus lives!" The man was so happy, so sure of himself that at first Jordan had taken the statement literally. It seemed true enough, for at Faith's house people were always laughing or dancing or praising God about something. If Jesus had to live somewhere, chances were he lived with the Moses family.

Jordan stayed for dinner that night and every now and then his eyes would meet Faith's and they would giggle. When he went home that evening he made an announcement to his mother. "I'm going to marry Faith Moses one day."

His mother smiled at him and pulled him close, the way she always did when he came through the door. "Are you now?"

Jordan nodded. "Yep. I like her, Mom. Jesus lives at her house."

Jesus lives at her house?

The memory was more than a little startling, and Jordan shifted, gazing at the tops of the trees along the park's edge. Was *he* the one who introduced Jesus to his family? He'd always assumed it was Faith's mother, Betty, who'd led them to the Lord. But that wasn't how he was remembering it now…

An arrow of regret pierced his heart. If he'd been the one, he was deeply sorry. There was no reason to believe Jesus was alive—not back then or today. Yet somehow his mother had fallen completely in love with Jesus Christ. And it had happened sometime after he'd come home from Faith's that night.

Another picture came into view of Heidi and him watching television with Faith in the den while their mothers talked quietly in the next room. The women had their Bibles out, as they did several times a week when Faith's mother came to visit. A few weeks later he and Heidi and their mother started attending church with the Moses family. And Jordan still remembered the highlight of their Sunday outings: As they walked from the car to the church building, Mr. Moses would put his arm around Jordan's shoulders and ask him questions.

"Did you have a good week, Jordan? Been talking to Jesus much?"

Jordan didn't remember his answers or even all the things Mr. Moses asked. Just the feeling of the man's arms around him.

Two months later, his mother got baptized at church, and after that there was something different about her eyes. She'd always been kind and gentle, quick with a hug and a kiss for him and Heidi. But that day she pulled them aside and told them what happened. "I gave my life to Jesus, kids. And one day I want you to do the same thing. He loves us all very much…and I love Him more than anything."

Jordan had bristled just a bit at that. More than *anything?* More than Heidi and him? His worries didn't last long, because whatever loving Jesus meant, it seemed to only make their mother more wonderful, as though it had accomplished something deep and lasting within her. There was a peace in her eyes, a joy that remained whether the welfare check came on time each month or not.

It was a joy that was still there two years later when she began to have a strange cough that wouldn't go away.

Jordan was twelve that year, Heidi just nine. Still his little sister picked up on their mother's condition and shared her fears with Jordan. "I'm worried about Mama," she told him one night. Their mother had gone to bed early, pale and tired, and Jordan was in charge of doing the dishes and making sure they were both in bed by nine. He pulled Heidi into a hug. "I know. Me too."

"You think we should pray to Jesus?" Heidi stared at him, her brown eyes glistening with sincerity.

Jordan thought of the way his mother loved God, the way she talked about Jesus as though he no longer lived only at Faith's house but at their house too. "Okay, let's do it."

Then Jordan and Heidi held hands and talked to Jesus as though He was right there with them, part of their circle. Jordan remembered keeping his eyes closed, wondering if he opened his eyes whether Jesus would really be standing there with them. "Mama loves you, Jesus. So make her better quick, okay? And thank you for giving us each other."

It was something he'd heard his mother pray and it seemed appropriate that night. Over the next few weeks she had several doctor's appointments and for a while the cough seemed to go away. It came back in the springtime when Jordan was thirteen, and this time she seemed worse than before.

One afternoon Jordan and Faith were walking home from the local junior high when he stopped and sat on the edge of the curb. His feelings were all jumbled that day. He'd seen Faith talking to another boy at school, and though they were too young to date, he couldn't fight the uncomfortable feelings squaring off in his heart. If he hadn't known better he'd have thought he was actually jealous. But it wasn't just Faith. He was worried about his mother, too. She seemed to be getting thinner, wasting away a little more each day. The combination of feelings was simply too much and as Jordan sat on the curb, he hung his head and choked back a sob as two teardrops fell to the ground.

"Jordan, what's wrong?" Faith was immediately at his side, her arm around his shoulders. "Are you sick? What?"

Worried as he was about his mother, his heart suddenly overflowed with thoughts of Faith. He sniffed once and studied her eyes. "Am I your best friend?"

She was so pretty, her pale blond hair framing her face as she nodded. "You know you are."

"Then why were you with Scott Milton today at lunch?" Jordan could still hear himself, hear the way his voice sounded as he asked the question. Not angry or accusatory, but wounded.

Faith's eyes danced. "Jordan Riley, you mean you're jealous of old Scott Milton?" She giggled and removed her arm from his back, punching him playfully in the shoulder. "I thought you and me were only friends." She raised her chin a notch. "Besides, everyone says you like Lorianne Wilcox."

It was Jordan's turn to laugh, and he bumped her playfully with his shoulder. "Don't believe everything you hear."

"It's true, isn't it?" She was teasing him, and he loved the way she made him feel. Even back then, when he was too young to know what it all meant.

"No, it isn't true. Lorianne has a big nose."

A knowing look filled Faith's eyes. "I'll be sure to remember that." She pretended she was taking notes on an invisible piece of paper. "Jordan Riley...doesn't like...big noses."

Jordan stopped laughing and his smile fell. Faith stared sadly at him, clouds dimming the twinkling in her eyes. "What is it? What's wrong?"

Jordan knew she was the only one he could talk to about his fears. Heidi was too young and he didn't want to scare her. Of course he could never tell his mother; she would be devastated to know his true feelings. "I think...I think my mom's dying."

Faith's eyes flew open and she shook her head. "No, Jordan. Don't say that. She's just sick. Remember, it happened last year, too?"

Jordan hung his head again. "I know, but this time it's different. Like she's not ever going to get better again."

Faith was adamant in her response. "Then we need to pray. Right away so Jesus knows what you're feeling."

Jordan nodded and waited for Faith to take the initiative. She reached out and held his hand in hers. "Father God, we come before You knowing that You hear us when we pray...please, Jesus, make Jordan's mom get better. He and Heidi need her so much. And please help Jordan trust You so he won't be afraid." She said some other things too, but Jordan didn't remember them. He was torn between trying to focus on the prayer and enjoying the way her hand felt in his.

When they were finished they looked up at each other, and Jordan realized all the other kids had made their way inside already. It was just he and Faith alone on the curb, a spring breeze washing over them. Without giving it another thought, Jordan leaned forward and kissed her on the lips. A simple kiss that was neither lingering nor rushed. The kind of kiss that meant they were more than friends, but still too young for anything serious. Faith's cheeks grew flushed, and for once she had nothing to say.

Jordan looked through her eyes straight to her heart that afternoon. "I'm going to marry you one day, Faith." He grinned and poked her in the ribs to lighten the mood. "So don't go spending too much time with Scott Milton."

There was a new shyness in Faith's eyes as she smiled at him. "Okay. And don't forget to pray about your mom. Jesus'll help her, Jordan. I just know it."

Looking back now Jordan wasn't sure if it was Faith's words that afternoon or his deepening sense that something was terribly wrong with his mother that had spurred him to start riding his bike to Jericho Park. He would sit on the very bench he occupied now and pray to Jesus about the thoughts that filled his heart. Usually his trips to the park were at night, after he and Heidi had finished their homework, after the two of them had cleaned dinner dishes and he was sure his mother was sleeping comfortably. Then he'd tuck Heidi into bed, jump on his old bicycle and head for the Jesus statue.

Jordan had no idea how often he'd visited Jericho Park during that time of his life. The only person who knew what he was doing was Faith, but even she didn't know the range of thoughts he brought before the Lord at the foot of the statue. He prayed for his family and his grades and his baseball game. Money was scarce and he wanted a scholarship to play baseball in college so he could get a good job and make a decent living. That way they could afford the best doctors for his mother. He even prayed about Faith, knowing that somehow the two of them would be together one day.

But most of all he prayed for his mother.

Faith had asked him about the statue before. "It's not like that's really Jesus. You know that, right?"

Jordan had laughed. "Of course I know that. It's just a good place to pray. It makes me remember Jesus is real, not just some imaginary person, you know?"

Faith grinned. "I know. I feel the same way. I'm glad we have the statue here. It must make Jesus happy that it's right there on Main Street for everyone to see."

As his mother's health worsened that summer, Jordan began making the trip to Jericho Park every night. Sometimes Faith would come with him and they'd sit on the bench together, holding hands as they prayed for Jordan's mother. Once in a while they'd share a brief kiss or two, but nothing more. When school started that fall, Jordan and Faith privately knew that they shared a relationship, but they also understood they were too young to make their commitment public. Whereas they'd held hands innocently in their younger, childish years, now they were careful to only do so when they were alone.

On several occasions, Heidi had caught them that way, hands linked as they talked outside on the curb. Once in a while she'd tease them, but most of the time she understood.

"You still love me too, right?" Heidi asked him one night before they went to sleep.

"Of course, silly. You're both my best friends."

By the time the leaves changed in October that year, Jordan's mother was at the doctor every other day for some kind of appointment, and she wore a scarf all the time. *Chemotherapy.* He understood now, but at the time he'd had no idea what that meant. Only that she looked worse all the time and with each passing day his fears grew stronger than ever. He began listening in to her conversations with Faith's mother. One afternoon he overheard her say something about telling the kids, choosing the right time. That night he found her alone in her room and knelt by her bedside.

"What do you want to tell us, Mom?" He whispered the words so he wouldn't startle her, and she turned her head weakly in his direction.

A smile filled her thin face. "Oh, hi, Jordan. Wasn't it a beautiful day?"

Panic worked its way through Jordan's young body. "Mom, I don't want to talk about the day. I want to talk about you. What did you want to tell us? You said something to Faith's mother about talking to Heidi and me. About what?"

Tears welled in his mother's eyes, and she breathed out for a long time. "I guess it's time you know." She hesitated as though she would have done anything in the world to keep from having to tell him this news. "I have cancer, Jordan." She swallowed and for several moments couldn't speak. "Do...do you know what that is?"

Jordan had the feeling he'd been plunged under a twenty-foot tidal wave. He felt the same way he'd felt when Jimmy Julep hit him in the stomach with a fast pitch back in fifth grade. He clutched his sides and nodded. "Faith's grandpa died of cancer."

His mother smiled. "Right." She struggled to catch her breath and wound up coughing for several seconds. "I have it in my lungs, honey. The doctors say that Jesus might be calling me home."

"No!" Jordan had to work to keep from shouting as anger and fear fought for position in his heart. "I've been talking to Jesus every day about you, Mom. You're going to get better!"

She reached out and took his hand in hers. Even now Jordan remembered how weak her grip was. "I want you to take care of Heidi, okay? And one day we'll all be together again...in heaven."

Jordan shook his head, raw terror strangling him as he fought the truth with every breath in his body. "No, Mom! God wouldn't do that. You're going to be fine."

"Jordan, it's time you knew the—"

"No!" He was on his feet, angry with her for reasons he didn't even understand. "Don't talk that way, Mom."

Without waiting for her response, he ran outside and climbed on his bike. Five minutes later he was on his knees, weeping at the foot of the Jesus statue. "Don't take her away from us, Lord, please. I'll do anything You want. I'll quit baseball or stop spending time with Faith. I'll do more chores and get better grades in school. Please, Lord...just let her live, please!"

Faith must have heard the same thing from her mother that night because she went looking for him. Thirty minutes later she showed up at the park and gently fell on the ground beside him. She wrapped her fingers around his and hung her head, sobbing softly alongside him. There were no words between them that night, only tears as they both raised their silent voices to God and begged Him to save Jordan's mother's life.

A wave of nausea came over Jordan now as he remembered how bad things had gotten after that, how terrified Heidi became at the thought of losing their mother, how she'd started to stutter because of the fear that welled within her. And most of all how their mother had suffered...

Suddenly the memories were more than Jordan could take. He took a deep breath and let go of all the images except one...him and Faith in this very park, fingers linked as they prayed for his mother.

What do you think of your Jesus now, Faith?

The thought filled his mind and anchored there. What could she possibly feel but disillusionment? Jesus had taken his mother, her father...and left Jordan and Faith grieving for the people they loved. He tried to picture Faith, wondering what she might look like now, what hand life had dealt her. And whether sometimes, when the leaves turned in the fall as they were about to do in a few weeks, she remembered kneeling beside him at Jericho Park and holding hands with a boy who was her very closest friend.

He stared at the statue, the outstretched arms and passionate eyes, and he was filled with an overwhelming, growing sense of purpose. Coming to see the statue, praying to Jesus every night...none of it had done any good. Not for Jordan or his mother. The words on the inscription, the statue's very presence, all of it implied promises that had nothing to do with reality. If there was a God, then He'd let Jordan down in his greatest hour of need. Certainly the same had to be true for other children in Bethany, children who had grown up in the shadow of this stone memorial to deception.

Well...no more. This was a public park, after all. A place where people had the right to laugh and run and play without being confronted with a fairy-tale Jesus who only pretended to care.

Jordan stood and made his way back to his car. He didn't need to look over the briefs. He knew the legalities so well he could recite them in his sleep. Before he pulled away, he saw three children skip toward the statue and stop near its base. In obvious wonder they stared up at the stony face, pointing and talking amongst each other.

He wanted to shout at them, warn them against putting their faith in a God who would take away everything that mattered in a boy's life—his closest friend, his sister, and his mother. Jordan worked the muscles in his jaw as he checked traffic, pulled onto Main Street, and headed toward the courthouse.

It was just before two o'clock; there was no time to waste. The lawsuit had to be filed before another hour passed.

The statue had to go.

7

At just after two o'clock that day, Charles and Heidi Benson pulled up in front of Jericho Park and killed the engine. "There it is." Heidi stared across the grass at the old play area and scanned the grounds until her eyes fell on the Jesus statue. "We used to play here every day."

Charles glanced at the clock and shrugged. "We have time. Wanna walk for a bit?"

"Good idea." Heidi patted her rounded abdomen. "It'll be a long drive home and the last thing I need is leg cramps."

They climbed out and Charles came up alongside her, tenderly taking her hand in his as they started walking. "So...do you think you could live here again?"

Heidi gazed out across the park. They'd taken the day off so Charles could interview at a medical clinic in the newest part of Bethany. He'd been working out of a busy office near downtown Philadelphia for two years—ever since finishing medical school. Now, with the baby on the way, they'd agreed it would be nice to get out of the city.

But Bethany...

Heidi sighed. "I have mixed feelings."

Charles was quiet as they walked, allowing Heidi to remember life the way it had been when she last lived in this same small town. She'd told him how she and Jordan and their mother had shared a house not far from the park, how the days before their mother got sick were little more than a happy blur. It was what happened afterward that made it hard to come back, hard to walk in the very park where they'd played back when each day seemed more charmed than the last.

Their mother died when Heidi was ten, and afterward someone from the state stepped in. Heidi held the memories at bay and watched a boy about twelve years old pushing his little sister on the swings. The two laughed as only children can...

That had been Jordan and her back then, hadn't it? Happy and sure that their time together would never end?

"You okay?" Charles bent his head so she could hear his words, soft and filled with concern.

"Just thinking…" She looked up, conveying with her eyes the fact that she needed this time, needed to remember again what had happened that year. At first she and Jordan had lived alone with the help of their neighbors…Mosely or Moss…Moses…something like that. But after a few weeks the state intervened, and she and Jordan were sent to separate foster homes.

She could still hear her brother's voice, see him standing there before her, tears streaming down his face as the people from Social Services waited to take them away in two different cars. "We won't be apart for long, Heidi, I promise. Just until they can find us a home where we can live together…"

There was no forgetting the way she'd clung to him that day, knowing he was all she had left in the world.

"Don't let me go, Jordan. Please!"

He had shaken his head, placing his finger to her lips. "Shh…it's okay. You can call me whenever you need me. We'll be together soon, you have to believe that."

But it hadn't turned out that way. She stayed in one foster home for a week and then was transferred to another. Even now she remembered asking about her brother but getting only vague answers in response. "It's difficult to place siblings your age," one social worker told her. "We're doing our best."

Then one day she overheard her foster parents talking. Something about Jordan running away and getting locked up at a boys' camp. Before they could finish Heidi burst into the room, screaming. "I want to see Jordan! He doesn't belong in a camp, he belongs with *me.*"

She was so upset at the thought of losing her brother that she threw a tantrum, screaming at the top of her lungs, her fists flailing. The next day she was transferred to a foster home across the state. Four weeks later her foster parents, the Morands, sat her down.

"There's been an accident at the camp where Jordan lives." Mr. Morand took her hands in his. Heidi remembered liking the Morands from the beginning. They were kind and gentle and somehow in their presence the tragedies she'd suffered seemed bearable.

Now though, her young heart raced with fear. "An accident?"

Mrs. Morand nodded. "An underground cavern collapsed and many of the boys were killed, Heidi."

She shook her head, her eyes wide with fear. Not Jordan…not her brother… "What…what about Jordan?"

"Honey, I'm sorry. He was one of the ones inside and he—"

"No! He would have gotten out. He's bigger than other boys and strong. He never would have died in there!"

The Morands held her close and let her sob away her grief long into the night as they stroked her hair and comforted her. Something Mrs. Morand said that night stuck with Heidi even to this day. "He's with your mother now…taking care of her in heaven until you can all be there together."

Now Heidi stared sadly at the Jesus statue. Once her family had come to believe in Christ, the statue had always been a beacon of hope. Her foster mother's words had been true; they had to be. And they were the only reason she survived that time at all.

A year later, the Morands adopted Heidi and raised her in a suburb north of Pittsburgh, where over time she was finally able to put the tragedies of her childhood behind her. The Morands loved her as if she were their own daughter, and in their care Heidi flourished. She was active in high school—involved in tennis and track. Her senior year at her church's fall kickoff she met Charles, a new boy whose family had just moved to town.

She and Charles dated through college and married before he started med school. Now they wanted a quiet place where Charles could practice medicine and they could raise their family. A place not too far from the Morands. When Charles got word that the clinic in Bethany was looking to hire a pediatrician, the two of them scheduled a day trip and he arranged an interview.

"They want me," Charles had told her when he found her in the hospital cafeteria after the interview.

She threw her arms around his neck and squealed. "I knew it."

"I can start November 1."

"Honey, I'm so proud of you." It was true. Charles was everything she'd ever dreamed of in a man. He took care of her the way…well, the way Jordan had when she was a little girl. She could hardly wait to have their baby and set up house wherever he got a job. Even in the town that harbored all her childhood memories.

Charles interrupted her thoughts. "Everything looks good to me, the offer, the hospital…the community." He slowed his steps and faced her. "I guess it's up to you. Whether you can be happy here or not."

Tears clouded Heidi's vision and she swallowed hard. "It makes me wish Jordan had lived. That we could have stayed close and somehow…I don't know…maybe been adopted together." She walked a few more steps, and he fell in beside her, silent, waiting for her to continue.

"My parents told me they would have adopted Jordan too. If he hadn't…" Even after so many years it was hard for her to picture her strapping brother, buried beneath tons of earth in the camp accident. Wouldn't he have found a way out? Couldn't he have heard it coming and run for daylight before it was too late? But her thoughts went unspoken.

"I like to think of him the way your adoptive mom does…up there in heaven taking care of your mother until you can all be together again." Charles put his arm around her shoulders and held her close.

A single tear made its way down Heidi's cheeks. "Me too. But I still miss him."

There were questions in Charles's eyes and Heidi understood. If she felt this way now, just walking near the Jesus statue, would it be impossible for her to live in Bethany? To walk the streets daily where she and Jordan once lived? To take their children to Jericho Park—a place where she and her brother once played?

Heidi sighed. "It's in the past, Charles." Her voice was quiet, choked by emotion. "I have you now…our life is everything I've ever wanted." She hugged him again. "I can do this. I can live here, raise our family here." She kissed him as two more tears fell onto her cheeks. "Call them and tell them yes."

8

The Monday night newscast was always busier than most because with it came the weekend wrap-up, stories that covered not only that day's events but also any loose ends from Saturday and Sunday. By the time Faith left the soundstage at just before midnight, she was exhausted in more ways than one.

She'd called the Social Services department earlier that day, and though the piece on Rosa had appeared several times during daytime broadcasts, not a single person had called about her. *Is there no one for her, God?*

I have appointed you for this, my daughter.

Faith made her way through the station's back corridors toward the rear parking lot. What had God appointed her for? Getting the news out about Rosa? If that was the case, why hadn't anyone called? At age six, she was a sweet-natured child, but give her three or four more years in foster care and Rosa was bound to grow jaded. The innocent faith that lit up her countenance would certainly grow cold in light of the truth that no one wanted her.

I'd adopt her myself if I wasn't single. The thought simmered in Faith's heart like an overcooked vegetable. It was true, wasn't it? She'd go through the process, work with the system and make Rosa her own daughter if only her personal life wasn't so uncertain. But Rosa needed a father, too…a real family.

I will supply all your needs. Wait for the appointed time.

Faith had no idea what *that* meant but she was sure of the message, felt it resonate deep within her soul. And for reasons she didn't understand, the holy whispers sent a ray of hope through her. If God said it would all work out, then somehow—against the odds—it would. For Rosa and for herself.

She pushed the heavy metal door open and was met by an icy wind. The parking lot was dark and she moved quickly, pulling her jacket close as she stared into the starry sky. Fall had arrived, all right. And with it the promise of colder days ahead. Football weather, really. Her father's favorite time of year.

"Faith…"

The male voice came at her from across the parking lot and it stopped her in her tracks. She backed up a few steps toward the building, staring into the darkness until she saw the shape of a man about twenty yards away. Her heart pounded. Was it a fan? A stalker? She didn't recognize the voice—and suddenly realized how vulnerable she was.

"Who is it?" She continued taking steps back toward the station door, determined to alert security before she became the victim of an attack. "Come into the light."

"Don't be afraid, Faith." The man took three slow steps into a circle of brightness that came from one of the station windows. "It's me. Jordan."

Faith felt her knees go weak. It couldn't be… "Jordan who?"

Step by step he moved closer, and Faith's breath caught in her throat as she made out his face. It wasn't possible, but it was him; her childhood friend…the boy who'd asked her to marry him the summer they were just thirteen. He was a man now, tall and dark with looks that likely stopped women in their tracks. His designer suit suggested he had done well for himself, and Faith was flooded with feelings she couldn't quite decipher. Whatever they were, she was glad for the darkness, glad he couldn't see the heat she felt in her cheeks. "Jordan Riley? How in the world did you find me?"

"I was in town…on business." He smiled, and there it was. The same eyes and grin he'd had as a teenager. It was Jordan, all right. Without giving it another thought, she came to him and hugged him.

"I can't believe it's you." She pulled back and looked at him. "Who told you I was here?"

"I went to your old house. A Mr. Joe Cooper told me you were a big star now doing the news for WKZN." Jordan grinned again, his eyes twinkling. "You looked beautiful tonight, Faith."

"You saw me?" Was she dreaming? Was this really Jordan Riley standing here, talking to her after so many years? To think he'd come into town and seen her on the news that night…

"I watched you for five minutes and I knew I had to see you in person. I have a few meetings tomorrow, then it's back to New York, so tonight was my only chance. I thought I'd surprise you."

How long had it been? What was he doing now? Was he married? And what had happened to his sister, Heidi? A hundred questions shouted for Faith's attention, and she tried to think of which was most important. "So, tell me about yourself…what've you been doing?"

Jordan put his hands in his pocket and studied her. "It's so good to see you, Faith. You have no idea…" He hesitated, glancing around. "Can we get coffee somewhere, sit and talk a bit?"

Faith shrugged. "Sure. My mom's visiting her sister in Chicago, so she won't notice if I'm late."

Jordan looked at her strangely. "Your mom? I thought…aren't you married?"

A short laugh escaped Faith's freezing lips. "Definitely not."

He tossed his hands in the air and laughed. "Well, me, neither. I guess that means it's a date."

Faith's heart soared at Jordan's words and she stepped back, surprised at herself. What was she feeling, an attraction? To Jordan? After so many years had gone by? She chided herself for letting her imagination get away with her. They'd been kids back then, after all. This was nothing more than an old friend checking up on her.

He angled his head, his eyes locked on hers. "So…not married, huh?"

"Nope."

"Long story?"

"Very."

Jordan took a few steps back toward his car. "I'll follow you."

Faith led him to a twenty-four-hour diner in the heart of Bethany, a place for people who worked the night shift or needed a quiet moment alone in the still of the early morning hours. When they were seated at a booth, Faith again felt the familiar draw to him. Just as she'd felt it all those years ago…

The waitress brought them coffee, and Faith studied him over the brim of her cup. "How long's it been?"

He smiled. "You mean since I kissed you and asked you to be my wife?"

They both laughed, and he took a swig of his coffee. "I was trying to figure it out on the way over here. Sixteen years I think. They took me away right after my mother died and that was just before Christmas 1985."

The mention of his mother put a deep sadness in the air between them. "Whatever happened to Heidi?"

Pain flashed in Jordan's eyes, and he looked down at his hands. "I don't know. We lost track of each other. That was part of what I wanted to do this week, but the records are sealed. I've been trying to find her since I graduated from law school."

Faith felt sick to her stomach. Jordan and Heidi had lost track of each other? Sixteen years ago? She pictured how Jordan had been with his sister, how he'd looked after her and played with her even though she was younger than his friends. "That's awful, Jordan. There must be someone who knows where she is."

He shrugged and when he looked at her this time it was as though walls had been erected around his heart. What had been transparent a moment earlier was now guarded, hidden behind a fortress of stone. "I haven't found anyone yet. The clerk today told me I could register a petition with the state's Social Services, but only people directly involved had the right to see the files."

"But that's you…you're as involved as you could be. For goodness sake, they took you out of your own house and separated you from her without giving either of you a choice."

Jordan smiled, but the gesture looked forced. "Those things happen. I'll look for her till the day I die, but I've accepted the fact that I may never find her."

"So what happened when you left here? Where did you go?"

"At first I was at a foster home. But one day I overheard the social worker say there was no way the state could keep Heidi and me together. So I ran away, tried to find the house where she was staying but wound up getting in trouble instead. I was thirteen and they figured I was unstable. Incorrigible, I believe they said. They sent me to a boys' camp in the foothills about six hours from here. Southridge, it was called."

"A boys' camp?" Faith could feel the blood draining from her face as a memory began to take shape in her mind. "But…weren't my parents thinking of adopting you both?"

"I don't know. No one ever said anything to me." His eyes locked onto hers and she saw concern there. "Faith, I'm sorry about your dad. He was a great man." Jordan's eyes grew wet. "He was the only father I ever knew…"

Faith blinked back sudden tears. "I miss him so much."

"I bet." Jordan hesitated. "He was practicing law in town, is that right?"

She nodded. "He and his friend Joshua Nunn opened a law office and took on religious freedom cases. They'd gotten off to a great start when Dad had his heart attack."

They fell silent, and Faith shook her head. "Imagine how different things might have been if you'd lived with us, if we'd adopted you and Heidi."

Now that she had remembered it, she could hear a conversation playing in her mind, one between her parents a few nights after Jordan and Heidi were taken from their home. "It's the only thing we can do, Betty…"

"I know, but I worry about Jordan. It might not be good to have a boy Faith's same age living under one roof."

Her father had been adamant. "It'll work out. God will see us through."

Yes, she was sure of it now. Her parents had contacted Jordan's social worker and asked about adopting both Heidi and him. "The more I think about it the more I'm sure. They wanted to adopt you both."

His eyes grew wide. "You're serious? Your family was really going to do that?" Awe and regret seemed to play out across his face simultaneously.

"I remember them calling about it." She studied him, frowning. "Did you ever hear anything?"

Jordan shook his head, his eyes a well of sadness. "They probably told your parents I was a risk. By that point they'd already moved me to the boys' camp."

How awful that Jordan had been sent to a camp for delinquent boys when all he'd wanted was a chance to be with his sister. "I'm so sorry, Jordan."

He drew a deep breath and smiled—but the smile didn't seem genuine. It had a polished, practiced look about it—as though he were familiar with masking his real feelings. "Enough about me, what about you?" He reached across the table and squeezed her hands gently before pulling back and finishing his coffee.

The feel of his fingers against hers sent electrical currents up her arms and down her spine.

"What's the long story behind not being married?"

Faith was completely flustered. The touch of Jordan's hands on hers had brought back feelings for him she hadn't known still existed. Logic told her that at twelve, thirteen years old one wasn't wise enough to understand love. But the reality lay in the feelings assaulting her heart. She had cared for Jordan deeply, with a whole-hearted innocent devotion that is possible only for young people. Indeed she had loved him at a time when life was most impressionable. Now that they were adults, the memory of those earlier feelings—combined with the heady closeness of sitting across from him—left her unsure what to say or do next. *Help me get a grip here, God....*

He was waiting for her response. "Okay, but tell me if you get bored." She grinned at him and the way he looked at her made her cheeks grow hot again.

"Trust me, Faith, nothing you say could bore me."

She inhaled and forced her heart to beat normally. Then she told him how she'd studied journalism in college and started as a sports reporter. Two years later she fell hard for a professional football player.

Faith hesitated and Jordan raised an eyebrow. "Anyone I'd know?"

Everyone knew Mike, but Faith wasn't ready to go into details about her relationship with him. Even now it was too hard to share over a casual cup of coffee. Especially with Jordan Riley. "It isn't important."

The warmth in his expression told her he understood.

"Then I had my accident."

Concern fell across Jordan's face. "Accident?"

She nodded. "Three years ago. I was driving home from work and a little boy ran out in front of me. I swerved and missed him, but hit a power pole. Wrapped the car around it. They pried me from the wreck, and I was in a coma for two weeks."

"Two weeks?" He ran his hand over his hair. "Faith, you're lucky you lived."

Faith pictured the people who had filled her room the day she came to, people who had been holding vigil since the accident. "Not lucky, blessed. I had people praying for me around the clock, Jordan." She hesitated, surprised at how emotional she still felt when she thought back to that time in her life. "My dad put together a prayer chain, and for two weeks people took half hour shifts praying for me. Not a moment went by when someone wasn't praying."

"Hmm." The muscles in Jordan's jaw flexed. "That's nice." Something hard flashed in his eyes, and Faith couldn't decide what it was—but she had the oddest feeling that she'd offended him somehow. Strange. Jordan was a believer; certainly he wouldn't have been put off by prayer.

"The doctors said it was a miracle. It took nearly a year of operations and therapy for me to learn how to eat and walk and be independent again. When I got out of the hospital, I moved back in with my parents, and two years ago I finally felt good as new. That's when I took the job at WKZN."

Jordan eased himself forward as they both accepted coffee refills from the waitress. "Lots of people are never the same after an accident like that."

"All credit goes to God. Without His help I wouldn't have made it. That's for sure."

"Right."

An awkward silence filled the distance between them, and Faith studied him closely. There it was again, a flicker of distaste or anxiety, as though she kept touching a sore spot somewhere near his heart.

"You okay?" Faith uttered the question before she could stop herself. Jordan was a man now, someone she barely knew. What right did she have to probe into the private places of his emotions?

Surprise filled his face but he glanced down at his coffee cup as the corners of his mouth lifted. "Yeah, sure."

He wasn't going to elaborate so Faith tried another tact. "How 'bout you? You left the camp at some point, obviously. What's God been doing in your life?"

She stretched out her legs and felt their feet touch. Without saying anything she discreetly moved hers to one side. He looked up at her again, and though his smile was back, the discomfort in his eyes remained. "I stayed at camp till I graduated from high school. Spent most of my time playing baseball and wound up with a scholarship to play at New Jersey State."

Finally some good news. Faith clapped her hands. "Jordan, that's wonderful. You always dreamed about playing ball in college. You have to tell me all about it."

He chuckled at her enthusiasm and spent the next half hour regaling her with stories of his playing days. She remembered then that he'd mentioned something about law school. "So after college you became a lawyer?"

He nodded and signaled for the check. "I should let you get some sleep; it's one-thirty."

Faith didn't care how late it was, she didn't want the night to end. It felt so good to share a few hours with him after all the years that had passed without him, without knowing what had happened to him. "What kind of law do you practice?"

Jordan let his gaze fall for a moment and then flashed her a smile plucked from their early days together. "This and that. Civil rights stuff. Nothing interesting."

"If you'd lived with us I bet you'd have been working right there alongside Dad. Don't you think?"

The walls in Jordan's eyes grew thicker, impenetrable. "It's late, Faith." There it was again. That artificial smile. "I have to go. I have a long drive tomorrow." He laid a five-dollar bill on the table and stood to help her with her jacket. As their arms touched Faith caught her breath at the jolt that went through her. What was wrong with her? She pulled her jacket on the rest of the way. Probably just adolescent memories playing tricks on her emotions.

Whatever the reason, she was strongly aware of Jordan beside her as they left the diner and headed for their cars. Before they said good-bye, Jordan pulled her into a hug then looked intently into her eyes. "It was good seeing you again, Faith." He ran his thumb along her eyebrow. "I thought I'd lost you forever."

Her heart skipped a beat, but she held his gaze. Was he going to kiss her? Here in the diner parking lot? He brought his face closer to hers and whispered against her face. "I never stopped thinking about you."

A floating sensation came over her, and she nuzzled her face against his. "I thought about you, too." She pulled away, wanting to ask him but not knowing how to word it without sounding blunt. "Want my phone number? So you can call me from New York?"

In response he brought his lips to hers and kissed her gently, tenderly—but this wasn't a young boy kissing a girl for the first time. It was the kiss of a man. A man who Faith knew for certain was as attracted to her as she was to him. They drew nearer to each other as the kiss continued, but before it could become more passionate, Jordan drew back. "I have to go. I'll call you."

A dozen emotions assaulted Faith and she searched his eyes. If he could kiss her like that, then he must still care for her. But if he was interested in her, he certainly hadn't said so. *Why are you doing this, Jordan? What's going on in your head?* She kept her concerns to herself, all but one. "You don't have my number."

"I'll call you at the station."

Then, in what seemed a poorly scripted ending to a wonderful evening, Jordan opened her car door and ushered her inside. "Good-bye, Faith." He bent down and their lips briefly came together once more.

He climbed into his black sports car and before she could turn the key, he drove away.

Jordan's entire body trembled as he pulled out of the diner parking lot. It had been heaven spending an evening with Faith, seeing her again, feeling her in his arms. She was more beautiful than he could have imagined, more intuitive to his feelings. He hadn't planned to kiss her, but after their hug, there was nothing he could do to stop himself. In all his life nothing had felt so right as having her in his arms, kissing her.

But it had been deeply wrong and he was furious at himself for letting his emotions get the better of him.

What right did he have listening to Faith talk about the miracle of her healing and the ways people had prayed for her? As though he still shared that same belief system? He had planned to tell her that he no longer bought into the stories about Jesus loving him and God having a plan for his life, but somehow the words hadn't come.

He eased up on the pedal and drove slowly back to his motel room. If only things had been different, if her parents had gotten word to his social worker earlier about their intention to adopt Heidi and him. Jordan couldn't imagine how things might have turned out, but they would definitely have been different. Maybe Faith was right. Maybe he would have wound up working alongside Bob Moses on the other side of the battle for religious rights.

But none of that mattered now.

He'd already made his decision, already filed the lawsuit. He'd taken a public stand against the very things Faith held dear, the things her father had devoted his final days defending. Jordan let out a strangled huff. Of course he hadn't asked Faith for her phone number. Angry tears stung his eyes as he let himself into his motel room. Faith represented everything good and pure and clean about life; ideals he knew nothing about and didn't believe in, anyway.

There would never be another date between them, never another kiss.

After tomorrow, Faith would learn what he'd done. What he'd become. Then he'd no longer be her old friend, a man who'd captured her heart in the parking lot of a Bethany diner.

He'd be her enemy.

9

One of the benefits of doing the eleven o'clock news was that unless Faith was working on a *Wednesday's Child* segment, she had her days to herself. When she awoke that Tuesday morning, after a night consumed with thoughts of Jordan, Faith knew there was only one way she could right her perspective.

By spending a day with Rosa.

Since the interview there had been one other time when Faith had contacted Rosa's social worker to arrange an afternoon with her. Over the weekend they'd seen the latest Disney movie and today...well, today Faith wanted to take her back to Jericho Park. Rosa had been drawn to the Jesus statue, and Faith couldn't think of any place she'd rather spend a few hours to sort through her emotions.

Faith planned to pick the child up at her foster home just before lunch. She brought a picnic and found the girl ready and waiting.

"You came!" Rosa ran down the sidewalk, her hair bouncing behind her, and flew into Faith's arms. "Did you see me on TV again?"

"I sure did." The girl's hair felt smooth beneath Faith's fingertips, and she and Rosa locked hands as they made their way to the car. Rosa's words rang in Faith's heart. *You came...you came...you came...* How many times had the child been let down if Faith's simple commitment—the mere act of showing up as she'd promised—meant so much?

"You sure looked pretty."

Faith pulled into traffic and headed for the park as Rosa grinned at her, her eyes huge and full of expectation. "Did my new mommy and daddy call yet?"

An ache settled around the base of Faith's heart and she swallowed a sigh. "Not yet, sweetheart, but that doesn't mean anything. Jesus has a plan, remember?"

Rosa's smile faded some and she settled back into her seat. "Uh-huh. My forever parents will come for me in His timing. Right? That's what my foster mom says and you too."

"Right, baby...that's right. Jesus has someone planned for you and one of these days you'll meet them and it'll feel as if they were there all along."

"One of these days..." Rosa sighed and stared out the windshield. There was nothing cynical or defeated in the little girl's tone. Only a resignation that as of yet there were still no parents for her, no one to call her own. *You know I'd take her if I could, Lord...*

Silence.

Faith felt the beginning of tears and forced herself to be cheerful. It wouldn't help Rosa if she were sad this afternoon. This was a day for playing and laughing and enjoying their time together. They arrived at the park and shared a peanut butter sandwich and homemade cookies. Faith was pushing the child on the swing, when she noticed the way two little girls nearby whispered about Rosa's missing fingers. Faith slowed the swing down and tickled Rosa.

"Okay, sweetcakes, get off."

Rosa grinned at her and slid down to the ground. Once the swing was empty, Faith sat down and pulled Rosa onto her lap.

"Hold on!" Faith waited until the child had a tight grip on the chains, then covering the girl's deformed hand with her own, Faith pumped the swing higher and higher, savoring Rosa's little-girl laughter.

Something about Faith's acceptance of her seemed to convince the other little girls that Rosa was okay. After a few minutes the two of them came and stood nearby. "Can she play with us?"

Faith felt a surge of hope as she slowed the swing, breathless from the cool fall air and the thrill of the ride. She leaned close and spoke softly in Rosa's ear. "Wanna play with them?"

Rosa bobbed her head up and down. "Yes, please..." And with that she and the other girls ran off to the merry-go-round. The tears were back as Faith silently celebrated the victory. *She needs a mom, Lord...someone who can help her win those battles every day of her life.*

No words of wisdom echoed in Faith's soul as she made her way to a nearby bench. She watched the children play and gradually her mind wandered once more to the night before.

Jordan Riley.

Was his return some part of God's plan? Faith thought about that and decided it could be. After all, they were both still single and whatever attraction had been there for them as kids had obviously lasted over the years. She sighed and tried to imagine what might have happened if Jordan hadn't disappeared for sixteen years of her life. There would have been no Mike Dillan to forget about, no broken heart.

What had she been thinking to date a man such as Mike Dillan anyway? Faith sighed and crossed her legs, enjoying the way the sun felt on her shoulders. Becoming Mike's girlfriend wasn't something she'd planned; it had just sort of happened. Faith hadn't let herself remember that time in her life for years, but now, watching Rosa play with her new friends, still basking in the memory of Jordan's kiss from the night before, Faith felt herself drifting back.

For years after Jordan left, Faith waited for him, asking her parents where he lived and imagining ways she might find him again. Through junior high and even high school she never had a boyfriend, because every time one of her peers was interested she compared him to Jordan. *Someday,* she'd tell herself, *someday God will bring us back together.* It was a sentiment she wrote in her journals and carried with her straight into college.

Her four years at Penn State were a blur of busyness and activities led by her involvement with the school newspaper and broadcast department. There was little time for boyfriends, but every now and then she'd spend a weekend at home and wind up at Jericho Park, on the bench near the Jesus statue where she and Jordan had spent their last days together. *Where is he, Lord?* She'd let her imagination run wild. Maybe he'd moved on to another state or another country…maybe he'd gone to college and was spending all his free time trying to find her. Wherever he was, he wasn't in Bethany, and the chance that Faith would ever see him again was practically nonexistent.

Faith stared at the Jesus statue now and tried to remember herself as she'd been back then, a senior in college, working as a broadcast intern for a small student-run station not far from campus. She'd been too busy to do much more than keep to her schedule and once in a rare while think about Jordan and what might have been.

Mike had come into the picture two years later when her internship led to a full-time sports reporting position at the Philadelphia CBS affiliate. Mike was a tight end with the Eagles, and from the first day Faith was assigned to do sidebar stories on the team, he'd made his presence known.

He had come up to her after the game, when her interviews were over and she was making her way to the car. "Hey, gorgeous."

Faith remembered not being sure how to answer him. He was good-looking, but she was on the job and determined not to date players. She wound up waving to him as though she hadn't heard his comment, relieved when he waved back but went his own way. *Good…keep him far away from me, Lord…pro athletes are nothing but trouble.*

That had been only the beginning. As she got to know the personalities on the team better she learned that Mike was a devoted Christian who gave both his time and money to local charities and churches. After her first five weeks covering the team, he began asking her out.

She would smile and change the subject, sticking to her professional list of questions and assignment objectives. "I don't date players."

"I'm not a *player,*" he'd grin at her. "Players hang out with different girls every week. I'm a professional athlete, and you're a professional reporter…"

His relentless pursuit of her chipped away at her resistance with one fine-sounding argument after another.

One sunny afternoon before practice, it was: "What are you afraid of, Faith? I don't bite."

Or after a game, when the locker room had cleared: "Why won't you go out with me? I think we have a lot in common."

And in the parking lot a week later: "We're adults, Faith. When are you going to take me seriously?"

After a month of saying no, Faith finally agreed to have dinner with him following a home game. They went to a little-known Italian restaurant, and six weeks later, Faith had fallen hard for him. They became expert at keeping their relationship a secret, sure that it would cast a questionable light on Faith's reporting if word got out.

Faith squinted and let her gaze settle on Rosa, enjoying the way she laughed and ran as she played tag with her two new friends. If only things hadn't gotten so serious between Mike and her. She would have been okay with a casual friendship, a dating situation with long-term potential. Instead, on their first-year anniversary they went to the same Italian restaurant and Mike tenderly took her hands in his.

"Faith, I've never loved anyone like I love you." There had been unshed tears in his eyes, tears that at the time seemed utterly genuine. He let go with one hand and reached into his coat pocket, pulling out a velvet box. As though he'd practiced for the moment, he opened it in a single move. There inside lay a diamond ring bigger than any Faith had ever seen. "Marry me, Faith."

The memory faded, and she gritted her teeth, noticing that her hands were clenched. Even now, when she was glad for not having made the mistake of marrying him, the anger and hurt he'd caused her still lay in the open places of her heart. If only she'd seen it coming back then.

Rosa caught her gaze and waved at her. "Hi, Faith!"

Faith's love for the child made her heart swell. "Hi, sweetie!"

Confident that Faith was there for her, watching her, Rosa returned to her play. Faith glanced down at her hands, remembering how she'd gone home a week after Mike proposed and shown the diamond ring to her parents. They'd met Mike by then, and though her mother was thrilled with the idea of their engagement, her father had been wary.

"Something about him doesn't ring true." Her father had stroked his beard thoughtfully. "I can't put my finger on it, but it makes me worried for you, Faith. I have to be honest."

She'd only given her father a teasing smile and a quick kiss on the cheek. "Would any man ever be good enough, Daddy?"

There was just one aspect of their relationship that caused Faith any private doubt. Mike hadn't wanted to set a wedding date. She could still hear his weak excuses. "I need to focus on my career right now, Faith. It'd be impossible to be married and keep up my performance as an athlete." He'd weave his fingers through her hair and pull her close, kissing her. "You understand, right?"

And she had. After all, he'd been a perfect gentleman, respecting her determination to stay pure, at least respecting it until his marriage offer. Faith had her own apartment, and certainly they'd had their moments of temptation, but always he found his way to the front door before midnight and without putting any pressure on her. They prayed together, attended church together, and talked of having a godly marriage, one that the Lord Himself would bless for all time.

Faith uttered a sad laugh.

In the end, her father's doubts had been more genuine than anything Mike had promised. The changes came after the engagement, and though they were subtle, they were persistent. "We're practically married, Faith…" he'd whisper as he kissed her neck, running his hands along her sides. "Do you really think God would care if I stayed the night? Just this once."

Week after week Faith could feel her resolve wearing thin, but still she refused his attempts. "We've waited this long, Mike. It's important to me. To both of us, right?"

"Please, Faith…just one time…"

Three months after getting engaged, when they were alone in her apartment well after midnight, she couldn't find the words to tell him no, couldn't hold back from welcoming his embrace and finally giving in to the physical love they'd both been resisting. Six weeks later a home pregnancy test confirmed what she already knew.

She was a Christian sportscaster carrying the baby of one of the players on the team she covered.

Faith felt nauseous as she remembered what happened next. She'd told Mike about the baby and suggested they set a quick wedding date, but he was distant and vague, careful not to make promises. *Why didn't I see it coming, Lord?* Faith's unspoken question hung in the rafters of her mind even now. It was behind her; it had to be. Forgotten as though it had never happened…

The sun was shifting and a chill passed over her. It was almost time to get Rosa back to her foster home. She blinked and tried to forget the way the story ended but there was no getting around it. For the next month Mike seemed always too busy to return her phone calls.

It wasn't until she saw a newspaper photo of him with one of the team cheerleaders that she figured it out.

She'd broken down and cried when he finally called her a week later. "How *could* you?"

"Listen, Faith, you're too serious for me. I'm not ready to settle down."

She had been so distraught she'd spent the afternoon fighting violent bouts of nausea and anxiety. The bleeding started later that night, and by the next morning she had lost everything that might remind her of Mike Dillan. At the end of the month she took his diamond ring to a pawnshop and hocked it to pay her hospital bills.

The only person who ever knew about the baby was her father, and his support had been exactly what Faith had expected. "I'm sorry, honey." He held her, stroked her hair and comforted her as he'd done when she was little, back when having an argument with a girlfriend was the worst thing that happened to her. No snide remarks or reminders about how he'd seen it coming, no chastisements on how she should have known better than to date a professional athlete. No digs about Mike's supposed belief in God and how that had turned out to be nothing more than good public relations for his high profile persona.

Only understanding and grace.

The same grace God Himself had extended her when the ordeal was over. Faith's throat was thick with the memories, and she swallowed back a wave of tears. God had never turned His back on her. Not then, and not years later when she had her accident. Not even when her father died.

No, God had been there through it all.

She thought about Jordan, how she had long since given up the idea that she'd ever see him again and somehow she knew the Lord had His hand in that too. Had she ever felt so at ease with another man? She knew she hadn't. Though she'd been attracted to Mike, she'd been cautious from the beginning. First because of their professional conflicts, then because of her father's concerns. Her subtle fears about Mike had been easy to bury, but now, in light of her time with Jordan, the difference was striking.

No one had ever made her feel the way Jordan did. Maybe because she had loved him back when they were so young.

Faith noticed the sun making its way toward the horizon and she locked her attention on Rosa. Poor, girl. *Lord, give her a family, please…*

She cupped her hands around her mouth. "Rosa, let's go, honey."

The little girl jumped up and waved at her new friends. Then she ran up and circled her arms around Faith's neck. "Is it time to go?"

Faith's heart felt as though it had slipped through a hole in her left sock. "Yes, sweetie pie. Your foster mom's expecting you back."

Rosa stared across the park toward the Jesus statue. "Know what I asked Jesus for today?" She angled her head in Faith's direction and grinned, her eyes filled with light.

"What?"

"I asked Him to let *you* be my mommy."

There was a choking feeling at the back of Faith's throat as she fought more tears. *What's this feeling I have, Lord? I can't be her mother, You know that. I can barely take care of myself.*

Be strong and courageous, my daughter. Life is not lived within the safety of walls.

Faith gulped back a sob as she knelt and hugged Rosa. After a moment she drew back, looking straight into the child's soul. "Oh, honey, I would love to be your mommy. There couldn't be any better daughter for me than you."

Rosa's eyes glowed with hope. "You mean you'll do it then? You'll take me home to live with you?"

"Sweetheart…I don't know." There was nothing she could do about the tears and Faith held the girl close once more so she wouldn't see them. Why was she feeling this way—as though she'd been born to love this little girl? Faith wiped her cheeks and looked at Rosa again. "I'll ask Him the same thing, okay?"

Rosa's smile took up most of her face as she tucked her small hand into Faith's. "My Sunday school teacher says that Jesus always hears us, even when we don't get the answer we want."

Discreetly, Faith wiped away another release of tears. "That's right, honey."

Rosa stared across the park again. "Know why I like the Jesus statue?"

"Why?" They walked without any sense of purpose, both reluctant to see the afternoon end.

"Because it makes me know how big Jesus is." Rosa released her grip on Faith's hand and stretched her arms as far as they could go in either direction. "Bigger than anything in the whole wide world."

Faith caught the girl's fingers again and squeezed them gently. "Don't you ever forget it, honey. Don't ever forget it."

Rosa's words still played in Faith's mind that evening as she got ready for work. The news didn't start until eleven, but she had to be there four hours early to write and edit her newscast. Ultimately Dick Baker had final editorial say over what aired, but Faith liked to think she played some role in shaping the flavor of Philadelphia's news.

I'd come in six hours early if they'd give me a little more influence...

She pulled a navy rayon blouse from her closet and slipped it on. Her bedroom was smaller now that she'd moved back into her parents' house, but it had been the smartest thing she could do at the time. Besides, she and her mom were agreeable roommates, and with Dad gone now and Sarah married, it made no sense for Faith to live across town alone.

Faith wished her mother were here now, but she'd gone to Chicago for eight weeks to help her sister recover from ankle surgery. Faith's mother had planned the trip months before her father's death, and they'd both felt the trip might actually do her some good, get her out of the house.

But her absence left the house too quiet.

Faith had located matching slacks and was about to slip them on when the phone rang. Maybe it would be Rosa's social worker calling to say that they found her a family...

Faith grabbed the receiver on her bedside table. "Hello..."

"Faith, it's me, Joshua." There was a pause and Faith sat on the edge of the bed. Why would her father's former law partner be calling her? "We've got a problem. I wanted you to know before you got to work and found out."

Her heart rate quickened in response. "What happened?"

Joshua drew a deep breath. "You've heard of the legal group HOUR?"

Faith searched her memory bank, but came up empty. "It sounds familiar..."

"Stands for Humanity Organized and United in Responsibility. They make their mark with religious freedom cases, you know—hassling churches, forcing Scout troops to act in violation of their guidelines, making sure nativity scenes don't crop up in public places—that kind of thing."

"Okay." Faith felt her shoulders drop as her body relaxed. Whatever it was, it didn't involve her.

"Anyway, yesterday afternoon they filed a lawsuit against the town of Bethany."

Faith could feel the blood draining from her face. "What for?"

Joshua's voice was thick with emotion. "They want the Jesus statue torn down."

Anger released into her veins like a dose of adrenaline. "What? Why would they want that?"

"It's a religious symbol in a public park. Precedence says they probably have a valid point, and Frank's asked me to work on the case. Could be the biggest I've done."

"Frank Furlong? Mayor Frank Furlong?"

"Right."

"He's worried about it?"

"Faith, we're all worried about it. HOUR sent an attorney to Bethany yesterday, and by this morning we were already fielding calls from three major newspapers and all the network affiliates."

"Even WKZN?" Faith was stunned. What would cause an outsider to drive to Bethany and attack the statue in Jericho Park? It wasn't hurting anyone; in fact it was part of the town's history, its heritage. Faith felt her anger rise another notch.

"It'll be one of your top stories." He hesitated. "I wanted you to hear it from me first. I know you're on...well, I know the station's watching you."

The realization of what Joshua had done finally dawned on her. Here he was, about to be thrust in the limelight of a case that would be the most controversial Bethany had seen in decades, and the thing he felt compelled to do was call her. Joshua was more than her father's friend and partner, he was her friend, too. And with her father gone, it meant everything to Faith to know that he'd chosen to look out for her.

You're so good, God...first seeing Jordan last night and now this. "Thanks, Joshua."

"It's what your dad would have done."

"So what happens next? When's the hearing?" The anger had turned to something altogether different, a sense of justice, of fighting for what was right. It resonated in Faith with a strength that was foreign to her, and she suddenly had to know more details, find out where she fit into the picture and how she could be part of the solution.

"The judge assigned us a date, four weeks from tomorrow. The last Wednesday in September." He paused. "The guy from HOUR tried to talk us into taking the statue down without a fight, met with us yesterday afternoon. When we told him no, he filed suit and headed back to New York."

New York? Faith's fingers began to tremble. *"I have to get back to New York...New York...New York...."*

It couldn't be. He would never have been involved with an organization such as HOUR, not in a million years. Still, how many other New York attorneys had passed through town yesterday? Her throat was suddenly dry and she had to work to find her voice. "Did you get the guy's name? The attorney, I mean?"

"From HOUR?"

"Yeah, the man from New York?" Faith held her breath as she heard Joshua shuffling through papers.

"Yeah, just a minute." There was a pause, and Faith didn't think she could stand the suspense. Even if she was right, if it was Jordan, she had no intention of telling Joshua she knew him. It was all too much of a shock.

"Okay, here we go…just a minute…let's see…it's right here."

No, don't let it be…it can't be…

"His name is Jordan Riley."

10

At five minutes before eleven Jordan tuned his satellite receiver to a channel he'd never watched before his brief visit to Bethany: WKZN out of Philadelphia. Since Philadelphia was a major market, it made sense that Jordan's satellite service would carry it, but he was surprised all the same.

Since seeing Faith the night before, feeling how she worked magic on his heart and soul, he'd been plagued by more doubts than he cared to admit. He had never experienced a connection that strong to any woman, never had the unexplainable urge to take a woman home right then and marry her…

Of course his feelings didn't matter. What mattered was that he and Faith had grown into adults who stood on opposite sides of a religious Grand Canyon. As strong as their opposing views were, he knew there would be no bridges to build, no earthly way to span the distance between them. Any chance that may have existed would be demolished after Faith learned the truth.

No, he'd never hold her again, never have the chance to tell her that he would remember last night as long as he lived…but he still had her news show. Once he found the channel, he sat stone still and waited for the broadcast to begin.

The music came first, then a gradual close-in on Faith and her coanchor. The man spoke first. "A second victim in last week's local gun battle is dead today as police continue looking for the suspect."

It was Faith's turn. "And in Bethany, a powerful law firm takes aim at the city's favorite landmark."

Jordan searched her beautiful eyes for any sign that the story had hit her personally, but he saw none. He could only imagine what sort of emotional turmoil was going on just beneath her polished veneer. He studied her eyes, her hands. *Don't hate me Faith…this has nothing to do with you.*

"Good evening everyone, I'm Ron Leonard…"

"And I'm Faith Evans, welcome to tonight's edition of WKZN's Nightly News."

Leonard talked a few minutes on the gun battle story; then the camera fixed on Faith.

"An attorney from Humanity Organized and United in Responsibility filed suit yesterday against Bethany claiming that the nearly hundred-year-old Jesus statue violates the Constitution's call for a separation of church and state." Faith kept talking but the camera cut away to a shot of the Jesus statue, with young children playing nearby. "For nearly a century the Jesus statue has stood as a landmark in Bethany, Pennsylvania, without a single complaint waged against it."

Jordan watched, his palms sweaty. Did she know he was the attorney?

"But all that changed yesterday when Jordan Riley, an attorney with the HOUR organization, filed suit asking that the statue be removed."

Well, that answered that. A strange sadness settled over Jordan. After spending more than a decade wondering about Faith, looking for her, they'd lost each other again in less than twenty-four hours. The camera cut back to her.

"There'll be a hearing on the matter Wednesday at which point Judge Randall Webster is expected to make a decision. Hundreds of citizens from Bethany and surrounding communities are expected to attend."

Oh, they are, are they? Jordan raised a single eyebrow. Despite his boss's warning that this case could gain national attention, Jordan hadn't really expected a fight. Case precedent on such matters was clear: Whenever a city had chosen to erect a religious display or statue, almost without exception the city had been made to take it down. Jordan wondered if maybe Faith was talking about herself or if she knew for a fact that citizens had already rallied against him.

Faith turned to her partner. "Quite a case, huh?"

Ron shook his head. "Bound to be in the news for a while."

The camera hadn't focused back in on her, but still Faith continued the conversation with her coworker. "I'm from Bethany as you know, and all I can say is that this Jordan Riley—whoever he is—doesn't know what he's getting himself into."

Jordan felt as though he'd been stepped on by an elephant. *Whoever he is?* Faith—his childhood best friend, the woman he'd kissed so gently the other night—had referred to him on East Coast television as *whoever he is?* She must be furious with him. The knowledge of that truth cast another strange layer of grief over him. What was wrong with him? Was he surprised that she was angry? He should have expected it the moment he realized she still lived in Bethany.

No, there was nothing shocking about Faith's reaction. After all, Jordan had always known how she loved Jericho Park and the Jesus statue in particular. But somehow he'd hoped she might understand, that she might see how God had let him down, how He'd taken his mother, his sister...even his chance at a relationship with Faith. Jordan wasn't the bad guy here, couldn't she see that? Jesus was.

The lawsuit was an act of mercy, really. No city in America should have a statue honoring such a cruel God.

The minute the newscast was over, Dick Baker marched across the soundstage, the capillaries in his temples purplish and threatening to burst through his skin. He pointed his finger at Faith's partner. "Leonard, out!" Dick's bellow echoed off the stage's fiberboard sets.

Faith gulped. *If he fires me, Lord, let me get out of here without crying.* Ron Leonard, his hair and stage makeup still perfect, scowled at their boss, looking as if he might argue the station manager's approach. But instead he gathered his things and stormed off the stage. When he was gone, Dick turned to her.

"I warned you, Evans. What you did out there tonight was over the top. I mean completely unprofessional." He was breathing hard, his face almost as red as the veins in his neck. "The story didn't call for you to talk about the citizens of Bethany. What…were you out taking a private poll this morning?" He barely paused to grab another mouthful of air before he answered himself. "Of course you weren't. You said hundreds of citizens from Bethany and other towns were expected to be at the hearing and that is simply a lie. A complete fabrication of the facts."

There were knots in Faith's gut but it was too late to back down now. She'd made the decision to express her opinion on the air because it was the least she could do. If people knew that Faith Evans didn't want the Jesus statue moved, they'd likely side with her. She had that kind of following. The elderly saw her as a pretty daughter they needed to protect. Women related to her freshness and lack of guile, and men, well, it had never been difficult for Faith to gain the support of men. Not since she was ten years old and won a beauty pageant at the county fair.

He was waiting for an answer, and Faith met his gaze head on. *Okay, God, give me the strength…*

"I live in Bethany, Dick. I know the way people think there. It'll probably be more like a thousand people. That's how much they love that statue."

"No one—" he shouted the words and then gritted his teeth as he struggled to tone his voice down—"no one at this station is free to present his or her own news without some kind of outside research. Otherwise we're reduced to a group of op-ed mouthpieces spewing *our* thoughts and *our* ideas and *our* take on the news as it relates to *us!"* He paced two steps out and then back again, his hand raised for emphasis. "And what was that ad-lib thing you did? The camera wasn't anywhere near you! It was Ron's turn to speak, and all of a sudden we hear little Miss Opinionated talking about how this attorney from HOUR doesn't know what he's gotten himself into?" Dick massaged his temples with his thumb and forefinger, then he peered over the top of his hand and his eyes locked on hers. "Who in the world gave you permission to make such a statement?"

Faith didn't blink. "Ad-libbing is part of the job. It sounds conversational and approachable and friendly. It makes viewers tune back in tomorrow. Remember, Dick? Those were your words from last month's editorial meeting."

Dick glared at her and slammed his raised hand down on the countertop between Faith and him. She started from the ferocity of it. "You know darn well what I meant in that meeting! I was talking about scripted ad-libs. The kind that bridge us from news to weather, and weather to sports. Not a free-for-all, utterly biased conversation where all of Philadelphia gets to hear Faith Evans's opinion of HOUR."

Faith sighed. "Listen, Dick, I'm sorry. I didn't think it was out of line."

The station manager threw his hands in the air. "Sometimes I can't believe the networks are considering you for a national spot. I mean, don't get me wrong, Evans. You're beautiful and bright and you connect with our viewers like no other female anchor in the last decade." He moved closer and the corners of his eyes narrowed. "But the network has made it clear that I'll lose my job if I let you or anyone else use airtime for their own agenda. I cannot—*will* not—tolerate your Christian posturing on my news program." He was so upset his hand shook and he drew it back. "I could fire you, Evans, you know that?"

She knew he was right. Her contract included a promise of no biased reporting, which meant that even though it might look to the public like religious discrimination if she was let go, the truth was it would be perfectly legal.

Do not be dismayed, daughter, I am with you…

The sudden silent reminder of God's presence in her heart caused a warm calming feeling to spread out from her gut. Baker was waiting for an answer, and Faith forced herself to reply. "Yes, sir. I know."

"You will take tomorrow off without pay and you're to see me before going on the air Thursday."

Thursday? That meant she wouldn't be there for the *Wednesday's Child* segment. If she didn't do it, no one would. She had planned on running the segment on Rosa again in hopes that someone, somewhere would fall as quickly in love with the precious child as Faith had. Making her miss Wednesday was the worst punishment her boss could have meted out. *Lord, see what happens when I try to stand up for my beliefs? What good did it do?* There were no words in response, only images. A candle under a bushel, a buried coin, and walls around something Faith couldn't quite make out. It didn't matter, the message was the same: God wanted her to be bold, no matter the cost.

Dick's voice was so loud Faith was sure most everyone at the station could hear him. "Tomorrow I'll write up a probation form, which we will both sign…and the next time you pull a stunt like this, Evans, you're fired. It's that simple. You can forget about any help from the network. The big boys like your talent, but pretty mouthpieces are a dime a dozen. If I don't keep the executives happy they'll have both of us gone before the weekend." He lowered his face so that he could stare straight at her. "Have I made myself clear?"

There was no point arguing. "Yes, sir."

Dick spun and walked away. Faith watched him go and knew she should have felt discouraged, and she was—about missing *Wednesday's Child* the following day. But as she left the station she felt strangely inspired, uplifted—as though she'd taken the first step toward a life that God had been calling her to for years. It was a small step, but it was in the right direction, and though her job hung in the balance, Faith was curiously unconcerned.

By walking the narrow path ahead of her she somehow knew she would be safer and more secure than at any other time in her life. Faith paused as regret hit her over one fact: Jordan had become an enemy overnight, someone attacking her home, and she wondered for the hundredth time since Joshua's call why her long-ago friend had filed the lawsuit in the first place.

And how he'd had the nerve to hide the fact from her that night at the diner—and later in the parking lot. He had filed suit that very day…he must have known she would be upset by it. Otherwise he wouldn't have been so evasive when she asked him why he was in town.

The thought of it turned Faith's stomach.

Had he only wanted to trick her, use her for a night of reminiscing? And what did he have against Jericho Park and the Jesus statue? Faith had no answers, but there was someone who did. As she climbed into her car that night she made a plan to get Jordan's phone number and call him.

Even if it was the last time the two of them ever talked.

The easiest way to find him, Faith knew, was to call the HOUR organization in New York, so at two o'clock in the afternoon the next day from her mother's kitchen she did just that. Once Faith had Jordan's number from the operator, she was connected to his secretary in less than a minute.

"Jordan Riley, please." Faith put on her professional voice, hoping to ward off any censoring by the woman.

There was silence for a beat. "Who may I say is calling?"

"Faith Evans. It's about a case we're working on."

Again there was a hesitation. "Just a moment, please…"

Faith sat back in the kitchen chair and forced herself to be calm. *I can't believe it's true, Jordan…you've sold out to the other side, given up the precious faith you and your mother and your—*

"Hello?" The voice at the other end lacked any of the warmth it had held the other night, back when he'd wrapped her in his arms and…

"It's Faith." She could hear ice in her own voice as well and she felt as though she were lying, as though the role of enemy didn't quite fit yet.

"Faith, I was going to call you tom—"

"Don't lie to me, Jordan." She was maintaining her cool exterior, not showing too much emotion. "You knew you weren't going to call from the moment you saw me at the station."

He was silent and Faith took the cue. "Listen, obviously you're upset and mixed up. You must have personal reasons for wanting our statue down, for suing Bethany over the Jesus statue…but I meant what I said."

"Which was?" He, too, sounded dry and businesslike. Gone was the man she'd connected with, the one whose voice had been heavy with years of memories and longing.

"The whole town will turn out." She was careful with her words. "I think you're making a huge mistake."

A laugh void of any humor came at her in response. "You really don't get it, do you, Faith?"

She hated his condescending tone. "No, I really don't. The Jordan Riley I knew would have loved God too much to attack Him in court."

"I've changed since then. Grown up. I thought you could see it that night…when we were together."

Faith felt her stomach tighten. "The man I was with was not someone different. He was the same boy I loved as a kid."

"The same—" Jordan's voice was softer this time, but he cut himself short. When he spoke again it was with fire. "I prayed to Jesus, Faith. The same Jesus honored by that stupid statue. And what did it ever get me? My mother died, my sister was sent off to live with strangers, and I never heard from her again. I never heard from you, either. I lost everything that mattered to me that year, Faith. And the reason it hurt so bad was because of the Jesus statue."

In the silence that followed, a light began to dawn in the shadowy places of Faith's heart. Jordan blamed God for the losses in his life. And now he was trying to get rid of the Jesus statue as his way of exacting revenge. "Why the statue?"

"Because—" his words were like bullets spewing from a semiautomatic— "because there's no such thing as a Jesus like the one in the statue. A Jesus with open arms, welcoming those around Him to come, to bring their troubles and lay them at His feet so that He might make things right again. God—if there *is* a God—is a hands-off, mad scientist. Someone who set the world in motion and then stood back to watch it self-destruct."

Faith leaned forward, physically ill at Jordan's anger toward the God they had once worshiped side by side in church and Sunday school. *Lord, how did this happen?* How had Jordan missed the point that God didn't promise a trouble-free life, just peace and joy and friendship through the troubles? "I'm sorry, Jordan. I…I didn't know you felt that way."

"Well I do, and you ought to feel the same way." He huffed. "The Lord took your dad, He took away your relationship with that football player, and because of the accident He took a year of your life. How can you defend a God like that?"

What struck Faith most was that Jordan honestly had no answers for himself. "I can defend Him because He loves me. He loves you too, Jordan."

"Wake up, Faith. He could care less about either of us."

She sighed. "I don't want to get into a theological debate. I just want to warn you. The Jesus statue belongs to the people of Bethany, and any battle you wage there is one you'll ultimately lose."

"Then I guess I'll see you and the rest of the town in court." His voice was sharp and cool, lacking even the anger it had held earlier. "Good-bye, Faith."

Jordan hung up before she could say anything else, and her own anger rose in her defense—then an image filled her head. Jordan Riley, thirteen years old, kneeling on damp grass in the freezing still of night a few feet from the Jesus statue, begging God to let his mother live.

Faith closed her eyes and felt tears spill onto her cheeks. She bowed her head and prayed for her father's old law partner, Joshua, and the people of Bethany, that they might have strength to fight the battle of Jericho Park. Then, with a full and broken heart, she prayed for the boy she had grown up with, the one she had once dreamed of marrying, the one who had lost so much the winter of his thirteenth year.

And for the bitter man he'd become.

II

Heidi and Charles were stretched out on their living room sofa enjoying the opportunity to chat about their move to Bethany. Charles had given notice at the hospital, and for the most part everything was in order. Heidi watched him now, the love in his eyes, the way he cared so much about her happiness. He put his hand on her belly and smiled.

"It's getting bigger."

She pushed her fist into his shoulder and giggled. "Not *it,* silly. *Her.*"

"Ah, another princess in the house!" He laughed. "Ultrasounds can be wrong, remember. Happens at the clinic every day."

"Not this time. I have a feeling about her." Heidi placed a protective hand over her abdomen. "She's our little sweetheart." Her eyes lifted to his and her heart felt light as air. "I can actually picture her."

The baby kicked, and a grin spread across Charles's face. *"Must* be a girl. She's feisty, just like her mother."

He snuggled in close to her, his arm around her midsection as though he were cradling them both. "You don't mind moving in November…right after the baby's born?"

She chuckled and ran her fingers through his hair. "As long as I've got you and God on my side, I can do anything."

There was a comfortable silence between them and Heidi stared out the window at the gold and maroon leaves on the tree. Fall was her favorite time of year. Summer's last hurrah—its shout that life is, and life will come again. It was the time of year her mother had gotten sick, a time when Jordan had been her greatest strength, her pillar of hope that God would work through their mother's illness no matter what happened. Even after their mother died Jordan had been strong for her, holding her, assuring her that one day they'd all be together in heaven.

Heidi sighed. Days like this it was easy to picture Jordan as he'd been back then, dark-haired and muscle bound, eyes glowing with sincerity. What if he hadn't been in the cave that terrible afternoon at the boys' camp? What if the state had kept them together instead of separating them?

"You okay?" Charles brushed her bangs to the side and looked into her eyes. "Feels like you're a million miles away."

"I am." She snuggled against his shoulder and resumed her study of autumn out their living room window. "Just thinking about Mom and Jordan."

Charles exhaled through pursed lips, and she could feel his concern for her. He understood the place in her heart that would always remember, always yearn for the people of her childhood days, for her mother and brother. An idea occurred to her and she turned her attention back to Charles. "What if we name her Jordan Lee?"

Charles cocked his head thoughtfully and then drew near and kissed her. "I like it."

"Really? You do?" Her mood soared with the possibility that her little girl might carry on her brother's name. The name of an uncle her daughter would never know.

"From everything you've told me about Jordan, he was kind and strong and loving. He cared deeply about God and his family. Our little girl couldn't have a better name."

Heidi buried her head in Charles' shoulder again. "I love you so much. Thanks for understanding."

He squeezed her once. "You make it easy."

A few minutes passed and he grabbed the remote control. "I want to see what the president said in his address last night."

They watched the opening story and after a few minutes Heidi stood up. "I'll get dinner." She moved behind Charles and massaged his neck and shoulders.

"Mmm." He closed his eyes and the corners of his mouth lifted. "Can't we just skip dinner?"

She laughed and gave him a final squeeze. "You might not need it, but I'm eating for two." She ducked her head in front of him, kissed him on the cheek, and left the room.

Charles craned his neck and watched her go. How did he get so lucky, anyway? Married to the perfect woman and about to be a first-time father? He turned his attention back to the television. It was good to see Heidi smile. Too often this time of the year she was lost in thought, remembering ghosts from her past. He sighed and flicked the channel. If there was one thing he was anxious to ask God, it was why He'd taken Jordan Riley so young. Hadn't it been enough to call Heidi's mother home without taking her brother too? A news program played on but Charles was too lost in thought to hear it.

He wasn't angry with the Lord, just curious.

It didn't matter that he'd never met Jordan. Charles had heard enough about him to feel like family, as though he could easily recognize him if he passed him on the street. Clearly Heidi had been crazy about her brother, and every fall her feelings for him came back stronger than ever. The reason was simple: During the hardest time in Heidi's life, Jordan had meant everything to her.

The news program moved onto another story, and Charles focused on what was being said. Something about a park in Bethany and a lawsuit to remove a statue. He tried to make sense of the story, but he'd already missed too many details. He wondered if Heidi knew about the case. Probably. He leaned back into the couch and yawned. Maybe he'd talk to her about it over dinner. His thoughts shifted to the playoffs and whether the National League had a team worthy of the World Series. For that matter, where the big games would be held that year and whether he'd have a chance to take in any baseball action before the move.

By the time Heidi called him for dinner, he'd completely forgotten about Jericho Park and the obscure news item regarding a legal fight over some statue, or the fact that he'd ever intended to bring up the story to Heidi in the first place.

12

In the small law office in Bethany, the weeks passed in a blur of case study and preparation for Joshua Nunn. But when the day of the hearing arrived, he felt no more prepared than the day he'd been given the case, the day he'd had the strange dream.

"You ready to beat this guy?" Frank had asked in a phone call that morning.

Joshua hadn't been sure how to answer him. Frank was the mayor after all, the one who had put such faith in Joshua's abilities in the first place. From the beginning he had known it would be a tough case to win. Now that he'd had a chance to study case precedent, he was fairly sure it was impossible.

A pain took root in his gut. "I'll give it my best."

"Don't worry about a thing, old friend. We've got the Lord on our side."

That much was sure, Joshua knew. Twice in the past week various churches had held prayer rallies at Jericho Park with as many as three hundred people—singing and agreeing with each other that the Jesus statue was part of who they were, a key facet of their town's history and personality. The gatherings had done a great job of making the townspeople heard. All three local network affiliates had carried stories about the public outcry on their nightly news, making Faith Evans look like a prophet.

"Think there'll be a group at the courthouse?"

Frank chuckled. "If you call a thousand people gathered on the courthouse lawn a group."

Joshua gulped. "A thousand people?" *Lord, I'm not up to this. I need Bob...*

Be strong and courageous...I will go before you.

The silent words reassured him, easing the kinks in Joshua's belly.

"At least that many. People are outraged over this. Lot of nerve that HOUR group has, messing with our statue. That's the message the people want to convey and I'm betting they actually get heard today." Frank offered a few more words of encouragement then wrapped up the conversation. "Gotta run if I want a good seat. See you there."

Joshua rubbed the back of his neck and leaned forward in his chair. "See ya."

If Bob were there they'd have had an early morning prayer time, bowed their heads together, and taken the issue straight to the throne room of God. Since that wasn't possible, Joshua was left with only one option: pray alone. The image of Bob's daughter came to mind, and suddenly he knew he would not be praying alone that morning. Wherever she was, Bob's daughter would be lifting her voice as well, asking God, even begging Him, to have mercy on the people of Bethany, Pennsylvania.

Even if case precedent and HOUR and everything else were against them.

Joshua folded his hands, stared for a moment at the photo of Bob Moses on the office wall, closed his eyes, and hung his head. "Okay, God, here it is: You know the situation…"

Faith pulled into a nearly full lot across the street from the courthouse, parked her car, and instructed herself to calm down. Her heart pounded as though it were trying to break free from her body and start a life of its own.

"God help us," she whispered as she climbed out of her car and locked the door. She'd gotten up earlier than usual that morning and prayed for nearly an hour, but still peace eluded her. In the weeks since speaking to Jordan, since hearing the determination in his voice, Faith's confidence that the city would win the case had eroded like beach property in winter. Now that the morning of the hearing had arrived she was more nervous than ever.

She wasn't covering the story for the station, but she'd be recognized all the same. Days earlier she'd been warned to stay out of the camera's view—keep her distance if she wanted to keep her job.

"You're recognized everywhere you go," Dick Baker told her. "No anchor of mine will be taking sides on a political issue like this one."

His words echoed in Faith's mind as she made her way past a peaceful demonstration on the front lawn, nodding at several people who waved in her direction. She entered the courtroom and found a seat near the back. The courthouse was located just outside Bethany in a newly renovated area designated for state government buildings. Judge Randall Webster would preside, and Faith was not at all comforted by the fact. Prior to taking the position as a jurist for the state of Pennsylvania, Judge Webster had been a defense attorney who earned a reputation for getting his clients the lightest possible sentences. He was a liberal man who'd made it abundantly clear he saw no place in society for religious icons, the Ten Commandments, or any mention of God whatsoever. Faith felt certain that if it had been up to Judge Webster, the dollar bill would say, "In us we trust." And that philosophy pervaded everything he said from the bench.

Faith spotted her father's partner across the courtroom and their eyes met. She smiled and discreetly pointed upward, mouthing the word, "Believe." Joshua nodded, his eyes filled with warmth even though uncertainty controlled his face. He returned his attention to his notes, and Faith shifted her gaze to the other side of the room.

Her breath caught in her throat as she spotted Jordan Riley. He moved easily from one end of the table to the other, his chiseled face masked in concentration, shoulders filling out his dark designer suit. She berated herself for being attracted to him. *God, help me remember he's on the wrong side.*

He moved toward what looked to be a team of attorneys, and they surrounded him the way athletes do in the final moments before a game. Clearly Jordan was in control of the meeting. He spoke commands to several of the men, and one at a time they peeled away and took their seats, either at the plaintiff's table or in the first row behind it.

She looked at him, hoping he would meet her gaze, but he was too caught up in his preparation. *God's on our side, Jordan... besides, nothing will bring back your mother.*

Faith saw that every seat in the courtroom was taken, but still people continued to stream in, lining two and three deep along the walls. Finally, security guards blocked the entrance and began turning people away.

Judge Webster entered the room and a hush fell over the crowd. He studied the mass of people, looked from perfectly dressed Jordan to the older Joshua and gently rapped his gavel. "Order... court is in session." His voice was deep and gravelly and carried with it an authority that sent a shiver down Faith's spine.

Please, God, be with us...

"This court will now hear the matter of Humanity Organized and United for Responsibility versus the city of Bethany, Pennsylvania."

Joshua watched as the judge lifted his chin and stared down the bridge of his nose. "I understand there are—" he made no effort to hide his sarcasm—"a few people interested in the outcome of this case." His voice boomed out from the bench. "Let's make one thing clear up front. No intimidation will take place in my courtroom. People are welcome to have an opinion." He gestured toward the window that overlooked the courthouse greens. "They are even invited to line up twenty deep across the lawn." He paused and glared at Joshua. "But nothing they say or do will influence the rulings I make in my courthouse now or at any other time. Is that clear?"

Joshua felt every eye in the room on him. "Yes, Your Honor, of course not."

The judge glared at Jordan next. "That goes for you, too."

Jordan Riley grinned at the judge as though the man were a favorite uncle. "Absolutely, Your Honor."

Judge Webster sat back in his seat. "In that case, let's begin. We'll hear from the plaintiff first." He motioned at the audience. "The rest of you may be seated."

Those who had seats did as the judge directed, and Jordan took the floor. He paced slowly in front of the tables, holding his notes as though if he studied them long enough he might remember what to say. Joshua knew that wasn't the case. He'd done his research on Riley. The man's memory was one of the best in the business. The notes in his hands were merely for appearances, a device intended to give the impression that everything he said—from his opening argument to his closing remarks—was strictly from case law and researched material. That way he wouldn't come across as having a personal vendetta against the people of Bethany or their Jesus statue. Rather he was simply a legal servant of society, doing his best to maintain the line between church and state.

Joshua wondered if he was the only one in the room who saw through the ploy.

"Your Honor, the HOUR organization has filed suit against the people of Bethany for what is clearly a violation of state law. In the center of Bethany is a park—owned and operated by the city. And at the center of the park stands a ten-foot-high statue of Jesus Christ." Jordan paused as though he might rest his case on that note alone. "We believe the statue represents a conflict between church and state and is therefore a violation of the Constitution." He stopped pacing and stood with his legs shoulder-width apart, the folder held at his side. "The law is clear that no state government shall endorse or suggest or force any religion on its constituents. Clearly Jesus Christ is the universal symbol for Christianity. And since the Jesus statue stands on public property, its presence suggests a religion that is not only government-sponsored and endorsed, but quite possibly mandated."

Jordan shrugged his shoulders and cast an easy smile at Judge Webster. "Very simply, we want the statue removed as soon as possible."

The judge nodded. The lines on his face had eased considerably. "Go on, Counsel."

Jordan nodded and resumed his meandering pace across the front of the courtroom, his eyes on his notes once more. Joshua watched him and was caught off guard by something in the young man's eyes. His face was familiar in an eerie sort of way…

"In addition to the law—which is clearly on our side—we believe we have ample precedent to prove our point. With us today we have research from dozens of past cases, both from the state and Supreme Court level. If it pleases Your Honor, I'll give a summary of that research at this time."

Judge Webster gestured toward Jordan in a way that was just short of rude. "Continue."

Across the room Joshua tried to read the feeling coming from the bench. Anyone who knew the judge knew where he likely stood on the issue of church and state. But Joshua knew the man also prided himself on not being biased. Joshua prayed that pride would work in their favor.

Jordan set his things down on the plaintiff's table and sorted through them for a few seconds before apparently finding what he was looking for. "Here we are…" And with that, Jordan neatly and succinctly cited exactly fourteen sources that were similar in nature, cases where a nativity scene or a Christian fish symbol or a cross was eliminated from the landscape of any place even remotely public. For good measure, he included two examples where private establishments were ordered to remove their Christian symbols as well.

After talking for less than an hour, Jordan set his notes down and looked at the judge. "That's all for now, Your Honor." A warm smile filled his face. "We are not looking to punish or in any way penalize the people of Bethany. We merely want the good citizens of this country to feel free to live and work around public areas without being forced to adhere to a specific religion. In essence—" he gestured toward his team of attorneys, and again Joshua had the strange feeling he'd seen the young attorney somewhere before—"we want to preserve the rights of the people to live free from the burden of state-sponsored religion. Now and as long as this great nation might stand. Thank you, Your Honor."

Jordan took his seat, and Joshua gathered his notes. He was certain his opponent had reams more of case precedent to support the idea that religious icons and displays ought not to be left standing on public property. That was fine. Joshua had prepared as well. He smiled to himself and felt a peaceful confidence come over him. God had promised to fight the battle, to go before him. Surely that meant victory, right? He stood up and headed toward the center of the floor, six feet from the judge's chair, praying for the right words.

"Your Honor, I appreciate the comments and concerns presented by the plaintiff. But I disagree that this is a case of the HOUR organization looking out for the rights of the people." He glanced at his notes and allowed a measured pause. The last thing he wanted was to appear rushed and flustered, as though he had to work to defend the city's position.

He took a steadying breath and continued. "The statue in question was given to the city of Bethany as a gift nearly a hundred years ago." Joshua squared up before the bench and met the judge's eyes straight on. "If the city had received a statue of Pocahontas or Christopher Columbus or Martin Luther King Jr., certainly no one would object to having it placed at the center of the city's oldest park. Like Columbus or King, Jesus Christ is a person of great historical significance, both in our United States history as well as the history of the world. Removing the statue of Him now is, in this city's opinion, a violation of the citizens' rights to cherish this gift, to look upon its considerable beauty and expression, to consider the historical significance of the man it represents." He made his way to the defense table and sorted through a series of files. If his opponent could look loaded with precedent, so could he. "I'd like to share some case law supporting that opinion."

The reality was Joshua had been able to find only two cases that even remotely upheld the idea that the Jesus statue should remain standing in Jericho Park, but he played them for all they were worth. One case involved a cross anchored on a hill that was—technically—part of the Texas state park system. It was also, however, a landmark by which those traveling the interstate could determine how far they'd traveled and how much time remained on their journey. Ultimately it was deemed more of a landmark than a religious icon, and the courts allowed it to stand.

The other case centered on the town of Camp Verde, Arizona, and an annual Christmas parade that culminated in a float depicting a living nativity scene. The parade entry included Mary, Joseph, an actual baby playing the part of Jesus, and an assortment of donkeys and sheep being tended along the parade route by Boy Scouts in shepherd garb. Since the parade was sponsored by the city, someone cried foul one year and filed a lawsuit requesting that the religious parade entry be excluded from the procession. After much bantering back and forth, a state court judge ruled that the parade was—in nature—organized around a Christmas theme, and that Christmas was, inherently, a celebration of Jesus Christ's birth. Therefore it was within the city's legal bounds to include in its Christmas parade the nativity scene, and the float was allowed to stay, right down to the babe in swaddling clothes.

Joshua did his best to make these cases look similar to the one involving Jericho Park. He played up the fact that government groups were involved in both cases and remained intentionally vague on his comparisons that a landmark and a Christmas float were almost exactly the same thing as having a Jesus statue in the center of a public park.

But as he spoke, even Joshua could hear the gaping holes in his argument. It was one thing to have a directional landmark or a holiday-themed parade entry. Joshua simply had no precedent demonstrating a city's right to maintain a religious presence on public property for no apparent reason. The landmark case was the most similar and the night before he'd decided to hammer on that one more than the other. Now as he neared the end of his remarks, that's exactly what he did.

"Your Honor, the people of Bethany use the Jesus statue as a meeting spot. They talk about it as though it were part of the town's landscape. Generations of Bethany citizens have held annual picnics around the base of the statue and found comfort in the fact that though things change with time, the statue remains. It stands regardless."

He set his notes down and faced the judge again. "It is our opinion that the Jesus statue is as much a landmark as the cross that stood in the publicly owned hills of Texas. We ask that you make a decision allowing it to stand. Thank you, Your Honor."

Joshua caught Faith's weak smile as he sat down. Was his case that lacking? *Come on, God…make it happen.* He winked at Faith, turned and took his seat.

The judge looked from Joshua's table to that of the plaintiff and leaned forward. "This court will recess for ten minutes while I consider both arguments. We will meet back here at ten-fifteen at which time I will give my decision."

Frank Furlong and several members of Bethany's city council surrounded Joshua, patting him on the back and assuring him he'd done a fantastic job. But Joshua thought their remarks seemed canned, contrived—as though they were trying to convince themselves of something that suddenly seemed almost impossible.

A noise began to build outside, and Joshua turned toward the window. People covered the grounds below, some of them carrying signs that read, Stay out of our park and It's HOUR statue. Many of them marched peacefully, while others formed prayer circles. Joshua watched, and the pressure he felt nearly suffocated him. He shuddered and turned back to the others. "You were right." He looked at Frank. "At least a thousand."

Frank and the others joined Joshua at the window, and the men watched as the group formed a single line and began marching around the lawn, singing what sounded like a hymn. Frank flipped a lock on the window frame and lifted the glass so they could hear more clearly. Immediately their song became audible, the words ringing over the voices in the courtroom, stopping conversations and gradually causing some people to join in the song.

"Great is Thy faithfulness, oh God my Father. There is no shadow of turning with Thee. Thou changest not, Thy compassions they fail not...as Thou has been Thou forever will be...."

Joshua felt tears stinging at his eyes and he blinked them back. The people were united in this, that much was sure. They didn't know what the outcome would be but they agreed on one thing: God would be faithful. Suddenly the pressure he'd felt a moment earlier lifted. It wasn't Joshua who would deliver victory to the people, but God. And whichever way the case went, He was in control. Faithful as He always had been, always would be.

The song grew louder as more voices joined from among those in the audience. "Great is Thy faithfulness, great is Thy faithfulness, morning by morning new mercies I see. All I have needed, Thy hand hath provided. Great is Thy faithfulness... great is Thy faithfulness...great is Thy—"

"Shut the window!"

Joshua started and turned to find Judge Webster standing near the bench.

"And stop singing! I will not stand for this type of disruption in my courtroom." He sat down and fanned his robe around him in a huff of anger as the voices around him died off one by one.

Joshua hurried back to his seat, certain deep in his gut that he'd lost the case.

Back at the window, Frank hesitated long enough to show his frustration toward the judge. Then in an angry motion Frank slammed the window shut, silencing the voices of the crowd midrefrain. He took his seat with the others from Bethany as Joshua prayed that the people outside—people protesting with praise—would not blame him or the mayor for the decision that was about to be made.

The redness in Judge Webster's cheeks lightened some, and he settled back in his chair. "That's better." He looked at the younger attorney and managed a crooked smile. "I have heard a variety of cases in my courtroom over the years, but I must say I've rarely seen one as clear-cut and simple as this one." His eyebrows lowered as he gazed across the room at Joshua. "I've had time to go over the case precedent cited by both parties and I have but one choice."

He sifted through several sheets of paper. "Our country ought to be grateful for organizations such as HOUR who come along and help us find balance in the public places of our national life." Judge Webster stared at Joshua. "To think that a public park has had a Jesus statue standing at its center for nearly a hundred years is appalling. It suggests that Christianity is the religion of the day and that Jesus Christ is to be worshiped and adored among the people. It is no better than the statues built back in Communist Russia or in Red China today, where public artwork represents a government-mandated mind-set. A mind-set that is inherently dangerous and in direct opposition to the freedoms for which this country stands."

In his peripheral vision, Joshua could see an HOUR attorney lean over and whisper something to Jordan. Both attorneys then looked across the room at Joshua and exchanged a smile.

We've lost. . . O God, we've lost.

You will not have to fight this battle, Joshua. The battle belongs to the Lord. . .

Okay, God, but we're running out of time. . .

Be strong and courageous.

He swallowed hard, keeping his eyes on Judge Webster. Waiting for what he knew was coming.

The judge was going on about the value of separation of church and state. Finally he paused and cleared his throat. "For that reason, it is my decision to side with the plaintiffs in this case and to order the Jesus statue removed at the expense of the city of Bethany." He narrowed his eyes and looked directly at Joshua.

Father, I know You're in control, but I don't understand this. . .

The judge continued. "You, Mr. Nunn, will instruct the city officials that they have thirty days to remove the statue. A hundred-dollar penalty will be exacted on the city for every day it continues to stand past the deadline." He motioned toward the crowd. "I will expect you to conduct yourself with decorum after court is adjourned. Anyone who protests in an unsuitable manner—" he peered over his wire-framed glasses—"and that includes singing—will be arrested and held in contempt of court." The judge hesitated only a moment. "Court is adjourned."

Immediately there was a rustling of whispers and people began moving about the courtroom. In the confusion, Joshua looked across the table and saw Jordan Riley staring straight at him, his eyes filled with a strange mixture of victory and sadness.

Joshua's heart skipped a beat as the pieces fell into place. He met Jordan's gaze and held it, studying the eyes of the man who had claimed victory over Joshua, the Jesus statue, and the people of Bethany. Suddenly he knew why the young attorney looked so familiar.

His was the face in the dream, the one he'd had the day he was packing Bob Moses' things at the office. When Bob's face had disappeared from the framed photograph hanging on the office wall, it had been replaced by the image of a younger man with angry eyes and a handsome, chiseled face. A face Joshua had never seen.

Until now.

The face of Jordan Riley, chief counsel for the HOUR organization.

13

*N*early two weeks had passed since the ruling, and Faith knew from Joshua that the Bethany city council had held several emergency meetings in recent days. There wasn't much to discuss. Since the judge had ordered the Jesus statue removed, there was little they could do but decide on a ceremonial way to watch it go. A farewell party perhaps, or a designated day where the town could gather at the park for a picnic and hear a few words from key members in the community. There was talk of selling the statue to J. T. Enley, a retired stockbroker who had made millions in the market in the late nineties. Or perhaps donating it to a museum in Philadelphia. They also talked about selling the statue in an auction and donating the proceeds to a local charity.

Still, a deep and angry sadness remained, a sense of astonishment that a single attorney could breeze through town, file a lawsuit, and summarily have a town treasure eliminated. The story had made headlines in both local papers and was easily the biggest item in the newscast for three nights after the ruling. Tonight would be more of the same. According to Joshua, reporters had attended the latest council meeting earlier that day.

Faith finished applying her makeup and pinned her hair up, certain she'd feel the smirks of several station employees tonight as much as she'd felt them for the past fourteen days. She'd made her views public and she'd lost. The statue was coming down, and there was nothing she could do to stop it.

She slumped back against the wall in the boxy dressing room and stared at herself. Her father would never have let the statue be removed. Not that Joshua hadn't done his best in court; he had. But Bob Moses was a man who refused to let life get the best of him. Faith didn't know how, but her father would have found a way to keep the statue standing.

So what did that say about her?

What good had she ever brought to the world around her? She woke up at her parents' house, washed and cleaned and shopped for her mother, and on occasion spent a day with Rosa Lee. Every night on the air she dressed the same and smiled the same and used the same polished voice to deliver news that people could have gotten from a dozen different sources. Newspapers, other networks, the Internet.

Her job didn't really matter to anyone.

Mike Dillan continued breaking hearts in every town he played, Rosa went without a family, the Jesus statue was ordered down. Through it all, she'd been little more than a meaningless bystander. A weak-willed, passive participant with none of the gumption and determination that had been the benchmark of her father's life.

"Evans, let's go!" The voice on the other side of the door snapped her out of her reverie, demanding her attention for yet another newscast, another series of stories she would read for the cameras. Faith Evans, expert mouthpiece.

Lord, make me a light...help me bring about change.

As if in response, an idea came to mind. A brilliantly simple, amazing idea that took shape in Faith's mind in less time than it took her to grab the door handle and turn it. She hesitated for a moment, staring at the wooden door as a smile filled her face. The idea was so solid, so sound, Faith knew it had to have come from the Lord.

And as she breezed out of the dressing room and headed for her place on the soundstage she knew something else as well.

It just might work.

The next morning Sandy Dirk, Rosa Lee's social worker, got a phone call from a man who said he was from WKZN. His conversation was quick and to the point: "Our Internet site isn't receiving nearly the hits we'd like it to get."

She rolled her eyes, reached for a pencil and began doodling on a notepad. Sandy had seen so many down-and-out kids come through her foster home that she'd lost track of the number. Rosa was destined for the long-term facilities. She was too old to draw the attention of a couple looking for a baby, and though Sandy loved the children in her own way, she no longer got sucked into relationships with them. Hers was merely a stopping ground, a place for children no one wanted until the state could figure out something else. Often the only thing better was a group home, and Sandy had never known a child yet who hadn't been hardened beyond recognition after spending a year in such a place.

There was nothing quite like the pain of watching officials from Social Services—and on some occasions even police officers—show up at the house, take a child and all her belongings, and haul her off to live at a group home for an indeterminate amount of time. Whatever a child's demeanor was when he or she left for group care, inevitably it would be worse six months later. People who knew Sandy understood that her gruff voice and no-nonsense approach was merely a front to prevent children from getting too comfortable in her care. And to keep herself from getting too comfortable with them.

Now as the man on the other end spoke, Sandy jotted the words *Internet site* and coughed into the receiver. "Okay, I heard ya. What's your point?"

The man drew a breath deep enough to hear over the phone lines. "We have advertisers, Mrs. Dirk. People who want to buy space on our Web site—especially the *Wednesday's Child* page."

"What's that have to do with me?" Sandy peered out the back window to make sure Rosa Lee was still playing outside with the other children.

"We're taking Rosa's picture off the site. To make room for other kids."

A flicker of understanding passed across Sandy's mind. "You mean because she isn't cute enough? What with her missing fingers and Asian blood, is that it, Mr. Baker?"

Sandy chuckled twice, though it sounded more like an exaggerated huff. She'd been against the *Wednesday's Child* program from the beginning, convinced it would do nothing to increase Rosa Lee's chances for adoption and would most likely wind up hurting her in the process.

"The children who are getting attention from online users are younger than Rosa." The man sounded as though his patience was running low, as though it was demeaning to talk to a woman of Sandy's stature. "The fact is, Mrs. Dirk, no one's even asking about Rosa. She'll be off the Web site as of tomorrow morning. I thought you'd like to know."

Sandy thought for a moment. "Does Faith Evans know about this?"

There was a long pause on the other end. Apparently her question had hit its mark.

"No…the *Wednesday's Child* Web site has nothing to do with the program anchor. Unless you have other questions, Mrs. Dirk, I have appointments to keep."

Sandy hung up the phone and stared at it a moment, knowing that after tomorrow, getting Rosa Lee adopted would be virtually impossible.

In fact, it would be nothing short of a miracle.

Dick Baker hung up the station phone and buzzed Laura Wade, the young woman who manned the station's Web site. She was twenty-three, possessed a Microsoft certificate and a brain that seemed even quicker than the station's lightning-fast computers. Normally he had little to do with the Web site, but this was something special. Three days earlier, an anonymous caller had asked for him by name, offering to pay ten thousand dollars for a spot on the site under one condition: Baker had to keep Faith Evans from making any more opinionated outbursts.

At first Dick had balked at the request, assuming the caller was a nutcake. But after further questioning him, Dick learned that the man was from HOUR—the same group that had won the lawsuit against the town of Bethany. "Any suggestions?"

There was a pause. "*Wednesday's child.* That's Evans's project, isn't it?"

Baker was impressed. The man had done his homework. "Okay…so?"

"Remove the photos of one or two kids she's particularly fond of. That ought to get her attention."

A strange rumbling began in the pit of Baker's stomach. "How do I justify removing a child? They all need homes. The staff'll ask questions."

The caller chuckled. "That's up to you."

Baker thought about the ad money and his mind raced. Certainly he could remove the little Asian girl's photo. The other featured children were younger, healthier. Not biracial. Certainly he could make a case that they would adopt easier. Besides, the Asian girl belonged on a Web site for special-needs kids, not in a showcase position such as WKZN offered.

"All right. I can take care of that." Dick informed the man that the cost for the ad space was only seven thousand dollars per month. What he learned next cinched the deal.

"We'll be sending out two checks. One for the first month and a three thousand dollar check made out to you. For...administrative expenses."

Dick hadn't needed any more information than that. He imagined the cruise he and his wife could take with the bonus. There'd even be enough for gambling money...souvenirs...time off.

The checks had arrived the day before, and he'd already spoken with Laura, the Web master, about the ad. HOUR's insignia and hot line number had been displayed prominently at the top of the *Wednesday's Child* Web page since last night.

Getting the Asian girl's picture removed had been another thing altogether.

The station's standard permissions form for children who appeared on the *Wednesday's Child* program and Web site stated that a child's guardian had to be contacted before his or her picture could be removed from the Internet page. Dick hated having to contact Rosa Lee's social worker, but there'd been no other way. At least he hadn't lied to the woman. The fact was, there *were* younger, more desirable children whose pictures belonged on the Web site. Rosa Lee was something of a distraction, a misfit. Dick held his breath as the phone rang in the station's computer lab.

"Yes?" Laura's voice was robotic, as though she'd spent too many years in the company of a computer.

"Baker here. I notified the social worker. Pull the photo of Rosa Lee."

Baker heard a series of clicking sounds as the woman's fingers raced over the keyboard. "Okay. She's gone."

As he hung up the phone he smiled to himself—but even as he did, Baker felt a twinge of regret. What heartless person at HOUR had sent in the request that Faith's favorite child or favorite children be removed from the site? He let the thought pass. The benefits far outweighed any damage to his conscience over the issue. WKZN would come off looking like it approved of HOUR, a fact that would help balance the conservative on-air views Faith Evans continually spouted. Baker could use HOUR to maintain an unbiased position, thereby pleasing the network executives in Philadelphia. His station had picked up an extra seven thousand dollars and he'd made a tidy bonus in the process.

Satisfaction filtered through Baker's veins. There was one other benefit, the icing on the cake, really. If the HOUR group was intent on pressuring Faith Evans to quiet her religious views, then that would take the burden off him.

In the end, it was a win-win situation for everyone.

⌒⊙⌒

At just past eleven that morning Faith sat by the fireplace in her parents' house sipping hot, steamed milk and second-guessing herself. She stared at the dancing flames, and though the warmth from the fire spread over her body, an icy wind resonated in her heart. The idea that had seemed so perfect the night before now felt impulsive and shallow and more than a little dangerous.

Faith curled her legs beneath her and considered the outcome if she went ahead with her plan. Certainly it could cost her a chunk of her savings—as well as any pretense of impartiality she might still have among her coworkers. She drew a deep breath and sank further back in her chair, her lips pursed together.

She had to be realistic about it…it could mean losing her job.

The image of Rosa Lee filled her mind, and she picked up the phone. Maybe an afternoon with the little girl would make Faith's decision more clear, help settle her priorities into place. She dialed a number she had long since memorized and waited while the phone rang.

"Yup." As far as Faith could tell, Sandy was an upbeat woman who dearly loved the children she cared for. The fact that she wasn't as tender or soft-spoken as Faith might have been didn't make her any less valuable in the lives of the kids. It merely underlined the fact that Rosa and the other children needed families.

"Hi, Sandy, it's Faith. Any calls for Rosa yet?" Faith held her breath. It was the same question she asked every time she called, praying all the while that someone had seen the Web site, a mom or dad who wanted to make Rosa their daughter.

"Nope, and it don't look like it'll happen any time soon."

Faith clenched her teeth and felt her heart sink halfway to her knees. *Poor Rosa. Why, God? Why isn't there someone for her?*

Silence.

There was no time to question the lack of holy reassurance. Sandy sounded more discouraged than usual, and a strange sense of alarm rippled through Faith. "Did something happen?"

"Yeah, something happened. That boss of yours down at the station called this morning and said they were pulling Rosa's picture from the Web site." Sandy paused, and Faith felt as though the fire had spread straight to her soul. "Something about her being too old."

Faith's hands began to tremble and her mouth went dry. "Dick Baker called you?"

"He's the one." Sandy's voice rang with cynicism. "Get the little girl's hopes up and then pull the rug out from underneath her. Don't tell me Rosa Lee's too old. If she were a white girl with a normal hand she'd be on the Web site as long as it took her to find a home."

Faith's mind was reeling. Why hadn't anyone from the station called to tell her about the decision? How come she hadn't known they were looking to keep older children off the site? "I'm sorry, Sandy. I'll see what I can find out and I'll give you a call back."

Five minutes later she had Dick Baker on the phone. "Why didn't you tell me you were pulling Rosa's picture?" She didn't bother masking her anger.

"Nothing says I have to contact you first." Baker sounded flip and unyielding. "I'm too busy to get involved with matters such as this."

Faith could feel her heart pounding in her throat. "Not too busy to call Rosa's social worker earlier today and get the child's picture removed. Why would the station manager have to take care of something like that? Isn't that the webmaster's job?"

"Listen, *your* job's on thin ice as it is, Evans. I don't need some two-bit anchor questioning my decisions." His anger came like a sudden storm and she felt her heart rate quicken in response. "Not that I have to tell you this, but it wasn't my call. We had complaints from advertisers, and honestly they had valid points."

"Complaints?" Faith pressed her fingers up along her scalp and let her forehead settle in her hands. "About Rosa?"

Mr. Baker sighed as though he could barely tolerate her. "About her age. She belongs on a special-needs Web site; not the WKZN *Wednesday's Child* page."

A dozen questions jockeyed for position and Faith tried to articulate the most important. "What advertiser could have possibly cared about that?"

"This conversation is over. I'll expect you in at the regular time this evening and I don't want to hear another word about the matter. It's your job to locate orphaned children; it's our job to manage the Web page." He might have been a rabid bear for the way he growled at her, but this time Faith's fear dissolved, leaving in its place a growing determination as foreign to her as the idea of arguing with her boss.

"Do I make myself clear?"

"Yes." Faith gulped silently, considering her options. She had to know who the advertiser was, what company would single out a lonely child such as Rosa and have her picture removed from the Web site. "I'll see you at the station."

Faith moved across the room to the computer and accessed the Internet. Typing in the correct address she pulled up WKZN's home page and clicked onto the *Wednesday's Child* link. What she saw made her sit back in her chair, her heart hurting as though it were bound and gagged.

Across the top of the page was a banner advertisement for HOUR.

The realization took nearly a minute to sink in. Clearly Jordan Riley had placed the ad, but why? Was this how he'd chosen to pay her back for her televised animosity toward him and his group? Faith felt the enormity of their differences more sharply than ever. To think he'd take out his anger on a little child—a child as desperately lonely as he himself had once been. Faith had the strong desire to call him at work and tell him how she felt. Instead she reached into the cupboard and pulled down the phone book. Flipping to the list of government offices her eyes searched the page until she found what she was looking for.

Mayor Furlong answered on the third ring.

"Hey, Frank, it's Faith Evans." Her body tingled from the adrenaline racing through her system. There'd be serious repercussions, no doubt, but nothing could stop her now. This call was for the people of Bethany, in memory of her father. It was for little Rosa Lee, and most of all it was for Faith herself.

She had lived in the shadows long enough; this time her mind was made up.

Suddenly she knew that this feeling—the odd sensation that her heart was in her throat, the way her body pulsed with conviction—this was what her father had lived for.

It was a feeling that what was about to be done was inherently right.

No matter the cost.

"Hello, Faith. What can I do for you?"

Faith cleared her throat. "I'm interested in buying a piece of property from the city."

14

The meeting took place after hours in a spacious, well-appointed office on the top floor of the headquarters for HOUR. In attendance were all three partners, as well as five of the firm's top lawyers.

The notable exception was Jordan Riley, whose case against the town of Bethany was causing more than a little concern.

A silence fell over the room, and Peter T. Hawkins, the oldest and most intimidating partner, rose from his seat and leaned against the wall. "Morris, tell 'em about the phone call."

T. J. Morris stood and slid his hands in his pockets. This was the year he'd been hoping to make partner and he knew he had no choice but to play the part asked of him in the Bethany case. There was the other detail as well…the bonus money.

What would Jordan think if he knew they were meeting behind his back? That they'd resorted to blackmail to make sure the press portrayed HOUR in a favorable light? He restrained a grimace, but not the thought that came with it: *What have I become?*

For a fleeting instant his thoughts nearly got the better of him. But with each man in the room waiting for him to speak, he had no time to answer his own question—and no answers, even if he'd had the time.

He stared at his notes and then lifted his eyes to meet those of his peers. "We received a phone call this afternoon from a reporter in Bethany. Apparently the city council held another of its emergency meetings today, and the reporter caught wind of something he thought we'd find interesting."

T. J. raised a piece of paper so he could see his notes more clearly. Beneath his shirt he could feel the perspiration building along his collarbone. The Bethany case was supposed to have been a natural winner, a simple, open-shut situation. Now he was at the center of what could wind up being a public relations nightmare. He exhaled slowly.

"Apparently a private citizen came forward yesterday and offered to purchase part of Jericho Park." He glanced at the stone-cold faces around him. "The piece where the Jesus statue sits."

There was a shifting of legs and glances about the room, and two of the partners whispered something to each other. T. J. waited until they were quiet again. "The city council chose not to inform the people of Bethany about the offer. Instead, they accepted it without question."

Steve Nelson sat forward in his chair. "What was the offer?"

"Ten thousand dollars." T. J. glanced at his notes again. "That includes the statue. Joshua Nunn, the attorney for the city, has requested a hearing for early next week, at which time we expect him to ask Judge Webster to throw out the case against Bethany. By that time the statue will no longer belong to the city, but to the private citizen, so there is no way a judge can rule separation of church and state." He looked at the others and tossed his notes onto the table.

Hawkins had stood throughout T. J.'s announcement and now he stepped out to the front of the room. "Tell them who bought it."

T. J. felt a drop of sweat roll down his right side underneath his dress shirt. "Faith Evans, the WKZN newscaster for the Philadelphia affiliate. Pretty girl with the whole town on her side."

Everyone spoke at once.

"That's a conflict of interest…"

"Reporters can't get involved that way…"

"Does the station know what she's done?"

Hawkins slammed his fist on a nearby desk and the room fell silent again. "HOUR simply will not stand for this debacle of justice. We cannot have it. The press will have a field day with us. Outsmarted by a bunch of bungling townspeople and some…some religious fanatic reporter!"

T. J. cleared his throat, and the attention shifted back to him. "Obviously Jordan Riley needs to know about this development. But for now—" he glanced at Hawkins—"we thought it was best to discuss this without him."

Hawkins's face contorted into a frustrated mass of wrinkles. "Jordan's got—" he waved his hand in the air—"a personal interest in this case. I think we all know that. He wanted the statue gone in the first place." Hawkins looked as though he'd swallowed something that was still moving in his stomach. "But he let something slip the other day in a conversation with T. J. It seems back when he was a boy he was in love with the very same girl who's giving us fits."

One of the other partners lurched forward, his face pale. "Faith Evans?"

"Yes." Hawkins spit the word as though he had a bug in his mouth. "Faith Evans." Hawkins shifted his gaze back to T. J. "I assume you took care of that little item I requested."

T. J. nodded. "Of course." He was still having trouble sleeping at night, wondering when HOUR had stooped to using orphans as pawns, but he kept that to himself. "I placed an ad on the WKZN Web site, paid off the station director, and got the photo of a young girl removed from the *Wednesday's Child* page. Apparently, the orphan was Faith Evans's favorite, and by now she knows HOUR was responsible for the child's removal."

"Excellent." He looked at the others. "I have nothing against this Evans woman personally, you understand. But she's taken up the wrong battle. In cases such as this, intimidation can make for superb warfare when the battle gets intense. And this figures to get downright ugly before it's all over." Hawkins looked at T. J. "Tomorrow I want you to call the news station and talk to Dick Baker; he's the station manager. Tell him you have something that might interest him. Then ask if he knows that his nighttime anchorwoman has purchased a piece of Jericho Park to help the town of Bethany sidestep Judge Webster's ruling." Hawkins chuckled and scanned the room again. "Something tells me there'll be an opening for an anchor on the WKZN eleven o'clock news by tomorrow night." He nodded at T. J. "Give us the rundown on the plan from here."

T. J. took a step forward, hoping he looked more together than he felt. *I'm only being a friend…it's for Jordan's good…* But the party lines felt as comfortable as thumbtacks in his gut and he cleared his throat. "We'll work on a solution tonight and then tomorrow get the information to Jordan, who will then file a secondary suit at the same time the city asks for a reprieve. That way the media will be less likely to focus on the people's defensive move—the sale of the park land—and more likely to highlight our next stage of attack." He looked at the eyes of the men and saw they were tracking with him. He raised his chin and his voice grew steady.

"In other words, we don't want the story to be the sale of the park land. Not for a single day. Obviously it'll be an aspect of the story, but the main point of interest must be whatever move *we* choose to make."

Hawkins stepped forward and waved his hand at the others. "That's where you all come in. No one, and I mean not one of you, will leave this room until an action based on case precedent has been decided on. At that point, T. J. will write up the plan as a single brief and give it to Jordan tomorrow."

T. J. blinked. He could just imagine Jordan's reaction when he learned he had not been one of the first to hear Bethany had sold the land to Faith Evans. Or when he found out that T. J., one of his best friends, had been part of the plan to leave him out. But then, business had to come first. And if Hawkins was being level with him, his work on the Bethany case could mean he'd make partner that much sooner.

Hawkins sat down and leaned back in his chair. "Jordan Riley must never know about this meeting, is that understood?"

The men around the room nodded, and three of them agreed out loud. As they began tossing out ideas and jotting down notes, T. J. tried to convince himself that such meetings were a necessary part of being a lawyer. That blackmailing reporters, getting an orphan's photo pulled from a Web site, and holding clandestine meetings behind the back of a coworker and friend were an understandable price to pay in the fight for human rights.

He tried to believe it was all in Jordan's best interest. Just a way of ensuring his friend's heart didn't get too involved—which would only render him ineffective.

But for the first time since T. J. took the job at HOUR he could only convince himself of one thing: This time he and his coworkers were going too far.

Hawkins waited until the others had filed out of his office before returning the call. The message had come in just before the meeting. An advisor to one of the top politicians in the state of Pennsylvania wanted to talk to him.

Hawkins felt his heart beat hard against his chest. Whatever this was, it ought to be interesting. He dialed the number and waited for the man to take the call.

"Hello, sir. Peter Hawkins here. With the HOUR organization."

There was a pause as the man switched off his speakerphone. "Thank you for calling me back." He hesitated and lowered his voice some. "I have some people interested in funding your Jesus statue case."

Hawkins sat up straighter in his chair. "Funding it?"

"Yes." The man chuckled quietly. "We've gotten wind that the statue's been purchased by a private citizen. Some of our…friends thought this might mean complications to the case." He paused. "I'm talking about an awful lot of money, Mr. Hawkins. But there's one catch…"

Hawkins's throat felt suddenly dry. Funding? From a political office? "What?" He grabbed a notepad and a pencil and poised himself, ready to write.

"You have to win the case. We want that statue down, regardless of the cost. Am I making myself clear?"

Hawkins doodled the word *clear* on his notepad. "Yes, sir, you are. You mind if I ask why your office is interested?"

"That should be obvious." The man's voice was so soft Hawkins had to strain to hear him. "Election year is coming up. Who wouldn't want to claim such a victory before hitting the campaign trail? The special interest campaign trail, that is." The man's voice grew serious. "As I said, we're talking about a lot of money."

Hawkins could no longer help himself. "How much?" He drew a dollar sign on the notepad and waited.

The man rattled off a figure, and Hawkins dropped his pencil, his breath trapped somewhere deep inside his throat. "I'm listening."

"Very well—" the caller chuckled again—"here's what we want to do…"

Jordan Riley paced his office like a caged jaguar trying to warm himself on a December morning in New York City. "Explain it to me again, T. J., because it doesn't make sense. I'm out of the office for one day researching some innocuous Bible club, and Hawkins asks you to write a brief on *my* case? A case that's been over for weeks?"

It was just after noon on Friday, the week before the Jesus statue would be down for good and suddenly everything certain about the case had dissolved in the time it took T. J. to sit him down and close the door. And why did his friend look so nervous? Something about this newest twist in the situation didn't ring true to Jordan and he was operating under a barely controlled rage.

"I told you. Hawkins got word that a private citizen bought the Jesus statue and the land where it sits. Joshua Nunn requested a hearing for next week, and Hawkins thought you could use some help. He asked me to write a brief and meet with you this afternoon." T. J. uttered an empty laugh. "What, no thanks? A guy spends a day writing a brief for his friend, and this is the appreciation I get?"

Jordan stalked from his desk to the large picture window behind it and stared outside, his back to T. J. "Who bought the land?"

"I told you, we're not sure."

Jordan whipped around. "You expect me to believe that? Hawkins doesn't know? He used to be an investigator before he turned lawyer, remember?" Jordan huffed and returned his gaze to the window. He wanted to ask his friend to leave so he could take a minute and collect his thoughts. Why wouldn't this case go away? He'd have to go back to Bethany now, which meant he might well run into Faith again. He hated the thought of facing those innocent, warm eyes of hers…of standing up under her questioning, accusing gaze.

Her words filled his mind, as they had often in the past weeks. *The Jesus statue belongs to the people of Bethany and any battle you wage there is one you'll ultimately lose…one you'll ultimately lose…one you'll ultimately lose…*"

How many times since the lawsuit had he wished he could call off the whole thing, run back to Faith, and tell her he hadn't changed after all? That he really was the same boy she'd been in love with all those years ago.

But he couldn't. He wasn't. It was that simple.

The person he was now could not be undone because of a jumble of teenage memories. He had taken his stand—armed himself for war—and there would be no going back, no convincing himself that Jesus was real or that the court battle he'd waged was not worth giving his life for.

No matter what Faith had done to his heart that night in the parking lot.

Jordan turned back to his desk and sat down, holding his conflicting emotions at bay. He had no idea why T. J. had been brought into this, but it was time to make sure Faith's words didn't turn out prophetic. And whether T. J. would be sent to Bethany with him or not, he needed a game plan. Even if it wasn't one of his own making.

"Okay." Jordan gritted his teeth as he leaned forward and met his friend's gaze straight on. "Tell me about your brief."

15

It was Monday morning, twenty-four hours before the Jesus statue was legally required to be removed from Jericho Park. The morning of the hearing that would end the case once and for all. Rain beat a steady pattern against the courthouse roof and a blustery wind howled through the trees on the lawn.

As always, the wet weather made Joshua's knees ache. A reminder of his cross-country days. Still, as he walked the hallways toward Judge Webster's courtroom, there was a definite spring in his step.

In fact, he hadn't felt so good since before Bob Moses died.

God had promised to go before him, promised His faithfulness, and indeed, it was coming to pass. The goodness and steadfastness of the Lord. To think that Faith would purchase the piece of Jericho Park where the statue stood. It was a move her father would have made, but not Joshua. Not in a dozen years of studying law briefs.

He rounded a corner and headed through the double doors of the courtroom to an inconspicuous spot in the back. He was glad he was the first to arrive. *How could I ever have doubted You, Lord?* He thought again of Faith, of her brilliant move and the change in her over the past few days. As though she'd somehow found the drive and determination of her father. Of course, if the station management discovered that *she* was the one who'd bought the land with the statue, the fallout would be devastating to her career.

Joshua glanced at his watch—he had forty minutes before the hearing began. Good. He'd need at least that long to pray for Faith, for the case, for a dozen other needs…

Finally he prayed for Jordan Riley—something he'd felt compelled to do every day since the last hearing, since he realized Jordan's was the face he'd seen in his dream. Joshua still had no idea what it all meant, but he was sure of one thing. The young man needed prayer.

Suddenly, Joshua's silent pleadings were interrupted by the sound of several people and a clanking of equipment making its way toward him. As the entourage rounded the bend and headed his way, Joshua felt the blood leave his face. What was this? Reporters? For a simple hearing? How had they gotten wind of the story?

And what would their presence mean for Faith?

The minutes passed slowly while the camera crews took up their positions. Jordan Riley appeared, followed by another dapper-looking attorney wearing a dark suit as expensive and tailored as Jordan's. Immediately the reporters were on Jordan, pumping him with questions, cameras running.

"Is it true you have a response for whatever happens today in court, Mr. Riley?"

"Can you tell us the details?"

"Who purchased the land, Mr. Riley, can you tell us?"

Joshua gritted his teeth. So they knew about the land… *Help Faith, Lord…please.*

Joshua's opponent exuded cool assurance as he answered their questions. Yes, he had a response; no, he couldn't discuss the details until the hearing was over; no, he had no idea who purchased the land.

"I'm assuming the city will reveal that information today." Jordan nodded politely and excused himself as he and the other HOUR attorney made their way to the plaintiff's table.

Joshua listened to them and chill bumps rose on his arms. As he stood to take his place at the defense table, the reporters turned their questions on him.

"Mr. Nunn…Mr. Nunn… Tell us, who purchased the land from the city?"

"Did the town have a vote in the sale of the statue?"

"Was this a ploy by the town of Bethany to circumvent Judge Webster's mandate?"

They acted like a pack of rabid dogs. Joshua held his hand up and repeatedly told them he was unable to comment until after the hearing. He took his seat near the front of the courtroom, his mind racing in silent prayer.

There was no time to think about the outcome. Judge Webster appeared from behind closed doors and took his place at the bench. He surveyed the reporters and cameramen and raised an eyebrow at Jordan. "Well, Mr. Riley, it seems whenever you come to town the local press is intent on capturing every detail."

Jordan nodded politely and allowed the slightest grin. "Yes, Your Honor."

Judge Webster banged his gavel once. "Court is now in session." He stared strangely at Joshua. "Will the counsel for both sides please rise?" He waited until they were standing, then he addressed Joshua. "I understand you come with new information regarding the case of the HOUR organization against the city of Bethany, Pennsylvania. Is that correct?"

"Yes, Your Honor."

"And you—" the judge looked at Jordan—"will be filing another suit in response, is that right?"

Joshua steadied himself against the news. What other suit was the judge talking about? There was no way Jordan Riley could have come prepared to file a counter-suit unless…

He closed his eyes briefly. Unless he'd been tipped off about the details of the hearing.

Be strong and courageous, Joshua...I will go before you always.

The holy whisperings still infused him with peace, but Joshua definitely could not see God's plan unfolding.

"Mr. Riley, you may be seated." Judge Webster leaned back in his chair and waved toward Joshua. "Present your brief, Counselor."

Joshua straightened his tie. *Give me the words, Lord...I can't do this alone...* He walked up to the bench and raised the document in his hand. "Your Honor, in the weeks since our last hearing, the situation at Jericho Park has changed considerably. It is my intention to inform you of those changes and then—once you understand them—I will request that you throw out your earlier decision."

Judge Webster raised a single eyebrow and shifted his lower jaw to one side. "Continue."

Joshua studied his notes for a moment and then looked at the judge. "Last week, a private citizen came forward and offered to purchase the piece of park property where the Jesus statue currently stands." Joshua moved to the second page. *Make him open to the idea, Lord...* "That citizen paid a substantial amount, the price of which is detailed in the brief I'll provide you. The price included not only the land, but the statue as well."

The judge leaned forward. "And so..."

Joshua nodded politely and continued. "Now that the land and statue in question no longer belong to the city, there is no conflict with the separation of church and state law. Therefore, we request that you throw out your earlier decision, since such a decision cannot be enacted on a private citizen."

There was a pause while Judge Webster stroked his chin and studied Joshua. He seemed less antagonistic than he'd been back when they'd had the first hearing, but something about the man's eyes—a knowing look, or perhaps a smugness—left Joshua anxious and uncertain.

He had the feeling the judge had known all along what this second hearing was about and was merely going through the motions.

"Mr. Nunn, I'd like the name of the private citizen, please."

Joshua's heart skipped a beat. *No, not with the press here...* "The private citizen?"

Webster raised both eyebrows this time. "Yes, Mr. Nunn. The private citizen who purchased the park property. I need a name, please."

Out of the corner of his eye Joshua saw reporters whispering to one another, their pencils poised, faces awash with anticipation. If the judge pushed, Joshua knew he'd have no choice but to present the documents that showed Faith as the buyer. Real estate dealings were public record. "Well, Your Honor. The citizen desires to remain anonymous. The city has chosen to honor that desire."

A ripple of slow laughter escaped Judge Webster's throat. Then just as quickly it faded, and he raised his eyebrows at Joshua. "It isn't optional, Counsel. Either you tell me the name of the citizen, or I'll have to assume this is nothing more than political posturing, a trick devised by the city of Bethany to avoid carrying out my order. You give me the name, or I'll hold you in contempt of court and have the statue removed anyway." He looked at his watch. "At this point you'd have less than twenty-four hours to get it down."

Joshua worked his jaw, desperately searching for a trick door or an open window, any way out of the jam he was in. But there was no escape…

There was an odd light in the judge's eyes, and Joshua wondered again if the man didn't already know the answer, if he was playing with Joshua, drawing out the hearing in anticipation of watching the press's reaction. Because finding out that Faith Evans had bought the property was definitely going to be news.

Just last night he'd spoken to her about this very thing—about the possibility that he'd have to give her name in court. She'd been adamant: "It doesn't matter what happens, Joshua. If you need to tell them it was me, then tell them. I want the statue to stand. If I lose my job, so be it. God'll take care of me. I'm not worried."

Joshua loved the girl for her attitude, and he knew her father would be proud. But it didn't make this moment any easier. He clenched his teeth and released them. "Very well, Your Honor. The citizen is Faith Evans."

A roar went up around the courtroom as reporters reacted to the news. Joshua closed his eyes for a moment and heard Faith's name uttered over and over, heard the whispered comments…

"Faith Evans? The nighttime anchor for WKZN?"

"*She's* the citizen who'd purchased the park property?"

"Faith Evans helped the city of Bethany avoid a ruling by a state judge?"

While Joshua felt certain someone had leaked the information to the judge, clearly the news took the press by surprise. He glanced at his opponent and thought Jordan looked paler than before. His eyes were glazed over, as though the revelation of Faith's name had sent him spiraling to some faraway place.

Did Jordan even know who Faith was? Joshua didn't think so. After all, the young attorney lived in New York, too far to recognize Faith as a WKZN news anchor. Besides, why would Jordan care who had bought the property? Joshua couldn't quite place the expression on Jordan's face, but it wasn't simple anger or aggression or the desire to win. It was all of those things, but Joshua could swear there was also regret.

Judge Webster banged his gavel twice and waited for the uproar to die down. "Order. I will not tolerate another outbreak. If you people—" he motioned toward the reporters—"can't keep quiet I'll have you all charged with contempt." He turned his attention back to Joshua. "So you're telling me that the land has been purchased by Faith Evans—the same Faith Evans who does the WKZN nightly news?"

Joshua's chin dropped several inches. "Yes, Your Honor."

There was a moment of silence while the judge considered this new information. "Very well, then. You have a point, Mr. Nunn. Since the property now belongs to a private citizen, there is nothing I can do to enforce the removal of the statue." He glanced at the others in the courtroom. "I hereby dismiss the earlier judgment against the city of Bethany and will no longer require officials of that city to remove the statue of Jesus, which now stands on private property." He cast a calculated look at Joshua. "You may be seated." His gaze shifted to Jordan. "If you have something to add, Counselor, please take the floor."

Jordan undid the lower button on his jacket and stood, approaching the bench with a practiced ease. Joshua watched him with a mixture of admiration and regret. *What an impact this young man would have made if he'd been fighting for Your side, Lord...*

"On behalf of the HOUR organization, I'd like to share with you details of another lawsuit filed this morning and brought up as an emergency matter before you today."

The judge nodded to Jordan. "Go ahead, Mr. Riley."

"It is our opinion that the spirit of the law in this case has been evaded. Yes, the people of Bethany seemed to have found a loophole by selling the public property in question to..."

Jordan stopped short of saying Faith's name, and Joshua was sure there was more to the story than he knew.

"To a private citizen." Jordan took several steps toward the judge but spoke loud enough for the reporters in the back to hear. "But Your Honor, we fear as a result that justice has not been served. In response, the new lawsuit names the city of Bethany as being responsible for subjecting park-goers to a blatantly Christian display— whether on private property or not. In the suit we are asking for a remedy, which we believe is reasonable and would serve the same purpose as Your Honor's original judgment. We will expect Mr. Nunn to have some type of response, of course, but not until we make our requests clear."

Jordan's jacket hung beautifully on his lanky, athletic frame, and Joshua had the sickening feeling that somehow—regardless of Faith's effort to put herself, her job, her reputation on the line—the HOUR organization was going to win. *I know You're here, Lord. Make Yourself known...please...*

Judge Webster nodded and motioned for Jordan to continue. "Explain the remedy you're seeking."

Jordan reached for a document and flipped past several pages. "Okay, here it is. HOUR is asking that Your Honor order the city of Bethany to build a wall around the statue. Since the statue is ten feet high, the wall would also be ten feet."

Joshua's heart ached at the thought. Was it possible? Would a judge really order a wall to be put up around the statue? He began scribbling notes, listening to every word the judge said.

"Hmm. A wall, is that correct?" Judge Webster actually smiled, as though he wished he'd thought of the idea.

Joshua let his gaze fall to his hands. So much for taking pride in being objective.

"Yes. It is our opinion—and quite obviously your opinion based on the earlier ruling—that the people who visit Jericho Park should not be subjected to the Jesus statue. We understand that although a small piece of property—along with the statue—now belong to a private citizen, there is still the problem of the statue seeming to be supported by the city of Bethany. In summary, that is our case and the remedy we seek."

The judge looked comfortable and happy, like a man enjoying a favorite movie for the fourth time. He shifted his attention to Joshua. "Mr. Nunn, normally I would postpone making such a decision, but since it's so closely linked to the previous matter, I will ask you to state the city of Bethany's position."

Joshua rose and locked eyes with the judge. "Your Honor, erecting a ten-foot-high fence around the base of the Jesus statue is a ludicrous suggestion. Not only would it be wrong to leave a private citizen with no access to her property, but it would also create an eyesore in a park that has been beautiful, generation after generation. A park in existence for more than a century."

For the better part of an hour, the two men debated the issue until finally the judge had heard enough. "I will take a brief recess and return in a moment with my decision on this new action."

Joshua buried his attention in the notes at his table and across the courtroom he could see Jordan doing the same thing. Joshua had expected him to use the time to entertain the reporters, to talk up the fact that Faith Evans had started this mess by purchasing the property. But Jordan was easily as intent on his notes as Joshua. The minutes flew by, and finally Judge Webster returned.

Once he was seated at the bench, the judge glanced at a sheet of paper in front of him and rapped his gavel a single time. "Court is back in session. I have made two decisions while in my chambers, both of which will affect all parties concerned in this case. First, I want to agree that Mr. Riley has a valid point about the people who happen to visit the park. It is wrong to assume the public will know that part of the park—the place where the Jesus statue stands—belongs to a private person. For that reason, most park-goers will believe the statue is supported and maintained by the city of Bethany."

His glasses fell a notch lower on his nose and he looked hard at Joshua. "My understanding on the ruling that separates church and state is very simple: We cannot have a city park giving the appearance of having sided with one religion over any other. For that reason there must be a wall erected around the statue."

Joshua thought about his short-lived victory and his stomach settled somewhere around his ankles. *God, where is this going? Faith put her job and reputation on the line, but for what? What victory is there with a fence around the statue?* There was no time for holy answers. The judge was moving on to his second point.

"However—" the judge shot a gaze at Jordan—"I've made another decision as well. I'm not sure that the statue requires a ten-foot high wall. That, Mr. Riley, I will leave up to you."

The man beside Jordan pointed to something in a file on their desk, and Jordan nodded. He stood and faced the judge. "Your Honor, it is the opinion of the HOUR organization that nothing short of a ten-foot high fence will successfully hide the statue in Jericho Park." He glanced at his associate, then back at the judge. "We don't feel we need thirty days to make that decision."

Joshua felt more like a silent bystander than a part of the proceedings, but he knew if he didn't say something now he might not have another chance. "Your Honor, may I interject?"

Judge Webster shot him a surprised look and seemed to consider Joshua's request for several seconds. "Very well, go ahead."

"Since the property now involves a private party, I believe another hearing—between that person, myself, and Mr. Riley—is essential. Certainly we cannot come up with a final decision without consulting the person who now owns that property." Joshua stepped back and resisted a smile. He hadn't planned on making that argument; the words could only have come from God. *Thank You, Lord...* He blinked and waited for the judge to respond.

The muscles in Judge Webster's jaw tightened and relaxed three times before he spoke. "We do have an unusual situation here, I'm afraid. Mr. Nunn is correct—we must involve the private citizen before I make a permanent ruling." He checked his notes. "At the same time, I have already stated that the people must no longer be subject to a statue of Jesus Christ in the center of a public park." He leaned his forearms on the bench and frowned. "For that reason I am ordering that a temporary ten-foot-high plywood wall be erected around the statue for thirty days, until our next hearing. At that time I will hear from Ms.—" he looked at his notes again—"Ms. Faith Evans, along with the plaintiff and defendant in the case. Only then will I make a permanent ruling." He leveled his gaze at Joshua. "You will inform the Bethany city council that they have seventy-two hours to build the wall around the statue, and that the city is to incur the cost of building it."

"Yes, Your Honor." Joshua did his best to hide his disappointment. At least the ruling was only temporary. Still...he was heartsick at the ground they'd lost. He'd come to court that morning certain the judge would throw out his earlier ruling, sure that Faith's decision to purchase the park land had been God's way of handing them a victory. Instead the city was now party to yet another lawsuit and in three short days the Jesus statue would be surrounded by a ten-foot wall.

The hearing was over and the reporters moved in with their questions, most of them directed toward Jordan Riley.

"Are you happy with the judge's ruling?"

"Do you think the wall will become permanent?"

"Is it right for a newscaster to get involved in something this political?"

The air of tension in the courtroom lifted as Jordan smiled at the cameras. "We won't be completely happy until the ruling is permanent, but it's the best we could hope for at this point."

"What type of wall are you going to request at the next hearing?"

He glanced at his friend and flashed another smile for the reporters. "Brick."

"Do you feel justice was served today?"

Jordan hesitated, and from where Joshua was gathering his legal files several feet away, he could see the air of professionalism in the way Jordan angled his head, his eyes suddenly serious again. "Justice will be served when we don't have to go to court to see that the Constitution is honored. There are still hundreds of thousands of citizens across America who hold to a dangerous belief that the government should advocate a state religion—Christianity, to be specific." He shifted his attention to another camera. "We attorneys at HOUR refuse to rest until that belief has been eradicated from the public conscience of these great United States."

Across the room, Joshua resisted the urge to roll his eyes. Jordan couldn't have sounded more polished if he'd been running for office. The reporters seemed to be finished with the plaintiff's point of view and the group of them migrated across the courtroom and fell in around Joshua. But whereas they'd smiled and bantered easily with Jordan, they seemed to have just one question for Joshua Nunn and the Religious Freedom Institute:

"How can we get in touch with Faith Evans?"

16

*J*ordan hadn't expected to be back in Bethany so soon, but now that he was there he planned to spend the night and return to New York in the morning. When the press had finished with him, he dismissed T. J., explaining he had to take care of paperwork at the local courthouse.

"I'll take a room next to yours," T. J. said as they made their way to the parking lot. The men had driven to Bethany in separate cars since T. J. needed to finish a case he was working on before driving up. "You never know, you might need help. Besides, that way we can find some all-night Italian diner and catch up on the other half of life—you know, the hours we actually spend at home."

Jordan looked at his friend, convinced again that something wasn't right. Without a doubt Jordan and his assistants could have handled today's hearing on their own. Dozens of times he'd handled more demanding hearings without the help of an associate. And now—instead of heading back to New York to be with his wife and baby daughter—T. J. wanted to spend the night in Bethany?

They walked in silence and arrived at their cars, parked side by side at the back of the lot. Jordan leaned back on his and faced his friend. "What's up, T. J.?"

Jordan had known T. J. for years. They were hired at the same time and had spent at least one Saturday a month fishing the rivers and lakes outside the city. They'd double-dated on occasion. In all of New York, T. J. was Jordan's best friend.

So why wouldn't his best friend make eye contact?

"Nothing's up. I mean, why hurry back to the office?"

T. J.'s voice lacked conviction, and Jordan felt a fluttering in his gut. What *was* this?

Jordan slid his hands in his pocket, leaned harder against his car, and crossed his ankles. "Level with me, buddy. I'm serious." He positioned his head so he could see T. J.'s eyes.

Even above the occasional gusts of wind in the maple trees that lined the parking lot, Jordan could hear the heaviness in T. J.'s sigh. "Hawkins asked me to stay."

Jordan felt the ground beneath him give way. "What do you mean? Why would he do that?"

T. J. shrugged. "I'm not sure anymore, Jordan." He looked up, his gaze level. "Maybe you should ask him." T. J. turned his head and stared across the parking lot, as though watching invisible monsters closing in. "Sometimes…I think we're losing our focus."

"What d'ya mean, buddy?" Jordan's voice was softer than before, and he searched his friend's face. What wasn't T. J. telling him?

T. J. gave a few quick shakes of his head and looked at Jordan again. "Nothing." He forced a laugh. "It's been a long couple days." He glanced at his watch. "Tell you what, you stay here and take care of business and I'll head home." The corners of his mouth lifted and he winked once at Jordan. "She misses me when I'm gone more than one night."

Without saying another word, T. J. fished his keys from his pocket and climbed into his car. Jordan was torn between relief that he had some time to himself and concern about whatever it was T. J. wasn't saying. "Wait a minute—" he grabbed hold of his friend's open car door and stooped down—"what aren't you telling me?"

T. J. looked at him, then pursed his lips and angled his head. "It's all for a good cause, isn't it, Riley? Isn't that what they tell us?"

A ripple of panic shot through Jordan. "*What's* for a good cause? You're losing me here, Teej."

"The whole thing." He motioned toward the courtroom. "The fight for human rights. Battling the little guys. It's all for a good cause." He put his hand on the steering wheel. "Look, I gotta get going or I'll never make it home for dinner."

Jordan got the message. He let his hand fall from T. J.'s car door and stepped back. He nodded at his friend as he turned the key and backed out of the spot. Maybe Jordan had been looking too deeply into things. Maybe Hawkins merely wanted to make sure they won the case. But something about that thought felt as comfortable as bad seafood in his gut. Jordan blinked, trying to see the bigger picture. Whatever it was, he knew he could count on T. J. If something was eating at him, Jordan would find out sooner or later. "Drive safe."

Not until T. J.'s car turned out of the parking lot and disappeared down a narrow side street toward the freeway did Jordan release the air that had been building up in him since the old lawyer's revelation. Faith Evans had purchased the park property? How was that possible?

He stared at the scant leaves still clinging to the branches above him. Why would Faith make so bold a move now, when she held a prestigious position with WKZN and sat poised on what could be a move to national television? He remembered something Faith had said back when they were kids, back when Jordan had spent every evening praying at Jericho Park: "*That statue isn't Jesus, you know that, right? It's just a picture of Him…*"

Surely she felt the same way today. So why the fight? What did it matter if the statue came down? He thought about all she could lose, the way she would likely be mocked and held up for ridicule before the public eye after today's hearing.

"Ah, Faith…" Her whispered name took to the wind like one more dead leaf. He'd spent sixteen years searching for some sign of his past, some remnant that would help him connect those early days with the life he was living now. His mother was gone; Heidi too. And until that fall, Faith had been little more than a distant memory, a symbol from a time when everything was as it should have been.

Before God had pulled the rug out from underneath him.

And now that he'd found Faith, there was more distance between them than ever before.

Jordan squinted and tried to see through the barren branches to the sky beyond. Was He there, that mighty God, the one Faith clung to so blindly? Did He know that the lovely Faith Moses was about to take a fall, about to be the sacrificial lamb in a media event that was far from played out?

Another breath eased its way through Jordan's clenched teeth, and he slid into his car. He was an attorney at the top of his game, a man who after tonight's news would be credited with single-handedly foiling the plans of an entire city. A human rights advocate to be reckoned with and admired in legal circles around the country.

But for all that, as Jordan drove out of the parking lot he had to fight an urge that made no sense whatsoever. An urge he could barely acknowledge and would certainly never voice. The urge to call the judge and drop the case. Then to find Faith, gather her in his arms, and love her the way he'd wanted to do since that magical, long-ago fall. Back when his mother was well, and Heidi was there, and everything good in life seemed to center around one very special girl.

Faith was at the station all of two minutes when she realized there was a problem. Cameramen and stage hands omitted their usual greeting and scurried out of the way when she entered the building. Before she even had time to hang her coat in the dressing room, there was a knock at the door.

"Yes…" She had no reason to be fearful. After all, she'd survived two newscasts since buying the property and still no one had said a word about it at the station. By now she'd decided that maybe they wouldn't find out; maybe she had the right to buy property like any other citizen. So what if she was an anchor for the nightly news?

Her certainty fell away like a poorly built house of cards when she saw Dick Baker's secretary at the door. "Mr. Baker wants a word with you." Normally the older woman was friendly, but this time her tone was curt and after delivering the message, she left quickly.

Faith made her way down the hallway and found the door marked Station Manager. The moment she knocked, Mr. Baker's voice boomed from behind the door. "Come in!"

Faith's stomach felt like it was being trampled by a herd of cattle. She crossed her arms tightly, gripping her sides with the tips of her fingers. "You wanted to see me?"

She expected him to be mad, but his face lacked any expression whatsoever.

Someone's told him. Dear God, give me strength. You promised You'd get me through this… Faith froze, unblinking, waiting for her boss to speak.

Mr. Baker leveled his gaze at her, and Faith saw that his features were hard and cold as steel in wintertime. "It came to my attention a few days ago that you'd done something incredibly stupid, something I hoped wasn't true." He paused, and she saw another emotion filter across his eyes. Disgust…even disdain. "As I told you before, the network has talked of bringing you up, giving you a reporter position on a national level. A move like that would have looked good for us, given the network moguls a reason to keep their eyes on the Philadelphia station."

Faith's knees felt weak and she shifted her weight. *Help me be calm, Lord…I can do all things through Christ who gives me strength…I can do all things through Christ who—*

"Today, however, I learned from several reporters—including ours—that the information I'd heard the other day was true." The man made *true* sound like profanity. Faith could see he was working to remain calm and though she was tempted to join the conversation to defend herself, she kept silent. There was no doubt in her mind that he'd found out about the Jesus statue. She kept her chin up, her eyes on his, and waited for him to continue. *I can do all things through—*

Mr. Baker suddenly stood and began pacing near his desk, rubbing the back of his head as he spoke. "When I hired you, Faith, I warned you that being an anchor would require your unbiased attention. That there was no room here for your religious views. You signed the contract promising as much." He stopped and pointed at her. "You're a public figure as long as your face is on television every night. I made that clear to you from the beginning."

He resumed his pacing, staring at his feet as he walked. "Our reporters must be intelligent, law-abiding citizens who, though they cover the news, must steer clear of ever *being* the news." He glanced up at her. "You understood that when I hired you, am I right?"

"Yes." Faith could feel God's peace working its way through her being, could feel God's promise for strength being fulfilled.

I can do all things through Christ who gives me strength…

The verse she'd relied on since her breakup with Mike had never felt more real than at this moment. Certainly this was not the worst situation a believer ever faced… How had John the Baptist felt when he was called in and asked to lay his neck across King Herod's dinner plate? And how about the martyr, Stephen, who refused to answer even one complaint lodged against him, not even when the rocks started to fly?

Of course, the greatest example of all was Jesus…called in and questioned about His identity, knowing full well the deadly fate that awaited Him before the weekend was through.

No, whatever Dick Baker might say or do, it couldn't compare to any of that. Faith steadied herself and waited for what was coming.

Her boss spun around and faced her. "The story I hear is that you bought the land where that Jesus statue stands. You contacted Bethany officials and paid ten thousand dollars for it so the city could avoid following the judge's order." His chuckle was bitter and filled with sarcasm. "Believe me, I'd like to look each of those reporters in the face and tell them they were wrong. Tell them there's no way any anchor of mine would do a foolhardy thing like that. Especially when I'd already told her not to do anything of the sort." He raised his voice. "But in this case, I had nothing to tell them."

The man walked four slow steps toward her, his eyes never leaving hers. "Did you do it, Faith? Is it true?" He stopped in front of her and crossed his arms, his glare boring into her like a drill bit.

"Yes...it's true." Her voice was kind but firm as she felt the Scripture continue to work its way through her heart and soul. "I am an anchorwoman, and yes, I promised to be unbiased. But I'm a Christian first, and a citizen second. I have a right to purchase property like anyone else."

Anger burned in Baker's eyes, but he neither shouted nor stormed about the office as Faith had seen him do on other occasions. Instead he jerked his head up, sucked in a deep breath though his nose, and studied the ceiling. When he looked back at her, his words were matter-of-fact. "Very well. And now I have the right to fire you."

I can do all things through Christ who gives me strength...I can do all things through... She forced herself to exhale so she wouldn't pass out. *Help me, God. See me through.* Faith knew there was no debating him on the issue. Instead, she endured the five minutes of paperwork in silence. Dick Baker gave her a final paycheck, then shook his head. "You could have been something special, Faith. The stars were all lined up in your favor."

She could feel tears in her eyes, but it didn't matter. Because in a part of her mind so close she could almost touch it, she could see her father's face, hear him telling her, "Well done, honey. Well done."

She gathered her dismissal documents and shook Mr. Baker's hand. Meeting his gaze, she let a smile tug at the corners of her mouth. "My life isn't guided by the stars, sir. It's guided by the One who made them. And whatever happens from here, He's got it perfectly in control." She hesitated for a moment. "I'm sorry about all this."

Her boss didn't seem to know how to take that, and Faith wondered what he'd expected. He scratched the back of his head and shrugged. "I have someone else filling in for you tonight. We'll hire a new anchor within the week." He seemed to be searching for the right words. "Good luck, Faith."

Fifteen minutes later she was on the doorstep of Joshua Nunn's office, the same office he had shared with her father. Joshua appeared in his suit jacket, and Faith guessed he'd been on his way home. It was after six, after all, so she was surprised to catch him there at all.

"Faith, what is it?" There was a pained look in his eyes, and almost immediately realization settled over his face. "The station found out?"

It was a moment her father would have understood perfectly, but in his absence, Faith felt as though she had nowhere else to turn. Joshua held out his arms, and she took a single step forward, collapsing against him and giving way to the sobs that had been building since she'd first gotten to work.

"There, there, honey, it's okay…" Joshua stroked her hair as he pulled her into the office and closed the door. "Did they fire you?"

Faith took three quick breaths and tried to control her tears. "Y-yes. I want so badly to be strong, Joshua. But it's too hard. I'm not as g-good at it as Dad and you."

The feel of Joshua's strong arms around her reminded her of her father, and Faith felt her tears start to subside.

"Sweetheart, there are times when I don't feel good enough, either." He smoothed her hair off her face. "But the truth is neither of us has to be like your dad. We can just be us, the way God made us to be. That's enough, understand?"

Faith swallowed hard. "I hated being passive, sitting by while bad things happened around me." She drew a steadying breath and wiped her cheeks with the back of her hand. "That's why I bought the land. It was something I could do, something I believed in." She eased herself into a nearby chair, and Joshua took the one opposite her. "You know why I did it, right? It isn't that the Jesus statue has some kind of magic powers or anything. It's just a piece of rock, really. But it *stands* for something, for the freedom of the people of Bethany. Freedom to have a statue of Jesus Christ in our public park, freedom to worship Jesus and talk about Him and not have to live in fear that the government will one day take away our right to do so." She lifted her chin and felt her strength returning. "Know what I mean?"

Joshua leaned forward and planted his elbows on his knees, his eyes filled with compassion. "I know exactly what you mean." He uttered a quiet laugh. "Faith, my dear, you're more like your father than you think."

She sniffed again and smiled. "My father was never unemployed."

"No, but he would gladly have given up a job if it meant standing up for what was right."

Faith studied Joshua for a moment and decided it was time he knew. "You know the attorney for HOUR, Jordan Riley?"

Joshua worked the muscles in his jaw. "I know him."

Faith sighed and shook her head, running her fingers up through her bangs. "We were friends as kids." She looked up again. "I thought you might want to know."

Understanding passed over Joshua's features. "Very interesting. I had a dream before I got this case…" He pointed to the photos on the wall, one of himself and one of Faith's father. "In the dream my picture was still on the wall, but your father's was missing. In its place was a picture of an angry young man—a man who looked exactly like Jordan Riley." Joshua eased back into his chair and stroked his day-old beard. "I've been praying for the young man, Faith. Why don't you tell me about him? Maybe this is the answer I've been waiting for."

Her eyes closed as she allowed herself to drift, allowed the hands of time to unwind, to take her back to the days when she and Jordan were barely teenagers, to the winter his mother got sick. As the images took shape, she told the story for the first time in more than a decade.

"Jordan was the kindest boy I'd ever known." She smiled. "A grown-up in a thirteen-year-old's body. He never knew his father, but he had the instincts of a dad, especially after his mother became ill. He made sure his sister, Heidi, was in before dark, helped her with her homework, and cooked dinner for their family."

She opened her eyes and blinked back fresh tears. "He was a wonderful boy, really."

He smiled. "It sounds like it."

Emotion filled her throat. "We were best friends, and when his mother got sick we spent hours talking on the porch, sitting side by side, sharing our feelings. That was when I told him about Jesus. Before long, Jordan and Heidi and their mom began attending church with us. They read the Bibles Mom and Dad gave them." She swallowed, letting her head fall back against the chair. "Oh, Joshua, in those early days—before we knew Jordan's mother was dying—it seemed like new life had been breathed into him...into his home."

Faith wiped at a trail of tears on her right cheek. "I always knew he wanted a father. But until Jesus became part of his life, Jordan's world revolved around his mother and Heidi and me. After finding that faith in God, it was almost like his life was complete. He had the three women he loved and a Father who would never leave him, never give up on him. A Father who would love him into eternity."

Faith hesitated. Should she tell Joshua about Jordan wanting to marry her? Immediately, she knew the answer. Telling Joshua would be like telling her own father. Besides, she needed to talk. She'd talked with her mother on the phone, of course, and Mom had been very supportive when Faith explained that she'd been fired from the station. They'd prayed and even cried together, and her mother told her how proud her father would be of the stand she was taking. And yet...for all that the call had helped, she needed to talk to someone face to face.

"Jordan wanted to marry me." She smiled through her tears and made a sound that was part sob, part laugh.

Joshua's eyebrows raised. "Jordan *Riley?*"

"We were so young back then. I think we both thought we'd live next door to each other and go to church together and grow up that way forever. It seemed only natural that at some point we'd get married. We—" she swallowed back another sob—"we had very strong feelings for each other."

She shared in detail the terrifying day she'd found out Jordan's mother was dying. How she'd overheard her parents talking and crept closer to the wall, still out of sight, so she could pick up every word.

"She isn't going to make it, Bob. The doctors told her this morning." It was Faith's mother's voice—and she was crying.

Faith's father had taken a long time to respond. "We need to pray for a miracle. That's all we can do."

Her mother wept then, her voice strained with sadness. "But…if she doesn't make it…what'll happen to those kids, Bob? It isn't right."

Most of the time Faith's father was upbeat, full of life and enthusiasm and had an answer for every dilemma. But that afternoon he released a heavy sigh, one Faith could still hear to this day. "We can't let them be separated, even if it means we take them in to live with us."

The whole conversation had scared Faith to death. Why Jordan and Heidi? Why their mother, when she was all those kids had? And what if she did die? Did that mean God wasn't listening to them? That He hadn't heard their prayers? Would Jordan and Heidi really come and live with Faith and her family? How would that make Jordan feel? He loved his mother with all his heart…

Faith sat back in her chair, the memory of those feelings making her uncomfortable and more than a little confused. As strong as her beliefs were, as devoted as she was to Scripture, as strongly as she loved her God, a God she related with personally, the questions remained. There were no more answers today than there had been back when she'd first felt them rise up in her heart.

"Jordan rode out to that statue every day. Every single day." Faith felt the sting of tears again and gazed out the window, remembering how Jordan had been singly determined to pray his mother back to health. "He'd ride his bike out to Jericho Park and fall to his knees, face flat to the ground on behalf of his mother. He'd pray and pray and…sometimes I'd join him. I'd kneel down in the wet grass beside him and hold his hand, and we'd pray together. Begging God to spare his mother."

Joshua shifted his position and leaned his elbows on the arms of the chair. "She didn't make it?"

Faith reached for a tissue from the desk that had been her father's and headed off the streams of tears making their way down both sides of her face. "No. She died before Christmas."

At the service, Heidi had grabbed onto the casket and wailed for her mother. Only Jordan had been able to pull her away, wrapping his arms around her and comforting her so the minister could carry on with the eulogy. As far as Faith could remember, Jordan never broke down in front of his sister. He saved that for his time with Faith.

"What happened to Jordan and his sister?"

At Joshua's question, Faith frowned. "They lived alone in the house next door for a while, maybe two weeks or so. No, it had to be less time than that. Three days, maybe four. Anyway, every evening following the funeral, I'd sit beside Jordan on his front porch and let him talk."

She could still hear his agonized cries today. "Why, Faith…why'd He let her die? Doesn't He love me? How can I look after Heidi on my own?"

Faith remembered struggling for the right words and usually failing. The best she could do was offer him her hand and once in a while her arm around his shoulders when the questions grew too great and there was nothing left but the quiet sobs of a brokenhearted teenage boy. A boy she had come to love.

But that wasn't the worst of it.

"I was outside the day the state workers came to the house…" Faith sucked in a deep breath. "They came in two cars, and I stood off in the distance while the first worker explained the situation. Jordan and Heidi were to pack their things in separate suitcases. Clothes, a few toys, special pictures. Anything they wanted to save. They would be going to different foster homes—" her voice caught, and she cleared her throat—"until the courts could find a way to get them back together."

Joshua stared at her, his stunned expression mirroring her remembered emotions. "They separated them?"

She nodded. "But not without a fight. Heidi panicked. She kept crying, refusing to go with them, to leave her brother." The way the girl had screamed and thrown her arms around Jordan's waist was as vivid a picture in Faith's mind today as it had been that fall so many years ago. Heidi's agonized words echoed through her again.

"No. I won't leave him! Mama wants him to stay with me. We have to be together… No! Nooooo!"

Faith closed her eyes and pushed her wet tissue against the bridge of her nose. She took several seconds to compose herself before continuing the story. "My parents weren't home when the social workers came. Maybe, if they had been, things would have been different somehow. I don't know." She swallowed hard. "In the end, Heidi's crying didn't change anything."

Left with no choice, Jordan and Heidi had done as they were told. They filled a couple of suitcases with all the belongings they would ever have from the place that had been their home. The social workers promised them that soon, very soon, they could come back home and people would help them get their other things—their beds and books, belongings that wouldn't fit in a suitcase.

"When they finished packing, they stood on the front yard clinging to each other, waiting while the workers whispered together. I crept up behind the adults and came alongside Jordan." She'd known from the look on his face that Jordan wanted to hug her, to pull her aside and ask her to pray for him or to promise her that he'd be back. But Heidi needed him, and all he said was, "This is only for now. We'll get it all straightened out, I know it."

Faith had nodded and kept her distance, giving Heidi the time she needed with her brother. After a few minutes, the first worker turned to them and held out his hand. "Heidi, why don't you come with me? We'll get you settled tonight, and by tomorrow we'll probably have the whole thing figured out."

"No!" Heidi had screamed at the man, clinging to Jordan, sobbing, much as she'd done at her mother's funeral. "I won't leave him!"

Faith remembered Jordan's pale face, how he'd looked decades older than his thirteen years. He seemed too terrified to cry, too shocked to do anything more than respond as an adult, the way he'd been responding ever since his mother had gotten sick. "Heidi, it's okay." He put his face close to hers and forced her to look at him. "It's just for a few days. They'll bring you to me as soon as they find a place for both of us."

Her screaming subsided, and she studied his face, her eyes wide with fear, her fingers clutching tightly to the sleeves of his sweater. "I d-d-don't want to go, Jordan. I need you."

Jordan had pulled her close, running his hand along her back. "Shh, Heidi, it's okay. Pray to Jesus…ask Him to work it out so we'll be back together soon."

The sound of Heidi's sobbing changed then and even at that age Faith could tell the fear was gone. In its place was a sadness that could simply not be measured. "I'm going to m-m-miss you, Jordan. I love you so much…"

The memories were devastating, and Faith fell silent, not even wiping away the tears coursing down her cheeks.

"Faith, are you all right?"

She met Joshua's concerned gaze and nodded, grateful for his care. "I'm fine. It was just a terrible time. Even the social workers were crying before it was over. Jordan kissed Heidi on the top of her head and on both her cheeks and promised, no matter what, that they would be together again. In the end, he had to walk her to the worker's car and hold her hand through the open window, clinging to her fingers until the car began to pull away and their hands came apart."

Faith closed her eyes and she could see them as clearly now as she had back then. Jordan, sobs jerking his shoulders as he reached out to his sister; Heidi, her arm still sticking out, reaching back to her brother, tearstained face pressed against the back window as the car drove out of sight.

"It was one of the most awful things I've ever seen." Faith opened her eyes and stared sadly at Joshua. "Something I'll remember as long as I live."

"What happened to Jordan?"

"After Heidi was gone, he fell against me, and I almost believed he might die from the grief. He kept asking me, over and over, if I believed they'd let Heidi and him be back together."

"What did you say?"

Faith shrugged. "The only thing I could say. I told him to pray that God would bring Heidi back to him. He just had to trust and pray."

She gazed at Joshua through another wave of tears. "You know what, though?"

Joshua bit his lip, and Faith saw that his eyes were wet too. "No one ever brought her back?"

Faith shook her head and glanced out the window once more. "He never saw her again, not once." Her eyes found Joshua's. "That boy prayed for his mother to live— I mean he *prayed*, like I've never seen before or since, Joshua. He prayed, and she died anyway." She swallowed hard. "He prayed that way for Heidi, too…that'd he'd see her again, grow up with her, and look after her the way he'd promised his mother.

But to this day he has no idea where she is or if she's even still alive."

She clenched her fists. "Maybe that'll help you understand Jordan Riley a little better."

Joshua seemed to consider his next words carefully. "You've seen him, haven't you?"

The memory of their kiss flashed across the surface of Faith's heart. "Yes."

"He must have been very special to you back when he was a boy…"

Faith angled her face in Joshua's direction. "Honestly, I think I loved him. We were just kids, I know, and our feelings for each other were innocent enough. But they ran deep all the same."

Joshua let that sink in, and Faith's gaze fell to her hands. "When he came to town that first time, back in the fall, he told me he'd changed, but I didn't know what he meant until I saw him in court. He's so angry at God…he doesn't know who he is anymore."

"Does he…" Joshua squirmed in his chair, as though he weren't sure he should continue.

"It's okay, ask. I'll tell you what I know."

"Does Jordan still have feelings for you, Faith?"

Sadness settled over Faith's shoulders like a lead blanket. "That first night I think we realized we both still have feelings for each other. But now…" She lifted her shoulders, wishing she could ease the tension that seemed to grip her neck. "It's like we're on opposite sides of the ocean."

She eased herself from the chair, stood, and stretched. "You need to get home."

"You'll be expected to speak at the next hearing, you know."

Faith nodded. "I'm organizing a prayer rally at the park the morning the wall goes up. Let's meet in your office after that."

Joshua agreed and walked her to the door. "I'm sorry about your job, Faith."

"God has a plan, right, Joshua? Isn't that what my father always said?" She leaned up and kissed the older man's cheek. "Even in this."

17

*S*omething was wrong.

Heidi knew it as surely as she knew the personality of the baby inside her. The pains were coming every five minutes now, and she was certain this was not another false alarm. They'd been to the hospital twice in the past three days and each time doctors had checked her and sent her home. But this was different. Something deep inside, where intuition mingled with holy whisperings, told Heidi there was trouble. She hadn't felt the baby move in nearly ten hours.

With shaking hands she picked up the phone and dialed Charles's number at the clinic.

"Heidi, honey, what is it? My nurse said you were crying."

"I'm scared—" Heidi's voice broke—"I can't feel the baby."

Charles had always been a rock, but in that moment he was silent. When he finally spoke, he had just one piece of advice. "Pray, Heidi. I'll get there as soon as I can. But until then, pray."

Heidi wrapped her hands around her abdomen and rocked as another pain seized her midsection. Minutes passed and she lay huddled on the couch. *Hurry, Charles...* Then she remembered what he told her. *God, You know I love You...hear me, now. Save my baby, Father. Please don't let her die.*

There was the sound of tires screeching around the corner, tearing into their driveway. Heidi struggled to her feet, stooped halfway over, and met her husband at the door.

"Honey, what happened? When did it get like this?" He swept her into his arms and hurried her out to the car. "We all agreed it could be two more days."

A string of sobs lodged in her throat as another pain sliced through her. "I n-n-need to go..."

Heidi's bag was already in the car, and in ten minutes they were at the hospital, where she was whisked by stretcher up an elevator to an operating room, Charles close by her side. Heidi clutched her husband's hand, and suddenly she could see Jordan's image. She'd lost her brother and now she was about to lose her firstborn. "No, God...please...let her live..."

Heidi's voice was barely a whisper but Charles heard it and lowered his head close to hers. "God, we beg You…be with our baby."

A technician worked furiously, taking Heidi's blood pressure and inserting an intravenous line into her wrist as a doctor hooked up a fetal monitor. Everyone seemed to be working faster than usual, and their serious faces only made Heidi more afraid. She craned her head up from the pillow and searched out the doctor's face. If only Charles were her doctor… "Is her heartbeat okay?"

Charles squeezed her hand and looked at the doctor in charge. "Heidi told me in the car that she hasn't felt the baby move in ten hours."

The doctor worked the sensors expertly around Heidi's belly. "I can't find anything yet." He met Heidi's eyes first and then Charles's. "That doesn't mean there's a problem, but I'm concerned enough to get her into surgery. I think the best course of action is to do a caesarean section and get that baby out."

"Dear God, no…" Heidi began to cry again, one hand firmly tucked in Charles's, the other gripped around her protruding stomach. "She can't die…"

The doctor was talking to Charles about anesthetic and epidurals and the process of a C-section delivery when Heidi began seeing black spots. They grew larger and larger until they took up most of the scope of her vision. The effect left her feeling as though she were floating above the gurney. The pain faded considerably…but an alarm sounded in Heidi's soul.

Something isn't right…get their attention…

The strange, silent warning demanded her response, and she used all that remained of her strength to find her voice.

"Help…me…"

Her cry was so faint the others in the room almost missed it.

"Get a line in! Her blood pressure's dropping! Quick, start the infusion, get a fluid bag and—"

"Heidi, hang on, baby. Jesus'll save you, honey! Don't go to sleep until you—"

"Get her into the operating room stat and let's get the—"

The voices jumbled together, making no sense. The black spots joined up, and she couldn't decipher the faces of the people around her, couldn't feel the baby or the pain or anything but a few gentle prods here and there.

The floating sensation grew stronger, and suddenly Heidi could see herself on the stretcher some three feet below. Charles was off to the side, his head buried in his hands, his shoulders shaking while a roomful of doctors and nurses worked on her.

I'm here, can't you see me? What's wrong with everyone?

The questions passed through her mind, but she couldn't seem to make them come from her mouth. In the place where she found herself, hovering above the room, the pain had stopped entirely and she could no longer hear the voices of the others.

Beyond them, beyond anything earthly, was a glow that grew brighter with every breath she took. Or was she breathing? Maybe she wasn't breathing at all, but rather existing in some other dimension, separate from any of the trappings of the body on the gurney below. Heidi was drawn to the light and she prayed for direction. *Lord…is that You?*

The voices in the hospital room grew barely loud enough to understand and again Heidi strained to make them out.

"We're losing her! Grab the paddles!"

"Let's get the baby, now!"

What about Charles? Heidi couldn't see him anymore…and there was something else, some reason why she was at the hospital in the first place…

An otherworldly peace came over her, and she realized why she was there. For the baby, of course. A sweet little girl, their firstborn. But where was she, and why was Heidi looking down at herself when she should have been breathing and pushing and helping in the delivery?

The light grew brighter.

Help me, Lord…I want to see my baby…

For I know the plans I have for you, daughter.

Heidi's head began to swirl, and her vision grew blurred. The light faded. *Father, help me…I'm afraid…I need Charles and my baby…my baby girl, Lord, let her live…please…*

The light grew brighter and brighter until it was all she could see. Then suddenly there was nothing but empty, quiet darkness.

She woke slowly, her eyelids feeling as though they were taped shut, and for the first few seconds Heidi thought she was alone. There were no sounds of hurried doctors, no desperate demands for fluids or blood pressure readings or assistance.

No babies crying.

"Charles?"

The voice that came from within her sounded like it belonged to someone else, like maybe she had cotton stuck to the inside of her mouth. Her hand rushed to her stomach and felt the flattened place where the baby had been just yesterday…or was it today?

"Charles!" Where was he? Where was the baby, and why was she alone in this hospital room?

"Honey, I'm here." Charles was at her side in an instant, and she forced her eyes open.

"Where were you?" Tears spilled onto her cheeks, and she searched his face, willing him to tell her the truth. "Where's the baby?"

He leaned over her, holding her close, his tears mingling with her own. "Thank God…thank God, Heidi. I thought I'd lost you. You've been in a coma for two days."

A coma? For two days? An urgency began to build in her heart, and she pulled away so she could meet his gaze. "What happened to her, Charles? Where is she?"

A smile filled his face, and his eyes glowed with a warmth she'd never seen before. "She's fine, sweetheart. She's down the hall in the nursery."

Heidi's tears came harder now, and she clung to him, giving way to the sobs that had been building in her heart. "I thought I'd lost her…"

"No, honey, she's perfect. Wait'll you see her." He nuzzled his face against hers and wove his fingers through her hair.

Odd images filtered through Heidi's mind. "I had the strangest dream…just as the baby came, like I was watching the whole thing from above."

Charles sat up straighter, his mouth open as he searched her face. "You were bleeding, Heidi. They lost your pulse, your blood pressure, everything. Clinically, you were dead." He searched for the right words. "It was God, Heidi. He brought you back, sweetheart. It was a miracle."

Charles took her hands in his and bowed his head. "Thank You, Lord. I will never forget this. Never." He kissed her tenderly and pulled back, his eyes dancing even under the glare of hospital lights. "You see a lot of amazing things as a doctor, but I've never seen anything like this. It's a miracle that either of you lived."

There was a sound at the door, and a nurse appeared pushing a small clear bassinet. As she drew closer, Heidi searched for her daughter's face—and what she saw made her eyes fill with fresh tears. The baby was more beautiful than any she'd ever seen. Charles moved to the small bed and carefully lifted the infant, shifting her straight to Heidi's waiting arms. The nurse smiled and left them alone to share the moment.

"Oh, Charles, she's perfect." A tear fell onto the baby's cheek, and Heidi laughed, wiping first her own face, then that of her tiny daughter. She took hold of Charles's hand with her free one and squeezed it. "She *is* a miracle. God is so good."

They admired the infant snuggled between them, trying not to imagine how different this day might have been if not for the grace of God and the second chance at life they'd been given. Charles broke the silence first. "So did we decide on a name?"

"Remember that day? The name I had then?"

Charles nodded, his eyes twinkling. "I wanted to make sure you hadn't changed your mind."

Heidi stared at her daughter again and smiled. "I haven't changed my mind. I've always known what I wanted to call her." Her heart felt like it might burst from joy as her eyes stayed fixed on her little girl's delicate features.

"Well, that settles it then." Charles tickled the baby's chin. "Your name is Jordan Lee—after your uncle Jordan."

Heidi smiled and ran a finger over the baby's eyebrows. "Hi, little Jordan Lee."

"Jordan Lee…" Charles's arm was around Heidi then, holding her close and whispering the baby's name over and over in a way that told Heidi he absolutely understood.

"It fits her, sweetheart."

She swallowed back a wave of sobs as she nodded. The moment was perfect except for one thing.

Jordan Lee would never have the chance to know the one for whom she was named.

Another two days passed and Jordan Lee was thriving beyond anyone's expectations. Heidi understood now what had happened. A tear in her placenta had caused internal bleeding, which in turn nearly killed her and the baby. Throughout her hospital stay, doctors who'd had nothing to do with her delivery made their way in and introduced themselves, curious to see Dr. Benson's wife and baby, a pair who'd literally come back from the dead. Heidi spent her time holding her daughter and reveling in the infant's sweetness and good health, and the intensity of her own feelings.

Charles had been right, their daughter's name fit her. She had Jordan's dark hair, his chiseled face. She was beautiful, and it grieved Heidi in a way she hadn't felt in years to know that this side of heaven Jordan would never see her.

It was after noon and the television played in the background as Heidi and Charles cooed and marveled over their little girl. There was a chance they could go home later that afternoon and they hoped the doctor might stop by any moment with Heidi's discharge papers.

She eased back onto a stack of pillows as her eyes fell on the TV screen. "Nothing but news…"

A reporter's voice was saying, "In other news a shocking development in the case of the Jesus—"

"I can't wait to get home." Charles smiled at her. "And know that both of you are right there with me where you belong."

Heidi smiled at him. "For a few days, anyway, until we pack up."

In the silence between them the newscaster continued. "…private citizen Faith Evans purchased the property from the city in what some people say is a conniving attempt at obstructing justice. The attorney for HOUR, Jor—"

"You mean the move?" Heidi groaned as a grin worked its way across Charles's face. "Just think, three weeks from today we'll be moved in, unpacked, and ready to put down roots."

She chuckled. "That's my Charles. The eternal optimist." She adjusted Jordan Lee so the tiny girl was nestled between the two of them. "Right now I can barely put my feet on the floor, honey. Putting down roots might take more than three weeks."

"True." They both smiled and glanced back at the television.

"Another hearing in less than a month to determine what type of wall would make the best permanent barrier. And in other news, the president told the public this morning—"

"What wall?" Heidi lowered her eyebrows.

Charles smoothed her bangs off her forehead. "I wasn't listening. It's a slow news day. Most of the stories are just filler."

Heidi reached for the clicker dangling on the side of her hospital bed and turned off the television. "I've got you and Jordan Lee and a new home waiting for me in Bethany, Pennsylvania…" She leaned up toward her husband's face and their lips met. The kiss lingered, and when he pulled away she knew she'd never been happier in all her life. "The last thing I need is filler."

18

It was just after seven o'clock in the morning and a thin layer of fog hung over the town of Bethany as Faith arrived at Jericho Park. She positioned her car so she could see the Jesus statue. In a few hours, ten-foot-high plywood walls would surround it, and Faith wanted to be there early, wanted to mingle with the locals as they arrived by van and bus for the prayer rally. They'd decided to march around the park, singing hymns and stopping every ten minutes to pray. This would go on throughout the construction of the wall, and Faith was certain their peaceful protest would make all the local news shows.

She leaned back against the headrest. How had things gotten so crazy? Her father's face came to mind, and she smiled even as she released a heavy sigh. "Dad, you wouldn't recognize me…" She gave a short, soft laugh. "Mom says I'm trying to take your place, but you know me, Dad." Her smile faded and tears filled her eyes. "I'm scared to death."

Memories drifted in on the fog and filled her heart with images from days gone by. A sunny afternoon began to take shape, the year she and her sister, Sarah, were seven and thirteen years old, and had been ordered not to play catch in the house. Their mother was in the backyard working in the garden when Sarah found a softball and grinned at Faith. Sarah was on a park-league softball team that year and was always looking for someone to play catch with.

"Let's pretend we're trying out for the World Series."

Faith could see her own little pixie face contorted in grave concern. "Outside. Mom says we have to play outside."

Sarah peered around the wall and gazed into the backyard. "Mom won't know. Besides, it's too hot out there. Come on, don't be a baby."

Faith remembered her stomach hurting from the conflict. Stay inside and risk getting in trouble, or refuse to play with her big sister and be labeled a baby. Finally Faith gulped back her fears and nodded. "Okay, but be careful."

Sarah grinned and grabbed the ball, tossing it at Faith. Her heart beating wildly in her little girl chest, Faith snagged it from the air and smiled. "Good throw." She remembered feeling better about the game after that. It wasn't so bad, throwing the ball in the house. What was their mother worried about, anyway?

They played that way for five minutes, but then Sarah caught the ball and held it. "Let's pretend I'm the pitcher and you're the catcher, okay?"

Faith shrugged. "Okay. I'm the catcher."

Sarah wound up like a mountain lion ready to spring and fired the ball straight at Faith's nose. In a split-second decision, Faith fell to the ground, missing the ball— and the spray of glass that exploded in her direction as the ball soared straight through the window.

The timing couldn't have been worse, for at that moment a key turned in the front door and their father walked in. At almost exactly the same time, their mother entered the house from the backyard and peeled off her work gloves. "Hi, honey, how was your day?" Her smile lasted only until she made her way into the front room and found the girls and their father staring at the pile of glass and a jagged, gaping hole in the window.

Their mother stepped around the broken pieces and stared outside. "What happened?"

"I was just asking that question myself." Their father set his things down, his face stricken with disappointment.

"Obviously they were playing ball in the house." She looked from Faith—still cowering on the floor—to Sarah, huddled against the opposite wall. "Whose idea was this?"

Faith looked at Sarah and waited, expecting her to come clean with the story. Instead, her sister was staring at her shoes as though she had no intention of saying anything. Their father was not a man who raised his voice except with laughter when he was playing cowboy or horsie games with them. But that afternoon he came close. He ordered Sarah and Faith to the sofa and stared at them long and hard.

"In this life we all make mistakes," he began, his voice a low growl. "But I did not raise my daughters to be liars. Someone better tell me what happened or you'll both be punished."

For three minutes—three whole minutes—he stood there, hands on his hips, his eyes shooting invisible guilt rays down upon Faith and her sister. They were quite possibly the longest minutes of Faith's childhood, and she remembered feeling like she might be sick all over the clean carpet. She was about to open her mouth when her father pointed a finger at Sarah. "Young lady, you're the oldest and I'll have to assume this is your fault. Now why don't you tell me what—"

"No, Daddy." Faith was on her feet and she threw her arms around her father, her eyes squeezed shut as though she couldn't stand his anger for one more minute. "It was my fault. I told Sarah we could play catch and I didn't catch the ball. Don't be mad at her, please, Daddy. Please…"

The memory made Faith chuckle under her breath as she wrapped her jacket tighter around her shoulders. She thought back to how Sarah had cast her a surprised glance, but it didn't matter. Their father's face relaxed, and he patted Faith's hair, running his hand down the back of her head and onto her back. "Thatta girl, Faith.

Thanks for being honest. Now you know the rules, and I'm still going to have to punish you. You'll spend the rest of the day in your room, but you told the truth and that should make you feel good about yourself."

Faith wasn't sure she'd told the truth, but she certainly remembered feeling better. Much better than sitting on the sofa squirming beneath her father's angry gaze. She gladly took the punishment, content because no one was mad at her anymore.

It had been that way as far back as Faith could remember. She hated conflict, couldn't tolerate people being angry with her or anyone else for that matter.

Another memory came to mind. Her father ran in fairly influential political circles and once in a while he'd have friends with opposing views over for dinner. Faith recalled several times when after the meal they'd gather in the living room over hot coffee and even hotter conversation.

"Aw, Bob, you lean so far to the right you'd make a minister look liberal."

Her father would raise his hand. "Now, wait a minute, don't forget about that tax you people invented to cover the—"

The longer they talked, the louder they grew. Faith understood now that the banter was all in good fun, and that her father's visitors left the house with their friendships intact. But back then, from her childish perspective, the discussions had made her worse than nervous. Typically she'd work her way into a corner of the kitchen and sit on the floor, her knees pulled up to her chin until her mother found her that way.

"Faith, honey, what're you doing?" She'd stoop down and place the back of her hand against Faith's forehead. "Are you sick?"

Generally Sarah would be helping with the dishes and she'd toss out a sarcastic comment about Faith finding any excuse to get out of doing chores. But that wasn't it at all. Faith finally explained herself one evening later that year when the conversation between her father and his friends again grew heated. That night, Faith ran from her spot in the kitchen to her bedroom upstairs, tears streaming down her face.

Minutes later her mother found her in bed, the covers pulled up over her head. "Honey, whatever is the matter? Is it something you ate? Don't you like it when Daddy has his friends over?"

Faith pulled the covers down a few inches so that only her eyes and the top of her head were showing. "It scares me..."

Mom pulled the blankets down further and looked at Faith's arms and neck. "Why, sweetie, I think you're having an allergic reaction. You have hives all over your body."

Immediately she summoned a doctor who confirmed the thing Faith understood better now. "It's nerves, Mrs. Moses. Is there something happening in the home, something that might be upsetting her?"

By that time, her father's friends had gone home, and Daddy stood alongside her bed, frowning his concern at both the doctor and her. "I can't think of anything; Faith's a very happy little girl, doctor."

But after the doctor was gone, her parents sat down with her and drew out the truth. "It scares me when Daddy and his friends fight."

Her father looked at her and then put his hand over his mouth. Just when she thought he might burst out laughing, his eyes grew sad and dark, like the deep places of the river that ran outside of town. "Honey, those men and I like talking about things we don't agree on." He cast his gaze at the ceiling as though he was searching for the right words. Then he looked at her once more. "We might sound like we're fighting, but we're only sharing our different views."

Mom stood off to the side, her chin lowered just so, a crooked smile on her face as her father leaned over and snuggled Faith close to his chest. "I'm sorry we upset you, honey. You should have told me a long time ago."

Faith knew he was right, but the idea of approaching her father and complaining about his conversations with his friends was almost as frightening as the visits themselves. After that her mother made a point of keeping Faith and Sarah busy when her father had friends over, and she never again remembered hearing them talk that way.

There were other situations—her relationship with Mike Dillan, her refusal to stand up to Dick Baker at the station, her inability to confront the HOUR organization over their request that Rosa Lee be removed from the Web site...

She had always managed to find the easy route, the path of least resistance, the road that might keep life calm and even keeled.

Several cars pulled into the parking lot, and people she recognized began piling out, forming a circle on the grass in front of the statue. Faith shook her head. How was it, considering her determination to avoid conflict, that God had her here, in the middle of a political hurricane? Her, the weak-willed Faith Evans Moses?

As the crowd began to build she found herself sliding down in her seat. *I can't do it, God. They think I'm their leader, and I'm not. I want to go home and hide under the covers...*

Be strong and courageous, daughter. You will not fight this battle alone. I will go before you...the battle belongs to the Lord.

The words washed over her, giving her a strength that was not her own. She drew a deep breath and sat up straighter. It was true. She would not fight the battle alone. She had God and Joshua and a thousand friends across the city. In the end, God's will would prevail, whether the statue remained fenced or not. All He wanted of her was loyalty and obedience. Suddenly her father's words came back to her, words he'd spoken days before he died. He and Joshua had been hired to take a case involving prayer in a public school and the media involvement figured to be considerable.

"If it doesn't go our way it could break us," Dad told her and Mom at dinner that night. His eyes shone with sincerity as he continued. "But you know I've learned something over the years of walking with the Lord. My best successes come when I am at my absolute weakest."

His words had seemed strange, incongruous, as though her father couldn't possibly have uttered them. He had never been weak, at least not as far as Faith knew. But he'd gone on.

"When I am weak, my God can be strong. And it's the battles He fights for me that end up being my greatest victories of all."

In the end, the school district in question had agreed to settle out of court, fearing they faced a losing battle. Her father had celebrated the news with them the day before his heart attack.

"See?" His cheerful voice filled their home with life. "I couldn't do it, so God went before me and look what happened. They dropped the case! Those students can go on praying, and the Lord wins a victory all because we were willing to step out on His behalf."

Her father's words soothed the restless places in her heart, and Faith sucked in as much breath as she could muster. She climbed out of her car and headed toward the crowd as dozens of people turned and motioned for her to join them. Across the park she saw a construction crew and cringed as two of them nailed the first piece of plywood around the base of the statue.

The battle had begun.

It was time to meet the people, time to acknowledge that she was out of ideas, out of options, and fully incapable of fighting.

Most of all, it was time to do whatever it was God had for her to do. Even if it put her squarely in the middle of the greatest conflict of her life.

Rosa Lee was putting together a puzzle on the kitchen table in the minutes before school started when she remembered something. "Faith told me I could see her today. Is she coming for me?"

Her social worker wiped her hands on a dishtowel and walked closer, smiling at the puzzle. "Nice job, Rosa. You're almost done."

Rosa brought her lips together and did a huffy breath. "Excuse me, ma'am, did you hear me? Is Faith coming to get me this afternoon?"

Sandy Dirk sat down at the table and looked sad for a minute. "Rosa, Faith's very busy today—" She stopped the way grown-ups do sometimes, and then kept talking. "Did Faith tell you about the Jesus statue, honey?"

Rosa's heart lit up and she could feel her face change into a giant smile. "Oh, I love the Jesus statue. Faith took me to the park lots of times and we looked at the statue and talked about it." Rosa felt a little worried for Miss Dirk, in case she didn't understand. "It's not really Jesus, you know that, right?"

Miss Dirk seemed to rub a smile off her face, and she squeezed Rosa's shoulder real soft like. "Of course."

Rosa nodded, glad Miss Dirk knew the truth. "It's just a reminder of Jesus. Sort of like when I draw a picture of Him in Sunday school." Her smile was back again. "I think it's the bestest picture in the whole world, Miss Dirk. Because my Jesus—"

she held out her arms so that her hands were stretched out toward heaven—"my Jesus is even bigger than the trees. And He always has His arms open for me to hug Him anytime I want."

Miss Dirk's eyes looked kind of wet and shiny, but she smiled. "Yes, honey, that's right. Anytime you want."

"Like when I'm thinking about having a mommy and a daddy and wondering when God's going to bring them to meet me. That's when it's really nice to remember just how big my Jesus is."

Miss Dirk blinked at Rosa. "Some sad people are trying to take the Jesus statue down. Did Miss Faith tell you that?"

A sick feeling filled up Rosa's tummy and she dropped the puzzle piece in her hand. "Take it down? You mean like take it away so it isn't in the park anymore?"

"Yes, honey." Miss Dirk covered Rosa's hand with her own. Rosa made herself think as hard as she could, but no reasons came to her. Why would anyone want to take the Jesus statue down? Then she got an idea, and her heart grew kind of jumpy. "Is Faith going to stop them? She likes the Jesus statue, too."

"Well, that's just it, Rosa. That's what Faith's doing today. She's meeting with a lot of people from the town who like the statue, and they're going to pray for the sad people who want to take it down. That's why she can't come and play with you today."

What? Faith would be praying for the sad people? Rosa sat up straighter and pulled her knees beneath her. "Then I need to be there, Miss Dirk. It's my statue too. Faith would want me there, praying with her, I know she would."

Her social worker smiled, and Rosa knew the answer was no. "You have school today. I can't keep you home so you can pray with Faith."

As soon as she said the words, Miss Dirk's face looked the same way it had one night when she burned the squash and ate a whole bite of it anyway. Rosa leaned closer. "But Faith told me there's nothing more important than praying. It's the whole reason we're here on earth."

Miss Dirk put her elbows on the table and slumped over a little. She stayed that way for a long time and finally she looked at Rosa, her lips squished together. "Oh, all right. What could it hurt?"

Rosa jumped from her seat, clapped her hands, and danced about the kitchen floor. She spun and twirled her way in front of Miss Dirk and stopped only long enough to get more information. "When can we go, huh? Is Faith already there?"

Miss Dirk looked at the big clock on the wall and nodded. "Probably." She tugged on Rosa's shirt, straightening out the wrinkles. "Go get your sweater, and I'll take you there now."

Rosa clapped some more and hurried her feet up the stairs to the closet she shared with two older girls. She grabbed her sweater, pulled it around her shoulders, and checked the mirror. A piece of her hair was sticking out above her ears, and Rosa tucked it in neatly and smiled at herself. Faith was right. Jesus had made her a very pretty girl. She waved at herself real quick and skipped back down the stairs.

If Faith was going to pray for the sad people who wanted to take the statue down, then Rosa was sure everything would work out just fine. God would see to that. She waited by the door for Miss Dirk to get her coat and keys and grinned quietly to herself. Even if it wasn't sunny outside, it was going to be a wonderful day after all. She was going to spend it talking with her two favorite people in all the world.

Faith Evans and her best friend, Jesus.

The six o'clock news used the protest at the Jesus statue as their lead story, and Joshua watched it closely in his living room, his wife at his side. Two of the three major networks chose to play Faith as the primary local angle, saying things like, "Former WKZN newscaster Faith Evans—who lost her job because of her role in the fight to keep the Jesus statue standing—led the protest at Jericho Park this morning..." and "The battle has already been costly to local residents, especially Faith Evans, who was removed from her position as anchor for WKZN because of her role in the fight to keep the Jesus statue..."

Joshua watched for many reasons.

First, he wanted to see the way the statue looked with walls around it. He hadn't been able to bring himself to drive by the park that afternoon, hadn't wanted to stomach the sight of the statue walled up with plywood, so the pictures on the news were his first chance to see the effects of the judge's ruling.

Also he wanted to get a feel for the residents' heart on the issue, whether they were tired of the battle or willing to go the distance to see their statue standing proudly the way it had stood for a hundred years prior.

Two minutes into the newscast, he could see that none of the city's supporters were losing their fervor. If anything, their numbers had grown, making the crowd a considerable force as they marched around the park while workers erected the plywood wall. Every station carried several sound bites from Faith and featured her in much of the taped footage. In several shots Joshua saw a little Asian girl at Faith's side, a child no older than five or six who looked at Faith with wide, adoring eyes. He tried to remember where he'd seen her before and it hit him.

She was the little girl featured a few weeks back on the *Wednesday's Child* program, the one Faith had hosted. Obviously Faith's love for the girl went beyond her role as an interested reporter. He watched as Faith's face filled the screen and a reporter asked her whether the battle of Jericho Park was worth losing her job over.

"Recently I've come to understand that there's nothing more important, more sacred than your convictions." She smiled in a way that was contagious among the reporters, disarming them, Joshua noticed, before they might realize what was happening. "I believe the people have a right to their statue...our statue. Even if it does depict the central figure in the Christian faith. This is the kind of battle that's worth fighting." She smiled again, a smile void of animosity. "My father taught me that."

There was something about Faith's openhearted smile that touched Joshua deeply. As though she held no anger toward the people at HOUR or the station manager who had fired her, but rather a deep compassion. It was not something that could be faked, and Joshua knew it was the same love for people her father had carried in his heart during his days battling for religious freedom.

The camera moved in on Faith once more as she bent to give the little girl a hug, and suddenly Joshua was struck by Faith's beauty. *Oh, Bob, if you could see her now... Lord if You could let him know...* How proud his old partner would have been of his daughter. Little Faith, all grown up. Joshua thought back and in his mind he saw her as a girl, running across the backyard with the other kids during a family barbecue. Now she was poised and confident, filled with a peace that Joshua knew could only come from one source.

The segment drew to a close, but the image of Faith remained in Joshua's heart.

She was simply breathtaking, both in appearance and in the purity of her convictions. He leaned back into the sofa and wondered if somewhere in New York City, Jordan Riley was watching the same newscast. And whether the attorney's desire to see the Jesus statue removed could possibly be stronger than the feelings he must be having for the very special young woman who'd once been his friend.

A woman who had risked everything to see the statue remain standing.

19

*J*ordan flipped off the television and stretched out on his leather sofa, his hands folded beneath his head. The newscast had clearly favored Faith, and that surprised him. Normally the media would take HOUR's side and make a woman like Faith look fanatic. Instead they'd given her ample time to share her point of view and done nothing to contradict it. The fact that the local networks had footage of the wall going up only made Faith look more like the persecuted victim.

The overall effect was that justice had been thwarted, not meted out on the public's behalf.

Jordan replayed the images of Faith again in his mind and felt a smile tug at the corners of his mouth. He knew he should be angry. What right did the people of Bethany have to demand a statue of Jesus Christ remain standing in a public park? A ripple of frustration worked its way down his spine, but only a ripple. Normally he'd be furious with the way the story was handled, ready to hold a press conference the next day with the walled-up statue in the background, and slam every angle Faith had chosen to discuss.

Instead the only reason he wanted to go back to Bethany was to find Faith and tell her what a great job she'd done, how successfully she'd managed to articulate her point of view without looking like a religious fundamentalist. He caught himself grinning again at the memory of her poise, of the beauty that seemed to come from somewhere deep inside. What was it about her that had worked its way so thoroughly into his heart? And why was it happening now, when they were on opposite sides of a national legal battle?

The phone rang, and Jordan blinked back the images of Faith. It was nearly seven o'clock and he'd been so caught up in the newscast he hadn't even considered fixing dinner.

"Hello."

"Jordan, it's T. J." His friend sounded nervous, and an alarm sounded in the sensory panel of Jordan's mind. Ever since the hearing the week before things had been strange at the office, as though people were carrying around some kind of secret and Jordan was the only one not in the loop. He'd tried to dismiss the feelings, chalk it up to the fact that he had a lot going on. But the signs that something wasn't right continued.

He sat up. "What's up?"

"I'm at the office still and…well, a bunch of us saw the Philadelphia news a few minutes ago."

A bunch of them? "What, Teej, a party and I wasn't invited?" He did his best to sound casual, but his concern rose a notch. Why were they so interested in his case? And why hadn't they included him?

T. J.'s brief laugh sounded hollow. "Not a party, just a chance to see how the local media's playing the story."

"Let me guess…there aren't a lot of smiles in the room." Jordan intentionally kept his tone light, not wanting to validate T. J's seriousness.

"Well…uh, Mr. Hawkins is here, and the other partners. They wanted me to call and see if you'd watched it."

"Yeah, I watched it. So what do they want me to do? Put a contract on the girl?"

There was silence on the other end. "They're not laughing, Jordan." T. J. had lowered his voice, and Jordan figured the others in the room had resumed talking. "The coverage was bad."

Jordan sighed, raking the fingers of his free hand over his knee. "I saw it, remember? I know it was bad. How does that involve me?"

Voices in the background grew louder and for a moment there was no one on the other line. Then, "Riley, this is Hawkins."

Jordan hung his head. Why were they so relentless this time around? Wasn't it like any other issue HOUR battled? Jordan's insides squirmed as though he'd developed an ant farm deep in his gut. Something just didn't add up… "Hey, Mr. Hawkins, I guess you saw the news?"

"That girl is killing us, Riley. She must be stopped."

Jordan released a sound that was part exasperation, part chuckle. "She has a right to be interviewed by the press, sir. You understand that, right?"

"So where's our presence, Riley? Why're you back here in New York while those religious do-gooders take up the entire six o'clock news?"

Jordan stood and paced toward a large window that overlooked swarming city streets far below. His stomach churned and he realized he'd lost his appetite. "Have you checked my caseload, sir? The Jesus statue isn't the only case I'm working on."

There was a pause. "Well, it is now. I'll get someone else on your other matters. Starting tomorrow I want you in Bethany, Pennsylvania, making yourself available to the media and seeing that this thing gets turned around." Hawkins voice was a study in controlled fury, and again Jordan was struck by a sense of incongruity.

What did they want? There were walls around the statue, weren't there? Besides, HOUR would carry on whether the Jesus statue stood or not. After all, *he* was the one who'd found it in the first place. How had it suddenly taken top precedence at the firm? "Fine. I'll pack tonight and leave first thing in the morning."

Hawkins seemed only slightly appeased by Jordan's answer. "We want a press conference tomorrow afternoon, a victory statement, something the rest of us can identify with."

Jordan leaned his forehead against the cool glass of the window. Why had he ever become an attorney in the first place? He should have been a fireman like his buddy Chip from the boys' camp. Fighting fires *had* to be less stressful than this. "Yes, sir…I'll schedule it as soon as I'm in town."

Hawkins uttered what Jordan figured was supposed to be a sigh, but it sounded more like the hiss of a snake. "You won't let us down, will you, Riley?"

No one had ever asked him that before, ever doubted that he gave everything to his work. Jordan felt his face contort as he tried to make sense of Hawkins's comment. "Of course not, sir. I'm the one who found this case, remember?"

"That's true." Finally there was a degree of confidence in Hawkins's tone. "And when it's over there'll be a bonus in it for you, Riley. Keep that in mind."

"A bonus?" The partners got healthy bonuses at the end of every year, and now and then a productive attorney, one who billed out more hours than his peers, might see a small bonus as well. But no one he knew had ever been offered a bonus for a single case.

"Ten thousand dollars, Riley. You get a permanent wall, ten feet high, around that statue and you earn yourself ten grand." He paused while the figures sank in. "Have I made myself clear?"

Jordan straightened and felt the blood drain from his face. Whatever had happened, it apparently involved a third party. A very wealthy, very influential third party. One that wanted the Jesus statue gone as badly as every attorney at the HOUR organization.

Jordan dismissed his earlier thoughts of Faith and pondered what Hawkins said. His eyes closed as he imagined what sort of deal might be hinging on this case. Bonus or not, he had to give everything to the battle now. The fight was more fierce than ever, and he was directly at the center of it. He nodded his head slowly, as though trying to convince himself of the words he was about to say.

"Yes, sir. Perfectly clear."

"Very good. Then you won't let us down." It wasn't a question.

Ten thousand dollars? Jordan opened his eyes, a new determination pulsing through him. "No, sir, I won't let you down."

In the executive offices of HOUR, Hawkins hung up the phone and smiled at the others. "I think I've convinced him."

One of the older men wrinkled his eyebrows together and shook his head. "Riley's nothing but a boy. We've got ourselves national interest in this case, and I think you men know what I'm talking about. It's time to hand it over to T. J."

T. J. uncrossed his legs and leaned forward in his seat. "Jordan's my friend…I could help him and not make him too suspicious."

Hawkins sat on the edge of the desk and considered that. "Everyone in this room knows what we're talking about. A million dollars, gentlemen. That's a hundred thousand for each of the partners, twenty grand for T. J." He stared at his feet for a moment then back at the others. "The problem is Faith Evans. Without her, the people have no voice, no sense of organization." He swore under his breath. "She's the one who bought the statue, after all." His gaze shifted and he studied each of the men around him. "We need to silence her; it's that simple."

T. J. shifted in his seat and blinked. "Meaning?"

"Meaning I need you here. Let Jordan handle the matter in Bethany. I have friends at the national network level. I'll put you in touch with them. See if there's any interest in bringing her up to the network, get someone to call her. Maybe we can lure her away from this ridiculous park situation."

T. J.'s eyes were wide, but he nodded. "Yes, sir, first thing in the morning."

"And if that doesn't work...well, there are other ways." Hawkins reached for a pencil and tapped it rapidly on the desk. "Find out who the little girl was. Maybe she's the key to Evans's conscience."

"The little girl?"

Hawkins felt his lips curl ever so slightly. "It's time to do whatever it takes." He glared at the others. "I will not have another public display of sympathy like we saw today. That statue is ours, am I making myself clear?"

There was a chorus of "yes, sirs" and a round of head nods.

They'd do as he said, Hawkins was sure. There was too much money riding on their success this time. And something else that only the partners would ever know about, something all the money in the world couldn't buy.

A four-year commitment of support from a primary team of very influential advisors. Advisors to a politician with more political power than anyone at HOUR had ever dreamed of having.

There was no way one crusading woman was going to cost them that.

Jordan finished packing and set his suitcase out in the hallway. It was a cool night, bordering on cold, and Jordan found his old parka, the one he used to use when he and his college buddies would go camping in upstate New York. It felt good on his arms, lighter and less confining than the suit jackets. He took the stairs down and welcomed the burst of fresh air as he strode out onto Twelfth Street and headed toward Second Avenue.

The air might not have been country fresh, but it was better than the boxy feeling he was getting in his apartment. The conversation with Hawkins, his promises and implied threats, played over again and again in Jordan's head, but after five minutes of walking the images changed. In their place Faith's face returned to haunt him. It was a sure bet her nights weren't spent walking city streets... How had she been fortunate enough to land a career that kept her in Bethany?

Then like a brick it hit him: Because of him, she no longer had a job. The thought settled like week-old pizza in his stomach, and he quickened his pace.

All around him the city hummed with activity, and Jordan suddenly longed for the nights when he would ride his bike to Jericho Park. Nights when the only sound was the whirring of his spoked wheels and the wind in the giant maple trees. Sometimes it had been so quiet at the park he could have sworn he heard the moon rising in the sky above him.

If only his mother hadn't died.

He thought of her now, her gentle spirit and loving touch. The way she had imparted to him her sense of wonder over a waxing crescent moon or a singing blue jay in flight or the distinctly vibrant colors in a monarch butterfly. It was no wonder there were times when Jordan thought he might suffocate if he lived another day in the city. With his mother, every day had a magical quality, a sort of expectancy that something small and ordinary would become a miracle. Jordan kept his pace steady and turned the corner, heading down another endless street, stepping over the occasional drunk passed out against the side of a building. The city air had a pungent smell to it, a mixture of rotten garbage, exhaust fumes, and air pollution that never went away. It made him miss the freshness of small-town air in a way he hadn't for years.

Jordan stared up at the sliver of sky between the converging buildings. When Faith's family had told them about Jesus, it had been as though everything in life finally made sense. Jesus had created everything, from the small wonders to the magnificent landscapes, all of it for their enjoyment. But there was more; He'd created them as well, and best of all, He had a plan for them to spend eternity with Him. All of it had been so believable.

Jordan stuffed his hands in the pockets of the parka and continued down the street. How blissfully peaceful those early days had been, back when it not only made sense to believe that way, but the Jesus rhetoric actually seemed true. A city park appeared in the distance, and Jordan headed for it. It wasn't grand like Central Park, or anything even close to resembling the quaint ambiance of Jericho Park. But it was a patch of grass with trees that might, for a few hours, help Jordan forget he was trapped in a city where butterflies and crescent moons didn't seem to exist.

He made his way across the street and found a bench. In the recesses of his mind he knew it wasn't the safest thing—hanging out in a park at this late hour in the heart of New York City—but he didn't care. Besides, the way he felt inside, his face was bound to scare away any unwanted company. He settled into the bench and stared straight ahead at a sickly tree struggling skyward. As gentle and loving as his mother had been, the end had been awful. A nightmare that no matter how many years passed Jordan couldn't forget.

Eventually the cancer moved to her lungs. As a thirteen-year-old boy he hadn't understood what was happening, but it made sense now. It started in her breast, moved into her lymph system, and wound up killing her when it took over her lungs. That was the only way he could explain her cough. Those last two weeks before she died, his mother coughed in a way that still sickened him today.

He and Heidi would be doing their homework at the kitchen table and they'd hear their mother wake up in her bedroom upstairs. At first she'd cough lightly, a few times, then a few more. After a minute or so, she'd be hacking so hard Jordan remembered fearing for her life. He'd jump from his chair, grab a cup of water, and rush to her room.

"Mom, are you okay?"

There she'd be, perched on the edge of the bed, little more than a skeleton. Her hair gathered in one hand, the other over her mouth, she'd cough with a convulsing force that sent her nose almost crashing into her knees. "Yes, Jordan…I'm okay…don't…worry about me."

He'd step from side to side, helpless, watching her, wanting to do something but knowing there was nothing he could do. Then she'd point to the floor. Her bowl. She wanted her bowl. He'd grab it as quickly as he could and hand it to her and although she'd eaten no dinner, although she'd probably eaten nothing all day, her coughing would turn to dry heaves.

"It's okay, Mom, I'm here." He'd stand beside her, rubbing her back and hiding the tears that made their way down his face. Once in a while Heidi would appear at the door, her eyes wide with fear.

He'd hold his finger to his lips, knowing that their mother was unaware of Heidi's presence. "Shh…it's okay," he'd mouth the words to his sister. "Go back downstairs."

No matter how long the spasmodic episode lasted, Jordan would stay there, putting his fingers over hers, helping her hold the hair off her face. When it was over, when her body finally released her to lie back down, Jordan would hurry to the bathroom and get a cool cloth for her forehead. "It's okay, Mom. It's all over. You're going to be all right."

How many times had he said those words? Every day, every hour? Jordan knew now, much as he'd known then, that the words were more for himself than anyone else. His mother had known the truth from the beginning. *God's calling me home, Jordan… He's calling me home.*

But Jordan and Heidi weren't ready for her to go. Hadn't God known that? Hadn't He cared?

He pulled the parka tighter, grateful he was the only person at the park that night. His mother's illness had gotten worse with each day until finally—the last day of her life—he hadn't bothered to ride to Jericho Park. He no longer wanted to spend time talking to Jesus; he wanted to be with his mother. Wanted to cling to her and stay by her side, to will the life back into her and love the cancer out of her body.

Faith's family was with them every day, nearly all day long that last week. Faith's mother would bring dinner and her father would sit by Mom, praying for her, talking to her. Not until sometime around eight o'clock, when his mother seemed able to sleep, would the Moses family go home. After that Jordan often led Heidi to her room and prayed with her. When she was asleep he would spend an hour or so at

Jericho Park, then come home and creep into his mother's room, taking her hand, kissing it as his tears fell onto the dirty knees of his jeans.

"Don't go, Mom. Stay with us. Please..."

A few times Faith had stayed with him, having been given a reprieve on her normal curfew in light of Jordan's mother's condition.

"Can she hear you?" Faith whispered one night.

Jordan remembered feeling angry at her question. "Of course she can hear me. She's sick, but she's going to make it, Faith. God's going to heal her."

Even after Faith had gone home, Jordan stayed at his mother's side, finally falling asleep on the floor, his hand clinging tightly to hers. He and Heidi had skipped school every day that last week, and time lost all meaning.

The morning of his mother's last day, he got up early and had a feeling she was already awake. He sat straight up on her bedroom floor and rose to his knees, peering over the top of the bed, making sure she was still breathing. When he saw that she was, he gently took her thin, bruised hand in his and smoothed his fingers over the top.

Her eyes opened and moved slowly in his direction and the shadow of a smile crossed her face. "Jordan..."

Heidi must have felt something different that morning, too, because she appeared at the bedroom door, and Jordan motioned her inside. His sister knelt beside him and he put his free arm around her as she reached over and linked her fingers between those of Jordan's and their mother's. "Hi, Mom...how're you feeling?"

Jordan had no trouble remembering his mother's face that morning, but the image of Heidi was less clear. Had she been fearful or sad or unaware? Had she known, like him, that their mother's time was running short? Did he take the time to tell her, to explain to his sister what was happening?

Jordan thought about that for a moment and decided he hadn't. Why would he have? Until that last day, he'd thought for sure God would heal her. But that morning there was a different look in his mother's eyes, a sadness and joy that Jordan still couldn't explain. As though she was about to take a much-anticipated journey and her only regret was having to say good-bye.

"Heidi..." Their mother's voice was clearer that morning. For days she would cough violently every time she tried to speak, but this time she was comfortable, at peace. "Heidi, you're so beautiful...you must...put Jesus first...always."

Heidi threw herself over her mother and hugged her, weeping and wailing over the prospect of what was happening. In that moment it must have been obvious to both Jordan and Heidi: They were saying good-bye to their mother. "Don't go, Mommy, please... I love you too much."

Heidi carried on for a long while, and Jordan could do nothing but rub her back with one hand and their mother's hand with the other while quiet tears coursed down his face. After a while Heidi sat up again and leaned into Jordan. There was silence while their mother seemed to summon what little strength remained. Jordan pulled

Heidi more tightly to himself as they watched, waiting for their mother's next words.

"I love you, Jordan...you're such a good boy...so...kind."

The memory of the moment was more vivid now than it had been since that awful morning, and Jordan felt the sting of tears in his eyes. He had cried so much that year, the year he lost his mother and Heidi and Faith. But tears had not touched him once in the time since then. Not since his move to the New Jersey boys' camp. He was a survivor, a loner, really. A smart and lonely kid who'd found a way to make it on his own.

But here, now—the memory of that last day with his mother so real he could almost touch her again—tears filled his eyes and spilled onto his cheeks. His eyelids closed and he saw her as she'd looked that day, so frail and weak her skin was practically translucent. She stayed very still in the bed, but her eyes darted between Heidi and Jordan. "Jesus...Jesus wants you to know...He loves you, Jordan. Keep praying, please. And one day...when you come home...I'll be waiting for you. Just like I used to wait for you here."

When you come home...when you come home...when you come home...

Why hadn't he remembered those words until now? The last thing his mother had said to him, the last thing that made sense amid her frenetic coughing and drug-induced incoherency was an invitation. When it was his turn to go home, she'd be waiting for him. Just like she'd always waited for him when he was a boy.

The thought was sadder than anything Jordan had considered for a very long time. To think she'd been so certain of God and heaven and eternity that it really had been like going home. In her mind, the cozy house they had on Oak Street wasn't home at all, but rather a temporary stopping ground. Heaven. That was home to his mother, and her last morning on earth had been spent trying to convince Jordan of the same.

Her words rang in his heart. *When you come home...when you come home...*

He wouldn't have struggled with the idea back then, back when his blossoming faith had been the only life preserver in a raging sea of tragedy. Had his mother known, somehow? Back then, with death mere hours away, had she known he would grow up to be an angry, cynical man who scoffed at the mere idea of a higher power and summarily dismissed the thought of eternity? Had she known?

The memories faded as Jordan caught something moving behind him, off to the side. He turned and saw three shabbily dressed teenagers heading his way. *Just try and mess with me tonight, punks.* They laughed and poked each other in the ribs as they came closer and stood in front of him, half-circling the bench.

"Okay, rich boy, what ya got for us?" The kid was tall and skinny, with ratlike eyes and bushy hair.

Jordan chuckled and let his eyes run the length of the boy and his friends. "Isn't it past your bedtime, children?"

A short boy with pants that sagged nearly to his knees kicked Jordan's shoe. "Bet we could get a couple ten spots for those leathers, what ya think?"

His redheaded, squatty companion yanked at Jordan's coat sleeve. "And a couple more for this." He looked at his friends, and they all burst into laughter.

Jordan felt his patience waning, but just as he was about to tell them to leave a glint of light reflected on a sizable knife in the skinny kid's back pocket. Just as Jordan had known his mother was going to die that morning sixteen years ago, he knew without a doubt what was about to happen.

He was going to be murdered.

They would rob him, maybe strip him of his coat and shoes, and stab him right there in the park. His lip curled. *So, God, is this Your way of showing You love me?* For a split second he wondered if there was time to reconsider, to analyze whether God's alleged promises might be true after all. *If You're there, God, now's the time to show me.* He sat up straighter and stared at the teens. "Get lost."

The skinny one moved in closer, and his eyes narrowed, the pupils black as flint. "Don't tell us what to do." He reached back toward the knife.

Jordan's mind raced in search of a plan, but all he came up with was a plea. *God, if You're really there, keep me safe. I'm not...I'm not ready to go home.*

"You're pretty stupid, rich guy." The teen's bushy hair shook as he jerked the knife from his pocket and pointed it at Jordan's throat.

The sirens came at that exact instant.

They couldn't have been more than a block away by the sound of them. The kid glared at him and shoved his knife back in his pocket. Then he and the others took off, running across the street, away from Jordan and the park. Before they could get to the other side of the road, several police cars converged on the area, and officers sprang from the cars, guns drawn. Using a megaphone, one of them shouted at the boys, "Police! Drop your weapons and freeze."

For a moment it looked as though the teens might try to outrun the officers, but then they came to a strange stop, almost as though their feet had gotten stuck in wet cement. No, that wasn't it. Almost as if someone unseen had grabbed them by their ankles. Jordan gawked at the unfolding scene as, one at a time, the teenagers dropped to the ground, their hands spread out in front of them. One of the policemen found the skinny kid's knife and tossed it to his partner. There were knives in the pockets of the other boys as well. In a matter of minutes, all three teens were whisked away in the police cars, leaving Jordan to absorb what had happened.

He had prayed to God for help...and for what felt like the first time in his life, the Lord had answered. He really and truly had answered his prayer. Not in a way that might be confused with coincidence or good vibrations or a strangely timed bout of luck. No, the teenagers being arrested seconds before they might have attacked him was something else altogether.

Even for a nonbeliever like Jordan, there was only one possibility. God had worked a miracle right before his eyes.

He began walking, and fifteen minutes later he was back at his apartment, assailed by doubts and doing his best to ignore whatever strange thing had happened back at the park. He must not be getting enough sleep. The teens were just punky kids. They weren't really going to harm him, were they? And if there was a God, He wouldn't have answered a prayer from someone like him. It was all just a strange set of coincidences...

Jordan put on a pair of sweats, flipped on his favorite sports channel, and sank into his leather recliner. Whatever had happened back at the park didn't matter. He was determined to make good on his word to Hawkins. He had a job to do in Bethany, a ten-thousand-dollar job.

And regardless of whether angels or God Himself had intervened on Jordan's behalf, he intended to do it.

20

The walls around the Jesus statue had been up for two full days and the outcry against HOUR was building across the city with each passing moment. It was nine o'clock at night when Faith returned home exhausted from another prayer vigil. She gazed around the empty kitchen.

Another night alone.

If only Mom were here…

Faith understood, of course. Aunt Fran's recovery required her to stay off her feet at least eight weeks, and since she lived alone, Faith's mother had been adamant about going to stay with her sister. No doubt about it, Mom was where she needed to be.

Faith tossed her coat on a chair, made herself a cup of tea, and sat at the kitchen table. As she sipped the warm liquid, she closed her eyes, remembering the conversation she'd had with her mother about the legal fight and the loss of her job.

"You have to do what God's telling you, Faith. I'm completely behind you."

Her mother had been shocked and then distraught to learn that Faith's opponent in the battle was Jordan Riley. She remembered him fondly as the boy who had been their neighbor all those years ago. "The walls around the statue are nothing to the walls that must stand around that boy's heart. I'm so sorry I'm not there with all this going on, dear."

"It's okay, Mom," Faith had assured her, though she wished her mother could be with her. Especially to talk through her feelings about Jordan.

Her mother had asked about how it felt to have Jordan as an adversary. "It hurt at first," Faith told her. "But I understand him better now. He's in too much pain to see what he's doing."

Faith cupped her steaming mug in her hands. It was true. She held no animosity toward Jordan, just a deep sadness that the tragedies in his life had caused him to think of God as an enemy.

Father, am I doing the right thing? Is the Jesus statue worth all this?

I will fight the battle, daughter… Go forward in My strength, not yours…

At the reminder, Faith drew a calming breath. She had no choice but to heed the words she continued to hear deep in her heart. The battle had grown more heated than ever. There were times she felt as if the expectations of the entire town rested on her shoulders, while she herself was balanced precariously on a tightrope two miles above the city. And if that hadn't been enough to consume her mind...

Jordan was back in town.

He'd held a press conference the day before, stationing himself in front of the walled-in statue and apparently inviting every member of the media within a three-state radius. Based on the number of vehicles that had congregated around the park for Jordan's statements, Faith was sure he considered the conference a success.

She took another sip of tea and spread the newspaper out on the table in front of her.

Like the first time she'd seen it earlier that morning, she couldn't help but laugh, even just a little. The photo on the front page was taken barely twenty-four hours after the wall went up, but citizens had begun to show their dislike for it by spray painting sentiments across the plywood. The photographer had captured Jordan speaking into a dozen microphones, the walled-up statue in the background. Taking up nearly half the photo were these words written across the wall: "God rules."

Faith stared at the picture and marveled at the goodness of the Lord. Obviously Jordan's press conference had been in direct response to the media coverage she'd received the day before. Even the daily paper captured the fact that the public loved Faith. "Media Darling Sides with People of Bethany," one headline read. Faith had expected to be persecuted, berated, and mocked for her stance. Instead the Lord seemed to be using her to bring the people together, to shed light on the public's right to keep the statue.

The night before, she'd watched the news segment on Jordan's press conference and winced when he made comments that seemed directed at her. "I won't smile and tell you a litany of lies intended to pacify the people." His face had been stern. Strikingly handsome, Faith had to admit, but stern. "The truth is this: People have a right to separation of church and state." He'd pointed to the walled statue behind him. "That wall is proof that every man, woman, and child in this country has rights, and that among those is the right to choose your own religion. Buddhists and Baptists—both are welcome in the United States and both should be welcome at Jericho Park. I can only imagine the outcry if, for instance, I donated a statue of Buddha to the people of Bethany. If a statue like that stood in the park, people would be lining up across the city to have it removed."

Jordan's voice rang with sincerity. "That's because there's a sentiment in this land that Christianity should be endorsed by the government." He paused—for effect—Faith was sure. "Tolerance toward this type of public Christianity leads to an endorsement. And an endorsement will one day lead to a mandated, state-sponsored religion." Jordan raised his voice. "We must preserve our freedom of religion...our freedom to choose. That's why HOUR is here in Bethany, fighting for every citizen in this country. Fighting to save us all from the tyranny of a state-sponsored religion."

Faith had watched the entire segment and sighed at the sadness in her heart as she turned off the television. Could Jordan really be that far gone? Was her childhood friend really the same man speaking out against God at a press conference? She studied Jordan's newspaper photograph, looking for anything remotely familiar—the earnest eyes, gentle heart, or dimpled smile. But there was nothing except the shape of his face, chiseled chin, and cheekbones.

Otherwise he looked like a stranger.

Images from the prayer vigil came to mind, and Faith considered the commitment of the townspeople who'd come that night. It had been obvious by their kindness that they were there as much to support her as to support the Jesus statue. If their favorite daughter were involved in the cause, then by golly they'd be involved too. Faith smiled at the memory. With each gathering the numbers grew, and people often asked what they could do to help. She thanked those who spoke with her, but the truth was frighteningly simple: They could gather the support of everyone in the state, but the decision would still be up to the judge.

Faith held her cup of tea closer to her face and let the steam warm her cheeks. It felt like days since she'd had a moment alone, time to talk with the Lord and seek His direction. She'd wanted to stay at Jericho Park after everyone was gone, to pray as she'd done when she was a young girl, back when she and Jordan would go there together. But dozens of people obviously planned to stay until she left.

She checked her watch and saw that a half hour had flown by. Surely the last of the prayer warriors had left the park by now. Faith considered the idea, pictured having the park all to herself and the chance to sit on her favorite bench and pray. Yes, it was just what she needed. The temperatures were expected to hit freezing that night so she bundled up in a full-length wool coat, gloves, and a scarf. Satisfied that she'd be warm enough she made her way out to her car. In five minutes she was back at Jericho Park.

She scouted the area before getting out of her car and found it empty. Without hesitating another moment she made her way across the familiar path toward the bench, the one closest to the Jesus statue. Her statue.

Faith sat down and pulled the coat tightly around her body. She thought about how busy she'd been earlier with the crowd gathered around. So busy she hadn't taken time to really look at the walled-in statue. In some ways it felt like some sort of bizarre dream, a surreal image of a fantasy future world where all signs of God might be forcibly eradicated from the public landscape. Faith stared at the plywood and half expected to look around the city and see churches boarded up as well. To think her father had devoted his final years to preserving religious freedom only to die months before the fight showed up on his own doorstep.

That was what coming to the park at ten o'clock was all about, really. Taking time to remember her father. "Dad…" Tears filled her eyes as she studied the covered statue. "You wouldn't believe the battle we're fighting." She uttered a sad laugh. "It's ridiculous."

She closed her eyes and imagined her father still alive, imagined him sitting beside her, holding her hand. Felt the way he would sympathize with her for losing a job she'd dreamed about all her life over the battle at Jericho Park. *Daddy, I need you here. Joshua needs you. God, how can You let us fight this battle without him?*

Faith tried to hear the Lord's answer, but the only sound was the faint rustling of a handful of stubborn leaves that hadn't yet fallen from the trees above. It didn't matter. She knew the answer already. God was with them; He'd go before them.

But at what cost?

The question whispered through her, much like the wind through the leaves. She hesitated. Would she ever find another job as an anchorwoman now that she'd become a key figure in a national legal battle? And what about Jordan? Win or lose, he'd wind up back in New York, never making peace with his mother's death or finding Heidi. Without any of the answers that might have restored his trust in God.

The tears that had been gathering spilled over and flowed steadily down her cheeks. As they did, Faith realized she'd been too caught up in the moment to grieve the changes that had happened around her, too busy to let down her guard and weep over all that had transpired in the days since her father's death. What she wouldn't give to be eight or ten again, running with Sarah and her father in the backyard of their home on Oak Street, certain that life would go on that way forever.

Faith allowed the tears, doing nothing to stop them, or the sadness that gripped her heart. With the Jesus statue walled up everything about her life seemed uncertain and hopeless. Yes, the town of Bethany supported her, but the people couldn't force the judge to make the right decision at tomorrow's hearing…they couldn't get her a job…or transform Jordan into the boy he'd once been.

And they couldn't bring back the man who had always been bigger than life, the man who had given everything for his convictions.

"Daddy, I'm here. I miss you…" Her words took wing and blended with a chorus of whistling wind gusts. Faith looked up and stared hard at the stars, dancing in the clear, cold, late-night sky. "God, please, tell Daddy I love him."

Jordan wasn't sure what he was supposed to do in Bethany for three days, but based on the media coverage and the size of the demonstrations against what he was trying to do, he knew one thing: He wasn't a popular figure. For that reason he holed up in his hotel room most of the day, aware that his photograph was on the front page of the paper. He'd spoken to Hawkins earlier and somehow the firm had seen a copy of the article.

"What's this, 'God rules' garbage?" Hawkins had blasted the question across the phone line, and Jordan had to ease away from the receiver to protect his ears. "Was that the only place you could set up a press conference? You might as well have been talking for the other side."

"I had no control over the photographer's angle." Jordan had never felt more insecure about his job. He'd figured out that the ten thousand dollars must have been only a fraction of the bonus money. Otherwise the partners would never have been so interested in the Bethany case. But none of that changed the fact that it was up to him to make sure public opinion was at least balanced in these final days before the hearing.

Hawkins had ended the conversation by asking Jordan the strangest question. "You haven't seen the girl, have you?"

"The girl?"

"The girl. Faith Evans. Have you seen her?"

For the tenth time in as many days Jordan felt as though his entire existence was founded on shifting sand. Why would Hawkins care about that? And why would he ask in the first place? Jordan hadn't told anyone about his childhood friendship with Faith Evans. No one but T. J., and Teej was his best friend. No way he'd say anything.

Before Jordan could muster an answer, Hawkins barked the question again.

"No, sir, I haven't seen her."

"Good. She's the enemy, Jordan. Don't forget it." He paused. "Don't let us down, we're counting on you."

Six hours had passed since then, and just after dark Jordan managed to sneak out for a bucket of fried chicken. Now that was gone, and he felt restless again. His time at the city park in New York had been cut short by the close encounter with the street thugs and besides, nothing in the city could compare with what Bethany offered. As he paced the boxy motel room he realized the only place he really wanted to go was Jericho Park. He'd allowed himself to journey down almost all the roads of his past, but there were a few he hadn't yet traveled and there would be no place like Jericho Park to allow the years to fade away.

He dug through his suitcase and came up with an old New York State sweatshirt and a Mets baseball cap. He slipped on a pair of tennis shoes and the parka he'd worn the other night, pulling it up close to his neck. Locking the motel door behind him, he set out on foot.

He realized there was no reason to walk fast—no sirens in the distance, no men with knives looking for solitary prey. Just the simple sleepy streets and suburban homes that made up the neighborhoods a mile from downtown. He took in every detail as he made his way closer to the park, noticing how little the area had changed in sixteen years. For a moment he pretended he was thirteen again, making his way home from Benjamin's Market with a quart of milk and a loaf of bread, confident that his mother and sister were waiting for him behind their nicely painted front door.

Jordan sighed and continued down the familiar streets.

That was the hardest part of being in Bethany. On the outside it all looked the same, felt the same. Even the cool early winter air was the same. But beneath the surface everything was different. It was the same feeling he'd had looking at his mother lying in a coffin. The shell of the woman was there, but none of what mattered most.

Jericho Park lay ahead of him, and he crossed Main, avoiding the circles of light from the street lamps. He was fifty yards from the bench when he saw a woman sitting alone, staring at the walled-up statue.

Fine. The other side of the park's as good as this one. He veered to the right, careful not to attract the woman's attention as he padded along a narrow strip of grass between the sidewalk and the curb. At the far end of the park, he turned left and walked in the darkest shadows until he reached a different bench. He sat down and allowed his eyes to adjust to the lack of light as he surveyed the park. The plywood around the statue stood out like a rusted Chevy on a neatly manicured lawn. He'd ask for brick, of course. Ten feet of dark brick, with a plaque explaining how the public had a right to choose. A nice touch to make the walls less of an eyesore, more of a message for the children of future generations.

Jordan let the words play in his mind and heard himself sigh. Who was he trying to kid? There were no cameras rolling now, no political posturing needed for the quiet hours of the night. The wall looked ridiculous and would look equally so made of wood or straw or the highest quality dark brick. He leaned back and stretched his feet out in front of him. Faith was right. The statue belonged to the people and they had a right to keep it standing—visible for all the world to see.

Staring at the strange-looking walls, he found himself missing the Jesus statue, the way the arms stretched out, the Scripture verse inscribed below. *Come to me all you who are weary and I will...*

Jordan blinked. What was he doing? How could he miss something that had played a part in the greatest deception of his childhood? He'd had more faith than all the people in the New Testament combined and *still* his mother died, still his sister had been taken away. He remembered the way his mother spoke so clearly to Heidi and him that last day, as though she'd known she had only hours to live.

He closed his eyes...feeling again his desperation as that awful day wore on and his mother's weakness returned. She coughed and gasped for breath, frightening them until finally Jordan ran next door and summoned Faith's family. Immediately Faith, her sister, and their parents took up their places at the Riley home, helping his mom and comforting Jordan and Heidi. Faith's parents took turns sitting beside his mother, while Jordan stood stiffly in the hallway outside and Heidi wept in the arms of one of the other adults. Jordan remembered staring at his mother through the open door, willing her to sit up. *Come on, Mom...get up. Talk to us...*

For a while she seemed to get better. Her coughing episodes grew less frequent and Jordan dared to believe that maybe...just maybe...a miracle was taking place before his eyes. "Mr. Moses—" Jordan had been hopeful as he came up behind Faith's large father and tugged on his sleeve—"I think the cough's going away. Maybe she's coming around some."

Mr. Moses clenched his jaw and led Jordan out of the room. Then, in quiet tones, he explained the situation. "She's coughing less because she has less air. Her breathing is slower and she's drifting in and out of our world here. Sort of like she's halfway to heaven, Jordan."

Jordan must have looked confused because Faith's father put a hand on his shoulder and stared deeply into his eyes. "It won't be long, Jordan. Your mother is dying, son."

As awful as the news was, Jordan remembered feeling some comfort in the way Mr. Moses had called him *son*. As though every shred of support and security wasn't slipping away from him and that even if his mother did die, he and Heidi wouldn't be alone in the world. Jordan nodded and looked around the man at his mother. "Should we…should we tell her good-bye?"

Faith's father had tears in his eyes. "Heidi said you already did. I guess your mother had a chance to talk to you earlier today, is that right?"

Jordan nodded, his eyes trained on the form of his mother in the next room. "We had a real nice talk."

Mr. Moses squeezed his shoulder again and pulled him close, hugging him the way Jordan had always imagined a father might. "I'm glad, Jordan. Really, I am."

Then, even though she could no longer hear them, Jordan and Heidi returned to the bedroom and sat on either side of the bed, holding their mother's hands and talking to her in quiet tones. Heidi was not ashamed to cry and she wept throughout the day, occasionally throwing herself across her mother and holding her close despite the fact that their mother was no longer able to respond. "Don't leave us, Mommy."

Jordan hadn't felt the same freedom. His world was changing with each passing hour, and any moment he was about to be the head of the household, the only person who could look after Heidi. He kept his back straight and his lower lip stiff as he squeezed his mother's hand again and again, praying for some sort of response. He had tears, for sure, but they were quiet tears. Tears that coursed down his face and made wet marks on the legs of his jeans. Now and then Heidi would come up behind him and take hold of his shoulders, resting her head against his back as she sobbed silently.

They stayed that way for hours, Heidi and Jordan on the bed with their dying mother. Finally, just before six o'clock that evening, she made three quick gasping sounds and then exhaled long and slow. Even now Jordan remembered the sound. It was the same sound his bicycle tire had made back when he was twelve and had run over a pop bottle on the way home from school. A long, slow hiss that seemed to last forever until there was no air left.

"Mom!" Jordan shook her so she might draw another breath, but as he watched, her features relaxed and a tranquillity came over her. One moment she'd been there, fighting for her life, and the next she was simply gone, leaving nothing but the shell of the body she'd once occupied. He remembered being sure she'd gone to heaven. Since then, though, he'd convinced himself that heaven didn't exist. The peace on his mother's face after drawing her last breath was merely death taking another victim. Heidi's reaction had caused an ache deep in his heart, like a bruise that never healed even to this day.

His sister realized what was happening at the same time Jordan did and she screamed, dropping their mother's hand and running across the room to Faith's mother, clinging first to her and then moving alongside the bed back to Jordan. "Bring her back, Jordan, make her come back!"

He winced and eased himself out of the memory. Heidi had been terrified of being alone, living without their mother. Only Jordan's presence in her life had given her the security she'd needed to survive that day and the ones that followed.

He felt tears stinging at his eyes and wondered how long it had been since he'd grieved the loss of his mother and sister. Of course, back then he hadn't imagined he'd lose Heidi the same week. Somehow he'd figured he could raise her by himself, that they might continue to share the house on Oak Street, eating an occasional meal with Faith's family and getting themselves off to school on time each day. He'd had no understanding of utility bills and food costs or that there might be a law against children living alone.

They'd been taking care of themselves for months, ever since their mother got sick. Why should that change now that she was gone? As they got through the next few days, it wasn't a problem either of them considered. Faith's mother was over often, taking them to the funeral home and helping them understand what was happening. Looking back, Jordan realized the church or Faith's family must have paid for his mom's funeral, the casket, and burial plot, because certainly his mother had no money. Once when he was old enough to search the records he looked into what had happened to their house. According to his file—which lacked any specific detail— the house was sold to pay his mother's medical bills.

Jordan guessed that the government took the rest.

The days after his mother's death were as much a blur now as they were sixteen years ago, but in the still and quiet darkness of Jericho Park, Jordan did his best to remember. They had worn their nicest church clothes for the funeral, and Heidi hadn't been able to pull herself away from him. She was so sad, so afraid at the loss of their mother that she wouldn't speak to anyone but Jordan. Especially the morning of the funeral service.

"She w-won't really be there, right Jordan? In the wooden box?" Heidi had found him in the bathroom that morning getting ready. She was so distraught she could barely speak. "Even though...even though her body will be there, right?" Tears filled her eyes, as they did all the time back then.

Jordan adjusted his white button-down shirt that the Moses family bought him and rubbed a dab of gel into his hair. It was the last time he'd see his mother and he wanted to look his best. "No, Heidi. She won't really be there. Having her body there is just a way of giving people a chance to say their good-byes."

"But...but she's already gone, right? Like if I talk to her, she won't be able to hear me, right?" Heidi stood inches from him, waiting anxiously for his hand to be free so she could take hold of it.

Jordan set the tube of gel down and pulled her close. "She won't hear you, but God will. Remember what Mom said? Don't stop praying...and one day when we go to heaven she'll be waiting for us."

Jordan frowned into the cool dark air. Had those really been his words? Had he truly felt that confident in the hours before his mother's funeral? He wasn't sure. He just knew he'd vowed to take care of Heidi until she was grown. Other than Faith and her family, Heidi was all he had and clearly she needed him.

The air was getting colder and frost was appearing on the park grass. Jordan looked across the field and searched for the woman he'd seen earlier. Whoever she was, she'd gone home. Jordan knew he should do the same. The hearing was scheduled for ten o'clock the next morning. But somehow he didn't want to leave this place—or the memories of those days after his mother's death, the last days with Heidi. Jordan remembered making breakfast for her and doing laundry and making sure they got to bed on time. Faith's mother was there a lot, and so was her father. But most of the time Jordan had been in charge, and though they were still reeling from the loss of their mother, there was comfort that went beyond words in the fact that they had each other.

How long had that time lasted? Jordan used to think it was a week or so, but now it seemed more like two or three days at the most. Either way, it hadn't been long enough. Faith's father had pulled him aside and promised he'd do all he could to see that Jordan and Heidi stayed together. Certainly he hadn't contacted the state and reported them living alone. But somehow the office of Social Services got wind of their situation and one afternoon—the day they'd returned to school—two workers came and asked them to pack their things. Heidi had been terrified about going away, even for a night, but the state workers promised she'd be back with Jordan in a day or so.

Promises that meant nothing at all.

He remembered Heidi's cries and wide-eyed terror as one of the workers drove her away from their home. Jordan had watched her go, believing he would die from the separation and helplessness of that moment. He had promised to take care of her and suddenly in an hour's time she was gone.

His heart felt tight and trapped at the memory, awash in an ocean of pain that still hadn't even begun to subside. "Heidi, where are you?" Jordan stared out ahead of him and wondered what she might look like now. Heidi…his little sister…the one who had depended on him for everything that last year they were together.

Another onset of tears burned his eyes. Jordan rarely afforded himself the chance to miss her this way, but here, with visions of that terrible afternoon as real as they'd been in the months that followed, he felt as though his heart would break from missing Heidi. He should have done more to find her, searched for her, refused to give up. Instead he'd made a series of bad decisions, choices that only cost him whatever hope he'd had of getting them back together again.

There was a rustling behind him and he whipped around. First New York City, now Bethany. Wasn't any place safe from the crazies who roamed the night? He scanned the bushes and a movement caught his eye. It looked like the same woman who'd been at his bench earlier that night, and she was walking toward him. Before he could clearly see her face she spoke.

"Jordan, it's me...Faith."

His heart skipped a beat as a series of emotions washed over him. Shock at seeing her here at the park, seeking out solitude at the same hour he'd chosen; guilt and sadness, and as she came into the light, a desire he hadn't known before in his life. She was so beautiful, her heart so clearly like it had been when they were kids living next door on Oak Street. It was all he could do to keep from meeting her halfway, taking her in his arms and apologizing for everything that had happened over the past few months.

He read her eyes as easily as he had sixteen years ago. She cared for him still— regardless of the war they were waging against each other, she cared. Then he moved to one side of the bench and patted the empty place beside him.

There were a dozen things he could think to say to her, but instead he held her gaze and hoped she, too, could see beyond the battle lines.

21

aith was still quite a ways off when she recognized Jordan. Something in the way he stretched out and stared off in the distance—the tilt of his head and the long legs that refused to stay bunched up beneath him—the same as when he was a boy.

For a moment she stopped and considered turning back. What would she say to him? After all they were enemies now, weren't they? But in the quiet of the darkened park the trappings of their current situation seemed to fall away. Here, in the shadows of the walled-in Jesus statue, they were merely two grown-up kids who'd lost each other a very long time ago when life was its most impressionable.

Looking at Jordan she saw him as he'd been in his mother's room the day she died, the way he'd held his head high at her funeral, the way he'd clung to his sister the day she was taken from him. Rather than fight him or berate him for his political views, she wanted only to take him in her arms and soothe away the years of hurt and anger and bitterness.

Jordan...her long-ago best friend...

When he finally spotted her she knew that she'd been right that first night in the diner parking lot. No matter what words came out of his mouth when the cameras were rolling, he was the same Jordan Riley she'd loved as a girl. When he patted the empty place beside him on the bench, she came to him willingly.

"I thought it was you." She took the seat, careful to keep her distance, angling her body so she could see him. Although they sat in darkness, the stars cast enough light so she could make out his features.

"I must have walked right past you. Were you sitting on the bench over there?" His voice was quiet and kind, and Faith felt herself relax.

"Yeah. It's been kind of crazy lately." She stared across the expanse of frosty grass toward the towering plywood walls. "I guess I needed some time alone."

Jordan followed her gaze and waited a moment. "I know what you mean."

There was an uncomfortable silence, and Faith could sense him searching for something to say. Something that didn't involve the statue or the fact that common sense said they were crazy to be sitting on a bench in a hidden corner of the park in the middle of the night.

He turned to her and seemed to force a smile. "Tell me about the little Asian girl."

Her gaze fell, and she tried to still her racing heart. "Rosa Lee?"

"I don't know…" He changed positions so that he was closer than before. "She was by your side at the protest the other day. I saw her with you on the news."

Faith gulped and tried to concentrate. Something about being in his presence was making her feel thirteen again, like they were only pretending to be adults locked in a legal battle. "She's…she's a foster child. Sometimes she reminds me of you." Suddenly her heart soared at the chance to share her deepest feelings with him. "She wants me to adopt her."

Jordan's smile seemed more genuine this time. "That's wonderful. Will you? Adopt her, I mean?"

"Oh, I don't know." She felt the corners of her mouth lift some. "Actually, I'm praying about it." Faith thought of the little girl and how close they'd grown in the past weeks. "I keep waiting for a real family to show some interest. You know, with a mom and dad. I think she deserves that." She hesitated, not sure if she should tell him. "Besides, my next job might take me away…"

He searched her eyes. "Away?"

She nodded. "I got a call today from the station's competition. A national network. They're considering me for a spot."

Jordan's eyes lit up, and for the first time that night his grin reminded her of the boy he'd once been. "For the national news? Faith, that's great!" He reached for her hands and squeezed them, then as the moment faded he let go and crossed his arms tightly against his chest.

Faith couldn't bring herself to tell him the rest of the conversation. The network executive had acknowledged that Faith was embroiled in a national legal battle. "Be careful," he'd told her. "Don't do anything too extreme. And keep a low profile. I have to be honest with you, prayer rallies, protests, that kind of thing won't look good, Ms. Evans."

She and Jordan fell quiet, and an icy breeze kicked up a pile of long-dead leaves. Faith angled her head, studying Jordan. She wanted desperately to know the thoughts that filled his head. Was he here to strategize his next move? Or was he drawn to the past the way she was so often these days? *Talk to me, Jordan…like old times…* "What are you thinking?" Her voice was soft, allowing him the right to refuse to answer.

He shrugged and met her gaze. "About Heidi."

Faith's heart melted. He was the same; deep inside he was still the same. "I think about her a lot. Especially since…"

"I know," Jordan finished for her. Their voices were quiet, like the night around them. Even the breeze had stilled, and time seemed strangely suspended. "Since that night at the diner."

Faith nodded. "She loved you very much, Jordan."

He sighed and narrowed his eyes. "It was my fault what happened. I let her down."

Faith shook her head. "None of it was your fault. The state took you to separate homes and even if you'd—"

"No." His tone was gentle but insistent. "You don't know the whole story."

Faith thought about that for a moment and angled her head, trying to understand. For all the success Jordan had managed to achieve professionally, she suddenly knew he had no one to talk to, no friend like she'd been to him that year before he was taken from his home. She thought of a hundred things she could say. *Talk to me, Jordan. Share your heart with me. So what if we're enemies in the morning? Right now we're thirteen again, and you can tell me whatever's on your heart.* She swallowed hard and let her thoughts fade. "Tell me, Jordan. I have all night."

And to her surprise, he did.

Drawing a slow breath he stared straight ahead and talked as though the events were only just now happening, as though he could see them unfolding before his eyes the way they had that terrible year. "They put me in a foster home, and every hour I asked about Heidi. Two days passed, and then three, and I overheard the lady on the phone. I don't know who she was talking to, but she said she didn't think they could find a place for Heidi and me, for both of us. She said it could be weeks before I saw my sister again."

Jordan paused, and Faith allowed the silence. He closed his eyes as though the events of the past were settling into their proper order. Finally he looked at her and exhaled, his breath hanging in the air. "On the third day I set out on my own. The man of the house had told me where Heidi was staying—with a family on Birch Street. I figured I knew my way to Birch Street and even if I had to knock on every door I'd find her eventually." He released a frustrated huff. "I should have known better. One call to my social worker, and I might have had a visit with her that night. Maybe they didn't know how badly I needed to see her."

Without thinking, Faith reached out and took Jordan's hand in hers, wrapping her gloved fingers around his. "That's why you got sent to the boys' camp?"

Jordan gripped her hand, his gaze still straight ahead. "I wasn't gone an hour when the police came cruising up behind me. I'd almost made it to Birch; I was so close I could practically see Heidi waiting for me, calling my name. When the police asked me to get in the car, I ran the other direction." He released a sad laugh. "I was thirteen. What chance did I have at outrunning two police officers? They caught me, cuffed me, and tossed me in the squad car. That afternoon I was shipped thirty minutes away to the Southridge Boys' Camp."

Faith felt suddenly awkward holding Jordan's hand and she quietly pulled it back. "You can't blame yourself for that, Jordan. You were doing what you thought was best."

"I should have been patient. Who knows?" He turned and locked eyes with her. "Everything might have been different." He paused, his eyes more intense than they'd been all night. "Absolutely everything."

Faith thought she understood what he was saying. If he'd had the chance to grow up alongside Heidi he would not have held the anger he held today. He might not have become a human rights attorney, and perhaps…perhaps she and Jordan might even have stayed friends or… She refused to dwell on the possibilities. "Did you…at the camp, did they tell you anything about Heidi?"

"Not a thing." The muscles in Jordan's jaw flexed and he fell silent. He turned his attention to the spread of grass in front of him. "The camp was like a prison. Up at seven, chores till nine. A bowl of slop for breakfast each morning, lessons through the early afternoon, and four hours of hard labor before dinner."

Faith felt tears in her eyes. That was the type of life he'd been forced to live in the months after losing his mother? After losing Heidi? After losing his home and Faith's family and everything that had mattered to him? The reality of it tore at her heart, and she pictured Rosa Lee…stranded in the system, without a family. Where would she wind up when she got old enough to have a bad attitude? At a similar camp, fighting for her place among a houseful of angry young women? The thought made her shudder. "Oh, Jordan…I had no idea."

He nodded, his expression unchanged. "The boys at the camp were tougher than I was—serious hard-core kids. Most of them were drug addicts or thieves, guys destined for prison. I thought about Mom and Heidi—" he looked at her—"and you…every day, every hour. But there was nothing I could do about it. It took all my strength just to survive."

She always believed he'd remembered her, that he thought of her in those days after he was taken from his home. But this was the first time he'd said so, and a warmth made its way from Faith's heart out across her body. "You thought of me, Jordan? Really?"

He stared at her, and there were tears in his eyes. "Every day, Faith. I kept thinking…" He swallowed hard. "I kept thinking you and your parents would show up at the camp and take me home, rescue me from that awful place and help me find Heidi."

"We wanted to…" Her voice drifted. "I talked to my mom… she's in Chicago helping my aunt. She said they hadn't called social services because they were afraid once the state got involved it would be impossible to adopt you." She looked at the tops of the distant trees. "I guess my dad wanted to talk to an attorney friend of his about adopting both of you privately. But the state stepped in before he could do anything."

Jordan shook his head. "It doesn't matter. Things happened the way they did for a reason, right?"

Again she wanted to take him in her arms and hold him until the hurt faded from his heart. But she had a feeling it would take a lifetime, and they didn't have that. Morning was fast approaching. In six hours this strange time between them borrowed from a place where yesterday lived would be all but forgotten.

Come morning, they'd take up their places on opposite sides of the battle once more.

She decided to be honest with him. "Jordan…"

He turned to her and smiled sadly. "I'm sorry. It's late and cold. I'm sure you don't want to hear all this."

"No, I do…I just…" He was looking at her, waiting for her to finish. "I thought about you, too. Every day."

He searched her eyes. "I always wondered if you heard about the accident. For a month after it happened I expected to see you and your family." He smiled and gazed up at the midnight sky. "I pictured your dad striding up to the front office, demanding they let me go, insisting that the camp wasn't a safe place for kids like me." He shook his head. "But the truth is you probably never even heard about it."

Faith's eyes grew wide. An accident? At the camp? "Wait a minute, I do remember something about it."

Jordan lowered his eyebrows and bit his lower lip, stuffing his hands deep into the pockets of his parka. "It was awful, Faith." Even in the shadows she could see heartache settle over his face. "There was a cave built into the side of a ravine, maybe a hundred yards from the main camp. Over the years people used it as a trash dump." He paused and released a long breath, gritting his teeth in a way that made his jaw more pronounced. "That afternoon…the owners of the camp decided it was time to clean it out."

Faith racked her brain, trying to remember where she'd heard these details before. She waited while Jordan found the strength to continue. "The cave was more of a tunnel…I don't know, maybe twenty feet straight into the side of the ravine. Trouble was it'd been raining for three weeks before they ordered the cleanup. We were an hour into the job when dirt began falling from the ceiling."

Jordan shook his head, and his features looked chalky white, even in the shadows. "I remember every horrifying detail." He paused and looked at her again. "Another boy and I were near the entrance. We barely got out. I mean, we had dirt on our backs and our legs were buried as the cave collapsed." He stared at the ground near his feet. "They used shovels and got me and the boy next to me out first. Then they started digging for the others. Seventeen boys. All of them trapped beneath tons of dirt."

He was silent for a moment, lost in the memory, and Faith barely noticed the tears that trickled onto her cheeks. *No wonder Jordan's so angry…* She wanted to ask the Lord why—why had He allowed the string of tragedies to happen to a boy so young, one so new in his belief? But something deep inside her lacked the confidence to even approach God with the issue. She shifted her attention back to Jordan. "I can't imagine."

Jordan nodded slowly, thoughtfully and brought his eyes back up to hers. "For ten minutes we could hear the faint, muffled cries of the trapped boys. The camp owner dug as fast as he could, and after a few minutes firemen arrived and joined the effort." He shook his head, his eyes flat. "There was nothing they could do; it was too late."

Suddenly she could see the headlines, hear her parents talking about the accident.

As she drifted back to that year, she gasped and her hand flew across her mouth. "I remember it now! The newspaper said you died!" She stared straight ahead, digging her fingers into the roots of her hair, searching her mind for details she hadn't remembered until now. Her eyes flew back to his. "My parents read the article and told me that night. They said they weren't sure it was true and the next day they made some calls and found out you were okay."

"The paper said I died?" Jordan's eyebrows lifted. "You're kidding?" He bit the inside of his lip and his eyes grew even wider. "Hey, what if Heidi heard the same thing?"

Faith caught his enthusiasm. "You know, you might be right. Maybe she thinks you're dead, and that's why she hasn't tried to find you."

"I've looked up her records, but never mine. What if somehow they got it mixed up and—" He stopped, and his shoulders slumped as he leaned back against the bench once more. Faith watched the despair settle over his face. "They wouldn't have gotten a thing like that wrong. The papers might have made a mistake, but not the state."

He looked at his hands. "I spent a night in the hospital while they looked me over. The next day I was moved to a boys' camp in New Jersey." He leaned his head back some and looked at Faith again. "I asked about Heidi every day for three months until finally the camp warden told me not to ask anymore." Jordan huffed, and Faith could see the bitterness in his tensed features. "He threatened to send me to a camp in Montana if I spoke her name again."

Faith pictured him, only months after losing his mother and sister, stuck at a camp so far from home with people who neither knew nor loved him. "I wish…I wish we could have found you, Jordan."

He shrugged, and she knew he was letting her see into the very depths of his heart. "I kept thinking they'd bring Heidi to me, find us a home together. But one year led to the next, and in no time I was finished with high school and playing college baseball. By that point I think I figured no one wanted to find me. I sort of had to let the old Jordan Riley die…" He studied Faith's eyes. "Know what I mean?"

She shook her head and felt her heart sink. This was his way of telling her he'd changed, at least from his perspective. But it wasn't true; the old Jordan hadn't died. She'd sat right next to him for the past half hour.

Jordan's heart raced deep within him at Faith's nearness, at the desire he felt for her. How had he gotten in this position? How had things gotten so mixed up, so far from what he wanted?

He wanted to pull her close and tell her the way he was feeling, but how could he? Nothing lasting could ever come from a relationship between them. They were complete opposites.

But, oh! What she did to him, sitting so close he could smell the subtle sweetness of her skin.

"What are you thinking?"

Jordan looked at her, and a flash of anger pierced his soul. What was he doing here, anyway? This was all about the court case. Faith didn't have feelings for him. "I know what you're trying to do."

She jerked back an inch or two and knit her eyebrows together as though he'd suddenly switched languages on her. "What's *that* supposed to mean?"

He expelled the air in his lungs and dug his elbows into his thighs. "I'm sorry. I'm not making sense."

Faith was quiet for a minute. Then in a voice soft as silk she whispered words that felt like balm to his empty heart: "The old Jordan isn't dead. He's right here."

Get up and leave! She's trying to change you, make you into something you're not! She's one of them, remember?

The silent, angry whispers pecked at his soul, but he ignored them. It didn't matter what her motives were, or what she was trying to do to him, or which side she was aligned with. He looked up and their eyes locked. Slowly she slid closer and slipped off her gloves. Then she lifted her hand to his face, framing his jaw with the most delicate touch he'd ever known. "He's not dead, Jordan."

He searched her eyes, painfully aware he was losing control at an alarming rate. His words slipped out before he could stop them. "Sometimes I think, maybe…maybe you're right."

Faith's eyes filled with tears, and suddenly Jordan was sure beyond any doubt that the woman before him had no ulterior motives. Rather the two of them were caught in a time warp, transported back to that long-ago summer when they were two kids learning about love.

"Until tonight," she went on, "I thought it might be true, that the old you really had died. But now…"

He drew closer to her, savoring the feel of her hand on his face as she talked.

"Seeing you here, like this, I realized that somewhere inside of you the old Jordan Riley still remembers."

The night air was cold and oddly calm. Jordan looked into Faith's eyes, trying to memorize the moment and wondering if it wasn't all some kind of a dream. Finally, when he couldn't hold back another moment, he took her chin in his hands, allowing his fingers to caress the sides of her face. "I wanted to win this battle, Faith. For a long time I've wanted to win it. But I never meant to hurt you. I had no idea…"

Her eyes clouded over, and she turned her eyes toward the Jesus statue. Again there was quiet between them.

"What're you thinking about?" Jordan tucked the loose strands of her hair behind her ears. "You looked a million miles away for a minute there."

She looked back at him, and he wondered if she was as distracted by his nearness as he was by hers. It was all he could do to keep from taking her in his arms and…

If only there weren't an ocean of differences between us—

"It's cold."

At her words, Jordan nodded and closed the remaining gap between them, moving so close to her that his heightened senses took in every place where their bodies touched. The length of their arms, their legs… "Better?"

Faith hesitated, and Jordan knew she had to be waging an inner battle as well. But he felt her relax and snuggle close to him.

"Better." She positioned herself so she could look into his eyes again. "Remember what you said? About this case meaning a lot to you?"

He nodded, barely able to breathe for her nearness.

"It means a lot to me, too." The reality of her statement cut like a dagger, though it did nothing to stop the way he wanted her, the way he was sure he'd never loved anyone like he loved the woman at his side, the connection they shared. She was the only one he had ever been able to share his heart with.

"You have to be true to yourself, Faith."

Their eyes locked, their faces no more than an inch apart, and Jordan knew there was no turning back. Faith brought her cheek up alongside his and he nuzzled her face. "I will be… It's something I promised my father."

He eased his arm around her and pulled her against his chest. Finally, when he thought he'd die from anticipation, he whispered into her ear, "I still love you, Faith."

Sitting this close in the shadows of the park where they'd spent so many hours as kids…it was more than either of them could bear. The statue, the legal fight…none of it mattered with her so close he could feel her breath, smell her shampoo.

She cupped his face with both hands this time, her eyes full of questions. "Jordan, I…"

"Shh. Don't say anything." He could feel the early sting of tears. "We're different now, we look at life from opposite sides of the ocean. I just…I wanted you to know how I feel."

Her hands quivered against his face and he caught them in his own, protecting her from the freezing night.

Faith looked deeply into his eyes. "But you agreed with me. A part of you—who you used to be—still lives inside you. Isn't that right?"

Jordan let go of one of her hands, tracing her eyebrows with his thumbs. "If things had been different…who knows where we might be now." He warned himself not to do something he'd regret, but without paying heed he brought his lips closer to hers. This time he kept eye contact as he whispered the feelings that were flooding his heart. "I always loved you, Faith. What I felt for you was…I don't know, pure. Right. I never loved anyone the way I loved you. The way I still love you."

Certain they'd found a ride upstream in the river of time, he touched his lips to hers and kissed her until they were both breathless. When he pulled back, a breeze blew across them and he was struck by the insanity of their actions. What was he doing? Where could this possibly go?

A thought quickly took shape. Whatever their differences, this wasn't fair to either of them.

He searched her face, taking in the honesty and integrity and desire he saw there. The love. Tears pricked at his eyes again. "You're so beautiful, Faith. So good and right. But what we have between us is borrowed from yesterday." Before he could stop himself, he kissed her again, then drew back. "It isn't real."

Faith's eyes clouded. She lay her hand over his heart, and he knew she must feel the way he was trembling. "It is real. As real as the boy you used to be." She framed his face with her fingers again and kissed him with a passion that took him by surprise and was almost his undoing.

"Faith," he whispered when their lips came apart for a brief moment. "What you do to me…"

Again and again she moved her lips over his until he thought he might scream from the feelings welling up inside him. When they came up for air, she searched his eyes for a long moment, her voice barely a whisper. "You can't have your mother and Heidi back. But I'm still here, Jordan. That's proof that God loves you, isn't it?"

A single tear spilled onto his cheek, and he shook his head. "No. Tomorrow we'll be enemies again. I'll do whatever I can to see your Jesus statue walled up forever and you'll do everything in your power to stop me. Don't you understand, Faith? The God you love, the God you serve…He's my enemy. I spend all my time trying to have Him eliminated from society."

She drew back from him, open-mouthed as though she'd been slapped. And in that instant a knife twisted in Jordan's heart—and he knew the moment they'd borrowed from time was gone.

Forever.

At Jordan's words, Faith felt like a bucket of ice water had been dumped down her back. *What am I doing here, God?*

She was still reeling from their kisses, convinced of the love she still had for him, but how could she stay when he talked about God being his enemy?

What should I do?

Go, daughter…I will be with Jordan.

Faith wrapped her arms tightly around herself and let her gaze fall to her lap. Though she ached for Jordan, she knew now she had no right falling for him. Not when he thought of God as his enemy. *Give me the words, God…restore him to You…please, Father.*

Words began filling her heart, and she looked at Jordan through wet, blurry eyes and began to speak. "'For I am convinced that neither death nor life, neither angels nor demons, neither the present nor the future—'"

The light in his eyes disappeared as though his heart had closed up shop. He began to shake his head. But still the words came and Faith could do nothing but speak them clearly, with all the love she felt in her heart. "'Nor any powers, neither height nor depth, nor anything else in all creation, will be able to separate us from the love of God that is in Christ Jesus our—'"

"Stop it!" He put his hands on her shoulders and shook her. Not hard enough to hurt her, but hard enough to silence her. Anger flashed in his eyes, and it tore at Faith's heart like nothing she'd ever felt before. "I don't want to hear that, Faith. I'm serious. God is my enemy and nothing you can say will ever change that."

Her tears came harder and she pulled loose from his grip. "I'm not the one who doesn't get it, Jordan. You loved the Lord once, and that's something He doesn't forget." A sob escaped from deep within her, and she covered her mouth with the back of her hand. "No matter what you do…whether you put a wall around the Jesus statue or not…Jesus will still love you." She stood up and took three steps back. "And so will I."

With that she turned and began jogging back to her car, crying harder, not caring that the icy night air was stinging her face as she ran. What had she been doing, kissing Jordan like that? Was she crazy? Even worse, was Jordan right? Did the boy she loved no longer exist? Jordan seemed to have grown into a man determined to remain an enemy of her God. And yet…

His kiss still burned on her lips, and she was suddenly furious with herself. How could she feel so deeply for him when she knew what he stood for? Her tears came in torrents, both for herself and the way she'd betrayed God. *I'm sorry, Lord. Help me pull myself together…help me find the pieces of my heart.* She ran faster and before she could analyze her actions further she reached her car, climbed in, and drove away.

She glanced once more toward the bench where she and Jordan had been sitting but it was empty. *Lord, help me be strong next time I see him. How can he be so wonderful and warm one minute and so intensely angry and bitter the next? And how could I let myself kiss him? Oh, Lord…I need to keep my focus. Don't let me be distracted by my feelings, please, Father…*

I have loved Jordan with an everlasting love, daughter. Even now I am calling him…

The words washed over Faith with holy reassurance. She nodded, grateful. Let God work with him; it was too hard a task for her.

She would continue praying for Jordan's change of heart, but she knew she needed to pray for her own as well. Especially since the memory of his kiss, his touch, was stronger than she cared to admit. After all, she would see him again in ten hours.

When they'd face each other as public enemies in the Pennsylvania State Court.

22

When Jordan didn't answer his motel phone all night, T. J. knew he had no choice but to drive to Bethany. The hearing was at ten that morning, and the partners had made it exceedingly clear that they doubted Jordan's intentions.

"If he spends more than thirty minutes outside his hotel room I want to know about it. If he's in love with the girl, anything could happen." Hawkins had waved his hand in the air and pointed it at T. J. "You understand me, Morris?"

T. J. had nodded. "Yes, sir."

Hawkins crashed his hand down on his desk, knocking a stack of papers onto the floor. "The last thing we need is Jordan settling for some partial wall or even no wall at all just so he and the girl can pick up where they left off, wherever that was." He stared at the others. "With all that's riding on this case, his association with this woman is flat dangerous."

Hawkins's words echoed in T. J.'s mind as he set out before sunup for Bethany. Whatever the situation, he feared Hawkins was right. Friendship notwithstanding, when the phone in Jordan's motel room went unanswered until well after midnight, T. J. felt he had no choice but to go.

He would meet Jordan at court just before the hearing and tell him he'd come for moral support. Then all T. J. could do was hope Jordan wouldn't dare make an unexpected move with his best friend and coworker watching over his shoulder.

At eight o'clock that morning the phone rang in Peter T. Hawkins's office. It was his hot line, the number he gave only to a handful of people, including his friends in influential political circles.

"Hawkins here." He sounded more confident than he felt. The blasted statue hearing was in two hours, and Morris had already called to inform him there was trouble. Jordan had been out all night, which only added to Hawkins's mounting doubts regarding the young attorney.

"Hello, Mr. Hawkins."

He sat straighter in his chair. The voice on the other end was one that would be recognized in many political circles. Had the statue case actually gained this type of attention? Hawkins had presumed the bonus money was something only the politician's advisors knew about, but apparently not. "Hello, sir. How are you this morning?"

"Good…and hoping to get better. I understand you have this Jesus statue case under control."

Hawkins gulped and struggled to find his voice. "That's right."

"Good, good." The man at the other end chuckled. Hawkins could only imagine the pressure this man must be under to make a deal like this with HOUR. He held his breath as the man began to speak. "People are watching this case, Mr. Hawkins. You and the crew at HOUR have always been our most powerful allies, but it's time to raise the bar." His voice grew less friendly. "We cannot have Jesus statues standing in our public parks. Not while I'm in office." He hesitated and his voice relaxed some. "You're aware of the bonus money?"

A thin layer of perspiration broke out on Hawkins's forehead, and he wiped it with his fingertips. "Yes. It's very generous, sir."

"There's more where that came from. Private money, you understand. Nothing illegal." He chuckled again. "Just make sure the wall goes up. We'll start with statues and work our way to the churches. Isn't that right, Mr. Hawkins?"

Hawkins forced a tight-lipped laugh. "Absolutely, sir. You can count on us."

"I always have. One of my advisors will be calling just before noon for an update. Make sure it's a good one."

"Yes, sir."

The phone call was over, and Hawkins felt several sharp pains in his left shoulder. Since when did political giants get involved in cases like this? The answer was simple: Since special interest groups had gained control of the man's office.

Hawkins kneaded his shoulder and the pains eased. It was all too complicated these days, too many people making deals and manipulating court cases behind the scenes.

The bonus money flashed across the checkbook in his mind. All one million dollars of it. Hawkins eased back into his chair. Maybe the job wasn't so complicated after all. Besides, the burden lay on Jordan Riley. If the walls fell in Jericho Park it would be Riley's fault. Certainly Hawkins had done everything in his power to see victory take place. He'd gotten the Evans girl fired and given her something to think about with the call from his friend at CBS. She had to know how much power the firm wielded.

They'd done as much as they could to eliminate Faith Evans as an obstacle—short of hiring a hit on her. Hawkins chuckled under his breath. Not that he'd ever be involved in something like that. HOUR *was* a human rights group, after all.

Besides, whoever was behind the money was interested in the firm long-term. Win this case, and there'd be plenty more "bonus" money down the road…that was the impression Hawkins had gotten.

He drew in a deep breath. They needed to win this case. Desperately. At the thought, his shoulder began to hurt again. For the first time in his life he found himself wishing the wacky religious freaks were right, that there actually was an almighty God. Because the way public opinion was tilting in Bethany, Pennsylvania, it was beginning to look like HOUR needed more than a little blackmail and string-pulling to pull this case off.

They needed a miracle.

The key players were gathered outside the courtroom—Jordan on one side of the hallway; Faith, Joshua, and the mayor of Bethany on the other—when the clerk found them and told them the news. Judge Webster had the flu. The hearing had been postponed for one week. A reporter from ABC, who had arrived an hour earlier, immediately sent a wire preventing what figured to be as many as a hundred journalists from wasting a trip. In addition, a bulletin went out across local television and radio, so that only a few people who failed to hear the news had to be sent home.

Jordan felt his heart sink as the clerk explained the situation. Another week. He'd have to stay in Bethany, hold press conferences, and attempt to sway public opinion for another week—all the while avoiding the one woman he couldn't stop thinking about. It was like being sentenced to a torture chamber.

He shot a discreet look at Faith, admiring the angle of her head, the way her eyes danced with life when she spoke to the older attorney. The compassion and kindness she'd shown as a child were still very much a part of her…but she had more fire now. His eyes traveled the length of her, taking in the way her elegant skirt swished about her ankles and clung to all the right places, the way her blond hair fell from a simple knot halfway down her back. Everything about her called to him, beckoned him in a way he was barely able to withstand.

Jordan didn't know why he was surprised. She'd always been beautiful—but back when they were friends and neighbors, he'd taken her beauty for granted. Now…when there was no way to bridge the distance between them, when the memory of her kiss the night before was more pressing on his mind than anything else—including the fate of the Jesus statue—now the very sight of her left him with a sense of longing and urgency he knew he could never act upon.

He let his gaze linger a moment longer, then frowned. She was keeping to herself, refusing to even glance in his direction. He didn't blame her. The things he'd told her were as true now as they'd been last night: regardless of the attraction they obviously felt for each other, there wasn't enough common ground between them to build a sand castle let alone a life together.

Jordan sighed and reached in his suit pocket for his cell phone. As he moved down the hallway, he dialed Hawkins's private office number. He leaned against the wall as the line rang twice, but before it could ring a third time he heard footsteps.

Jordan looked up. "T. J.?" At the sight of his partner, he felt the blood leave his face. What possible reason would T. J. have for showing up at the hearing? *He must've left New York before sunup.* His cheeks grew hot and anger like a mounting storm began to build. He disconnected the phone call and waited for an explanation.

"Hey, Jordan." T. J. looked around as he closed the distance between them, breathless from the walk. "Where's the crowd?"

Jordan's mind raced. One of two things had to be happening back at the office. Either the partners had suddenly lost confidence in him and sent T. J. to baby-sit, or there was a serious lack of communication between him and the others. Either option made Jordan's skin crawl.

One thing was certain: he had no intention of holding a conversation with T. J. in earshot of Faith and the others. He motioned to his friend and they found a place at the end of the hall, near a boxy windowsill. Both lawyers set their briefcases down as Jordan stared at T. J. and swore under his breath. "Here to take over?"

T. J.'s eyes were unnaturally wide and his smile looked painted on. "Of course not. Hawkins just thought you could use a little support. This is the big day, right?"

Jordan didn't blink. "It was postponed a week. Judge got sick." He paused, his eyes never leaving T. J.'s. "Don't lie to me, Teej. You didn't get in your car at four this morning and drive all the way to Bethany to wave at me from the back row. Tell me why you're here."

For the briefest moment it looked like T. J. was going to keep up the charade. He opened his mouth and was about to speak when his smile faded. Then, like a week-old helium balloon, his shoulders sagged and he thrust his hands in his pants pocket, shifting his gaze so that he stared out the window. "You weren't in your room last night." His voice was monotone, a statement of resignation more than anything else.

Jordan leaned in close, wondering just how much about this case was being discussed behind his back. "Teej, buddy, I didn't tell you where I was staying."

T. J. nodded, his eyes still locked on something outside the window, a faraway look on his face. "Hawkins told me."

Jordan felt like he was trapped in some strange dream. He hadn't told Hawkins where he was staying, either. Of course there were only three motels in Bethany, so Jordan wouldn't have been hard to find. But the idea of a partner at HOUR—one of the top legal talents in all the country—trailing him like some two-bit private investigator sent a chill down his spine. He grabbed T. J.'s arm, tightening his grip until his friend made eye contact with him. "You drove down here because I was out last night?" Jordan released a single chuckle as he let go of T. J. "Call me crazy, but I'm not seeing the connection."

"If you tell Hawkins I told you, we'll both be fired."

T. J.'s flat voice told Jordan his suspicions were right. Hawkins—and maybe the other partners—didn't trust him with the Bethany case. The truth made his blood boil, and he could feel his face growing hot.

He spoke in a barely contained whisper, sliding the words through lips tight with fury. "I'm waiting."

T. J. sighed and leaned against the windowsill. He was still having trouble making eye contact. "They want this case bad, Jordan. There's a lot of...*bonus money* at stake."

Jordan remembered the ten thousand dollars he'd been promised. "You know about it?"

"Yeah." T. J. huffed. "I know about it."

Jordan felt like a man in a foreign country trying to understand a language he'd never heard before. "Where's it coming from?"

"From the top, Jordan." T. J. narrowed his eyes, and Jordan could see his friend's reluctance to talk.

"Hawkins?"

"A lot higher than that."

"Meaning what? And how much is there? Why this case?" Jordan fired the questions as quickly as they came to mind. He glanced down the hallway and saw Faith and the others leaving, making their way toward the stairs. *Can't you even turn around and look at me, Faith?*

But she was caught up in a conversation with the mayor and never glanced his direction. When she was gone, Jordan turned his attention back to T. J. "I need answers, Teej. Tell me what you know."

His friend shrugged again and shook his head. "It's political."

"Political? You mean someone from the state?"

T. J. nodded. "Someone very high up the ladder."

Again there was no way Jordan could make sense of the situation. High up the ladder? What stake could anyone at the state level possibly have in the Jesus statue case? "Okay, give me the name."

"I don't know. Honest, Jordan." T. J. squirmed and shifted positions. "You gotta believe me."

Jordan exhaled slowly and gazed out the window before turning back to his friend. "So you're saying the money came from an elected official?"

"I don't know how much HOUR's getting, but you have to win the case." He hesitated, and Jordan had the distinct feeling he was being lied to. "A permanent wall needs to go up around the Jesus statue or the whole thing's off."

"And that's why you're here?" His anger burned still hotter. If someone with significant political influence and financial backing felt it was important to win the Bethany case, Jordan should have been in meetings with Hawkins daily. It made no sense that T. J. was involved in those meetings instead. After all, the Jesus statue was Jordan's idea.

"Hawkins asked me to call you last night, but you were out. He got worried and told me to come. Wanted to make sure...you know, someone hadn't gotten to you."

Jordan's astonishment came out as another laugh. "You guys watch too many movies, Teej. This is a small-town case. I don't care how much national attention it gets, no one's hiring a hit on me." He crossed his arms. "What's the real reason? Hawkins didn't think I could pull out a victory?"

"No, Jordan. I swear. That wasn't it…" T. J. sounded like a bad actor, and Jordan was suddenly out of patience with him.

"Look, friend, why don't you get in your car and drive back to New York. Tell my boss that I've got things perfectly under control, thank you. And that I'm single and can stay out all night if I want to. Tell him if he thinks I need a backup he should say so to my face. If not, he should keep his nose out of my cases. The only reason I'm here at all is because he ordered it."

T. J. looked like he had pebbles in his shoes. "And…uh…what about the woman?"

Jordan lowered his eyebrows and felt the knot in his stomach grow. "Faith? The woman who bought the park property? The newscaster?"

His friend nodded. "Is she…you know, are the two of you seeing each other?"

A feeling of betrayal worked its way through Jordan's veins. "Is *that* what this is all about? Hawkins thinks I'm siding with the enemy?"

T. J. grimaced. "No, not at all. I was just asking. You told me you two used to be friends."

Jordan pictured himself kissing Faith in the park the night before. "Yeah, when we were thirteen. Obviously the word back at the office is that I'm caving in, lost in love, and suddenly inept at pulling off a simple separation case." He leveled his gaze at T. J. "Tell me something, Teej…how did Hawkins know about the girl? Because he asked me the same thing last week."

A knowing look took over his friend's features. "You don't think I…Jordan, I wouldn't have told him something like that. He must have guessed. Everyone knows you used to live here…Faith's a local girl…it wouldn't have been a stretch to think you might have known her."

Again Jordan had the strong sense T. J. was lying. He gestured toward the stairs. "Go home, Teej. And don't forget something…"

T. J. was already starting to retreat, taking small backward steps toward the stairs as though being around Jordan was more stress than he could handle. "What? Just say the word, buddy. Anything I can do for you…"

Jordan paused, assaulted by doubts, and studied T. J. one last time. "Don't forget you're supposed to be my friend."

Considering the way she'd come into the world, little Jordan Lee Benson turned out to be a sweet, content newborn, sleeping through the night almost from the beginning and giving Heidi's body time to recuperate from the traumatic delivery. She and Charles moved to Bethany on schedule, and Charles hired a housekeeper to help unpack the boxes and keep up the dishes and laundry. That Wednesday morning was the woman's first day off, and Heidi had decided to take it slow.

She'd already fed Jordan Lee, and the baby was down for her morning nap, giving Heidi a couple hours to herself. She sipped a cup of decaf and looked for something to read in yesterday's pile of mail. Junk mail…coupon flyers…advertise-ments… She scanned each item and tossed the stack in the trash. Then her eyes fell on the local paper. Photographers had been by Charles's office and taken pictures of him for a clinic ad announcing his arrival on staff. Wasn't that supposed to run on Wednesdays?

She slid the paper closer and tried to make sense of the photo on the front page. It looked like a construction site—some sort of partially finished building made of what looked like plywood. She found the headline and read it out loud: "Hearing on Jesus Statue Postponed."

She knit her eyebrows together and found the first paragraph. "A hearing to decide whether or not walls around the Jesus statue in Bethany's Jericho Park will become permanent was postponed yesterday. The hearing was rescheduled for Tuesday at which time court officials expect to have nearly a hundred members of the media and more than a thousand local residents in attendance for the final decision on what has become a case of national interest…"

Heidi sat up straighter in her chair. The Jesus statue had walls around it? Why hadn't she noticed? Who had put them up, and how had the case drawn national attention when she was only reading about it now? The answer was obvious. She hadn't so much as watched a news program or looked at a paper since having Jordan Lee.

Sadness like a dark storm cloud came over Heidi's morning. Was that what life had come to? A statue that had stood practically forever in a city park had to be removed because it depicted Jesus Christ? She thought about her brother, about how much time he'd spent at the park, staring at the statue. He would have been devas-tated to see it surrounded by plywood. She rested her head on her fingertips as she continued reading the article.

The information was both awful and fascinating. Joshua Nunn, a local attorney who headed up an organization called the Religious Freedom Institute was involved, as well as a former newscaster, Faith Evans. She had come forward and purchased the park land in an effort to keep the statue standing. The article said Faith had lost her job as a result of purchasing the land.

She thought about that. *Faith…Faith…Faith.* Hadn't Heidi and her family known a Faith back when they lived in Bethany? It began coming back to her, and she suddenly remembered. Faith Moses, that was it. She was the girl who lived next door, Jordan's friend. Heidi's eyes darted back to the place in the article where it listed the woman's last name and her heart sank. Faith Evans. It had to be someone differ-ent. Too many years had passed and besides, there were lots of women named Faith.

Heidi found her place in the article. The entire situation started because of a law-suit filed by an attorney from the HOUR organization. Heidi rolled her eyes and huffed softly. The HOUR organization was always meddling in other people's busi-ness and calling it human rights. What *right* was it of theirs to come to Bethany and sue the city over something that had never involved them in the first place? She con-tinued reading. The attorney's name was…was…

Heidi's breath caught in her throat. She felt as though she were free-falling from thirty thousand feet. It took ten seconds to remind herself to breathe, to assure herself that it was only some strange, twisted coincidence. Obviously it wasn't him. Her brother had been killed sixteen years earlier in the camp accident. But that didn't change the way her body reacted to what she was seeing in print before her.

The attorney who wanted the statue walled up was a man who worked for HOUR. A man named Jordan Riley.

Jordan Riley.

Heidi let her eyes settle on his name as the memories came back again, images of her brother sheltering her in his strong arms at their mother's funeral, of him holding her that awful afternoon on Oak Street when the state social workers took her away. Of the terrible moment when her foster father told her about the accident. She looked at the attorney's name again.

Jordan Riley.

Heidi blinked and looked away. It was an odd coincidence, but that was all. Her Jordan was dead. And if he *had* been alive, he would have been fighting alongside Faith Evans, whoever she was. He loved the Jesus statue as much as anyone in Bethany.

Besides, there was no way on earth Jordan would have represented a law firm like HOUR. Not after the way he'd loved the Lord, the way he'd trusted in Him that last year they were together. Jordan's faith had been rock-solid, no doubt. It was something Heidi remembered most about her brother.

She finished reading the article, folded the newspaper, and bowed her head.

Lord, the people of Bethany need Your help. Please be with the judge as he has an important decision to make. Let him see with Your eyes, reason with Your heart at the hearing next week. And be with this Jordan Riley, whoever he is. Help him to know that You're real and that You love him. Most of all work in his heart so that—

Jordan Lee's hungry cry interrupted the prayer, and Heidi finished quickly as she headed toward the baby's room. Ten minutes later she was feeding her tiny daughter, cooing at her and reveling in the joy of their shared private moments. When the feeding was finished she changed the baby's diaper, did laundry, and fixed herself a chicken sandwich. By one o'clock, as Heidi finally fell into bed for a much-needed nap, the walled-in Jesus statue, the woman named Faith, and the confused young attorney named Jordan Riley, were the farthest things from her mind.

23

$\mathcal{R}$ain beat a steady rhythm on the town of Bethany that Wednesday. With almost a week before the rescheduled hearing, Faith decided to take in an afternoon movie with Rosa. That left the morning with nothing to do but imagine how the next few weeks might play out. With any luck, the time would pass quickly. The peaceful protest wasn't scheduled until Friday night, when a dozen churches from the Philadelphia area had promised to join the people of Bethany in an effort to pray together about the judge's decision.

Things had been so crazy that Faith had found little time to read her Bible—something she'd enjoyed doing since childhood. Reading Scripture might be a chore for some people, a duty that went along with the calling to follow Christ. But for Faith it had always been more than that. The Bible was alive and active, and no matter what issue she faced, God's Word had something to say about it. She couldn't remember how many times as a little girl she'd run through the house looking for her father to show him some Scripture he'd probably seen a hundred times.

"Can you believe it, Daddy? Like Jesus wrote it there just for me!"

Faith's fervor hadn't diminished any during the years Jordan lived next door. In fact, until his mother got sick, Jordan seemed to share her enthusiasm. Faith could hear him still, commenting on various Bible stories while they sat side by side on her parents' sofa. "When I read the Bible it's like I have this calm feeling. Like God has everything in control."

Faith had already showered, and her damp hair hung loosely down her back. That was it really, wasn't it? God had it all under control. She thought about the sermon that past Sunday. They'd been reading in the book of Luke, the twenty-second chapter, where Judas made plans to betray Jesus and Jesus made plans to have the Last Supper with His disciples.

Faith settled into her father's favorite rocker and opened her Bible to that section of Scripture again. On the surface, it looked like everything was falling apart for Jesus. Days earlier He'd come into town on the back of a donkey to the shouts of praise from hundreds of thousands of people. Crowds openly calling Him King and acknowledging Him for who He was. But now His entire ministry seemed to be unraveling. The devil—who had been looking for a chance to bring down the Savior since Jesus' birth thirty-three years earlier—saw a weak link in Judas Iscariot. And so, as Scripture taught, Satan caused Judas to accept a bribe from the chief priests in exchange for betraying his Teacher.

Faith loved the way Pastor Todd Pynch taught the story. He smiled often and even laughed on occasion, so that Faith and everyone in the small congregation felt as though they were there alongside Jesus, walking near the donkey, sitting across the table in the upper room.

Immediately after Judas's decision to betray Jesus, the Lord made plans with two of his trusted followers to prepare for the Passover meal. Faith smiled as she recalled Pastor Pynch's comments: "Notice how Judas was left out of the loop as they prepared that meal. Nothing happened that weekend that wasn't exactly as Jesus had planned it. His life wasn't taken from Him. He gave it up willingly."

The story brought Faith as much comfort now as it had last Sunday. Especially given her current situation. She was a marked woman, with no likely prospects for a television news job unless she was willing to somehow back out of the Jesus statue case—which she wasn't. There were no signs of potential adoptive parents for Rosa Lee, and Faith's childhood friend had not only turned on God, but because of his bitterness, was willing even to stand against her in court. Meanwhile a statue of Jesus Christ, her loving Lord, could very likely wind up hidden behind a brick wall.

Indeed, things seemed to be spinning in all the wrong directions.

But the truth was something altogether different. Something Joshua had tried to explain to her, the very point the minister had reiterated at church last Sunday.

God was in control.

Wherever there were people who loved Him, who lived according to His truth, God would continue to work all things to the good. Even in this.

Faith closed her Bible and stared outside at the garden her father had planted. Shrubs and rosebushes stood barren but for a few tenacious buds. *You were in control back when Jordan's mother died too, right, God?*

She flipped to the very last page in her Bible, the blank space after the concordance and maps and historical facts. The place for personal notes. Faith had gotten the Bible for her thirteenth birthday, and back then, back when the Lord didn't seem to be hearing Jordan, she'd written her thoughts on that last page.

It had been years since she'd read what was written there, but today, in the silence of her parents' house, she was drawn back the way a moth is drawn to a porch light. She was suddenly desperate to remember her little-girl heart and the way she'd felt when life was falling apart for Jordan Riley.

She'd written dates next to her earliest entries; her words scribbled in the smallest print possible. *Nov. 3, 1985—Why is this happening, God? I told Jordan to read the verse that says, "Whatever you ask in my name, I will do it..." But his mom is still sick. Help me understand...*

And another entry six weeks later: *Jordan's mother died…his sister got taken away… Didn't we pray hard enough, Lord? Didn't You hear us?*

Faith let her eyes read over those entries again and again until tears clouded her vision. Suddenly she understood her own motive for waging battle on behalf of the Jesus statue. It was as clear as if someone had lit a match in the darkest cavern of her heart. The losses Jordan suffered that fall had changed her as much as they'd changed him. Indeed, they'd affected everything about their lives since then.

For Jordan, the unanswered questions and bitter seeds of doubt had sprouted into a full-blown war that raged in his heart to this day. He'd taken up his position, deciding that God either didn't exist or He was the enemy.

Faith's reaction had been the exact opposite.

At first, with no answers to anchor to, Faith had lived life with a lack of conviction. She spoke like a believer, attended church, and read her Bible, but her life choices bore out something altogether different. The hard decisions—what to do when Mike Dillon pressured her, when to take a stand in her role as television anchor, whether to adopt Rosa Lee—were decisions she made without seeking God. Instead they were decisions she made out of fear. Fear of losing Mike, losing her job, failing Rosa Lee.

And now, for the first time, she understood why.

Deep down in the hidden places of her heart Faith had been afraid that if she depended on God, He would let her down…just as He'd let Jordan down the winter of 1985. Without consciously acknowledging it, she'd decided long ago it was better not to ask much of God. And she'd built her life around that philosophy…until the Jesus statue came under attack.

In light of her father's death and the judge's mandate that the statue be removed, Faith had unwittingly recognized it was time. Time to take God out of the closet and see what He might do in response to her prayers.

That was why this case meant so much to her. She desperately wanted to believe again, the way she'd believed in the days before Jordan's mother got sick. The Jesus statue wasn't the only thing with walls around it. Faith had put walls around God Himself. Protective walls, so that the Lord of her childhood might never be called upon to do anything miraculous, anything that might not come to pass and cause Faith to be disappointed. Anything that might put Him in a bad light.

The rain was coming harder now, and tears came from the depths of Faith's soul. She ran her fingers over her neatly written words, the painfully penned cries that had come from her childlike heart. She would never know this side of heaven why God had taken Jordan's mother, why life had been so hard on him back then. But she knew what Scripture taught. She closed her eyes and let the verse from John wash over her soul: "In this world you will have trouble. But take heart! I have overcome the world."

That was it, wasn't it?

Jesus had overcome the world. Regardless of how things turned out here and now, He was in control. Just like He'd been back when Judas agreed to betray Him.

Nothing, not death or anger or lawsuits or lost jobs or homeless children, nothing could derail God's plans. The revelation felt like someone had lifted a truck from Faith's shoulders, and she desperately wished the same for Jordan.

A knock at the door pulled Faith back to reality. She closed her Bible, thanking God for letting her finally understand the fear that had eaten at her all her life, the poor decisions she'd made as a young adult, and her current determination to fight for what was right. She padded across the living room and opened the front door.

What she saw sent her heart spinning into her throat.

"Jordan…" He was so handsome, so much like the boy he'd been all those years ago. And this time the hard edges around his eyes were gone. She composed herself and held his gaze for a moment before speaking. *God, I don't know why You brought him here, but use me…give me the words to say so that maybe he could understand You better.* She swallowed hard and motioned toward the living room. "Come in."

Jordan had debated long and hard about making the trip to Faith's house, but in the end he knew he had no choice. With her skills as a reporter and her status as the town's most favorite person, she was possibly the only one who could help him find the files. And they needed to be found. Ever since their conversation the other day he'd wondered if somehow Heidi had gotten wrong information. If she believed—wherever she was—that he was dead, buried these past sixteen years. The visit would be purely informational, he'd told himself. He'd ask Faith for help, but avoid anything else.

Then she opened the door—and he had to order his emotions back into place. What kind of fool was he to fight against a woman like Faith Evans? Her eyes were so blue he felt sucked into them, and he struggled to remember why he'd come at all. She interrupted his thoughts with her invitation.

"Thanks." He wiped his feet on the outdoor mat and stepped inside. "Sorry to bug you at home."

Faith crossed her arms and lowered her head, her eyes lifted to his expectantly.

Jordan felt like a blushing schoolboy in her presence and he forced himself to speak. "I'm…sorry I didn't talk to you the other day at court."

She shrugged, her face still full of questions. Obviously he hadn't come to tell her that.

"Is your mother home?" Through all that had happened those past few months in Bethany he was sorry he hadn't seen Faith's mom, the woman who had been so helpful those last weeks before his own mother died.

"No." Faith's voice was quiet, guarded. "She's still in Chicago."

He nodded and studied his wet shoes as the tension between them grew. He wanted to take her in his arms and apologize for the other night, tell her that he needed her, and beg her not to hate him for his views against God. But he knew the idea was ridiculous. If he was going to get her help with the files, he'd better ask her now, before she kicked him out. He lifted his eyes to hers and held her gaze. "I need your help."

She stepped back and something in her features softened. "Take off your shoes." She leaned against the wall, her head angled in a way that reminded him of the young girl she'd been. "We can talk in the living room."

Jordan slipped off his loafers and followed her, waiting until she settled into the recliner before taking the chair beside her. "I want to see Heidi's file…in case the state gave her the wrong information."

"About the accident?" Faith's tone was hesitant, but at least she hadn't asked him to leave.

"Right. I've been to the courthouse and the records are sealed. I guess the file might even be at a different office now." He shrugged. "No one gives me a straight answer."

Faith nodded and shot a look at the ceiling. After a moment her gaze returned to his. "What about *your* file? Have you looked at that?"

Jordan settled back in his chair and stared at her. "Why my file? There wouldn't be anything there about Heidi."

"No, but there'd be information about you. Like whether the state thinks you died."

Jordan shook his head, trying to follow her reasoning. "No, because the state sent me to the next boys' camp."

"Right, but it was in a different state. It's possible they opened a new file on you there and never corrected the one in Pennsylvania."

Jordan felt the smallest ray of hope pierce his heart. "I have nothing to do today or tomorrow and I thought…" He exhaled slowly and dropped his gaze to the floor. Why should she help him now, after he'd been so rude the other night, letting her run off without even trying to stop her.

Before he could voice his question, before he could excuse himself and tell her to forget he'd ever come, he felt her hand on his. He caught her look and saw a love he hadn't known since leaving Oak Street. A love for which he had no earthly explanation. "Jordan, I understand your political stance. I know we're public enemies at this point, but that doesn't change who I am inside. Or who you are." She smiled through eyes wet with tears. "I'll do whatever I can to help you."

They took his car and entered the courthouse thirty minutes later.

Faith was careful not to let her emotions get the upper hand, not to let Jordan too close. She did not want a repeat of the tender, stolen moments they'd exchanged the other night—not when she knew there was no future for Jordan and her. Not together, anyway.

As they parked the car, Jordan turned to her, and she could see the apology in his eyes. "This could be uncomfortable for you."

She understood. People would recognize them and wonder why they were together. Faith refused to acknowledge her concerns about the matter. "For you, too."

The muscles in his jaw tensed, and he caught her gaze and held it. "I couldn't care less what people think about me."

Faith wondered at the strength of his statement. She'd seen him talking to a man who was obviously a colleague the other day at court. Clearly the case held great significance to him both professionally and personally. But that wasn't her concern. She cast him a guarded smile and opened the car door. "Okay, let's go."

Jordan wore a sweatshirt, blue jeans, and a baseball cap, and Faith figured the lack of a suit would help hide his identity. He kept his gaze on the floor, the bill of his cap down as they made their way to the front desk. Faith recognized the woman at the counter and smiled. "Hey, Cheri, how're you doing?"

The woman's eyes instantly lit up, and she grinned at Faith. "I've seen you on TV and in the papers, Faith. Everyone's so proud of you…giving up your job and all." The woman leaned forward as though she had an important secret. "The whole town's rooting for you."

The woman's words warmed Faith's heart, and again she thought of the revelation she'd had earlier that morning. No matter how it looked, God was in control. "Thanks, Cheri."

The woman glanced at Jordan, who was standing a ways off looking at a pamphlet he'd picked up from the counter. Faith was quick to explain. "He's an old friend."

Apparently Cheri didn't recognize him, and she turned her attention back to Faith. "So what can I do for you?"

"Well…" Faith moved as close as she could against the counter. She didn't want one of the other clerks to hear her request. Cheri was an acquaintance from high school, and Faith was fairly certain the woman would get whatever files Faith needed. Even if it meant bending a rule or two. "I need to see a couple foster care files. They might be sealed, but I'll only take a few minutes with them."

Nervousness flashed in Cheri's eyes, but she nodded. "Okay, I'll see what I can do. What're the names?"

Faith paused. "Heidi and Jordan Riley. They were brother and sister."

As soon as Faith said the names, Cheri's eyes opened wide. "The same Jordan Riley who's attacking our town?"

Faith had hoped the woman wouldn't ask, but now she had no choice but to be honest. She tried to sound confident. "Exactly."

Cheri's eyebrows bunched in the center of her forehead. "Does this have something to do with the Jesus statue case?"

Adrenaline flooded Faith's bloodstream as she searched for an honest answer. Did it have something to do with the case? Well, if the files helped Jordan find Heidi and if that, in turn, helped him get past his anger with God…then it would have everything to do with the case. "Yes." She nodded her head firmly. "Yes, it does."

That was all she needed to say. Cheri's eyes danced, and Faith could see she was grateful to be part of Faith's plans to outdo Bethany's enemy. "Two separate files, right? One for each of them?"

Faith nodded. "Right."

"Okay, wait here." She cast a glance at the workers stationed on either side of her and lowered her voice to a whisper. "I'll see what I can find."

Cheri disappeared, and Jordan was immediately at her side. "You asked for both?" He kept his gaze fixed on the voting brochure still in his hands but she could hear the disbelief and gratitude in his voice.

"Can't hurt." She nodded toward a counter with other pamphlets and information. "Keep busy. The last thing I want is her recognizing you."

Several minutes went by before Cheri returned. She had two folders tucked under her right arm. She approached the counter with a forced air of nonchalance and slipped them over to Faith as quickly as she could. "Twenty minutes, Faith." She gave Faith a wink. "The supervisor'll be back after that, and I need them put away. She'd have my head on a platter if she found out what I was doing."

"Thanks." Faith swept the folders up against her body and turned to leave. She didn't check to see if Jordan was behind her, but she could feel him there, a few steps back. As she made her way back outside she kept her face focused on the ground ahead of her. Now that she had the files, she wanted to avoid being recognized. Two minutes later she and Jordan were back in his car.

Jordan's features were pale. "I can't believe it was so easy. I've tried getting my hands on Heidi's file every year since I was twenty-two."

"Drive to the back of the side lot. No one parks there." Faith kept the files tightly on her lap while Jordan did as she said.

When they'd found a spot far from other cars, Jordan turned to her, his eyes filled with wonder. "No matter what these files contain…you'll never know how much this means to me, Faith."

She could feel her heart getting sucked into the moment and she steeled herself, giving him only a quick smile and pushing the folders into his hands. "Read them. We have less than twenty minutes."

Jordan looked at his file first. There were several entries beginning with the report from what appeared to be a neighbor. It stated that Jordan and Heidi were living alone after the death of their mother. He'd always wondered who'd reported them, but the man's name didn't look familiar. It didn't matter. The neighbor wasn't to blame; certainly he'd had good intentions. State officials would have figured it out eventually.

Jordan scanned the pages as quickly as he could, flipping past the report detailing the day Jordan and Heidi were brought into care and the one that came a few days later: *"Jordan is a very unhappy boy. He talks about his sister constantly and threatens to run away. He appears to be a troublemaker."* For a brief instant, Jordan wanted to cry for the boy he'd been and the way the state officials had wrongly labeled him. There hadn't been a trace of troublemaker in him. Just a brokenhearted boy who had promised his dying mother he'd take care of his sister.

He flipped a few more pages and saw the entry when he'd finally made good on his threat to run away from the temporary foster home: *"Police say Jordan was belligerent and borderline violent. He kept insisting that his sister lived nearby and she needed him. Social worker says the girl is adjusting fine and that a visit will be arranged sometime in the next two weeks."*

"Anything good?" Faith's voice brought him back to reality, and Jordan shook his head. He'd almost forgotten she was still in the car.

"Not yet."

"Fifteen minutes, okay?"

"Okay." He skipped a few entries and found the one marked Accident Report. The hairs on his arms stood up as he searched the tiny fields of information looking for a sign, something to confirm that his condition had been wrongly reported. Finally, at the bottom of the document, he found what he was looking for. In a section marked Condition of Child was written one word: Deceased.

Deceased...deceased...deceased...

Jordan's eyes moved over the word again and again until he felt sick to his stomach. A note was attached after the report: *"Collapsed cave accident claimed the lives of numerous boys at the camp including Jordan Riley. State to investigate. Case closed."*

It was the last notation in the file.

"It's right here..." He pointed to the sheet and angled it so Faith could read the important parts. "They...they think I'm dead."

Faith stared at the report, her face a mask of concern. "Your active file must be in New Jersey." She sighed. "That happens sometimes. The system has too many files and when someone gets something wrong—especially if the subject moves out of state—sometimes the error is never found."

Jordan stared at the entry and his hands began to tremble. The real answers lay in the other folder—Heidi's file. He closed his own and handed it back to Faith. Then he did what he'd wanted to do for sixteen years—open the document that would give him a window to Heidi's other life, the one she had lived since that awful afternoon when the state worker took her away.

He drew a steadying breath and began reading. The reports were arranged in chronological order, stapled to the inside so that they could be read correctly. He saw entries similar to those in his file—a report from the neighbor stating that a brother and sister were living alone, the report when she was taken into custody, and a report from the first foster home where she'd been taken. Jordan read every word, soaking it in, desperate to know what had happened to her.

"Heidi is very cooperative. She is sad about the loss of her mother and talks of wanting to see her brother. But she has made great strides in getting along with her foster family. She is agreeable and despite her age would make an excellent candidate for adoption."

She was always such a good girl. Of course she'd been compliant. She'd been promised a reunion with Jordan, guaranteed that the two of them would be together again. She'd probably figured it would happen faster if she got along with her foster parents. Tears burned at Jordan's eyes and he blinked them back. He had no patience for blurred vision. Not now when he needed to see every stroke of the pen.

He scanned over three more similar reports and found one that coincided with the date he'd been sent to the boys' camp: *"Heidi's brother, Jordan Riley, was caught after running away from his foster home. He is considered unstable and a threat to his sister's security. He has been placed at Southridge Boys' Camp until further notice. This worker no longer recommends that Jordan have scheduled visits with his sister."*

Jordan gritted his teeth as a tear landed squarely on the report. How *dare* a stranger make a recommendation like that? What did a social worker know about Jordan or the relationship he and Heidi shared? He wished he could find the man today…he'd grab him by the collar and—

Jordan dismissed the thought. There wasn't time to waste hating people who no longer existed. This was about Heidi and him and no one else. He flipped the page and saw an entry marked Special Report. His heart thudded in his chest as he let his eyes work their way down the page. The report detailed how Heidi had been given the news that her brother had been in an accident at Southridge Boys' Camp: *"Heidi cried for several hours and asked if she could go to the hospital to see her brother. At this time Jordan Riley's status—whether he survived the accident or not—is unclear."*

Jordan turned the page, barely aware that he was holding his breath. The next page told him all he needed to know. It was another special report and it indicated that Heidi had been told the news: Her brother had been killed in a collapsed cave incident at Southridge Boys' Camp. *"Heidi is very upset and had to be sedated in order to sleep. State worker recommends extended counseling to deal with issues of grief and loss."*

The words seared Jordan's heart like a branding iron, filling in the places that had only been chasms of darkness and uncertainty. So it was true after all; so soon after losing their mother Heidi had been forced to deal with Jordan's death as well. Tears coursed down Jordan's face and he let his head hang for a moment. When he looked up again, he showed the report to Faith.

She read it and then looked up at him, her eyes wet too. "Jordan, it's awful. All this time—" She reached for his hand, much the way a friend might reach out in the face of bad news. "No wonder she hasn't looked for you."

The missing pieces of his past were filling in quickly, but still there was a part Jordan wanted. "How much time?"

"Seven minutes."

Jordan nodded and flipped quickly through the reports, scanning the entries describing how well Heidi was responding to counseling, how she appeared to be bonding with her social worker, and how a placement had been suggested. Then abruptly he was at the last entry: *"Transfer was made to a permanent foster-adopt home. State workers believe Heidi will make a complete and successful adjustment and that adoption will be completed within the year."* In the place designated for the adoptive parents' names, there was just one word scribbled:

Morand.

"Morand?" Jordan practically shouted the word. He closed the file and smacked it against his thigh. "How is *that* supposed to help me find her?"

Faith squeezed his hand, released it, and folded her fingers together in her lap once more. "It isn't much to go on."

Jordan turned to the back of the file and scanned the last entry one more time. "No address, no phone number. For all I know they live at the other end of the state or halfway across the world." Frustration grabbed him like a vise grip and he felt like he was suffocating under a blanket-sized piece of plastic wrap. "That was fifteen years ago. There's no way I could find her now."

For all the answers the files provided, in some ways it was worse for Jordan than if he'd never seen them at all because now there truly was no hope. Heidi was gone from his life forever. Another wave of tears came, and he closed his eyes. Without warning, his mother's voice came back to him. *"Pray, Jordan...don't ever stop praying...don't ever stop praying."*

"Jordan—" Faith's voice interrupted his memories—"I know you don't believe in what I'm about to do, but it's all I know."

He opened his eyes and watched her bow her head, her heart and mind focused on a God he'd spent half his life fighting against. How had she known what he was thinking? That his mother's dying words on prayer had been rattling through his mind?

"Lord, we're out of options. You know Jordan's heart...the loss he's already suffered."

She paused, as though searching for the right words. The idea of Faith praying when it could not possibly do any good reminded Jordan of his mother again, her unwavering beliefs even on her deathbed.

Faith's voice rose a notch. "We have nowhere to turn now, no way to find Jordan's sister. Please, Father, bring them back together. I don't know how You're going to do it, Lord, but right here...right now...I thank You for what miracle You're working in this. No matter what happens, God, I trust You. And I'll always love you. In Jesus' name, amen."

She opened her eyes, and the light he saw there was too much for him. He shifted his attention to the folder in his hands. "I appreciate what you're trying to do, Faith, but there's no point."

Faith sighed hard and leaned back against the headrest, her eyes fixed somewhere on the ceiling of Jordan's car. "I don't understand why your mother died, Jordan. Or why Heidi was told you were killed in the accident. But I know the God I believe in is real." She was crying now, and the gentleness of a moment earlier was replaced by something Jordan couldn't quite identify. Anger maybe, or a deep, unquenchable fear. She stared at him, her eyes begging him to understand. "If I'm wrong about God, if your mom was wrong...what have we lost?" She let her question sink in. "But if you're wrong, Jordan..."

There was no need to finish her statement; he'd heard it before both from high school and college acquaintances, and always he'd had an answer for them: *"I'd rather live a truth that was doomed than a life of hope based on lies."*

This time, though, the words wouldn't come. It was as though the combination of reading about Heidi and remembering his mother while sharing the intimate space of his car's front seat with Faith was too much for him. He handed Heidi's file back to Faith and gripped the steering wheel with both hands. Then he looked at Faith and said the only thing he could think to say.

"Let's get the files back."

24

On the surface there wasn't any reason why Joshua Nunn should think the phone call strange. After all, Faith was at the center of one of the most fascinating religious rights cases ever. In fact, it wasn't so much the type of call or even the caller's voice that stuck with Joshua hours later.

It was the timing.

He'd been having a midday quiet time with God, alone in his office, wondering what more he could possibly do to convince the judge that a ten-foot high wall was unreasonable. The Scripture that day was from the book of Joshua, and it confirmed everything the Lord had been laying on his heart since he'd first heard about the case: "Be strong and courageous. God will go before you. You will not have to fight this battle…the place where you are standing is holy ground."

The verses all seemed to run together, lifting Joshua and taking away his fear. He had no idea how God was going to pull off a victory, but he believed with all his heart that somehow the Lord would come out a winner. Even if it didn't look that way to the public.

That afternoon he'd felt compelled to pray for wisdom. Like he'd done so many times in his life, he slid to his knees, closed his eyes, and raised his hands as high toward heaven as he could. "Lord, show me the way. I've done all I can do and still HOUR has the advantage. If there's something I'm missing, some way that victory might belong to You, Your people, show me now, Lord. I'm almost out of t—"

The phone rang before he could finish the word. Joshua did not immediately see the interruption as an answer to prayer, but rather as one in a series of distractions that were a regular part of his life lately. He quickly finished his talk with God and answered the phone.

"Religious Freedom Institute, Joshua Nunn."

"Uh…yes, I'm looking for Faith Evans." The woman seemed nervous, not sure of herself. "I got your number from information and thought maybe…is there some way you could get her a message?"

Joshua scooted onto the edge of his chair and forced himself to change gears. "Faith doesn't work here, if that's what you mean. But I can get a message to her."

"Are you the…the attorney representing the city of Bethany?"

The woman was obviously a fan of some kind, calling to wish them God's blessings or offer prayer support. Joshua inhaled slowly. "Yes, ma'am." He didn't want to seem rude but he had no time to waste on the phone. "Why don't you give me your name and number, and I'll give Faith the message?"

There was a pause and again Joshua had the sense the woman was uptight about something. "My name's Heidi Benson." She rattled off her phone number with what seemed like a sense of urgency. "I'd really like to talk to Faith about the case. I…I used to live in Bethany a long time ago and the statue meant a great deal to my mother."

Joshua's heart went out to the woman. "I'll give her the message this afternoon."

Long after the phone call ended, Joshua was haunted by something in the woman's voice. It was a feeling that was completely unfounded, yet it remained. Joshua tried reaching Faith seven times before she finally answered the phone at just before five o'clock.

"Hello?" She sounded relaxed and upbeat, and Joshua was relieved. Faith had been under too much pressure lately, and he knew she was operating on sheer Holy Spirit power.

"You've been busy today." Joshua didn't want to question her about her absence. With everything going on, she deserved time to herself. "I've been calling you all afternoon."

"I took Rosa to the movies." She seemed breathless, as though she'd just come in the door. "It's snowing outside, Joshua. It'll be a perfect Thanksgiving."

The holiday was just eight days away and until Faith's mention of it, Joshua had barely considered how quickly it was approaching. He glanced out his office window and saw Main Street covered in an inch of powder. "Well, I'll be. First real snow of the season."

"Okay, what's so important?" Faith had caught her breath and sounded ready to chat.

"A woman called you. Wants to talk about the Jesus statue. She used to live here and the statue mattered a lot to her mother. I have her name and number for you."

"Just a minute." It wasn't the first time such a conversation had transpired between the two of them, and after several seconds Faith returned with a pen and paper. "What is it?"

Joshua gave her the phone number and hesitated. "I don't know, Faith. Something about this one feels strange. The Lord kept putting it on my heart over and over again."

Faith chuckled. "You're just an old softie, Joshua. Now tell me her name so I can call her back."

"Her name? Oh, right." He looked at his notepad again. "Heidi…Heidi Benson."

When Joshua said the woman's first name, Faith about fell from her seat. But as she wrote down the last name she knew it couldn't be the same Heidi. By now Heidi

Morand—or whoever she was—could have been anywhere. Besides, the phone number had a Bethany prefix. If Jordan's sister had lived in Bethany all this time she would have come forward a lot sooner, wouldn't she?

Faith thought back over the day and how Jordan had closed down after reading Heidi's file. Especially in light of her prayer that God help them find Heidi. They'd gone back to the courthouse, and she'd returned the file while Jordan waited in the car. After that he hadn't spoken much until he dropped her off.

"Like I said, I'll never forget this. You took a risk for me, Faith. It means a lot." Jordan's eyes were still teary, but he stopped short of hugging her or doing anything that could have been misconstrued.

After he was gone Faith was grateful for her plans with Rosa Lee. The time with Jordan had been hard on her heart and she needed a distraction. An old theater in town was showing reruns of favorite kids' movies throughout November, and they ended up seeing *The Prince of Egypt*.

Faith had to smile at the way God drilled a message home. First the sermon on Luke and Jesus' final days, then her realizations about her own life, and finally the animated movie. There the Israelites stood, toes in the water, enemies charging at their heels, and Moses did the only thing he could do: He raised his staff to heaven and begged God for a way out. He never would have asked God to part the Red Sea. It would have been beyond Moses' understanding. But God...ah, God didn't need Moses to figure it out. The answers belonged to the Lord all along. When things looked their worst—in fact, *especially* when they looked their worst—God was busy putting in overtime, making marvelous things happen.

Faith could feel it in her gut: He was going to do that in the Jesus-statue case as well.

She stared at the woman's name and phone number and decided to call her back. Faith could carry on a conversation while making dinner, and later she would call her mother and catch her up on all that had gone on in the past few days. Suddenly Faith remembered being with Jordan in the park the other night, the way he'd kissed her.

Well, most of what had gone on.

She dialed the number and waited while it rang several times. Finally there was a click and an answering machine came on. "Hi, this is Faith Evans calling for Heidi." She left her home number, confident that the woman wasn't a wacko. After all, she lived in Bethany and had a fondness for the Jesus statue.

The irony of the woman's name struck Faith again as she hung up. If only it *was* Jordan's sister. Wouldn't that be something?

Faith checked the boiling water and dropped in a handful of pasta. Even though the woman wasn't Heidi Morand, her name was a reminder that Faith still needed to pray.

While she stirred the spaghetti sauce she spent the next fifteen minutes praying fervently for Jordan and his sister. That wherever Heidi was, she and Jordan might

find each other again. The prayer brought about a freedom in Faith she hadn't felt in
months.

The answer to the battle of Jericho Park wasn't strategies or case precedent or vig-
ils in which they took turns talking about their rights. It was something Christ
Himself had done, something she knew she must continue to do if there was any
hope of seeing God glorified in the process. The very thing she'd been doing since
seeing Jordan on her doorstep that morning.

Praying for her enemy.

Heidi was strangely energized when she and Charles got home at ten-thirty after their
first date since the baby was born. With all the talk about feedings and diaper changes
and nap schedules, they'd realized several days earlier that they needed adult conversation.

Together.

Charles's nurse at the office had baby-sat and in what seemed like a perfect ending to an already wonderful evening, Jordan Lee was sleeping peacefully in her
bassinet and the house was cleaner than when they'd left.

"Wow..." Heidi wandered into the kitchen and found Charles digging through
the cupboards for cereal. "What a great night."

He reached for a box of Grapenuts, set it on the counter, and pulled her into a
lingering hug. "What I want to know is where that baby in the other room came
from."

Heidi knit her brow together. Even after several years of marriage there were times
when she wasn't sure if Charles was kidding. "What do you mean?"

His gaze wandered lazily over her green sweater and new black jeans. "There's no
way that body of yours just had a baby. You look better than you did the day I met
you."

After weeks of feeling tired and frumpy, Charles' comment made Heidi's heart
soar. "Why, thank you, sir." She kissed him, nuzzling against his rough cheek, then
rested her head on his shoulder, her eyes closed as she savored the feel of him. "I love
you, Dr. Benson."

"Mmm. I love you, too."

She opened her eyes and noticed that the answering machine was blinking. "I
wonder who called? No one knows us yet."

She made her way across the kitchen as Charles returned to his cereal. There was
a click as Heidi pushed a button and stood back to hear the message. "Hi, this is Faith
Evans calling for Heidi... I'm returning a call you made to my friend Joshua Nunn
earlier today. Give me a call when you get a chance." Heidi scrambled for a piece of
paper and scribbled the number as the caller rattled it off.

"Who was that?" Charles looked at Heidi from his place on the stool at the center island. He took another bite and waited for her answer.

She remembered then that she hadn't told him, hadn't even mentioned the story she'd seen in the newspaper earlier that day. She looked at her watch. The news was set to begin in five minutes. "We have to watch the news tonight. You won't believe what's happening in Bethany. It's big time, Charles. National news."

He was working on another mouthful of cereal. "You mean that whole mess about the statue at the park?"

Heidi let her mouth hang open. For a moment she considered telling him about the attorney for HOUR, how strange it had been to see her brother's name in print. But that wasn't the point of the story. "Yes. That's not just any statue, Charles. It was one of my mother's favorite places in town. My brother's, too."

"So who's Faith Evans?" He finished his cereal and set the bowl in the sink. "Her name sounds familiar."

"She was a newscaster at WKZN, but she was fired because she got involved in the Jesus-statue case."

Creases appeared on Charles's forehead. "They fired her for that?"

Heidi nodded. "I called the city's lawyer and asked him to give her the message to call me. I felt like she might need help."

Charles took Heidi's hand and led her into the den. "And what—my sweet, still-recuperating love—could you do to help?"

She knew he was teasing and she tilted her head, her gaze fixed on the ceiling as though she were trying to figure out a difficult mathematical formula. "Let's see, I could go door to door getting people involved, or stand at the park all day handing out flyers with one hand, feeding Jordan Lee with the other. I could..." She broke into a laugh and punched Charles lightly on the arm. "I'm not an invalid, you know."

He grinned and tickled her until she let out a light scream. Across the room Jordan Lee sighed and shifted positions. "There you go, wake up the baby..." he whispered. He was still chuckling, but a curiosity filled his eyes. "No, I'm serious, honey. What are you thinking of doing?"

Heidi stared at the television set. The news was just coming on, and she shot a knowing glance at her husband. "I could tell her I'm behind her 100 percent, and that we'll pray for her." Her shoulders lifted twice. She wasn't even sure why she'd called, just that she'd felt compelled to do it. "I don't know, Charles. I care about that statue. I had to do something."

"That's my little activist." He kissed her on the top of her head and stretched lazily. "I'll be in the shower if you need me. Let me know what I miss." He winked at her and disappeared up the stairs.

Heidi watched him go and thought, as she often did, how blessed she was. She turned her attention back to the television and the top story—a newsbreaking item about a banking crisis in Philadelphia. Heidi absently bit the nail on her forefinger as she waited. There was a reason she wanted more information, a reason she wasn't ready to admit even to herself. It had everything to do with the attorney's name.

Maybe they'd show his picture...maybe...

Heidi forced herself not to get worked up. Her brother was dead, the state had notified her foster parents, hadn't they? That wasn't a detail people got wrong.

Was it?

Since television news would have reported the postponement of the hearing the night before, Heidi wasn't sure they'd carry another story about the case. But sure enough, three items into the lineup a female anchor stared into the camera, her face serious. Heidi leaned forward in her seat. *Come on, give me something…*

"The countdown has begun for the people of Bethany, Pennsylvania, as they await the final hearing in a case that will decide whether ten-foot walls must remain standing around a statue of Jesus Christ." The reporter droned on, recapping details that even Heidi knew already. The story ended with an update on the attorney for HOUR. "Sources say Jordan Riley will remain in Bethany until the hearing, making himself available for press conferences and other media events involving the case." The anchor reminded viewers of Mr. Riley's press conference earlier in the week, and as she spoke, the station aired footage of a man talking before a dozen microphones and cameras.

Heidi was on her feet, her next breath forgotten. "Dear God….it can't be…"

Though her blood ran cold and her head was spinning, she moved trancelike across the room to the television screen. Falling to her knees, she touched the image of the man on the screen.

Jordan Riley.

"He's alive…" She whispered the words as the man's picture was replaced by the anchor. Then Heidi's voice became a shout. "He's *alive!* Charles, come here! He's alive!" She was overcome with a dozen different emotions, and she felt like she'd slipped into some far-too-real dream. The baby began to whimper, and Heidi held a hand up in her direction. "Shh, honey, it's okay." Heidi peered over the edge of the bassinet, relieved to see Jordan Lee's eyes closed. "I'll be right back."

Don't let it be a dream, God…please… He's alive! Jordan's alive! "Charles!" She darted upstairs as quickly as her feet could take her, into their bedroom and around the corner, where she found Charles wrapped in a towel, his hair still dripping from the shower. "Charles…" She froze in place, her knees knocking, heart stuck in a beat she didn't recognize. The tears came then, quickly and in rivers, warm with the mixture of pain and elation. "He's alive, I saw him!"

Her husband's blank expression told Heidi he had no idea what she was talking about. "Who's alive?" He ran the towel across himself, slipped into a robe, and was at her side almost instantly. His damp fingers came up around the sides of her tear-soaked face as he searched her eyes. "Honey, what is it? What's wrong?"

Her voice was a whisper this time, and it was hard to draw a deep breath. "My brother…Jordan…" Spots danced before her eyes and she backed up. *Help me, Lord…I can't faint. Not now.*

Charles held her steady and eased her down onto the bed. Concern screamed from his eyes, as though he thought perhaps Heidi had lost her mind. "You're white as a sheet, baby, put your head between your knees." He kept hold of her shoulders as she followed his instructions. Though her body had no idea how to handle the shock of seeing Jordan alive, her husband did. And in Charles's presence, aware of his years of medical experience, she felt herself beginning to relax. *Thank You, God…help me get a grip…*

"I'm okay." The words sounded muffled as Heidi moved to sit up again.

"Slowly. Come up real slowly, babe." Again she did as she was told, grateful that Jordan Lee had slept through the ordeal. When she was upright again, she felt another wave of tears, but this time when she spoke her voice was steady and certain.

"My brother's alive."

The sense of shock belonged to Charles now, and Heidi watched his eyes change from confusion to utter disbelief. He put a hand on her shoulder and sat beside her. "Honey, that's impossible. He's been dead more than fifteen years."

She shook her head and wiped her cheeks with the back of her hand. "I saw him on TV." There was no way she could convince Charles without an explanation. This time her lungs allowed her to breathe, and she inhaled deeply. "This morning when I read about the Jesus statue case I came across the name of the attorney from HOUR who started the whole thing, the man who sued the city of Bethany to have the statue removed." Heidi locked eyes with her husband. "His name is Jordan Riley."

It took a moment, but eventually a knowing expression filled Charles's face. "Honey, there are bound to be other—"

Heidi put her hand up to stop him. "I know that. I told myself the same thing." She pointed downstairs. "But a few minutes ago I was watching a news story about it, and they showed a picture of the attorney talking to a crowd at Jericho Park the other day." New tears pooled in her eyes and spilled over. "It was Jordan, Charles. I would have recognized him anywhere, case or no case."

The sadness in Charles's eyes told Heidi he wasn't convinced. "Sweetheart, Jordan was just a boy when he died. A lot of grown men might look the way he would have looked." He hesitated. "If he'd lived."

Heidi knew Charles didn't mean anything by his doubts, but they angered her all the same. After all these years she'd found her brother. He wasn't dead; he was alive! She pursed her lips and stood up. There was only one way to prove it to him. Without saying a word she headed out of the bedroom and toward the stairs.

Charles was on his feet, close behind her. "Where're you going?"

She glanced at him over her shoulder and saw in his hurried steps how deeply he cared for her. But she couldn't wait another moment to know she was right. "I have to make a phone call."

"But it's eleven-thir—"

Heidi was already dialing the number. A woman answered on the second ring, her voice wide awake. "Hello…"

"Did I wake you?"

"No…who is this?"

Charles came up behind her, wrapped his arms gently around her waist and drew her near, laying his head on her shoulder and waiting. There was a pause, and for a moment Heidi thought the woman was going to hang up on her. "I'm sorry, it's Heidi Benson. I shouldn't have called so late, but, well…is this Faith Evans?"

"Yes, it is, and don't worry about the hour. I stay up late." Heidi drew a breath. Certainly the woman would know the details about the attorney from HOUR. *Please, God…I need to know now…*

"You're calling about the Jesus statue case, right? I left a message with you earlier?"

Heidi could feel herself beginning to shake again and she willed her heart to remain calm. "Yes…I, uh…I have a question first, Mrs. Evans." She closed her eyes and pulled her fingers in tight against the palms of her hands. Charles still stood behind her, and she was suddenly desperate to know the truth. "What can you tell me about Jordan Riley, the attorney for HOUR?"

Faith paused. "What did you want to know?"

"Everything." Heidi said the word quickly to keep herself from screaming in frustration. "Whatever you can tell me…why he's suing the city and whether he ever lived in Bethany?"

Again Faith was silent, then, "Yes, as a matter of fact, he did live in Bethany a long time ago. Back when he was a boy."

There was nothing Heidi could do to calm her heart now. "How old was he? When he lived here, I mean?"

Another pause. "I'm not sure I understand what this has to do with the case."

Heidi heard uneasiness in Faith's voice. *Let her hear my heart, Lord.* "It's very important. I think maybe I know the man." Heidi's voice broke. "Please, if you know anything about him, help me—"

"Are you…are you serious?" Faith's tone was suddenly as breathless and anxious as Heidi's.

"Yes, please…"

"Okay, Heidi. I'll tell you what I can." Faith's voice was kind, and Heidi knew instinctively she'd found an ally. She held her breath as Faith continued. "Jordan and I were friends…we lived next door to each other for several years before he moved away. He was thirteen that year."

The shock of Faith's words sent Heidi backward, against her husband. She lowered her head and was seized by a wave of sobs that had been building for fifteen years. Ever since she received the news that Jordan was dead. "Faith…then it's you?"

"I'm…I'm not sure I know what you mean. Look, Mrs. Benson—"

"Riley…I-I'm Heidi Riley."

Heidi heard the gasp on the other end. *What?* "I can't believe it…Heidi Riley… it's really you?"

A sound escaped Heidi that was part sob, part relieved laughter. "Yes, it's me. So my brother isn't dead?"

Faith was crying now as well. "No, Heidi. He's alive! He's alive and he's been look-ing for you ever since the state took you away. Where do you live?"

Heidi rattled off the address as she turned to Charles, grinning madly through her tears.

"Can you come over?" Faith sounded like she was crying too. "Right now? I think we have a lot to talk about."

Heidi agreed, and the two hung up. She grabbed her jacket from the back of a kitchen chair as Charles waited.

"What'd she say? Is it Jordan?"

She smiled through her tears. "You always wished you could have met Jordan, right?"

Charles nodded, his eyes glistening in stunned disbelief.

"Well—" she hugged him close, then pulled back just enough to see his face— "how 'bout this week?"

25

Faith leaned against the wall to keep from collapsing. Heidi Benson was Jordan's sister? The shock jolted through her, making her feel she was in the very presence of God.

Stunned, she moved into the front room and sat on the edge of the sofa, watching and waiting. She was just about to get into bed when the phone rang. At first she'd thought it nervy that the woman had chosen to call so late, but when she heard the urgency in her voice, Faith had silently prayed for patience. Whatever Mrs. Benson had to say mattered deeply to the woman.

And now...

Faith shook her head. Now, she knew she'd been witness to a miracle.

Her father had loved moments like this, when it was blatantly obvious they were treading on holy ground. He would smile and say, "Looks like God has something up His sleeve." There was a lump in Faith's throat and she swallowed hard as her thoughts drifted back to the last time she'd seen Heidi, the little girl's arm reaching desperately from a stranger's car as she was separated from her brother.

The noise of an engine snapped her out of the memory and Faith watched through the window as a car pulled up and a woman climbed out.

Heidi Riley...the very person she'd prayed for earlier that day in Jordan's car... *No one but You could have done this, God. No one but You.* Faith opened the door. Jordan's little sister had grown into a beautiful woman, with Jordan's striking features and hair—but that wasn't what made Faith's heart skip a beat.

Heidi Benson looked exactly like her mother.

There were no words needed as Heidi and Faith came together, eliminating the years between them in a single hug. Faith felt fresh tears sting her eyes and she laughed to keep from breaking down. "I can't believe it's you. It's too amazing."

"I read your name in the article, and I had the craziest feeling...but your name was wrong. So I knew you couldn't be the same Faith who'd lived next door to us." Heidi pulled back and took Faith's hands in hers. "But here you are."

Faith led her inside, and they took seats next to each other in the living room. Normally she'd offer Heidi tea, but given the circumstances there was simply too much to talk about first. A smile lifted the corners of Heidi's lips. "You're so pretty, Faith. Just like I pictured you."

Faith laughed and dried her eyes. "And you look so much like your mother I could barely believe it wasn't her. Jordan's going to be amazed."

A look of raw pain flooded Heidi's face. "All these years...I thought...I thought he was dead."

"I know. We looked at the state foster care files today."

"Today?" Heidi's eyes grew wide. "You mean you were with him today? I thought with the...well, the two of you are on opposite sides of this thing." She stared at her hands. "I didn't think you'd be talking."

Faith saw a pink tinge shade her cheeks. Was she ashamed of her brother's involvement in the case? Compassion flooded Faith's heart.

"It's a long story." Faith's voice grew somber as Jordan's words flitted through her mind again. *The God you serve is my enemy..."*

"Your brother's very hurt, Heidi. He spent most of his life looking for you. And after today..."

"What'd the files say?" Heidi's eyes grew dark.

"That Jordan was killed in the camp accident. There wasn't enough adoption information in yours for Jordan to have any hope of finding you." Faith could still see the sorrow on Jordan's face as he read the report. "After that he figured he was out of options."

Heidi's face twisted. She sat back in the chair, covered her face with her hands, and cried as though her heart were being ripped to shreds. She spoke through the spaces between her fingers, her voice was little more than a muffled cry. "All those years...thinking he was dead. We've lost so much time." She wept harder than before. "And now...he's not the person he was."

Faith dropped to her knees and embraced Heidi, smoothing her hand over the back of her head. "His views, his beliefs are different—but deep down, Jordan's still the same." She wanted to be honest, but Heidi had to believe there was hope. Faith remembered her night with Jordan at Jericho Park. "Sometimes when we've been together...I've felt like he was exactly the same."

Heidi leaned back and reached for a tissue on the coffee table. She held the paper to her face, letting her head rest in her hands for several seconds. When she looked up she gave Faith a weak smile. "I'm sorry. I didn't plan to break down."

"Don't be sorry. It's right to grieve the years you've lost. You must have been devastated when you thought he was killed."

Lines of confusion appeared on Heidi's forehead. "So what happened? At the camp, I mean? How did they get it so mixed up?"

Faith exhaled and moved back to her chair, her eyes fixated on a crack in the ceiling. "A cave collapsed. Nineteen boys were working inside and Jordan was one of them. He could easily have been killed, Heidi. He and another boy were the only ones who got out alive." She met Heidi's questioning eyes. "He spent a day in the hospital, but he was fine." She paused, knowing the details wouldn't help Heidi with the fact that she'd been given wrong information. *Lord, give her strength...please...* "I don't know where the error came from—the camp officials or the hospital. But it doesn't matter now. Someone from the camp contacted another camp—out of state—and Jordan never returned to Southridge. My guess is his records are active somewhere in New Jersey."

"New Jersey?"

Faith's heart sank. She'd forgotten how much of Jordan's story Heidi didn't know. "Yes. He spent the rest of his school years in New Jersey. He went to college there on a baseball scholarship. He was never adopted but he did very well. He went to law school, passed the bar exam, and took a job with HOUR." Faith pursed her lips and glanced down. "He's one of their best attorneys."

"And you think it's because he's hurting, maybe even mad at the Lord?"

Faith looked at Heidi through a fresh layer of tears. "I know that's why. He told me so himself."

Heidi shook her head and closed her eyes. "I've been praying for him ever since you told me...the whole way over here."

Praying for him? A surge of hope worked its way through Faith. "So you're...you still..."

"Believe?" Heidi opened her eyes again. "My relationship with Christ pulled me through. Without Him..." Faith could see her struggling to control her emotions. Heidi swallowed hard and straightened. "I never would have made it."

The bond between them was growing, and Faith was glad. "I'm so glad for you...I hoped your love for God was strong. Something in the way you spoke, the light in your eyes..."

"My husband's the same way."

"Husband?" Faith realized there were still lots more details to be discussed.

"Oh, Faith, he's wonderful...my perfect match."

My perfect match. For some reason as Heidi said the words, Faith was surrounded by invisible images of Jordan. She saw him talking with her at the diner, sitting with her on the park bench, making her feel flustered and more connected to him than anyone in the world. Just like he'd made her feel that long-ago winter. She shook off the memories and the bittersweet feeling that wedged itself in her heart. While Heidi and her husband had been building their life together, she'd wasted years with Mike Dillan and spent months learning to walk again after her car accident.

Where's my perfect match, Lord? Obviously it isn't Jordan Riley. And where is Rosa Lee's match?

Be strong and courageous, daughter. I know the plans I have for you.

A sense of peace washed over Faith at the silent reassurance, and she smiled at Heidi. "Tell me about him."

Her eyes sparkled, like a little girl about to describe her favorite birthday gift. "He's kind and loving and it breaks his heart that I lost my mother and Jordan when

I was ten years old." Heidi's eyes grew softer. "We just moved to Bethany this fall. He's a pediatrician at the new clinic." Her eyes lit up. "Oh, and five weeks ago we had our first baby. A little girl."

"Five weeks!" Faith hadn't even considered the idea that Heidi might have a child or children, that Jordan was an uncle. "Wow, Heidi, you look great...you'd never know. What's her name?"

Heidi's eyes lifted to meet Faith's. "Jordan Lee."

More tears fell as both of them wept again, and something inside Faith swelled at the thought of seeing Jordan with his baby niece, an infant named after him. "Well, that settles it. You'll have to dress her up tomorrow."

"Why?" Heidi lowered her eyebrows.

"Because—" Faith grinned as she imagined the next day—"tomorrow's the day Jordan Lee gets to meet her uncle."

At nine o'clock the next morning Jordan was lounging in bed, watching an old Western on cable. He had plans to join the local leader of a small, human-rights group for dinner—a meeting that would give him a window to the area's less popular viewpoint regarding the Jesus statue. Jordan remembered the conversation he'd had with the man—Wally Walters—after the last press conference.

"We've hated that statue as far back as I can remember. In fact, we wrote a petition asking the city to tax anyone who wanted to keep it standing." Walters had gone on, describing his frustration in language littered with four-letter words.

Jordan had doubts about the productivity of such a dinner, and bigger doubts about the man himself. He was a lumbering hulk who towered six-five and had a tendency to spit when he talked. Jordan had wanted to know how many people were in Walter's local group and how many of those were opposed to the Jesus statue. The first three times Jordan asked, Wally avoided answering. Finally, when pressed for a specific number, Wally admitted he and a beer-drinking buddy of his were the group's only two official members. And both of them wanted the statue removed or walled up for good. "There are others, though, mark my words. They're just afraid to share their viewpoint what with the whole town ripe full of Jesus freaks."

Jordan rubbed his cheek, recalling the spray of saliva that had accompanied Walter's complaint. He stretched his legs to the end of the bed and yawned. What a waste of time. He thought of the cases he could be researching, the hours he could be billing back at the firm. The only good thing that had come from spending a week in Bethany was the fact that he finally knew the truth about Heidi.

For all the good it would do him.

He doubled the pillow behind his head and sat up straighter. Since reading his sister's file he'd made a decision. This time when he left Bethany—regardless of the outcome of the case—he was finished looking for her. After all, it wasn't as though Heidi was longing for him to turn up, searching for him, desperate to be reunited.

She thought he was dead.

Jordan pondered that and realized it wasn't far from the truth. The Jordan Riley she had known and loved had been dead since the day they took him to Southridge.

He flipped the channel to ESPN and stared at the screen absently, remembering Faith and her prayer that God help them find Heidi. He huffed under his breath and flipped back to the Western. How naive Faith still was after all these years. Couldn't she see it? God hadn't been there when that football player raked her over the coals…He hadn't been there when she gave up her safety for the life of a child and wound up in a coma for two months…He hadn't been there when her father died decades younger than he should have, and in the middle of doing God's work, no less. He chuckled lightly and shook his head.

Faith was a fool.

Oh, there was no denying the power she still held over him, the way her presence made him long to run off with her to a mountain retreat where politics and religion didn't exist. But that wasn't possible. If Faith was still able to cling to her beliefs after all she'd been through, all she'd watched Jordan go through, then nothing would make her let go. She'd be a believer to the day she died, and that counted Jordan out completely.

"Ah, Faith…"

He remembered the way he felt with her so close to him. "If only I could change your mind. You and I would be so good togeth—"

The phone rang, and Jordan stared at it strangely. Was it Hawkins again? Didn't the man ever rest? Jordan tried to decide whether his boss would be frustrated that he wasn't holding another press conference that morning or grateful he wasn't out fraternizing with the enemy. He picked up the phone, his mood suddenly sour. "Hello?"

The caller paused, and at first Jordan thought it was a wrong number. He was about to hang up when he heard her. "Hi…it's me, Faith."

Jordan closed his eyes and felt his body relax. Even if he never saw her again after this week, nothing would change the way she made him feel. "Hey, what's up?"

"I need to talk to you…today, say around one o'clock?" There was an urgency in her voice.

"Why?"

"Something's come up. I can't talk about it on the phone."

Jordan opened his eyes, sat up on the edge of the bed, and rested his elbows on his knees. As emotional as he'd been the past month it probably wasn't a good idea to spend time alone with her. Each time it was more difficult not to touch her face, to pull her close and…

He inhaled sharply. "It just so happens I have an opening at one."

She laughed, and the sound was like music from a favorite song he hadn't heard in years. "Okay, see you there."

"Wait…" A grin tugged at the corners of his mouth. "Where?"

"Oh, right." She was suddenly in a hurry. "Jericho Park, near the swings."

"Jericho Pa—" In the full-length mirror opposite the bed, Jordan watched his face grow dark. "If this is some kind of media event I need to know what's hap—"

There was a pause. "You should know me better than that." Hurt rang loud and clear in Faith's voice as she cut him off. "This has nothing to do with the case."

He felt his shoulders slump. "I'm sorry. It's just…there's been so much pressure from the office to stay on top of the media." He rubbed his forehead. "Why am I telling you this?"

There was silence for a moment. "Because deep down, where your heart lives, you still trust me."

He uttered a nearly silent laugh. *Faith, if only you knew… What I feel for you goes much deeper than trust and friendship.* "You think so, huh?"

She picked up on his teasing tone. "Yes, and besides, I'm probably the only friend you have in town."

"That's not true." His grin was back. "I'm having dinner with Wally Walters."

"You and old Wally?" Faith laughed again, and Jordan felt warmed with relief that she wasn't mad at him for doubting her. "I didn't know they let him out at night."

"Very funny."

She was giggling harder now. "Let's just say your one o'clock appointment will make up for it."

"Okay." He stood up and wandered toward the closet area. The day looked a hundred times brighter than it had before her phone call. "But Faith…"

"What?"

"You'll have to prove it to me."

She didn't laugh. "I don't think that's going to be a problem."

26

*H*eidi's heart raced as she sat in the parking lot at Jericho Park and waited for Faith to show up. It was almost one, and Faith had promised she'd be there before Jordan. Heidi glanced at her baby daughter sleeping so peacefully in the backseat, and then at the driveway. She willed Faith's car to appear.

Come on...get here...

Her breaths came in short bursts, and her hands were sweaty against the steering wheel. She couldn't remember being this nervous about anything in her life. Conversations with the Lord had done nothing to ease her anxiety, and in the twelve hours since seeing Faith the night before, she'd had only a few moments of restless sleep. After crying herself to sleep weeks on end as a child and living with a hole in her heart since Jordan's supposed death, she could hardly believe she was about to see him again.

But there was a nagging doubt she couldn't quite shake. The last time she and Jordan were together, he'd been her hero, her protector. Now, he was the one hurting and they had moved miles apart in their walks with God.

What if Jordan didn't like her? What if all they had was surface talk and promises of Christmas cards? How would she handle that?

"And we know that in all things God works for the good of those who love him, who have been called according to his purpose." The words from the book of Romans played over and over in her mind ...*those who love him, who have been called according to His purpose...called according to His purpose...called according to His purpose...*

Her heartbeat slowed, and she felt peace come over her like a protective shield. Jordan might be fighting God now, but the Bible was full of such men. Paul, for instance. Paul had overseen the killing of Christians, and yet God had still used him. Certainly Jordan had been called by God. He had given his heart to the Lord long before their mother got sick. Heidi leaned back in her seat and smiled.

Okay, God, I believe You... There's a plan in all this. But please...hurry up and show me.

Faith pulled into the driveway ten minutes before one and immediately found

Heidi's car. Her heart soared as though it had wings. *Lord, You're so good. I can't believe this is happening.* Heidi and Jordan would want time alone, so Faith had decided to bring Rosa. School was out and the child loved spending an hour or two at Jericho Park. She shot a look back at Rosa Lee and grinned. "Honey, we're here. Get your coat."

Rosa did as she was told while Faith parked the car next to Heidi's, and climbed out. In the spot next to them, Heidi took Jordan Lee from her car seat and strapped her into a stroller. Faith held Rosa's hand, weaving her fingers between the child's. Then she led Rosa to the stroller where they peeked at the baby.

Tears filled Faith's eyes as she marveled over the infant's perfect peachy skin and dark hair. "Oh, Heidi, she's beautiful." Faith leaned in closer and ran her fingertips over the tiny girl's downy-soft forehead. The resemblance was striking. "She looks just like Jordan." Faith stood up and hugged Heidi. "I can't believe the two of you are really going to see each other…after all this time."

Heidi dabbed at her own tears. "I promised myself I wouldn't break down. Not yet." She uttered a cry that was part laugh. "I don't want mascara running down my face when he sees me."

"He's going to love you, Heidi. Stop worrying." Faith ran her thumb under Heidi's right eye. "There. No mascara." She grinned and looked down at the child beside her. "Rosa, I'd like you to meet Mrs. Benson. She's a friend of mine."

Rosa stuck out her good hand. "Nice to meet you, Mrs. Benson."

"What nice manners, Rosa." Heidi shook the child's hand and smiled, casting Faith a quick grin. "It's a pleasure to meet you, too."

The four of them made their way into the park and found a picnic table near the swings. Rosa was singing happy songs, soaring halfway to the trees in a matter of minutes.

"What a beautiful little girl. Is she family?"

Faith shifted her gaze to Rosa and sighed. "I'd like her to be, but no. She's a foster child up for adoption." Faith looked at Heidi once more. "I think I'm in love with her."

"I see that." Heidi smiled, and her eyes danced with the possibilities. "Is there a chance you'll…?"

"Adopt her? I don't know." Faith could feel the tears again and she blinked them back. "I've prayed about it every day for weeks now, and it seems like God's telling me to wait." She glanced back at Rosa. "Deep in my heart I feel she deserves two parents—a mom *and* a dad." Faith felt the corners of her mouth droop a fraction. "And that's something I can't give her."

They were quiet for a moment as Heidi rocked the stroller back and forth and they watched Rosa swing.

"I wish we were sitting over there." Faith broke the silence and pointed to the bench closest to the walled-in Jesus statue. "That was Jordan's favorite spot when he was a boy." She let her gaze settle on the plywood walls and her heart felt heavier than before. The walls were starting to break away in a few places, no doubt pulled at by teenagers or people frustrated with the mandate. The whole situation was too sad for Faith. She turned back to Heidi. "But I promised Jordan this wasn't about the statue, and it isn't." She patted the wooden table. "This'll do fine."

Heidi was about to say something when a car pulled into the parking lot.

"That's him." Faith drew a deep breath and squeezed Heidi's hand. "I'll meet him halfway and explain what's happening."

She stood up just as Jordan climbed out of the car and shut the door. He wore casual dress slacks, a white button-down shirt, and a navy cardigan sweater. Even from fifty yards he was easily the most handsome man Faith had ever seen.

Jordan spotted Faith as soon as he pulled into the parking lot and felt a frown crease his brow as he slid from the vehicle.

Who was she talking to? Just his luck someone would see her there and cut into their time together. Faith knew just about everyone in town...and he was painfully aware that neither of them wanted people talking about their friendship.

He slowed his pace and waited for her.

As she came closer, he savored the sight of her and wished for the hundredth time she wasn't so dogmatic about her beliefs. Could the young woman before him really be his enemy? He dismissed the thought, forcing himself to keep a businesslike attitude. "Okay, this better be good." He slipped his hands in his pocket and smiled at her.

Her eyes lit up in response and she stopped a foot from him, crossing her arms and lowering her chin playfully. "It will be."

The woman Faith had been sitting with was watching them. "Should we find a better place?" He was serious now. It was important neither of them were seen together. "We can drive somewhere outside of town..."

Faith shook her head. "No. She's okay."

Jordan glanced at the woman again, then searched Faith's eyes. "Who is she?"

There was hesitation in Faith's face, as though she wasn't sure where to begin. Finally she drew a slow breath and locked onto his gaze. "Remember yesterday in your car when I prayed we'd find Heidi?"

He blinked. Why was Faith bringing that up now? "Okay, so..."

"Last night I got a call, Jordan. From a woman named Heidi Benson." She paused, and he felt as though his heart had taken leave of his body. He couldn't breathe. Couldn't think. All he could do was wait for her to continue. "At first I thought she was just another townsperson. You know, someone wanting to help keep the statue up."

"But..." Jordan forced the word through suddenly numb lips. His head was spinning. Nothing about the conversation fit neatly into any of his mind's file drawers.

"But...she wasn't. She saw you on television yesterday, Jordan. She lives right here in Bethany. Moved here a few weeks ago." Faith's eyes filled with tears, and they spilled onto her cheeks as she reached out and laid her fingers on his arm. "She came to my house last night. Jordan, it's her. Heidi."

He could feel the blood leaving his body—first his face, then his chest and arms. His legs trembled as he looked again at the woman sitting at the picnic table. "But...who is *she?*"

Faith's voice was little more than a whisper and her lip quivered as she spoke. "She's your sister, Jordan. And she wants to see you."

His gaze dropped to the ground and he clenched his teeth. When he looked up, he found Faith's eyes once more. "You're serious. You found her?" He gazed at the woman in the distance again. "That's...Heidi?"

"Yes, Heidi and her baby." Faith came to him then and hugged him, and he couldn't decide whether to run the distance between him and Heidi or fall to the ground and weep. It had been so long...and after finding her file he was sure he'd never see her again. Now...

"She...has a baby?" He folded his arms across his chest, squeezing his hands together in tight fists. "Faith, I can't believe it...I..." He looked at her, stunned, still not believing it was true, as tears welled in his eyes. "How can I ever thank you?"

"That's just it, Jordan." Faith leveled her gaze at him, her eyes unblinking. "God brought her back to you." She paused. "I had nothing to do with it. Remember that when you hit the pillow tonight."

Jordan nodded absently, and Faith moved her face inches closer to his. "I'm serious. You can't stay angry at God forever."

Her last remark left something unsettled deep in his gut, but he shifted his attention to Heidi. She was looking at the baby in her arms, and suddenly he needed to see her, hold her, be with her as desperately as he needed air. "Sure, Faith, okay." He hugged her again, truly grateful for her role in this. Finding Heidi had been nothing short of providence and good luck, mixed with Faith's kindness and determination. But it would only upset Faith to say so now. "Come with me?"

She shook her head. "I'm watching Rosa. I'll hang out with her while the two of you talk."

Jordan stared at his sister again, and this time Heidi caught his look. She waved, though she was too far away for him to make out her face. "Hi..." He silently mouthed the word as he waved back.

"It's really her!" Jordan brushed away a tear and smiled. He began walking briskly toward Heidi, Faith still at his side. Dozens of images filled his mind...his sister walking home from school beside him...the two of them doing homework at the kitchen table...Heidi holding his hand as they crept into their mother's room in the days when her sickness first got bad...Heidi throwing herself over their mother the day she died and Jordan pulling her gently back, assuring her that no matter what, they'd have each other.

Heidi being torn from him that day in their front yard and begging to stay.

The look in her eyes as the car drove out of sight.

I promised I'd take care of her, Mom…but I never could because I couldn't find her. But now…I'll watch over her forever. Though his sister couldn't hear him yet, he talked to her anyway. "I'm coming Heidi. And I'm never, ever going to lose you again."

Heidi wanted to take Jordan Lee and race across the park to where her brother stood with Faith, but she couldn't do it, couldn't take her eyes off of him for fear he would disappear and everything about the past twenty-four hours would turn out to be nothing more than a haunting dream. She studied him, surprised at how tall he was, how he'd filled out. From the place where he stood, she couldn't tell if he looked the same, only that he'd become a man.

God, I'm not sure I'm ready for this… Please, heal him of his anger and bitterness…let my light, Faith's light, be enough to make him want to come home.

Do not be troubled, daughter…I know the plans I have for Jordan.

Heidi exhaled softly. "Okay, Lord. I'm ready."

Jordan slowed his pace as he neared her, and Faith veered off to the play area where Rosa was waiting for her. Heidi watched silently as her brother nearly stopped twenty feet from her. He looked like he was seeing a vision. Heidi understood exactly how she felt.

"Heidi…"

She nodded, and her words came out like trapped cries escaping the recesses of her very soul. "It's me, Jordan…" She set the baby down in her stroller and stood to face him.

There was no stopping him after that. He ran the remaining steps that separated them and swept her into his arms, lifting her off the ground and spinning her around in a full circle before setting her down. They hugged again, and he pressed his face against hers. "Heidi, I can't believe it's you."

She was sobbing and smiling all at the same time, and she took hold of his face, studying it through her tears. "You look the same." Her hand flew to her mouth, and she nearly fell from the power of her weeping. "I…th-th-thought you were dead."

Once more he pulled her close, wrapping her in his arms, and smoothing his hand over her back, her hair, just as he'd always done when they were kids. In the place where her memories lived, her brother had never died. Birthdays, special occasions, times when she remembered her mother…always Jordan was there. But now…to have him hold her like he'd done when she was ten years old…

It was more than she could take. "Don't let go, Jordan… please."

"Shh…it's okay, Heidi. I won't." His voice was a hoarse whisper, choked by the immensity of the moment. "I thought I'd never find you."

Heidi had no idea how long they stood there, holding each other. It could have been hours or minutes. All she knew was she was transported back to the winter of

1985. No longer were they adults who'd spent half their lives apart, but a sister and brother certain that though the whole world might let them down, at least they had each other.

Eventually Heidi's sobbing eased, but she stayed in Jordan's arms all the same. How many times had she ached for his protection, cried for his loving assurance in the months and years after hearing about his accident?

And now…here he was. Alive.

She closed her eyes. "Thank You, Lord…oh, thank You…You're so good." She realized she'd whispered the prayer out loud, and pulled back some and grinned at him. "I told myself I wasn't going to cry." She laughed and caught two quick breaths. Her eyes were nearly swollen shut, but she smiled all the same. "I wanted you to think I was pretty."

Jordan searched her face and his fingers came up to frame her cheekbones. "You're beautiful, Heidi. And you're…" She saw that his eyes were red, his cheeks wet. "You're all grown up." He took in all of her and smiled even as more tears came. "The sister I lost was a little girl…but you…you look just like Mom did."

"That's what Faith said." Cooing sounds came from the place where Jordan Lee lay, and Heidi motioned with her head in that direction. "I have someone I'd like you to meet."

Her brother's eyes danced, and he linked arms with her, leading the way to the stroller.

She looked from her baby to her brother.

"Jordan, meet Jordan Lee." Heidi grinned at him as she saw the surprise in his eyes.

"You…you named her after…"

A sound that was part laugh, part cry came from Heidi. "Yes, we wanted her to always know about her Uncle Jordan."

He looked at his niece for the first time. His mouth opened and he stared at her, speechless. "Oh…" The last part of the word lingered in the cool November air. Several seconds passed and finally Jordan looked at Heidi, his face full of questions. "Can I…would you care if I held her?"

Heidi giggled, wiping an errant tear as she gently lifted the infant and set her in Jordan's arms. Again the resemblance was wonderfully clear. Heidi stood behind him and studied her daughter over Jordan's shoulder while he clutched the baby in a stiff embrace, holding his niece as though she might break in two.

"She looks just like you." Heidi put her arm around Jordan's back and pressed her cheek against his.

He turned and gave her a crooked grin. "Yeah, she does, doesn't she?" His eyes lit up. "Hey, you haven't told me about your husband." He gestured with his elbow at her wedding ring. "I saw it from the parking lot."

Heidi laughed again. "His name is Charles. He's wonderful and charming and he loves me more than life itself. He's a pediatrician at the local family clinic and he can't wait to meet you."

"You've told him about me?"

Heidi angled her head and locked eyes with him. "I never stopped talking about you, Jordan. He feels like he knows you."

They heard voices drawing near and they turned at the same time to see Faith and Rosa walking toward them. Heidi watched Jordan's reaction, noticed the way his eyes locked onto Faith's, and she had the sense that whatever it was the two of them shared, it was deep. Lasting. Heidi smiled as she remembered how Faith and Jordan had been as kids.

Whatever had gone on between the two of them since Jordan had been back, it hadn't been all bad.

"I've gotta take Rosa home." Faith was breathless from playing with the girl, her cheeks red and striking, her smile all for Jordan. No doubt about it, Heidi thought. There was a definite attraction between Faith and her brother…

Faith led Rosa up to Jordan. "Rosa, I'd like you to meet someone else." Faith's eyes lifted and connected once more with Jordan's. Without looking down, her face lit up and she continued. "His name is Mr. Riley." Her eyes filled with warmth. "He's my friend."

"Nice to meet you, Mr. Riley." Rosa held out her hand.

For several seconds Jordan seemed unable to break eye contact with Faith, then he looked down and smiled. "Nice to meet you, too. You're sure a pretty girl, Rosa." Jordan did a little bow. "I understand you're a foster child."

Rosa's dark, silky lashes moved up and down as she blinked twice and looked from Jordan to Faith and back to Jordan again. "How'd you know?"

"I told him, honey." Faith stood behind Rosa, her hands on the girl's shoulders.

Jordan nodded. "She wanted me to know because I used to be a foster child, too…a long time ago." He shot a glance at Faith and slipped his arm around Heidi. "Mrs. Benson is my sister."

Heidi leaned around Jordan and winked at Rosa. "We were both foster children."

Rosa's eyes grew wide. "Really? Wow…" Her expression seemed instantly infused with hope. "And you both found families, right?"

Heidi felt Jordan's pain at the child's comment as strongly as if they shared one heart. She resisted the urge to wince as Jordan struggled for the right words. "Everything worked out, if that's what you mean, sweetie."

Faith pulled Rosa gently back from the others. "Well, we've got to get going."

Rosa bid Heidi and Jordan good-bye, a grin still plastered across her face. She reached out for Jordan again but this time with a hand that was misshapen and missing fingers. As though realizing her error, the girl froze. Heidi forced her face to remain unmoved by the sight and watched while Jordan hid his reaction as well. At first Rosa seemed unsure what to do, her hand suspended in the space between her and Jordan, her eyes filled with questions.

Then carefully, tenderly, Jordan took her hand in his. He held it, closing his strong fingers over her entire hand while he stooped closer to her. "Hope to see you again sometime, okay?"

Relief flooded Rosa's face and she nodded, her head angled sweetly. "Me too."

Without hesitating, Jordan leaned over and kissed her hand the way a king might kiss the hand of a princess. Heidi shot a glance at Faith and saw tears in her eyes. Something special was happening between the two of them.

No, she thought, studying the scene once more. It was something special between the *three* of them.

When Faith and Rosa were halfway back to the car, Heidi took a chance. "You're in love with her, aren't you?"

Jordan slid himself onto the top of the table and anchored his feet squarely on the bench beneath him. "Rosa? She's a little young for me…"

Heidi peeked at Jordan Lee and saw she was sleeping. Then she took her place on the table next to Jordan and linked her arm through his. "You know who. Faith Moses…Faith Evans, whatever. You're in love with her."

Jordan shrugged and cocked his head so he could see Heidi better. "It wouldn't matter if I was." His eyes grew sad, and Heidi sensed he didn't want to broach the next subject. Finally he sighed and stared back out in front of him. "If you saw me on the news you must know why I'm here."

Heidi held her breath. *Lord, give me the words…* "Yes. I know."

He studied her again and exhaled slowly. "Something tells me you're just like Faith and Mom and the other believers. You love God more than reason, right?"

"What makes you say that?" She tried to see into the depths of his soul.

Jordan sighed and gazed at a passing cloud. "I don't know. Something in your eyes. A glow or a warmth I can't really explain. I saw the same thing in the eyes of this teacher I came up against in court…and in Faith's eyes. It's what I remember seeing in Mom's eyes." He looked back at her and Heidi ached for him. "Am I right?"

She slid an arm around him, leaning her head on his shoulder like she'd done when she was little. "You are. I love God, I've never stopped. And deep inside, you haven't either." She paused. "Sometimes our walk with the Lord gets a little confusing, that's all."

Jordan uttered what sounded like a frustrated sigh, and Heidi felt his shoulder tense beneath her. "We have a lot to catch up on, Heidi. The whole religion thing isn't…I don't want to talk about it."

His reaction shook Heidi. *Lord, he's as bad off as Faith said. Maybe worse.* "Okay, fair enough. Let's catch up, then." She asked him about the accident at camp, his school days in New Jersey, and what it was like to play collegiate baseball. She even asked about his position at the HOUR organization. It broke her heart to imagine him sold out to a firm that was so obviously against the very beliefs the country was founded on, but she was careful not to share her feelings with Jordan. That was God's territory, not hers.

All she wanted to do was let him know he was loved—regardless of his opinions.

They were an hour into the conversation when she pulled an envelope from her pocket and held it out to Jordan. She noticed how time had yellowed it and made the creases sharp and pronounced, but the letter was still safely inside. Just as it had been that long-ago day. Scribbled across the front in their mother's handwriting was a single word: *Jordan.*

Heidi felt the tears again. "Here…it's for you." In all her life she hadn't imagined she'd get the chance to do this. But now that they were together, she wasn't about to wait another minute.

He looked at it. "What is it?"

"A letter. From Mom."

Jordan took it from her slowly, as though it were made of gold dust. For a long time he stared at the envelope, running his finger over his name. Then his eyes rose to meet Heidi's. As he spoke, his voice was thick with emotion. "How'd you get it?"

The answer was bound to make Jordan sad. After all, he'd never had a chance to come back to the house for any reason. "My social worker said I could go through my things and save what I wanted." Heidi paused, remembering the moment. "I checked my bedroom, and he went into Mom's room. He looked through the drawers and stuff. The letters were in her nightstand. Right on top. I always thought about opening yours, but I…"

He looked at her, his eyes wet again, too. "You what?"

She blinked and stared at her hands. "I guess a part of me always hoped I might find you again. Even after they told me you were dead."

Jordan drew her close and hugged her for a long time. When he pulled back he stared at the envelope and then at her. "You got one too?"

She sniffed once and nodded. "I've read it so often the folds are starting to wear out."

Jordan's eyes were flooded by what looked like an ocean of grief as he tucked the letter into his back pocket. "Thanks, Heidi." His voice was tender, his eyes even more so.

They heard someone approaching from behind. Heidi turned and saw Charles, his eyes full of questions. She nodded toward him, assuring him it was all right to come closer. He had told her that morning he might stop by sometime around two if they were still at the park.

Now here he was, and Heidi felt happy enough to float. She climbed down to meet him, hugging him and leading him by the hand to meet Jordan. Then she looked into her brother's eyes and spoke the words she'd only dreamed of speaking. "Jordan, this is my husband, Charles. Charles, my brother, Jordan."

The men shook hands, and Charles grinned. "You look pretty good for a dead guy."

All three of them laughed, and what little tension had existed dissipated like morning dew on a summer sidewalk.

They made small talk for a few minutes before Charles's beeper went off. He glanced at it. "Looks like my time's up." He reached for Jordan's hand again and for a brief instant caught Heidi's eye. "Listen, we'd love to have you come for Thanksgiving dinner if you can make it."

Even after all the years that had passed, Heidi knew Jordan well enough to know he was choked up. Too much so to speak. Instead he nodded, swallowing hard, his eyes focused at something on the ground.

Fresh tears nipped at Heidi's eyes and she slid an arm around both of them. "What he's trying to say is, 'Yes, thanks, I'd love to come.'"

Jordan looked up and shifted his gaze from Charles to Heidi and back to Charles again. "She's right." He grinned, though his eyes glistened with tears. "That's exactly what I'm trying to say."

27

Joshua Nunn turned in early that night and almost immediately slipped into the strangest dream. He was in front of a crowd of supporters at Jericho Park, and everyone had an instrument of some kind. "We are here to represent God's people," he heard himself say. Then all at once instruments appeared in everyone's hands and they began to play. The sound was more beautiful than a hundred concert choirs, and not only that but someone was singing. Joshua gazed into the sky and saw hundreds of golden men circling above the park—just like the one who'd appeared to him that day in his office.

A voice boomed from the heavens, and Joshua fell to the ground. "See, Joshua, I have delivered Jericho Park into your hands..." The words faded, absorbed by the music of the people, who were now forming a line and looking to Joshua. *What do I tell them, Lord? I don't have the words.*

This time the voice was silent, echoing loudly within the chambers of his heart. *Be strong and courageous, Joshua. I will go before you. Tell the people to march around the walls.*

Joshua opened his mouth to give the command, but the people were already making their way around the perimeter of the park, playing music as they went.

"Can we shout?" a man yelled from the back of the line.

"Yeah, can we shout yet? Tell us when..."

"We want to shout..."

The voices grew into a chorus of grumbling that silenced the music. Joshua raised his hand high in the air. A surreal silence came over the park, and Joshua looked from person to person, realizing for the first time that he could see into their hearts...the condition of their souls.

"Do not give a war cry, do not raise your voices, do not say a word until the day I tell you to shout." Joshua smiled, for the hearts of the people were good. "Then...shout!"

The music resumed and the people began marching, only instead of their moving around the park, the park and its walled-up statue seemed to be revolving beneath them. At the end of one full rotation the sun disappeared and heaven's golden men shone like stars in the sky. Just as quickly, the sun returned and the people set out around the park again. This happened six times. On the seventh rotation, the sun remained in the sky and the people marched around the park seven times.

"Wait a minute, this isn't right." Joshua yelled out the words, but no one was listening. "This is the story of Joshua in the Bible. Stop! Can't you hear me? Stop! We need real answers here, not a bunch of people marching in place!"

Joshua's hands and legs trembled and suddenly he was falling to his knees, about to cry out to God for help, when there was the loudest, most convincing sound Joshua had ever heard.

Immediately his eyes flew open and he sat straight up in bed. Beside him, Helen stirred and looked at him, eyes blinking. "What was that?"

He stared at the room around him, but it took several beats of his heart before any of it looked familiar. He shot a glance at the alarm clock—it was only 11:30. "I don't know. A dream, I guess…"

Helen snuggled up against her pillow. "That's strange—" she yawned—"I thought I heard something."

Joshua's hands felt clammy, and he shifted his attention to his wife. "Like what?"

She was already drifting back to sleep. "I don't know, something loud. Almost like a shout."

His blood couldn't have felt any colder if he'd been standing in a freezer. Slowly, he settled back into bed and lay there, his eyes open, staring at the ceiling. *What's going on, Lord? What are You trying to tell me?*

But all he received in response was an image that seared its way into his consciousness, keeping him focused and denying him any sleep whatsoever.

The image of plywood walls falling to the ground.

Jordan pulled his car up along the side of Jericho Park at 11:31 that evening and stared into the darkness, allowing his eyes time to adjust. He'd stayed with Heidi and her husband until ten minutes ago, and now he needed a quiet place to think. As driven as he'd been that ill-fated winter when his mother lay dying years earlier, Jordan felt compelled to find his way to Jericho Park.

Especially in light of the task that lay ahead.

He fingered the fragile envelope in his hand and reached up to flip on the car's dome light. All that had happened that day was overwhelming, almost more than he could bear. His sister had found him, and in one afternoon they'd recaptured the closeness they'd shared as kids. He'd found Faith, too…and despite his determination to see walls around the Jesus statue, she'd been nothing but kind and loyal to the memory of their friendship.

And now this.

A letter from his mother, words straight from her hand intended for his heart alone. Jordan felt himself tense at the thought of opening the letter and he searched himself, trying to understand his reluctance. Was it because of her beliefs? Because he'd turned his back on the One who had mattered so desperately to her? Was that why his hand trembled now?

He gritted his teeth and slid his finger carefully under the flap. The paper inside was pressed thin from years of being unread, and Jordan pulled it out slowly, careful not to rip it. As he opened the folds he thought he caught a faint whiff of his mother's perfume, and his hands fell to his lap. He closed his eyes and allowed himself to go back. Not to the days when his mother lay wasting away in her bedroom, but before that…

Back when she would put on a baseball cap, sweatshirt, and jeans and play catch with him in the front yard…or sit behind home plate at his games, flashing a thumbs-up whenever he had a good hit. Back when she and Heidi would do handclaps on the front porch, their sing-song voices ringing out while Jordan and his friends played ball in the street. Happy days, memories that almost seemed to belong to someone else entirely. Times when going to church and loving God Almighty made perfect sense.

The fragrance of her perfume faded. It was getting late, and the temperature in his car was dropping. He tenderly lifted the paper, as though it were his mother's hand in his and not her penned words, and in the brightness of the car light held the letter up and began reading.

Dear Jordan…

He could hear her voice, see her face again—and he missed her more than he thought possible. Tears came, and he closed his eyes, not wanting to break down. He could do this—he could read the letter and allow himself to feel her loss as he hadn't done in years. From somewhere deep in his soul he found the strength. Clenching his jaw he drew a steadying breath through his nose and opened his eyes once more.

Dear Jordan,

As I write this I already know what will happen. God, my eternal Father and yours, is calling me home. I've prayed otherwise, asked God to let me stay with you, but He's made it clear to me that—for whatever reason—it's time. I want you to know I'm not afraid to die. I know this will sound strange to you, but I'm actually excited. I've been doing some reading on heaven lately and I understand it as well as I will this side of eternity. Here— this place we call earth—is not our home, Jordan. It's a waiting room, really. The place where we live together until we're called into the grand palace—the place where real life will begin. Our forever home.

And so my fears are not for myself.

Rather they are for you and Heidi. You are young, Jordan, and though you love God now, I fear deeply that you will change your mind. Life as you know it is about to change, and the world will want you to blame our loving God. But Jordan, it's not His fault death and disease reign here in the shadows. He's not the cause of bad things. In reality, He's the only way out…the only life rope, the only path from the darkness to eternal light.

The only way home.

Jordan blinked, and what felt like a bucket of tears fell down his cheeks. When his vision was clear again he continued.

You see, Jordan, I love you and Heidi so much that I've asked God for something very special. If He wants me to be with Him now, fine. I'm comfortable with that. But I feel in my heart He's promised me this: You and Heidi will live a life of faith. You might stray from Him at first, but eventually…in His perfect timing…you will come back. And one day we will be together again in Paradise.

By the way, I want to say a word about Faith Moses. Her family has been wonderful to us, Jordan. In ways you could not possibly know or understand. If you were older I'd explain in detail how we might not have had food and electricity if it hadn't been for them. As for Faith, I know the two of you care about each other and that you're young. But if…just if you should choose to marry her one day please know this, son: Somewhere up in heaven I'll be giving you the happiest thumbs-up ever.

I'm tired and I need to get some sleep, but I wanted you to know my heart. I may stop breathing, Jordan, but I'll never stop praying for you and Heidi. Begging God that no matter where you journey from here, you'll find your way home again. Because when you do…I'll be there, waiting with open arms. I love you more than you know…Mom.

The sorrow that welled inside Jordan was so great it was as though someone was standing on his chest. His hands trembled as he read the note again, and finally a third time. His mother had known all along…

Forget the fact that Jordan seemed strong and able to handle her loss, that he seemed willing to take on the responsibility of Heidi's well-being. His mother had seen something else, even back then.

She'd seen his heart. And his weakness.

"How could you know me that well?" Jordan's question came in a broken whisper, and he wished with everything inside him he could reach across the seat and hold his mother's hand, hug her like he'd done as a boy. He stared at the letter again, though the tears made it impossible to see. Before he could analyze his thoughts, he began to speak. "Thank You, God…for letting me hear her voice again. How can I thank You?"

Return to Me, son. I have always loved you…let down the walls…

The words that flashed across Jordan's heart were so foreign that he sat up straighter in his seat and glanced around. Switching off the dome light, he inhaled sharply and folded the letter. Then he slipped it back in the envelope and set it squarely on the dashboard, staring out into the evening.

What was he doing? Had that been his voice, praying to God, thanking Him for his mother's words?

Jordan gulped and clenched his hands on the steering wheel. Something felt different, something in the neighborhood of his heart. As though thick, stony walls had surrounded it for years…and now…now they'd crumbled to the ground, and all in the space of a heartbeat. He sat back in the seat and marveled at the lightness of the feeling. Was it his mother's prayer that had done it? Heidi's prayer? Faith's? Jordan wasn't sure, but he knew one thing. He'd come to Bethany a month earlier longing for three women he'd once loved: Faith, Heidi, and his mother. And now…here in the cold darkness of his sports car, alone at Jericho Park, he'd found them all.

His eyes adjusted to the night, and the image of the walled-in Jesus statue came clearly into view. Walled-in just as his heart had been. To people. To God.

Suddenly, more than anything in his life, he wanted to see those plywood walls—walls he'd been instrumental in erecting—come down. He wanted to see the image of Jesus, arms outstretched, beckoning all who had a willing spirit to come to Him…

Come, and He would give rest for even the hardest heart, the coldest soul.

Even a sinner like Jordan.

The truth dawned on him then, and his head spun as he struggled to take it in. God wasn't his enemy. No, the only enemy he'd had these past sixteen years was himself. He'd spent all his time, his talents, waging a battle against the Lord as if that could somehow erase the losses in his life. But in the end that battle would have cost him everything.

Jordan blinked…it was as if he could feel scales falling from his eyes.

God was real. Of course He was. What other explanation could there be for the way Jordan's mother had found His saving grace before her death? Image after image filled Jordan's mind, and he saw the Lord's hand at work throughout his life—even in the darkest hours. He'd survived the cave incident, hadn't he? And what about the other day in New York City, when the trio of muggers was arrested moments before they would have attacked him? What about Faith's victories? And Heidi's? What about the fact that he'd found his sister after all these years only hours after Faith's prayer?

Even little Rosa had reason to believe: God had given her one good hand, after all, and a devoted friend in Faith.

All of it was proof. Proof he'd avoided with a lifetime of hiding behind walls of anger and bitterness. Walls of fear.

Why hadn't he seen it before, the trustworthiness of God?

His gaze lingered on the plywood walls, and he began to shake his head as a heavy mourning swept him. "I'm sorry, Father…I've gone against You at every turn." He began to cry, deep, guttural sobs that worked their way up as the sorrow and regret he felt for a lifetime of wrong attitudes and actions threatened to consume him.

"I'm sorry…I'm so sorry, God…"

The words of the three women he loved most echoed in his heart. He could see Faith, her beautiful eyes filled with sincerity as she whispered, *"You can't stay angry at God forever…"* Heidi's image appeared in his mind and he took in her tearstained face in the hour after they'd found each other, heard her earnest words: *"Sometimes our walk with the Lord gets a little confusing."* The picture faded and his mother's words appeared, words from years ago, words God had saved for this time and place…a message that Jordan understood now was absolute truth: *He's the only way out…the only life rope, the only path from the darkness here to eternal light.*

The only way home…only way home…only way home…

His mother…Heidi…Faith…their wisdom echoed again and again in the core of his being, and Jordan knew he couldn't last another minute. No matter what he'd said before, no matter how he'd bought into a lifetime of lies since his mother's death, a few truths remained. Deep down inside, Jordan Riley still loved God.

And he could wait no longer.

Compelled by a force greater than anything he could remember, moving with a strength that was not his own, Jordan climbed out of the car and began jogging toward the statue.

The cold air burned his lungs, his loafers slipped with each step, but Jordan moved on, determined, energized with a supernatural desire. He reached the statue, and his eyes darted from one board to the next until he saw several areas where the wood was loose. Working his hand into a crack between two panels, he gripped the plywood and pulled. He cried out from the effort as a section of the wall fell to the ground.

Then he moved to the next piece.

One by one, he gripped the wood, tearing the panels from the place where they stood, barely noticing the splinters that pierced his skin. There wasn't a person in sight, but Jordan wouldn't have minded if there were. They could pack the place with people and air what he was doing live on national television for all he cared.

The walls had to come down. The Jesus statue in Jericho Park deserved to be seen.

Faith wasn't sure what lured her to the park that night, whether it was her desire to soak in all that had happened between Jordan and Heidi, or whether she wanted to pray about Rosa Lee and the upcoming hearing. Whatever it was, she hadn't been able to sleep and at almost midnight, bundled in her thickest winter coat, she stepped out of her car, gazed across the park, and considered whether she wanted to find a bench or get back inside where it was warm.

She'd been standing there only a few seconds when she heard loud cries and frightening noises, as though some terrible fight were taking place. She spun around and stared into the darkness. What she saw made her mouth fall open, her eyes widen with a mixture of emotions. Someone was ripping down the walls around the Jesus statue, tearing at them and pulling them down with a brute force Faith had never seen before. She watched, mesmerized, as the panels of plywood fell in heaps of scrap around the base of the statue. The entire process seemed to take no more than five minutes, and when the man was done, he fell back on his heels and stayed there, unmoving.

Lord, what should I do? A ripple of anxiety coursed through Faith, and she glanced around, making sure no one else had seen what happened. She wanted to hurry over and thank the man for doing what she'd wanted to, but a voice of reason told her what she had just witnessed was wrong. The judge had ordered the walls up, and they should have stayed that way until—by God's design—they were ordered down. She pulled her coat tight around herself and began walking toward the man. Whoever he was, he was on her side and he apparently had a deeply personal interest in the Jesus statue.

The man remained on the ground and finally, when she was ten feet from him, he whipped around to face her.

Faith gasped. "Jordan! What are you doing here?" Her heart pounded and she took slow steps in his direction until the gap between them closed. He stared at her, and there was a light in his eyes that hadn't been there before. "You…I didn't see your car."

"I parked on a side street." He was breathing hard, and a layer of sweat glistened on his forehead.

She stared at the statue, at the piles of broken plywood, then her gaze met his again and her voice was barely a whisper. "Why, Jordan?"

He reached out and took her hands in his, searching her eyes as though he was only now seeing her for the first time. "Faith, I'm so sorry…"

The ground beneath her seemed to fall away. "I…I don't understand."

Jordan motioned to the statue. "The lawsuit, the walls…all of it was wrong, Faith. I must have been crazy…"

She couldn't decide whether to laugh or cry, and in the end she did both, coming to him as he stood and wrapped her in his arms. It was a miracle beyond anything Faith could have imagined or hoped for. Jordan had torn down the walls around the Jesus statue, but not before God had torn down the walls around his heart. "What happened…what changed your mind?"

He drew back several inches and met her gaze. "Heidi gave me a letter…from my mom." He shrugged, looking from the statue back to her as though he were still confused himself. "Something happened while I read it, Faith. I don't know how else to explain it." He looked up at the dark, starless sky above them and Faith's heart beat high in her throat from the nearness of him.

God, is it true? Have You really restored his love for You?

Jordan uttered a quiet laugh and shook his head, his eyes still focused on the heavens. "It was all so amazing. I kept hearing you tell me I couldn't be angry at God forever…and Heidi saying sometimes our walk with the Lord gets confusing…and then my mom's words…set aside for me until this exact moment. Right when I needed them most."

He looked at her, and a shiver ran down her spine. "I've been a fool, Faith." He eased his fingers along the sides of her face and drew her gently toward him until their lips met. When they pulled apart, breathless from the cold air and the desire Faith knew they both were feeling, he ran his thumbs gently over her brow, her cheekbones. "Faith, I love you. I always have."

She wanted to shout aloud from the joy that welled up inside her. "I prayed you'd come back, Jordan." She smiled and kissed him tenderly once more. "And now here you are." Her eyes searched his. "Welcome home, friend."

He cupped her face with his hands, framing her with his fingertips as though she were the finest treasure. "I have so much I want to tell you…" He grinned, and she saw the depth of love in his eyes. "So much I want to ask you. But there're some things I need to do first. Can you give me a few days?"

Faith didn't stop to consider his words. It didn't matter what he wanted to tell her. Instead, she let her head fall back a bit and laughed softly before meeting his eyes once more. "Are you kidding? I'm so happy for you, Jordan…whatever you want to talk about, take as long as you'd like."

Jordan brought his face to hers once more, and kissed it in a way that made Faith's knees go weak. "Come on, little Miss Town Favorite," he whispered near her ear. "You need to get home before you freeze to death."

He put his arm around her shoulders, and they were halfway to her car when he stopped and turned to look back at the Jesus statue. Faith did the same and smiled at the way it glistened under the dim park lights. Jordan sucked in a breath through clenched teeth and cast her a hesitant look. "You think God'll forgive me for destroying public property?"

Faith hugged him and they started walking again. "To tell you the truth—" she grinned at him—"I think He already has."

Joshua was up earlier than usual the next morning.

He sipped a mug of French vanilla roast as he flipped on the TV and turned it to the local news. He still couldn't shake the strange dream from the night before or the way the shout had seemed so real.

Real enough that Helen had heard it, too.

A commercial break ended and a newscaster appeared on the screen. "In other news, vandals apparently tore down the walls around the controversial Jesus statue in Bethany, Pennsylvania's Jericho Park last night…"

Joshua was on his feet, his coffee forgotten. *Dear God, did she say what I think she said?* The picture changed and suddenly Joshua was staring at the statue, standing victorious amid a pile of scrap wood. It was true, the dream he'd had the night before…the walls really had fallen!

"Helen! Get in here, quick!" Joshua kept his eyes trained on the screen and in that moment he had the distinct feeling that the walls around the statue weren't the only ones that had fallen the night before.

Father…thank You…I'm sorry for ever doubting…

The battle is Mine, Joshua… I will go before you as I always have. Your prayers have crossed My Jordan and now he and the land are both yours.

Joshua drew his eyebrows together as the strange thought drifted across his heart. Jordan and the land were his? It didn't make sense, but then nothing had since he'd first heard about the case. The day he'd seen the golden man in his office. It didn't matter. The Lord would make everything clear in the end.

"Helen!" He shouted again, his voice filled with celebration. The news segment was almost over and he didn't want her to miss it. "Helen, get in here! You won't believe it… It's just like my dream…"

28

Twenty-four hours before the hearing and with everything that mattered to him waiting back in Bethany, the last thing Jordan wanted to do was drive east to New York. But he knew with every fiber of his being he couldn't move forward without first tying up the loose ends back home.

He walked into T. J. Morris's office just before noon and shut the door.

His friend was working on a file. He whipped around, his features instantly frozen. "Jordan, what the—"

Jordan held up a hand. "Don't talk. Just listen."

T. J. started to stand, started to open his mouth, but Jordan pointed to his friend's chair. "Sit. You owe me that much."

A look of resignation flashed across T. J.'s face. Slowly, silently he sat back down.

Jordan took the chair opposite him, folded his hands, and rested his chin on the tips of his forefingers. "You look nervous, Teej. Why do I get the feeling everyone in my office is somehow doubting me these days?"

T. J. turned and looked out the window, studying the towering office buildings fighting for position in the city skyline. "This is all because of Faith Evans…"

Anger began to boil in Jordan's blood, but he was careful not to let it show. "Her again, huh?"

T. J. sighed and stood up, shuffling toward the window, and then turning to face Jordan again. "I can't believe she's still fighting this thing…I mean, Hawkins thought for sure she'd pull out after the network called."

Jordan had the strange sensation he was dreaming. Almost immediately he could see in T. J.'s eyes that he knew he'd made a mistake by mentioning Faith at all. "How'd Hawkins know about the network call?" Jordan leaned back in his chair and stared unblinking at T. J. "And why do *you* know about it?"

T. J.'s expression went flat. He moved to his chair once more, sat down, and slumped back. "Hawkins knows all about Faith." T. J.'s cheeks puffed out as he exhaled through pursed lips. "You can't tell him I told you, but he's…he's worked hard to make her change her mind about fighting for the statue."

Jordan clenched his teeth and again forced himself to appear unaffected. "What's he done?"

T. J. crossed his arms and studied his feet. "He got her fired—at least he said he was going to—and he pulled some strings at the network…had someone call her and tell her they were interested in her for a national spot if she stayed out of the political limelight." T. J. looked up. "Oh, and that kid she likes, the orphan. Hawkins had her picture yanked from the Web site the day our ad began to run. Just to send Faith a message…to warn her there'd be a price if she got too involved in the case."

T. J.'s eyes clouded with shame, and Jordan felt sick to his stomach. He'd always known Hawkins was ruthless, but this… He thanked God for opening his eyes to all that had been going on around him.

T. J. leveled his gaze at him, and Jordan had the feeling this was maybe the last conversation he'd have with his old friend. In the past week friendship had taken on a deeper meaning for Jordan, one that left him little in common with someone like T. J. Morris. Jordan watched the man struggle for words to fill the awkward silence between them.

"I should have told you sooner… I don't know…things have changed around here, Jordan. There's a lot at stake."

Jordan wanted to stick around and find out what T. J. meant, but he knew he needed to get back to Bethany. And he still had one more stop to make. He studied T. J. It made sense, he supposed, that his friend had been quiet about the attack against Faith. HOUR was made up of a determined group of attorneys bent on seeing justice done the only way they understood it. Even if it meant betraying one of their own.

Jordan stood, and T. J. did the same. For a moment neither of them spoke, and finally Jordan reached out and shook his hand. "I've got a case to finish." He held T. J.'s eyes for a moment, praying that one day the man would understand the decision Jordan was about to make. "See ya, Teej." With that, he turned then and walked out into the hallway.

Jordan expected T. J. to protest or stop him, but as he made his way from his friend's office there was nothing but silence behind him. Two minutes later, Jordan stood in front of Hawkins's secretary, an older lady who had been a prison warden in her younger days—and who still carried the same charm and demeanor. She scowled at him as he approached. "I thought you were supposed to be in Bethany."

Jordan wanted to ignore her and head straight into Hawkins's office, but that would ruin his plan. It was important he play his cards perfectly. He smiled at the woman. "The hearing's not until tomorrow. I need a moment with Mr. Hawkins, if you don't mind."

Her frown eased some and she hesitated. Jordan thought she might decline his request, but then she stood and disappeared down a series of hallways. In less time than it took Jordan to rehearse his game plan, Hawkins came into the foyer, a smile pasted on his face. "Jordan…come on back."

Jordan followed him into the plush, spacious office, the place where they'd cele-brated numerous legal victories in the past. He felt a pang of regret. Those legal victories had put Jordan on the map of human-interest law—and taken him miles from the things that mattered most.

Jordan had sometimes felt intimidated by Hawkins, but this was not one of those times. He understood too clearly the path he needed to follow, the choices he must make in order to finally be true to himself and the God who had never stopped lov-ing him.

Hawkins slammed his forearms onto his desk. The smile was gone. "You're sup-posed to be in Bethany."

Jordan chose his words carefully. "Sir, I had some things to take care of here."

Hawkins waved his hand toward the door. "Well, take care of them and get back to Bethany. We have a case to win there, Riley. You worry me." He searched Jordan's eyes, as though looking for signs of weakness. "I don't know if you understand how important this case is to HOUR."

"Yes, sir," Jordan smiled. "I think I do know."

Suspicion darkened Hawkins's face. "So what do you want? A vote of confidence? You already have that or you wouldn't be there in the first place." Hawkins's voice was gruff. Clearly the man was unsettled over Jordan's unexpected visit.

"I have a question, sir. I thought you'd be the one to ask."

Hawkins gestured as though a fly were buzzing near his face. "Go ahead."

"About the bonus money…" Jordan was guessing, going out on a limb, but it was something he needed to know. "I want to know if the person in public office has promised additional funds for future cases?"

Hawkins eyed him carefully. "Who told you?"

"Same way you heard, sir." Jordan paused. "Found out the other day."

The scowl on his face deepened. "Look, Riley, what happens behind the scenes at HOUR is none of your business. All you need to do is win the case. The partners will take care of you after that, and one day—" his smile was small, forced—"one day you might have an office on this floor." He chuckled, but the sound made Jordan's skin crawl. "You'll make a fine partner, Riley." The room was silent for a beat. "Now get back down there to Bethany and do the job."

Jordan felt a chill pass over him. So he'd been right. Funds were coming from an elected state official. And if Hawkins had been willing to play Faith like a puppet, what else might he have done? What might he still do? Jordan resisted the urge to end the conversation then and there.

He and Faith were going to pray with Heidi and her husband at Heidi's house that night. Jordan hadn't told them yet what he planned to do, but he had told them about the change that had come over him. They knew, as did he, that whatever hap-pened in court the next day, the former Jordan Riley was gone forever.

He glanced out the window, reminding himself to be patient. His heart was already halfway down the highway, but he had one thing to tell Hawkins first. After that…well, if HOUR chose to sue him for what he was about to do, so be it. "Sir, I want you to know that the Bethany case is very important to me. I…well, I have a personal interest in it. And you can be sure tomorrow, when you hear the outcome, it'll be just the way I want it to go." Jordan stood and shook Hawkins's hand. "After tomorrow, I want everyone to know how I feel about that statue."

Hawkins looked like a man warmed by a sudden burst of sunshine. "That's my boy, Riley. You go get 'em."

On Tuesday morning Joshua Nunn arrived at the courthouse an hour before the hearing. A crowd had already gathered on the lawn, and a quick glance showed they were in support of the statue. Joshua nodded at them, waving and pointing a single finger heavenward. "Pray!" he called as he headed into the building. In front of the double doors to the courtroom he found Frank Furlong and several city council members, concern etched on their faces. Frank motioned Joshua aside.

"I got a call this morning from the HOUR organization." Frank wiped a layer of perspiration off his brow. "It isn't good."

Joshua set his briefcase down and crossed his arms. Since his dream about the walls he wasn't even a bit concerned. Faith had told him there was something different about Jordan now. He'd had an awakening, she'd said. Joshua had no idea what Jordan was going to do that morning, but he believed without a doubt that God was in control.

Joshua smiled at the mayor. "Did the person from HOUR give you his name?"

"Peter Hawkins, one of the partners." The others were far enough away not to hear the conversation. "Joshua, he offered me twenty thousand dollars to make a statement in court…to insist that permanent walls go up." Frank raised his eyebrows. "I told him no, but he said he knew for a fact the city was going to lose. He'd seen to it personally."

Joshua took hold of his friend's shoulder. "It's too late to panic. Believe me, the battle of Jericho Park is under control." He patted the mayor on the back and led him toward the others. "In fact, it's already won. No matter what it looks like."

While they were talking a man approached them, someone Joshua had never seen before. In his hand was a stack of papers more than an inch thick. "Sorry to interrupt, Mr. Nunn." He handed the papers to Joshua and smiled. "The townspeople have been working on this for a few weeks. We thought it might help."

In that instant, Joshua knew that everything God had promised from the beginning was about to happen. He would present his case with strength and courage, and no matter what happened, no matter what was said, God Himself would go before him.

29

Jordan was still reveling from the feeling of praying the night before, but even now, fifteen minutes before the hearing, he wasn't exactly sure what he was going to tell the judge. Charles had shown him the Scripture that said not to worry about words…God would provide what to say.

He had two assistants nestled in the row behind him, young attorneys clearly out of the inner loop of happenings back at the office. They were there to make copies or read through case precedents should he need help. Jordan could picture them getting star status as they replayed for Mr. Hawkins the events that were about to play out.

A chorus of whispers and movement filled the courtroom as reporters squeezed into the back and townspeople filled the spectator rows. Jordan made eye contact with Faith, and she nodded to him. He refrained from smiling or winking in response. *She knows my heart, Lord. I can see it in her eyes.*

As he took in the rest of the courtroom, Jordan realized he wasn't nervous. In fact, he felt wrapped in a cocoon of peace that surpassed anything he'd ever known.

Judge Webster appeared at the bench and took his seat. Rapping his gavel twice he shot a frustrated look at several noisy groups. "Order! This court will come to order." Immediately the reporters fell silent.

They don't want to miss the townspeople's tears, Jordan thought. Then he swallowed hard and focused on the judge.

"Very well." Judge Webster looked from Jordan to Joshua and back again. "I have given you thirty days to determine what type of permanent fixture will best keep the people of Bethany, Pennsylvania, from feeling forced to view a statue of Jesus in the middle of—" he checked his notes—"Jericho Park."

A holy presence seemed to settle around Jordan, and he knew instinctively that Faith was praying for him. Faith and Joshua and Heidi and Charles. Most of the people in Bethany for that matter.

The judge cleared his throat. "At our last meeting, counsel for the plaintiff recommended a ten-foot-high, permanent brick wall to resolve the matter." He looked at Joshua. "But before I can order anything, I promised to give the defense and the—"

he arched his eyebrows—"new owner of the statue a chance to speak before this court."

Joshua Nunn, the city's attorney was first. The older man looked ten years younger as he took the floor and moved slowly to a spot in front of the judge. "Your Honor, the people of Bethany believe their voice has not been heard in this matter. It is *their* park and they have enjoyed the statue in question for decades without incident." He pulled out a thick stack of papers and handed it to Judge Webster. "I'd like to introduce these documents as Exhibit A."

The judge wrinkled his nose as though he'd caught whiff of a bad odor. "What is it?"

Joshua smiled. "The signatures of more than five thousand citizens of Bethany and the surrounding towns. People who do not want walls around the Jesus statue." He hesitated.

Across the room Jordan masked the way his heart soared within him.

I'm right there with them, Lord…thank You for letting me see…

"If I may read the opening paragraph, Your Honor?"

Judge Webster rested his forearms on the edge of the bench and sighed. "Very well, proceed."

"Thank you." Joshua held the paper out in front of him and studied it. Then he raised his voice so even the reporters in the back row could hear him. "We, the people of Bethany, Pennsylvania, believe it is important for our voices to be heard. The statue of Jesus Christ in Jericho Park neither offends us nor threatens our religious freedom, as some have contested. Rather it is our privilege as Americans not to be subjected to censorship."

Joshua hesitated, and Jordan could sense a chill making its way down the spines of all in attendance. "Placing permanent walls around a statue given as a gift and now belonging to a private citizen—just because it depicts the central figure of the Christian faith—is censorship and it is discriminatory. We are, for that reason, asking that common sense and true freedom prevail in your decision." Joshua looked up at the judge. "The signatures begin at the bottom of the page."

The only sound in the courtroom was that of Judge Webster turning the pages of the petition. Page after page after page…apparently until he was convinced the signatures were valid. He cleared his throat and adjusted his glasses, his eyes still on the document. "Obviously I'm unable to count the names, but I'm willing to admit this as Exhibit A and stipulate that it appears to have the signatures of some five thousand people." He looked at Joshua. "However, as I said when hearings first began in this case, I am not obligated to pay heed to this exhibit or the protests or the opinions of newscasters. It is my decision alone." His eyes narrowed. "Anything else, counselor?"

The attorney folded his arms in front of him and cocked his head. "I had an argument prepared, Your Honor." He shook his head once, as though even he couldn't believe the strength in the voice of the people, a voice that Jordan knew would resonate in his heart forever. "But I believe in a government that is of the people…by the people…for the people. A government our forefathers would have recognized as constitutional." He waited a beat and a smile filled his face. "They elected you, if I'm not mistaken."

Jordan glanced at the judge and thought he looked less confident than before.

"As far as I'm concerned, Your Honor, the people have spoken. Anything I might say at this point would hardly be relevant." He looked at Jordan and back at Judge Webster. "The defense rests."

Jordan considered all that hung on the next few minutes. Members of the press held their collective breath, waiting to share the story with the nation. Hawkins no doubt was pacing by the telephone in his plush office, and somewhere a room full of advisors to a shady politician stood by anxiously awaiting the outcome as well.

Despite all of that, Jordan could not remember ever feeling more relaxed.

It was Faith's turn. Judge Webster scanned the spectator section and leaned into his microphone. "The court would like to hear from Ms. Faith Evans."

Faith made her way to the front of the courtroom, and Jordan joined the others watching her as she took the witness stand. She looked professional, like she'd just walked off the studio set at the station, and Jordan wondered if she knew how proud he was of her.

Although Faith made an undeniable presence, Judge Webster did not look affected by it. "Miss Evans, as a landowner and party to this matter, I will allow you to voice your concerns." He sounded unemotional, as though his dialogue were scripted. "You may proceed."

Faith smiled at him. "Thank you, Your Honor." Her eyes shifted to the courtroom and locked onto Jordan's. His pulse quickened. How had he survived sixteen years without her? She looked away, her eyes dancing as she searched the faces of the spectators. "The reason I purchased the property in Jericho Park is because I think the people of Bethany deserve to see the Jesus statue. Every hour, every day of the year. Anytime they'd like." Jordan was struck again by both her beauty and eloquence. He stifled a chuckle. Even a crusty old guy like Judge Webster had to dread making a decision against her.

"When the statue belonged to the city, it was a liability the people were unaware of until the judge's earlier ruling." She turned back to Judge Webster. "But now that it belongs to me, I believe I have a right to see it, to access it like any other property owner. By placing a permanent wall around it, that would of course be impossible." She shrugged lightly and looked back at the spectators, this time bypassing Jordan.

"Ultimately I agree with Joshua Nunn and the citizens who signed the petition. Let the people decide. And in this case, my purchase of the property has helped to do just that. The mandatory placement of a permanent wall around my property would be a violation of my right to access it." She leveled her gaze at the judge in a way that was just short of angry. "And that would defeat the whole point, Your Honor. Because you told this court at the first hearing that you were concerned for the *rights* of the people. I'm assuming that means my rights as well." She smiled politely. "That's all, Your Honor."

In the silence that followed Faith's testimony, it hit Jordan that no matter what argument he might present today, God's plans would prevail. Based on the statements by Joshua, the valid points by Faith, the fact that the statue was now clearly private property, and the signatures of five thousand local voters, Jordan was sure he wouldn't have had a chance. He swallowed and looked down at his hands, humbled by the enormity of it all. He would have lost the case—and possibly his job. Maybe even the relationships he'd rekindled with Heidi and Faith.

Most of all he would have missed a chance at new life, the life God planned for him to live all along.

The judge was rambling on about the decision being his no matter what anyone else brought to the table. Jordan's thoughts wandered for a moment and almost immediately his stomach twisted. The loss of this case would cause fallout from the lowest levels of HOUR to the highest levels of state government.

It was entirely possible Jordan might never work as a lawyer again after today. What firm would trust him after what he was about to do? *See me through it, God...please. Give me the words to say.*

Faith had returned to her seat, and Judge Webster smiled weakly at Jordan. He knew the judge wanted him to save the day, to give an irrefutable argument strong enough to quell the voice of the people. "The plaintiff will now state his position. Mr. Riley?"

He thought of the hours he'd spent preparing for his career, his fervor at winning battles for the wrong side—and he was assaulted by warring emotions. *These are my last few minutes as an attorney for HOUR...*

Jordan took the floor, and his anxiety dissipated, as though he were sailing on a reservoir of peace. He had no idea what he was going to say, but he wasn't worried.

God was in control.

"Thank you, Your Honor." He slipped his hands in his pockets and made his way closer to the judge. "Several years ago when I first became a lawyer, I had one thing in mind." He stopped and locked eyes with Judge Webster. "Find the wrongs and right them."

Jordan exhaled heavily. "For years I thought those wrongs centered around Christianity, around the people who insisted on being public about their religious beliefs." An image came to mind of Mr. Campbell, the high school teacher Jordan had gotten fired for praying with a student. He cringed inwardly. *Lord, if only there was some way to make it up to him...*

And suddenly Jordan knew that there was.

"I thought those things, but that was before I filed suit against the city of Bethany." He turned and faced the curious eyes of the spectators and the concern on the reporters' faces. "I've found out a lot since I started this case." A smile tugged at the corners of his lips. "I found a friend I thought was lost forever..." He let his gaze linger on Faith for an instant before looking around once more. "I found a sister who thought I was dead...and I found the heart's cry of my mother, who I buried in Bethany when I was just a boy. But most of all I found this."

Jordan faced the judge and took another step closer. *Let him hear me, Lord...let all of them hear me...* "Most of all I found out that putting walls around myself, or walls around Jesus Christ isn't righting a wrong."

A wave of whispers washed over the courtroom, and from the corner of his eye, Jordan saw several townspeople break into grins and grab hold of the hands of someone next to them. There was no turning back now.

"Order!" Judge Webster was furious. "There will be no talking, no—" he waved his hands in the air—"no outbursts like that, or I'll have everyone thrown out."

Quiet fell over the crowd, and Jordan waited until he had the judge's full attention before resuming. "I could tell you that I concede here this morning. That Mr. Nunn's speech about government of the people, by the people, for the people was right on, or that Faith Evans made a valid legal argument by requesting that her right to access and view her property not be denied." He cocked his head and paced a few steps toward the spectators. "I could tell you the HOUR organization has no right removing a landmark from a city where five thousand people want it to remain." He stopped and gazed past the people to Joshua, sitting serenely at the defense table not ten feet away. "But I don't want to concede."

The courtroom seemed to hold its collective breath, waiting for Jordan's next word the way a retriever waits for a tennis ball. He smiled at them, praying they could see the difference in him. "Instead, I want to add my voice to those who have already spoken today by saying this—" he spun slowly around and stared at Judge Webster— "please, Your Honor, put a *three*-foot-high wrought iron rail fence around the base of the Jesus statue, but don't wall it in. I have no right, and neither do you nor anyone else, to censor a park statue because it depicts a religious figure."

Jordan folded his arms and looked down for a moment, overcome with emotion. When he felt strong again he looked up and continued. "My days of attacking the very beliefs this country was founded on are over, Your Honor."

Judge Webster's face was chalky white, and an air of stunned amazement hung in the courtroom. Nearly a minute passed before the judge spoke. "Am I to understand that you are revoking your earlier request, counselor? That you no longer want this...this Jesus statue surrounded by walls?" His voice was quieter than at any time since earlier that fall when the proceedings first began.

Jordan felt a twinge of pity for the judge. It wasn't his fault God had opened Jordan's eyes, and now he had little choice but to rule in favor of the people—a ruling he was clearly against. *Help him see the truth, too, God.* "Yes, Your Honor. I'm revoking my earlier request."

For a moment, Judge Webster did nothing but stare at Jordan. Then he rolled his eyes, looking like a man disappointed in a favorite son's bad decision. "Very well. I will take the information shared with the court this day and make my decision. Court is adjourned for fifteen minutes." He rapped his gavel once and then quickly left the room.

Jordan saw the reporters pressing in toward the front of the courtroom, each of them desperate for an interview with him. He looked to the spot where Faith had been sitting, but she was gone. He moved back to the plaintiff's table, sat down, and rested on his forearms. There was a tap on his shoulder and Jordan braced himself. After today, the public sector would never again view him the same way.

He turned around, expecting to find a microphone in his face. Instead he saw Faith, eyes glowing with more feeling than Jordan had ever seen before. Unconcerned about the cameras aimed on him, despite the fact that the entire country would know his feelings by tomorrow, he stood and came to her. A railing separated them, but he drew her close anyway, hugging her, certain that somehow—despite the camera flashes lighting up the room—everything was going to work out.

He pulled back and saw there were tears in her eyes.

"That was perfect."

He lifted his eyebrows. "It wasn't planned." He squeezed her hands, still mindful of the crowd closing in, watching them. "I told God I'd let Him do the talking."

A reporter wedged herself between them and stared at Jordan. "Mr. Riley, did someone pay you to revoke your earlier request?"

"No, of course not, I—"

"Mr. Riley—" Another reporter, this one with a microphone half the size of his face, angled in closer and took Jordan by the sleeve. "Now that you've become religious, are you resigning from the HOUR organization?"

"I didn't become religious. I've always known God…I just got sidetracked for a few years because of personal—"

"Mr. Riley, what is your relationship with Faith Evans?"

"Did you change your mind about the statue because of your feelings for her?"

"Mr. Riley, tell us why you no longer think human rights are important?"

The questions came at him like bullets from a semiautomatic. Faith cast him a quick look of sympathy and allowed herself to be squeezed back by the media. Her eyes told him they'd talk later. As she moved to the back of the courtroom, a vision filled the screen in Jordan's mind. Faith and him and Rosa Lee in a church full of people. And something else. His mother smiling down at him from heaven, giving him the biggest thumbs-up he'd ever seen.

His heart grew warm with compassion for the throng around him. After all, he'd been just like them a week ago. He turned his attention to the reporters. "Rights are very important to me, but I understand now that I've been *attacking* human rights, not defending them. People have a right to freely express their religious views whether in this court or…"

Jordan continued to answer questions, and the fifteen minutes passed quickly. Judge Webster needed only one rap of his gavel to bring the courtroom to order. Reporters hurried back to their spots and a hush gave way to utter silence. The judge looked about, and there was humility in his eyes. "This court is now in session." He glanced at the piece of paper in his hand. "I have reached a decision in the case of the HOUR organization versus the people of Bethany, Pennsylvania."

Jordan clenched his jaw and prayed.

A heavy sigh drifted from the judge's mouth. "Honestly, I had my mind made up about this case long ago. From a personal standpoint, I agreed fully with Mr. Riley's earlier argument." He cast a discouraged glance at Jordan. "But this is not a case I can decide based on my personal viewpoint. Instead I must—according to the law— make my decision based on all possible evidence and points of view." His eyes shifted to the spectators. "As Mr. Nunn reminded us, this is government of the people, by the people, and for the people. And I believe in this case the people have spoken."

He tapped his finger on the paper and looked from Joshua Nunn to Jordan and back again. "For that reason, I hereby rule that a three-foot high, wrought-iron rail-ing shall be erected around the Jesus statue in Jericho Park, along with a plaque declaring it to be private property."

Jordan wanted to raise his fist in the air, jump on the table, and shout to all the courtroom about God's faithfulness. Instead, he glanced up toward the window, at the blue sky beyond, more grateful than words could express. How awful it would have been if...

Jordan banished the thought. Things had worked out, just as the Lord had prom-ised.

A wave of excited whispers rose through the courtroom, but the judge said noth-ing. He glanced at Jordan, but refused to make eye contact, allowing his eyes to settle on Joshua instead. "If there are no further questions—" he waited for a moment— "this court is adjourned."

Judge Webster left in less time than it took Jordan to stand and start loading his briefcase. The moment the judge was gone, a cheer rose up across the courtroom, the kind usually reserved for game-winning touchdowns or buzzer-beating three-pointers. The cheers filled Jordan's senses, and he had the distinct impression that the applause of heaven itself was mingled in the sound. He looked behind him and saw that Faith was gone, but that was okay. She and Heidi had agreed to meet right after the hearing since Heidi had stayed home with the baby.

"Jordan..."

He turned and saw Joshua Nunn. He reached out his hand, aware that the reporters were closing in again. "Hello, Mr. Nunn. Great job."

Joshua smiled, and Jordan had the strange feeling he'd spoken to the man before. Something about his eyes. Then it hit him. Shining from the older man's eyes was the same peace and warmth and certainty he saw in Faith's, the same he'd seen in his mother's eyes back when he was a boy. Wasn't there something about that in the Bible? The eyes being the window to the soul? Jordan wasn't sure, but he knew one thing. He had a friend in Joshua Nunn.

One that he felt sure had been praying for him.

"Faith tells me you've had an interesting week."

Jordan nodded. "Yes, sir." He dropped his gaze for a moment and then found Joshua's eyes once more. "I'm sorry about all this. I was wrong. There's no other way to say it."

Joshua put his hand on Jordan's shoulder and grinned. "I didn't come over here for an apology, Jordan. I have something to ask you. Now let's get out of here before the press eats you alive..."

30

The warm smell of fresh roasted turkey filled the Benson home, and Joshua Nunn could hardly wait for the meal. In the days since the hearing, he and Jordan had talked at length, and finally Jordan had promised an answer by Thanksgiving Day.

"It's a lot to think about," Jordan had said the night before. "I'll give you my answer tomorrow. Over dinner."

Now, as the others bustled about the kitchen and Joshua and Helen watched the final minutes of a football game, he smiled to himself. The idea that Jordan would tell him over dinner was a good sign. Especially given the group of people gathered there. Heidi and her husband and baby daughter, Jordan and Faith. Even Rosa Lee had been able to come for the day. They were a tight group with everything in common and every reason to celebrate, even if Jordan had been fired the day of the hearing. Jordan hadn't gone into details, but apparently his conversation with the partners at HOUR had not been a pleasant one. He'd planned to quit anyway, and Joshua had a hunch God had better plans for the young attorney than any of them could imagine.

Faith's news had been better. The media groundswell of interest surrounding her had continued to be positive—even after Jordan's statements in court and the photographs of their hug had made the front page of every newspaper for a couple hundred miles. As a result, WKZN made an executive decision to hire her back on a part-time, feature basis. She'd work out of the same Philadelphia studio as before, but her feature pieces would run nationally. It was a dream position that paid twice as much as her previous job and allowed her more time off.

In addition, the previous station manager, Dick Baker, had been relocated to an affiliate in Los Angeles.

Joshua smiled. It was just one miracle after another.

He remembered again the dream he'd had in his office back before Jordan had filed suit, back when he couldn't imagine lasting another day without Bob Moses' help. *You're so faithful, God.* And he realized the Lord hadn't merely brought down the walls in Jericho Park, He'd torn the walls down from their hearts as well. All of them.

His and Faith's, and especially Jordan's. He saw again the portraits he'd seen in his dream. One of himself, and one of a handsome, angry young man. Joshua chuckled softly.

God had done everything he'd promised.

And now that Jordan was smiling more, his picture was going to look absolutely fantastic on the office wall.

Faith set the mashed potatoes on the table and caught Heidi's eye. "I think we're ready."

From across the kitchen, Jordan smiled first at Faith, then at Heidi. He had Rosa Lee by the hand and he bent down and whispered something to the child before the two of them took their places on either side of Faith. Rosa's entire face was lit up, a grin spreading from ear to ear as she took Faith's hand.

Thank You, God. I've never been so happy in all my life. Daddy, if only you could see me now…

Over the past two days, she and Jordan had spent hours together, much of it with Rosa. There was no denying the feelings she and Jordan had for each other, and though she wasn't exactly sure of Jordan's intentions, she could see how completely he'd fallen for the little girl as well.

"Okay, everyone, time to eat." Heidi's voice rang across the room, and in the den Joshua turned off the television. The group gathered around the table and held hands. Heidi smiled at her brother. "Jordan, would you say the blessing for us?"

Faith squeezed Jordan's hand as a hundred memories danced across her heart. Memories of Jordan and Heidi and her as kids, believing that somehow they'd be together forever. And now, against all the odds, on a day devoted to giving God thanks, here they were.

Jordan returned the squeeze and bowed his head. "Lord, we come to You this day with full hearts, hearts of gratitude for all You've done." He paused and Faith knew he was struggling to find his voice. "Thank You for the people we love, for bringing us back together. And thank You for this food. Help us to stay close to You now and always, in Jesus' name, amen."

Faith slipped her arm around Jordan's waist and hugged him, letting him know that she understood how deep his feelings were. Laughter and conversation broke out as they sat down and loaded their plates. A full thirty minutes passed before Jordan stood up and grinned, waiting for the others to notice him.

Faith's heart skipped a beat and she put down her fork. He'd hinted that he had something important to announce at dinner, and with all the whispering he'd been doing with Joshua and Rosa, she had no idea what it might be.

When everyone was quiet, Jordan looked across the table at Joshua. "I won't take too long, but I have a question to answer and a question to ask. I wanted all of you to witness both because, well—" his eyes lit up and he smiled at each of them before continuing—"this is one of those moments you remember forever."

People put down their forks, and across the table Faith could see tears in Heidi's eyes. She could hardly believe that a few months ago Heidi had thought Jordan was dead, and now here they were, celebrating Thanksgiving together.

Jordan set his gaze on Joshua again. "Joshua has asked me to team up with him at the Religious Freedom Institute here in Bethany."

Faith's breath caught in her throat. Why hadn't she realized that was what he and Joshua had been talking about? She waited while Jordan continued.

"After praying and thinking through my options, I'm absolutely sure that I want the job."

Joshua stood and reached his hand across the table to Jordan. Their handshake had the definite air of finalizing the deal. "I never had a single doubt." Joshua dropped Jordan's hand, circled the table and gave him a hearty hug. "Welcome aboard!"

Faith clapped her hands, then joined the men, reaching an arm around each of their necks and kissing Jordan on the cheek. "I didn't know you were thinking about working here!"

He squeezed her, his eyes shining with new life, new hope. "Let's just say I've had a lot on my mind and wanted to wait until—"

"Okay," Heidi interrupted. Faith and the others turned to look at her, and Faith lowered her eyebrows curiously. What was that look on Heidi's face? Like she was keeping a secret that was about to burst to the surface. Heidi raised a single eyebrow at Joshua and then leveled her gaze at her brother. "You said you had a question to answer and a question to ask. You've answered the question about the job. So what's the question you want to ask?"

"Give me a minute." Jordan grinned and motioned for Faith and Joshua to sit down. When they'd slipped back into their seats, he asked Faith and Rosa to turn their chairs out from the table. They did as he asked, and he positioned himself between Faith and Rosa, dropping to one knee.

Tears stung at Faith's eyes and she had to remind herself to breathe. Was this what she thought it was? Was he...could he be...? She blinked and two tears slid down her cheeks as she uttered a sound that was part laugh, part sob. "Jordan?"

He took hold of her fingers in response, then reached out for Rosa's hand with the other. "All my life I've searched for a special kind of love..." His eyes grew watery and they stayed locked on Faith's, as though they were the only two people in the room. "The kind of love I'd known only once in my life, back when I was thirteen and shared a special friendship with a girl named Faith."

Fresh tears filled her eyes. Was this really happening? Was he going to ask her to...?

Jordan swallowed, struggling to keep his emotions at bay. "And now that I've found you again, I know that I could never share that kind of love with anyone else. Faith, with all my heart I want to love you and cherish you, laugh with you and grow old with you." He looked at Rosa and nodded. She pulled a velvet box from a pocket in her dress and handed it to Jordan.

Faith watched, eyes wide, mouth open. Rosa had been in on the secret the whole time? Her head was spinning, and she felt as though she were dreaming, but she held her questions at bay. Jordan released the hold he had on her fingers and opened the box. From inside he pulled out a diamond solitaire ring. As the others watched—and Heidi cried softly from the other side of the table—Jordan locked eyes with Faith once more. "So my question is this: Faith Evans Moses, will you marry me?"

Across the table, Joshua's wife, Helen, gasped, and her hands flew to her mouth. Her smile lit up that corner of the room, and Faith knew that her parents' friends were as sure about Jordan as she was. She directed her focus on Jordan. Surely there would have been a hole in her chest if she'd looked down, because her heart was gone, given completely to a man she'd wondered about most of her life. Deep in the core of her being Faith knew that this was the holy plan her father had spoken of for so many years. Finally, here in Bethany, when it seemed all hope was lost, God had shown her His most excellent reality for her life.

Jordan held the ring out, and she lifted her hand, allowing him to slide it on her finger. It glistened, casting a spray of light across the dinner table and causing the others to lean closer, looking over the turkey and stuffing and green bean casserole to see how it shone and to wait for her answer.

Faith met Jordan's gaze, praying he could see the way she felt for him, the way she'd always felt for him and always would feel. All the days of her life. "Yes, Jordan Riley, I will marry you and love you, laugh with you and grow old with you."

There was a chorus of cries and applause as Jordan stood and eased Faith into his arms. He moved his mouth near her ear and whispered, "I love you, Faith."

Her words were equally quiet, equally private. "I love you too. Forever, Jordan."

Rosa stood at their side clapping and smiling and tugging on Jordan's sweater. "Is it time, is it?"

He patted her head and helped Faith back to her chair. The others remained standing, wondering what Jordan was going to do next. Faith still felt as though she were floating, but she sat down and took Rosa's hand as Jordan pulled another velvet box from his back pocket. This time he took a small locket from the box and opened it. Inside were two single pictures, one of Jordan and one of Faith.

Faith hadn't thought she could possibly feel happier until now, but as she watched Rosa's face, she knew she was wrong. Jordan was on his knee again. "Rosa, now that Faith has agreed to marry me, we have a question for you." He winked at Faith, and took her fingers in his. "Faith has been praying for a family for you, honey. And now that the two of *us* will be a family…" Jordan let go of Faith's hand and leaned forward. He put the locket around Rosa's neck, and when it was clasped, he leaned back on his knee again. "We want to ask you to be our little girl."

Rosa squealed and threw herself into Jordan's arms. Faith couldn't hold her tears back any longer. She wept for God's goodness, for the amazing way that only He could have worked this miracle between the three of them. Faith wished her mother could have been there to share this moment with them, but it would be fun sharing every detail with her by phone that night. With her arms around Jordan and Rosa, the three of them formed a hug. They stayed that way as her father's partner stood and circled the table, putting himself directly behind them.

"I say we all gather around this family-to-be and ask God to bless them."

Heidi was crying, using her Thanksgiving napkin to dab at the mascara beneath her eyes. With Charles by her side, the two of them joined Helen and the others in a circle around Faith, Jordan, and Rosa. Before they could pray, Joshua began to sing. It was Faith's favorite hymn, the one the people had sung on the courthouse lawn back when everything about her life, about all their lives, looked like it was falling apart. She could think of no other song that so aptly fit the moment. She choked back her tears and joined in while Jordan did the same.

"Great is Thy faithfulness, oh God my Father, there is no shadow of turning with Thee…Thou changest not, Thy compassions they fail not, as Thou has been Thou forever will be…"

Heidi and Charles and Joshua and Helen added their voices as the song grew. "Great is Thy faithfulness, great is Thy faithfulness…morning by morning new mercies I see."

Rosa's eyes lit up and she added her voice as well. "All I have needed Thy hand hath provided. Great is Thy faithfulness…great is Thy faithfulness…great is Thy faithfulness, Lord unto me."

As the song ended, Joshua led them in prayer, and Faith tried to believe it was all true. Jordan had really found her after all these years, he'd really asked her to marry him and asked Rosa to be their daughter.

It was beyond her comprehension. *Lord, Your faithfulness knows no limits. How have You pulled this all together, worked this out?*

My daughter, I have always known the plans I had for you…and it is My pleasure to do more than you can ever ask or imagine…

God's words echoed in Faith's heart, and she allowed herself to be wrapped in them, covered by them, loved by them. She tuned back in to Joshua's prayer and held tight to the people who would soon be her family, the people she loved more than life itself.

"Finally, Father, we thank You because You work all things to the good for those who love You, for those who are called according to Your purpose. And together, as a family united in Your truth, we look forward to the wonder You have in store for us today…and all the days of our lives. In Christ's name we pray…"

With the smell of pumpkin pies baking in the oven and refrains of Joshua's favorite hymn ringing in their hearts, they finished the prayer together with a single word:

"Amen!"

31

*J*oe and Jenna Campbell led their three children into Jericho Park and set up their blanket not far from the famous statue, the one that had caused a national commotion almost a year earlier.

"Okay, kids, there it is. The Jesus statue."

Their ten-year-old son cocked his head and stared up at the eyes of the statue, taking in the way Jesus' hands were outstretched, welcoming, beckoning all who were weary to come. "That's exactly how I picture Jesus, Dad."

Joe stared at the statue, liking the way its presence dominated the park. "Yes, son. Me too."

The family moved closer, and Jenna put their picnic basket down as the five of them formed a circle on the ground.

"Why are we here again, Dad?" Their six-year-old daughter smiled through curious eyes. Joe knew she was unaware of all that had gone on since the trial, back when he'd been fired by the New York school district.

"Well, honey, about a year ago Daddy lost his job because he wanted to pray with one of the kids at school." He looked at his wife and saw tears glistening in her eyes. "Mommy and I wanted to come here to celebrate how good God is for taking care of us and getting me a new job."

Their eight-year-old daughter nodded as though she understood the situation completely. "That's why we moved here, right, Daddy?"

Joe grinned and tousled the child's hair. "Right, sweetheart. A few months ago a nice attorney here in Bethany, a Mr. Riley—" he caught Jenna's gaze—"called me and told me about a teaching job at the high school here. He put in a good word for me, and I got hired." He looked at the faces of his family and felt his heart swell with gratefulness. "We're here today to celebrate God and all He's done for us, for His provision and love and care."

Jenna took his hand and finished the thought for him. "And for sending Mr. Riley at just the right time."

Joe thought back to that awful day in court, when Jordan Riley had fought so hard against him and he'd lost his job. He could see it as clearly as if it had happened yesterday. There they were, Jenna and him, immediately after the judge's decision, bowing their heads together in prayer, scarcely aware of the chaos that reigned in the courtroom. Joe drew a deep breath and searched the faces of his children, wondering how much they understood. "The day I lost my job, your mom and I prayed very, very hard."

Their oldest daughter angled her head, curiously. "Did you pray for a new job, Daddy?"

"No, we didn't, honey." He smiled at his wife and gently squeezed her fingers. "We weren't worried about that because God always takes care of us." He paused. "We prayed that Mr. Riley might love Jesus one day."

"That was a good thing to pray, right, Daddy?" Their youngest nodded confidently.

"But does he?"

"Yeah, Daddy, does he love Jesus now?" The kids spoke at the same time, and Joe and Jenna laughed.

"Yes." Joe's eyes were suddenly wet. He remembered Jordan's phone call a few months earlier, the tears in the man's voice as he apologized for costing Joe his job…and the joy as Jordan shared the fact that he had joined the ranks of believers. "Yes, kids, he loves Jesus very, very much."

"That's kind of like a miracle, isn't it, Dad?" Their oldest waited for an answer.

"Yes." Joe gathered his family close and gazed up at the Jesus statue. "It's the best miracle of all."

FEDERAL COURT RULES CITY NOT REQUIRED
TO HIDE STATUE OF JESUS

(Marshfield, Wisconsin)—An atheist group's request to erect a ten-foot-high wall around a statue of Jesus was denied May 9, 2000, by U.S. District Court Judge John Shabaz. The decision came as a result of a lawsuit filed by the Freedom From Religion Foundation, whose goal was to remove or hide the statue, which has stood in a Marshfield city park since 1959.

The case was dismissed by the U.S. District Court after the city sold the statue to a private landowner in December, 1998. On appeal, the U.S. Court of Appeals for the Seventh Circuit held on February 4, 2000, that the sale of the statue was valid and appropriate, but ordered the city to take steps to differentiate between the property owned by the city and the private property where the statue is located.

Judge Shabaz in his final decision said the Constitution did not require what he called "visual separation" of the statue from the rest of the park. He accepted the proposal from the city requiring the erection of a four-foot-high, wrought-iron fence that will not block the view of the statue. The city will display a sign signifying that the statue and the land it sits on is privately owned.

The city of Marshfield was represented by the American Center for Law and Justice (ACLJ), and by Harold Wolfgram, assistant city attorney for the city of Marshfield. The ACLJ specializes in First Amendment law and focuses on pro-family, pro-life, and pro-liberty cases.

Although *On Every Side* was inspired by this true event, it is not intended to accurately depict any aspect of either the ACLJ, the Freedom From Religion Foundation, or any other person or event involved or associated with the actual incident as it took place.

Dear family and friends:

It's good to meet with you again and as always to thank you for traveling with me through the pages of this, my latest book. I must tell you how much I enjoyed writing *On Every Side*—both the heart-stopping research and the way God worked in me, bringing down walls of my own as He brought Faith and Jordan and Joshua to life.

As with all my books, there is a nugget of truth nestled between the lines of this story. The truth is that walls have been around since the beginning of time, whether they belonged to Adam and Eve, who allowed a barrier between themselves and God, or the people of Jericho, who believed they could keep God out by building a wall around their city.

Before I wrote *On Every Side,* I thought walls were more of an Old Testament issue. Walled-in cities; walled-in, stubborn people; temple wall, that kind of thing. But as the story came to life, God began to make something very clear.

Walls are a part of our lives to this very day.

Oh, we may not think we've put walls between God and us. I certainly didn't think so. But I discovered that without meaning to, I had allowed schedules and responsibilities and the busyness of life to put distance between the Lord and me. In a sense, I allowed walls to form. I'm guessing that this is true for you as well. Though your intentions may have been good, though they may still be good, somewhere along the way you've allowed space to come between you and the Father.

It is my prayer that in reading this book you've had a chance to take stock of your faith life. That where you've recognized walls, you've found time perhaps even now to draw nearer to God, to tear down the walls and enjoy once again that intimate walk with Him.

Of course, for some of you the walls have been in place as far back as you can remember. People might have told you about God, and in the back of your mind you knew you'd have to deal with Him someday. But not yet, not while you were busy with life and planning your agenda without Him. For you, I pray this will be a life-changing moment, here, now. That you will recognize as long as walls exist between you and God your situation is desperate. And that you will beg His forgiveness. Ask Him to knock down the barriers, brick by brick. Believe that He will take you into His loving arms and grant you mercy and grace so long as you take the first step.

If this is you, and if here and now you've made a decision to accept Christ for life and allow the walls to fall, please do this: Get connected with a Bible-believing church and plant yourself in the fertile soil of God's Word. That way you will be sure to grow deep roots, roots that will prevent anything from ever coming between you and the Lord again.

On that note, I'd like to ask for your prayers for our family. We have adopted three precious little six-year-old boys from Haiti. Many of you have journeyed with me through all my books and know a little more about how we came to this decision. For those who don't, let me say it was a two-year process. We began by believing God wanted us to take into our hearts and homes one or two children who were orphans. And so we searched social services' photolisting files online from across the United States.

What we found was sad indeed.

Generally, if a child was up for adoption, and if there weren't already ten or twenty families waiting in line for a child, then our social worker would simply say, "That child can't go to a family with young children in the home." Or, "There are severe anger issues with that child, making him unsafe around other children." Or, "That child has a considerable number of special needs."

In the end, we nearly gave up.

Then God led us to a wonderful Christian orphanage in Haiti called Heart of God Ministries. We found our little boys on a photolisting on their Web site (www.hgm.org) and prayed for God to open the door for us to adopt them if it was His will. Let's just say God has blessed us indeed, opening the door so wide it came off the hinges! Our three birth children are thrilled about the arrival of their new brothers and have talked about them for nine months as though they're already here.

A few days ago, three-year-old Austin said, "Mommy, will you pick up E. J. and Sean and Joshua from their house?"

I said, "No, honey. They don't have a house."

He blinked. "Do they have a castle?"

I smiled at him and smoothed a finger over his cheek. "No, buddy. They don't have anything. Not even a mommy and daddy."

With that, baby tears filled his eyes, and this normally rough-and-tumble child said, "Can we be their mommy and daddy?"

Yes, I believe God has all our hearts ready. We anticipate a God-directed transition, safe travel, and a closer walk with Him because of the privilege of caring for these three in addition to our three birth children. Still, there are bound to be speed bumps along the way (for instance, they speak Creole and we don't). Because of that, please pray for us. I'll give you another update at the end of my next book. Until then, blessings to you and yours, humbly in Christ,

P.S. As always, I'd love to hear from you. Write me at my e-mail address: rtnbykk@aol.com

DISCUSSION QUESTIONS

1. Have you ever prayed for something or someone and felt as though God didn't hear your prayers? How did it make you feel? How do you feel now?

2. Did it surprise you to learn that there really was a Jesus statue case? Why or why not? Where do you think our country stands today in terms of religious freedom issues?

3. How are you or your family and friends affected by restrictions on religious freedom in the United States?

4. To which character in the book can you most relate? Why?

5. Consider the main characters. How did they change over the course of the story? In what way is God trying to change or grow you at this stage in your life?

6. Read Joshua 5:13–6:20. What are the parallels between that story and the story in this book?

7. Jordan lost much as a young teen. What losses have you dealt with and how have you responded to them?

8. Have you ever been angry at God because of those losses? Have you ever walked away from God? If so, how are things now between you and God? Why are they that way?

9. Read Romans 8:28. God always has our situation under control. His control, not ours. Has there been a time in your life when all seemed lost, but God—in His timing—worked things out for your good? What was that like? How did you feel about God during that time?

10. Why did the letter from Jordan's mother change his life? Has anyone ever written you a letter that changed your life? Describe that situation.

THE
FOREVER FAITHFUL SERIES

WAITING FOR MORNING—*Book One*
A drunk driver...a deadly accident...a dream destroyed. When Hannah Ryan loses her husband and oldest daughter to a drunk driver, she is consumed with hate and revenge. Ultimately, it is a kind prosecutor, a wise widow, and her husband's dying words that bring her the peace that will set her free and let her live again.
ISBN 1-59052-020-3

A MOMENT OF WEAKNESS—*Book Two*
When childhood friends Jade and Tanner reunite as adults, they share their hearts, souls, and dreams of forever—until a fateful decision tears them apart. Now, nearly a decade later, Jade's unfaithful husband wants to destroy her in a custody battle that is about to send shock waves across the United States. Only one man can help Jade in her darkest hour. And only one old woman knows the truth that can set them all free.
ISBN 1-57673-616-4

HALFWAY TO FOREVER—*Book Three*
Matt and Hannah...Jade and Tanner—after already surviving much, these couples now face the greatest struggles of their lives: Parental losses and life-threatening illness threaten to derail their faith and sideline their futures. Can Hannah survive the loss of an adopted daughter? Will Tanner come through decades of loneliness only to face losing Jade one final time?
ISBN 1-57673-899-X

ABOUT THE AUTHOR...
Karen Kingsbury is an award-winning author and former reporter for the *Los Angeles Times* and *Los Angeles Daily News*. She is also a recognized author with the Women of Faith Fiction Club. Kingsbury lives with her husband and six children in Washington.

KAREN KINGSBURY
AND PRISM COFOUNDER TONI VOGT

THE PRISM WEIGHT LOSS PROGRAM

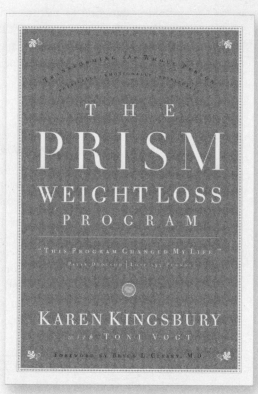

The PRISM® Weight Loss Program, founded in 1990, has helped more than 60,000 people transform their eating behaviors with a sensible, lifestyle-change approach. Now available in *The Prism Weight Loss Program* by bestselling author Karen Kingsbury and PRISM cofounder Toni Vogt, the book shows readers how to not just "tame the monster" of food addiction, but destroy it through simple eating strategies and biblical principles. It includes testimonials, descriptions of the authors' personal struggles with food addiction, details of the program, and a fabulous recipe section that will help readers become the fit people God created them to be.

ISBN 1-57673-578-8 HD